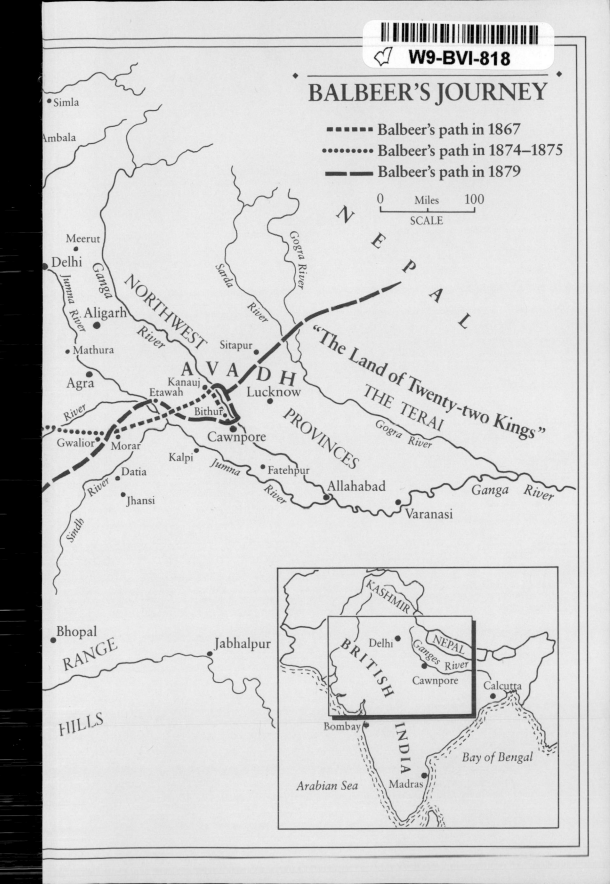

BALBEER'S JOURNEY

- - - - - - Balbeer's path in 1867
- - - - - - Balbeer's path in 1874–1875
— — — Balbeer's path in 1879

0   Miles   100
SCALE

Simla

Ambala

Meerut

Delhi

Jumna River

Ganga River

NORTHWEST

Aligarh

Mathura

Agra

River

Gwalior

Morar

Sindh River

Datia

Jhansi

Kalpi

Kanauj

Etawah

Bithur

AVADH

Sitapur

Sarda River

Lucknow

Cawnpore

PROVINCES

NEPAL

Gogra River

"The Land of Twenty-two Kings"

THE TERAI

Gogra River

Jumna River

Fatehpur

Allahabad

Varanasi

Ganga River

Bhopal

RANGE

Jabhalpur

HILLS

KASHMIR

BRITISH

INDIA

Delhi

NEPAL

Ganges River

Cawnpore

Calcutta

Bombay

Bay of Bengal

Arabian Sea

Madras

THE BLOOD SEED

ALSO BY ANDREW WARD

Fits and Starts:
The Premature Memoirs of Andrew Ward

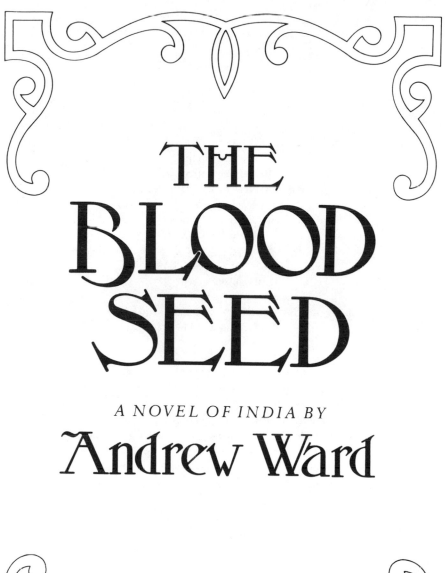

THE
BLOOD
SEED

A NOVEL OF INDIA BY

Andrew Ward

VIKING

VIKING
Viking Penguin Inc.
40 West 23rd Street,
New York, New York 10010, U.S.A.

First American Edition
Published in 1985

LIBRARY OF CONGRESS CATALOGING IN PUBLICATION DATA
Ward, Andrew, 1946–
The blood seed.
I. Title.
PS3573.A69C6   1985   813'.54   83-40661
ISBN 0-670-58934-9

Printed in the United States of America by
R. R. Donnelley & Sons Company, Harrisonburg, Virginia
Set in Sabon
Map by David Lindroth

For Debbie

CONTENTS

PROLOGUE

On that heartbreaking morning in 1947 when my family and I left India for good, as the lift van rumbled to the Jullundur station and the Wolseley, piled high with baggage, purred in the porte cochère, our staff lined the bare verandah, holding garlands and sweets and assorted quaint gifts to present to us on our departure. These we accepted from our servants without hesitation, and had it not been for proprieties of caste and class I could almost have reached out and embraced them all.

All, perhaps, but one: an old, abstracted man who stood dry-eyed at the very end of the line, a step or so back from the others. He had been known to us only as Moonshi and had served as bearer's assistant in my household for fifteen years. Moonshi was not the sort of servant one would have been tempted to bring home to England, but he was a reliable old fellow: honest and, by Eastern standards, clean and punctual. His posture left something to be desired, and when he served tea on a summer afternoon he could appear alarmingly chapfallen. But he was quite vigorous for his years, which we numbered about seventy, and never lost a day to illness. I had been far more attached to my manservant and even to our cook, despite his petty pilfering, but Moonshi nonetheless had his own special place in my family's affections and his experience was a resource upon which we all drew.

I had inherited Moonshi's services from B. D. Cox, my predecessor as magistrate in the district of Jullundur, as Cox evidently had from his, and none of my other servants was old enough to know precisely when Moonshi had first settled in the compound, but I now realize that something more than age separated Moonshi from his colleagues.

For one thing, he was the only member of my staff who did not come into my employ trailing wife, children, parents, grandparents, washed-up uncles, widowed aunts, ne'er-do-well brothers, and abandoned sisters — the whole catastrophic complement of the Indian extended family. He lived entirely alone in a small brick structure Cox had had built for him on the roof of the old stable so that he would not waste a full suite in the servants' quarters. A local woman brought him his meals for a fee, but in all the years I employed him he had no other visitors. This did not surprise the rest of our servants, for his manner was always distant and his fellow Hindus in the compound deplored his indifference to their rituals.

Perhaps at this remove my curiosity seems a lame old thing not to have been roused by Moonshi's singularity. But he was only one of the twenty servants which our life required and he was never a cause of trouble in the quarters. He had, besides, the gift for making himself all but imperceptible that is the mark of a natural domestic.

When I reached him on that morning of sad farewells he wished me a safe journey and without lifting his gaze from the floor presented me with a crude bundle wrapped in coarse cotton cloth and bound with string. His was not one of those elaborate expressions of longing one might have expected from a kitmadgar bidding farewell to his sahib of fifteen years, and, irritated, I suppose, that even these poignant circumstances had not unsettled Moonshi's reserve, I told him that though the gesture was much appreciated we simply could not add so cumbersome a package to our surfeit of baggage.

But when I attempted to return it to him Moonshi stepped back and glared at me with such ferocity that, startled, I reflexively tucked the parcel under my arm before climbing into the car and waving a final goodbye to our staff, our compound, our one true home.

I did not open Moonshi's gift until later, on the train, when the girls insisted. I had been tempted to dispose of it at the station; one should have been safe in assuming that it contained one of those horrid chalky confections of which the Indian is so proud. But, haunted by Moonshi's sudden, defiant scowl, I had held onto it.

So, in short, I opened the thing and found it to contain a great

heap of paper covered with writing. I could see that the writing was
Hindustani, but since most of my native contacts had been conducted
in Urdu and Punjabi I could barely understand it and was soon
stumbling over what turned out to be an elegant and vivid vernacu-
lar. It was not until I was aboard the P&O boat for home that I
began to realize that what Moonshi had pressed upon me with such
uncharacteristic insistence was the autobiography of one Balbeer
Rao, a Hindu born in Cawnpore shortly after the great Indian
Mutiny of 1857. And it was not until our ship entered the Gulf of
Aden that it finally dawned on me that Moonshi and this mysterious
Balbeer Rao were one and the same, that the frayed and soiled
manuscript was the record of Moonshi's own life, spanning ninety
years of Indian history.

Of course, to begin with, it was difficult to believe that Moonshi
was ninety years old; it had been remarkable enough to think that an
Indian of such vigor could have been seventy. And more doubtful still
was Moonshi's contention that his domestic service had been a ruse.

But the first few chapters, or what I could understand of them,
were written with such specificity and conviction that I could not
simply dismiss Moonshi's tales as senile apocrypha. By the time our
ship entered the Red Sea I was under Moonshi's spell. All through the
voyage I struggled with his manuscript, forgoing the society on deck
for the musty confines of the ship's library, where I tried to confirm
Moonshi's assertions. Those events which I could check against the
records of the period proved plausible in their context, and since he
had presumably written his memoirs by lamplight in his little brick
room, without reference to records of the past, my belief in his
contentions deepened with each turning of a page.

I am no historian, nor much of a literary man, but I was soon
convinced that Moonshi had entrusted a treasure to me. Here was no
static, caste-bound life but an adventure propelled by quests and
incarnations, each more astonishing than the last and none more
astonishing nor more tragic than his finally coming to rest in our
compound.

When I reached home I tried to find a scholar willing and able to
take on the formidable task of translating Moonshi's story into
English. But the more learned gentlemen I approached the less
eagerly I tried to press this burden upon them. During the weeks I

waited outside academics' offices, only to be patronized for a half hour by men whose knowledge of India was abstract and second-hand, I became as protective of Moonshi's story as a hen of her eggs. At last, when my wife Judith suggested with some exasperation that I do the job myself, I surprised us both by accepting her challenge.

Now my work is done. However vividly he may bring himself to life in the pages that follow, try as I may I cannot remember Moonshi himself except in the most fleeting glimpses: his distracted gaze as I handed him his wages, his bony fingers on the tea tray. What became of him in the end I shall save until his story closes. Now I must leave it to you to judge whether I have honored his trust.

Hugh W. Cuthbertson
I.C.S., Retired
Cheltenham, Gloucester
October 1955

PART ONE

CAWNPORE

CHAPTER

1

I was born to a widow in 1858 and named Balbeer Rao: *Balbeer* meaning 'valiant,' because I'd pulled through a hard birth, *Rao* being the name of my mother's family back in Rajputana. She and I lived with our servant Moonshi in a room over a confectioner's stall in the city of Cawnpore in the Northwest Provinces.

Ask most Indians what year they were born in and they couldn't tell you, though they could tell you a lot else about the phase of the moon or the disposition of the stars. But I can place my birth on your calendar because I was conceived during a great historical conflagration which the British call the Sepoy Rebellion of 1857, or the Great Mutiny of 1857, or just the 1857 Mutiny, but always with *1857* tagged onto it, just to be specific. Patriots like to call it our First War of Independence, as if it had been a real revolution, with the little people rising up, but I know it was a fever, and I call it the Devil's Wind.

This is to be the story of my search for my father in the years that followed the Devil's Wind; of the strange, comical and terrible circumstances of that search; and of the people who helped and hindered me along the way. If I sometimes seem to tease and trick you with the truth, remember that I too was teased and tricked, and for a lot longer than it takes to read a book. My whole youth was haunted by the question of my father's identity, and the rest of my life has been hostage to the answer.

For most of my life I've been disguised, even to myself, as a servant, thus confounding the destiny prescribed at my birth almost ninety years ago. It's only now when I can set these past sixty-five years of safety and routine against my first twenty-five years of danger and adventure that I dare to record my early life.

I've got to keep everything in order so that this follows that, just as it happened. But what should I do with the first dim images I come up with when I try to go as far back as my memory can reach? For a moment I see my mother massaging my infant limbs in the sunshine. For an instant I hear her lullaby in a heavy rain. But in these images I see myself too clearly – stretched out on a charpoy or pressed against my mother's breast – and I wonder if I'm confusing my mother with my wife, myself with my son, my infancy with the time, not much less long ago, when I raised my own family by the River Sindh. And sometimes I wonder if these images are memories at all, or just the shards of an orphan's dream.

So I shall begin where my memory first gains its footing: eighty-two years ago in the city streets.

My mother was taking me to the temple. I was five years old and followed in the flutter of her widow's sari as she led me along the Street of Silver. It must have been early evening, because the swollen sun grazed and gilded the city's jumbled rooftops and my nose itched with the dung smoke from a host of cooking fires. For all the noise along the street – the peddler's pitch, the beggar's whine, the taunts and laughter from the tea stalls and coolie stations, the roll and clop of bullock carts and ekkas, the chants and grunts of the palanquin bearers as they toted their masters home – I could hear my mother's anklets clinking.

She balanced a little brass jug of milk in one hand, held my hand in the other, kept the veil of her sari tight across her face with her teeth. Pausing in the shadow of the bullet-pocked arch, she bought a few blossoms from a flower vendor, and I remember how the dust around his basket was spattered with betel juice and he gave my mother a crimson smile.

We crossed a road lined with cotton bales, and I could see the Ganga and the Bridge of Boats. The stink from the harness factory followed us as we made our way to the Sati Chowra Ghat, where Shiva's priests had raised a tall, lopsided adobe temple to house the few relics that had survived the conflagration just six years past.

My mother left me to sit by a rickety gate festooned with banners and circled the temple a few times before going inside to make her offerings. I suppose I must have been used to waiting for her by then. I'd been going along on her expeditions ever since I was old enough to ride her hip. A widow of dwindling means, my mother would walk two miles to save a few pice on some eggplant, wait behind the Moghul serai to sneak a purchase from the cook, buy her spices from thieves in the Gola Ghat bazaar. So I waited peaceably outside the temple that evening, squatting by the gate.

On the old worn steps leading down to the river, pilgrims, penitents, cripples, and holy men sat chanting their evening prayers, some at the top of their voices, as if Shiva were hard of hearing, others in whispers. Beside me an old man wearing nothing but a length of thread around his waist and someone's discarded spectacle frames on the bridge of his nose sat beating time on his thigh with his open hand and chanting:

> *Shiva is my father*
> *Shiva is my father*
> *Praise God*
> *He reaps the field with fire and flood*
> *So it may be sown again*
> *Father*
> *I have sprung from your loins*
> *I shall fall beneath your feet*
> *In your shadow I shall be reborn*
> *Shiva*
> *My father*
> *Shiva*
> *My father*
> *Shiva*
> *Protect your son*
> *Shiva is my father . . .*

He went on and on in that vein, even through his inhalations, and I decided I had to try it too. So, keeping my eyes on his jaw as it rose and fell, I began to chant along with him – *Shiva is my father, Shiva is my father*, and other words to that effect. At first I only meant to pass the time, but it must have put me into a kind of trance, because after a while I closed my eyes.

I know I sat that way for quite some time because when I opened my eyes again the sky was a good deal darker. But I don't know when it was that tears first began to trickle down my cheeks, nor when I first came to believe the innocent blasphemy that the chant was literally true: that Shiva *was* my father, the father I had never known: that I was sitting outside my father's house and somehow, before nightfall, I had to find him.

I only remember that suddenly I was on my feet and moving as if on a tide through the gate and under Ganesha's gaze. Bells rang, drums rattled, and moans rose from the black mouth of the temple as I approached, but I wasn't going to let anything stop me, not the noise, not the dark, not the stench of camphor and soured milk and decaying blossoms; so I entered Shiva's house.

As in a dream I seemed to walk not so much through the scattering of worshippers as over them, and no one made a move to stop me as I passed beneath a bell, climbed three steep steps, and walked through a curtained archway and into the inner chamber where the priests tended Shiva, my father, in the dark. The floor was tamped and hard and crowded with Brahmins, and the black walls, which glistened as if they were bleeding wherever an idol had been installed, loomed so high into the gloom that I couldn't see the ceiling.

In the center of the floor was a deep pit surrounded by a low clay wall. Around this cavity the priests sang and beat their drums and sprinkled blossoms and water and ghee, while a few old priests sat along its lip dipping smoldering chunks of sandalwood into the pit and, like body servants preparing a bath, reaching in to stir the blue currents of smoke.

The priests didn't notice me and I was barely aware of them. They didn't matter; I'd come to find my father. Still chanting to myself, my little voice drowned in the din, I slipped between two busy priests and peered down into the fuming hole.

At first I couldn't see anything but smoke and gloom. The pit looked empty and endless, like an overturned sky, and I seemed to lose all sense of scale, so that the sandalwood smoke looked to me like subterranean banks of clouds. I tried to fix my eyes on something to get my bearings, but the harder I tried the more the pit lost its scale and substance until I became so giddy that I began to waver on my feet.

But suddenly, in just the way you might make out a lizard on a wall or a leopard in the dappled bush, I saw a gargantuan worm, all smeared and ghastly, beckoning to me like a finger.

I cried out and hurled myself back so hard that I sent an old priest tumbling to the floor in a storm of jasmine petals. He made an awful noise when he landed, and I think he must have broken his hip, though I never knew for sure. All the racket came to a stop in that black chamber as the other priests froze where they were and stared down at the two of us sprawled on the floor.

'Oh God!' the old priest cried out, curling up on his side. 'Somebody help me!'

I got to my feet slowly and stared down at him with the others and saw that in his shock and pain he had wetted himself, as old men will (including myself, for lately I've begun to leak like a mali's hose).

Now you would think that the younger priests at least might have rushed to the old man's assistance, but you have to remember that these priests were Brahmins, and Brahmins aren't men of action or famous for aiding the fallen. Emergencies present them with a lot of knotty problems to straighten out. First of all, Brahmins don't want to do anything rash that might endanger their station, which is why they're so deliberate in their travels and slow to reform. It takes nothing more than a sweeper's shadow or a fleck of pigeon feather to defile them and set them to bathing, fasting, meditating, despairing for weeks on end. Even if the defilement doesn't sicken them the penance will.

And beyond the inconvenience there's the problem of motivation. If you put yourself in their position — if you had reached a lofty status only after a millennium of rebirths and were convinced that you were already in what a Christian might call a state of grace, like an angel or a saint — then you might also believe that doing something kindly wasn't worth the risk. And since your exalted position is supposed to be a reward for all the good things you must have done in your past lives, you might decide you shouldn't have to put yourself out any longer for your fellow man.

So even the best men among that little squad of priests were paralyzed, for though the old man was a Brahmin and a comrade he was now soaked with piss, and, Brahmin or no Brahmin, piss is piss and a defilement to the touch. I think those priests might have stood there all evening in their pitiful predicament had the old man not blinked open his eyes, pointed a crooked finger at me like a stick, and cried, 'Get him! Get the boy!'

The other priests looked at me with relief, for here was something they could do, and with sudden shouts and unpriestly curses they closed in on me like beaters in a hunt.

I have never been one to take my punishment lying down, and I began to dart among the priests to escape their clutches. A plump priest blocked the archway as the others chased me, but I was small and quick, and after two laps around the pit I dove between his knees and tumbled down the three steep steps outside the door, bringing the curtain with me. The priests ran after me, but as I struggled to free myself of the curtain they all skidded to a halt and shrank back, waving their arms like old women shooing birds off laundry, for it had finally occurred to them that they didn't know my caste and that my touch, my breath, even my shadow might be vile.

Over the noise as worshippers jumped to their feet I could hear my mother calling for me outside. At the sound of her voice I sobbed and tore loose from the curtain, scrambling for the doorway and the evening light. There, by the festooned gate, my mother slung me up onto her hip and turned toward the temple with a glare.

The Brahmins all crowded together in the doorway and shook their fists, still shouting and cursing.

'Bastard!' one called out in a high, hooting voice.

'You son of a whore!' another lisped, and soon the faithful took up the cry – even the naked old man in the spectacles – and began to hurl stones.

The first stone clattered at my mother's feet, and she turned to run. More stones followed and one struck her leg, but she kept hold of me as she raced across the sandstone rubble, and it wasn't until we were out of range and earshot of the temple – not until we had safely crossed the river – that she finally put me down, collapsing against a cotton bale and coughing up blood.

CHAPTER

2

The priests were wrong about my mother. She was a widow, not a whore. But in those days there was shame enough in that. The ghat we'd been chased off was called Sati Chowra because it was where widows used to break their wedding bangles (chowra) and commit sati (immolate themselves on their husbands' pyres) in the days before the British. I've been told that sati was invented by kings centuries ago to rid their courts of the bloody scheming of their predecessors' widows, but it appealed so much to men's self-esteem and became such a popular public spectacle that it caught on with even the low-caste poor.

When my mother was a little girl in the Rajput court at Harigarh, her father made her watch the mass sati of the Raja Jagatjit Singhji's harem. Whenever she described it to me she made it sound awesome and beautiful, like the metamorphosis of butterflies, as the Raja's wives and concubines, my great-aunt included, filed up to their master's pyre and silently burst into flames.

You won't find sati in the sacred books, and God knows womanhood is well rid of it, but when the British wiped it out thirty years before my birth they created a new breed of outcaste so useless and despised that many of its numbers chose to starve themselves to death. Those widows like my mother who elected to live were branded cowards and sluts and shamed their husbands' memories.

I suppose it's possible that if my mother hadn't had me to look after she might have starved herself or drowned herself in the Ganga, but I don't think suicide was in her nature. Every son should believe that his mother is beautiful, and I did, but I also know that it wasn't Natholi Rao's features that caught the eye but the spirit that shone through.

She was a Rajput noblewoman, and if her pride didn't always make her easy to live with, it had seen her through the lifetime of misery and persecution that fate had compressed into the few years between her birth and mine.

Sometimes her pride took the form of vanity, for she'd been born into a world where, besides producing sons, a woman's paramount duty was to preen. Widows were supposed to look shamed and shabby, like the walking dead, but my mother kept her sari so clean and groomed herself so exquisitely that she could scandalize the neighborhood just by walking across the street.

She had removed her rings and earrings and bracelets when her husband died, but she still wore two silver anklets and kept all the rest of her finery in a trunk. I remember the nights when I used to watch her from my bed as she sat by her open trunk in the wavering light of a mustard lamp, smoothing her saris, polishing her jewelry, and inhaling the scent of her forbidden perfumes.

After the calamity at the temple my mother led me home in silence, hurrying through the dark streets and dragging me along behind her. When we'd passed through the sweet steam from the confectioner's stall, climbed the little stone stairway to our room, and bolted the door behind us, she sat me down before her and gripped me by the shoulders.

'What did you think you were doing?' she wanted to know, trying to stay calm as she caught her breath. 'What could have possessed you?'

Bone-tired, still whimpering, I could only shake my head.

'Answer me, Baloo,' she said, for that was her name for me. 'Why didn't you stay where I left you?'

'I – I was only – '

'Only what?'

I glanced around the room, afraid and confused as her fingers tightened on my shoulders. How could I tell her that I'd been looking for my father when she'd commanded me a hundred times never to speak of him?

'I can't,' I said, closing my eyes and squeezing tears onto my cheeks. 'I can't tell you.'

'You'd better tell me,' my mother said. 'I order you to tell me.'

'But you'll only be angry.'

'I'm *already* angry. Now what were you doing? What were you looking for? Why did you disobey?'

I turned my head away and braced myself. 'I was – '

'Yes?'

'I was only looking for my father.'

With a gasp my mother stiffened and released my shoulders so suddenly that I almost fell back onto the floor. For a moment she stared around her with a wild and hunted look, as if wolves had slipped into the room to devour her. She raised her hand over me with another sharp breath, but just when she seemed about to strike me she slumped back onto her bed and stared into the empty space in front of her.

'You mustn't do that,' she said slowly in her hoarse voice. 'You can't go looking for him like that. He doesn't exist.' And then, almost in a whisper, she said, 'He never existed.'

Well, this was either a lie or I was in need of more information, so when I thought the danger had passed I said, 'Mataji, how can that be?'

But the danger had not passed, and before the words were out of my mouth my mother had risen up again and glared at me with what I can only call hatred. I shrank back from those fierce, dark eyes, and when she pushed by me now and hurried out into the streets something withered inside me.

All through my boyhood, up until her final decline, my mother made regular forays into the night streets, and I used to rise from my bed and watch her slip through the shadows like a ghost and disappear on her westward course into the shuttered-down bazaars of Ram Ganj. I always promised myself I would keep watch for her, and just as invariably I would fall off to sleep by the window and when she returned that night that is where she found me.

I awoke in her arms as she carried me back to my bed, and it seems to me now when I recall her fond gaze as she smoothed my blanket all around me that in that instant when she'd glared at me it wasn't me she'd hated, but someone or something I somehow evoked.

By morning word about my banishment from the temple had reached the streets, and when I came outside to play the neighborhood children faced me like an army.

I'd always been peculiar to them. To begin with, I was an only child, while they all seemed to come from huge families with brothers and sisters and cousins tumbling after them into the street. And since my mother was all I had in the world, my deepest allegiance was to her, while my playmates thought of adults as foes to be tricked, opposed and overcome.

My mother didn't like my playing with the children of clerks and craftsmen, and I suppose some of her snobbishness must have rubbed off on me. No matter how eager I was to join up with them I could never put my heart into their games, especially when they involved playing pranks on lame or elderly passersby. I blame this on a trepidatious, not a kindly, nature, because my mother had somehow convinced me that if I behaved badly the sky would collapse upon me.

Whether my playmates thought of me as the son of a Rajput noblewoman or the son of a disgraced widow, I was clearly not their equal, so for one reason or another they persecuted me. As a result I developed a knack for deflecting abuse which has stood me in good stead ever since; for instance, I learned never to position myself in the center of a group but always on the periphery where I could wait out their abuse until something came along to distract them: the bear walla with his toothless beast, Kacha the naked and somersaulting lunatic, Rhandawa the limbless veteran of the Sikh Wars, Har Pyari the songbird peddler. I also always kept in motion, for I'd learned that in human affairs as in hunting the standing target doesn't stand a chance.

But none of that would do me any good this morning.

The children faced me in a long line before which strutted their commanders, short and stocky Sikh twins named Mohinder and Bhagat. The grown-up Sikh is a fearsome sight with his turban, whiskers, bangle, and sword, but the juvenile Sikh is a clown. His oversized turban presses down on his brow, all he's got for whiskers is a haze of fuzz, his bangle looks feminine on his delicate little wrist, and the only sword he's allowed to wear is a penknife. To compensate for these indignities a Sikh boy will develop an aggressive disposition and steep himself in the warrior legacy of Guru Gobind Singh, who turned their peaceful little sect into soldiers back in Moghul times.

Mohinder and Bhagat regarded play as training for the warrior's life, though their father was only a nightwatchman and they were certain to follow in his footsteps. In any case, keeping up their image gave Mohinder and Bhagat a sense of urgency about street games that made them reckless but natural leaders.

'Look!' Mohinder shouted back to his troops. 'It's Balbeer! Balbeer the Bastard!'

'Balbeer the Bastard!' Bhagat echoed his brother.

'Only now he isn't just Balbeer the Bastard any more,' Mohinder said as all the others, from Sanjay, the huge idiot son of the pahn seller, to the toddler offspring of the livery man, sniggered and jeered behind him. 'No, that wasn't enough. Now he's Balbeer the Damned, too!'

'Balbeer the Damned!' shouted Bhagat.

'Balbeer the Blasphemer!'

'Balbeer the Blasphemer!' everyone shouted.

I stood stock still, not knowing for sure what a blasphemer was though it didn't sound good, and then I took a step forward, still smiling as if nothing had changed.

'Get back!' Mohinder cried, bugging his eyes and waving his arms around. 'Make way! Don't let him near you! Make way for the damned!'

The others circled around me, laughing and jeering, as I stopped and tried to step sideways and lose myself among them. But they kept moving just out of reach, trapping me in the center, circling like rags in a whirlwind.

'That's enough,' I said as a strange new dread began to spread through my stomach.

'That's enough?' Mohinder sneered. 'You little son of a whore —' he said, leaning toward me with his fists clenched.

'Take that back!' I heard myself shout. 'My mother's not a whore!'

'Then how come you're a son of a whore?'

'Son of a whore!' shouted Bhagat.

'You stop it!' I said, lurching toward Bhagat. I tried to grab his shirt in one hand, but someone shoved me from behind and sent me stumbling to my knees.

The laughter surged around me, and when I got to my feet with my knees scraped and my eyes burning with tears, someone threw a fistful of dirt in my face and another tripped me over as I recoiled and all I could see now was a blur of limbs reeling around me.

I tried to find Mohinder through the tears and dust and strike at him again, but he wove so quickly among the others that my blows just fanned through the air. 'I'll get you!' I snarled at him, but God, I sounded small, and hearing myself I felt something give way inside me, and at last I ran for home.

'That's right,' Mohinder called after me. 'Go home! Go home to the whore that bore you!'

'And stay there!' Bhagat cried as the others jubilated.

'Never mind them,' my mother said as she cleaned the muddy tears from my face. 'They're just ignorant urchins. They can't hurt a boy like you. You're too good for them.'

But was I? I wondered that afternoon as I sat on the roof of our home, watching the city's shadow slip across the Ganga like a stain. The priests had been wrong about my mother. But were they wrong about me? Who was it my mother had seen in my face the night before? Was it my father? Had he been cruel to her? Had she hated him? Or had I simply reminded her of her miserable lot, the fruit of her misfortune?

But even if I'd had the wit and mettle to ask such questions I would never have found the answers in the Cawnpore of my boyhood, for it was as desperate as my mother to bury the recent past.

CHAPTER

3

Cawnpore had no ancient past to speak of. None of our gods had romped along the riverbank, none of our kings had warred upon its plain. The old city was just a clump of huts and cenotaphs, the new city was a British garrison and trading center: a watchful and drudging sister to the elegant, sleepy city of Lucknow across the Ganga.

But in the summer of 1857 when the native troops of the East India Company's army rose up against their British officers and plunged North India into war, Cawnpore finally came into its own. For forty days it was the rebel capital of the Nana Sahib, the last heir to the Mahratta throne, at whose orders every white in the city had been put to death.

By the time I was born the Nana Sahib had disappeared into the Himalayas with what little was left of his rebel army, leaving the city in ruins. Though my mother would never tell me anything about the first months of my life, our servant Moonshi said that for many of those months the roads in and out of the city were littered with the remains of the people who'd been shot, hanged, and blown from guns by British troops crazed with grief and outrage. Even around the time of my first birthday Indian citizens kept out of sight of the Highlanders who occupied the city. And I have heard since that the British had considered razing Cawnpore and leaving its rubble as a memorial to the women and children the Nana Sahib had massacred.

But the city was a British invention, after all, and by the time I became aware of the world, Cawnpore was being reconstructed to serve its old purposes, with armories, warehouses, and mills rising out of the rubble.

Only one of us in that haunted place tried to keep the past alive: a blackmailing Bengali named Nanak Chand. The Bengalis of Cawnpore had been the Company's most loyal clerks and errand boys, but for sheer sycophancy no one could compete with Nanak Chand. An agent for a grain-contracting firm, he affected all sorts of English ways, even going so far as to don a bowler hat and live among the sahibs and memsahibs in the civil lines.

When the rebels came to power the Bengalis were the first loyalists to suffer, and to escape being dismembered by the Nana's soldiers, Nanak Chand fled into the countryside, eluding his enemies for two long months with bribes, threats and disguises. He understood the English well enough to know that they'd come back in force and he made certain he'd be ready when they did. Every day, no matter how uncomfortable his situation, he made an entry in his diary, recording every rumor that might suit his schemes.

When the British did sweep back and set up their tribunals, Nanak Chand humbly stepped out of the shadows to offer his services. For many months he was their chief witness against the rebels and their sympathizers, his diary their principal evidence. On the strength of his word, hundreds were condemned to death or imprisonment, and Nanak Chand soon became Cawnpore's most feared, and thus most powerful, native citizen.

Nanak Chand did not take long to realize that the tribunals had such an appetite for retribution that they would forgive his diary its inconsistencies and even, on occasion, permit him to make revisions as new misdeeds occurred to him. This placed temptations in Nanak Chand's path which he had no intention of resisting, so that should, say, Bector the silk merchant become too insistent about his bill, Nanak Chand would suddenly recall – how could he have forgotten? – that it was Bector who'd been seen making sport of Mrs. Harris's corpse; and hadn't it been Bector – or had it been his son? – who presented a bolt of brocade to the rebel minister Azimullah?

I've sullied these pages with this scoundrel because my mother was one of those temptations Nanak Chand could not resist. After I was born and my mother regained her youthful contours Nanak Chand came to court her with his gifts and threats. All Nanak Chand had to do to get invited into our little room was suggest that my mother's past might be of some interest to his English 'colleagues,' as he called them, for my mother had a special horror of the British. Of course, her past was probably as much a mystery to Nanak Chand as it was to me, but a widow was in no position to call his bluff.

Around Englishmen Nanak Chand was a model of humility and murmured his concurrences like a shy, adoring suitor. But around his own kind, especially those of us he called 'Hindustanis,' he puffed himself up like a bullfrog. In the manner of all low and lucky men of sudden wealth he was forever lecturing people on the virtues of patience and hard work, even as he rewarded their patience and hard work with extortion. He was the muck which rises to the surface when a pond is waded through, and all we could do was wait until, of his own weight, he sank back down to the bottom.

My first clear memory of Nanak Chand is of a stout man with a heavy brow and protruding lower lip, pausing winded on the stairway. He must have been at the height of his influence, because he was dressed in silks and travelled around town in a six-man palanquin. I was always sent down to greet him and help him up the stairs, for which he sometimes rewarded me with a few grains of anise he would filch from the confectioner's stall downstairs. He pretended to like me just to feed his self-esteem and because I was pale he called me Little Turnip.

'We'll wait here,' he said in his thin voice, leaning against the stairwell wall and gasping for breath, 'to give your mother a moment more to ready herself for me.'

He pinched my cheek and bared his crooked brown teeth in a grin. 'Ah, women – eh, Little Turnip? They always keep you waiting but they're always worth the wait.'

Then, seeing that I didn't understand or maybe remembering that, after all, this was my mother he was talking about, he frowned, gripping my shoulder and leaning forward to complete his ascent.

At the landing he stopped to compose himself, removing his bowler and wiping the sweat from the crease it left on his brow. From behind the door I could hear my mother's coughing, which always got worse on the days Nanak Chand came to call.

'All right, Little Turnip,' Nanak Chand said, reaching for the latch. 'Vanish.' And with that I climbed the ladder to the roof.

After that morning when I was chased home by the neighborhood children I never played in the streets again and spent my free time in lofty exile on the roof, where I could play my solitary games in safety and out of my mother's earshot. I tried to pretend that I was doing this not out of fear or shame but in order to punish my old playmates by depriving them of my company, but even from that altitude I could tell that they didn't miss me much. I would always ache to join them, but sometimes I could soothe the pain of my banishment with fantasies of kingly power. As I watched the children dart through the bazaar below I imagined myself their emperor and pretended to command them, as on a field of battle, with furtive nods and gestures. I became so skillful at anticipating their routes and destinations that I sometimes convinced myself that I could control them, like a capricious god, and when they strayed from the paths I'd set for them I would obliterate them into the roiling dark of my closed eyes.

But from my perch I could also fly my kite, watch the city rise from its devastation, and, through a gap in the skyline, count the boats on the distant river. From Cawnpore one thousand miles to the Bay of Bengal the Ganga was navigable, and boats of every description stopped at the city's ghats to deliver grain and take on passengers and goods from the mills and tanneries. There were big three-masted pinnaces; clumsy old budgerows with their teetering sterns; baulias gliding along like swans; granary barges like floating haystacks; the stray pleasure craft of a cruising prince built in the shape of a heron or a fish, regally drifting along the riverbank. And, with perfect regularity, the English touring steamers, towing flats, would dock by the Bridge of Boats, white and reproving amid all the dusty clutter.

After a while Moonshi joined me on the roof, having served Nanak Chand his limeade and milk cakes, and squatted near the ladder, where he could hear my mother if she called for him.

'Is he still down there?' I asked, walking along the rim of the roof.

'He is,' Moonshi replied with a solemn look. 'It pleases Shri Chand to spend all afternoon in your mother's company.'

Moonshi wiped his hands with the little tattered towel he carried with him everywhere and then slung it over his shoulder. He'd been my mother's servant ever since her wedding and had stuck by her through all her misfortunes, as servants did back in those days, I suppose because they didn't know what else to do. As far back as you could trace my mother's family there you would find one of Moonshi's ancestors hovering around, scolding the punka walla, flicking away flies, serving rosewater after summer meals. The youngest son of my grandfather's chief bearer, Moonshi had been a chinless, wall-eyed disappointment to his family. He overslept, daydreamed, forgot half the errands my mother had him run; and what little money we could afford to pay him he gambled and lost on partridge flights.

But I loved Moonshi, and he loved me, and I came to owe him my life. It infuriated me to think that he had known my father, but wouldn't tell me anything about him, no matter how much I begged or threatened or tried to trick him. But at least I knew that I could trust him with my secrets when the time came, just as my mother could trust him with hers.

Moonshi must have understood why Nanak Chand came to visit my mother, but he never let on to me. His way of making the most of his mistress's disgrace was to treat Nanak Chand with extravagant respect, as if to transform the calumnious scoundrel into a proper, benevolent figure, like a kindly uncle checking up on an indigent niece.

'I wish he'd go away,' I said to Moonshi, balancing with one foot on the edge of the roof.

'He's our guest,' Moonshi replied, setting what passed for his chin. 'And he's a most important personage, Little Master. A very influential dignitary. We owe him our affection and respect.'

'But why does he have to come here all the time?' I asked. 'Why is he always visiting my mother?'

Moonshi looked my way and sighed a little. 'Because your mother is a dignitary herself, Little Master, and dignitaries hang together.'

'Am I a dignitary?'

'Of course you are,' Moonshi said gravely. 'You come from a line of diwans in the land of kings. That's why Shri Chand likes you so much.'

'They why don't I like him?'

Moonshi put a finger to his lips. 'But it is never a matter of liking or disliking, Little Master,' he said softly. 'Shri Chand is your mother's guest, your elder, and a man of influence.' Moonshi paused and lowered his voice. 'And Shri Chand is the Feringhee's eyes and ears. He could make life very hard for us.'

'What can *he* do?'

Moonshi moved closer to me, smiling and shaking his head. 'Little Master, don't you know what influential men do all day? They exercise their influence. They decide our fortunes. Fat or thin, dark or light, it doesn't matter; they can wreck your life with a nod and a whisper. That's why you've got to tread a little more lightly around Shri Chand, Little Master. It comes naturally to me, but you're going to have to learn these things yourself.'

Moonshi suddenly got to his feet. 'Look,' he said, pointing upward. 'Someone's challenging you.'

Even before I saw the crimson battle kite bobbing and soaring in the deep blue winter sky I could hear it crackling on the wind.

'He slows down before he dives,' Moonshi said as I hurried over to get my kite from its hiding place under Moonshi's charpoy. 'He must be somewhere near the old Savada House. Get him from below and you can take him, Little Master.'

My kite had been a gift from heaven that had crashed to the roof on a dusty morning, trailing a hundred feet of line. Moonshi and I had lashed its broken bow with thread and patched its tears with rice paste and tissue from the vegetable seller's stall. Moonshi had brought me scraps of string to add to the line and a carder's spool to roll it on, and then, when he thought I was ready, he'd spent his own money on ten yards of the best glass-encrusted battle line and coached me to victory after victory in the kite wars that raged high above the city.

I set my spool of string under one foot and tossed my kite up until it caught the wind off the river and rushed with a sharp flap just over the rooftops of the city, out of sight of the Savada House ruins.

'That's it, Little Master. Stalk him. Sneak up on him,' Moonshi murmured, moving his hands in imitation of my kite. 'Get him while he's showing off.'

Gingerly playing out the sharp, rasping foreline, I steered my kite over Faithfulganj and the British graveyard, and not until it was over the parade ground did I hoist it directly into the sky, crossing my challenger's line as he paused to attack.

'Get him now, Little Master. You've got him!'

Pumping my kite high into the air, I sawed at his string with my foreline, and severed it with a few hard strokes.

'That's it!' Moonshi exclaimed, punching at the air as the crippled kite zigzagged back to earth. 'That's it, Little Master. I tell you, there isn't a flyer in all of Avadh who can get the best of you.'

'*Boy!*' came a high desperate voice from below.

Moonshi froze for a moment and then rushed to the ladder, replying, in the abject whine he affected for professional purposes, 'Yes, excellency. Coming right away, excellency.'

Wrapping my line around the leg of Moonshi's charpoy, I rushed after him and looked down the length of the ladder to see Nanak Chand, his hair tangled and his eyes wild, shoving Moonshi into our room.

I scrambled down the ladder and ran through the doorway to find Moonshi standing over my mother. Half clothed and doubled over, she lay on her charpoy coughing with such violence that she couldn't seem to catch her breath.

'I didn't do anything! I didn't do anything!' Nanak Chand cried out as I ran to her. I tried to embrace her, but Moonshi pulled me away to give her air.

'Mistress,' Moonshi said softly, covering her shoulders with her blanket.

'We were just talking, passing the time of day,' Nanak Chand said as I glared up at him. 'That's all we were doing. And all of a sudden she starts to choke. What's wrong with her. Is she sick? If she's given me a sickness,' he said, grabbing Moonshi by the arm and spinning him around to face him, 'I'll have you all – '

For an instant Moonshi glared at him too, and seeing the hatred flash in Moonshi's eyes, Nanak Chand cut his threat short and gaped at him. 'You – you won't breathe a word of this, boy,' he stammered, releasing Moonshi's arm.

'Don't worry, excellency,' Moonshi said, leading Nanak Chand toward the door as my mother hacked and cringed into her bedding. 'She'll be all right. It's just the winter chill these past few nights. The dust, too. My mistress is delicate.'

'Not a word of this, I'm warning you,' Nanak Chand growled, flustered and insulted by Moonshi's assurances.

'No, no, excellency. You've got nothing to fear from us. We – '

'Nothing to fear?' Nanak Chand cried, angrily tying the sash to his tunic. 'Nanak Chand fears no one!'

Moonshi bowed low with a pained look, but continued to lead Nanak Chand to the door. 'Of course not, excellency. I only meant that your secrets are our secrets.'

Nanak Chand stood on the threshold, scowling at us.

'So perhaps if your excellency would find it in your heart to let her rest now so she may be refreshed for your next visit?'

'She'd better be,' Nanak Chand said, shaking his finger at her. 'I've no time to waste on sickly women.' And with that he flung a few coins to the floor and turned to go.

At that I ran at him, intending to push him down the stairs, but

Moonshi caught me and threw me back onto the floor, saying, 'No, no, Little Master. We mustn't delay his excellency further with our gratitude. Save your thanks for later.

'Go to the roof, Little Master,' Moonshi said, once Nanak Chand had bobbled down to the street.

'But I – '

'Do as he says, Balbeer,' my mother told me in a whisper. 'I'm all right.'

She smiled to show me she was all right. But I could see that she was not all right; something was missing in her eyes, as if a flame had been snuffed out.

'Go on, now,' Moonshi said, shooing me out the door. 'My mistress will be fine.'

I didn't remember about my kite until I reached the top of the ladder, but by then it was too late. In the still of the evening the kite had fallen onto the distant plain and my line had settled across the rooftops like a spider's strand.

CHAPTER

4

My mother's attacks grew much worse that winter, until she was too weak to manage the stairs. Nanak Chand still made his weekly calls, but he never stayed very long and always left with a haunted look, muttering to himself.

Moonshi did what he could to care for us, but without my mother's help he was soon overwhelmed, and certain chores began to fall to me. It became my job to build the cooking fire on the roof each evening, to keep the lamps filled with mustard oil, to settle with the dhobi when he brought our laundry. But the only chore that took me away from the safety of my exile was fetching my mother's medicine in the Moslem bazaar across the bridge.

For as far back as I can remember my mother had been a patient of a hakeem named Sayideen who had left his family's practice in

Lucknow a few years before the Devil's Wind and had set up shop in Cawnpore to treat the Moslem soldiers of the garrison. But when the British returned to punish the rebels, they killed or chased off Sayideen's patients and filled the ranks of their new Indian Army with low-caste Hindus, among whom Sayideen had to drum up business by adding cow's urine and Ganga water to his venerable Grecian remedies.

Fetching my mother's medicine meant I had to sneak through the stalls to avoid the children of my neighborhood, but it also meant freedom, and I remember dashing across the footbridge that spanned the Ganga Canal and rushing through the Moslem bazaar with a thrill of release.

Sayideen was a deliberate, bespectacled man with the henna beard of a Mecca pilgrim and a physician's air of disappointment in his fellow man. I had learned early that the more I tried to hurry Sayideen, the more I slowed him down.

'Do you suppose your mother is the only sick woman I have to care for?' he would ask me over his spectacles. 'We have a whole city full of sick people, and I have to take care of them one at a time.'

'But Hakeemji, she told me to run to you. She's choking.'

'It will pass, Balbeer. Now sit quietly beside me and I'll get around to your mother's medicaments when I can.'

Most of what kept Sayideen so busy seemed to me to be commerce. The patients who waited outside his stall for their treatments were always outnumbered by the patients waiting to settle their debts. I used to sit beside him for hours as sepoys, merchants, peddlers, and servants filed by with their installments, their indignant threats, or their abject excuses, all of which Sayideen equably forbore. He'd managed to convince all his patients that if he deprived them of his care they would all die, so he never had to employ badmashes to collect his fees; sooner or later everyone paid him.

Only after the last debtor had slumped out of his stall did Sayideen smile down at me and ask after my mother's health.

'She's worse,' I told him. 'Her cough's worse than ever.'

'A contradiction,' Sayideen said, shaking his head.

'But she just seems to be getting sicker.'

'No, no, no,' Sayideen said, removing two vials of powder from a studded wooden chest. '*She*'s not getting worse. *She*'s getting better. Her *cough* is getting worse.' He sprinkled a little of each powder onto the dish of a scale.

'But how — '

'Let me try to make you understand,' Sayideen said with a sigh peculiar to medical men. 'You see, when your mother was in hiding she — '

'In hiding?'

Sayideen put his hand on my head to quiet me. 'Never mind. A slip of the tongue. We're discussing your mother's ailment,' he said, removing the dish from the scale and stirring the powders together with a silver spoon that hung on a chain from his neck. 'When she was starved and alone and carrying you in her womb the vapors from the unburied dead of the city penetrated her bones and chilled her to her marrow.' He pointed to a skeleton painted on the wall behind him, around which vile humors in the forms of bats and snakes swirled and slithered, and he uncorked a little glass bottle.

'Ganga water,' he said with a sneer, holding the bottle in front of my eyes. 'And who can say,' he said in a mocking singsong, 'how many miracles it's performed?' He grudgingly sprinkled a few drops over the heap of powder. 'Anyway, to rid your mother of these deathly vapors we must help her body expel them, so I have devised a remedy which will intensify her coughing and rid her of her impurities.'

Sayideen rolled the wetted powder into a ball and wrapped it first in an edible leaf of silver and then in blue tissue. I tried to snatch it from him, but he held it out of reach and peered at me over his spectacles. 'Ah, ah, Balbeer. Have patience. Now, tell your mother to swallow this pill after sunset and tell her she's not to eat a scrap of food tomorrow, nor sip a drop of water if she can manage it, so the medicine can go to work. Can you remember all that?'

I nodded.

'Very well, then,' Sayideen said, slowly placing the pill in my hand. 'And Balbeer,' he called after me as I dashed down the street, 'I'll just put it on her bill.'

CHAPTER

5

Holi must have started out as a rite of spring before it became a festival of Krishna, but all it meant to the children of my neighborhood was a rampage in the streets and an end to the cool winter weather. As people doused one another with colored water tossed from buckets or pumped from brass syringes, the summer sun struck like a hammer.

Back in the Rajput court of Harigarh my mother and her sisters had celebrated Holi with decorum, squirting colored water at each other and giggling among the fountains of the Maharao's garden. So she regarded the brawling celebration in the city streets as beneath our dignity.

Before she became so sick she hadn't been above watching with me from the window as children ambushed each other in the alleyways, youths strutted about singing lewd songs at the top of their voices, and stern and disapproving elders were splashed and soiled with crimson dye. But during the last Holi I would spend with her she was too weak even to watch, and lay curled on her bed with her hands over her ears to block the din that arose from the streets.

'Look, Mataji,' I called down to her from my perch atop her trunk. 'The whole city's gone crazy!'

But she sat curled at the end of her bed with her hands over her ears and her eyes shut tight.

'Little Master,' I heard someone whisper from the doorway. It was Moonshi, dyed half yellow and half red, hiding from my mother in the hall. 'Come with me.'

I turned to ask my mother's permission, but Moonshi put a finger to his lips and shook his head. 'Come on,' he said, beckoning me toward him.

I slowly climbed down from the trunk and padded past my mother.

'Let her rest,' Moonshi said when I reached him. 'We've got

work to do.' He held a pail of water in one hand and now pointed up to the roof with the other.

I climbed up ahead of him and took the pail from him when he reached the top. 'Moonshi,' I said, 'what are you trying to – '

'Shh!' Moonshi said, creeping toward the rim of the roof. I looked down into the pail for a moment and then tiptoed along behind him, wondering why we had to be so quiet in the din from the streets.

'Look,' he said, pointing directly over the edge at the turban tops of none other than Mohinder and Bhagat, who were poised behind a coolie's cart to ambush a passerby below.

'Aren't they friends of yours?' Moonshi whispered, nudging my shoulder. 'It seems a shame to leave them out of the fun just because they're Sikhs.'

I peered down at them for a moment and felt my mouth go dry. 'But what if they – '

'Come on, Little Master,' Moonshi said. 'They'll never know what hit them.'

I looked at Moonshi, and when our eyes met (or anyway when my two eyes met one of his, for you remember he was wall-eyed) I held my breath and nodded.

'Careful,' Moonshi said as I brought the rim of the jug into position. 'Wait until I give the signal. Are you ready?'

I took a deep breath again. 'I'm ready.'

'All right then,' Moonshi said, cupping his hands and leaning over the edge of the roof. 'Ho sardarji!' he shouted down as loudly as he could. 'Sat sri akal!'

And just as the twins looked up to see who was shouting Sikhdom's sacred war cry I tipped the pail and the heavy blue tongue of water caught them full on their faces and knocked their turbans into the dirt.

If I hadn't been so eager to savor my little victory they might not have known who had ambushed them, but I couldn't stop staring down at them as they stomped and spat like fouled cats and clawed at the ground for their unravelled turbans.

A few days later, Nanak Chand travelled in his palanquin through the dye-splashed city and stopped at our home for a visit. If I reckon right I was almost seven years old by this time and I'd known Nanak Chand for at least two years – long enough, in any case, to see a decline in his fortunes.

A new Collector had been appointed to get the city back to normal, and the civil administrators who took over from the army were eager to put the Mutiny behind them. Consequently, Nanak Chand was less and less welcome around the government compound. He tried hard to keep the authorities' minds on the Mutiny by making more and more dramatic and outlandish accusations, even going so far as to drag an old sadhu in from the countryside and pass him off as the fugitive Nana Sahib himself.

These escalations backfired, of course, and Nanak Chand became a grim joke around the Collector's office – a sad, sputtering waiting-room fixture. It didn't take long for word of his disgrace to spread to the native quarter, and little by little his victims began to defy him. At first he hired badmashes to enforce his old arrangements, but his victims hired their own badmashes to oppose him, and soon his old arrangements were costing him more than they were worth.

Only a few of the weakest of his victims, or 'clients,' as he liked to call them, still kept up their payments or forgave him his debts, and none was weaker and more isolated than my mother. I don't know what brought Nanak Chand to our house even after my mother was too weak to greet him in her finery or attend to his needs. It may be that he loved her in his twisted fashion, or that he was too demoralized for lust, but all he wanted that day after Holi was someone to talk to.

'Stay with us, Little Turnip,' he said as I led him up the stairs. 'We'll all be one happy family.'

Though Nanak Chand never touched my mother during his last visits to her, the very sight of him crossing the threshold and spreading himself out on her bed was enough to send her into prolonged bouts of coughing, and as he launched into one of his self-pitying monologues she seemed to shrink before my eyes.

'Gratitude?' Nanak Chand began almost at once, as if we'd asked him a question. 'You think they're even capable of such a thing? Not the English,' he said, removing his bowler and setting it beside him on the bed. 'Gratitude's *beneath* them, you see. *Every-*

thing's beneath them, Little Turnip,' he said, motioning to me to sit beside him. 'You, your mother, even me – who knows? – even God when you get right down to it. You risk your life for them, you endure the envy and the bitterness and the hatred of your own people, you renounce your own father's ways to serve them, and do you know what they'll tell you? Are you listening, Little Turnip?'

I looked toward my mother and nodded.

'They will tell you that you're merely doing your *duty*. Your *duty*! And they don't reward you for doing your duty. Oh, no. Duty is what's expected. "Duty," says the Collector Sahib, "is its own reward." '

Seeing me next to Nanak Chand was making my mother anxious, and she directed me to bring her a cup of water.

'Water?' Nanak Chand exclaimed, sharply clapping his hands together. 'Are we reduced to water? Boy!' he called out, and when Moonshi appeared in the doorway he said, 'Bring limeade for everyone!' and smiled around at us as if he were our host.

'Pardon me, excellency,' Moonshi said, giving my mother an imploring look. 'I'm afraid we – '

'At once!' Nanak Chand commanded, still clinging to his smile.

'I'm sorry, Shri Chand,' my mother said in a small voice, 'but what Moonshi is trying to say is that we don't have any limes for – '

'Then get some!' Nanak Chand snapped at Moonshi, his feeble good nature exhausted. 'For God's sake, it's only a little trip downstairs.'

'But we – ' my mother began.

'*But we* what?' Nanak Chand blustered. He looked at my mother, at me, at Moonshi, and back at my mother again. 'Is it the money?' he exclaimed, catching on at last. 'Is that it? You can't afford to serve your guest a measly glass of limeade?'

'Well,' my mother said weakly, pulling her veil across her face to cover a cough, 'this time of year they're more than we can – '

'So,' Nanak Chand muttered, pouting and frowning as he fumbled among the folds of his dhoti for his change purse. 'It's up to your guest, is it? Hindustani hospitality, Little Turnip,' he said to me, throwing a coin in Moonshi's direction. 'Get used to it.'

My mother stared grimly at the floor and coughed into her fist as Moonshi hurried off to fetch the limes.

'And the money I left for you last time, Natholi?' Nanak Chand said, rolling his eyes and waggling one fat foot in irritation. 'What became of that? No, no. Never mind. A silly question,' he said with a sour smile. 'Forgive me. I can guess what became of it. Frills. Am I right? Trinkets. Gewgaws. My God, am I the only soul in this miserable city who has any respect for money?'

My mother's coughing worsened, and she turned toward the wall until she could regain her breath.

'Natholi,' Nanak Chand said, as if he'd been interrupted with a triviality. 'Natholi, I'm trying to talk to you.' Her coughing went on a moment longer, and Nanak Chand turned to me with complicitous exasperation. 'Your mother could waken the dead with all that hacking, couldn't she, Little Turnip?'

As my mother's coughing at last subsided, Nanak Chand's gaze lingered on me and he grasped my chin and turned my face toward him as if he'd found something new in my eyes: something of value.

'What's to become of my Little Turnip?' he wondered aloud. 'How are we going to provide for him, Natholi?'

My mother turned toward us again, wiping her lips with her veil and catching her breath. 'I have family in Rajputana, Shri Chand,' she said in a hoarse voice, her eyes narrowing at the sight of Nanak Chand's hand upon me. 'As you know.'

'Well, of course I know,' Nanak Chand said, releasing my chin. 'I know all about your family in Rajputana. But what good are they going to do him?'

'I've been in touch with them,' my mother said. 'I'm expecting word from them any day now.'

'A fairy tale,' Nanak Chand said with a dismissive shrug.

'They'll care for him.'

'Mataji?' I asked from Nanak Chand's side. 'Who do you mean?'

'Nonsense,' Nanak Chand interjected, putting his hand on my head to quiet me. 'If they cared about him they'd have taken you back years ago. Why should they care about him if they don't even care about you?'

'Baloo,' my mother said firmly, 'go see if Moonshi's returned.'

'No, no,' Nanak Chand said, throwing his heavy arm over my shoulders as I tried to rise. 'The boy should hear this.'

'Please. Shri Chand,' my mother said through her teeth.

'He has a right to know about his future, Natholi. And you can't just trust his future to a sentimental dream. Natholi, you and I both know you can't have much longer to – '

'Shri Chand!' my mother exclaimed, rising to her feet.

Nanak Chand slid back slightly on the bed and blinked up at her. 'Natholi,' he said uncertainly, 'I don't think I like your tone. You have no right to – '

'I am not going to discuss my son with you, Shri Chand,' my mother said, the old fire rising for a moment in her eyes.

'But,' Nanak Chand said, pointing at me, 'I insist we talk about it. I think you'd better start facing up to the facts, Natholi. It's a cruel world out there, and the boy is going to need all the friends he can get.'

My mother stiffened and the veil fell from her head and she stood as I now remember her best, with her long neck straight and her chin upraised, like a frail and defiant queen.

'I will not discuss this with you, Shri Chand,' she said calmly and firmly, as if addressing a child. 'Balbeer is my son and I will determine his future.'

Nanak Chand gaped up at her for a moment and then heaved himself off the bed and began clumsily to place his thick, spreading feet into his chappals. 'All right,' he said, grabbing his sweat-stained bowler. 'That does it. That's it. I show a little interest in your little bastard's future and you talk to me like this? Well, I don't have to put up with it. The disrespect,' he said thickly, his eyes reddening. 'The ingratitude. Don't you understand what the world is like out there?' he asked, pointing out the window with a pleading look, as if begging her not to send him back out into it.

'I think I do,' my mother said, slowly replacing her veil.

'Well, that's just fine,' Nanak Chand said, jerking his bowler onto his head. 'If you think you can survive it on your own, that's just fine with me. I'm not going to put up with this any longer. Not from you. Not any longer.'

'As you wish,' my mother said, taking my hand as I stepped toward her.

'I mean it this time,' Nanak Chand said with a hesitant step toward the door. 'This time you're on your own.'

'I have always been on my own,' my mother said, looking down at me.

'Have you really?' Nanak Chand sneered. 'Surely not *always*. Not from what *I've* heard.'

'Good day, Shri Chand,' my mother said with a slight bow.

'Don't you know about your mother, Little Turnip?' Nanak Chand said, grasping the door latch. 'Don't you know what sort of company she's kept?'

'*Goodbye*, Shri Chand,' my mother said, her grip tightening on my hand.

Nanak Chand opened his mouth to speak, but just then the door swung open and struck Nanak Chand's shoulder, and Moonshi appeared on the threshold with three limes in his hand.

Regaining his balance, Nanak Chand shoved Moonshi aside and stepped out the door, but just when we thought he was gone he turned about, grabbed the limes away from Moonshi, and shook them at us.

'Go on, then,' he called out as he heavily stomped down the stairs. 'Live without my protection for a while. See how you like it.

'But I'll be back!' he called out as he reached the street. 'You haven't seen the last of me!'

CHAPTER
6

I used to blame my mother for shielding me from the truth, but now I know better. Knowledge, like money, should be acquired a little at a time. Children should never have to look into their futures nor fathom their helplessness; if we were all told where our lives will lead us, how many of us would bother to finish the trip?

As Nanak Chand's bearers hoisted his palanquin onto their shoulders and trotted his bulk off into the simmering city, my mother kept hold of my hand and gazed down at me with her large, grave eyes. If Nanak Chand's insinuations had stirred up all my old, forbidden questions, my mother's sweet regard settled them down again.

But after a moment her grip went limp and she staggered backwards. Moonshi rushed to her side and helped her toward the bed, where she collapsed like a severed puppet.

'Mistress,' Moonshi said, looking panicked. 'What can I do?'

'Baloo,' my mother whispered back. 'Baloo, where are you?'

'*Here*, Mataji,' I said, still holding her arm.

'Yes,' she said, smiling weakly. 'There you are.' She reached forward, and I could see the veins risen up on her outstretched fingers.

'Baloo,' she said, her cold hand passing across my face like a shadow, 'don't you have any tears for your mother?'

'Mistress,' Moonshi said, moving me aside, 'I'll get Sayideen.'

My mother sighed, and her hand fell from my face. 'What for?' she asked vaguely, closing her eyes.

'Little Master,' Moonshi said, grabbing my arm and leading me away from the bed. 'Go get the hakeem.'

'But he won't come. He's too busy to – '

Moonshi shook me slightly. 'You *make* him come,' he said, pushing me toward the door.

'But how?'

Moonshi stopped for a moment and stared at my mother, biting his lip with indecision. Then, with a sharp intake of breath, he lunged toward my mother's bed and extracted a key from beneath her blanket.

'You'll keep your promise, Moonshi,' my mother said in a deepening whisper.

'Yes, mistress,' Moonshi replied as he worked the padlock on my mother's trunk.

'You'll take him back with you.'

Moonshi slowly lifted the trunk's lid.

'Moonshi!' my mother cried out, raising her head slightly, her long neck trembling. 'Promise me! Promise me again!'

'I promise, mistress,' Moonshi said, reaching into the trunk and fumbling through it.

'No matter what happens,' she said, easing her head back down.

'No matter what happens; yes, mistress,' Moonshi replied as he brought out a small painted wooden box.

'They'll take him back,' my mother whispered, rocking slightly on her side. 'They can't refuse him. Not once they've seen him. They can't blame him, Moonshi. It isn't his fault.'

'No, mistress,' Moonshi said, opening the box and delicately extracting a tiny stone.

'None of it is his fault,' my mother said, her voice fading off. 'You've got to make them understand . . . '

'Here,' Moonshi said, pressing the stone into my hand. 'Give this topaz to the hakeem. Say there's another for him if he comes. Now, hurry!'

I rushed to the door, but something told me to pause a moment and look back at my mother, whose voice had trailed off into a soft, almost musical moan.

'I said, *Go!*' Moonshi barked, pushing me forward, and I ran down the stairs.

The streets were almost empty in the afternoon glare, and I ran through them as fast as I could, praying I wouldn't be spotted by the neighborhood children. When I finally turned off my street and onto Bithur Road a pariah dog, crazed by the heat, ran behind me, snapping at my heels, but after a few yards he fell back and stood barking after me in the dust I kicked up from the street. As I neared the canal bridge I was light-headed and soaked with sweat but I kept running, fighting for every breath, my eyes fixed on the blur of the road before me, the little topaz nestled in my fist.

'Look!' a child's voice suddenly cried out as I loped along the bridge. 'It's the bastard!'

I stopped so suddenly I almost fell forward. Ahead of me at the end of the bridge stood Mohinder with his brother Bhagat and Sanjay, the oversized son of the pahn seller, all eating pakoras they'd probably filched from a tea stall.

'Who let *him* out?' Mohinder asked as loudly as he could.

The three stood side by side, blocking my way, and began to walk toward me, Bhagat and Sanjay grinning, awaiting Mohinder's command.

My mouth went dry and the sinews in my gut tightened like bowstrings. I began to back away with the intention of outracing them to the canal bridge further up the road, when I remembered a trick I'd watched Mohinder himself play on the indignant merchants who were always chasing him away from their wares. So I turned and began to run back off the bridge, and looking behind me, I saw that my three foes had taken up the chase.

'Make way!' Mohinder called out like a king's page. 'Make way for the bastard prince of Rajputana!'

I slowed the pace a little as the others took up the call, and soon they were only a yard or so behind me, their feet pounding in the dusty street, and just as I could feel Sanjay's hand brushing the back of my fluttering shirt I hurled myself sideways to the ground.

The ploy worked fine as far as it went; I sent them all sprawling into the street. But on his way down Bhagat struck me on the head with his foot, and for a moment I was too dazed to spring back to my feet and get away.

Sanjay was the first to recover and leapt upon me, followed by Bhagat, who took hold of my arms, and before I could regain my senses they had pinned me to the ground.

'Now we've got you,' Mohinder said, straightening his turban still stained blue from a few days before. 'Now we've got the little bastard.'

'I'm not a bastard,' I said, struggling in vain to free myself. 'Stop calling me that!'

'Of course you're not a bastard,' said Mohinder. 'Your father was – your father was – I forget. What was his name again?'

The blood flushed my face and my mind began to race in crippling confusion. 'You'd better shut up,' I said, the tears springing to my eyes.

'Who's going to make me?' Mohinder asked, his grin vanishing.

For a moment, as I had done so often on the roof, I tried to annihilate them by closing my eyes, but when I opened them again they still clung to my limbs and grinned down at me like demons. I groaned, and Sanjay chuckled at my despair, but for an instant I could feel his grip relax on my legs, and baring my teeth I shouted, 'Let me go!' and kicked one leg free with all my strength.

My foot flashed up and caught Mohinder on the bridge of his nose, and he fell back with a yelp as Sanjay regained control of my thrashing legs.

Mohinder fell back out of sight, but I could hear him moaning, and suddenly he was standing over me, his eyes burning and his nose bubbling blood.

'You'll pay for that,' Mohinder whimpered as he reached into his shirt and brought forth his penknife.

'What'll it be?' he asked, his pained face cracking into a grim smile as he dropped to his knees beside me.

A small crowd had gathered around us, and one old woman was crying out from the shade of her stall for someone to help, but no one made a move.

'Shall I pluck out your eye?' Mohinder asked, brushing my forehead with the tip of his blade. 'Or how about your tongue?' he asked, running the blade across my lips.

'I know what,' Bhagat said brightly. 'Let's write something on his forehead.'

'Good idea, brother,' said Mohinder, gripping the knife handle with both hands and steadying it over my brow. ' "Balbeer the Bastard" in nice, big letters.'

I strained with every fibre against Sanjay's and Bhagat's grip, and as the tip of Mohinder's blade neared my forehead I shut my eyes and screamed.

Suddenly I could feel Mohinder, Bhagat, and Sanjay being torn from my limbs and hurled into the air above me as if by the force of my cry, and when I opened my eyes I saw that a huge, homely, pockmarked face had passed across the heavens like a cloud.

'Get up!' it commanded in a voice like faraway thunder.

Weeping, I rolled over onto my side and saw Mohinder and his allies limping back toward our neighborhood.

'Here,' the giant said, gripping my arm and lifting me to my feet. His hand encased my entire forearm, and as he put me down I could only gaze up at him in astonishment. He was as tall as a camel, with the bulk of a bull. His face was long and drooping, with a protuberant brow and a great jaw that thrust his lower teeth forward.

'Stop crying,' he said sternly, releasing my arm and straightening to his full, impossible height. 'You can never let them see you cry again.'

I blinked hard and wiped my tears with my forearm.

'You are Balbeer Rao,' he said carefully, lowering his voice, as if 'Balbeer Rao' were a title and not a name, 'And you aren't your father's son just so you can shame him.'

I slowly nodded up at him, trying to calm my breathing.

'Those brats won't bother you again,' he said, turning and clearing a path for me through the little circle of onlookers which had formed around us. 'Now they know that Genda's your protector.'

And before I could thank him or ask him how he'd known my name, he'd rushed off in a few long strides and disappeared around a corner of the street.

I wanted to run after him, ask who he was, show him that despite my tears I had still had the mettle to keep my mother's topaz locked in my fist, but the stone itself then reminded me of my mission, and I rushed across the bridge again and dashed through the Moslem bazaar.

By the time I reached Sayideen's stall he had shut it up for the night and was inside performing his evening devotions.

'Hakeemji!' I shouted, banging on the shutters with my fists.

'I'm not here,' came his weary voice from within.

'Hakeemji, it's Balbeer. My mother, she's – '

'Sick,' he interjected. 'She's always sick. Go away.'

'But she's worse. She wants you to come.'

'To her? Now? Don't be ridiculous. Go home. I'll try to fit her in tomorrow morning.'

I stopped hitting the shutters with my fists and began to kick at them until they loudly rattled on their iron hinges. 'No,' I shouted back. 'I won't go home!'

'Stop that!' Sayideen shouted, but I kept kicking, a vision of Moonshi's panic-stricken face, of my mother's collapsed form, taking hold of me, although I suppose I had the twins to thank for the depth of my rage.

'Not until you see my mother!'

'Forget it!' Sayideen bellowed, and I kicked even harder. Another set of onlookers gathered, some of Sayideen's debtors among them, and they began to cheer me on.

'Stop it!' Sayideen shouted from just behind the shutters.

'No!' I shouted back, and a cheer went up around me.

For a moment all was silent inside Sayideen's stall, and I stood back, my feet aching. 'Very well, very well,' Sayideen finally said, undoing the latch from inside. 'Just stop kicking.'

Another cheer rose up as the shutters opened and Sayideen appeared in his lounging robe, putting on his spectacles.

'Now then,' he said, looking down at me and affecting a sheepish grin. 'What's the problem?'

'I told you,' I said, emboldened by the crowd. 'My mother needs you and you must come.'

'Yes,' Sayideen said, grinning around at the onlookers and stepping down from the platform of his stall. 'Yes, I suppose I must.'

And then suddenly he reached out and grabbed me by the ear and shook me, and the fickle crowd began to howl with laughter.

'You dare to interrupt my prayers, you little infidel son of a bitch?' he hissed, his glasses slipping down his nose. 'You dare to tell Sayideen the hakeem what to do?'

I tried to move with him as he sharply tugged at my ear. 'But I have something for you,' I said through gritted teeth. 'Look.' And I held out my fist and opened it.

Sayideen stopped shaking me and pushed his spectacles back into position to look at the little stone stuck to the sweat of my palm.

'What's this?' he asked, plucking it away and releasing me.

'A topaz,' I said, rubbing my ear and wincing.

'A topaz?' Sayideen said, holding it up in the evening light. 'Where did *you* get a topaz?'

'It's for you,' I said, 'and there's another for you if you come.'

'It *is* a topaz,' someone exclaimed in the crowd.

Sayideen closed his hand over the stone. 'Can it be true what they say about her?' he muttered, peering down at me through his spectacles.

'Hakeemji?'

'So she's sick, you say?' he asked aloud, giving me an appraising look.

'Yes,' I said. 'Please, Hakeemji. Hurry.'

'Very well,' Sayideen said, tucking the topaz into his change purse and patting the sash of his robe. 'Just give me a chance to get my case and lock up in here.' And as the murmuring crowd drifted away he brought out a papier-mâché box and hung it on his shoulder with a tasseled strap, closed the shutters to his stall, and secured them with a padlock.

'Come on then,' he said, turning to face me. 'We don't have all night.'

CHAPTER

7

I strutted ahead of Sayideen through the streets like a triumphant general with a captive king. There was no sign of my three foes as we reached my neighborhood, and the few children who still hung about the street watched me pass in sullen silence, just as Genda had promised. Tomorrow, I told myself as we neared my home, I would play in the streets again.

'I got him!' I called out as I hurried up the stairs. 'Moonshi, look! I got the hakeem!'

But there wasn't any answer, and stopping halfway up the stairs I saw something move in the gloom of the landing.

'Moonshi?' I said, slowly taking another step.

I heard a shuddering exhalation of breath and then Moonshi stepped forward in dismal silhouette.

'I brought him,' I said, pointing down at the plodding and muttering hakeem.

Even when I reached the landing I still couldn't see Moonshi clearly, and he backed away, his movements quick and urgent, like a bird's.

'Up here, Hakeemji!' I called down.

'I'm coming,' Sayideen said. 'Be patient.'

Moonshi bowed low, still keeping his distance as Sayideen

joined us on the landing. 'Hakeemji,' he said thickly. 'Thank you for coming.'

'I'm a hakeem,' Sayideen said. 'This is my duty.'

'Yes, Hakeemji,' Moonshi began, 'but I'm afraid you – '

'This way, Hakeemji,' I interrupted, stepping toward the door. 'My mother's in here.'

'Wait,' Moonshi said, covering the latch with his hand.

I stepped back and peered up at him. 'But Mataji needs – '

'Hakeemji,' Moonshi said, turning away from me, 'we were wrong to trouble you.'

'But,' I stammered, 'you sent me. You *told* me to get the hakeem.'

'Hush, boy,' Sayideen said, placing a hand on my shoulder. 'What happened, Moonshi?'

Moonshi's hand went up to his brow. 'She . . . fell asleep,' he said with a deep breath.

'What about her medicine?' Sayideen asked.

'We ran out,' Moonshi said, his voice trailing off.

'Then why didn't you come to me for more?'

'The money, Hakeemji,' Moonshi said, disguising his irritation with a slight bow.

'The money?' Sayideen exclaimed. 'What was a couple more rupees going to do? She owes me a fortune already. Typical,' he said, turning toward the wall. 'Just when we start getting somewhere she starts worrying about the money.'

In my heart I understood what you by now must know had happened. My chest would only admit the shallowest breaths, and I felt as if Moonshi's and Sayideen's shadowy forms were engulfing me, as if the walls were closing on me like the doors to a vault. But I told myself that I didn't understand, and I threw my weight against the door.

'Mataji!' I cried out as I hurtled into the room. 'Mataji, I'm home!'

Moonshi lunged forward to stop me, but seeing he was too late he collapsed to his knees by the door and covered his face with his hands.

The only light in the room was a mustard lamp whose flame fluttered and shrank in the burst of air fanned up by the door, and only after it flared up again and cast its faint aureole did I catch sight of my mother's recumbent form stretched out in the middle of the floor.

'Oh, Little Master,' Moonshi sobbed as Sayideen stepped by him and entered the room.

'Mataji?' I said, dropping to my knees beside her. 'I brought the hakeem for you.'

Sayideen stood beside me and stared down at her as he reached into his little sack of cures and brought out a small glass bottle.

'She can't hear you,' Sayideen said, unstopping the bottle and handing it to me. 'But give her this.'

I gave him a puzzled and hopeful look.

'It's Ganga water,' Sayideen said with a slight shake of his head. 'It's your custom.'

But I still refused to understand. 'Here, Mataji,' I said, tugging on her sari. 'Here's something to drink.'

Baloo? Is that you? my mother asked, her eyes fluttering open as I tugged on her blanket one thunderclapped night.

But now as I jostled her and brought the bottle to her lips, her head merely rolled toward me slightly with a small noise, like the sound of a breaking thread. She stared beyond me from beneath her half-closed eyelids, and her face was the face of a stranger – indifferent, remote, content; the flesh clinging to her skull like wet silk. My hand began to shake so much that I spilled a few drops from the bottle onto her temple, and they crept along the slant of her jaw and gathered in the hollow of her cheek.

I fought my tears a moment longer and swallowed back the sob that welled up at the base of my throat, as if by staving off my grief I could confound my mother's death. I reached forward to brush the water from her face, gently, so as not to disturb her sleep; but once I had felt her cold, imperturbable flesh against my fingertips I fell back weeping into Moonshi's embrace.

Moonshi didn't have much time to comfort me. Sayideen, who dabbled in astrology, told us that if we intended to cremate my mother we had to get it done before the moon reached its zenith, for the next day the most treacherous caprices would prevail.

So Moonshi gathered a handful of precious stones, and leaving Sayideen behind to guard the rest of my mother's goods, rushed off with me in tow to do the needful. First we hunted up three able-bodied brethren of our Rajput caste to officiate at her cremation, women mourners to prepare my mother's corpse, and a barber to shave me bald for the procession to the ghats. Such was my mother's reputation, as both prostitute and princess, that Moonshi had to pay everyone double the usual rate, which left him little with which to purchase the paraphernalia ritual required: poles, a shroud, a magenta coverlet, incense, flowers, rice, curds, thread, sandalwood, and a dozen other bits of junk.

When we brought everyone and everything back up to our room we found Sayideen still waiting, sitting atop the trunk with his arms folded, like a faithful old guard, barely acknowledging our return.

While the mourners washed my mother's face with milk curds and wrapped her in the shroud, the brethren fashioned a stretcher for her out of a palm-frond mat and the two bamboo poles.

'Is he all there is left of the family?' one of the Rajput brethren asked, looking down at my tear-streaked face and working a fingernail between two of his teeth.

'Yes,' Moonshi said, still weeping himself as the mourners covered my mother's body with the coverlet and scattered flowers on her breast.

'No brothers left? Not even a cousin?'

'In Rajputana,' Moonshi said hopelessly, gripping Sayideen's receipt in one hand and gathering me to his side with the other. 'Not here.'

The Rajput shook his head slightly and made a smacking sound with his lips. 'Then he'll have to do,' he said, turning to the scowling old barber. 'Get him ready.'

Sighing heavily, the barber brought a folded straight razor out of his waistcloth and grabbed me by the arm. 'Put your hands on your knees, boy,' he said, opening the razor and pressing his fingertips onto the top of my head.

I did as I was told, and the old man's razor began to scrape across my scalp, leaving a strange chill in its wake, and as my hair tumbled to the floor I began to whimper and tremble.

'Damn it, boy, get a hold of yourself,' the old man said as his blade nicked the rigid edge of my ear. 'Look what you made me do. Now hold still,' he said, dabbing at the little blossom of blood with his sleeve.

The brethren began to debate the proprieties of burning a Rajput widow. The oldest of them believed that widows could only be properly disposed of on their husbands' pyres, as in the old days. But the others reminded him that women were frail creatures and no husband could expect his wife to break British laws in order to obey divine prescriptions. Just the same, the old man replied, his own mother had committed sati, and as far as he was concerned she'd been the last true Hindu wife he'd ever known.

So what was left? the others wondered. Did my mother's sins disqualify her from sanctified cremation?

'We'd better agree among ourselves about that before we get to the ghat,' the youngest said.

'Well,' the barber grumped, shaking my hair from his sleeve, 'if you aren't agreed about that, what did you take the boy's money for?'

'Because we're her brethren, and you're nothing but a barber,' the third one snapped.

The barber chuckled bitterly and shook his head.

'Did any of us even know her?' the third said. 'She used to pass our women on the street like *they* were the sinners. Too good for them. Too refined. A rani. And here we are fussing over her like she was our sister.'

The youngest looked at me for a moment. 'Well, she *was* our sister. We're her brethren, and we seem to be all this little fellow has left.'

'But she was a whore, wasn't she? Or are you forgetting the fat man's visits?'

'I'm not forgetting anything,' the youngest Rajput said as I looked up into his kindly eyes. *Be my father*, I wanted to beg him. *Take me as your son.* 'You're forgetting how we wept over old Barfi when she passed on, how we fawned upon her corpse.'

'That was different,' the third replied without conviction.

'That *was* different, wasn't it?' the young one said. 'You were one of her best clients.'

'She was my friend, not just a whore.'

'And so was Natholi Rao. Maybe not a friend to you, but a friend to somebody, and this little fellow's mother. Besides, all we're doing is taking her to her judgment.'

'That's right,' the oldest said, watching as the barber worked the blade across my temple. 'Let's let God worry about her sins.'

Out of the corner of my eye I could see Moonshi press his palms together and bow down with relief.

'Done,' the barber said, standing back and closing his razor.

I slowly straightened and reached up to feel my smooth and alien scalp.

'Let's go, then,' the youngest Rajput said, laying the stretcher down beside my mother. 'Are you women ready?'

The mourners daubed a crimson line across my mother's forehead and stood, gathering their veils across their faces.

'Well, then,' the young Rajput said. 'Let's hear you.'

The mourners ducked their heads and cleared their throats. 'Ram, Ram, Ram,' one of them whined, and then, as if displeased with her delivery, she swallowed hard and started again, this time at a higher pitch, punctuating her whine with calculated sobs. 'Ram, Ram, Ram, hai Ram, hai Ram, Ram, Ram . . . '

The brethren lifted my mother onto the stretcher, and with Moonshi taking the end of one pole, they all hoisted her onto their shoulders.

'Light as a bird, isn't she?' the youngest said, grinning at the oldest, who stood grunting and glowering as he tried to fit the pole into a hollow of his bony shoulder.

'Go on, boy,' he said to me. 'You go first.'

I looked around the room for a moment, and met the gaze of Sayideen, still perched atop my mother's trunk and now gravely waving me forward.

'Let's go, boy,' the oldest growled, and I led everyone out the door.

The sweets seller was working late that night, and his bubbling cauldrons of milk and syrup sent a dense, sugary steam up the stairwell. Moonshi and the brethren descended the stairs with difficulty, trying to keep the stretcher flat, my mother rocking upon it like an effigy in a procession.

Once outside, they carried her at a near-trot, the two stooped mourners lagging behind, Moonshi calling out directions as we wove through the black streets. We passed a few people along the way, but the brethren didn't pause to give them the customary look at my mother's face, and in any case the passersby seemed hurried and indifferent as they rushed home through the treacherous shadows and sidestreets of the city.

My feet fell heavily and my body was bathed in sweat, but my shaven head felt cold and giddy in the night air, as if I were holding it at a frigid altitude. I rushed along in a daze, determined not to look behind me, trying not to hear the brethren's muttering and the mourners' faltering chant.

As we crossed the footbridge the Ganga Canal sparkled with the reflected lights from the houses leaning along its banks and the voices of families gathered inside for supper and sleep echoed off its surface. Marching toward the river road, I began to entertain the most fantastic notions: of my mother passing us on the street; of my father as I imagined him – lean, soft-spoken, grave – stepping out of a doorway to claim me; and later, where the street was lined with ruins, I was gripped by the inexplicable fear that if I turned around I would not see Moonshi and the grunting brethren but a great bejewelled and smirking pig joggling along behind me.

CHAPTER
8

'Let's rest here,' the oldest of the Rajputs wheezed as we neared the river road.

'Rest?' laughed the youngest. 'Come on. We're almost there.'

'Straight down to the river!' Moonshi called out to me breathlessly.

I led them over the ruins of a tomb, and at last we reached the burning ghat a few yards from the familiar and forbidden Shivaite temple. The ghat was deserted and unilluminated but for a few faint embers from the ashes of a pyre and the halfmoon climbing through the haze over the water.

Moonshi and the brethren put my mother down on a step and stood for a moment, stretching their arms and groaning.

'Ram, Ram, Ram, hai Ram ... ' the mourners were still chanting when they caught up with us, too winded to wail properly.

'Where is everybody?' one of them asked, cutting the chant short, 'Where are the domri? Where's the priest?'

'Didn't you notify them?' the youngest Rajput asked Moonshi.

Still trying to catch his breath, Moonshi slumped down onto a step and hopelessly shook his head.

'Brilliant,' said the oldest, rubbing his shoulder. 'You mean I've wrenched my back for nothing?'

'Oh, leave him alone,' the youngest said with a sigh. 'That was our job, anyway.'

'*Your* job, maybe,' said the oldest. 'Not mine.'

'All right – *my* job, then,' the youngest exclaimed, cupping his hands over his mouth and taking a few steps up toward the temple. 'Domriji?' he called out, his voice sailing up into the gloom. 'Ho, domriji!'

I sat beside Moonshi and leaned my head against his shoulder. In the dark my mother's shrouded form looked too small to contain her.

'Moonshi?' I asked in a halting whisper.

'What is it, Little Master?' Moonshi miserably replied.

'What are we going to do?'

'The domri will come,' Moonshi said, patting my shoulder. 'Don't worry.'

'No,' I said, watching the mourners squatting like dark, plump birds by my mother's corpse. 'I mean after. What are we going to do after tonight?'

Moonshi's patting slowed, and he straightened slightly. 'We're going to go back, Little Master,' he said without conviction. 'Just like I promised your mother.'

'To Harigarh?' I asked, sliding my head onto his chest.

'Yes, Little Master. To Rajputana, far away.'

'But how are we going to get there?'

'We'll get there,' Moonshi said. 'We'll just get there.'

'But how?' I persisted, if only to sustain the soothing resonance of his voice against my ear.

'We'll walk if we have to,' Moonshi said. 'But we'll get there.' And then he added, as if to remind himself, 'I can't go back on my promise.'

A little distance along the riverbank we saw a torchlight wavering toward us, and as it approached we could hear a chinking noise, like a dull bell being tapped.

'I got them,' the young Rajput announced cheerfully as he came into view. 'A little sleepy, maybe, but ready to do the job.'

Beside him stood two tall men holding long metal poles like cowherds' staffs. Their arms and legs were pale grey with ash, and their eyes were so deeply set in their skulls that all I could see of them was a faint glint, like moonlight on a tear.

'Where's the body?' one of them asked in a voice like rustling leaves, holding up his torch.

'Over here,' said Moonshi, standing and bowing slightly, for though the domri were outcastes this was their territory and their unspeakable duties gave them a peculiar power.

The two domri walked to where my mother lay and stared down at her for a moment.

'How long has she been dead?' one of them asked, walking around my mother's bier and stroking his chin.

'Since this afternoon,' Moonshi said, pulling me to my feet beside him.

'What do you think?' the dom said to his partner. 'We got enough left over from the last job?'

'Depends,' said the other. 'How quickly do you want this over with?' he asked, turning to Moonshi and me.

Moonshi pointed up to the halfmoon climbing in the hazy sky. 'Before the zenith.'

The dom leaned against his pole and thought for a moment. 'That'll take ghee,' he said. 'Lots of it. You bring any with you?'

'Of course he didn't,' the oldest Rajput said with a sneer. 'You're lucky he remembered to bring the body.'

Moonshi bowed his head. 'We didn't have any ghee to bring,' he said softly.

'Then that'll cost you extra,' said the dom with the torch. 'Plus you reckon we're going to be here all night . . . '

'I know,' said Moonshi. 'I expected that. How much more, though? Quickly.'

The unhurried dom stroked his chin again. 'It'll cost you thirty all together,' he said.

'Yes,' said his partner. 'Thirty ought to do it.'

'Then take these,' Moonshi said, bringing two more of my mother's gemstones out of the folds of his dhoti. 'I don't have any cash.'

'And no wonder,' said the youngest Rajput, snatching one of the gems away before the domri could get hold of it and pressing it into my hand. 'One of those stones is more than enough,' he said, closing my fingers over it and winking. 'Don't be so eager to turn this boy into a pauper.'

The dom snatched the remaining stone from Moonshi's palm and glowered at the brethren. 'Emerald,' one of them muttered, peering at the stone in the torchlight. 'A few carats. Too smoky. Badly cut . . . '

'Not enough,' the other said, turning toward me. 'We need more. Give us the other stone.'

'Don't do it,' the youngest of the brethren said. 'They're trying to cheat you.'

I held the stone for a moment, looking around at everyone, then my eyes fell on my mother's form again, waiting in the shadows cast by the domri's torch. 'Here,' I said at last, handing the dom the stone and shrinking back as he plucked it away with his long, ashen fingers.

'Well,' the Rajput said with a sad shake of his head, 'I did what I could.'

'All right,' said the dom, 'this will do it. Do you have a priest?'

'No,' the youngest said. 'They refused to come.'

'We should have a priest,' said the oldest. 'What's the point without a priest?'

'Look,' the youngest answered, his good humor exhausted. 'You want a priest? *You* go get one. We're lucky we got the domri to come at this hour. We're lucky they've even let us onto the ghats.'

The domri lit a little fire under a pitcher of ghee and began to drag firewood down to a stone ramp that extended into the black water.

'All right,' one of the domri said as he piled a final armload of twisted roots and branches onto the little heap of wood. 'Bring her down here.'

'Come with me, Little Master,' Moonshi said in a cracking voice, stooping down to help lift up my mother's bier.

He and the brethren hoisted it to their shoulders once again, and I followed them as they gingerly stepped down through the shadows to where the domri waited. They set her down gently, but a branch gave way beneath her and left her lying at a precarious tilt, which the domri had to correct by poking at the pyre with their poles.

'Now,' Moonshi said as the brethren stood back, 'you're going to have to be strong, Little Master. Just do as I tell you, all right?' he said, beckoning to the dom with the torch. 'Hold this,' he commanded, taking the torch and passing it to me. 'Now repeat after me: *God's name is truth, God's name is truth . . .* '

'But why should – ' I asked, gripping the torch with both hands and holding it over my head.

'Just do as I say,' Moonshi said. '*God's name is truth, God's name –* '

'*– is truth,*' I whispered back at him as the torch sputtered above me.

'That's good,' Moonshi said, taking my hand and leading me around the pyre. 'But keep it up, Little Master. *God's name is truth, God's name is truth . . .* '

'*God's name is truth, God's name is truth,*' I said after him as we circled the pyre once, twice, until I was stumbling beside him and the chant had become a question on my lips: ' . . . *Is truth God's name? Is truth God's name?*'

After another circuit around the pyre Moonshi stopped me and, taking hold of my shoulders, turned me around to face my mother.

'We're almost done now, Little Master,' he said as one of the domri tucked a pillow of bundled twigs beneath my mother's head and stepped off the pyre.

His partner began to pour hot ghee in a thick, golden trickle over my mother's form, turning her crimson shroud black in the dim light.

'Keep chanting,' Moonshi said as the domri spread a few more branches atop my mother.

'*God's name is truth*,' I repeated once in what was left of my voice.

'Now all you have to do,' Moonshi whispered, his hands tightening on my shoulders and pushing me forward, 'is drop the torch.'

But as I looked down at my mother's glistening, spattered shroud my voice left me soundlessly mouthing Moonshi's chant and my limbs began to tremble.

'Go on, Little Master,' Moonshi said. 'Quickly. Before the moon descends. You can do it.'

'*Now!*' the youngest of the brethren barked, and with a gasp I finally dropped the torch at my feet.

Flames leapt up from the ignited ghee and with a hungry roar spread across my mother's shroud.

'Good,' Moonshi said, his voice cracking as he pulled me away from the flames. 'You did it, Little Master. Now she's free.'

Through the forest of flame I saw my mother's shroud explode and her black form begin to peel away, flying off layer by layer like papers in a sudden wind.

'Don't look, Little Master,' Moonshi said, trying to turn my face against his stomach. 'It's forbidden.'

But I twisted my face back toward her and for an instant saw, as her last garment disintegrated in the flames, her abeyant, oblivious face.

'Mataji!' I cried into the sour folds of Moonshi's shirt. 'Mataji, please! Mataji, don't go!'

'Stop it,' Moonshi said as his chest began to heave with sobs. 'Please stop, Little Master. Please don't cry.'

The three brethren took leave of us then, and the mourners followed after them up the steps, leaving Moonshi and me to keep our vigil as the sparks that bore my mother's soul soared up toward the divided moon.

All night long the domri tended my mother's pyre: coaxing it, feeding it, poking at the core of the blaze beneath her bones. By the time I finished weeping the moon was slipping behind the temple's dome on the riverbank's rim, and Moonshi had fallen asleep. At first

I tried to waken him, but he slept so soundly and looked so tired, slumped back against a rise in the embankment, that I gave up and let him be. After all, the vigil was mine to keep, so I sat near him with one hand on his arm, comforting myself that I was his guardian and my mother's sole protector.

Staring into the fire I promised my mother that I would stay awake until morning. But it was a child's vow and quickly broken. The forbidden flames put me into a trance, and through the night I ferried back and forth between consciousness and sleep, so that to this day I can't disentangle my memories of that night from my dreams. You would think that when I heard paper crackling high above me and looked up to see my mother hovering over the river in the bow of a golden kite, waving down with a sad smile to her earthbound son, I must have been dreaming; and that when her skull came loose and rolled down from the pyre's summit, spewing sparks at my feet, I was probably awake. But on that night my mother was burning and I had set her on fire, and if that was true then anything was possible: even the kite, even the urgent, incomprehensible whispering of my mother's skull as it was chased back into the flames by the domri's poles.

CHAPTER

9

'This is the poor lad?' someone was saying as I opened my eyes to the morning light.

'Yes, Reverend Sahib,' a thin, familiar voice answered. 'My poor Little Turnip.'

I blinked up through the smoke and saw Nanak Chand, unmistakable in his bowler, standing with a tall figure dressed in black from head to foot.

'And this was his mother's pyre?' Nanak Chand's companion asked in crisp, formal Hindi.

'Yes, Reverend Sahib,' Nanak Chand replied lugubriously. 'Such a good woman. Such a humble woman.'

'And a *widow*.'

'Yes, yes, Reverend Sahib. Just as I told you.'

'And no family left at all?'

'None,' said Nanak Chand with a shake of his head. 'My poor Little Turnip is an orphan.'

No more than a wavering shadow through the dense smoke, the figure looked headless for a moment, like a ghost, so closely did the color of the smoke match his face and whiskers. But when he stepped through the smoke and looked down at me I could see at last that he was no ghost but an Englishman.

'Moonshi!' I whispered, shaking his arm, 'Moonshi, wake up!'

Moonshi only groaned a little and turned his head away.

'Stand up, lad,' the Englishman said, staring at me with his colorless eyes as he held his hand out toward me.

'Do what the Reverend Sahib tells you,' Nanak Chand said, standing behind the Englishman.

I kept shaking Moonshi, my eyes fixed on the Englishman's pale hand with its sharp red knuckles and long crooked nails.

'Little Turnip,' Nanak Chand said, leaning around the English-man's shoulder. 'Where are your manners?'

'No, no, my friend,' the Englishman said with a smile. 'Don't be so harsh with the lad. Not after what he's been through.'

'You're too kind, Reverend Sahib,' Nanak Chand said with grim sincerity, glowering at me as he bowed.

Still prodding at Moonshi with one foot, I finally stood up and pressed my hands together in greeting.

'I am Reverend Weems,' the Englishman said, still holding out his hand.

'Take his hand, Little Turnip,' Nanak Chand growled.

But I only stared back at him with my palms still joined before me.

'No, no,' the Englishman said with a thin smile. 'Like *this*, lad,' and he captured my right hand in his and squeezed it.

The Reverend probably thought he was doing me an honor, but I was so horrified by the touch of his skin (if it was skin at all and not some abominable membrane, like the hide of a worm) that I pulled my hand away and stumbled backward over Moonshi's form.

'What is it?' Moonshi called out, scrambling blindly to his feet. 'Little Master! Where are you?'

'Who is this?' the Englishman said as I rushed over and threw my arms around Moonshi's legs.

'Just a servant,' Nanak Chand hissed. 'He won't affect our arrangement.'

'What is your name?' the Reverend asked Moonshi, sniffing slightly in the smoke.

For a moment Moonshi stood dumbfounded, trying to keep his balance in my fierce embrace. 'Moonshi Lal, burra sahib,' he said in his best servile whine, folding his hands together and lowering his gaze to the black, ash-strewn stone at our feet.

'Moonshi Lal, is it?' the Reverend said, raising his chin and giving Moonshi a suspicious squint. 'And who are you, Moonshi Lal?'

'I'm – I'm – '

' – a servant,' Nanak Chand interjected. 'Believe me, Reverend Sahib. That's all he – '

'Shri Chand,' the Reverend said, holding up one hand. 'We must do this properly. Now, Moonshi Lal, you were about to say?'

Moonshi lowered his head still further. 'A servant,' he said, subduing his whine.

'A servant to whom?' the Reverend asked, now tucking in his chin and clasping his hands behind him.

'To my mistress,' Moonshi said. 'Shrimati Natholi Rao.'

'To your *late* mistress, if I am not mistaken?'

Moonshi shut his eyes for a moment. 'To my late mistress, burra sahib.'

'My sympathies.'

'And now to my Little Master,' Moonshi said. 'Shri Balbeer Rao.'

'You mean the boy?' the Reverend said, looking down at me with one eyebrow arched.

'Yes, burra sahib,' Moonshi said, unfolding his hands and placing them on my head.

'Just as I said,' Nanak Chand muttered. 'He's just a servant, Reverend Sahib. No more.'

'Shri Chand,' the Reverend said without looking back at him, 'I must satisfy myself.'

'And what became of the boy's father?' the Reverend asked Moonshi. 'Is he still with us?'

I looked up at Moonshi, waiting, too, to hear his answer. 'No, burra sahib,' Moonshi replied at last.

'Then may I ask what your plans are for this boy now?'

'He hasn't any plans,' Nanak Chand said. 'He can't have. He's only a servant. The Reverend Sahib shouldn't have to bother – '

'Shri Chand,' the Reverend said, his lips barely moving, 'stay out of this.'

Moonshi looked down at me, his wall-eyed gaze even more unfocussed than usual, as he stammered to reply. 'I – *we* – are going back to Rajputana.'

'To where?' asked the Reverend.

'This is nonsense,' Nanak Chand grumbled, turning away and pouting at the yellow river.

'To Rajputana, burra sahib,' Moonshi said.

'Look me in the eye, Moonshi Lal,' the Reverend said. 'Let us discuss this man to man. Now, why do you plan to go to Rajputana?'

Moonshi warily lifted his gaze, glanced for an instant at the Reverend's face, and ducked his head again. 'Because I promised my mistress, burra sahib.'

'She was out of her senses toward the end,' Nanak Chand muttered, craning toward the Reverend's sunburned ear.

'And what's in Rajputana?' the Reverend asked, ignoring Nanak Chand.

'His family,' Moonshi replied.

'Family?' the Reverend exclaimed, scowling at Nanak Chand.

'Proof!' Nanak Chand cried, stepping toward us. 'Ask him for proof!'

'Shri Chand,' the Reverend snarled, turning his back on us and clenching his fists, 'if you've brought me out here to no purpose . . .'

'What sort of family?' Nanak Chand demanded.

'My – my mistress's brother,' Moonshi answered, dropping his whine and glaring at Nanak Chand. 'The Little Master's uncle.'

'Uncle? Brother?' asked Nanak Chand. 'Then what's his name? Eh? Tell me that!'

Moonshi's hands jumped from my head, and for a moment he fidgeted with his shirt.

'Well?' Nanak Chand persisted.

'His name is Shri – '

'Not *you*,' Nanak Chand barked. 'The *boy* has to tell us. Tell us, Little Turnip. What is this uncle's name?'

I didn't know, of course, and before I could summon the wit to invent a name, Nanak Chand had whirled around to retrieve the Reverend, who was making an elaborate show of walking away.

'See, Reverend Sahib?' Nanak Chand said. 'It's a fairy tale. There's no uncle in Rajputana. You didn't know this woman,' Nanak Chand said, kicking aside an ember. 'She was deranged. Lived on dreams. Thought she was a princess.'

The Reverend stopped and slowly turned around, poised above us on the stone steps.

'If she was a princess, why did she live in such squalor?' Nanak Chand went on. 'If she had family in Rajputana, why didn't she seek them out herself? And even if she does have a brother somewhere, what sort of man can he be if he let his own sister – and his own nephew – live like paupers, live in such disgrace? I tell you, burra sahib, uncle or no uncle the boy has no family.'

As the Reverend pondered Nanak Chand's exposition, Moonshi gave me a despairing look and pressed my shaved head into the hollow of his stomach.

'Shri Chand does have a point, Moonshi Lal,' the Reverend said, stepping down to us again.

'My mistress was a noblewoman,' Moonshi said softly. 'From the court of Harigarh.'

'And so every servant will claim his mistress is a noblewoman,' Nanak Chand said with a sneer. 'The bazaars are full of maharanis.'

'I want to believe you, Moonshi Lal,' the Reverend said, rubbing his chin and gazing off at the low, veiled sun. 'But I'm afraid the authorities are going to demand proof. Don't you have papers of some sort? A will, perhaps?'

Moonshi shook his head after a moment. 'I – I don't think so. But they were her last words, burra sahib,' he said. ' "Promise me," she said. "Promise me you'll take him home." '

'She was very sick, wasn't she?' the Reverend asked gently.

'Yes, burra sahib,' Moonshi replied, his voice breaking.

'And she suffered terribly,' the Reverend said, his eyebrows upraised.

'Yes, terribly, burra sahib,' Moonshi said, weeping openly now.

'And when people are so sick they say strange things, don't they, Moonshi Lal?' said the Reverend. 'Delirium sets in. Phantoms speak to them. But God forgives them for what they say, because He knows the flesh is weak. And I think we must do the same, Moonshi Lal.

'Boy,' the Reverend said, squatting down in front of me like a great blond crow, 'do you know what I do?'

I hugged Moonshi's legs more tightly, terrified that the Reverend might touch me again.

'I help boys like you – boys who have lost their mothers and fathers, their homes, their whole families. I come to them at their darkest hours and I take them by the hand and bring them home with me and they become a part of my family. And where there were tears I bring laughter, and where there was darkness I shine an eternal light. Do you understand?'

I turned my face away and shuddered.

'I have a home for you, Bambeer Rao – '

'Um, *Bal*beer Rao,' Nanak Chand gently corrected the Reverend.

'What's the difference?' the Reverend snapped back, and then, softening his voice again, continued. 'I have a new home for you, and you won't have to march across the desert to find it, either.'

'But – ' Moonshi said, steeling himself. 'I promised my mistress, burra sahib.'

'Yes, yes,' the Reverend said, 'but think about it, Moonshi Lal. Do you know who awaits you in Rajputana, what dangers may stalk you along the way? Do you even know if this "uncle" you talk about will take the boy back?'

'Exactly,' said Nanak Chand.

'But I promised . . . '

'And you want to keep your promise,' the Reverend said. 'I entirely understand. Very admirable, indeed. But should we put your promise, even your honour, ahead of this boy's welfare?'

'But my mistress – '

' – is dead,' the Reverend said with a nod. 'And if she were alive would she deny her son a safe and happy life so you could drag him off into the wilderness? Looking down upon us now, would she stand in her precious son's path to prosperity, fellowship, and salvation?'

A hot wind began to ripple the river. The Reverend cut himself short, as if afraid he'd given himself away, and anxiously glanced at Moonshi.

'Excellently put, Reverend Sahib,' Nanak Chand said with an appreciative shake of his head. 'I think we all now know what must be done . . . '

'So,' the Reverend said, rising to his feet, 'will you come with me, boy? Will you give me the joy of calling you my son?'

I slowly turned my face toward him, and though I was still horrified by the angry pink of his skin, the words 'my son' from a man's lips, tempted me. Family. Laughter. Home. The Reverend knew his business.

I gaped up at Moonshi, hoping he might protect me, but he was too lost in his grief to notice.

'Well?' the Reverend asked, taking out his pocket watch. 'What do you say?'

Moonshi's voice was now a strangled whisper. 'But what will I tell his uncle?'

'What uncle?' Nanak Chand said with a triumphant grin.

'You may tell him that you did your duty by his nephew,' the Reverend said, snapping his pocket watch closed. 'You may tell him that you left his nephew in the best of hands. And you may tell him that if *he* wishes to do *his* duty by the boy he can always send you back with the proper papers and we can all proceed from there.'

Moonshi stifled his sobs and dared to look down into my eyes for a moment. 'Little Master,' he began in a whisper.

'No!' I cried, knowing what was coming.

'Little Master, please,' he said. 'It's for the best.'

'No!' I cried again, shutting my eyes and tightening my grip on his legs. 'I'm going to go with you, Moonshi! Just like you promised!'

'But it's for your own good,' Moonshi said, prying my arms away from his legs. 'The burra sahib is a dignitary, Balbeer. Remember what I told you about dignitaries?'

'I want to stay with you!' I said, as the wind blew across my scalp.

'You can't,' Moonshi said, turning away from the Reverend and lowering his voice. 'Not now, Little Master. You have to go with the burra sahib. But' – and here Moonshi leaned close to me – 'I will come back for you, Little Master. I promise.'

I struggled against his grip for a moment and then stopped and glared at him. 'Liar!' I growled at him. 'You take me back! You have to take me back! I'm your master!'

A shadow passed across Moonshi's face, for I had never spoken to him like that before. 'I can't,' he said stiffly, standing to his full height. 'But I will keep my promise.'

'Promise?' I shouted back at him. 'You promise? Like you promised my mother? Liar!' I cried, kicking at him. 'Liar! Liar!'

Moonshi gripped my shoulders and shook me slightly until I was quiet. 'I didn't lie to your mother,' he said, glaring at me so hard that his eyes nearly matched. 'And I'm not lying to you. I will come back.'

I wiped at my tears with the back of my hand.

'Do you hear me, Little Master?'

'I – I hear you.'

'And do you believe me?'

I looked up at Nanak Chand and at the Englishman and then back at Moonshi again in the dim morning light. What choice did I have but to believe him? Who was I to throw away this last scrap of hope?

'Do you?' Moonshi said, one eye wandering off again from the other.

'Yes,' I said, swallowing back a sob.

'Good,' Moonshi said, drawing me to him again. 'That's good, Little Master.'

'Very touching business,' the Reverend muttered behind us as we embraced.

'Now,' Moonshi said, taking my hand, 'I have to leave you for a while, Little Master. So I want you to be brave, as your mother's son should be brave, and say goodbye.'

I don't know if it was because Moonshi had invoked my mother or because I had caught sight of Nanak Chand smirking in the background, but I did manage to still my sobbing before Moonshi led me over to the Reverend.

'Goodbye, Little Master,' Moonshi said as the Reverend took my hand.

'Goodbye, Moonshi,' I said, shutting my eyes to the sight of the Englishman's pallid fingers closing on mine.

'You're doing the wise thing, Moonshi Lal,' the Reverend said. 'Your mistress would have been very proud of you.'

'Not that he had any choice in the matter,' Nanak Chand said, taking hold of his bowler in the stiffening wind.

But as Nanak Chand, the Reverend, and I climbed up the steps, a limb of the river wind reached around and caught us for a moment in a swirl of smoke and ashes.

PART TWO

BASTARD
BHAVAN

CHAPTER 10

'Once more I am in your debt, Shri Chand,' the Reverend said as he led me northwestward along the river's edge.

Nanak Chand shrugged, replying in a language I couldn't understand.

'In Hindi, if you please, Shri Chand,' the Reverend interjected. 'I must try to keep in practice.'

'Of course, Reverend Sahib. Forgive me, but it's such an unworthy tongue, if I may say so, for the nobility of your sentiments.'

'Oh, Shri Chand,' the Reverend said, pursing his lips to mask his satisfaction as he paused in the heat to mop his forehead with his handkerchief.

'But I was going to say that our arrangement is never a matter of debt. Your friendship is an honor worth an infinitude of my meagre services.'

They exchanged these civilities for another half mile, Nanak Chand's flattery coiling along our path like a vine, the Reverend demurring with elaborate displays of embarrassment which only served to egg Nanak Chand on, until we came upon Nanak Chand's palanquin bearers resting by a tea stand.

'Now I fear I must exile myself from the beneficent aura of your presence,' Nanak Chand said, looking grief-stricken as he motioned his bearers to their feet with one brisk wave of his hand. Now reduced to three, they rose slowly and stood with shabby insolence in their frayed and dusty uniforms.

'Very well,' the Reverend said. 'But I must find a means of repaying you for bringing this boy into our fold. We owe Shri Chand our thanks, don't we, Bambeer?'

'*Balbeer*, if I may presume to correct you slightly,' said Nanak Chand, half-covering his mouth with the back of his hand.

'*Balbeer*, of course. How will we ever repay Shri Chand, eh?'

I turned my face away. I would find a way to repay him, I told myself, glowering at the ground.

'Shy,' the Reverend explained, giving my hand a squeeze.

'There's no need for thanks, Reverend Sahib. Merely to be seen having a stroll and a chat is payment enough,' Nanak Chand said with inadvertent candor. 'Farewell, then, Reverend Sahib,' he said, grasping the Reverend's free hand in both of his and bowing down to touch it to the brim of his bowler. 'And give my regards to the rest of the boys.'

'I shall do that, Shri Chand,' the Reverend replied, his nostrils flaring as he freed his hand and wiped it on the tail of his coat. 'Goodbye.'

'And goodbye to you, Little Turnip,' Nanak Chand said, holding out his hand. 'Behave yourself, boy,' he said when I made no move. 'Do what the Reverend Sahib tells you, Little Turnip,' he said, his eyes narrowing, 'and don't ever dare to shame me.'

'I'm certain he won't,' said the Reverend, looking down at me with his transparent eyes. 'I'm confident Bambeer will do himself proud.'

As Nanak Chand plumped down into the cushioned shade of his palanquin and his muttering bearers hoisted him to their shoulders, the Reverend and I continued along a broad dirt road lined with the ruins of shops and factories. Against the few walls left standing, construction workers had erected fragile, tented lean-tos in which their children sat, out of reach of the punishing sun, watching us pass with their great, grave eyes.

Here and there new buildings were under construction amid mazes of bamboo scaffolding, along whose connecting ramps and ladders skeletal men and women trudged with baskets full of bricks and mortar. We passed a procession of gypsy smiths in their studded carts, a trio of water carriers with their bulging, glossy goatskin sacks, a brickworks, an expanse of abandoned, weed-ridden racquet courts, the Reverend humming tunelessly and looking straight ahead.

◆———————◆

You would have thought the Reverend was leading me to my doom the way I staggered along beside him, but he was merely taking me to school. In those days just about every Englishman in India had his own little Empire. The Reverend's was the Mission Society for the Propagation of the Revealed Word Asylum for Orphan Boys, locally known as Bastard Bhavan.

Bastard Bhavan had been founded by the Reverend Horace Dunbar to minister to the orphans of the Great Famine of 1837. It was said that Dunbar had been a zealot who'd taken, in his later years, cheerfully to condemning passersby to hellfire and delivering midnight sermons outside the sepoys' barracks, so it was no wonder that when the Devil's Wind began to blow, old Reverend Dunbar was one of the very first white men the rebels dismembered.

When the young Josiah Weems arrived to replace his martyred predecessor, there wasn't much left of Bastard Bhavan. The school had been fastidiously razed and all but one of the boys had either been converted to Islam or executed. And the military authorities, who blamed missionaries like Dunbar for provoking the Mutiny in the first place, were not welcoming.

But all of that added up to the sort of predicament Christians cannot resist, for like some of our most fanatical ascetics, they take root where they're despised and thrive where they're persecuted. Where I would have seen only scorched rubble and devastation, the Reverend Josiah Weems saw cheap land and a new beginning.

Reports of heathen atrocities during the Mutiny had swollen the Mission Society's coffers, so Weems was able to purchase a sizable plot of ground northwest of the city, and convert a battered old warehouse into a school.

The challenge lay in finding boys. The British had avenged themselves randomly on the surrounding villages, producing a good many orphans in the process, but the truth was that my countrymen took care of their own. (Even I, whose mother had died in disgrace and whose father was an unspeakable mystery, evidently had family waiting somewhere.)

The Reverend looked everywhere – the courts, the famine camps, the burning ghats – but all to no avail, until at last he made the acquaintance of Shri Nanak Chand, the Englishman's friend, who, for a modest fee, recruited unfortunates like me, and saw in

Weems's predicament an opportunity to retrieve, in some vague and desperate fashion, a little of his lost prestige.

Run, I tell myself now as I watch the Reverend lead me away from the miscellany of the river road, through a grove of charred trees, and up a little rise in the scrubby ground. And I suppose I could have broken free and escaped into the countryside if I'd had the strength, or the courage, or the will. But the Reverend looked like fate itself in his tight black clothes, and if his eyes were as clear as glass and his skin was the color of bone, how could I be sure that he couldn't sprout wings and fly if he wanted to, or hear my thoughts, or flick out his arm like a lizard's tongue to catch me?

'There it is, boy,' the Reverend said, stopping at the top of the rise and pointing into the distance. 'We're home.'

The hot breeze carried the sound of children's voices plodding along in unison, but there was no one in sight: just a long, white-washed building set on a deep green island of vegetable plots and grass. It was the cleanest place I'd ever seen, though its walls looked a little wrinkled here and there, like paper that's been crumpled up and straightened out again. There was an uneven row of windows just below the wavering line of the roof, along whose ridge jutted several bent iron chimneys. To one of these had been strapped a towering, sun-bleached cross.

'Your new brothers are already at their studies,' the Reverend said, squinting again at his pocket watch. 'But come along now. They're eager to meet you.'

The path evened out as we approached the school, until it was as straight as the fall of a stone, and here and there along the way the Reverend stooped to pluck a weed or a broom bristle from the uniform sporran of grass.

'Here we are, then,' the Reverend said, stepping up toward the double-door entrance and releasing my hand. 'Now look about you, boy. Take it all in. See what we've raised up out of this violated ground. A garden. An orchard,' the Reverend said, waving his arm toward a row of small, doubtful trees whose trunks were wrapped in burlap. 'A meadow,' he said, directing my gaze to three fenced-in, tethered cows. 'And a sanitary station,' he said with an extra measure of pride, turning me around to admire a closet-sized structure.

'And a house of God,' he said, taking my hand again and leading me inside.

'Most Reverend Weems Sahib,' a youth with a missing leg and an addled manner greeted us as we entered the school.

'Good morning, Dhanda,' the Reverend said without a pause. 'I've brought a new brother into the fold.'

'Oh, excellent, Reverend Weems Sahib,' Dhanda said, rushing alongside us on his crutch and scrabbling at my sleeve with his fingers.

'Go back now, Dhanda,' the Reverend said, leading me to the end of a short hallway lined with bamboo screens and pulling me through a curtain. 'There'll be time enough to make friends later.'

We thus entered a room filled with tables, around one of which sat a dozen boys of various sizes hunched over little black books as a small Indian man dressed like the Reverend paced around, reading aloud in a harsh tongue.

'Please, Mr Peter,' said the Reverend at the top of his voice, 'don't let us interrupt.'

'Not at all, Reverend Sahib,' replied the little man, snapping his book closed and bowing. 'We were just nearing the end of our lesson.'

'Good,' said the Reverend, positioning me in front of him and placing his hands on my shoulders.

'You all may be seated, my sons,' he said, quietly, and with more shrieking of benches the boys sat down again.

For a moment there was total silence, and then the Reverend said, 'When I have everyone's attention . . .' and Mr Peter glowered at a tall boy seated near me who had momentarily taken his eyes off the Reverend to close his book.

'Dileep!' Mr Peter barked. 'Pay attention!'

Dileep smiled up at Mr Peter for a moment and slowly turned his attention to the Reverend.

'Today – ' the Reverend said with an irritated snort, 'today is a day for rejoicing, my sons, for look what God has given us.'

The boys looked at me warily: even Mr Peter, who stood in his black suit beside the Reverend like a foreshortened shadow, nervously fingering his book.

'Misfortune has given birth to a new brother,' the Reverend went on, squeezing my shoulders, 'and a new son.'

I could feel the Reverend's breath gusting across my scalp. 'Tell me your name again, my boy,' he said in a near whisper.

Gooseflesh rose along the back of my neck and the walls of my stomach closed on themselves as I struggled to find my voice.

'Your *name*, boy,' the Reverend said, his voice tightening like a fist.

'Balbeer,' I said at last, trying to stand erect but unable to lift my eyes from the floor.

'Louder,' the Reverend said, 'Nice and loud so we can all hear you.'

'Balbeer,' I said again, afraid my name might crack like an eggshell if I spoke it too loudly.

'Yes, good,' said the Reverend. 'Balbeer? Balbeer what?'

I put my hand to my chest, trying to calm my breathing. 'Rao,' I said.

'Balbeer Rao!' the Reverend announced. 'That's the name he brings with him and a fine name it is. But who knows what name he will *take* with him, right, my sons?'

'Yes, Reverend Sahib,' the boys replied in perfect unison.

'So let us welcome Balbeer Rao properly,' said the Reverend. 'Are you ready? Three cheers for Balbeer Rao! Hurrah!' the Reverend cried out, standing on his toes, and the boys cheerlessly joined in.

'Hurrah! Hurrah!'

Now an urgent need to urinate was added to my gooseflesh, my nausea, and the rapid pounding of my heart.

'I know what all of you must be thinking,' the Reverend said. 'You're remembering when you yourselves first came here, aren't you?'

'Yes, Reverend Sahib,' the boys replied.

'I thought so. And because you've been through this before, your hearts are going out to him, are they not?'

'Yes, Reverend Sahib,' the boys answered in a drone.

'Good boys,' said the Reverend with a satisfied smacking of his lips. 'But I wonder why we should pity little Ban – Bam – what's your name again?'

'Balbeer,' the boy named Dileep answered for me before I could open my mouth.

'Balbeer,' the Reverend said, squinting at Dileep. 'As I was saying, I wonder why we should pity little Balbeer, my sons. Should we pity him because his mother's just died?'

'No, Reverend Sahib,' the boys replied as if they'd been marched down this path before.

'Quite right. For all our mothers must pass on eventually, just as we all must die, in God's wisdom, by God's will. Well then, are we to pity him because he comes to us so destitute and hungry?'

'No, Reverend Sahib.'

'Correct again. For he will learn that poverty is a state of grace. Better save our pity for the rich who will never know the kingdom of heaven. And yet we *should* pity this lad, shouldn't we?'

'Yes, Reverend Sahib.'

'Our hearts demand that we pity him, don't they? But why?'

A small dark boy with a furrowed brow frantically waved his arm near the head of the table.

'Let's give someone new a chance to answer,' the Reverend said, and all movement in the room ceased. 'Dileep?' the Reverend asked, jutting his chin. 'Perhaps you would like to answer for a change.'

Dileep slowly stood, pressing the edge of the table against his stomach. 'Sahib?' he said with an air of studied conscientiousness.

'Why do we pity little Balbeer?' the Reverend asked with one eyebrow raised.

'Well, sahib,' said Dileep, shaking his head slightly.

'Speak up,' the Reverend said, cupping his ear. 'Speak up so everyone can hear you.'

'Well, sahib, I don't think I know, sahib, unless – '

'Yes, Dileep? Nice and loud. Unless what?'

'Unless we should pity him,' Dileep said with a light shining in his eyes, 'because he's ended up here.'

There was some inadvertent giggling along the table as the Reverend frowned. 'Was that a joke, Dileep?' he asked, putting his hands behind his back now and tucking his chin against his chest.

'A joke, Sahib?'

'Yes, Dileep. A joke. Were you making a joke at my expense?'

'Sahib?'

'Because if you were it couldn't have been a very humorous joke or we would all be laughing.'

'Sahib, I – '

'Because if you were making sport of this poor lad's predicament I would be very disappointed in you.'

Dileep shrugged, his face a mask of bewilderment.

'But then I'm often disappointed in you, Dileep. You may be seated.' The Reverend scowled at Dileep a moment longer and then turned toward the eager boy at the head of the table.

'Now, then, John Christopher,' he said with a heartened look. 'You've been very patient. Will you be good enough to answer my question? Why ought we to pity this lad?'

The Reverend patted my shoulder and nodded as the boy jumped to his feet. He was grave and wizened, like an elderly dwarf, and briefly smirked in Dileep's direction.

'Because he hasn't heard the Good News,' he declared woodenly, as if reading it off the Reverend's forehead.

'Which is?' the Reverend asked with a confident nod.

'That God loves the world so much that He gave His only Son, and whoever believes in Him can live forever.'

The Reverend mouthed along to John Christopher's answer as if listening to a beloved song. 'John, Chapter Three, Verse Sixteen,' he murmured, closing his eyes for a moment. 'Yes, John Christopher. Excellently said. And without the bread of life he's gone hungry, my sons, and without the light of the world he's gone blind. But let's put pity behind us, and envy little Balbeer for what lies ahead of him. The lessons, the fellowship, the revelations, and in the end?'

'Salvation, Reverend Sahib,' everyone answered.

'Salvation from the sins of his birth, the sins of this cursed land which has abandoned you, which has cast you all away. And just as he finds a place at our table,' the Reverend said, leading me to the table and motioning two boys to make room for me between them, 'let him find room in our hearts.

'Mr Peter?' he said as I sat down with my bald head bowed. 'I think this calls for a prayer of thanksgiving.'

Everyone around me shut his eyes and clasped his hands together on the table before him.

'Oh God,' Mr Peter began in a lugubrious voice, 'we – '

'In English, if you please, Mr Peter,' the Reverend interjected without opening his eyes. 'Just to be certain that God will hear us.'

And Mr Peter began again in a gibberish, in a spray of razor-sharp consonants and starved vowels, his mouth wrestling with each word as if trying to work a hair off the floor of his tongue.

With a final, drawn-out unison drone everyone blinked his eyes open again, and when I looked over at Reverend Weems his nose was leaking and there were tears on his cheeks.

'Welcome home, Bambeer,' he said as he wiped his tears away with his handkerchief, and blowing his nose like a trumpet he turned around and left.

CHAPTER

11

For the rest of the morning I sat like a ghost through Mr Peter's lessons, resisting sleep and grief and the call of nature as he maundered on, now in Hindi, now in gibberish. I was too scared to sleep and my tears were all dried up, but I gave in to the call of nature long before I dared asked to be excused, and as I stood up from the table and everyone saw the stain on my dhoti they began to laugh — even Mr Peter, who laughed with a scowl, like a mordant crane.

John Christopher was entrusted with leading me out to the proud Reverend's privy, which he did in a silent rage, furious that I'd interrupted his studies. As he paced around outside like a warden, I closed the privy door behind me and stood dizzy and bewildered in the befouled dark. Had the lid to the privy been open I might have figured out what was expected of me, but in my shamed confusion I could only guess that as part of some inscrutable English ritual I was supposed to stand on the box and press myself against the wall and urinate through a knothole, which is what I did.

'Horrible! Horrible!' I heard John Christoper cry after a moment, and I hurried out of the privy to find him shaking his trouser legs as if they'd caught fire.

'You horrible boy!' he piped at me, staggering off on his wetted legs. 'I'm telling! I'm telling Mr Peter on you!'

I hurried after him, trying to explain, but like the flame on a fuse he raced inside, and I heard the explosion of his classmates' laughter, his own indignant demand for vengeance, and Mr Peter's angry call for silence before I could reach the door.

'So,' Mr Peter said, grabbing me by the arm as I came to a halt in the doorway, 'we have a troublemaker on our hands, do we?'

'No sir,' I said as he shook me. 'Please, sir. I was only – '

'Silence!' Mr Peter shouted, as much to the rest of the boys as to me. 'I'll teach you not to play your filthy tricks in my class,' he said, raising his hand to strike me, and just as the first blow landed I fainted dead away.

It was night when I came to, and I squinted into the darkness, trying to focus on my mother's slumbering form across the familiar length of our room, until, with a start, I realized that I was staring at the barren plane of a wall.

'Mataji?' I called out, whirling about in my bed and finding myself lying in one of a row of double-decked bunks in a long and unfamiliar room.

'Are you all right?' someone whispered from above me, and with a gasp I saw a boy's face hanging upside down from the upper bunk, only inches away from my face, and grabbing my blanket to me I shrank back from him as if from a bat.

'You've been out cold,' the boy said, swinging down onto my bed. 'I was afraid you'd never wake up.'

Now that I saw him right side up I could see that he was Dileep, the insolent boy with the mischievous answers.

'He really let you have it, didn't he?' Dileep said, reaching toward my face.

I pressed myself against the wall and raised my hand to defend myself, but felt a strange bulge on my left cheek that burned to the touch.

'See what I mean?' Dileep said as I winced. 'Hit you even after your lamp went out. Just like the son of a toad, too. You watch out for Mr Peter, Diwan.'

'Diwan?' I asked, relaxing slightly against the wall.

'What?'

'You called me *Diwan*.'

'I did?' Dileep whispered.

'Yes,' I said, scowling at him. 'That's not my name. My name's Balbeer.'

'I know,' Dileep said calmly, 'but I like *Diwan* better.'

'What do you mean?'

'Well, it just seems to suit you better, that's all. Better than the names Redeemer Walla has planned for you.'

'Redeemer Walla?'

'The Reverend. I call him Redeemer Walla. He's going to want to name you Thomas, or Samuel, or Joshua. You'll see. A nice Christian name, like John Christopher. *Hey*, you got John Christopher good,' Dileep said, nudging my leg. 'That was beautiful.'

I opened my mouth to protest that I hadn't meant to drench John Christopher, but Dileep gave me such an admiring look that I thought better of it and shrugged. 'You mean that wasn't his name before – '

'No, no. Which of us ever started out with a name like that? His name was Ram Kali when he came here. Nice little fellow, too. A little too serious. Not much spark. But all right. Used to follow me around like a little brother. But not John Christopher. He follows me around like a spy, like a little brown Redeemer Walla. "*I'm telling Redeemer Walla*," he says. "*I'm telling Mr Peter*." ' Dileep's impersonation was so exact that I gaped at him. '*I'm going to tell and you'll be sorry*,' Dileep continued with a grin. 'Just like that.'

I laughed with him for a moment until it awoke the ache in my bruised cheek. 'And does he?'

'Does he what?'

'Tell on you.'

'Yes,' Dileep sighed. 'I'm afraid he does, the poor little mouse. He thinks it's his duty.' Dileep shook his head. 'Imagine that.'

'And what happens if you get caught? Do they beat you like they beat me?'

'That depends on what you've done. I mean, you're always going to do *something* wrong here. Redeemer Walla's seen to that. It took me a couple of weeks to figure him out. He stays in control by changing the rules all the time, because if he didn't change the rules then the *rules* would be in charge. See what I mean?'

I didn't.

'You will.'

'Shhh!' someone exclaimed from a nearby bunk.

'Sorry, brother John,' Dileep whispered back, rolling his eyes at me. 'We holdouts don't know any better, do we, Diwan?'

I nodded back, but asked. 'What are holdouts?'

'We won't be converted. Redeemer Walla can't have our souls. He can't have *mine*, anyway,' Dileep said, frowning slightly.

'But we've got to be careful,' he said as much to himself as to me. 'I've seen boys come in here with their sacred threads and their caste marks and their mantras and oppose Redeemer Walla like little Mahratta warriors. And then one morning they wake up singing *Nearer My God to Thee.*'

Dileep saw my puzzled look. 'It's one of their songs. One boy started weeping like a baby one morning right in the middle of chapel and climbed into the baptismal font, begging Redeemer Walla to convert him.'

'Why?'

Dileep shook his head. 'I don't know. Something happens. Something gets to them. It's like a fever.'

Dileep wrapped his arms around himself and then abruptly turned toward me and grinned.

'Where'd he get you?' he asked, leaning back against the wall beside me.

'Off the ghats,' I said, and my eyes began to tear. 'By my mother's pyre.'

'Just like Puran, eh?' Dileep said, nodding toward a heavy youth slumbering in a nearby bed. 'They brought him in a couple of weeks ago. Redeemer Walla's been hanging around the ghats all spring. Was the babu with him?'

'You mean Nanak Chand?'

'Who else?'

'You know him?'

'Oh yes,' Dileep said grimly, biting at his thumbnail. 'The Bengali ass with the English bray. He was in on it, wasn't he?'

I looked away and nodded.

'They make quite a pair, don't they? What'd they do? Did they even wait until the fire was out?'

I thought about my mother's ashes then, of the domri sweeping them into the river, and didn't reply.

'In a way you're lucky,' said Dileep.

I turned and glared at him.

'I don't mean *lucky*, exactly. None of us is lucky. But at least you're a real orphan. At least they've brought you to the right place.'

'But isn't everyone an orphan here?' I said a little too loudly, for a boy in the next bed groaned.

'Not everyone,' Dileep whispered after a pause. 'Not me. I'm no orphan. My mother's still alive.'

'Then why —'

'I *know* she's still alive,' Dileep said, shaking his head. He seemed to withdraw for a moment and then looked at me and took a deep breath.

'I come from a village near Kanauj. My father was a tenant farmer. Our landlord was a Moslem who became one of the Nana Sahib's ministers. So when the British came through they hanged all the men of the village. Strung my father up from the sisal tree with all the others and set fire to everything: huts, carts, even the crops in the field. My brother was trampled by their horses, and when the rest of us fled toward Bithur my sister was killed in a hailstorm. That left me and my mother. We tried to get past Cawnpore and make our way to Fatehpur, where we have kin. But we were stopped and put in a camp with some other refugees, and my mother caught a fever. She told me to get out before I caught it too. I didn't want to go, Diwan, but she made me promise, commanded me to flee to Fatehpur and never look back.

'I did what I was told. I didn't plan on going through Cawnpore. Wanted to go around. But I was only six years old, and one night I lost my way and passed through an evil part of town.'

'The Gola Ghat bazaar?'

'Yes,' Dileep said. 'The Gola Ghat. Anyway, a gang of bad-mashes caught me there and abused me, and when they were done they took me to Nanak Chand, who bought me from them with an English umbrella with a silver handle. Nanak Chand pretended to be my friend, soothed my injuries, told me he'd saved me so he could send me home safe and sound to my mother. And I fell for it, Diwan. Like a fool, I fell for it. I told him my mother's name and where she was and exactly how to find her. And of course right away Nanak Chand changed. Picked me up by the hair. Told me he was going to hand me over to an Englishman friend of his and that if I ever tried to run away or tell his friend the truth he would send his men to the camp and they would find my mother and cut her throat.

'So he brought me here the next morning and told the Reverend some story, and I've been here ever since.' Dileep looked at me carefully for a moment, and his face broke into a bitter smile. 'So you see, I'm no orphan, Diwan, and Redeemer Walla can never have my soul.'

'Be quiet!' John Christopher's crisp little voice exclaimed, setting off a chain of shushings down the whole row of beds, until we could see the Reverend's nightcapped head pop up from behind a partition and blearily peer at us.

'Settle down!' he called out in a husky voice, and after a moment his head sank back down behind the screen.

Dileep slowly shook his head with grudging respect and whispered, 'The Very Reverend Josiah Weems.'

I squinted through the slanting beams of moonlight that shone through the row of windows above us, and once the others had settled back into their bedding I could hear a muffled pounding noise from the Reverend's direction, and I gave Dileep a questioning look.

'He's beating his pillow,' Dileep whispered. 'Redeemer Walla wrestles himself to sleep.'

'Why?'

'He hates to sleep. Thinks it's a waste of time, or anyway that's what he says. I think he's afraid of his dreams. I used to clean his room every morning as punishment for something or other until he decided to make it a reward and handed it over to John Christopher. You should see his bed. It looks like he drags it all over Avadh,' Dileep said with a nudge. 'And some nights he drops his seed.'

'His seed?'

'*You* know,' Dileep said, making a circle with his hand and shaking it over his lap.

I didn't know.

'Never mind,' Dileep said with a shrug. 'But look, Diwan,' he said, moving closer to me for a moment and speaking with great earnestness. 'Don't feel too bad about all this. This isn't the worst place in the world, or even in Cawnpore if you think about it. You'll have a roof over your head and enough food to get by on and people who don't think you're a freak just because your parents are dead. You might come out of here reading and writing. And now,' Dileep said, placing a hand on my shoulder, 'you've got a friend.'

I appreciated the gesture, and all the advice, but I couldn't help but feel sorry for Dileep, because I knew that in a day or two Moonshi would come and take me away, leaving Dileep behind.

'Now, get to sleep,' he said, crawling back to the edge of the bed. 'And remember tomorrow that there're lots of ways of getting your way around here without getting whipped for it.'

'I know,' I said, looking away with my nose in the air.

'Goodnight, Diwan,' Dileep said, hoisting himself up onto the bed above me.

'Goodnight, Dileep,' I whispered, too softly for him to hear me, and lay awake for a time in the vaporous dark, listening for Moonshi's footsteps.

CHAPTER

12

The next morning, before the sun rose, Mr Peter passed along our row of beds, clapping his hands to rouse us.

'Follow me, Diwan,' Dileep said, dropping down from his bed and yawning. 'I'll show you what to do.'

I followed Dileep and the others out into the dim dawn light and, keeping an eye on Dileep all the while, washed my face and arms in a long trough and joined the queue at the privy.

'Watch out for the Golden Avenger!' Dileep called out as I went in, and everybody but John Christopher laughed. But this time I guessed right, and though I was horrified by the privy's putrid depths, I managed.

Back at my bed I found a bundled-up uniform waiting for me: rope-soled sandals, leggings that reached to just below my knees, and a shirt with a high collar and sleeves that buttoned well above my wrists.

'This is too small for me,' I told Dileep as I fastened my trousers.

'No, no,' Dileep said, lowering his voice as Mr Peter bustled by us, barking commands. 'See? They're just like mine. They just *look* and *feel* too small, Diwan. Redeemer Walla designed them himself. Very scientific. "Ventilation and retention," you see. They're all-weather uniforms. You'll only *think* you're burning up in the summer. You'll only *imagine* you're freezing in the winter,' Dileep said, shaking his head as he buttoned his shirt and tucked it into the waistband of his trousers. 'I tell you, Diwan, the man's a genius.'

'Well, *I* think they're quite comfortable,' John Christopher piped up, loud enough for Mr Peter to hear. But Mr Peter was too busy dragging Puran outside with one hand, Puran's wetted bedding with the other.

'John Christopher,' Dileep said, casually stepping into his sandals, 'you'd be "quite comfortable" if Redeemer Walla stuffed you into a sack of thorns.'

'Redee – *Reverend Sahib* would never do such a thing,' John Christopher said, buttoning his shirt up to the throat.

'No, of course not,' said Dileep. 'He's too kind to do a thing like that, isn't he? Unless, of course, it was for your own good.'

'That's right,' John Christopher replied, turning his back on Dileep.

'And if he did it for your own good you'd be "quite comfort-able," wouldn't you?'

John Christopher brought his Bible out from under his pillow and held it against his chest like a shield. 'That's right, too,' he said, walking away with his head upraised.

The others laughed and lined up behind John Christopher at the dormitory door.

'Another joke, Dileep?' the Reverend asked as he appeared in the doorway holding a great studded, leather-bound book in his arms. 'I'm sorry I missed it.'

Everyone stopped laughing, and not until the last smile had been wiped off the last of our faces did Weems smile down at us. 'Good morning, my sons,' he said quietly. His coral face was still marked by the creases of his sheets.

'Good morning, Reverend Sir,' we all replied – even I, my voice trailing behind like a lame stray.

'And who's going to carry the Good Book to chapel this morning?' he asked, beaming around to us.

Several boys volunteered at once, but the Reverend peered through their upraised arms and looked at me.

'I think I know just the man for the job,' he said, moving toward me. 'And how are we getting along, my son?' he asked, leaning down slightly and placing the fingertips of his free hand on my shoulder. 'You got off to a sticky start yesterday, didn't you?'

I looked down at the floor, saw the shine on the Reverend's sharp black shoes.

'Well,' he said, lightly touching my bruised cheek, 'I'm sure you've learned your lesson. And you'll soon learn too that here, my son, your transgressions will always be forgiven when they are followed by sincere repentance. Are you very sorry for what you did?'

I swallowed hard and glanced at Dileep.

'Yes, Reverend Sahib,' I said as quietly as I could, for I knew I was lying and didn't want my mother to hear me.

'I know you are,' the Reverend said. 'And just for that you shall have the honor of carrying the Good Book for me.'

He held the huge book out for me to take, and I gripped it with all my strength as he led us off to a large partitioned room at the opposite end of the building which served as a chapel. As the others took their places along a row of benches the Reverend had me follow him up onto a platform at the front of the room and place the book, with a loud, dust-raising thud, atop a tall wooden box which looked to me to be a smaller version of the privy outside, though this was decorated with a cross in carved relief.

'Now you may rejoin your brothers,' he said, hurrying me off the platform, and I took my place with the others.

'To begin,' the Reverend said, ceremoniously opening his book and smoothing its pages, and he promptly lapsed into his native tongue.

Over the next hour I had to keep a sharp eye out to see when I was expected to kneel, rise, sit, bow, mouth songs, and clasp my hands, but there were long stretches when I could just sit and stare about at my surroundings. The walls, floor, and benches were all the same muddy green as my uniform, and the only color in the room was a red stripe along the base of the Reverend's platform, the gold bookmark that hung from the Reverend's Bible like a tongue, and a blue-and-white pedestal opposite the podium atop which a cannon-ball was perched. From the upper reaches of the wall behind the altar a ragged shell hole stared down upon us like a mad, sky-blue eye, preserved by the Reverend, Dileep would tell me, as a symbol of God's and England's wrath.

Pigeons burbled in the windows along the top of the walls, exclaiming and ruffling their drab feathers as the Reverend's voice rose and fell. And toward the end of the Reverend's morning lesson, as he pointed a quivering finger at the breach above him, a stark crow suddenly flapped through it and cawed among the rafters, menacing the pigeon's nests.

Our breakfast consisted of milky tea and boiled lentils, also the same equivocal green, and despite my hunger I could barely force it down, fumbling with the wooden spoon with which we were each provided. When we were finished, Mr Peter rang a bell and we filed outside to rinse our bowls and cups in the bathing trough.

I tried to rejoin Dileep at the table for morning lessons, but as the Reverend bellowed his instructions Mr Peter had me sit at a separate table with Puran, the other newcomer, who was already busy at his slate, biting down on his tongue in concentration.

Mr Peter gave me a little stack of books, all in English but one: an abridged and paperbound Sanskrit Bible. Though my mother could read and write three languages, she had taught me little more than the Sanskrit alphabet, and I could now barely spell out the words on the Bible's cover.

In fact, the little English textbooks made more sense to me, because they were filled with engravings: a bird, a rabbit, a forest cottage strangling in vines, and a tiny and portly Englishman kicking what appeared to be a melon. I reckoned that this was how Englishmen looked back in their island home, and it wouldn't be until days later that I would realize that the plump little fellow was a boy, for I'd never seen an English child and supposed England must have been a nation of adults, hatched full-grown from gourds or tumbled down out of the sky in thunderstorms.

Mr Peter returned with my slate, a warped and whitewashed plank on which I was instructed to copy down the English alphabet with a stick of charcoal. It shouldn't have been hard for me, for I've always been good with my hands, but under Mr Peter's impatient gaze, with the threat of another blow hanging over me, I couldn't get the hang of it, even when he gripped my hand to guide it, and by the end of the morning all I'd produced was a hedgerow of crossings and loops.

After a long blessing and a short lunch we continued our lessons through the heat of the afternoon, until our slates were spattered with sweat and the stench from the older boys forced Mr Peter, who was no rose himself, into walking around us in ever widening circles. In yet another blessing the Reverend assigned us our afternoon chores, dedicating our labors to the glory of his god as we filed out into the sunlight.

I stuck close to Dileep and was assigned to help him empty out the washing trough into a drain that was connected to the pit beneath the privy and then refill it for the evening ablutions. It should have been a repulsive task for a boy of my caste, but if it meant that I could be in my new friend's company I would have scooped up excrement with my two bare hands.

'Take your time with the alphabet,' Dileep said as we hoisted the trough together. 'That way you can set your own pace. You don't want them to get a good grip on you.'

I wanted to tell him that I wouldn't be there long enough for anyone to get a grip on me, not even Dileep, but I only nodded to spare his feelings.

'But don't take it too far,' Dileep said, raising his end with my help and tipping the water out. 'You don't want them to give up on you completely.'

'Why not?'

'Well, do you want to end up like Dhanda over there?'

Dileep nodded over to the crippled boy who'd greeted the Reverend and me the morning before. Dhanda looked back with his mismatched eyes and grinned at us.

'No,' I said, picking up my end of the trough again. 'But what happened to him?'

'To Dhanda?' Dileep replied. 'Old Dhanda's been here longer than anybody, even longer than Redeemer Walla. He was here before the war. Saw it all. Saw the old Reverend get it. Saw all his friends wiped out. Lost his leg in a cannonade, but somebody's servant took him in and nobody finished him off. Anyway, he's real friendly and helpful and all that, and he wants Redeemer Walla to convert him — he's been hounding Redeemer Walla to convert him for as long as I've been here. But he just can't get a grip on himself in class. Keeps answering out loud every time Redeemer Walla asks a question just to hear himself talk, and you've got to hit Dhanda over the head with a hymnal to get him to stop singing in chapel. He's not even allowed in chapel any more. He just hangs around with nothing to do, talking to himself and real eager to please, and nobody pays attention to him.'

'But why won't the Reverend Sahib — '

' — Redeemer Walla.'

'Redeemer Walla then. Why won't Redeemer Walla convert him?'

'Good question,' Dileep said, leading me over to a water pump and handing me a bucket. 'I think Redeemer Walla would convert a chicken if he could. But you see, he could hold up that chicken and say, "I brought this chicken to Jesus," ' Dileep said, pursing his lips, his impersonation impeccable. 'But the *old* Reverend's the one who pumped Dhanda full of all this bunk, not Redeemer Walla. The old Reverend did all the work and would get all the glory if they ever dunked Dhanda in the font, so what would Redeemer Walla get out of it?'

'But isn't that all he wants? To convert us?'

'Sure,' Dileep said. 'Only it's got to be on *his* terms. You can't satisfy him by pretending you want to be converted just so he'll leave you alone. It's trickier than that. So he says, "No, Dhanda, not today, Dhanda, but someday, perhaps. Someday." '

'Someday?' came the Reverend's voice from behind us like an echo. 'Someday what, if I may ask?'

Dileep began to jerk at the handle of the pump, gushing water into the bucket. 'I was just telling the new boy that someday —

someday he'll learn the truth about Jesus.'

'Will he?' the Reverend said, approaching with a trowel in one hand, a potted seedling in the other. 'And what is that?'

Dileep stopped pumping for a moment and tilted his head slightly. 'I would never presume to tell the Reverend Sahib the truth about the Redeemer,' he said, clinging to his smile.

The Reverend frowned, a droplet of sweat bobbling on the tip of his nose.

'Bambeer,' he finally said, turning toward me. 'Come this way.'

At last, I thought as Dileep winked behind the Reverend's back, Moonshi has come for me. I wanted to tell Dileep that I was sorry that our little friendship had come to an end, but all I could manage was a mumbled goodbye as the Reverend led me away.

'Well now, Bambeer,' said the Reverend, leading me back into the school building, 'I see you've found a friend.'

'Yes, Reverend Sahib,' I said, looking around for Moonshi.

'Friends are important, Bambeer,' the Reverend said a little grimly, as if conceding a point. 'But beware false friends. Charming friends who delight in leading you astray, who rejoice when you stumble, who jubilate when you fall.'

He led me to the door of his office and unlocked it with a key. The room was almost pitch black, its windows shuttered up against the sun, and the air inside smelled like stale bread. A large desk occupied the middle of the floor, covered with piles of papers, pamphlets, ledgers, and books. The shelves behind the desk were only half filled, and the walls were bare but for a little engraved portrait set in a frame between two windows.

The Reverend opened the louvers, and tiger stripes of orange light spread across the room. It would not have made sense for me to have expected to see Moonshi somewhere in the shadows, but I looked for him anyway.

'Over here, Bambeer,' the Reverend said, walking toward the shelves and pointing to three half-opened wooden boxes on the floor.

'Bibles, Bambeer,' he said as I approached. 'I want you to help me shelve them. But no task here is without its lesson. I thought that from this you might come to understand what blessings lie before you to be harvested, if you will only stoop to reap them.'

The Reverend began to pull stacks of Bibles out of the boxes, trailing excelsior. 'Come along then, Bambeer,' he said when I made no move to join him.

In my disappointment I began to worry that my name might disappear into the order of the Reverend's universe. 'It's *Bal*beer,' I said weakly.

'Yes, yes,' the Reverend snapped back, 'Now let us get to work.'

'False friends,' he said as I lifted a little stack and reached up to place it on the shelf. 'How easy it is to make them. They'll befriend you in a twinkling. And why? Do you know why?'

'No, Reverend Sahib,' I said, standing on the tips of my toes and sliding the Bibles into place.

'Why, because they are so desperate, for no one who truly knows them will have anything to do with them.

'But *true* friends,' the Reverend said as I went to fetch another stack of Bibles, '*true* friends are another matter. It takes time to make true friends, because true friendship must be *earned*. Respect is a flower that needs faithful tending. You cannot merely pluck it and expect it to last.'

I hefted a taller stack of Bibles this time, impatient with the task.

'Do you understand what I'm trying to tell you?' the Reverend said, stepping out of my way.

But I could barely answer him, for I'd balanced my stack of Bibles in my arms and held them steady with my chin.

'But there's only one true friend for any of us, Ban – *Bal*beer, that is. Only one true friend for all mankind.'

Now I had a problem. I knew that if I tried to let go with one arm and remove the Bibles one by one from the stack and place them on the shelf, my other arm wouldn't be able to handle the load. So there was nothing for it but to try to set the whole stack down on the shelf at once.

'And do you know his name?' the Reverend asked, lifting the lid off the second box.

Keeping one hand hooked under the stack, I placed the other on top and with all my might endeavored to hold them sideways, like a pump organ, and set them on the shelf in one heft.

'His name is – ' the Reverend said, but the rest of it was lost in the avalanche of Bibles that now roared down upon me, knocking me to the floor.

'Pick them up!' the Reverend began to shriek as I lay in a daze amid the fallen Bibles. 'You clumsy boy! You wicked, wicked, clumsy boy!'

He dragged me to my feet, and I began to reach for the Bibles again, but before I could set them on the shelf the Reverend snatched them from me and began frantically to clean them off on his shirtsleeve.

'Oh, what's the use? What's the use?' he asked himself. 'What in heaven's name is the use?'

But then he took a deep breath and seemed to listen for a moment as if someone were answering him, and he appeared to force himself to stare at me, as if looking for some little thing of value.

'Never mind, never mind,' he said, lowering his voice again. 'The Holy Gospel has withstood worse punishment than that, and still it lives, still it abides. You hand the Bibles to me, Balbeer,' he said, standing by the shelf, 'and I shall place them one at a time.'

I don't know if it was my disappointment at Moonshi's delay or if I'd swallowed what the Reverend had said about false friends, but at supper that evening I was cold to Dileep, even after he broke his biscuit in two and handed half of it to me. I eyed the biscuit for some time, and the Reverend, who sat at the head of the table delicately chewing little mouthfuls like a great pink mouse, nodded to me with an approving smile.

But Dileep wouldn't be put off so easily, for he always knew that whatever the Reverend did he could undo, and after more parables, prayers, and benedictions, after the lamp had been snuffed out and we all lay abed in the lingering summer dusk, Dileep dropped down onto my bed again to visit.

'So what do you think of the place now?' he asked, leaning toward me and whispering.

But I only shrugged back at him.

'You did better than I did my first day, Diwan,' he said with a shake of his head. 'You should have seen me back then.'

Dileep looked to me for encouragement to go on, and, getting none, he sighed and changed the subject.

'Can you read already?' he asked. 'Did you know how before you got here?'

I shrugged again. 'A little.'

'I couldn't when I got here. Wouldn't learn, either, for the longest while. I figured, why bother if I'm not going to be around more than a day or two? Only of course the days kept going by and I never could figure out a way to get out of here without Nanak Chand finding out. So after a while I gave up. Figured I might as well learn something useful, something that might get me out of here someday.'

'Not me,' I said.

'Not you what?' Dileep asked.

'I mean, not me – I don't have to learn anything. I'm – ' I looked at Dileep for a moment, wondering if I could trust him with my secret hope. 'I'm getting out of here tomorrow.'

I was afraid I had devastated him with this news, but when I looked over at him again he was smiling calmly.

'You are?'

'That's right,' I said. 'My servant's coming for me. He's getting the papers.'

'Ah,' Dileep said with a mild nod.

'And then we're going to go find my uncle in Rajputana.'

'I see,' Dileep said.

'I – I'm sorry, Dileep,' I said as he began to crawl off toward the edge of the bed. 'I wish we could take you with us.'

'Oh well,' Dileep said, reaching up toward his bunk.

'Maybe we could get the Reverend Sahib to let you go with us,' I said.

Dileep nodded with a distant smile. 'I don't think so,' he said. 'but good luck, anyway, because,' he said as he lifted himself back up to his bed, 'if you do get out of here you'll be the very first.'

'Then I'll be the first,' I said to him aloud as the weave of his bed above me creaked under his weight.

'That's all right with me,' Dileep said after the creaking had stopped. 'But if I were you, Diwan, I wouldn't hold my breath.'

I sat in my bed for a while after that, trying to still the doubts that Dileep had awakened. Looking down the row of beds, depth after depth to the far end of the room, I saw the Reverend's head risen over the partition again, and his eyes upon me like an owl's.

CHAPTER 13

You would suppose I might have thought about my mother more that first day at Bastard Bhavan, or at least that I might evoke her more in recounting it. But much as I would like you to believe that I've always been alert to the proportion of things, I can't say that my mother's death figured in my thinking very much until that night after Dileep had returned to his bed.

I suspect I have the Reverend to thank for having kept me too cowed and busy to dwell on my bereavement. Whatever the reason, it wasn't until I lay down in that dark, angular room full of slumbering strangers that it occurred to me that my mother was only two days dead. And I couldn't get that to sink in until I cast my mind back, hour by hour: watched Weems retreat into the smoke, doused the flames of my mother's pyre, carried her home, restored the light to her eyes, heard her speak to me again, followed her through the streets, rode on the bone of her hip.

I cried as quietly as I could so as not to awaken Dileep and the others, sobbing with my mouth and throat wide open and my face buried in my arms. I still couldn't help but make a few wet noises like bubbles bursting in my gullet, but they were lost in the general mumble and snore around me.

Even before I fell asleep I began to feel her presence, as if something of my mother – her scent, her breath – had survived the pyre and still abided, as if the flames had circumfused her: dissipated her into the air, diluted her in the Ganga's flow. But if that was her touch I felt in the air around my ear, if that was her voice I heard among the night songs outside the window, her touch was too equable to comfort me and she spoke in a language I could never understand.

When at last I did fall asleep, watching and listening for her as the tears dried on my cheeks, she came to me, fluttering toward me along the surface of the river with the same easy grace with which she used to walk across the street. It was the beginning of a dream I would have all through my childhood, almost as soon as I closed my eyes. It became so predictable that even in sleep I always knew what would happen next, though knowing what would happen next only deepened my terror.

She approached with her head uncovered, and in the yellow haze I could see she was smiling. I waded out a little way to greet her, but as she drew nearer her features grew dark and her cheeks seemed to shrink against her skull and her smile became a white-eyed, horror-struck stare. I tried to back away, but it was as if my legs had dissolved in the thick opacity of the river water, and by the time she was close enough to touch me, flames had begun to rise on her hair and clothing.

She raised one arm and pointed over my shoulder where her stare was fixed, and when she opened her mouth to speak a great rush of smoke howled out toward me. I fell back out of the water and onto the shore, and as I scrambled to my feet I saw that someone had been standing behind me all along. I looked up to see who it was, but I would never find out, because always, no matter how many times I dreamed this dream, no matter how many times I promised myself I would see it to its resolution, just as my gaze reached the stranger's face I would awaken with a shout in a tangle of bedding.

I slept badly when I managed to sleep at all, when I wasn't listening for Moonshi's footsteps or too terrified of my dreams to close my eyes. The days and nights passed and still there was no sign of Moonshi, but I clung to my hope that he would come for me. It was my shield, for no matter how many times I was bellowed at, punished, bullied, or ignored, I could always tell myself that none of it mattered, that tomorrow or the next day or the day after, Bastard Bhavan would evaporate like a dream.

As a consequence, I was a poor student – obstinate, fumbling, and distracted. I was probably never destined to be a scholar; maybe because my mother had filled me up with so much nonsense about how superior I was to everybody else, I always pretended that I knew more than I did, and supposed that what I didn't know was probably beneath me. And it didn't help that I now believed that none of it mattered, anyway. Of course, it's easier to believe that nothing

matters than it is to try to learn something, so maybe that's why I
tried so hard to keep believing in Moonshi, day after day, night after
night, during those first weeks at Bastard Bhavan.

But I probably wasn't as hopeless a case as the Reverend and Mr
Peter made me out to be. A good teacher understands that you can't
teach children anything they don't already know one way or another,
but Weems supposed that we didn't know anything at all, that we
were blank slates upon which he could write whatever he wanted.
And Mr Peter, with the self-hatred peculiar to the converted, believed
that what we did know, what he once knew, was so vile that it had to
be burned out of us with punishment and prayer. They both had
staked their souls on the notion that if they couldn't persuade us with
the righteousness of Christian thinking then they could at least
oppress us with its bulk.

Mr Peter's technique was to read a page aloud from one of our
textbooks, then have one of us read it aloud, then all of us, and then
he would make us copy it down on our slates, from which, taking
turns, we would read it aloud again. At last, to test us on it, he would
turn each sentence into a question which we were supposed to
answer in unison.

Thus, a paragraph might read, 'A fox passing by a garden, one
day, saw some very sweet and ripe grapes hanging in clusters from
the vine. But the vines had been trained, as vines should be, on a tall
trellis, and he could not reach them.' And after we'd tromped across
it all morning, Mr Peter would ask, 'A fox passing by a – what?'

And we'd respond, 'A garden, sir.'

' – a garden, yes – one day, saw some very – what?'

'Sweet, sir.'

' – sweet, yes – and?'

'Ripe, sir.'

' – ripe, yes – ripe what?'

'Grapes, sir.'

' – grapes, yes – hanging from the?'

'Vine, sir.'

' – vine, yes. But the vines had been – what?'

'Trained, sir.'

Even the Reverend was a welcome change when he deigned to
visit our class and check up on our instruction. The Reverend had

taught Mr Peter his numbing technique, but allowed himself to depart from it occasionally with a definition, an anecdote, or a moral, which Mr Peter lacked the personality to bestow.

'And what *is* a trellis?' the Reverend might ask, peering around us. 'You there, Keri. Tell us what a trellis is.'

'I don't know, Reverend Sahib.'

'Then kindly be seated and I shall tell you,' he'd say, and proceed to define a trellis and thus eventually remind himself of his boyhood, which, if you were to believe his recollection of it, afforded him a moral lesson every hour, and then finally he would liken a trellis to something holy – God's law, maybe, without which we could never grow toward the light and bear fruit.

I wasn't all that hard a nut for the Reverend to crack, especially when he launched into his attacks on the Brahmins. There'd been no love lost between me and the priests who'd banished my mother and me from the temple, so it pleased me to hear them vilified. And there was a lot about Hinduism, at least the surface of it that Weems understood, that didn't fit into my way of thinking the way a philosophy should if it's going to stick.

I don't mean to make it sound as though I knew all this from the start. Some of it I knew only by intuition and can articulate only now that I'm old and don't have to answer to anybody. And the rest of it came from Dileep.

If I'd had only the Reverend and Mr Peter to teach me I might never have learned a thing at Bastard Bhavan. But Dileep was a real teacher. Schoolwork came easily to him, like everything else, maybe because he didn't care very much about it. Unlike John Christopher, who had to labor all day long and into the night to memorize a verse from the New Testament, Dileep could read an entire chapter twice, slam the book shut, and recite it from memory. This amazing facility only enraged the Reverend, because none of the Gospel Dileep recited had any effect on Dileep's belief, unless it was to deepen his disbelief.

Everything I retained from Bastard Bhavan Dileep taught me on the sly, swinging down from his bunk after everyone else had fallen asleep and fixing scientific principles, the times table, English words and phrases in my memory with tricks, rhymes, jokes, and riddles, pulling the Reverend's lessons out of the clouds and down to earth where I could manage them. I remember his explaining English punctuation as follows: a comma was a cloud of breath, a question mark was a quizzical eyebrow, an exclamation point was the spittle on a shouting man's chin, a period was a nail upon which you hung a thought to dry. I think such devices as those were all that stood in the way of my turning into a helpless lackey like poor old Dhanda.

Dileep didn't seem to have much more use for Hinduism than he had for Christianity. He just naturally didn't take a liking to authority. When he talked about his soul he didn't mean it in a religious way; he meant his essence, his self.

I think he was the first person I ever knew who could hold two thoughts in his mind at the same time. Just because Christianity was bad didn't mean that Hinduism was good, and vice versa. Without Dileep's interventions I might have been converted in a fortnight, for I did think that if two ideas were in opposition, you had to choose one and discard the other. I guess I was like Weems in that regard, which was probably what gave the Reverend hope.

A friend like Dileep could be exhausting company. He was always making me stretch myself. He was a lot smarter than I could ever have hoped to be, and sometimes he hurt my pride intolerably. His way of thinking took more clear-headed independence than the Reverend's and though I stuck with it as best I could, it was lonely sometimes.

I remember one day in the late monsoon when the Reverend delivered a sermon based on his Redeemer's promise that the meek would inherit the earth. Maybe I was feeling especially meek that afternoon, or maybe it was the lightning which punctuated the Reverend's sermon outside the shell hole in the chapel, but the idea took hold, and when Dileep dropped down into my bunk that night to talk I brought it up.

'And won't that be wonderful?' he asked with a little smile. 'I don't know about you, but I can't wait.'

'Well,' I said. '*I* think the meek *will* inherit the earth.'

'You do?'

'Well, why shouldn't they? They deserve it, don't they?'

'I suppose so,' Dileep said, 'Only what about all the others in line ahead of them?'

'What do you mean?' I asked halfheartedly.

'Well, first you've got Christ – '

'But Christ was meek.'

'Meek? Oh, sure. Meekest fellow you'd ever want to know. Thought he was the only son of the only god, but everyone's got his crotchets.'

I leaned back and sighed.

'And then you've got the Queen, of course. Meekest old lady in the world. Never meant to take over. Never meant to hang my father.'

'All right, Dileep,' I said.

'And then of course you've got the rajas up ahead of you too, but they're such a generous bunch I'm sure they'll let you butt in ahead of them.'

'I said *all right, Dileep*.'

'But wait,' said Dileep, who was never above rubbing it in. 'We don't want to leave out Nanak Chand, do we? Or the badmashes? Or Mr Peter. Or, heaven forbid, Redeemer Walla himself. I tell you, Diwan, the meek are going to inherit the earth any day now, just as soon as the bloodsuckers are done with it, just as soon as their bellies are full.'

I guess what Dileep got out of our friendship was a means of formulating his ideas, for I think he was someone who didn't really know what he was thinking until he said it aloud. But all in all I know I got more out of our friendship than he did.

'Listen, Diwan,' he said, softening his voice a little, 'you've got a lot of sense. A lot more sense than all the rest of them, but like all the rest of them you've got a weakness for dreamy notions. Well, dreamy notions are fine if you're asleep, but when you're awake you've got to trust a little more in your eyes and ears, in the here and now. Why do you think Redeemer Walla spouts all this nonsense about being meek and having a childlike faith and waiting for a heavenly reward and all the rest of it? He doesn't want you to trust yourself. He wants you to – '

'And what about you?' I muttered with a scowl. 'What do you think *you're* doing?'

'What do you mean?'

'You don't trust me either.'

'That's not true. You're my friend. You're my Diwan.'

'It *is* true. You think I'm stupid for believing all that stuff about the meek.'

'I do not. I just said you've got a lot of sense. What are you talking about? Look, I live here too. I know what it's like. I'd like to stop fighting too sometimes. But I can't. And neither can you. We've got too much to lose.'

I was startled to realize that I'd begun to cry. '*What* have we got to lose?' I sobbed back at him. 'We don't have *anything* to lose. We don't have anything . . . '

Dileep stared at me for a moment, and I could hear the rain spattering on the roof above us. 'Whenever you forget what you've got to lose, take a look at John Christopher,' Dileep said, reaching toward his bed. 'I gave up on him, Diwan, and he gave up on himself, and now look what's become of him. One of these days while you're lying around dreaming about your servant, Redeemer Walla's going to snare your soul. But if you want to become another one of his mynah birds that's your business, not mine. I'm going to sleep.'

I stopped sobbing and looked for a moment at John Christopher as he lay sleeping on his back, as rigid and symmetrical as a corpse.

'Dileep?' I whispered up along the wall.

'What is it?'

'Are we still friends?'

I could hear him pause and sigh. 'Yes, Diwan,' he finally whispered, barely audible in the noise from the falling rain. 'Friends forever.'

CHAPTER
14

My weeks at Bastard Bhavan turned into months and somewhere along the way I gave up on Moonshi. Not all at once, but little by little, as I ran out of excuses for him, and acknowledged, in the end, that Bastard Bhavan was now my home, Dileep and the boys my family. My life with Moonshi and my mother hadn't been all that enviable, after all, even from the dismal perspective of Bastard Bhavan, and though there was no forgetting my mother, as she reminded me every night in my dreams, my errands in the Moslem quarter and my long and solitary afternoons on the roof became ever more strange and distant.

Not that my present situation was any less peculiar. Looking back, I think the strangest thing about my time at Bastard Bhavan was how little I learned about the Bible. I must have read most of it, or heard it read aloud, but never in sequence. Dileep used to say that the Reverend didn't really want us to master Scripture, since it was his mastery of Scripture that gave him his power, but I think the Reverend believed in the Bible too much to teach it very well. One little phrase – 'The Lord will smite thee with the botch of Egypt' is one I remember for some reason – could set him off on a whole afternoon of sermonizing until it lay at his feet like a wrung-out rag.

What I liked best about the story of Jesus was the virgin birth. The mystery of his paternity was like a bond between us, and I could never blame Jesus, as Dileep did, for choosing God as his father.

But now I'd better return to my daily routine at Bastard Bhavan, which underwent a change in the early winter of my eighth year, 1866. One evening at chapel, just as the cool weather was approaching, the Reverend read a letter to us that he'd received from Sir Harry Billings, the newly elected chairman of the Society for the Propagation of the Revealed Word. Owing to an unspecified scandal involving the society's former treasurer, donations were off and all its missionaries were directed to make their operations self-supporting by the time the board took its tour of the society's missions the following September.

'It is up to each of you, by God's grace,' Sir Harry concluded, 'to sink or swim.'

What this meant, the Reverend explained, was that we had to find some way of making money without at the same time slowing down our rate of instruction. Mr Peter suggested that we manufacture rope, sandals, or baskets like the other missions in Cawnpore, but the Reverend pointed out that none of these missions ever really made any money, and besides, he didn't want to engage his boys in work that wasn't educational.

No, Weems told us, the problem would require divine inspiration and penetrating cogitation, and he asked that we devote all our prayers to its solution. What we needed was an industry that was profitable but uncorrupting, material but also spiritual: that would harness our individual talents and ambitions for the good of the whole and the glory of God.

It may not sound like a fascinating problem to you, but to us it meant a break from the slow death of Mr Peter's teaching, and that evening during chores we were all animated by it. Besides Dileep, Dhanda, Puran, John Christopher, and myself, there were nine or ten other boys in the Reverend's keeping. There were three converts besides John Christopher when I arrived at Bastard Bhavan, each named after one of the three remaining Gospels: Matthew, Mark, and Luke. They weren't as priggish as John Christopher and probably didn't like him any more than Dileep and I did, but they also didn't like Dileep and me any more than John Christopher did, and thus tended to keep to themselves.

The youngest of us was a haunted Moslem loner named Jahangir – after the Moghul – who'd lost his family in a fire he'd accidentally set himself. I think there were four more Moslem boys, the oldest of whom had hair on his shoulders and was missing all his teeth. He liked to get attention by contorting his face in an astonishing fashion, so that he looked as though he'd swallowed his entire jaw.

The rest of us were Hindus, if you counted Ralph, who was no convert but the issue of a sweeper girl and an Irish soldier. He had red hair and strange black freckles and the meanest disposition at Bastard Bhavan. He once got into a fight with one of the Moslems and bit right through his ear before the Reverend knocked him cold with a blow from his leather-bound Bible.

And then there was Bhanu, Bastard Bhavan's reluctant saviour, a tiny and ricket-stricken Hindu boy whom we called 'Copy' because he could draw a perfect likeness of whatever you set before him.

Copy was an even worse student than I. When he wasn't daydreaming he was sketching things on his slate, and when he wasn't sketching he was standing in a corner of the room or silently receiving Mr Peter's ruler on the palm of his hand for his efforts. Dileep regarded Copy's talent as a miracle and tried to protect him from Weems and Mr Peter, but it wasn't easy; Copy was too candid and hapless to keep out of trouble for long.

Copy didn't remember his parents in what we called the 'Real World,' having been orphaned as an infant, adopted by a British couple, and orphaned again when they returned to England, so Dileep invented Copy's family for him. He maintained that Copy came from a long line of court portraitists, that his father had been decapitated for including the King of Avadh's warts in a royal portrait and his mother killed waving a scimitar at the side of the rebel Rani of Jhansi: his father a martyr to truth, his mother to freedom. Copy, in return for this genealogy, drew indelicate cartoons of Weems and Mr Peter on the backs of the Reverend's discarded papers.

After the Reverend announced the emergency he spent the next two days in conspicuous meditation. In fact, he was the most ostentatious thinker I ever saw. He wandered among us like a ghost, staring off into space, bumping into furniture, adopting all sorts of contemplative poses while we bustled around him. Sometimes he'd break into a sweat or begin to tremble and we'd all stop what we were doing to see what was percolating, but then it would pass and we'd go back to work.

One night soon afterward we heard what sounded like gunfire outside the windows and climbed up to the top bunks to see what it was. One of the converts, believing the Devil's Wind was blowing again, hid under his bed and lapsed into a mantra, and Dhanda, under the same misapprehension, rushed about on his crutch, singing a hymn.

But it finally dawned on us that it was Diwali that was filling the night with sparks and percussion, that the festival of lights had sneaked up on us and caught us unawares. As we watched, excited by the display but reminded by it of our isolation from the natural world, from Rama's welcome home, a rocket veered off its course and arched toward us, fizzling around on the Reverend's precious grass for a moment before exploding with a terrific bang.

But oddly enough there was no sign of the Reverend that night: only Mr Peter, who darted out onto the lawn with a bucket of water to douse the rocket's smoldering remains.

The next morning when we went outside to wash up we found a team of bricklayers at work in the dim dawn light, digging a pit a little distance from the privy, and as we washed our faces over the trough a potter arrived in a horsedrawn cart and began to set up his wheel under one of the Reverend's trees.

'What's going on?' I whispered to Dileep.

Dileep shrugged. 'It looks like Redeemer Walla's got a plan.'

'But what is it?' I asked. 'What do you think he's up to?'

'Pots, probably,' Dileep said with an unconvincing shrug. 'Probably pots for the memsahibs' gardens out in Generalanj.'

'Ha!' said Mr Peter, hurrying us inside. 'Pots indeed. You think you know so much? You wait until Reverend Sahib speaks to you this morning. Then you'll see how much you know. Now everyone get dressed for chapel.'

The Reverend waited until we were all seated in the chapel before making his entrance, striding up to his pulpit with his hair dishevelled and a strange light burning in his eyes. He rushed through the usual morning service, barely bothering to sermonize at all except to say that he was feeling especially thankful that morning; and after the benediction, looking as relieved that it was over as the rest of us, he stepped around in front of his pulpit, rubbing his hands together.

'My sons,' he said with a beneficent look, as if he were about to bestow a great gift, 'my dear, blessed sons. Last night amid the hellfire of heathen rites, God spoke to me, or more correctly perhaps I should say that I finally opened my ears up to Him, for surely He had been speaking to me all along and I was too deafened by the grumbling of profane despair to listen, as we all must listen if we are ever to know Him who made us.'

Talking like that worked fine for the Reverend when he didn't have anything in particular to say, but I could see that it bothered even him now that he had something to impart. Making a long story short, or keeping a short story short, was not his speciality, so perhaps I'd better have a try.

It seems that during the night as he paced around the ghats looking for orphans he got to thinking about the Mutiny. Everyone had thought the Mutiny had been a terrible calamity, Weems told us, but maybe God had had something else in mind. Before the Mutiny people never included Cawnpore on their Indian tours if they could help it, but now so many visitors came to the city to see the sights — the Nana's demolished palace at Bithoor, the entrenchment, the ghat where the sepoys had opened fire on the surrendered garrison, the house where the survivors had been slaughtered, and the well into which their bodies had been flung – that new hotels were being constructed to house them and a whole new industry of souvenirs and guided tours had sprung up.

But what this industry lacked was direction, a divine and uplifting purpose. The tour guides led their groups around, leering and haranguing as if Cawnpore were a bloody carnival sideshow while along their route peddlers hawked the most grotesque mementoes; here the Reverend held up some examples for us to deplore: an effigy of the Nana Sahib filled with firecrackers, a lock of blond hair supposedly scavenged from the House of Sorrow where the women and children had been massacred.

Surely the martyrs of Cawnpore deserved better than that, as did those sincere Christians who toured the sites to honor them, and better than that was what we were going to give them. Looking at the sky the night before, the Reverend had seen a vision in the pulsing glare from the whizbangs and fizgigs: a mounted sepoy with his gory cutlass upraised over the pleading figure of a half-drowned memsahib with her baby at her breast, the water around them littered with corpses and stained with blood. It was a vision to break the heart and sear the soul, and that, the Reverend told us, was precisely why God had revealed it to him. It was to be the hallmark of a new enterprise which would turn tourists into pilgrims, battlefields and slaughterhouses into shrines, while at the same time meeting the requirements of Sir Harry Billings and his board.

The solution to our problem, Reverend Weems finally declared – and if you think I've failed to make a long story short it's because you didn't sit there all morning through the Reverend's version – the answer to our prayers was plates.

Yes, plates. Memorial plates dedicated to the Nana Sahib's victims, emblazoned with pertinent quotations from the Bible, and illustrated by our own dear Copy with a rendering of the Reverend's vision. Imagine, Weems exclaimed; wholesome mementoes for Cawnpore's visitors to take home with them, decorated with a vision bestowed directly by God, preserving the memory of the Mutiny's martyrs forever (or for as long as the plates lasted, anyway) and spreading the name of the Mission Society for the Propagation of the Revealed Word Asylum for Orphan Boys throughout the Empire.

I suppose the Reverend had expected us to burst into applause or carry him around on our shoulders for his stroke of genius, but we'd been trained to be unresponsive and merely looked at each other in bewilderment.

'Plates, my sons!' he shouted at us, the light dying a little in his eyes. 'I tell you, it's our only hope!'

'Yes, Reverend Sahib,' John Christopher said, but his lone voice only seemed to make the Reverend, already feverish from lack of sleep, more desperate to convince us.

'Already, even as I speak, measures are being taken to ensure our success. A kiln is rising out of the ground and a potter is already turning out plates by the door. This very afternoon we will begin to train you at the glazing tables, and in a week, if we all pull together, we will be producing plates worthy of Wedgwood. Now, what do you say?'

We didn't know what to say, never having heard of Wedgwood or even glazing, until Mr Peter stepped between Weems and us, ordered us to our feet, and led us in a little cheer that seemed slightly to revive the Reverend's spirits.

'You'll see,' he said, walking past us and out of the room. 'You'll see what God can do.'

CHAPTER
15

That afternoon our study tables were arranged into one long line leading right up to the door. The Reverend tested our artistic abilities by having each of us copy a portrait of Queen Victoria on our slates. I surprised myself with my effort, for though I might have exaggerated the Queen Empress's eyeballs, I thought it bore a crude resemblance. It didn't impress the Reverend, however, and when he lined up our work in order of accuracy mine was not placed near Copy's, which was almost a duplicate of the original, but near Ralph's, which was a scrawl.

So Copy was seated at the head of the table, Ralph and me at the opposite end, Dileep and the others lined up in between. The plan, the Reverend explained, was for the potter's sun-dried plates to be dipped in white glaze and handed to Copy, who would pencil in a drawing of the Reverend's vision. This would then be handed to John Christopher beside him, who would brush a quotation from the Bible along the rim in his fastidious hand. Then it would be passed along to the next in line, who would color in the memsahib's face with pink glaze, then to his neighbor, who would color in her yellow tresses, and so on down the line in order of decreasing intricacy until it finally reached me. My job was to color in the blood on both the river and the sepoy's upraised cutlass in the hope that my artlessness would lend authenticity to the gore. Ralph wasn't allowed near a brush, but he was to take the completed plates out to be baked in the kiln and bring in fresh plates to be decorated.

It took all that afternoon for Copy to draw the Reverend's vision to Weems's satisfaction. At first he tried to go by the Reverend's description, but it only confused him, and always the memsahib would look too homely or the sepoy too heroic. Finally the Reverend fetched a book from his study and opened it to an illustration that depicted his vision with bewildering precision, right down to the corpses floating in the water. Dileep said that it proved that the Reverend had lied to us about his vision at the ghats, but now that I look back I don't think Weems had lied, exactly; it was just that even his visions were secondhand.

With the illustration to go by, Copy did his job perfectly, and John Christopher dutifully brushed on a quotation from Matthew that the Reverend had selected: 'Do not throw your pearls before swine lest they trample them underfoot and turn to attack you.' But the rest of us had a harder time of it, and during the first few days the plates got bogged down somewhere along the line. The first results weren't encouraging. After firing, the glaze corpses became loglike lumps, the sepoy's leer dissolved into a little brown blob, and the memsahib's face sprouted a snout where the pink glaze bled into the river.

But the Reverend would not be discouraged. He borrowed ceramics manuals from memsahibs in Generalganj and began to experiment scientifically with little samples of glaze on numbered clay squares. He had the potter make the plates larger so they could better accommodate the detail his vision required, and he had us thin down our glazes so they wouldn't globulate in the kiln. After a week or two we began to turn out saleable plates, the first of which the Reverend had us pray over and hang on the wall above the door.

At first even Dileep took pride in his work at the glazing tables, and Copy, of course, acquired an exalted status at Bastard Bhavan; if he injured himself with so much as a splinter the Reverend would fuss over him like a nursemaid and excuse him from his studies to rest.

While we were still perfecting our technique, Weems actually consulted us about the work: Were we comfortable? Were our brushes holding up all right? Did we think the pace of production was too fast? And every night before sending us to bed he would lead us outside to stand in the warmth from the kiln and watch the potter remove the plates and admire the results of our labors.

But there was a strange principle at work in that job: the better we became at it the less we liked it. As our work improved, the pace quickened, but the Reverend's expectations always outran us until his pride in our early efforts had soured into a general dissatisfaction. Some days we worked faster than others, which was inevitable, but the Reverend didn't admit to inevitabilities and regarded as a failure any day in which we didn't exceed the production of the last.

He stopped consulting us and varying our work with his experiments and began to berate us instead: Why was this plate chipped? Where was the ribbon in the memsahib's hair? Why did the sky look so muddy? Why couldn't we work faster?

Weems never bothered Copy, but I think he was the one who suffered the most. The rest of us had nothing in particular to lose by turning out those plates day after day, but Copy had his gift, and after a while he stopped drawing cartoons for Dileep at night or sketching in class, and during chapel his small, articulate hands would lie motionless in his lap.

The work became so automatic that we could have managed it with our eyes closed, and in fact when I close my eyes now I can still see that bloody scene. Floating in the foreground is a beheaded corpse in a British uniform, behind which a memsahib in a halo of light stands waist-high in the bloody water, pleading with the mounted sepoy to spare her and the child she holds to her bosom. The Reverend liked to believe that painting such a scene was teaching us about the barbarity of our people, but instead it made us wonder about the British. As Dileep put it one afternoon, 'What kind of people would eat off such plates?'

The answer was 'No one,' or so it seemed at first, for the Reverend wasn't having much luck finding customers for our gruesome merchandise. A pious hotelkeeper had agreed to sell the plates in his lobby, but his establishment was in a state of decline, reduced to a native and Eurasian clientele which had no use for such mementoes. The first-class hotels ran tours of their own and peddled their own souvenirs – maps, pamphlets, and lithographs.

As our stacks of platters multiplied along the wall of our workroom, Weems became desperate enough to send a reluctant Mr Peter out to sell our wares from a cart near the entrenchment. But Mr Peter had no more talent as a salesman than he had as a teacher and so infuriated his competitors with his haughty manner that they once overturned his cart and chased him home in a shower of broken plates.

There was no way around it; the Reverend was going to have to sell those plates himself. Of course, Weems would never do anything unless he could devise two or three righteous reasons for doing it. Getting our plates sold should have been noble enough, since it fit right in with Sir Harry's directive, but the process had to be further ennobled to serve the Reverend's purpose, for nothing was worth doing if it didn't ingratiate Weems with God.

So, after another one of his searching periods he came up with the idea of running his own tours. To that end he and Mr Peter distributed leaflets around town, inviting all true Christian Englishmen (and all true English Christians) to join him on a pilgrimage, boxed lunches suggested, which would begin at the entrenchment and proceed by palanquin to the Sati Chowra Ghat (Massacre Ghat, as he called it), then to the site of the House of Sorrows and the memorial well. The tour would finally end on a hopeful note at

Bastard Bhavan itself, where Weems could demonstrate how through rigorous Christian teaching and disciplined industry he was taming the heathen beast, and where pilgrims would be encouraged to aid in this effort by purchasing our memorial plates, available in the outer office, with substantial discounts on quantity purchases.

The Reverend took John Christopher and me along with him that first day, ostensibly to help him with various props – a map, a Bible, a flimsy folding podium – but really to act as props ourselves: John Christopher an example of what could be done with the heathen, me of what remained to be done. To play up the difference, Weems dressed John Christopher in a brand-new uniform starched and ironed by the Reverend's dhobi and clad me in a strange caricature of native dress: oversized slippers with spiralled toes, a great drooping dhoti wrapped around my legs, a frayed red tunic and a crude turban the Reverend fashioned himself out of handkerchiefs he'd knotted together into one long roll. I looked like no Indian you've ever seen, but I suppose that's what it took to make me look more ridiculous than John Christopher.

All this pleased John Christopher, who smirked at me along the way out of the compound as he rehearsed a scriptural recitation with the Reverend. And it was all right with me because it meant I would have my first glimpse of the Real World in nine months, for I hadn't set foot outside Bastard Bhavan's confines since the Reverend had brought me there, unbelievable as that seems to me now.

It was a cool winter day for those parts, but the sun was sharp on my turbaned head and we walked in a bank of the dust we kicked up in the steady, contrary breeze.

'So,' the Reverend said to John Christopher as we neared Bastard Bhavan's outer limits, 'you know what to do?'

John Christopher nodded up at him. 'Oh yes, Reverend Sahib.'

'The crucial thing is that you listen closely for your cues. But then I don't have to worry about *you*, John Christopher, do I?'

'No, Reverend Sahib,' John Christopher replied, beaming.

'It's Balbeer here I have to worry about,' the Reverend said as I walked along beside him, drinking in my first glimpse of the Real World. Already, where there'd been only scaffolding and workers' huts two years before, the Muir Cotton Mill was in full operation, its grounds carpeted with flecks of fuzz cast off by the carding machines.

'Balbeer isn't even listening to me now, is he, John Christopher?' the Reverend said.

'No, Reverend Sahib,' John Christopher sneered, peering around at me from behind the fluttering tail of the Reverend's coat.

'Reverend Sahib?' I said.

'*Listening,*' the Reverend said. 'You haven't been listening.'

'But I have, Reverend Sahib,' I said, though I still couldn't stop hungrily staring around me.

'Have you indeed?' The Reverend removed a sheaf of paper from the inside pocket of his black coat, 'Balbeer,' he said, squinting at his notes in the sunlight, 'I have brought John Christopher because he is such a source of pride to me, but I have brought you along only because of all my boys – and I exclude Ralph and Dhanda, of course – you were the least necessary at the glazing table, so do not pride yourself on this excursion. It is John Christopher's reward, not yours.'

'Yes, Reverend Sahib,' I said, staring back at a grim, wide white woman who stood on the verandah of a charitable dispensary with her arms folded.

'Good day, madame,' the Reverend called out, removing his hat in the peculiar English fashion and showing her the top of his head.

But as we passed, the woman stared at us without speaking, her little eyes rolling like marbles along the tops of her great red cheeks.

'Bless you, poor woman,' Weems muttered, replacing his hat, as the woman stepped back inside.

Nothing looked familiar to me. Every building we'd passed so far had been so new and bleak, tin-roofed and whitewashed and uniform, that it was as if Bastard Bhavan had somehow extended itself across the entire city since my mother's death and overwhelmed the Real World.

But then I remembered that we were still on Cawnpore's outskirts, for as we approached the Moslem quarter the Real World submerged me like a flood. The spectacle in the street suddenly became so dense and outlandish that like a cavebound beast flushed into the sunlight I had to shield my eyes.

We passed a penitent wrapped in chains, a dhobi straining under a laundry sack thrice his size, a chaprasi walking ahead of his master's palanquin and singing its occupant's praises in florid Urdu, an Akali sikh with his turban encircled by razor-sharp hoops, a family of Marvaris driving a herd of yearling bullocks, two Baluchis with muskets as long as lampposts, a kite peddler, a knife sharpener, a juggler, a jogi, and lining the streets like paintings in a gallery were the stalls of tailors and grain merchants, calico printers, tattoo artists, stonecutters, jawsmiths, each sending his own noise out into the general cacophony.

So the three of us passed through my old haunts: John Christopher clutching his Bible to his chest and staring straight ahead; the Reverend consulting his notes and mumbling to himself, his nostrils flaring in the scents and stenches from the street; and I in my costume, my arms wrapped around Weems's podium and rolled-up map, drawing stares from the idle and the curious, who must have thought they'd seen everything until I came into view.

As we neared the footbridge across the Ganges Canal I looked for Sayideen's stall in the last block of the Moslem quarter, but it was closed, and not just closed but boarded up and padlocked.

'Careful there, Balbeer,' the Reverend said as I stared back at Sayideen's abandoned stall and stumbled slightly in the street.

Now I began to wonder if Moonshi was still somewhere in the city or if he too had disappeared. I searched among the crowds that passed us as we neared the turn for my old street, but hopelessly, for I'd given up any real expectation that he would return to rescue me. He was probably destitute by then, or even dead, and I confess to thinking it would have served him right.

The Reverend paused at the corner of my old street to replace his notes in his pocket and blow his nose, and a small voice told me to escape from him and run off into the city. But as I stood with John Christopher at the crossroads a woman passed us with her head covered by the veil of her dingy sari, and then another passed in another direction, and I began to look around me in a mysterious panic, as if among the veiled passersby in the Hindu quarter my mother was materializing in fragments: in this woman's posture, in that one's gait, in the shape of another's veiled head.

'What is it, Balbeer?' the Reverend asked, scowling at me as he tucked away his fouled handkerchief.

'Sir?' I asked, startled and short of breath as I stared down my mother's street.

'What's the matter with you? Are you ill?'

'N–no, sir,' I said, looking down at my feet and trying to catch my breath.

'Then come along,' the Reverend said, striding forward, 'before you make us late.'

We passed under a convergence of wires at the telegraph office, and almost with relief I found myself back on the sanitary outskirts, out of sight of the haunted bazaar. The road took us past a row of barracks, where British soldiers were sleepily lining up in their red uniforms.

'Reverend!' a heavy, scarlet-whiskered soldier shouted with a peculiar leer. 'Yoo-hoo! Oh, Reverend!'

'Disregard him, my sons,' Weems said, grimly setting his jaw and quickening the pace.

'I say, Reverend!' the soldier persisted as his mates laughed behind him. 'Taking the little niggers to Jesus, are we? Leading the wogs to God?'

'Corporal!' a short man with a curlicued moustache shouted. 'Return to ranks!'

We turned off the road and walked out onto the parade ground, a long flat field of dust and dying grass. At the far end, where the field turned into a rubbled waste, twenty or so English men and women in full touring regalia stood waiting for us. A variety of ekkas and palanquins were parked nearby; their drivers and bearers squatted around in a circle nursing a hookah.

I wished Dileep could have seen the Reverend then. Weems became strangely agitated when his audience came into view. He stopped in his tracks, dropped his hat, fumbled a comb through his hair, retrieved his hat, and with his eyes darting about asked us how he looked. Then before we could answer he pulled his hat back onto his head and hurried us forward, muttering to himself and bellowing greetings in alternation, his walking stick upraised like a cutlass.

It was an odd performance, and several of the women backed away as we approached.

'Good morning, Reverend,' one hearty man in thick spectacles exclaimed with a bucktoothed grin. 'I know I speak for everyone when I express how very pleased and honored – '

But Weems was in such a dither that he didn't seem to see the man and rushed by into the center of the group, digging into his pocket for his timepiece. 'Well, then,' he said, consulting his watch with a frown. 'I see we're all on time.'

'Yes,' the toothy man said, 'and may I say – '

But again Weems didn't seem to hear him. He roughly retrieved the folding rostrum from me and began to set it up in everyone's midst. A contraption of his own invention, it was supposed to unfold like a tripod, but for a full minute Weems couldn't get its legs to lock, and when he set it down it fell over like a drunken spider. At last, after the most frenzied effort, he managed to erect it properly and stood before it with an impatient look, the sweat streaming down his forehead, though a cold wind scudded across the parade ground, kicking up dust.

Downright frightened now, Weems's customers gathered into a little bunch in front of him, their eyes never leaving his, and when they seemed arranged to his satisfaction, Weems spread his notes out on the rostrum's top and began.

He asked that everyone bow his head in prayer and then dedicated the tour to the glory of God and the men and women who were martyred in His name, expressing the wish that the story he was about to unfold would make his little windblown congregation ever mindful of their sacrifice, et cetera, et cetera. As his prayer stretched on his voice gathered strength until he was his old self again, and when he reached the proper pitch he cut his benediction short and with barely a breath between he launched into the lecture that follows, set down as best I can recollect it.

[Note: The following chapter is composed not of Balbeer's imperfect rendering of the Reverend's lecture, but of a pamphlet written and distributed by Weems himself, a copy of which has been very kindly loaned to me by Mr Samuel Swanson Weems, the Reverend's grandnephew. H.W.C.]

•CHAPTER•
16

Remarks
of the
Reverend Josiah Weems
of the
Mission Society for the Propagation of the Revealed Word
Asylum for Orphaned Boys
Delivered at the
Major Sites
of the
Great Mutiny
at
Cawnpore
and
Humbly Dedicated
to the
Christian Martyrs
Who Died for the
Glory of God
and the
Advancement of Civilization
in the
Cruel Summer of 1857

The Entrenchment

Dear ladies, distinguished gentlemen, fellow citizens of this glorious empire, true believers all in Christ our Lord and Saviour: we are gathered today on sacred ground: as sacred as any beyond the boundaries of the Holy Land. Looking around us at this dusty scrub and rubble, it might seem that in all the world there were no less likely stage for the sacramental drama of tragedy and triumph we are gathered here to commemorate; no city more forlorn and profane than Cawnpore. And yet is it so unlike our Maker to choose such a place? Is Cawnpore so different from Golgotha, or Sinai, or even blessed Bethlehem?

We may grieve for our fallen countrymen here so pitilessly slaughtered, but we owe them more than our tears. We owe them our lives, our honor, our rededication to Christianity's cause for which they gave their precious lives. It is for the sake of such recent and tragic sacrifice that we of the Mission Society for the Propagation of the Revealed Word Asylum for Orphan Boys have inaugurated these tours so that no longer shall the saga of our martyred dead be reduced to grist for the barker's mill, and so that *all the people of the earth may know that the Lord is God and that there is none other.*

I shall speak of the blood of innocents shed not ten years ago in this city of melancholy fame; but by this I cannot suggest, however devoutly I might wish I could, that nothing could have been done to avert the Great Mutiny of 1857. For the lives we honor were not lost in a natural calamity but in a disaster of man's own devising.

The first of our countrymen to reach these shores boasted many laudable qualities: among them grit, vitality, pertinacity, and vision. But we are agreed, I trust, that they were not, on the whole, the finest representatives of Christian civilization our race has produced. Impatient with the pace of Western commerce they sought the rich, tempestuous markets of the East; and discontented with the cohibitions of decent social intercourse, they lived lives of decadence and debauchery rivalled only by the vile indulgences of their heathen hosts.

But for all their faults they were Englishmen, and demanded order of their universe: a requirement the crumbling Empire of the Grand Moghul could not meet, besieged as it was like a toothless lion by the Mahratta and the Sikh. So our countrymen enforced their own order, bit by bit, frontier by frontier, Islamic barony by Hindu principality, until the East India Company's dominions stretched from Bombay to Assam, and from Kashmir to the Gulf of Mannar.

In this these adventurers were the instruments of God, but once their empire was won they proved ill suited to govern it, and a new breed of Company man emerged: temperate, domesticated, determined to bring the institutions of Western civilization to the benighted millions who were now their subjects. The order the Company had imposed on India it now proposed to impose on itself: a system of laws modelled on England's own was set down; administrative procedures were devised; taut lines of command were laid through the whole of the Company's irregular, ragtag army. Governors-general instituted social reforms: eradicated sati, wiped out infanticide, annihilated the dreaded Thugs, redistributed land to the peasantry, and annexed the kingdoms of profligate kings.

Who among us could but applaud such reforms, or be blind to the benefits of the Company's rule? But the house they built was set on a foundation of shifting sand, for it was their calamitous misapprehension that they could introduce these institutions into a barbaric society without the very light from which those institutions burst forth in the first place: Christianity itself.

For how could India's people, who believe themselves to be the descendants of insects and reptiles, who immolate their widows and propitiate their multitudinous and depraved deities with the sacrifice of their own children, or who, as in the case of the fanatic children of Islam, believe the Lord God chose a murdering bigamist as His messenger – how could such a people have been expected to embrace us? For every virtue we espoused they churned with a multitude of vices, *like the troubled sea, when it cannot rest, whose waters cast up mire and dirt.*

There is no peace, saith God, to the wicked. The subject races could not fathom the Company's fatuous reassurances that for all its reforms theirs was a government above religion which would never interfere with native custom and belief.

But the native's custom is suspiciousness, superstition his belief. Without the guidance which only a Christian firm in his evangelism could have provided, the heathen had no defense against the calumnious rumors spread through the villages and bazaars by those who had lost the most to the Company's governance: landlords, overthrown princes, disgruntled holy men, outraged mullahs, and querimonious Brahmin priests. It was whispered that the Queen herself had ordered that all natives be converted at gunpoint, that three hundred thousand heathen holy men were to be slaughtered, that all princely states were to be annexed and all their citizens' castes defiled. However grotesque and outlandish these notions may seem to us today, it is not difficult to imagine the effect they had on minds intoxicated by millennia of extravagant falsehood.

But none of these baseless calumnies proved more disastrous than that which reached our native soldiery via the whispered taunts of nautch girls and prostitutes to the effect that the paper cartridges for the newly issued Enfield rifles had been saturated with pig grease, so that when, before loading, the sepoys bit into them, as their officers commanded, they would be irrevocably defiled: the Moslems thereby losing their admission to paradise, the Hindus consigning themselves to an eternity of monstrous incarnations.

Once the pride of the Company, its annals charged with glorious deeds and adventures in the field, the native army had long been taken for granted by its English officers, who themselves had grown weary of the petty routine of an idle army and yearned for appointments elsewhere. In their longings for commissionerships, staff positions, or service on the Northwest Frontier, our officers grew remote from their men, allowed discipline to slacken, lost that personal allegiance which had been the underpinning of their past glories, and fell into a condition of inert despair.

Which brings us to the immediate particulars. Commanding the garrison here at Cawnpore was Major-General Sir Hugh Massy Wheeler, an aging soldier of the old school, wishfully tolerant of his sepoys' insolence and nostalgically confident of their loyalty, who had allied himself in marriage with one in whose veins flowed heathen blood. The garrison he commanded was three thousand strong, but it was a force in which his English soldiers and officers were outnumbered ten to one by native sepoys: a gross imbalance which, however, never seems to have given General Wheeler pause, even when word reached Cawnpore of the sepoy uprising at Meerut on the tenth of May.

Indeed, it was not until late in the month that he permitted his officers to make furtive preparations for a siege, and even then, out of some muddled hopefulness that no true disaster could befall his benign command, he chose for his entrenchment not the magazine –

three acres impregnably fortified and within a short distance of the river — but a pitiful row of barracks that once stood where we now stand, surrounded by no more than a low clay wall, over a mile from the Ganges's banks.

It was into this sorry enclosure under the scorching sun of early June that one thousand people poured: two hundred of them soldiers, one hundred officers, one hundred and twenty-five musicians and nonmilitary personnel, perhaps thirty loyal natives, a dozen or so faithful sepoys, and the rest women and children, precious to their husbands' and fathers' hearts; all, all destined for a worse fate than the greatest pessimist among them was despondent enough to apprehend.

Their hope was that the mutinous sepoys would not bother laying siege to so pitiful a garrison and might, after some minor mischief in the city, press on instead to join the fellows around the Moghul banner of Bahadur Shah, the King of Delhi.

And indeed such might have been the eventuality had it not been for the pernicious intervention of one embittered, ruthless, and ambitious man whose name I can scarcely bring myself to record, synonymous as it has become with the basest treachery and the most bestial atrocity: Dhundoo Pant, the Nana Sahib, the bloody Beast of Cawnpore.

'The so-called King of Delhi is a shadow of his exalted ancestors,' the Nana Sahib told the sepoys as they set off for Delhi along the Grand Trunk Road, 'but I am the true Peshwa, son of the great Baji Rao the Second, whose Mahratta warriors long ago chased the King of Delhi's forebears into their red fortress like mice. Why should you sepoys waste your valor on so frail a king as Bahadur Shah when here in your very midst is a courageous Hindu emperor, born to lead his people to victory against the exhausted magic of the English monkeys?'

That he was merely the adoptive and not the natural heir of old Baji Rao's throne; that the throne itself had been no more than a relic since Sir John Malcolm overturned it in 1818; that when it had served the Nana's purposes he had fawned upon the British in his palace at Bithoor; that he now opposed his former dinner guests and billiard partners not out of racial pride or patriotism but because they had refused to enrich him further by extending to him his late 'father's' yearly allowance – all this he left out of his exhortation on the Delhi Road, and with promises of treasure, glory, and adventure, he lured the sepoys back into the city.

But *the heathen are sunk down in the pit that they made: in the net in which they hid is their own foot taken.* Even with his thousands of mutineers, brigands, and badmashes to do his bidding the bejewelled coward faltered, fearing our countrymen even as they huddled nigh helpless on the all but open ground, and instead of laying siege to the entrenchment commanded his men to set fire to the city and murder every stranded European man, woman, and child they could find, hoping with such a spectacle of carnage and destruction to frighten our garrison into surrendering without a struggle.

But how little he knew the Christian faith, the English will. Though the night air carried the screams of the Nana's first victims to our countrymen's ears and lo! the horizon was lurid with the fire and smoke of advancing devastation, they did not falter, for they knew with King David that the Lord *trieth the righteous, but the wicked and him that loveth violence his soul hateth.* They would resist the Nana Sahib and his demonic army until every hope had been exhausted.

His own hope of easy victory dashed, the Nana raised up his war banners – one Moslem, the other sporting the Hindu monkey God – and he and his minions gathered *themselves against the soul of the righteous,* condemned *the innocent blood,* and opened fire on the entrenchment.

As you stand here, imagine the roar of the Nana's guns in your ears, the sky above you peppered with iron and lead, the air choked with sulfurous smoke, the children's screams of terror – nay, like so much of what happened here it is beyond imagining. Women nursing their fallen menfolk were decapitated by cannon shot where they knelt, babes were shot through as they suckled at their mothers' breasts, young men's hair turned white in a twinkling, others were driven mad by grief and the summer heat which climbed to 140 degrees at midday. Fever, apoplexy, cholera, dysentery, and insanity took their toll over the weeks our countrymen withstood the Nana's onslaught. Each morning deepened the concavity in the youngest cheek, added a new furrow to the fairest brow. There, where now you see that little hollow marked by a stone cross – but atop which will someday stand a great cathedral – was situated a weli into which the victims of the Nana's merciless bombardment were thrown at further cost of life, with no time for prayer and ceremony under the shroud of night.

By the end of the first week every artilleryman had been killed or gravely wounded; on the eighth day the roof of one of the barracks caught fire, consuming the wounded convalescing beneath it and illuminating the garrison for the sepoy snipers' sights.

But for all the horror, alarm, and dismay, such was the courage of that shrinking congregation that when, on June 23rd, the centenary of Clive's victory at the Battle of Plassy, the Nana ordered an all-out attack on the garrison (for it had been one of the incendiary native divinations that the English had been destined to rule for but one hundred years), our countrymen held their ground – *this* ground – and sent the Nana's soldiers scrambling for cover.

Woe to him that buildeth a town with blood, and stablisheth a city by iniquity! The Nana's rule would have been fit for comic opera but for the horror of its repercussions. Such order as there was was enforced by the Nana's brother, who dispensed justice from atop a requisitioned billiard table and for the most negligible misdemeanors condemned prisoners to amputations of their noses, lips, and limbs. The Nana's deputy, a former waiter named Azimullah, reassured the Nana's subjects that the British Isles had run out of men and that as soon as the wretched souls in the entrenchment were dead, India would be free of the English forever. A common prostitute patrolled the lines, exhorting the sepoy troops with offers of her poxy charms. The Nana's ministers lounged about in the Duncan Hotel – that charred shell in the western distance – drawing up exorbitant pay schedules for themselves to take effect when the Nana's conquest of India was complete. And up in his rooms the archfiend himself gave rein to every fleshy vice and corruption, deigning to show himself only when European prisoners were brought before him to be executed for his evil delectation: beheaded at his very feet, boiled in oil, tortured with fire, or given over to be rent asunder by the rapacious mob that haunted the Nana's door.

A true soldier with such superiority of numbers and firepower could have overrun this entrenchment in a day – as you can see from the remnant of earthwork still extant, an active cow could have cleared it – but such is the impotence of wickedness that in the end the Nana had to resort to the basest perfidy to accomplish his infamous fancied 'victory.'

After three weeks of merciless bombardment, after half the garrison had perished from the torments of the Nana's siege, the villain ordered his men to cease firing and sent one of his women prisoners across that far field to the entrenchment here with a message composed by Azimullah and promising the surviving garrison, should it agree to surrender, safe passage to Allahabad.

In other circumstances English officers would have spat upon such a proposition in defiant disgust, for no one in his heart of hearts could have truly trusted the word of so low a pretender to the Peshwa's throne. But in that blistering heat there were the women and children to consider, now ragged, hollow-eyed, and faint with hunger. And before them lay little hope of deliverance, only the certitude of the advancing monsoon whose deluge would wash away the feeble walls, flood the trenches, and turn their powder to paste. So, at last, shielding their children and womenfolk from their doubts, they accepted the Nana's offer, under the proviso that the survivors would be allowed to march to the river under arms, and that waiting for them at the ghats would be sufficient boats and provisions for the voyage to Allahabad.

Can we, knowing what would befall these heroic survivors of twenty days' hideous assault and deprivation, bear to think on their jubilation as they prepared to quit these melancholy premises, prayed around the well to which so many of their comrades and loved ones had been consigned, sang songs to their children as they gathered their most precious belongings together?

As we ourselves climb into our ekkas and palanquins and travel the route our doomed countrymen followed to the waiting boats in the river shallows at the Sati Chowra Ghat, imagine that the garrison's ghosts march with you, many of them wounded, all of them sunstruck, blistered, dressed in rags, and especially conjure the gentlewomen among them: unshod, unkempt, haggard, and squalid, their nakedness exposed to the jeering heathen throng that lined this Via Dolorosa of the Empire. And let us not forget the few surviving soldiers who marched behind them with their guns cocked and their sabres drawn; a martinet might have deplored their ragged appearance, but let who might incline to disown those weary warriors in the remnants of their dingy uniforms; their foes knew them for what they were and in their wake the jeering stopped.

Massacre Ghat

How often I have come here to meditate and pray, and always have I been moved to mark the contrast between the demonic turmoil of Sati Chowra that morning of June 27th and its peaceable near-solitude today! Sole vestiges of the great crime that was here perpetrated are the dints of bullets in the moldering temple in whose shadow dhobis now wash their masters' linens along a stream once crimson with the blood of sahibs, memsahibs, and their fair babes. One can but pity the man whose eyes are dry and whose heart pounds its normal throb when he first stands here by the Ganges's brink at the Sati Chowra Ghat.

Our people wearily waded out through the muck of the shallows and climbed onto the feeble, listing craft the Nana provided. Native boatmen helped lift the infant and the wounded aboard, and soon all was ready for the journey. The men laid down their muskets and blades and removed their shirts and jackets to assist in poling the boats out into the current of the stream, and for a sweet moment one longs to suspend in the imagination, it seemed at last that they were to be delivered out of the hands of their enemies.

Oh! were this a fiction and I a teller of tales how could I but spare that noble, ragged flotilla and, waving to them from the shore, wish them a safe voyage home? *Why standest thou afar off, O Lord? Why hidest thou thyself in times of trouble?*

For, lo, the wicked bend their bow, they make ready their arrow upon the string, that they may privily shoot at the upright heart. Arrayed along the riverbank, concealed like vermin in the interstices of town and temple, the Nana's sepoys lay with their muskets charged and their bayonets glinting in the morning sun. For the Beast of Cawnpore, *like as a lion that is greedy of his prey, lurking in secret places,* set out now to earn his infamy.

In the morning stillness a rebel general raised his hand; a bugle sounded; the native boatmen, flinging embers into the tinder of their vessels' roofs, leapt out into the water; and from along this height there came the spark and roar of a thousand muskets and a hail of lead threshed the river shallows.

O God, *why doth thine anger smoke against the sheep of thy pasture? O, deliver not the soul of thy turtledove unto the multitude of the wicked!*

Schoolgirls, their hair and clothing in flames, fell into the stream. Mothers leapt out clutching their babies to their breasts, only to be hacked to death by the Nana's mounted pandics who now galloped into the shallows, trampling the wounded into the Ganges's muck. Men and boys were beheaded where they stood, or casually shot to death by snipers as they swam to the aid of their families. Soon all were engulfed in the black smoke from the ignited boats until at last, out of perverted pity or wily craft, the Nana called a halt to the slaughter and a mere hundred and twenty-five survivors, out of the five hundred who had set out that morning, were dragged by their hair and clothing onto the blood-lapped steps.

How hard, oh, how hard to bend to the Almighty and say, *Thy will be done.* Four of the young women among the survivors were carried off for the lascivious sport of the jubilant sepoys; the rest – a few among them gravely wounded men and boys, many of them children, but most of them the flowers of English womanhood – were marched back up these crumbled steps, the faint and lame among them prodded forward by the sniggering gauntlet of black and blood-crazed rebels. Back they stumbled; back along the route paved with promise just an hour before but now strewn with the shards of their dashed hopes; back through the crowds of townspeople who jeered and spat at them and tore their ornaments from their ears and wrenched the rings from their fingers; back, back into the fiery night of the Nana's reign they staggered, Despair going before them, Grief keeping pace, Death following after in the suspended dust.

They were all of them brought before the archfiend himself, who sat in the shade of a lime tree, gloating upon his perfidious triumph. Because he was a goodly king, he declared to the victims of his remorseless wickedness, he would spare the women and children, whereupon he ordered that the men be executed on the spot, before the very eyes of their loved ones. Thus the few men left among the forlorn company, the youngest of them but a lad of fourteen years, bade farewell to their womenfolk and children, bowed their heads in prayer, shook hands goodbye all around, and prepared themselves for eternity. But just as the sneering sepoys raised their guns, several of the women rushed into their husbands' embrace again, declaring to the impatient and confounded Beast that they were resolved to die with their menfolk. But no, the Fiend had another fate prescribed for these heroines and their babes: a doom so terrible that it causes one to wish they had never survived the siege or risen back up out of the crimson waters of the Massacre Ghat. And so they were pulled away, and in a storm of bullets the last of their protectors were dispatched.

For four days the widowed women consoled their trembling babes in the Nana's anarchical court while sepoys trooped past to taunt them with the booty looted from their husbands' corpses. But, dear friends, what sorrow has yet gone unexpended, what tears may yet linger in the reservoirs of your grief, save, *save* for what follows two miles hence. For the time then came for them, as it has now come for us, to be moved to a place now known variously as the House of the Ladies, The House of Sorrow, and the Chamber of Blood, but which was known only as Bhibigar before our precious women and children sanctified it with their sufferings.

Bhibigar

Man knoweth not his time: *as the fishes that are taken in an evil net, and as the birds that are caught in the snare; so are the sons of man snared in an evil time, when it falleth suddenly upon them.*

Is it possible that in a mere ten years' time a scene of the utmost horror, the sight of which reduced the bravest warriors of our epoch to tears and retching and whose memory still smokes and smolders in the Empire's breast, could now be so carpeted with tended grass and ornamented with varicolored blooms that a stranger chancing upon it might mistake it for a mere city pleasance, a picnic spot, a rendezvous for innocent lovers?

But *the voice said, Cry. And he said, What shall I cry? All flesh is grass, and all the goodliness thereof is as the flower of the field: the grass withereth, the flower fadeth: but the word of our God shall stand forever.*

Here where there is but a verdant swelling in the ground to mark the spot, the ladies were brought with their children and imprisoned in a dingy little building erected in the old days by a Company officer for his heathen mistress. And to their numbers were added forty more women and children of their race and faith who had been languishing in the Nana's captivity for three weeks: refugees from the uprising at Fatehgarh fifty miles upriver who had fled with their husbands for illusory safety in Cawnpore, only to fall into the hands of the Beast and lose their husbands to his murderous wrath.

Bhibigar was a low, smutchy structure built around an open court. Its occupants were permitted no clothing with which to replace their gory and mud-encrusted rags, and no furniture: only bamboo mats and a few heaps of mildewed straw for bedding. A courtesan's handmaid they dubbed 'the Begum' for her haughty posturings and imperious cruelty was entrusted with their keeping, and over the next nineteen days she devised ever more humiliating measures with which to torment her helpless charges. Outcastes were herded together to prepare the watery gruel and coarse chapattis that comprised their diet, and each day two of the women were forced into the Nana's stables to grind corn and wash their clothes in the livery's filthy trough.

And as they suffered in the stifling swelter of Bhibigar, their tormentor revelled in the trappings of his bogus reign. Proclamations were issued announcing the 'delightful intelligence' that all 'yellow-faced and narrow-minded people' had been 'destroyed and sent to hell,' and commanding the natives to obey him as they had once obeyed the Christians. A grand review was staged, at which the Nana received the twenty-one-gun salute he had been so justly denied by the Company, and his nights were filled with orgiastic debasements, feasts, and entertainments, at which a jester reduced his crapulous monarch to helpless laughter by imitating an English officer's upright gait.

But trouble lurked on the fiend's dark horizon. In the second week of their captivity, his prized hostages began to succumb to his ghastly abuse. By the fifteenth day, eighteen of our women and seven of our poor children had died of dystentery and cholera, and one young mother had given birth to her dead husband's son, only to lose the infant two days later.

In a mockery of pity, the Nana ordered that his languishing prisoners be provided with rum and wine and brought outside each dusk to partake of the evening air. There, as they cowered with their children on a row of benches, our women were ogled by the Nana and his licentious brothers and tormented by the 'Begum' and her rebel lovers, who brandished swords before them and boasted of the torture, degradation, and death awaiting them.

But there was more to trouble the Nana's dreams of glory, for on the 15th of July one of his brothers limped back into the city, his arm bleeding, to report that avenging Highland troops under the command of General Havelock had captured and crossed the bridge at Pandu Nadu twenty miles to the west and were fast advancing upon the city, sweeping all in their path as if death held no terror for them, life no value.

'Yes,' the Nana replied, 'but does not my fearful brother know why the English fight so bravely? Is it not to save the memsahibs and babalogues? Would they press down so hard upon the city if there were no memsahibs and babalogues left to save?'

Now some among even that blood-crazed pack shrank back from the Nana's meaning. A wailing rose up from old Baji Rao's widows, who vowed to fast unto the death if the English mems were harmed. But it was no use, of course, for like the deaf adder he stopped up his ears, and as the afternoon shadows lengthened across the ash and dust of Cawnpore the Nana Sahib summoned his vile squad of sepoy executioners and issued his flagitious command.

But even these bloody men, who had not blinked at the massacre of helpless, wounded, and unarmed men and boys, had no stomach for the Nana's bidding, and at four o'clock that afternoon, as they stood with their muskets poised in the windows of Bhibigar, they could not bring themselves to fire upon so wretched and helpless a prey and merely emptied their guns into the ceiling.

Can we bear to imagine our ladies as the roar of musketfire echoed around them and the dust and splinters sifted down from the bullet-ridden ceiling? What could they have thought when they realized that they had none of them been shot, when all that could be heard from outside were the furious insults the 'Begum' now hurled at the departing shamefaced rebels? We know that one gallant lady stood before the 'Begum' and demanded to know if they were all to be killed, and if so, if it were to be done cleanly, and with dispatch. But the 'Begum' only sneered back at her and set forth to conscript a second squad of murderers less scrupulous than the first.

Some among the ladies now tore strips from their clothing with which to secure the doorlatch against their executioners, while others contrived to hide their toddling babes beneath their skirts. And yet others passed among their sisters, assuring them that the gunfire and the threats were nothing more than the 'Begum's' cruel tricks again, for was that not cannonfire they could hear in the far distance? Were not their deliverers but a night's march away?

Oh, would that the sepoy gunmen had had the heart to get the killing over with and quickly! O Lord our God, how *the bloodthirsty hate the upright! How vain is the help of men!* For now as a hymn rose in quaking unison from within the House of Sorrow, the 'Begum' returned with five coarse men: two of them dimwitted peasants, two of the butchering caste, and one an idler from the Nana's own bodyguard. In the short gloaming of Hindustan a crowd now gathered around and watched as the five brutes followed the 'Begum' to Bhibigar's door, swords and cleavers bristling from their fists.

They made quick work of the feebly bound latch and burst into the house. For a moment, as the door closed behind them, they silently passed their eyes across their shuddering prey, and then a gallant lady stood up before them, demanding to know their business.

O! horror hath taken hold upon me! Arise, O Lord; O God, lift up thine hand! Give us help from trouble!

Is the heathen's tenebrous evil so loathsome that even our Maker must shut His eyes to it? And if His children's sufferings are too grievous for His sight, are they not beyond all mortal forbearance? Oh! now, as the butchers begin their bestial work, stop up your ears to the wails, the shrieks, the pitiful pleas, the desperate patter of tiny feet running along the floor, the collisions of blade and bone, lest the sound derange us all.

Now the bodyguard staggers back out for a moment with his

sword broken to its blood-caked hilt and borrows a replacement from the crowd, only to re-emerge minutes later with his blade broken again, arm himself afresh, and return yet once more to his ghastly labors.

And by and by the screaming stops, and then the wailing, and then the last few stumbling footsteps, and for a moment all that can be heard is the stray blow of a blade against some vagrant sign of life. And when at last the five step out into the darkness and close the door behind them the crowd gasps and runs away, for the five are now soaked in gore from head to foot, like the hideous demons they have become, and only their infernal 'Begum' remains to embrace her abominable champions.

A silence now falls over Bhibigar as the five lock the door behind them and depart, leaving their bloody footprints in the dirt. And surely this must be the end of all horror. Surely now we may look to morning, to a paradise *where the wicked cease from troubling and the weary are at rest.*

But hark! what is that noise that disturbs our lugubrious vigil? Do you not hear a stirring, a rustling from within that abode of death? And there! is that not the gasping of a human breath?

But the night passes, and soon it is morning. Accompanied by a band of scavengers the five murderers return and open the door to the Chamber of Blood. A crowd gathers along the courtyard wall and watches as the ladies' lacerated corpses are now dragged by their fair tresses through a cloud of flies, roughly stripped of their last rags, and thrown into the abyss of a nearby well.

One by one they make the melancholy journey to the oblivion of a mass grave, when suddenly out of the dark portal of Bhibigar a fair young lad of five years darts, lunatic with terror and smeared with the blood of his mother beneath whose skirts he had taken refuge. He runs along the base of the courtyard wall, imploring the crowd to help him. For a moment the butchers merely gape in astonishment, but then another child runs sobbing into the light, and another, and seeing that their work is not yet finished the butchers now give gleeful chase.

Was it little Willie Duton they pursued around the yard and dashed by the heels against the trunk of this very tree? Was it young Master Samuel Gilpin that they then ran through with their swords?

And was it little Jimmy Reed they flung still living into the well's bloody depths?

Oh, how stubborn is the spark of life! O Lord, cannot Thou yet release these Thy children from their earthly torment? Why must Mrs Probett still live as they drag her out and leave her to die on the well's gory lip? Why dost Thou save young Isabella White for a lingering death amid a heap of corpses now engorging the well's infernal cavity to a depth of fifty feet?

Yes, weep. Ye may weep, for that at last is the worst of it. And when the last tear has scalded your cheek, imagine the passions of Havelock's Highlanders two days later when, having chased the Nana Sahib and his demon army northward into the Himalayan wilderness, they burst into the city. See how they search in an ecstasy of hope for the captive ladies and their precious children. See how doubt begins to trouble their rugged brows. See the first of them stumble into Bhibigar's courtyard, and step toward the gore-splashed door with flowering dread. See him enter now, and as his eyes accustom themselves to the dark, watch how he realizes that the sticky sheen underfoot is blood, that the stockyard stench is death's sickly redolence. See how he stumbles backward into the light, reeling in horror. See how he turns away to recover his senses, only to find himself leaning over the edge of the sepulchral well and looking down its throat into the black bowel of horror.

He weeps, he wails, he retches, and his anguish draws his comrades to him, and by the evening's end every soldier has passed through these portals and peered into the jaws of death. Here they find a lock of hair stuck to a dint in the bloody wall, there a frayed leaf from a prayer book, there a scrap of lace tied around the door's broken latch, and with these as tokens of their wrath, they swear a terrible vengeance upon the rebels.

Dare we judge the whirlwind that began to blow that day? Nay, *for God shall bring every work into judgment, with every secret thing, whether it be good or whether it be evil. Upon the wicked he shall rain snares, fire and brimstone, and an horrible tempest;* this was to be the portion of the Nana Sahib's cup.

Any native found to have witnessed these things without protest, to have honored the Nana's claims, to have so much as shared a hookah with the Demon's soldiery; any sepoy who was captured in the pitched battles between Cawnpore and Lucknow and who was not executed on the spot; any camp follower, rebel sympathizer, relative or friend; all, all were brought in chains to this place and made to clean a portion of the gore-caked floor with their tongues before hanging by their necks from the limb of this cursed tree. The Hindus were buried, the Moslems burned (not one of the rebels was a Christian), so that all went to their deaths in a certitude of eternal damnation. And our wrath was not spent until at last God was made *known among the heathen in our sight by the revenging of the blood of thy servants which is shed.* And by campaign's end each of our warriors could say with the Psalmist, *I have pursued mine enemies, and overtaken them: neither did I turn again until they were consumed.*

Only one of the rebels eluded our vengeance: the Fiend himself, the Beast of Cawnpore, the bloody Nana Sahib. Like Cain he became a fugitive on the face of the earth, begging for sustenance among the aboriginal tribes of the Himalayan foothills, condemned *to wander in the wilderness, where there is no way.* O God, *set Thou a wicked man over him: and let Satan stand at his right hand. When he shall be judged, let him be condemned: and let his prayer become sin. Let his days be few . . . Let his children be fatherless and his wife a widow. Let his children be continually vagabonds, and beg . . . Let his posterity be shut off; and in the generation following let their name be blotted out.*

But hold, let us not be *afraid of sudden fear, neither of the desolation of the wicked when it cometh.* Nay, it is not for us today to prolong the vengeance, nor devise his punishment, but to rest secure in the knowledge that God's punishment is more terrible than any chastisement we may propose.

It is for us to rejoice, yes, *rejoice* in the sacrifices of our countrymen, in the wonderful mercy of God. *In a little wrath I hid my face from thee for a moment; but with everlasting kindness will I have mercy on thee, saith the Lord thy Redeemer. With great mercies will I gather thee.* For God's anger *endureth but a moment; in his favor is life; weeping may endure for a night, but joy cometh in the morning,* for *whilst we are at home in the body we are absent from God.* Yes, whole families were extinguished in but a fortnight and by the brutalest of means, but in paradise their souls exult in divine and eternal reunion.

As we now enter the sacred precincts of the Memorial and encircle it in prayer beneath Marochetti's mournfully vigilant angel, let us remember the words of the 141st Psalm: *Our bones are scattered at the grave's mouth, as when one cutteth and cleaveth wood upon the earth.*

But mine eyes are unto thee, O God the Lord.

CHAPTER
17

I didn't know what Weems told his congregation after they'd passed through the gates of the Memorial Garden, for no native was allowed to set foot in there, not even we lambs of the Reverend's mission. But it must have been more of the same, because by the time they returned to their ekkas and palanquins for the last leg of the tour, the women were inconsolably weeping and the men angrily barked commands to their drivers and bearers and glowered at John Christopher and me as though we'd done something terrible.

It caused a strange, vaporous bloom of shame to rise in my throat, and looking over at John Christopher I could see he was even more perplexed than I, for he'd worked so hard to please them.

A few of the tourists returned to their hotels, but most of them stuck with us as we marched back to Bastard Bhavan. Mr Peter greeted us at the gate as best he could, although he didn't seem to make much of an impression. They all filed past him with nary a nod, for it seemed that the hatred and suspicion that Weems had so skillfully engendered in them had survived the little ride to Bastard Bhavan and extended even to Mr Peter, despite his suit and Bible.

After a tour of the grounds, Weems led everyone into the workroom, and as all the boys stood gravely at their stations along the glazing table, barely daring to sneak a look at the assembled whites, Weems launched into his summation, featuring the virtues of industry, the urgency of converting the heathen, England's sacred mission to India, and a scattering of Bible quotations which he delivered, as always, with his eyes rolled back and his bombilating voice worrying the pigeons along the rafters.

The time of vengeance had passed, he told them; it wasn't enough to damn the heathen for their savagery. The glory of God, the salvation of mankind, the survival of the Empire (not to mention their own safety) required that the infidel be raised from this – and here he pointed to me in my perverse and ill-fitting costume – to *this* and here he put his hand on John Christopher's shoulder and had him recite a few lines from Psalm 94 in his flat little voice:

Lord, how long shall the wicked triumph? . . .
They slay the widow and the stranger and murder the fatherless.
Understand, ye brutish among the people:
and ye fools, when will ye be wise?
Blessed is the man whom thou chastenest, O Lord, and teachest him
out of thy law.

John Christopher's recitation seemed to soften up our visitors a little, and the Reverend rewarded him by popping a sugar cube into his mouth before leading everyone into his office to peddle his plates.

When Weems emerged a half hour later we could tell right away from his triumphant smirk that his expedition had served its purpose. His visitors followed after him with their arms laden with little boxes of plates packed in straw, and left Bastard Bhavan looking almost as pleased as Weems.

That evening at chapel the Reverend gloated and boasted like a self-made man. He announced that one among the tour group had placed an order for a hundred plates for his brother's Calcutta bric-à-brac outlet, while another had promised to display his set of plates to the various colonial merchants with whom he did business in the south.

And thus was born the Mission Society for the Propagation of the Revealed Word Asylum for Orphaned Boys Memorial Plate Works, for with each new tour group the Reverend thrilled and horrified, a new market for our plates would open up.

Soon the demand became so great that we had to work through our class time to keep up with it. Those of us who remained unconverted were even put to work on Sabbath afternoons, and looking out of our windows at night we could see the hot bricks in the walls of the overworked kiln glow in the dark like blocks of gold.

Of course, the Reverend never believed in doing anything for a single purpose, and especially not for one so worldly as profit, so he set out to make our labors as educational as possible. Bible quotations were painted upon the table tops and read aloud by John Christopher until he was hoarse, at which point we would all sing hymns until *we* were hoarse. Then Mr Peter would circle around us firing grammatical and mathematical problems at our backs, and some afternoons the Reverend himself would settle into a chair at the head of the table and weave tales of come-uppance for our betterment.

And all the while we would sit hunched over the stream of plates, filling in the gaps with our little brushes dipped in glaze.

It wasn't long before the orders began to back up in the Reverend's office. He blamed us for this, for he'd come to regard our industry as a holy thing and it never occurred to him that he could actually refuse orders for more plates. So deeply did he believe in the sanctity of our labors that he even began to hold our chapel services in the workroom so as not to interrupt the flow of plates. But no matter what new methods Weems introduced and no matter how many hours we spent each day on our aching nates at the glazing table, we could never turn out more than a couple hundred plates in a day, and as the summer heat returned we could barely produce half that number. The potters lagged behind at their wheels (Weems must have fired a dozen of them in those first few months) or the kiln would run out of fuel, and of those hundred or two hundred plates at least a third would come out chipped, bubbled, cracked, globbed, or altogether exploded.

It took him three months to realize that no matter what he did we could never produce enough plates to keep up with the demand, not even in the hot season when the tourist traffic thinned out, for of course the heat affected our production as well and every day at least one of us along the glazing table would let the Reverend down by fainting from exhaustion.

What he needed was more boys. But as I've said, orphaned boys were hard to come by, and it was just beginning to look as though the

Reverend was going to have to give up on his dreams of expansion when out of the rain one afternoon stepped no fewer than five orphaned boys in the company of none other than my calumnious old benefactor, Nanak Chand.

I didn't recognize him right away, for he was pounds lighter than when I'd seen him last, and stubble-chinned, ill-clothed, and looking generally the worse for wear. But as he stood stamping his feet in the doorway, the water splashing off the brim of his mildewed bowler, his eyes caught mine and we seemed to recognize each other at the same instant.

'Little Turnip!' he exclaimed with a tight, furtive smile. 'How are you?'

But when he saw the hatred flare up in my eyes his smile vanished, and like a man coming out of a foolish dream he shook his head with a self-berating scowl. 'Get me the Reverend Sahib,' he said, turning away from me and drying his hands on his tunic. 'And be quick about it.'

I did as he said, and the Reverend came with me out of his office, peering over the rim of his spectacles, irritated to be interrupted in his bookkeeping.

'Yes, Nanak Chand?' he said abruptly. 'What is it?'

'Reverend Sahib!' said Nanak Chand. 'Ah, it does me so much good to see you again.'

'Yes, yes,' Weems said. 'I too, I'm sure. However, I *am* rather busy this afternoon with my – ' But he stopped himself and removing his spectacles entirely gaped out beyond Nanak Chand to the five boys who stood waiting in the rain. 'Nanak Chand?' he asked softly. 'Nanak Chand, are these – '

'Allow me,' Nanak Chand said, waving the boys in through the door and beaming with self-satisfaction. 'Children, come in and meet your new father.'

As the Reverend stood paralyzed, the five boys stepped into the room, soaked to the skin, a puddle of rainwater forming at their feet.

'Nanak Chand,' the Reverend muttered. '*Five? Five* boys?'

'Yes, Reverend Sahib,' Nanak Chand said, extending his arms to encompass the little herd of children. 'Five precious lads. Five new sons for the esteemed Reverend Josiah Weems Sahib.'

'But where did you find them? How did you manage?'

'Oh, there's been much hardship in the countryside, Reverend Sahib,' said Weems. 'Many have died from the floods. And these have been left behind. But out of hardship, Reverend Sahib, et cetera, et cetera . . . '

Falling on one knee and extending his arms, Weems seemed to be on the verge of tears. 'Oh, welcome!' he exclaimed. 'Oh, welcome, ye answers to my prayers!'

I suppose in his ecstasy he expected the five boys to come rushing into his embrace, but of course they just stood there staring at him, and the youngest, who could not have been more than four years old, sobbed weakly and wrapped his arms around the legs of the boy beside him, who stood like the others with limp resignation. They could all five have been brothers, for they looked so much alike with their strangely deep-set eyes and hollow cheeks.

'Greet your new father,' I heard Nanak Chand mutter, nudging one of the boys forward, but the boy looked to the floor and shivered. 'I must beg your pardon for their behavior, Reverend Sahib,' Nanak Chand said, suppressing his anger, 'but after what these dear boys have been through I hope you will understand.'

'Understand?' the Reverend said, grinning now at the youngest. 'Of course, of course. Why, they must be exhausted. Aren't you exhausted, my little one?'

'They have not eaten for some time, I must confess,' Nanak Chand said. 'I'm afraid there was not much to be had on our way here, and besides, they were all so eager to meet you that they wouldn't stop for sustenance anyway, would you, lads?'

'Well, you shall eat now,' Weems said, reaching his arms out toward the littlest. But the boy turned his face away, gripping his companion's leg more tightly.

Still grinning, for he was not going to be thwarted by the little heathen, Weems rose to his full height again and snapped his fingers. 'Dileep, Puran, Balbeer,' he said, 'fetch some victuals for your new brothers.'

'May I perhaps ask that I too may take some nourishment, Reverend Sahib?' Nanak Chand said, holding up one finger. 'I fear I shared all I had with the boys and there is nothing left.'

'Of course,' Weems said, 'of course. It's a small thing to ask when through you the Lord God has answered all my prayers. Bring bread and the soup – and spoons and bowls for six!' Weems commanded. 'And hurry!'

Dileep and I rushed off to the corner room that served as our kitchen, with Puran lumbering after us, and awakened Dhanda, who'd been taking his morning nap in the cool canyon between the water jars.

'Wh-what are you doing?' he stuttered, pulling himself up onto his crutch.

'Fetching food for the new boys,' Dileep said with a troubled look, untying a bundle of chapattis from where they hung by the window.

'New boys?' Dhanda asked, swinging his way toward the door. 'How many?'

'Five,' I said, handing a stack of bowls to Puran.

'Five!' Dhanda exclaimed, hurrying out to see them. 'So many!'

'Too many,' Dileep muttered, waiting for me as I fetched the bucket of leftover gruel still bubbling thickly on the stove.

'What do you mean?'

'I don't know,' Dileep said with a frown, 'but there's something wrong.'

'With what?'

'I don't *know*,' Dileep snapped back at me. 'But nobody's ever brought five boys in here all at once. And besides, there haven't been any floods this season,' he said as I heaved the bucket of gruel off the stove. 'The kiln walla told me this was a dry monsoon. Not enough rain for the crops.'

'Then where did they come from?' I asked as we hurried out of the kitchen. But Dileep had no time to reply, for already the Reverend was bellowing a blessing over his soaked and shivering lambs and making room for them at the glazing table.

·CHAPTER·
18

Nanak Chand could barely contain his disappointment in the food we brought for him, but redirected his irritation by requesting, for caste reasons, that he be permitted to dine at another table in a corner of the room, with myself to wait upon him.

'I hear you've been a stubborn Little Turnip,' he said through a mouthful of chapatti, too softly to be overheard above the patter of the rain and the Reverend's ecstatic exclamations. 'What's the matter, Balbeer? Is my prince unhappy with his accommodations?'

I had resolved not to speak to the scoundrel, no matter what he told me, but merely to stare back at him, and understanding this he shrugged and smiled and scooped up a little puddle of gruel in a section of chapatti. 'I suppose you'd rather be begging in the streets, Little Turnip,' he said, and popped the chapatti into his mouth. 'Or maybe you'd rather be lying dead on the road to Harigarh?' He glared at me for a moment as he chewed. 'Just like your mother, aren't you, Balbeer? Won't make the best of things, will you? Don't even know who your friends are.'

'*I* know,' I said, and then cursed myself for answering him.

Nanak Chand grinned at me. 'You do, eh? Then why do you resist the Reverend Sahib? Tell me, Balbeer. What other friend do you have in the whole world?'

But this time I kept silent.

'Where does all this — this *obstinance* get you? What do you care if he wants to turn you into a Christian? What does anyone care what becomes of you?'

I stood as straight as I could and swallowed hard as Nanak Chand peered up at me, licking the gruel from his fingers.

'Do what you like,' he finally muttered, wiping his hands on his tunic. 'It doesn't matter to me.' He suddenly scowled at me and snatched my wrist in his left hand. 'But if you ever dare try to leave this place, if you ever bring shame on my head,' he snarled, furtively glancing in the Reverend's direction, 'I'll send your skull to the

Harigarh court and feed your bowels to the jackals.'

'Catching up on old times?' the Reverend piped, approaching the table in quick, long strides.

'Yes, yes,' Nanak Chand said, releasing my hand and rising from his chair.

'Please don't bother to get up,' said Weems, gingerly placing a hand on Nanak Chand's shoulder and pushing him back down. 'Don't trouble yourself any further on my account. Oh, Balbeer, how may we ever thank this man for everything he's done for us, eh? Five new brothers for the mission! Five new lambs!'

'And very hardworking, too,' said Nanak Chand, 'Country boys are always – '

'I do not doubt it for an instant,' Weems cut in. 'Oh, I cannot help but think that God bestowed these floods in answer to my prayer . . . By the way, where exactly were these floods? I had heard that – '

'Oh, some distance from here, certainly,' Nanak Chand said. 'And not your usual flood, either. A little dam collapsed where a canal was being dug. Foolish people had set up their lodgings in the gully. Along comes one little rain and – '

'Devastation. Typical, all too typical. But look what it has brought us! And only two weeks before the board's visit. Plenty of time to teach them our ways, eh, Balbeer?'

The Reverend escorted Nanak Chand into his office and Mr Peter took the five boys off to find them some dry uniforms, leaving Dileep and me to clean up after them.

I don't know how the Reverend paid off Nanak Chand, but the swine made a great show of gratitude on his way out of Weems's office, only to slog off into the rain muttering ever more loudly to himself with each step, and there wasn't a boy at Bastard Bhavan who didn't breathe easier when he'd faded from sight.

The five boys sat so mute and vacant-eyed as the Reverend set the rest of us back to work that Mr Peter wondered if they understood Hindi at all or spoke some village dialect instead. But that evening, though they were only a little more responsive to Dileep's questions, we could tell from their shrugs and nods that they could understand us. Dileep tried to find out where they were from, but they wouldn't tell him, nor would they describe the catastrophe that had brought them to Bastard Bhavan.

'Give up,' John Christopher said as he climbed into his bed. 'They're just stupid heathen bumpkins.'

'They're not stupid,' Dileep said, looking searchingly into the eyes of the oldest. 'They're scared.'

'Oh, really?' John Christopher sneered. 'Scared of what?'

'Of everything, probably,' Dileep said. 'But most of all of that Bengali mucker. Who knows what he's threatened them with.'

That night as we fell off to sleep we watched the five boys settle in, each of us – even John Christopher, I imagine – remembering for a moment his own first night at Bastard Bhavan, though the memory of it affected each of us differently, casting Dileep and me into silent reflection but churning up evil feelings in Ralph, who hissed vile threats to the youngest weeping in the bed above him.

Though they never spoke except to say yes or no and always hung together, the five new boys caught on fast at the glazing table and, as Nanak Chand had promised, proved to be hard workers. After a couple of days they began to make a difference to our production and in each of Weems's blessings and benedictions he would bless Nanak Chand for sending him such diligent reinforcements. None of them would tell us his name, so we made up names for them, Mohan, Sohan, Nirmal, and Kihal, and the littlest we called Chota Chuha, for like the others, only more so, he resembled the gaunt rats that plagued the Reverend's fields.

In late August of 1867, two weeks before Sir Harry and the Mission Board were due to visit, Weems began to realize that however many orphans he'd gathered or plates he'd produced, there were going to be those among his sponsors who would only be interested in knowing how many of us he'd managed to bring to Christ. In the three and a half years I'd spent at Bastard Bhavan, only one boy – Puran – had been converted. Thus, out of eighteen boys, the Reverend had only five little brown Christians to show off.

Finding a sixth was simple enough, for under the circumstances there was obviously no use in the Reverend's holding Dhanda back any longer. So, in the briefest and most gingerly ceremony Weems ever conducted, he immersed Dhanda in the bathing trough and watched, appalled, as the delirious boy threw off his robe and hopped stark naked about the grounds, shouting 'Jai Ram! Jai Ram!' in addled jubilation.

But finding a seventh wasn't going to be so easy, for excepting the five new boys, who still seemed as deaf and dumb as stones, the rest of us holdouts had developed quite a resistance to the Reverend's evangelism. Nonetheless, Weems was determined to bring at least one of us into the fold before his day of judgment, so he began to call us into his office, one by one, for 'little talks,' as he called them, 'about this and that.'

I was among the last he summoned that week, rousing me from bed after darkness had fallen and leading me in his nightdress to his office.

'Isn't this a treat?' he said, showing me to a chair. 'Imagine, Balbeer. My allowing you to stay up later than any of the others! I fear I'm going to spoil you at this rate.'

Dileep had been the first boy the Reverend had summoned, and had told me to expect a perfunctory session, but I suppose Dileep's interview had been so brief because the Reverend had given up on him; Weems obviously held out more hope for me.

'How about a nice fresh glass of milk?' he said, pouring from a clay pitcher as he sat behind his desk. 'Now that would taste delicious, wouldn't it?' he asked, handing the mugful to me.

'Thank you, Reverend Sahib,' I said, holding the mug in both hands and sitting back down on the chair: or maybe I should say sitting back *up* on the chair, for it raised my feet some inches from the floor and the arms reached almost to my shoulders.

'In fact, it looks so good I think I shall have some myself,' Weems said, pouring again from the pitcher. 'To progress,' he said, raising his mug, and together we drank the warm, half-turned milk.

'There now,' he said, putting down his mug. The milk had left a moustache of scum on his upper lip. 'Balbeer,' he said, half smiling at me, 'I have called you in here tonight so we may have a discussion, just you and me, man to man. How does that suit you?'

'Fine, Reverend Sahib,' I answered, checking to see if my upper lip was dry.

'Good, good,' the Reverend said, sweeping his arm through the air to clear away some of the moths and beetles that flapped and whirred about his lamp. 'You know, my son, it seems like only yesterday that I came upon you at the ghat and brought you home to care for. But do you know how long it has been?' he said, flicking an overturned beetle off the paper unfolded before him and consulting it briefly. 'According to my records, it's been three years and . . . six months. Three and a half years, my son. More than a third of your life, if I am not mistaken. But still it seems like only yesterday to us, doesn't it?'

'Yes, Reverend Sahib.'

'Isn't that odd?'

'Reverend Sahib?'

'It struck me as *very* odd, Balbeer, until I began to wonder if perhaps it seems like only yesterday because there's been so little *change*,' he said with a concerned frown. 'And I suppose that's why I've called you in. To find out why.'

'Why, Reverend Sahib?'

'Yes, *why*, my son,' Weems said, bringing his fist down on his desktop. 'Why you are deaf to my entreaties, blind to my example. *Why* you've closed your heart to me.'

As the Reverend stared at me I averted my eyes from him and gazed at the great black cliff of bookshelved Bibles that stood in the gloom behind him.

'You aren't a stupid child,' the Reverend continued, his voice tightening. 'You're no scholar, certainly, but by each week's end you've usually learned your lessons after a fashion – *some* of your lessons in any case. But are you perhaps a wicked little boy? Could that be it? I should hate to think you resist me out of wickedness.'

I now ducked my head and looked into my half-filled mug of milk.

The Reverend turned his chair sideways and leaned back, drumming his fingers on the desk. 'No, *I* don't believe you are wicked. I might get an argument from Mr Peter about that, and some days I confess I do wonder if Satan has a hold on you. But no, I don't think you are a wicked boy. So what is it? Why aren't you buckling down? Why aren't you taking a bird's-eye view?'

I kept my head bowed. 'I – I don't know, Reverend Sahib.'

'I'm going to tell you a story, my son,' the Reverend said, turning back around to face me and folding his hands before him on his desk. 'Perhaps in it we may find an answer, a path we may follow to the light. Are you listening?'

I nodded sleepily through the swirl of bugs between us.

'Good,' said the Reverend, clearing his throat.

'Once very long ago a shepherd was trying to teach his sheep their names so that he could call for them, one by one, when the need arose. And all the sheep learned quickly, and came to honor and cherish the names the shepherd had given them. All, that is, but one: one proud little sheep who refused the name Joshua which the shepherd gave him, saying "I am a sheep and you are a man. What right have you to name me?" So he would not come when the shepherd called, but moved about on his own impulse and often strayed from the flock.

'One night the shepherd heard the cry of a panther in the distance and rose from his resting place and called each of his sheep, one by one, to gather with him around the campfire, and they all obeyed. All, that is, except Joshua, for when he heard his name on the night air he remained in the valley saying, "I'm not like those other fools. I'm a sheep and I know my name."

'But,' the Reverend said, tilting his eyebrows high, 'when morning came, the shepherd led his flock into the valley, and what do you think he found?'

I shifted slightly in my chair. 'The little sheep.'

'The proud little sheep, yes. The proud little sheep who refused to be named. And how did he find the sheep?'

'Dead?'

'Dead. Yes, indeed. Torn and lifeless, its little limbs crushed and bloody from the voracious panther's jaws.

'*Pride*, my son,' the Reverend said with an upraised finger. 'Pride is what killed him. Stupid, stubborn pride. Do you know what the Bible says about the Good Shepherd?'

'No, Reverend Sahib.'

'The Bible says, "The sheep hear his voice and he calleth his own sheep by name and leadeth them out. And when he putteth forth his own sheep, he goeth before them and the sheep follow him, for they know his voice."

'Do you know the Good Shepherd's voice when you hear it, my son?'

I looked down at my fidgeting hands. 'I don't know, Reverend Sahib,' I said.

'The *Lord* is the Good Shepherd, my boy. *You* may not know your name, but He does. He calls for you in the night, but you won't listen. He's given you a name, but you refuse to answer to it. What are you afraid of losing? Why are you such a stubborn little stray when He's calling you into His fold? What are you going to do when the panther comes?'

I stared into my mug of milk, trying to look humble and confused, but I had an answer – Dileep would stand by me when the panther came.

'Well?' the Reverend asked, placing his hands flat on his desk and leaning toward me.

'I – I don't know,' I said slowly.

'Is it just pride, then? Rajput pride?' Weems asked. 'If so it's a very silly pride, Balbeer. Think of it: a pride born of petty heathen princes standing in the way of God Almighty. We can't have that, can we, Balbeer? That doesn't make much sense, does it?'

I sighed and supposed not.

'Then will you promise me this much? Will you promise me you will at least open your ears to the Shepherd's voice?'

'Yes, Reverend Sahib.'

'That isn't too much to ask of one of my sons, is it?'

'No, Reverend Sahib.'

'Good,' the Reverend said, abruptly slapping the top of his desk with both hands and rising to his feet in an upward swirl of bugs. 'Do that much for me and I will flood your world with light.'

CHAPTER

19

That very night as I lay listening to my mother's fitful whispers, a great stink arose in the hot, moonless dark. Worse than Ralph's fetor or the acid stench from Puran's wetted bedding, it awakened all the boys at once, and our noise roused Mr Peter and the Reverend, who came in with his lamp, squinting into the darkness.

'Get back to bed!' he barked. 'What is the meaning of this?'

'But Reverend Sahib,' said John Christopher.

'Do as I say,' Weems snapped back, holding the lamp in front of John Christopher's face. There was a strange sheen to John Christopher's flesh and his eyes seemed to swim in their hollows.

'But Reverend Sahib,' he said again, though weakly, 'there's a smell – '

'A smell?' the Reverend said, sniffing twice. '*I* don't smell any – ' But then the stink must have reached him at last, for he recoiled, swinging his lamp around. 'What *is* that stench?' he said, holding one hand over his mouth.

'It's coming from up there,' Dileep called out, pointing to the bunk above John Christopher's bed.

The Reverend raised the collar of his nightshirt over his mouth and stepped up onto the edge of John Christoper's bed. 'Dileep, if this is another one of your tricks,' he started to say, lifting his lamp high above his head, but he stopped short with a choking noise and jumped back down, swinging his lamp about.

'Get back! Get back!' he said with a gasp. 'Oh, dear God, no! Oh, no!'

'What is it, Reverend Sir?' asked Mr Peter as he herded the rest of us away from John Christopher's bed.

Weems stood gasping for a moment and steadied the lamp, trying to compose himself. 'Mr Peter,' he said, 'fetch the doctor. It's one of the new boys. The oldest, I think. I'm afraid he's – he's –'

But he couldn't bring himself to say it. The boy was dead, and lying in a pool of his own filth. And when Weems, Puran, and Dileep wrapped his body in his fouled bedding and hoisted him down and took him out into the night, John Christopher began to vomit. At first everyone thought it was because of his delicate sensibilities, but his vomiting didn't stop until he lay twitching on the floor and the doctor came and proclaimed him sick with cholera.

By the middle of the next day, Bastard Bhavan had been quarantined, with soldiers posted at each corner of our compound. Two more of the new boys fell sick and lay in a row of beds with

John Christopher among the deserted potters' wheels on the verandah.

I have to admit that Weems rose to the crisis, judging by his own
lights. He nursed the four boys with wet sheets and bowls of broth,
and prayed over John Christopher until his voice was a rasping
whisper. But Mr Peter floundered and could barely conduct classes
now that our plate production had come to a halt. As we sat at our
table listening to our schoolmates retching and groaning outside the
door, he sat staring off into the middle distance and muttering to
himself in Hindustani.

It didn't take a genius to figure out what had happened, but
Dileep put the pieces together before any of the rest of us could. To
begin with, cholera was no stranger to him, for he'd seen it as a little
boy.

Toward the end of each monsoon, when the damp still fusted
your clothes and the paths were troughs of mud, cholera came
visiting the countryside surrounding the city. Some blamed it on
moldy produce, some on the overuse of yeast, some on the fear of the
disease itself, for cholera seemed to share all the symptoms of terror:
cold sweats, fainting, vomiting, diarrhoea, bug-eyed delirium.

But the English blamed cholera, like everything else, on squalor.
In those times the government believed hardship was an Indian's
traditional and therefore his natural lot, so when a local famine or
epidemic struck it was usually allowed to take its course. But here
and there an ambitious young district officer would get it into his
head to try to contain the pestilence by penning up an infected
village's population in a quarantine camp and burning down its
infested huts.

It was a risky business, because unless the camp was situated on
high ground and the villagers kept themselves clean, only the
strongest would come out of it alive. And it could be risky for the
district officer, too, for every now and then a farmer, blind to the
officer's good intentions, might attack him with a shovel.

And it didn't take much imagination to fit the last piece of the
puzzle together, either: to picture Nanak Chand circling one of these
camps like a vulture's shadow. Dileep believed Nanak Chand and his
badmashes must have sneaked in and snatched the boys away at

knifepoint and silenced them, as they'd silenced Dileep, with threats to their families. It appealed to my taste for melodrama back then, but now I imagine that when Nanak Chand came along with his frayed chits and phony documents the desperate officer in charge was probably only too glad to release a few orphans into the eventual safekeeping of Nanak Chand's close personal friend and colleague, the Reverend Josiah Weems.

'Either way,' Dileep whispered that night when he dropped down to visit, 'what's Redeemer Walla going to do now?'

But Redeemer Walla wasn't uppermost in my mind. 'What if *we* get it?' I asked with a shiver.

'We won't get it.'

'Why not? I've been feeling bad all day. Hot. Tired.'

'You're always hot and tired,' Dileep said, 'We're not going to get it.'

'We might.'

'*You* might, then, if that's the way you want it. *I* won't get it. I had it when I was small and I heard the doctor say you can't get it twice.'

'*You* had it?'

Dileep looked away for a moment. 'Yes.'

'And you didn't die from it?'

'That's a stupid question. Do I look like I died from it? Not everybody dies from it, you know.'

'*I* know,' I said.

Dileep smiled at me, for he always seemed to enjoy bringing out the fraud in me; it somehow endeared me to him. 'No you don't,' he said evenly. 'But I do think John Christopher's going to die. He's not getting any better out there.'

'Did you hear him this afternoon? The way he was chanting things?'

'That wasn't John Christopher,' Dileep said as if letting me in on a secret.

'It was too.'

'No, Diwan,' Dileeep said with a slight shake of his head. 'That was Ram Kali talking. Ram Kali reciting his mantra.'

And Dileep was right. No matter how firmly the Reverend tried to quiet John Christopher the next morning, no matter how many hymns he sang or prayers he uttered, Ram Kali would rise to the surface of John Christopher's being and emit his heathen cries into the saturated air.

The doctor came around every morning after that first day. I don't remember his name – I probably didn't know it even then – but he was a rushed, heavyset old Englishman with a wild shock of white hair, eyebrows as thick and black as a Rajput's moustache, and a voice like doom.

Before his rounds on the verandah he would always pass among us and peer into our eyes and mouths for signs of the sickness. In this fashion he determined that Copy had caught the fever, and Jahangir, and I think it must have been the third day of our quarantine that he paused a while by Dileep, ordered him to stand, and with a shake of his head led him out to join the others.

If I remember that as Dileep followed the doctor outside he turned to look at me from the doorway with a sad smile and a little shrug, it's a memory I don't trust, for I think the mind invents such things when friends must part without a chance to say goodbye.

I don't know where Dileep had been wrong – maybe he'd never really had cholera before, or perhaps you can get cholera twice – but by that evening he was voiding and vomiting along with the others. And that night, at the time when he would have come down to visit me, I lay in my own fever of grief and terror, certain that I too had succumbed to the sickness, almost wishing it so Dileep could keep me company again. But then as I listened to him moaning and retching out in the night I reached the core of my shame: that if one of us had to die I was glad it wasn't me.

It was a truth so unbearable that all I could do to restore my pride was to slip out of bed after everyone else had gone to sleep and visit Dileep at his bedside.

At first, in the dim light from the single guttering candle set on one of the verandah's crooked struts, I couldn't distinguish Dileep from the others. They had all wasted away so quickly that it was like trying to identify them by their skeletal remains. There was so little left of Copy that he seemed about to evaporate, and Jahangir and John Christopher looked like twins, but at last I identified Dileep by his size and then, looking more closely, by the angle of his brow.

'Dileep,' I whispered. 'It's me – Balbeer.'

His body had lost all its moisture, and his flesh clung to his bones like a web. He was wrapped in a stained, wet sheet against his fever and in the verandah's shade his eyes were as listless and remote as clouds in a calm.

I was afraid to touch him, but I willed my hand onto his arm and squeezed. 'Dileep?' I asked, leaning toward his ear. 'Can you hear me?' His arm was cold and damp, and when I released it his flesh retained my fingers' imprint like the potter's clay.

For a moment he only groaned a little, his breath settling over him like a fog, but as I repeated his name his eyelids twitched and his lips, straining against his jaws' dead weight, seemed to try to form words out of his moaning.

'What, Dileep?' I said, turning my ear toward him. 'I can't hear you.'

He made a strangling sound, and in a whisper so faint it barely reached past the shell of my ear, he said, 'Get,' and then, 'Get,' again and finally, in one last effort, 'Get *away*.'

My friend's breath was putrid, and though his lips fell limp and his eyes rolled back I didn't turn away. For a moment he seemed to be suffused in a golden light, but it was merely the flicker from the Reverend's lamp as he came up behind me and placed his chill hand upon my shoulder.

'Come, Balbeer,' he said in a broken whisper. 'We shall pray for him together.'

I stared up at Weems for a moment and wondered if he'd slept at all since the quarantine had been imposed.

Despair, or exhaustion, had humbled him. He'd tended to Dileep as faithfully as he'd ministered to the others, wiping his brow with a wetted cloth, toting his offal to the privy, receiving his vomit on his own prying fingers as he trickled water through Dileep's parched lips.

And now there was an imprecation in his eyes as he bade me pray beside him. I instinctively glanced at Dileep for instructions, but he was but a shadow, and my knees doubled down to the verandah floor.

'O Lord God,' Weems whispered with his eyes shut tight,

'Dileep hath sinned against Thee with a stubborn, troubled spirit. He hath mocked Thee with the gifts Thou gavest him. He would never answer to his name. But his gifts are proof of Thy Love, and it is but my weak voice that could not call him to Thine Altar. Call to him, O Lord God, and he might yet praise Thee. Ask of us some offering that he might save his immortal soul. Reveal to us Thy pleasure, O Lord God of Hosts, as we sing to Thee with our hearts,' and here he began to mouth the Lord's Prayer, with a yawn that trembled his shoulders in the lamplight.

And I confess that I prayed with him, and offered up my soul to the Reverend's god, mixing up all the prayers I'd ever heard: benedictions, my mother's chants and lullabies, even the old pilgrim's ode to Shiva – whatever I could recall and modify for the occasion. So I suppose it's no wonder that whoever was listening got my prayer garbled. Bring back my friend, is what I meant to say, and my soul is yours, dear Jesus.

Poor John Christopher died that night, and was already in his coffin by the time I awoke. It wasn't a real coffin, just a packing crate from the plate works, but the Reverend had painted a cross atop it and set it out in the rain. Weems announced his passing as he roused us, and though some of us had trouble making the appropriate noises, I'll admit I felt a peculiar secondhand grief. My heart still kept its vigil for Dileep, but in his delirious reversion to Ram Kali – his old self – John Christopher had become my brother.

Weems seemed to have transported himself somewhere beyond grief as he led us out to John Christopher's little coffin, plodding along in his soaked black suit, stooped and trembling, as if stumbling toward his own doom. We stood around a shallow pit half filled with water as the Reverend croaked a prayer, and if there were tears on his cheeks they were lost in the rivulets of rain that poured down from the top of his bare head. Maybe it was just pity I was feeling, but looking up at Weems as he bade farewell to his little convert, I was as close as I had ever come to liking him.

The Reverend said that since John Christopher was high and dry and there we were standing below in the mud and the rain, it wasn't we who should feel sorry for him, but he who should feel sorry for us. I suppose that by his own lights the Reverend had a point, but it was hard to envy John Christopher in his little shipping-box coffin, packed in straw like a stack of plates, as we lowered him into the pool of rainwater at the bottom of his grave. His coffin bobbed there for a moment, and as Weems cast ashes and mud atop it 'in sure and certain hope of the Resurrection unto eternal life,' his voice finally broke.

I don't think I'd ever seen a man look more miserable, for it seemed as though he'd buried all his hopes at once. But it was to last for only a moment, because just as Ralph and Puran began with their shovels to tumble the heaped banks of John Christopher's grave onto his sinking coffin, someone shouted 'Hallelujah!' from the verandah.

We all wheeled about on the muddy ground and peered through the rain at an exultant figure wrapped in a sheet.

'Hallelujah! Hallelujah!' he shouted again, stepping toward us with his hands clasped high above his head and his eyes as bright as fireflies, but it wasn't until he was halfway to us that I realized he was Dileep.

With a yelp I leaped away from the circle of mourners and ran straight for him, my heart about to burst, and embraced him as he stumbled forward.

'You're alive!' I remember crying out as I pressed my face against his ribs. 'Oh, Dileep! You're alive! You're alive! I knew it! I knew you wouldn't die!'

But what did I know, for Dileep didn't answer me, nor return my embrace, nor even stop plodding toward the Reverend. His eyes seemed to be fixed on something distant, and when he'd shaken me off he fell forward at the Reverend's feet and lay flat out in the mud, crying out that he was saved.

I sat in the rain and gaped up as the old certitude coursed through the Reverend's frame, the old steel glinted from his blood-shot eyes. He stood there a moment, not content with Dileep's prostrate, vanquished soul, and beckoned to me with his out-stretched arms.

Now it was true that I had made a bargain, but in the event I could not keep it. What would the Redeemer want with my poor soul anyway, now that He had Dileep's?

So I rose to my feet, turned tail, and ran.

CHAPTER
20

I didn't have any idea where I was running to, but knowing what I was running from was enough to get me across the Reverend's fields and over the compound wall. Someone must have alerted the sentries, for one of them took the quarantine seriously enough to fire his rifle, but the bullet whirred by and he must have lost sight of me as I scrambled through the brush.

I was a fair fugitive at first as I snaked my way toward town. Discarding my uniform, I fashioned a dhoti for myself out of a rag I found tangled in the bushes behind the Muir Cotton Mill, and when in the afternoon soldiers approached as I finally set foot on Bithoor Road, I immersed myself in a group of pilgrims and the soldiers passed by me without curiosity.

The stubborn core of myself was all I had left, for the rest of me was a shambles of grief and fear. I knew Weems must be looking for me, and the soldiers, and now probably the police as well, but it wasn't until evening, when I darted into the crowds on the Street of Silver, that I remembered Nanak Chand's threat.

In any other city I would have been quickly found out and dragged back into the Reverend's clutches, but Cawnpore was a city of strangers seeking jobs in the mills and factories, displaced villagers toiling in a uniformity of woe, each looking as lost as I in the swift, commercial flow of the streets.

I kept myself in motion all evening, running from shadow to shadow, searching the crowds for my enemies, shrinking from the idle glances of passersby, moving as much to avoid facing up to the hopelessness of my situation as to confound my pursuers with a moving target. The last place I should have chosen to hide was in my old neighborhood, but nevertheless when I at last came to rest in the dark beneath a parked coolie's cart I caught a familiar sugary fragrance on the damp breeze and saw that I was only five doors away from my mother's house.

As evening gave way to night the rain returned, and little

estuaries snaked out from the brimming gutter and ran among the paving stones. Even as feet slapped and splashed by me, hurrying home in the downpour, I tried to sleep, but it was useless. As I squatted in the cart's shadow, wondering what was to become of me now that my Christian phase was over, now that my mother was dead and in all the world I had no friend, I found myself staring with hopeless longing at the door to my old home.

A strong light, as from an oil lantern, glared out from the window where my mother's mustard lamp had once gently glowed, and I could see from the shadows that passed before it that Lalyat Prasad the sweetseller had new tenants in the apartment above his stall. The rain emptied the streets and Lalyat Prasad closed down his shop. For an hour or so the neighbourhood was still, and I wondered if I should sneak through the streets then, or if I would be less conspicuous in the morning throng.

But my thoughts seemed to circle back and mock me, now in Weems's voice, now in Nanak Chand's, now even in Dileep's. Where did I think I was going? Despair seemed to seep into my bones, and squatting in the gutter's stinking overflow I wrapped my arms around my knees and wept.

I may have imagined I'd escaped Weems in the nick of time, but he'd left his mark. For the first time since fleeing Bastard Bhavan I allowed myself to grieve for Dileep, but it was Christian grief, for I blamed myself for his downfall, blamed my incompetent prayers, and asked the pattering darkness to forgive me; and all that kept me from taking on the shame of fate itself was the sudden grumble and cough of two figures approaching on the dim, deserted street.

I sank deeper into the shadow of the coolie's cart as they passed, and over the trickle of the gutter below me and the fall of the rain above, I heard them speaking.

'I tell you, I've looked here three times already!' insisted the first, hunching under his torn umbrella.

'So what?' the other replied, leaning into the rain. 'Babu tells us to look again, we look again.'

'All right,' the first said as they passed directly by me, 'but this is the last time I'm looking for the little bastard. Do you hear me? The last time!'

They stomped up to Lalyat Prasad's shop, wrestled the umbrella closed, and ducked into the doorway. Sitting up and drying my eyes, I could make out the sound of someone rapping on the door, then a chorus of indignant shouts, and in a moment they were stumbling back out into the street.

'See?' the first said, struggling to open the umbrella again as they hurried by, their wet, spread feet splashing water on my legs. 'What did I tell you? Nothing but trouble all day. I don't care what he's promised us – I'm going to bed. Let *him* find the little son of a bitch.'

I wasn't so far gone that I couldn't guess that these were Nanak Chand's men and that I was the bastard son of a bitch they sought. As they disappeared down the dark street I decided I had to move from my hiding place – though it had concealed me well enough so far – and as I crept out of the shadows I had another one of those inspirations that kept visiting me back then, and whose recollection makes me marvel that I ever survived into manhood. For it suddenly occurred to me that if the two men had already sought me out in my old haunt four times that day and, besides, had given up the chase for the rest of the night, then the cleverest hiding place in town had to be my old haven, the roof.

And so, with my heart pounding its objections to this idiot plan, that is where I climbed: past the shutters of Lalyat Prasad's stall; up the old stone stairs; past the door to our room, which now seemed to wheeze in the stillness; and up the creaking rungs of the old bamboo ladder and into the little lean-to where I used to keep my kite.

The lean-to leaked in a dozen places and the roof's floor was slick with rainwater, but I felt protected on those familiar few square feet, and for the first time all day my breaths and heartbeats slowed. When I was certain that no one had heard me making my ascent I crept to the edge of the roof and dared to look around me. Only a few lights glittered in the surrounding gloom, and the river was a black void beyond the rooftops, but I could see that the skyline had changed: a great row of buildings had risen like a range of mountains and now superimposed themselves upon my memory of the view, with smokestacks and water towers reaching into the drizzling sky.

But immediately below me the bazaar was as I remembered it from the summer nights when I slept outside, seeking the weak breeze from the depleted Ganga. It had been more than three years since I'd last looked down on my mother's street, but I still remembered where Mohinder and Bhagat's nightwatchman father slumbered through his duties, where naked Kacha spent the night beneath the floorboards of the pahn seller's shop, where the sandal maker's cart was parked and locked. The only difference was that at my own new height it all looked smaller, and that as I stared, soaked to the bone, at the familiar streets, I heard no coughing from my mother's room below.

In my reverie I must have sat up too straight against the night sky, for out of the shadow of the produce stall across the street a figure emerged, staring up in my direction and plodding toward the house.

I pushed myself back and gasped, the flesh prickling along my brow. Where could I go? Where could I hide? I scrambled over to the ladder, but as I placed my foot upon it I heard my pursuer's footsteps on the stairs, and I leapt back into the blackest corner of the lean-to. I reached around me in the dark for a weapon, and could find only a piece of brick from the remains of our old cooking stove, and as the top of the ladder trembled with my intruder's slow ascent I gripped the shard and held my breath.

Perhaps in the calm and comfort of your chair you've already guessed who it was, but I didn't until two hands had appeared on the ladder's poles, cautiously followed by a head hooded against the rain, and a small voice I never expected to hear again called out, 'Little Master?'

It was a good thing Moonshi thus identified himself, because in another moment I might have brought my brick down upon his skull.

'Little Master?' he said again, peering around him like a mouse at the mouth of his den.

'Moonshi?' I finally replied when I found my voice, slowly lowering my weapon. 'Is that you?'

'Little Master!' he exclaimed, climbing out onto the exposed roof. 'I *knew* you'd be here.'

But he still didn't see me, so deeply had I buried myself in the lean-to's shadow, and though a part of me wanted to rush over and embrace him, my newfound fugitive's circumspection held me back.

'Keep away from me,' I said, raising my weapon again, and all at once my relief gave way to my old fury at Moonshi's betrayal at the Sati Chowra Ghat.

Moonshi stood and squinted in my direction and I could see his disjointed gaze puzzling out my dim form in the dark. 'But Little Master – ' he said aloud.

'Quiet!' I whispered back at him. 'And get down!'

Moonshi squatted down immediately and looked around him for a moment. 'Little Master,' he asked, 'are you all right?'

But I wasn't to be won back so easily. 'How did you find me?' I said.

'Shri Chand told me,' Moonshi blurted, 'and I – '

'Shri Chand?' I exclaimed, pressing myself againt the lean-to's damp thatch. 'What did he tell you?'

'That you'd run away, Little Master.'

'So you're here on Shri Chand's business?'

'No, no,' Moonshi said. 'I've come to see you. He told me you'd run away and he was looking for you and if I – '

' – and if you led him to me he would pay you. Is that it?'

Moonshi ducked his head in the rain. 'May I join you in there, Little Master?' he asked. 'I'm going to drown out here if – '

'You keep away,' I said, 'or so help me I'll – '

'Little Master,' Moonshi said, 'it's *me*. Old Moonshi. *I'm* not going to hurt you.'

'That's right,' I snarled back at him. 'You're going to get away from here. You're going to leave me alone.'

Moonshi gave me a long, searching look. 'Little Master, what's happened to you? What have I done to deserve your hatred?'

'You – you left me, Moonshi,' I said, and as I spoke his name my voice broke like a twig. 'and now you've come to give me up again.'

'No I haven't, Little Master. I've come to – '

'I can't *trust* you any more, Moonshi. You left me there and you never came back. You never came back to get me.'

As a sob bubbled out of me, Moonshi too began to cry and squatted as I had squatted on the street beneath the coolie's cart, with his arms wrapped around his legs. 'I tried, Little Master,' he said, pressing his face against his knees. 'I tried so hard to keep my promise.'

'Tried?' I exclaimed. '*How* did you try? You never came for me. You never even came to visit.'

'But you've got to believe me,' Moonshi said, lifting his face. 'I couldn't visit you. How could I visit you when I was – ' But here Moonshi hid his face again and shook his head.

'When you were what?' I asked, trying to keep a hold on my indignation, though Moonshi looked even smaller than I remembered him, huddled and sobbing in the rain.

'When I was in jail,' Moonshi replied.

'In *jail?*'

'Don't send me away, Little Master,' Moonshi said quickly. 'It wasn't my fault.'

'In jail for what?' I asked, laying down the brick.

'Does it matter? It matters only that I couldn't come to see you, and afterward – '

'It matters,' I said. 'Answer me, Moonshi. In jail for what?'

Moonshi sighed and gave me an imploring look. 'Can't I please come in out of the rain? Look,' he said reaching toward me. 'My hands are shaking.'

'All right,' I said finally, gripping the brick again. 'But only if you answer me.'

Moonshi nodded and ducked in to squat near the ladder, removing his hood and wringing it out by his feet. 'I didn't want to tell you,' he said. 'But now I see I must. Of course I must. I imagined you to be the same little boy I comforted at my mistress's pyre. But you've changed, Little Master, haven't you? The English have changed you, haven't they? And look at you,' he said, peering at me. 'Look how you've grown.' He nodded to himself and stared out at the rain. 'So Moonshi must do as he's told. Yes.' He began to move closer to me, but I stiffened and raised my brick slightly, and with a sigh he remained where he was, catching in his hands a trickle of rainwater from the thatch above him and drinking it.

'I meant what I promised you, what I promised my mistress,' he said, swallowing and shaking his hands dry. 'But how could I oppose your Englishman? Not without papers, letters, some kind of proof you had family. So Moonshi had to let his Little Master go. And after my mistress's ashes were scattered in the Ganga – and I did it properly, Little Master, with all the right observances – I went home to search your mother's trunk for a little bundle of papers I remembered she kept there. I figured I could take them to this bania I know and have them identified and maybe they would contain the proof I needed. But when I got there the trunk was gone – and not just the trunk but everything else, cooking utensils, blankets, even my mistress's Ganesha, all gone. And Shri Prasad told me who had taken it.'

'Nanak Chand,' I said with a grim nod.

'No, no, Little Master. It was the hakeem. As payment, he'd told Shri Prasad. So I went to the hakeem and I faced him, Little Master. I stood up to him. You give it back, I told him. You give it back or I'll call the police. But he refused, and I caused quite a scene. He said my mistress's goods barely covered half the debt she owed him. I called him a thief. And then he began to say shameful things about my mistress. I won't say what, but they were *shameful* things, and while her ashes were still floating on the river, too. So I called him a great many names and pulled down the awning above his door and the people gathered and cheered me, Little Master, for defending my mistress's name. And when he shut the doors to his stall and ordered me to go away I obeyed him, but only to summon the police. I got so full of myself that I forgot I was just Moonshi, a servant, but the police brought me back to my senses. They believed everything the hakeem told them. And why not? They were Moslems, and the hakeem was a dignitary. I had no proof to offer, no legal arguments to make, and when the police were done they struck me with their latthis and that was that.

'But I'd promised you, Little Master. And I'd promised my mistress. So I couldn't give up, not even then. I had to get my proof. So I went to the ghat and washed my wounds and when the moon began to fall I made my way back into town and travelled the rooftops to the hakeem's stall and climbed through his window. Can you imagine me doing such a thing? I can't believe it myself. But I did, somehow.

'It was dark in the room upstairs, and before my eyes got used to it I knocked over a jar of something on a shelf and it fell to the floor with a crash and raised a stink – must have been one of the hakeem's pickled organs he was always collecting – and I figured I was about to be found out for sure.

'But there wasn't another sound for the longest while and I guessed the hakeem must either be out or a deep sleeper. So I pumped up my courage again and looked around for the trunk. The rooms were filled with all kinds of stuff, and after bumping into skeletons and coming upon jars filled with eyes swimming in brine and all sorts of unwholesome things the hakeem collected, my nerves were gone, and my knees just barely had enough strength left to get me downstairs into Shri Sayideen's stall. As I made my way down, though, I noticed that the stall was flooded with moonlight, which didn't make sense since the hakeem always shut it up for the night. And when I got down to the stall I looked across the room and saw that one of his shutters was open, and hung askew from a busted hinge, and in the moonlight from the street, staring up like a frozen devil, lay the hakeem in his lounging robe. He was folded up like a piece of laundry, with his spine bent back on itself so that his head – and I swear to you this is true – lay back upon his buttocks.

'Well, I couldn't help myself, Little Master. I'd never seen such a thing, and after everything else I'd gone through it was just too much. So I screamed, and I couldn't stop screaming, and the chowkidor came running, and the police soon afterwards. And there they found me and the hakeem, and you can imagine what they thought after what had happened the day before. It was as clear as day to them. I had murdered the hakeem.'

Moonshi looked at me and shook his head. 'So that's why I went to jail, Little Master,' he said. 'Have I answered you?'

I looked back at him now, my anger spent. 'But you were innocent,' I said. 'You didn't do it.'

'Of course I didn't do it!' Moonshi snapped, and then hung his head, as though afraid I would strike him. 'Me break the hakeem's back? Me, Moonshi Lal, a murderer? But try reasoning with the police when they've made up their minds. They tried to get me to confess by beating me, and I've got to admit I came pretty close. But I kept my mouth shut, and finally they threw me back into my cell and arranged for a trial, but it was months before I got one, with nothing but the lowly and the vile as my companions, with nothing to look forward to but the gallows, and all the while I was wondering to myself, oh, what has become of my Little Master? How will he ever forgive me?

'But then came the trial, and this very distinguished English personage, the magistrate, Shri Harris Sahib, listened to all the evidence and weighed it carefully in his mind and came back and announced that I couldn't have broken the hakeem's back like that, it must have taken someone twice my size; and that though I'd had no business breaking into his shop like that, the hakeem had had no business stealing my mistress's trunk, and in any case I'd served enough time in jail already to pay for whatever crime I'd done and that speaking for himself he wished he could find servants as loyal as me.

'So he let me go. Oh, Little Master, this Harris Sahib is a very just and beneficient dignitary. A very good gentleman. And when I followed after him to pay him my most grateful respects he took an interest in me and told me I could work for him if I wanted, but that I would have to give up my notions of freeing you – for I'd told him about you, Little Master, and he took a great interest in you, too, and talked to your Reverend Sahib about you. He told me you were being looked after and you were contented and in any case I had no legal right to your custody, no hope of claiming you. But he promised to write to your uncle on your behalf. So what else could I do? Where was I to go if not to him? And he kept his promise, too, though he's never received a reply in all the time I've served him, Little Master. Not one.'

'You mean you work for him?'

'Oh, yes,' Moonshi said with a proud smile. 'For these three years now. And he has been a most generous sahib, Little Master, and so too the memsahib. Always looking out for my welfare. Always assuring me that you are thriving in the Reverend's care. How a gentleman with all he has to think about and do – how he can take the time to – '

'Then what about Nanak Chand? You said he told you I'd run away.'

'Yes, he did. He came to me this afternoon with two of his employees.'

'Badmashes, Moonshi,' I said. 'I saw them.'

'Yes, well, anyway, he told me you had run away, that you had done something very wrong and were very sick and that if you didn't return to the Reverend you would die, or at least that's what he told the Memsahib Harris, for she was standing there with me when he came to see me. And he asked if I'd seen you and I said no, and he said that if I did I was to tell him, for the police were looking for you, too, and if you fell into their hands you might be beaten or maybe even killed.'

Moonshi paused as if to let me explain, but I kept silent.

'So the memsahib let me go for the afternoon so I could search for you, and finally I came here and waited, for I know my Little Master. I knew you'd come here. I knew you'd come looking for your old Moonshi.'

'I wasn't looking for you,' I said, still trying to scold him, though my heart wasn't in it any longer.

'You weren't?' Moonshi said, his eye growing large. 'Then why – '

'And I don't believe your story. I don't believe –'

'Please, Little Master,' Moonshi said, raising his hand as if to ward off a blow.

'How can I believe you when – '

'Please, Little Master,' Moonshi begged again. 'Please don't be angry with me. I tried. I know I failed you, but I tried so *hard*,' and his shoulders began to shake as he covered his face with his hands.

I couldn't keep a grip on my suspicion, for my heart broke with his, and as the rain ceased pattering on the saturated thatch I crawled over to him and touched his shoulder.

'Never mind, Moonshi,' I said. 'Don't cry. I believe you.'

But just when I'd finished speaking, Moonshi looked up at me with a strange, hunted look, covered my mouth with his hand, and pinned me to the puddled floor of the roof.

CHAPTER
21

No, it's not what you're thinking, or at least not what I was thinking as he held me down, which was that he'd tricked me and captured me for Nanak Chand's reward. No, it was only that at the very same moment that I spoke, Moonshi heard something on the street below that made his blood freeze.

'*Shush*!' he whispered as I struggled against his grip. 'Listen.'

But I could barely breathe beneath him, and finally pulled his hand away from my mouth. 'Get *off* me!' I said, pushing at his shoulder.

'Be *quiet*, Little Master!' he whispered back, craning around in the dark to listen.

Realizing at last that Moonshi was trying to protect me from something, I caught my breath and listened to him. As the last drops of rain dripped off the fringes of the lean-to, the crickets began to saw, and in the distance I could hear someone coughing and spitting his way out of sleep. But then I heard another noise rising out of the ladder's well, a plodding rhythm as heavy and leisurely as a camel's, ascending the steps below.

'Come!' Moonshi whispered, crawling off me and ducking out of the lean-to to hide behind its thatch. I scrambled after him, and the two of us watched through the shelter's weave and listened as the footsteps stopped on the landing below and something struck the door.

Someone cursed from inside, but then a voice as deep and muffled as the strum of a rope replied and the door was opened and a conversation ensued, so subdued that the particulars were lost to us. The door closed, the conversation ceased, and it was silent for a moment, but then we heard those footsteps again, rising in volume until they paused at the foot of the ladder.

'Oh God,' Moonshi whispered to himself, holding me to him, as the top of the ladder shifted in its well.

We could barely hear the creak of the ladder over the pounding of our hearts as whoever it was took the first rung. But then there was a cracking noise and a great thump, as if the rung had broken. Whoever it was then took the second rung, and for a moment the top of his turban appeared in the opening, but then the second rung must have broken, too, for there was another crack and the turban disappeared back down with a louder thump and a curse like a tiger's distant grumble.

The ladder itself rose a foot or so out of the well for a moment, and then skyrocketed up as if heaved in a burst of rage, and landed with a clatter on the roof. Moonshi and I looked at each other, daring to hope that the danger had passed, but then, impossibly – for the ceiling at the landing was nearly ten feet high – fingers as thick as my wrists appeared along the lip of the hatch and a head as big as a water jar arose and peered briefly around the roof before his fingers slipped and he sank out of sight like a drowning bull.

'Genda,' I whispered as he limped back downstairs.

Moonshi snapped his head around and glared at me. 'How do *you* know his name?' he whispered back.

'I've met him. On the street. He saved me. He said he was my friend.'

'*Friend*,' Moonshi said with a grim nod. 'Well, forget what he told you, Little Master. He's not your friend.' Moonshi narrowed his eyes. 'What else did he tell you?'

'About what?'

'About – about anything.'

'He – I don't remember, Moonshi. He said I shouldn't cry. He said I shouldn't shame my father.'

Moonshi stared at me a moment longer, then crawled to the edge of the roof and watched the giant stride off into the bazaar. 'Little Master,' Moonshi said, 'you must forget what he told you. He's your enemy. Your worst enemy, no matter what anyone says.'

I crawled over to the ladder and examined its broken rungs. 'We've got to get away from here,' I said, sliding the ladder back toward its well, but Moonshi placed his foot on it to stop me.

'Not that way,' he said. 'They may be watching the door. We'll go down the back way,' and with that he carried the ladder to the rear of the building and set its feet down on the roof of an adjoining shed.

'Come on,' he said, climbing down ahead of me, and I followed after him and leapt with him from the top of the shed to the muck of the alleyway.

Moonshi hunched over and ran off down the middle of the muddy lane, peering around him like a soldier on patrol. I'd been a fugitive only since morning, but I'd learned enough to know that if Moonshi kept ducking around like that we were done for.

'Moonshi!' I whispered through my teeth, pulling him out of the dim light of the advancing dawn and into the shadows along the walls. 'Where are we going?'

'Never mind,' Moonshi said, pulling away from me but keeping clear of the light. 'Just follow me.'

We startled a Gujarati woman squatting with her skirts gathered up over a storm drain, relieving herself in the half light, and Moonshi managed to step on a dog as we ventured out onto the main street, but no one took special notice of us. We hurried north to the river's edge and followed the road along the Bargudiya Ghat and on past the Sarsiya Ghat, and when two men I mistook for Nanak Chand's men came into view we ducked down and crept along the water's edge. It was there that my lack of food and sleep caught up with me, for the bones in my legs seemed to bend beneath me and I reached out and tugged at Moonshi's shirt to stop him.

'Moonshi, wait,' I said. 'I've got to rest.'

'But we're almost there, Little Master,' Moonshi panted, hurrying forward.

'Almost where?' I asked, slowing my steps behind him.

'Come on. There's no time to lose. I can't be late.'

'Moonshi,' I said, stopping in my tracks. 'Where are we going?'

'To safety, Little Master. Please, don't hold us up.' Moonshi turned to face me and took a few more steps backward along the water's edge.

'Where are we going?' I asked again, and then for the first time saw that we were near the road to Bastard Bhavan, the route I'd followed on the last leg of Weems's tour. 'Moonshi,' I said, 'if you think you're taking me back to – '

'No, no, Little Master,' Moonshi said. 'I told you I was taking you to safety. Now let's go before we're too late.'

'Tell me, Moonshi,' I said, sitting down and folding my arms, 'or I won't follow you another step.'

Moonshi looked at me a moment longer and sighed. 'I'm taking you to Shri Harris Sahib, Little Master. He's a good man. He'll know what to do.'

'Harris Sahib?' I exclaimed, rising to my feet.

'He wants to help, Little Master. He – '

'He wants to help? Another Englishman? You want to give me over to another Englishman? So he can give me back to Weems?'

'He'll know what's best, Little Master,' Moonshi pleaded. 'Believe me. It's our only – '

'No,' I said, stamping my foot. '*We* know what's best. *I* know what to do. We have to get away from here. We have to go back to Rajputana.'

'What?' Moonshi said, slapping his brow.

'To Harigarh,' I said. 'To mother's family.'

'But Little Master, that's impossible. How can we – '

'*Moonshi*,' I snarled at him, 'You promised. You promised me you'd take me back.'

'But that was long ago. So much has changed.'

'Nothing's changed,' I snapped back.

'No, Little Master. You don't understand. I have a new master now. A new life. If you met Shri Harris Sahib you'd understand. He's not like the others. He's – '

' – an Englishman, Moonshi. And he's *not* your master.'

'But he is,' Moonshi said. 'He shelters me, he pays me, he protects me. He's so good to me, Little Master. I can't just leave him – '

'You left me,' I said, trying to keep from striking him.

'But I told you. I tried to come to you. I couldn't.'

'You can now,' I said, tightening my fists at my sides.

Moonshi held his head as if to keep it from spinning, then suddenly raised his face with a hopeful look. 'But what about your uncle? He never answered the sahib's letters. How do you know he'd even take us back?'

'He'll take us back,' I said, concealing my doubts with a hard glare. 'Your sahib never even sent any letters. My uncle doesn't even know I'm alive.'

Moonshi began to wring his hands. 'Oh, Little Master, please let me take you to my sahib. *He*'ll take you in. He'll embrace you like a son.'

I paused to gather my strength and said, with what little majesty I could muster in my ragged dhoti, 'He's *not* your sahib, Moonshi. *I* am your master. You're my mother's servant. And I'm telling you to take me back to Harigarh.'

'But I can't, Little Master,' said Moonshi with his head bowed. 'I just can't.'

'I *order* you to!' I cried out, though my voice cracked in the morning mist.

Moonshi straightened up and stared over my head like a scolded soldier. 'Then I won't,' he said, barely moving his lips.

I felt the blood rise to my ears and tears slip over my aching eyes. 'Tell *her* you won't!' I shouted, and I scooped up a handful of gray mud from the water's edge and flung it at him. 'Tell my mother you won't take me home!'

Moonshi tried to duck, but the mud fell across him like a lash. 'Please, Little Master,' he began to cry. 'Please don't make me – '

'Tell *her*!' I screamed at him. 'Tell *her* you won't keep your promise!' And I threw another handful at him and then another, as Moonshi fell to his knees and seemed about to melt back into the earth like a clay idol left out in the rain.

'Tell her! Tell her! Tell her!' I kept crying, still flinging the ashy muck at him, until all my strength had been expended, and I lay on the riverbank and wept.

Moonshi finally raised his head and miserably wiped the mud from his face, reaching out to stroke my back.

'All right, Little Master,' he said. 'I'll keep my promise. I'll take you home.'

'You will?' I asked, looking up at him, for I'd finally run out of commands.

'Yes, Little Master,' said Moonshi, gravely lifting me to my feet. 'I serve the Raos still.'

'You won't be sorry, Moonshi,' I said, wiping some of the mud from his shirt. 'You'll see.'

But Moonshi didn't look reassured as we set off together to find my mother's people, and why should he have, for with my persistence I had sealed his doom.

CHAPTER

22

Moonshi did go back to Harris's compound that morning, but only to sneak out a little purple sack of money he'd saved from his wages; evidently his new sahib had somehow cured Moonshi of gambling them away on partridge fights.

With half this money he bought us passage upriver to Fatehgarh on a battered old budgerow, handing the few folded rupees to the head boatman with an aggrieved look, as if he were feeding precious food to some menacing and insatiable beast. We purchased provisions for our journey in the old city and set sail in the late afternoon, stepping aboard from the Magazine Ghat a mile or so west of Bastard Bhavan. Our progress would be slow, the boatman warned, for the wind was weak and westerly, and the opposing current on the rain-gorged stream was strong.

I hadn't eaten anything for a day and a half, but I couldn't bring myself to eat the chapatti and ghee that Moonshi offered me until the Bridge of Boats had receded from view. I was leaving my birthplace, after all, and though common sense tells me now that I was well rid of the place, I suppose that no matter how squalid your birthplace might be a part of you will always long for it, for I watched wistfully then as the smokestacks from the Elgin Mills faded into the undulating haze.

Moonshi and I had decided to pose, if anyone asked, as a father and son returning from a funeral, but when the boatmen did ask, we floundered around for details. Soon Moonshi had us posing not only as father and son, which was unlikely enough, but as farmers from Gwalior – a poor choice, since anyone could tell just by looking at our hands that we were city folk, and neither of us had ever set foot in Gwalior State.

But the boatmen were indifferent, and kept their eyes on the patched sail's billow and the offal that floated toward us in the stream: uprooted trees, a cartwheel, a buffalo's bloated carcass. And the only other passenger was a Moslem peddler, with a trunkful of leather goods from the city's tanneries, who, though unconvinced by Moonshi's tangled replies to his idle inquiries, lost interest in us as we drifted toward Bithur.

But for the swift flow we might have been on a great gray sea, for the river was so wide in places that it reached to the horizon, and the wind rippled the water across the current as if to disguise its direction. The budgerow zigzagged upstream like a fish, and the light became a dim glow among the clouds beyond the western bank.

When we approached Bithoor the boatman prepared as if to tack across the river, but instead they brought the boat up to a narrow stone pier that jutted out from a ruined ghat, mooring it fast to an iron ring.

'Why are we stopping?' Moonshi asked as the boatmen secured the lines.

'We spend the night here, brother,' one of the boatmen answered, 'and pick up another passenger.'

'But we're in a hurry. We can't stop here. I thought you were taking us straight up to Fatehgar.'

'And we will,' the boatman said, lashing his sail to the boom. 'In the morning.'

'But why not now? You said you'd take us there tonight.'

'*You* dodge the sandbars in the dark if you want to, brother,' the boatman said, stepping into the lopsided cabin. 'But I need some sleep.'

Moonshi stared around him, strangely agitated. 'But – but where will *we* sleep?' he sputtered as the other boatman followed him inside.

'On the deck,' one of them called back, shutting the door behind him.

Moonshi and I gazed up at the town, but all we could see of it was a broken silhouette against the dismal, churning sky, and a few charred trees standing like skeletons along the strand.

'What is it, Moonshi?' I whispered up to him.

'*Father*,' said Moonshi. 'You've got to call me Father, Little Master.'

'Then you call me Balbeer,' I snapped back at him. 'Are you afraid they'll catch up with us here?'

'No, Balbeer,' said Moonshi. 'We've escaped them for sure.'

'Then what's wrong with sleeping here?'

'This place,' Moonshi said, pulling me into a dark corner of the sheltered deck. 'It's evil.'

'Why is it evil?'

Moonshi brought out his purple change purse and squeezed it into a tiny ball in his fist. 'Never mind, Little Master,' he said.

'Call me *Balbeer*,' I reminded him again.

'Never mind, Balbeer,' he said with a sigh, tucking the purse back into his waistcloth.

No lamplight pierced the gloom above us, and no human voice or footstep broke the silence. The storm which now began to flash and rumble far beyond the riverbank shunned the Ganga and the town and bore with it the last faint breeze, so that even the fringe on the budgerow's boom was still.

The leather peddler set out his prayer rug and began to praise his prophet in a muffled drone as Moonshi and I lay down for the night. Moonshi closed his eyes and tried to sleep, but with each creak of the deck beneath the peddler's knees, each fishtail's slap on the water along the hull, he would pop them open again and fret.

But I was too exhausted to share for long in Moonshi's anguished vigil, and when I closed my eyes my mother came to me again, hovering just above the river's yellow sheen, smiling, then beckoning, then approaching, and in her approach smoldering and decaying and with her smoking, skeletal arm and horror-struck stare, driving me out of the ashen shallows and up to the feet of a stranger.

I awoke from the dream in my usual panic, with my heart pounding and my quick breaths struggling in the heat, to find that Moonshi was asleep at last, and the peddler too, but that an old Rajput had boarded and sat now against the budgerow's rail, his one eye staring upon me like a star.

The light I saw in the old man's eye couldn't have been a reflection, for there was no moon, star, or lamplight to reflect, but I swear to you on my mother's ashes that it glowed, because when I shut my eyes its after-image lingered like an ember. I tried to go back to sleep, but even when I rolled over and turned my back to the old man I could feel his gaze like a breath upon my shoulders.

I turned around to face him again and stare him down, but he returned my gaze with the equable persistence of a corpse, until at last I lowered my gaze, balking as if stepping back from a precipice.

'Can't sleep?' came a voice from the gloom beneath his turban. It was the voice of someone who hadn't spoken for days, weeks, maybe even years. It faltered out into the dark like a cripple and scrabbled against my ears.

'Me neither,' he said as if I'd answered him. 'Sleep's a waste of the night, if you ask me.'

At last he broke his stare and fished around for something in his sack. 'Here,' he said, bringing forth a stack of brass food tins and snapping them apart. 'Eat with me.'

I looked over to Moonshi for guidance, but he merely twitched and whimpered like a sleeping dog, clutching at the bulge in his waistcloth.

'Come on,' the old man said. 'Look, I've got roasted eggplant and – what's this? – ah, yes, it's cauliflower and peas and potatoes and fresh-baked chapattis, of course. I can't possibly eat all this. You've got to help me.'

The aroma of eggplant and spices gathered like a ghost around my nostrils, and I finally crept toward him across the tilting deck.

'There we are,' he said as I cautiously sat down to his left and looked up at him. But when he began to turn his head toward me there was a blank where his left eye should have been – a puckered, crisscrossed pit – so that before his right eye had appeared I had already given out a strangled cry.

'Ah, the eye,' he said, pointing up to his face and smiling. 'I forgot. Didn't mean to startle you. I'll tell you what,' he said, moving his sack away from his right side, 'Move over here if it bothers you.'

I shook my head, afraid I'd hurt his feelings.

'No, go on,' he said, patting the deck to his right. 'It'll be easier on both of us. I won't have to crane my neck around to see you.'

So I did as I was told, moving slowly so as not to awaken the peddler, who lay nearby, chained to his trunk and gripping a pistol in his fist.

'Some people just can't stand the dark, can they?' the old man said softly, placing his brass food kit between us. 'Scares them to death. But I never could understand that. Light, dark – what's the difference?'

He tore his chapatti and handed half of it to me, and together we gathered up mouthfuls of potato. It was wonderful food – the best I'd eaten in three years – but my palate must have lost its tolerance at Bastard Bhavan, for the chilis brought tears to my eyes.

'Good, isn't it?' the old man said. 'Comes from a widow I know who cooks for the soldiers. Gives it to me on the sly for old times' sake. Don't have to make do with the garbage they sell in the street. Not me.'

We sat together for a moment, chewing and swallowing, and the old man said, 'And what about you, boy?'

I gave him a questioning look, another mouthful poised by my lips.

'What about you? You scared of the dark like everyone else?'

There was a challenge in his question, as if a wrong answer might expel me from his feast, so I shook my head to please him.

'Good boy,' he said with a firm, proud nod. 'That's the spirit. You know,' he ventured, peering at me for a moment, 'you've got quite a forehead on you. Anyone told you that?' He chewed for a moment, staring above my brow. 'Yes sir, quite a forehead. Great things written on it. Great good fortune – long life, anyway. And great adventures,' he said, reaching toward me and gently brushing my hair from my forehead. 'Remarkable adventures.'

He swallowed and leaned closer. 'So tell me,' he said, his lip slithering into a serpentine smile, 'you on the run, boy?'

I swallowed a whole mouthful of eggplant, and as it plunged down my gullet I tried to move away from him, but he reached out and closed his hand on my shoulder.

'I knew it,' he said, leering at me with his surviving eye. 'I know a brother when I see one.'

I tried to free myself, but his hand held me down beside him like a clamp.

'Relax, boy,' he said, reducing his whisper to the faintest breath. 'I'm not going to harm you. We're in the chase together.'

I grabbed his wrist and looked up into his face. It was a craggy wasteland: the nose broken and askew, the lip rimpled along the gapped teeth, the one eye lost in the quicksand beneath his brow. Maybe it was just the contrast between his gruesome features and his generous manner, but I saw something kindred there, and under his gaze again I let go of his wrist and ceased my struggling.

He smiled and, slowly releasing my shoulder with one hand, passed me the bowl of cauliflower with the other.

'You got a voice, boy?' the old man asked, dabbing at his mouth with the tail of his waistcloth.

I nodded back at him again and scooped up some cauliflower with my fingers.

'Then prove it. Tell me where you're headed.'

I popped the morsel into my mouth and tucked it into my cheek like a squirrel. 'Fatehgarh, sir,' I said aloud.

'*Quietly*,' the old man whispered, watching as the peddler snorted and rolled over onto his side. 'That crazy bastard's going to kill somebody with that stupid pistol. Useless, telltale contraption,' he grumbled to himself. 'Noisy, bloody, hit-or-miss piece of junk.'

The old man scowled around at me suddenly. 'You've been here before, haven't you, boy?' he snarled at me.

'Sir?'

'Here,' he said, putting a finger to his lips to quiet me. 'You've been to Bithur before, haven't you?'

I looked for a moment along the dismal bank and shook my head.

'You haven't?' he said with a dismayed look. 'But I just divined that you had. I must be losing my touch. Well,' he said, settling down again, 'never mind. It doesn't matter. Bithur's not exactly a garden spot, is it, boy? Not since the Devil's Wind. Used to be the Peshwa's capital, you know. Had a palace as grand as Jaipur's. Chandeliers as big as elephants. Gold plate. Had his own menagerie of wild cats, and enough whores to service the whole damn Indian Army. But,' he said with a shrug, 'it's all gone now. British must have burned it up three times over. Nobody'll live here but the domri. I like it, though. Come here to relax,' he said, looking around him and taking a deep breath of the heavy air. 'It's peaceful.'

The old man belched and dug a finger in among his teeth, and as I ate the remaining scraps he watched with a look of such proud satisfaction that it was positively motherly. And as I restacked the trays of his kit and snapped it closed he spat out a shred of food, stared at me for a moment, and set his pocked jaw as if he'd arrived at a momentous decision.

'Boy,' he said, clearing his throat, 'I'm going to tell you my name.'

I looked up at him with what I hoped was a receptive expression.

'My name – ' he said, and then took another deep breath, as if to brace himself. 'My name . . . is *Baroo*.'

Immediately he shrank back a little, as if he'd just lit a fuse, but when he saw how calmly I was taking this information he looked offended and said, '*Baroo. Baroo Singh*.'

I tried to look impressed, but I must have faked it badly, for as I nodded back at him he dropped his hands to the deck and gazed hopelessly up the budgerow's mast.

'Well, boy?' he asked after a moment, gritting his teeth to suppress his irritation.

'Sir?' I replied, watching as his oversized hands closed into fists.

'I told you *my* name,' he said, glaring back at me. 'What about yours?'

I almost told him my real name, but I reined myself in, for with such strange lurching from mood to mood I supposed there was a chance, unlikely as it seemed, that the old man was in Nanak Chand's employ. 'It's – uh – *Leela*,' I finally blurted. 'My name's Leela.'

'Leela, eh?' Baroo said without interest. 'Not much of a name, is it, boy?'

'No sir,' I said, looking away.

Baroo pouted and sighed as if giving up on a fond old dream. 'Go back to sleep, boy,' he said finally, staring out toward the water.

'Balbeer,' Moonshi suddenly whispered from across the deck. 'What are you doing – uh, son?'

I raised my hand to shut him up, but when I looked at Baroo he was already scowling at me in bewilderment.

'*Balbeer?*' he asked, tilting his head. 'Your name's *Balbeer?*'

'No sir,' I said as Moonshi scrambled toward us.

But Baroo was not to be fooled any longer. 'You *lied* to me, boy?' he snarled. 'I share my supper with you and you pay me back with a *lie?*'

'N-no sir. I was only – '

'He *lied* to me,' Baroo said, pounding one knee with his fist, but just when he seemed to be about to strike me he let out a loud guffaw and beamed down at me with the old light rising in his eye again. 'Beautiful!' he exclaimed, striking his knee again. 'Exquisite! *You* deceived *me*! Me, *Baroo Singh*! What a clever boy! And – and what a noble name!' he said earnestly, raising one twisted finger. 'Balbeer,' he said slowly, as if tasting a delicacy. '*Balbeer*. It suits you, boy. But Balbeer what? What's your last name?'

'Uh – Rao, sir,' I said.

'Rao,' the old man exclaimed aloud. 'Balbeer Rao! A Rajput! I knew it! And from where? Not from Jodhpur itself, am I right?'

'No, not from Jodhpur,' Moonshi replied with a mystified look, as if assisting in a magician's trick.

'No, not from Jodhpur,' Baroo muttered, shaking a fist and frowning slightly. 'And not from Bikaneer, either. No,' he said, staring up into the sky for a moment. 'I've got it!' he finally exclaimed, rising to his feet and clapping his hands together. 'Harigarh! You're from Harigarh!'

And as Moonshi and I gaped at each other the peddler started up out of his sleep in a tangle of chains and fired his pistol into the dark.

CHAPTER

23

Moonshi and I flung ourselves into a corner of the deck as the shot echoed off the bank. There were shouts of alarm from inside the cabin, and the peddler dropped his pistol with a cry, as if it had scorched his fingers. But through it all Baroo stood motionless above us, staring down at the peddler with an affronted look, and it wasn't until the echo had died away and he slowly picked up the pistol and flung it into the water that he seemed to realize that the bullet had passed through him.

He tore at his shirt and thrust his hand into his left armpit and with a sigh and a nod, as if this were just one more mishap in a long run of bad luck, he slumped down to the deck.

'Allah protect me!' the peddler cried, fumbling out of his chains. 'I've killed him!'

In his panic he tried to escape over the side, but he ran into the boatmen instead, who now emerged from their cabin with knives drawn.

'What's going on?' one of them demanded to know, holding a lantern up to the peddler's face.

'I didn't mean to do it!' the peddler cried as the boatmen trapped him in a corner. 'I swear on my son's head – I thought he was a thief!'

'Do I look like a thief?' Baroo called back, pulling his shirt down over his shoulder.

(Of course, he *did* look like a thief, and worse besides, but this was no time to quibble.)

'I was asleep!' the peddler whined. 'He woke me up! He – he *scared* me!'

'*I* scared *him*,' Baroo muttered as Moonshi and I crawled over to him. 'He goes to sleep with a gun in his hand and *I* scared *him*.' Bunching his waistcloth in his hand, he dabbed at the thin trickle of blood dripping from the loose flesh of his breast.

'I'll go get the police,' the younger boatman said as they pinned the peddler to the budgerow's mast.

'No!' the rest of us shouted back at once, the victim himself included.

'That is,' Baroo quickly added as we all looked around at each other, 'what's the use? It was just an accident.'

'Th-that's right,' the peddler piped, wriggling free and straightening his clothes. 'I didn't mean to do it. You're all right, aren't you, old man?'

'Oh, just splendid,' Baroo replied with a sour smile. 'Couldn't be better.'

In fact, Baroo didn't seem to be suffering much. Within an hour the bleeding stopped altogether, and he registered more anger than pain. Moonshi kept trying to quiet him down, convinced he was giddy from shock, but the old man remained mysteriously cheerful all through the night, chatting about this and that, even, at one point, bursting into song.

He told us he was a Bhatti Rajput from the desert kingdom of Jeysulmere. I now know that among the Rajput states Jeysulmere was one of the least, notable mainly for its isolation and famines, but as I said before, people can yearn for the most miserable places, and that night when Baroo spoke of Jeysulmere you would have thought that its phog bushes were shade trees and its shifting sands were fields of wheat.

But what Baroo told us was nothing compared to what we told him about ourselves, which was most of the truth, leaving out cholera and Bastard Bhavan and our multiplying foes. By morning he'd learned my mother's name, my father's mysterious absence, our intended destination, and many more specifics, while all we'd really learned about him was a few Jeysulmere legends and a general fact or two about his remotest ancestors.

How he accomplished this I don't exactly know. Everything we told him about ourselves seemed to endear us to him further, which of course encouraged us to tell him more. But his most inexplicable trick was to take whatever direct question about himself we might ask and turn it back on us, as with a mirror, so that no sooner had we asked him about his childhood than we'd be telling him all about ours. His guiding principle in conversation seemed to be that people's favorite subject was themselves. Whatever his secret was, by dawn we had so fallen under the old man's spell that Moonshi had fashioned an arm sling out of his own waistcloth and I found myself massaging his scrawny legs like a disciple.

As the sun glowed dimly in the congested eastern sky, the boatmen forced the peddler off onto the ghat and left him there with his trunk and chains. His threats and curses turned to pleas as the sail caught the damp wind, until he was a tiny, kneeling figure in the distance and his cries were lost to us in the gurgle along the budgerow's strake. Baroo made a great show of protesting the peddler's banishment, but he smiled to himself as he watched the little man recede, and, pulling a cloth over his head, he fell asleep with a satisfied chuckle.

So the truth about Moonshi and me – or most of it, anyway – was out, and since it seemed to make no difference to the boatmen, accustomed as they were to fugitive passengers where the Ganga passed beneath Avadh, we were relieved to be rid of our clumsy masquerade. I relaxed for the first time since I'd jumped over Bastard Bhavan's wall, and dreamlessly slept through the morning.

By the afternoon we were halfway between Cawnpore and Kanauj, and I awoke shivering in the light rain that soaked the sail and pocked the Ganga's sheen.

'I've decided,' Baroo said as I rose from sleep to find him staring at me as before from across the pattered deck.

'S-sir?' I said, wiping the rain from my face and shuddering with a chill.

'I say I've decided,' he called back.

Moonshi now began to stir beside me.

'Decided?' I asked as the chill seemed to sink into my belly.

'Yes, Balbeer,' Baroo said. 'I've made up my mind. I'm going with you.'

Moonshi's eyes popped open, and he raised his head. 'Going with us?'

'Going with you.'

'But,' Moonshi said, sitting up.

'I know, I know,' Baroo said, raising one hand. 'it's out of my way, I realize. But I tell you, I've *taken* to the two of you, so don't try to talk me out of it. I'm going to lead you to Harigarh.'

Moonshi and I looked at each other.

'Got our route all mapped out up here,' Baroo continued with sly pride, tapping a finger against his forehead. 'Get us there in no time. Haven't been back to Harigarh in – must be twenty years at least. High time I returned for a visit. Be sort of like a pilgrimage. Temple there I'd like to see again before I die. Might even help you find your uncle, Balbeer. Got some connections at court. At least I used to.'

'Oh, that's very nice of you sir,' Moonshi began, 'but you see – '

'Call me *Baroo*,' the old man said. 'No use being formal if we're going to be travelling together.'

'Baroo, then,' Moonshi said with difficulty. 'But what I was trying to – '

'Save your thanks,' said Baroo. 'It's my pleasure. Been travelling alone too long, anyway. It'll be good to finally have some company.'

Moonshi drooped a little and looked at me.

'You know what the trouble with people is?' Baroo said with a shake of his head. 'People just won't admit it when they're lonely. Spend all their time trying to look busy, preoccupied, burdened by human society, when company's what matters the most. Well, not to me. I won't lie to you, Moonshi. I'm all alone in this world,' he said cheerfully. 'Nothing waiting for me at home but the lizards on the wall. So when I come upon such worthy companions as yourselves I think to myself that I'd better make my feelings plain.

'Besides, it's fate that has joined us sons of kings together on the Ganga.' Baroo gave me another one of his burning looks. 'And who are we to question fate, eh, boy?'

There was something contradictory in his stare, but it was the contradiction that made him so hypnotic, and I blamed my uneasiness on the effects Baroo's supper seemed to be having on my tender stomach.

'Mind you,' Baroo said when we made no reply, 'I'm not one to join up with any little runaway who crosses my path. This is something new for me, too: something different. But I'm willing to take a chance on it if you are.'

Of course by then there wasn't much question but that Baroo was coming with us, for already we were considering the matter on his terms. But if only for our own pride's sake we had to make some show of independence, so we asked that we be allowed to discuss it between ourselves before deciding. Our asking his permission seemed to please him, and with a confident shrug Baroo turned around to give us a little privacy and gazed out at the river, upon whose surface the raindrops seemed to bounce like pearls on a marble floor.

'What do you think, Little Master?' Moonshi asked, ducking his head anxiously.

'I don't know, Moonshi,' I snapped back, surprising myself with a sudden anguished impatience that seemed to press down on my bowels like a fist. '*You* decide.'

'He seems to be a nice enough old fellow,' he said. 'And brave for a Bhatti. But he's going to slow us down with that shoulder of his.'

In answer to this, for Baroo could plainly hear us, he removed his arm from his sling and rotated it about, sniffing in the air with ostentatious vigor.

'On the other hand, he does know the route,' Moonshi continued. 'And there's safety in numbers, Little Master. What harm could it do? If it didn't work out we – '

'Just *decide*, Moonshi,' I snarled at him, closing my eyes now and gripping my stomach, as if to keep it from melting away.

'I just don't know,' Moonshi sighed, staring at the old man's bloodstained back.

I now began to rock on my heels, still bent double, and realized that something more was wrong with me than heartburn or a rainborne chill. I felt as though my belly were about to give way, and Baroo, hearing my groans, turned around to see what the matter was.

But Moonshi was still too caught up in the novelty of making a decision to notice my condition, and finally, in a loud but fragile voice, announced, 'We've decided, Baroo Singh. You are welcome to join us.'

But Baroo ignored him, and as I toppled over and my bowels leaked water on the slippery deck, he caught me in his arms.

'Balbeer?' he asked as my head fell back into his lap. 'Balbeer! What ails you, boy?'

His voice was so charged with alarm and affection that I think I may have smiled, even as I seemed to slip into the depths of a black and turbulent sea.

PART THREE

BHONDARIPUR

CHAPTER
24

It's plain enough that Dileep's corrupted breath had at last suffused my vitals. But I can't recall exactly what happened next. The boatmen must have thrown us off on the western bank somewhere south of Kanauj. I know Baroo stayed with us, but the rest of my memories are brief and fitful, like a drowning man's gasps.

I think that Baroo and Moonshi carried me between them for some distance in a sling, that at one point we were chased out of a field by a fat man with an ax, that it rained so hard one night we were nearly buried in a mud slide, that we rode for a time on the back of a cart loaded with sugar cane, that Baroo kept feeding me chunks of salt as a cure, that when we stopped to rest one afternoon Moonshi had to swing a stick over me to scare off the kites and vultures.

Everything else is tangled in my fevered dreams and delusions. I saw Dileep, his hands upraised and punctured, walking toward me on the Ganga's surface and then slowly sinking with a shrug. Then I seemed to be lying on the riverbank watching the budgerow, its sail ablaze, spinning and floundering in the current. A black goddess with breasts like eggplants bathed me in the shallows, embraced me in her many arms like a mother crab, and flew off on the back of a squawking crane. Genda set a golden tray before me and fed me living toads that bumped and jibbered against my cheeks as I chewed and swallowed them down.

And just before my fever broke I dreamed that Moonshi, Baroo, and I were sitting together around a campfire in the middle of a crimson lake, except that the bonfire was really the blazing budgerow and the lake's surface was firm where we sat, like earth. Baroo rose and began to pace about, telling a story, and at its conclusion he plucked a star out of the sky and handed it to Moonshi with the delicacy of a jeweller. At this Moonshi began to laugh, and we laughed with him, except that Baroo and I exchanged winks and seemed to laugh out of some unaccountable complicity, even as a serpent flew from Baroo's sleeve and coiled itself around Moonshi's neck. It choked off his laughter and pulled him down, and the red murk gave way beneath him, but as he began to sink he tossed his purse into the air and looked at me with such cross-eyed bewilderment that my laughter rose and would not stop and roared and echoed across the bubbling lake.

When I emerged from this delirium I was lying in a field of sesame blossoms, staring up into a clear blue sky dotted with little grey rags of cloud. A cool breeze skimmed over me, and the earth was dry between the rows of sesame stalks. The monsoon had passed; the world and I had broken our fevers together.

'Moonshi?' I tried to shout, but there was so little breath behind it that it came out like a hen's cluck and barely broke the stillness. I seemed to be alone, but over the crows' cries and wasps' whine among the crimson blooms, I heard a faint jingling, like temple bells. It seemed to flirt with rhythm for a moment: three evenly placed points in time marked by brief, muffled chiming, then a pause, two more beats, another pause, and then the rhythm took hold and gained in volume somewhere behind me.

I tried to raise my head, but it was like trying to heft a boulder with a twig. Looking down the length of my body, I saw ribs where the muscles of my breasts had been, a hollow where I should have seen my belly rise, and legs that looked like long brown bones stretched out beyond.

'Moonshi!' I called out again, louder this time, though the effort dizzied me and I sank back down with an exhausted sigh.

A head suddenly loomed over me, its face lost in the shade of a veil, and paused as if to gaze down at its own reflection.

'What's he saying?' it asked in an old woman's smoky voice.

A second head hovered over me, topped with a turban, its silhouette ornamented by sharp curlicues of moustache.

'He's calling his servant,' it said in a familiar voice.

'Moonshi?' I asked dimly. 'Is that you?'

'He looks terrible,' the old woman said, spitting off onto the ground behind me.

'He's all right,' the man said, and when I'd caught my breath and closed my eyes for a moment I realized he was Baroo.

'Please, sir,' I gasped, weakly raising one hand. 'Where's Moonshi?'

'Been like this for days,' Baroo said, rising to face the woman. 'But the fever passed last night, and this morning he took the broth you gave me.'

'Where *is* this Moonshi?' the old woman asked, straightening up with more jingling sounds as her silver ornaments shifted. I could see the undersides of her drooping breasts beneath her choli, the gaps in her teeth as she spoke.

Baroo didn't answer her, but instead knelt down and pried open my mouth as if inspecting a horse. 'It's passed,' he said, wiping his fingers on his shirt. 'Balbeer?' he asked, leaning close to my face. 'Can you hear me?'

I was so weary by then that I could only grip his sleeve in one hand to hold him still long enough to ask him again, 'Where's Moonshi?'

'Never mind Moonshi,' Baroo said gently. 'How are *you*, boy? That's what matters now.'

My fingers slipped from his sleeve. 'How long – how long have I – '

'Too long,' Baroo said, placing my hand upon the ground beside me. 'So long I've lost count. You've had quite a time of it, Balbeer. Thought you wouldn't pull through for a while there. But deep down I knew you would beat the fever. I could tell you had grit the first time I laid eyes on you.'

'He needs a bath,' the old woman said, looking me over appraisingly. 'And a meal or two to flesh him out.'

'Well, why do you suppose I brought him here, Amma?' Baroo snapped back, rising to his feet. 'Now grab hold of his arms and let's get him home.'

I felt them lift me up and carry me out of the crimson field, past a mound of earth studded with banners, a hardaur the old woman had erected to protect her village from my fever. The sounds on the breeze became distinct as they carried me through a stone gate and set me down on a charpoy under the dappled sprawl of a great tree. I was half faint but I could hear voices, the exhalation of a bullock, the chatter of birds in the treetop, a child's giggle as someone gently unwrapped my dhoti, the old woman's rebuke, quick footsteps padding away, and then nothing but the minute music of the old woman's ornaments as she passed a warm, wet cloth over my exhausted limbs: soothing, cleansing, healing.

In the evening the old woman covered me with a blanket and gave me dahl to eat, which Baroo fed me from his own fingers. My swollen tongue could barely convey the food and as the lentils seeped down my throat, my stomach twitched and trembled like the withers of an exhausted horse. But the food stayed down, like the warm sugared milk that followed, and the old woman gravely thanked Hulka Devi, the goddess of vomit, for letting me be.

Baroo winked at me, as if he and I were above such nonsense, and with a damp cloth cleaned off the food that I had dribbled on my chin.

'What is this miserable boy to you?' the old woman grumbled from where she squatted, waiting to carry away my bowl.

'This miserable boy,' Baroo said softly, with a fond smile in my direction, 'is everything.'

The next morning I managed to keep down a strip of chapatti smeared with ghee, and Baroo decided I was well enough to be told about Moonshi.

'Servants, Balbeer,' Baroo began, sitting by my bed in the clear morning light as men in carts and women carrying scythes passed on their way to the fields. 'They'll break your heart if you let them. And you're in no condition to let them, Balbeer, so try to control yourself, and listen to me.

'I tell you, after those swine threw us off, your Moonshi tended to you bravely. It was a privilege just to be around a servant so devoted to his master. Like something out of the old days. Nursed you, cleaned you, and when my back gave out he carried you around on his shoulders, even when all he got in return was crap down his back and your yellow drool in his hair. He must have carried you for twenty miles like that.

'But as the days went by you just kept getting worse and worse. We'd get some water into you at one end and it would just seep out the other. Pretty soon you were so far gone we hardly dared to move you. Couldn't hear your heartbeat, your lungs were rattling so. And your skin! It felt like a lizard's jowl. You smelled so bad we had to keep you downwind. I hate to say it, boy, but you were disgusting – something even your own mother would've been hard put to love.

'So when it seemed to Moonshi that you were done for, can you blame him for starting to wonder about his prospects? I mean, if you look at it from his point of view, what choice did he have? He got sentimental, which is always a bad sign. Began to tell me about this sahib of his he said he had back in Cawnpore, some Feringhee judge who'd done him a good turn. All very confusing stuff for me, boy. You'll have to fill me in on the details when you're up to it.

'Anyway, I tried to cheer him up, Balbeer. Tried to set his mind on Harigarh. Fed him some stories. Sang him a song or two. Didn't seem to matter, though. He just kept mooning around about that Feringhee. Was always checking to see if you'd died yet, fretting, cursing himself for coming with you.

' "Come on, Moonshi," I told him. "It's not as bad as all that. You did the right thing. Just doing your duty, after all. Can't blame yourself. It's all fated anyway. And besides, your Little Master might pull through yet."

'But it was no use, Balbeer. He didn't listen. He went to sleep one night with this faraway look, and in the morning he was gone.

'Look, Balbeer,' Baroo said as I turned my face away and began to weep, 'this whole trip of yours has been a shaky proposition from the start. You can't expect a poor, hapless soul like Moonshi to have stuck with it when a rich sahib awaited him in Cawnpore.'

But that was exactly what I'd expected of Moonshi, and soon my grief had given way to rage, and I imagined every kind of calamity befalling Moonshi on his craven retreat to Cawnpore. Let a tiger tear him to pieces, I told Baroo. Let vultures dine on his cocked eyes, if they'll have them. And I know I imagined much worse things, too, that I'm too ashamed to recollect.

Baroo heard me out, but when my voice was gone and I lay panting on the charpoy he slowly shook his head. 'I know it's hard, Balbeer, especially in your condition, but you've got to rise above these petty emotions. They're beneath you and a waste of strength.'

I weakly wiped my eyes and tried to calm myself, or at least tried to *look* calmer for Baroo's sake.

'That's my boy,' Baroo said. 'That's more like the Balbeer I know. Now then,' he said, packing his hookah for a smoke, 'let us consider your position. I think if we look at it carefully we'll see that it isn't all that bad.'

A small boy approached us with a smoking stick and lit the dung and tobacco in the hookah's bowl.

'Your servant has abandoned you,' Baroo said before drawing for a moment on his pipe. 'Let's face that one right away. And of course your mother's dead, too. And your father's – well, who knows about him. In any case, he's not in the picture. And for some reason you haven't told me you can't go back to Cawnpore, which it seems to me is just as well. And without Moonshi to vouch for you you can't necessarily go to Harigarh, either. At least, not yet. Now stop me if I've got any of this wrong.'

Baroo was going a little fast for me, but I shook my head as he drew again from his bubbling pipe.

'But on the other hand,' he said, so quietly that the smoke seemed to leak from his lips like milk, 'you've just eluded your enemies, you've beaten a terrible fever, and you are not entirely without friends.'

He paused as if to let me acknowledge this last point. But I suppose I believed I *was* entirely without friends, and I could only manage a groan.

'I mean *me*, Balbeer,' he said almost in a whisper. '*I'm* your friend, aren't I? Haven't I proved that?'

'Yes sir,' I said vaguely, for though he had borne with me where Moonshi had failed, Baroo's devotion seemed then, as it would seem for years to come, entirely unaccountable. I was in no position to reject it, but I seemed to be the object of unrequitable love.

'My protection is no small blessing, Balbeer,' Baroo snorted, spitting back over his shoulder. 'You ask anyone here and he'll tell you. But there's more to the positive side of things than that.

'We've been travelling together now for days and days, and do you know that in all that time I never divined a single ominous augury? Not *one*! It didn't seem possible. I kept trying to see if I was hearing right, if my eye wasn't failing me, if my nostrils could still pick up a scent. But nowhere on the whole journey did a dog shake his head at us or a cripple cross our path or a crow call from the back of a cow. As a matter of fact, the omens are positively jubilant. I saw kite dung falling to our right one day, and a bare-breasted woman walked by us with pitchers full of milk, and we passed like ghosts through a herd of buck. And do you remember how the crane sang to us on the riverbank? I tell you, I never experienced anything like it. Kept trying to tell Moonshi about it. Just seemed to make him more skittish. But I knew you were going to be all right. The whole world was telling me so.'

In his excitement Baroo had let his hookah die out, and he waved the boy over again to relight it. The boy looked to me like all the other village children I had glimpsed peeking at us from the doorways to their courtyards. He had a broad nose and high cheekbones and slightly sunken eyes, which he averted from us as he prodded with his stick at the embers in the hookah's bowl.

'So I said to myself I'd been right about you all along. There *was* something writ on your forehead. No piddling fever was going to rob you of your destiny. No sir. And when you'd put the fever behind you I wanted to be there to help you.

'So here I am,' said Baroo, swinging the pipe away for a moment, 'and here you are, with your whole life ahead of you.'

'But where *are* we?' I asked, rising up for a moment, for it had begun to occur to me that we hadn't come to rest in this village by chance. The scowling peasants who silently passed by us weren't trusting folk who welcomed strangers, so why did they care for us? What was Baroo's hold over them?

'I was getting to that,' Baroo said, laying me back down again. 'Let's not get ahead of ourselves. Seems to me you're going to need a few months to recuperate, and what with Moonshi gone you're not going to have much luck convincing your kin back in Harigarh that you're who you say you are.'

'But I am,' I said, rising up again. 'They've got to believe me.'

'Balbeer, Balbeer,' Baroo said, shaking his head. 'You have

many fine qualities, but you've got to learn to see things from other people's points of view. I know you're who you are, and you know you're who you are, but how are you going to convince anyone else? The journey to Harigarh's a hard one – we'll be at least five days on the sands of the Thar before we get there. So imagine how you're going to look to the dolts who guard the palace gates. You'll be even dirtier and scrawnier than you are now. You think they're going to read your forehead as I have? And when you puff out your chest and tell them you're the Diwan's nephew, what do you think they'll do? Fall to the ground and touch your feet? Open the gates and carry you to your uncle on their shoulders? Why, they'll laugh in your face, and why not? They'd be fools to believe you.'

I suppose I had assumed that though Moonshi had abandoned me, Baroo, out of his mysterious devotion to me, would lead me the rest of the way home to Harigarh. It hadn't occurred to me that all that awaited me now in my family's court was mockery and rejection, that now I not only didn't know who my father was but had no way of proving who my mother was, either. I felt as though someone had laid a great stone on my breast, and I sank back down against the charpoy's weave.

'But,' Baroo said, raising his finger, 'there's more to it than that, of course, for when Kali gives a boy a forehead like yours she's not going to let a few formalities stand in the way. She doesn't work that way. So we're not going to despair, Balbeer. We're going to find a way around these difficulties.'

But of course I was despairing already, and even wondering for a hopeless moment if the Reverend would take me back.

'Now,' Baroo said, standing and stretching, the bones in his back grinding together like stones. 'I know this place must not seem like much to a city boy like yourself, and I confess when I first laid eyes on it I was blind to its charms. But I think you'll find it has its own little virtues if you give it a chance. As a matter of fact, after a few weeks here it starts to feel like home.'

'But I'm not going to stay here,' I said as a tethered bullock urinated nearby. 'I don't even know these people.'

'Yes,' Baroo said, signalling again to the boy, who now darted out again from among the high walls, 'but I do. Don't I, Santosh?' he asked the boy, who stooped now at Baroo's feet and began to clean out the bowl of his hookah.

'Yes sahib,' the boy muttered in a voice as smoky as the old lady's.

'Yes sahib,' said Baroo with a satisfied grin. 'These people know Baroo Singh.'

'They do?'

'Of course,' Baroo said. He pointed now toward the cane that stood in a field just beyond the well, rising up from behind a tangle of thorn bushes. 'You can't see it all from here, but it amuses me to be the proud owner of forty acres of Bhondaripur's land, yielding a fair little profit for an old widower like myself, and some of the finest hemp in the world. In fact,' he said, leaning toward me and lowering his voice, 'that's what lured me here in the first place. In my younger days I happened to save a man from a gang of poisoners on the Etawah Road, and out of gratitude he gave me the deed to this land. Seemed like a headache to me at the time, what with keeping the tenants in line and keeping an eye on the patwari's books and all the other nuisances of the landlord's life. But it has turned out pretty well in the long run. Gives me a little income to put away for the future, and by now these people are practically like kin to me – like children. And like grandchildren, eh, Santosh?' Baroo said as the boy picked up his hookah.

'Yes sahib,' Santosh replied, backing away, his eyes never rising from the ground.

'Good boy, Santosh,' Baroo said, turning toward me and rubbing his eye. 'His father owes me so much grain by now he would have to live ten lifetimes to repay me, but Santosh and his heirs'll be good for it. Hardworking lad. Never let anyone tell me about lazy peasants. They work like bullocks, these people – and for the profit of men like me! I tell you, Balbeer, it's a mystery.'

Baroo pondered this for a moment, and shrugged. 'But some things aren't supposed to be questioned. I'm just glad that I'm on the right end of the arrangement. And you should be too, Balbeer, because it means I can do you some good.

'Now then,' Baroo said, sharply patting his knees, 'here's what I propose. You've got some recuperating to do, and it's going to take you a good long time to restore yourself to your original condition. Now, I would love to stay here with you and watch over you all that time, but I'm afraid I've got business elsewhere. So it's my intention to leave you here for a few months in my tenants' keeping while I proceed to Harigarh – after a few intermediate destinations – and prepare your way into your uncle's good graces. So, Balbeer,' Baroo said, gripping his knees and bending toward me, 'what do you say to that?'

What could I say? I was so mightily tired of being abandoned by my would-be protectors that I could barely rely on the sun to rise in the morning, but Baroo's plan made a kind of sense, and if he'd wanted to abandon me he would have done so back on the budgerow's deck. Baroo might well be out of his mind, but at least he was on my side. So, expending my last scrap of trust, I believed Baroo Singh and agreed to wait for him in Bhondaripur.

CHAPTER
25

That evening I met the farmers who tilled Baroo's land, receiving them from my bed like a frail potentate as they trudged home from the fields. These were the sons and grandsons of the old woman Baroo called Amma, and though they were polite enough they greeted me without enthusiasm.

It's not easy for me to recollect that first meeting for you, because these people were soon to compose, for better or for worse, the only real family I ever had. I wonder how we could ever have been so shy with one another: so clumsy, so fearful and mistaken. Only Baroo understood what we were to mean to each other, but he only made things worse with his hearty insistence that before we knew it we would all be the best of friends.

As Amma's oldest son passed by he must have seemed brutish to me with his broad shoulders, bowed legs, and crooked, broken nose. But that's just a guess, because I find I can't look back on Pyari Lal now without remembering his equanimity, his crotchety wit, and his grave, abiding poise. Nor can I envision Ramesh, his youngest brother, without looking past his sweet smile and his untroubled brow and remembering his gullible and envious nature and the demons and ghosts that plagued his nights. And the frowning middle son, Channa, who bowed his head and averted his eyes and worked his lips like a mad mute when Baroo spoke to him, must have seemed to me a dark and menacing imbecile as he limped by on his twisted foot, because no one – not even Baroo, for all his mysterious divinations – could have guessed at first glance that Channa was the wisest and the kindest of the three.

As the brothers stood by, Baroo shepherded the children past me, commanding them to shout out their names as they greeted me, but it was a useless exercise. Did Baroo really expect me to keep track of them all as they filed by? And what were they supposed to make of me, this living skeleton wrapped in blankets? They'd been looking me over from a distance ever since I got there and had tired of me already. In my daze they all looked as alike as stalks of wheat, and I doubt if I even saw Rambir among them, though he would become my brother; nor heard Ahalya speak her name, though she would become my wife.

Amma said some prayers over me, not to Hulka Devi this time, but to Agni, the god of fire, imploring him to protect her home from whatever demon it was that held me in its grip. Loudly coughing and clearing their throats to warn the women of our approach, the three brothers lifted my bed and carried me to their compound.

We walked through a maze of lanes banked by the walls of a score of courtyards, dodging the charge of a bullock calf panicked by the crowd, and before we reached the entrance to Amma's compound I wondered if I would ever be able to find my way out when the time came. The compound walls stood taller than Pyari Lal and blocked the soft orange light from the descending sun. The courtyard thus lay in a drab shadow, in an atmosphere of cooking smoke and dust. We passed the men's yard, a low terrace of clay where Pyari Lal's bathing stool, bucket, and hookah awaited his evening ablutions. Its backdrop was the men's sleeping hut, against whose doorway a newly carved and half-woven charpoy leaned, the replacement for the bed I was defiling. Beside this was a small storehouse with a bolted door and high, mean windows against whose bars newly harvested gourds pressed like the pale, bald heads of prisoners.

A dog barked at us as we crossed the courtyard, and Ramesh kicked it in the ribs, sending it rolling and yelping into an oblivious, hooded figure who sat like an idol by the storehouse, working a string of beads with his fingers. Baroo clapped his hands to announce our approach and led us through a doorway so narrow that the brothers had to tilt my bed a little and hook its legs around to get me through. We thus passed through a second sleeping hut littered with blankets and a few toddling children, and entered the women's yard.

In the center of the court a cooking stove raised a ribbon of pale smoke that stretched straight up to the tops of the surrounding walls. Above the walls the smoke was stirred by a faint breeze which permeated the yard with a haze smelling of dung, scorched wheat, and spiced onions simmering in ghee. As we entered, four women rose to their feet and stood back, covering their faces with their veils, and Baroo, without looking at them, exclaimed, 'Here he is, ladies. Where shall we set him down?'

Amma stepped from behind us and joined the four women as they turned their heads away in a show of modesty.

'What do we care?' Amma answered for them in an impatient squawk. 'Just put him down and get out of here.'

'That's right,' another piped in. 'How do you expect us to get supper ready with all this fuss?'

The three brothers bowed their heads and sighed, but Baroo, courteously averting his gaze, smiled philosophically. 'Sorry, ladies,' he said. 'We'll try to be out of your way in a twinkling.'

He quickly pointed to a spot near the doorway to the second sleeping hut, and there I was set down, under the fresh thatch of a lean-to roof and amid a jumble of jugs and bowls.

'There you are,' Baroo said, straightening my blanket as the three brothers waited for him in the doorway. 'How are you feeling?'

I looked up at Channa, who seemed to scowl at me as he worked his shoulders and stretched his back. 'I'm all right,' I said.

'Good boy,' Baroo said, straightening up. 'Now you do what these ladies tell you. I don't want to hear about you giving them any trouble.'

'Hurry up,' Amma snapped behind him. 'The chapatti's burning.'

Baroo looked heavenward for a moment, as if searching for the strength to hold his anger in, but failing to find it in the gloaming, he looked straight at all five women with his burning eye and said, 'Then sit on it.'

There was a gasp from the women, but their menfolk only shifted on their feet a little and stared at the ground, pretending not to have heard a thing.

'I'm leaving this boy with you, Amma,' Baroo declared, pushing out his chest. 'With you and your sons. I want you to treat him like one of your own. I want him on his feet when I get back, and if I hear you've abused him or neglected him I'm going to come down on this house like a thunderbolt! Do you hear me, Amma?'

The old woman squatted down at her stove, whose coals were glowing now in the faint light, and nodded her head.

'Amma!' Baroo called out. 'Do you hear me?'

The old woman paused and rubbed her veil across her nose. 'Yes, yes,' she muttered. 'I hear you.'

Satisfied, Baroo turned back toward me. 'That's telling her, eh, Balbeer?' he said, straightening his turban. 'She's a wonderful woman, you understand, but she'll caw at you like an old crow if you let her.

'Now then,' he said, putting his hand on my forehead and brushing back my hair. 'It's time to say goodbye, boy. I won't be seeing you for a while. You behave yourself and eat what you're given and by the time I get back you'll be a foot taller and fit for the trek to Harigarh.'

'But aren't you going to say goodbye to me in the morning?' I asked, beginning to sense, from the beat of my pulse at the base of my throat, how much I'd come to depend on this old man, how lost I was going to be without him.

'In the morning?' Baroo said. 'I'll be long gone by then, Balbeer. I travel by night. You know that.'

I looked away from him then and peered for a moment at the veiled women by their stove, huddled like the mourners who'd prepared my mother's corpse. A chill panic began to come over me, but I was not going to beg Baroo to stay, not because it was beneath my dignity but because it hadn't worked with Moonshi all those years before. All I could hope to do to ensure Baroo's return was to put up a brave front.

'So, goodbye, boy,' Baroo said, straightening my blanket, 'and take care of yourself. And when you begin to feel afraid, just remember your debt to destiny.'

'Yes sir,' I said with what little conviction I could muster. 'I'll be well enough to travel in no time.'

'Then that's when I'll be back,' Baroo said with a little wave of his hand, and he abruptly followed the brothers out of the courtyard.

I lay back trying to figure out what to do next. It seemed fitting to me that the night was falling then. The deepening gloom made me feel a little less ashamed of my self-pity, as though I could blame it on the atmosphere. I stared up for a time at the swallow's nests that hung from the thatch overhead, afraid to look over at the women again lest I catch them glaring at me and plotting my downfall in whispers.

But the only voices I could hear over the slap of chapatti patties and the dull rustle of the coals was the men's rumble beyond the doorway. Hoping to catch one last glimpse of my protector, I painfully leaned over the edge of the bed and craned my head around the doorframe. And there in the twilight hush of the men's courtyard sat Baroo Singh among the brothers, handing out coins from a purple purse.

CHAPTER
26

And so my fitful flight from Cawnpore had brought me to Bhondari-pur, east of Gwalior and a few miles north of the River Sindh. Moonshi must have carried me past scores of villages just like it: low mud fortresses against the tax collector's quota, the raja's fancy, the brigand's whim: each on its drab carpet of parched crops; each with its low shrine and crumbling mosque, its caste wells, its dung heaps, its diadems of thorns.

I ate the chapatti Amma served me and wrapped myself in my blanket for the night. I slept badly, and every time I popped open my eyes the surrounding walls seemed to have moved a little closer. Before the morning light reached the tops of the sisal trees I woke up to a fluttering overhead as the swallows rushed out of their mud nests and up into the sky to hunt the stray night midges straggling home. The swallows slipped out of their nests so fast and raced so high into the air that if I hadn't peered out from under the thatch to follow their flight I might have mistaken them later for flecks of windblown ash.

I lay back, wondering how far Baroo had travelled while I slept. Was he still close enough to see these same swallows peppering the dim sky? Was he already out of reach? Could I still catch up with him if I tried?

Pretty soon I was racing along that line of thinking like a fugitive, and every question I asked myself disguised a challenge. Wouldn't Baroo admire my pluck if I caught up with him? What if he never came back? What if he died on the road somewhere? What would become of me then?

My aching body tried to ignore these dares, but they finally engaged my will. So, with a groan, I flung off my blanket, swung my feet over the edge of the bed, and sat up, already short of breath. My dangling legs looked as fragile as chimes, and the veins on my hands were as plain as rivers on a map, but I gritted my teeth in the morning chill and began to push myself forward.

My feet found the ground all right, and my knees locked straight when I reached my full height, and for a moment I stood as if on stilts and took in a breath of air. But the momentum kept carrying me forward, leaving my feet behind, and I fell to the ground like a pole. I didn't really hurt myself, and I landed with a grunt that was as soft as a rabbit's fart, but I was so weak that it terrified me, and it was only out of bald panic that I found the strength to heave myself back onto my bed, like a drowning man clambering aboard a raft.

Wrapping myself in my blanket again and nearly choking on the crisp, cold air, I closed my eyes and saw Baroo disappear at last over the curve of the earth.

◆———◆

When the sun's rays had reached down to the peaks of the roofs the swallows began to return, stopping here and there to bob and preen on the straws bristling up from the fresh thatch. And as their twittering grew louder and sparrows began to fly down out of the sisal tree and hunt for scraps on the courtyard floor, the women began to stir.

First there came the youngest of Amma's daughters-in-law, Ramesh's wife, emerging bare-headed from the curtained doorway to the women's sleeping hut. Standing on rough, spread feet set apart as if against a strong wind, with her braided hair clinging too tightly to her skull, in beauty and bearing she was no match for my mother. But I'd seen so few women during my years at Bastard Bhavan that for all my fears that first morning alone in Bhondaripur, I drank her in like water.

She looked around her with her great dark eyes, as if reminding herself where she was, and then she stretched up on her toes and yawned, reaching out with her slender arms and pivoting her wrists around, her choli rising to reveal the dark nipples of her breasts.

I mistook the rush of feeling she raised in me for fear, and shrank back into my blanket. She seemed to gaze for a moment in my direction as she finally lowered her arms again, and I could feel the flesh prickle along the back of my neck, but her eyes passed over me casually, as if I were no more than another heap of rags on the courtyard floor.

Channa's wife joined her then, rubbing her eyes and muttering, and then Amma's maiden daughter appeared, shaking her hands to dry them, followed by Pyari Lal's wife with an infant on her hip, and at last Amma herself emerged, blowing her nose into a basket of ashes and squinting up into the morning light.

She walked with a stoop to the cooking stove, commanding the others to fetch their water pots and proceed to the well. I shut my eyes as they passed by, but I doubt if they even noticed me. They entered the children's hut, rousing their sons and daughters, and when I dared to open my eyes again only Amma remained, breaking up dung cakes for the breakfast fire.

Children began to emerge with blankets wrapped around their heads and shoulders, stumbling out on their little black legs like ungainly birds, to warm themselves by their grandmother's stove.

They took no notice of me, not even the littlest ones, though I don't think anyone had ordered them to leave me alone. They were like the demon who couldn't see what he couldn't eat. I was so strange and useless that it made me invisible.

At the time, however, I took it personally, and feared that now that Baroo was gone they would all ignore me to death. It worried me especially when Pyari Lal's wife dropped a scrap of chapatti on my blanket, for it was less than I'd been getting when Baroo had been around, and she never spoke to me or so much as looked my way.

And that's the way it went for the rest of the day. A dog sniffed up to me, looked at me with clouded eyes, belched a little, and proceeded past. A swallow fetched a straw from the foot of my bed, and a sweeper woman paused to clean out my chamber pot in a fog of dust. But that was all the attention I got.

Over the days that followed I developed a contemplative nature. Under the circumstances I didn't have much choice, lying around while everyone worked in the fields, but the place itself had something to do with it, too. Bhondaripur's backdrop – walls, floors, lanes, and fields – was dirt, and objects seemed as isolated and abstract against it as diagrams in a book. Maybe it was the objects themselves – the few crude possessions the family felt safe in leaving around – but it gradually seemed to me as though I were surrounded by animate beings with their own histories and personalities.

The seams in a shirt hung up to dry, the potter's marks on a water jar, the swirls of abrasion on one of Amma's polished pots seemed to give each object a physiognomy, somehow. I suppose many of the implements lying around seemed to me all that much more individual because I didn't have any idea what they were for. The sowing pipe baffled me especially, with its woven funnel and hollow bamboo trunk. It took me hours of holding it this way and that to figure out that seeds were dropped down it into the furrows of the fields, but by then I had come to think of it as something imbued with mysterious powers, which, as you will see, I eventually tried to put to use.

All this seems strange and worrisome to me now when I think about it, but these objects were my only companions, so I suppose it's no wonder that they took on a life of their own in my imagination.

Some people – healthy ones, mostly – like to think that sickness is good for the character, but it never brought out the best in me. A contemplative nature wasn't all I developed while the family was out harvesting Baroo's cane, for if you leave a boy alone in bed long enough with nothing to do he will begin to fidget with whatever's handy. When I wasn't conversing with scythes and walking sticks and other pieces of junk, I was thinking about Ramesh's wife and watching her every move with an unwholesome thrill.

She was a married woman of sixteen or seventeen years and I was only nine, but boys are idealists, and the distance only made her more exalted. When she was around, working the noodle press or outlining her eyes with charcoal, I ached for her purely, like an imprisoned, lovesick suitor. This was a little peculiar, certainly, but there was no harm in it. It was only when she was away that my thinking turned nasty. At those times she became no more than a collection of delectable parts among which I would root in my imagination like a swine, fiddling with myself beneath my blanket all the while.

During my first week in Bhondaripur, Bastard Bhavan began to seem warm and welcoming in retrospect. At least Weems had spoken to me that first day, and Mr Peter had called me by name. I was never so far gone as actually to miss Bastard Bhavan, but I did begin to entertain outlandish notions that I was better off dead, or that I was already dead, or that everyone else in the world was dead but me. I could snap myself out of these delusions only by reminding myself that I was a Rajput and shoring myself up with my city boy's pride. These villagers are brutes, I told myself over and over, and I am Balbeer Rao, nephew of the Diwan of Harigarh, with greatness writ across my forehead. If these peasants won't be my friends then they can be my servants; it's all the same to me.

I wish I could say that I did everything in my power to get back on my feet, but the truth is that lying around all day began to grow on me. The accommodations may have been crude, the service grudging, the food revolting, but still it all added up to special treatment, and I regarded it as my due.

So I began to apply myself not to getting better so much as to getting more comfortable. For a long while I was afraid to complain about anything, but as I got used to the place and as the scraps they threw me every morning and night grew smaller, I figured I didn't have much to lose. So at last, in a small, hoarse voice, I spoke up for myself one morning when Pyari Lal's wife passed with her tray.

'That,' I said as she dropped a measly shred of chapatti on my lap, 'isn't enough.'

Well, it was as if a tree had spoken. Pyari Lal's wife jumped like a rabbit, and all the others dropped what they were doing to turn and gape in astonishment.

'What did he say?' Pyari Lal's wife called out when she'd found her voice.

I looked around me, wondering if I had the courage to repeat it. 'I said, that isn't enough.'

Pyari Lal's wife looked at Amma and Amma looked at her, and finally, with a twisted grin, she gave a great bow, touched the ground before her, and said, '*Forgive* us, my lord. How may we serve you better? Have we displeased Baroo Singh's little prince?'

Everyone laughed, and Amma herself couldn't keep from cackling, but having even less to lose – now that I'd made my move – I sat up and glared back at all of them. No flock of ignorant hens was going to make fun of Balbeer Rao.

'You promised Baroo Singh,' I said coldly as Amma returned to her stove. 'I can't live on scraps. I'm sick. I need food.' And for good measure I called her 'old woman' with a regal sneer.

The children stopped laughing and looked over at Amma, for obviously no child had ever spoken to her so sharply.

I could see a dozen calculations fly across her eyes like digits, and the line of her mouth grew straight and thin. The children moved out of her line of fire and waited for the explosion, but after a long pause Amma merely pouted at the coals with a pained sigh and signalled to Pyari Lal's wife to give me more chapatti.

'And some ghee,' I demanded, for I was never above pressing an advantage, and again Amma nodded, and Pyari Lal's wife handed me a whole chapatti smeared with ghee.

No doubt Amma was merely protecting her family from Baroo's displeasure, but that's not the way I looked at it. I figured that she had gone along with me out of some dim recognition of my nobility. One command led to another over the days that followed, and pretty soon I'd turned into a proper little tyrant, ordering women and children around as if they were my slaves, and though they bitched and bristled under my capricious rule, they obeyed me.

I don't enjoy recollecting what a spoiled brat I fast became, but I have to remind myself, and you, that life had been especially unkind to me until then and so maybe it was natural for me to have believed that it owed me some special consideration. Bad as it was for my character, it worked wonders on my spirits, and before I knew it I was putting on weight.

CHAPTER
27

A month passed since Baroo left Bhondaripur: not exactly the 'no time' in which I'd promised I would recover and he'd promised he would return, but as I grew wider around my middle I got more and more narrow in my thinking and his absence didn't torment me so much. I'd been alone before, and though I wasn't immune to loneliness, I believed I could live with it. I made a great show of enjoying my own company, muttering and chuckling to demonstrate what a high old time I could have all by myself. And if my hosts took any notice I glared back at them as if they were crazy.

I took to pretending that my bed was a kind of magical throne: a perfectly ordinary fancy for an invalid boy to entertain, except that somewhere along the line the fancy became a conviction. I came to believe that my bed protected me from my foes, that it made me invisible, and transported me when I closed my eyes. Lying back in the afternoon with my eyes shut I could feel the bed tremble and strain beneath me, and then a rush of wind as I was lifted off the courtyard floor and carried up to fly among the swallows. That I always found myself back on the ground whenever I so much as blinked my eyes open never shook my conviction, for my delusions had their own logic, and I guessed that my spells worked only on the sly.

I got most of my sleeping done during the afternoon and had a hard time falling off at night. The dark made me giddy instead of sleepy and I felt more and more at home in it as time went on, but my daytime delusions were nothing compared to the ones I cultivated at night. I began to think of the whole village as my kingdom and all its sleeping occupants as my subjects. I figured my throne's powers were amplified in the darkness and its protection extended everywhere, like an aura.

I didn't want anyone to see me up and around during the day, lest it signal the end of my rule, but after a while I itched to try my legs out somehow, and decided to do it at night. I waited until everyone seemed to be fast asleep, and then, with my blanket still wrapped around me in the night chill, I set my feet on the courtyard floor.

I was as wobbly as a newborn calf, and almost fell forward as before when I took a step, but it felt good to operate at my full height again, and little by little as the nights went by I ventured further from my bedside and skulked around in the shadows like a thief.

These excursions were good exercise, of course, but they didn't exactly clear my mind of its delusions. Creeping past the family's sleeping forms only made me feel that much more separate and powerful. I began to poke around all over the place, even among the children sleeping in a tangle in their hut. I walked within a finger's length of the hooded old fellow who slept seated on a mat by the doorway that led through the children's hut and into the women's courtyard, and I even dared to peek into the women's hut in the vain, imbecile hope that Ramesh's wife slept in the nude. I always made a point of looking in on the brothers, too, for I never saw them during the day. They made an enormous racket in their hut, buzzing and snoring through their dreams, and I never visited them for long, because always one or another of them would cough or grumble so loudly that I would race back to my bed and lie as still as a stone until morning.

I usually didn't get to sleep until midnight, and for a long time I would wake up even before the swallows did, with the distinct sensation that someone had been standing over me and watching me sleep. I never saw who it was — couldn't even be sure if I hadn't imagined him, like the faceless riverbank figure who brought my nightly dream to a close. One night when I thought I'd felt a hand pass across my forehead, I rushed up out of sleep to see the curtain to the children's hut swaying in the still air. I lay awake for the rest of the night, afraid to move, wondering if Baroo had returned or if he'd been with me all along, permeating the atmosphere like smoke.

You may think these were ordinary notions for a lad to entertain. In a way, I had earned them. But they kept multiplying. I believed, for instance, that I could destroy things by staring at them, that the motes that swam across my eyeballs were spirits only I could see, that I could converse with dogs and swallows, that I could change the weather with a wink. These notions were all of a piece with my lonely fancies back on my mother's roof, but this time I couldn't shake them loose. They seemed to set like plaster, and like setting plaster gave off a mysterious heat.

Children kept away from me as much as possible for fear I might enlist them in my phantom campaigns, but when two or three boys would chance by on an errand I made them carry my bed around the courtyard like a palanquin while I waved my sowing pipe – which had become, in my mind, a kind of sceptre – and shouted my battle cries.

'Charge, my monkeys!' I shouted, pointing up at Maharaja Scindhia's distant fortress. 'Beware the Prince of Bhondaripur!'

And sometimes I would make the children shout these things too, which they would, but in abashed and hesitant little voices.

It's amazing how long Amma's family put up with its repulsive guest. I suppose they tried to think of me as an unhappy act of God, like a crop blight – only one of a whole series of jokes the divinities were always playing on them. But as you will see, even a peasant's patience has its limits.

By the beginning of my third month in Bhondaripur I had picked up a lot of local lore listening to the women gossip at their cooking stove. This was easy to do, because village women were so used to making themselves heard over great distances that they tended to talk at the top of their voices.

Amma and her womenfolk never had any use for a story that wasn't at least thirdhand. It was as if they believed that each mouth that passed a story along gave it additional validation. This is what is known as the folk tradition, which is fine if you've got a taste for the quaint, but hard on the truth. By the time a story had made its way around the village it would get so stretched and twisted and chewed up that it would be unrecognizable even to its originator. This eventually gave events in Bhondaripur mythological proportions, and now that I think about it I would suppose that you could trace all the world's legends to this process.

The barber's wife was the source of most of the stories that reached the women's courtyard. A lean woman with a fixed grin and a harsh philosophy, she carried gossip like the pox. Her supposed job was to wash, oil and comb the women's hair, but her stock in trade was rumor-mongering.

One afternoon she came to minister to old Amma, and as she slipped her cake of soap through Amma's grey scrags she passed the word along that Chawla, the Brahmin landlord of the fields north of the village, had arisen from sleep the night before and seen a ghost on Pyari Lal's rooftop.

Amma took the news calmly, for ghosts were believed to be as thick as flies in Bhondaripur. In fact, you were almost certain to become one for a while after you died, especially if you died in pregnancy, or on an unlucky day, or by your own hand, or in delirium, or with your cravings still unsatisfied. In fact, the spirits that managed to go straight from pyre to eternity were few. Most had to hang about, and with their mischief goad their families into releasing them with the proper rituals.

So Amma said, 'That's all we need. Did he say who it was?'

'It was dark,' the barber's wife replied, working up a weak lather with her long fingers. 'But he said it looked to him like your brother's boy, Jasbeer.'

'How could he tell?'

'Forgive me, but it was the nose, I think. Hard to mistake your nephew with a beak like he had.'

'O God,' Amma said wearily, 'What's *he* doing back?'

'Well,' the barber's wife said with the strange lilt that affected her speech whenever she had a scandal to report, 'I heard that the weaver told Barfi that Kurbatti overheard Kamla tell Sarupi that it was Jasbeer's ghost that got Angori's daughter pregnant.'

Ghosts could do this, by the way. In fact, they came in handy in all kinds of ways. Not only could an adulterous wife blame her pregnancy on a lustful spirit, but a drunken husband returning from a two-day revel could claim that a ghost had snatched him up in the middle of the night and dropped him in some distant place in the morning. Of course, not everyone swallowed these stories, but even a skeptic would now and then find it convenient to employ ghosts in his excuses and alibis, and they took some of the edge off everyone's culpability.

'That's not like Jasbeer,' Amma said, leaning forward as the barber's wife rinsed her hair. 'Why, he couldn't even keep his own wife satisfied.'

I won't go into the details these two dredged up about Amma's dead nephew's lovelife, but their conclusion was that Jasbeer had returned to satisfy his thwarted lust.

This was all new to me, of course, so I didn't take it as calmly as Amma did. I wondered why I hadn't bumped into Jasbeer's ghost on my nightly rounds, and took it as an affront that it should have trespassed on my territory.

I was as crazy as a sunstruck dog by then, and as the evening approached, a thought got snagged in my tangled thinking. If I were King of Bhondaripur, I told myself, then I had a duty to protect its women. It seemed to me that if I didn't do something fast, no woman would be safe from Jasbeer's ghost. I suppose it was Ramesh's wife I was worrying about especially, since if even a noble young prince like myself could have such lewd thoughts about her, then who knew what effect she would have on a rampant spirit.

So I resolved to chase the ghost away. How I would do this didn't worry me very much, for I was convinced by then that I had tapped an inexhaustible wellspring of divine and magical powers in my nature, to which my regal impersonation owed its mysterious authority. I was, in short, intoxicated with pride, and knew that nothing, not even a ghost, could stand up to me. And thus, holding my sowing pipe before me in one hand and keeping my blanket around me with the other, I arose from bed in the middle of the night to stalk Jasbeer's lustful ghost.

It was a clear, cold night, lit by a crisp halfmoon that gave the walls and floors of the courtyard a silvery sheen. I made my way to Pyari Lal's sleeping hut and lurked in the velvet shadows there for an hour or so, keeping my eyes fixed on the roof and waiting for Jasbeer to materialize. With every little creak of a beam in the cold air or jackal's cry beyond the walls, the hairs would stand up on the back of my neck, but the rest of me, being crazy, was calm. One wave of my sceptre, I told myself as I paused to urinate behind the hut, and I could vanquish the foe.

But as I was about my business I heard footsteps padding out into the court and hurrying in the direction of the women's yard. By the time I'd emptied myself out and rushed around to the front of the hut Jasbeer's ghost was gone, but it had left a sparkling wisp of dust over its path, pointing directly into the women's courtyard.

Praying that I wasn't too late to save the women, and holding my sowing pipe overhead like a sword, I charged across the men's court on my tiptoes, darted through the dark of the children's hut, and bounded out into the women's yard.

There was no sign of him anywhere and the air was deathly still, but just when I was about to give up the chase I heard muffled noises from the little room adjacent to the women's quarters, and with a sinking but noble heart I marched forward and stood in the doorway with my sceptre upraised.

It was just as I had feared — I was too late. My eyes took their time adjusting to the dark, but the beam of moonlight through the single window passed across Ramesh's wife as she lay on a charpoy, and who else could it have been pressed between her upraised legs but Jasbeer's hunched and bobbing wraith.

The sight of them together seemed to suck the breath out of me, but I did not forget my duty, and lunging forward I began to beat at the ghost with my sowing pipe. It took a moment for the ghost to realize what was happening, for Ramesh's wife had been beating at its back with her fists when I came in, but finally the spirit gaped up at me, let out a whoop, and with a wet, popping noise, leaped off its whimpering prey. It ducked around stark naked, trying to shield its pud with one hand and its head with the other, as Ramesh's wife — coming to her senses a little late, it seemed to me — began to scream, 'The ghost! It's the ghost!' at the top of her voice.

Well, I knew that, of course, and was already pursuing the spirit as best I could, beating at it with my sceptre, until it finally turned on me, knocked me down with unghostly substantiality, and rushed out into the night. Before I could stop her, Ramesh's wife followed after, and from where I lay sprawled in the dust I could hear her rousing the women next door. I decided that it would be unkingly of me to bask in my triumph over Jasbeer's ghost, especially under such delicate circumstances, so I returned to my bed and lay down, a little worse for wear, but satisfied by a job well done.

It didn't surprise me that, in all the hurly-burly that followed, the event got twisted around. The story was not that I had saved Ramesh's wife from Jasbeer's rampant ghost but that Jasbeer's ghost had attacked her and her husband as he was enjoying his conjugal rights. That Ramesh himself would go along with this version I attributed to his modesty or just to the general panic and confusion. Needless to say, I didn't try to clear it up for them, for it made no difference to me what they believed. Just knowing that I had done my duty by my sheep was consolation enough for me.

Only one of my subjects seemed to sense that I might have played a part in the events of that night, and that was Channa, Amma's crippled middle son. I caught sight of him watching me for a while amid the shouting women, barking dogs, and crying children, and as everyone returned at last to bed he limped out of the courtyard, stroking his chin.

I slept a peaceful, hero's sleep that night, as if I'd scared away my own ghosts, too, but as I awoke to the swallow's flutter I had the sensation again that someone was watching me.

And someone was: all three of Amma's sons, as it happened, standing like body servants around my bed. As I blinked up at them, Channa stepped forward, bowed slightly, and asked if he and his brothers might have the honor of carrying me about on a tour of the village.

Well, this was a nice surprise. I decided that Channa must have figured out the truth about my battle the night before, but out of a humble regard for his feelings I said nothing about it and only nodded my acceptance of his quaint and gracious offer. And so, as the women watched from their doorway, the three brothers lifted my bed up onto their shoulders and carried me out into the dim purple light.

It was a slightly rocky ride, what with Channa's limp, but it was peaceable, for no one spoke. I was grateful to the brothers for this, since I much preferred my own musings to their peasant conversation, and sitting up in my blanket with my sceptre in my lap I took in the sights of Bhondaripur.

We travelled along the narrow lanes, past bleary tethered bullocks, past a sweeper herding his scavenger pig to the crapping fields, past wells and dung piles and heaps of harvested sugar cane. I smiled beneficently at the passersby, and even bestowed a nod or two on the children who stumbled out of their compounds. Looking around as we neared a buffalo pond I was gratified to observe that I was now at the head of a small, silent parade, composed for the most part of Amma's family, but also including some stray onlookers we'd picked up along the way.

What a pleasure it is when the world conforms to your own exalted self-regard. It put me in an expansive mood, so that by the time the three brothers paused at the edge of the buffalo pond, lowered the bed from their shoulders, and began to swing it – and me – back and forth between them, I smiled up at the brightening sky like a baby in a cradle.

But just when I was about to suggest that they were beginning to rock me a bit too high and that perhaps it was time I returned to my court for breakfast anyway, the little crowd that had followed us gave a shout, and the brothers, on an upswing, let go of their grip.

I rose up over the pond with my throne, robe, and sceptre, and for a moment it seemed that we might rise into the air forever. But then we reached a little zenith and began to separate. I hit the water first, and the bed followed, striking the crown of my head. I sank straight down, spewing bubbles into the frigid, liquid gloom, and lay for a moment in the mire at the pond's bottom, as my blanket settled upon the silvery ceiling overhead.

I might have drowned there – it seemed the natural thing to do – but as I sank down, one of my hands passed across something hard and symmetrical. I looked over and saw a turbulence of mud rising like a cloud and beneath it an eye, a face, my mother's face glaring at me through the murk.

I screamed the last few bubbles from my lungs, thrust my legs into the mud, and launched myself up to the surface. I managed to get entangled in the heavy shroud of the blanket, but in my ecstasy of terror I thrashed my way free and snatched a breath from the morning air.

I began to sink again, and again I pushed myself out of the mud and back up to the surface, and by this means worked my way to the shallows and flung myself up onto the sloping bank. I lay there gasping with my eyes shut tight, hoping that somehow, like a fugitive taking refuge on the far bank of a bounding river, I had eluded Channa and his brothers. But when I opened my eyes again I found myself at Channa's feet, and looking up his twisted legs I saw that he was holding a bamboo staff over me.

I knew at once that, having failed to drown me, Channa was now going to beat me to death. I didn't try to run away but merely closed my eyes again and braced myself for the first blow.

'Wait!' a voice commanded from the distance. 'Wait, you people!'

It was a man's voice, but just barely: a tremulous bleat that faltered at full volume. But it had its own peculiar authority and in the silence that followed I opened my eyes, daring to hope that I'd been rescued somehow.

Channa and his brothers turned away from me to watch someone approaching beyond the disappointed crowd. I wiped the mud from my eyes and blinked at a little figure that now moved toward us through the throng. He was about my height, and had a child's proportions, too, but he moved with a man's rigid pretension, swathed in a pale red robe with ink-stained sleeves. He held a knotted cotton bookbag in one hand like a shield, a peacock whisk in the other like a sword, and though his face was as smooth as a child's, his jowls were swollen like a hoarding squirrel's and his eyes were sidelong and elderly.

'Now *what* do you *think* you're *doing?*' he asked, stopping a few feet from us and shaking his whisk.

Channa sighed and lowered his pole.

'Isn't this typical?' the little man asked no one in particular. 'I leave you people for one week – *one week* – and look what happens! Anyone mind telling me what's going *on* here? Do you people have any *idea* of what you're doing?'

'This isn't any of your business, Mangal Singh,' Ramesh called out from the crowd. 'This is a family matter.'

'And I suppose I'm not one of the family?' the little man shot back with a wounded look. 'I suppose your patwari hasn't been like an uncle to you?'

There were jeers and bitter chuckles from the crowd.

'Really,' the little man said, rolling his eyes and smacking his lips. 'I don't know why I bother helping you people, for all the thanks I get. But if I didn't, what would become of you? Can you answer me that? If Baroo Singh – your zemindar, in case you've forgotten – came back now, what do you think he would do? Have you thought about that? Now let him up this instant.'

Channa stood over me, scratching at his neck.

I peered cautiously over at Mangal Singh, who squinted down at me, stroking his cheek with his whisk. 'Get up, then,' he said to me with a little stamp of his foot.

I slowly stood up and took a step away from Channa.

'Just *look* at you,' Mangal Singh said as the crowd behind him began to melt away. 'You've been a very naughty little boy,' he said, tilting his head. 'And I think you owe these people an apology.'

I swallowed and nodded. 'I'm sorry,' I said, barely glancing toward Channa, who stood glowering at me and tightening his grip on his herder's pole.

'Of course, it's no wonder he's been strange,' Mangal Singh said as Ramesh and Pyari Lal stood by. 'Why, he's had absolutely nothing to *do*. You've let him lie around so long it's no wonder he turned into such a monster. The boy needs something to keep him out of mischief. You've got to put him to work.'

'Work?' Channa said, reaching out and pinching the loose flesh of my arm. 'What *kind* of work?'

'Do I have to think of *everything*?' Mangal Singh said with an impatient smirk. 'What about the buffalo? He could chase them around for a while, couldn't he? Work with Santosh until he gets the hang of it? And when he's done with that, I could always use some help. That would free Santosh for the planting. Isn't it time he took his place beside you, Channa?'

As I stood shivering and Mangal Singh idly examined his nails, the brothers conferred, and here I should explain why they put up with the little man's meddling. Mangal Singh was the patwari, the village clerk, who, in a tradition stretching all the way back to Akbar, kept the landlord's accounts. And it was part of that tradition that with the omission of a digit in his record book or the straying of a boundary on his map he could ruin a family for generations. No patwari worth his salt was above such things, for there was really no point in being a patwari in those days if you weren't ruthless and corrupt. The official pay and the social status were as low as the esteem in which his victims held him, so all the job could promise was the rewards of embezzlement and graft.

Of course, I didn't know this at the time, however much Mangal Singh may have reminded me of Nanak Chand in epicene miniature. All I knew as I looked over at him beyond the muttering brothers was that he had saved me from a beating and maybe even death.

Channa stepped forward and approached me now, suddenly raising the herding pole as if to strike me. Mangal Singh let out a little shriek, and I covered my head and dropped to my knees with a whimper, but when Channa brought the pole down it was merely to place it in my hands.

'W-why,' Mangal Singh exclaimed, slapping his whisk against his chest as the brothers laughed around him, 'you nearly frightened me to death!'

'Santosh!' Channa called out, ignoring Mangal Singh. 'Come!'

Santosh stepped out from among what was left of the crowd and approached us.

'Get up,' Channa commanded as I knelt gaping at the pole in my hand. I slowly got to my feet again, trembling with what I suppose was rage, though it felt like fear. 'Now you understand this, Balbeer,' he said, and I gaped up at him, for it was the first time I'd heard my name in months. 'You go now with Santosh here and do as he does. From now on you earn your bread.'

Mangal Singh set his whisk against his shoulder and began to whistle, as if bored by the inevitable outcome of his intervention.

'And Balbeer,' Channa said, pushing me forward, 'any more of this raja business and I'll break that pole over your head.'

Now that he'd rescued me, Mangal Singh wouldn't deign to so much as glance at me as I stumbled past him, nor answer when I tried to mumble my thanks.

Those I'd abused the most – Amma, Ramesh's wife, and some of the children – openly celebrated my downfall with hoots and cackles as I passed among them. I trembled as I staggered after Santosh, my bones as cold as lead, but there was something reassuring about my shame, for it was proof at least that I'd finally come to my senses.

CHAPTER
28

So the people of Bhondaripur drowned their king in the buffalo pond, and now all that was left of him was me, Balbeer Rao, a shivering waif with a herder's pole. If you'd tried to tell me that I was about to enter the happiest time of my life as I stumbled after Santosh that cold morning, I would have taken you for a fool. The best I could have told you was that I was lucky just to be alive, but that would have been saying more than I could have realized, for back then just being alive still engaged the hope that someday I might be delivered from my tribulations.

Santosh dragged his pole behind him, as if to lose me in the fine red dust he raised as he hurried ahead. But I managed at least to keep him in sight as he made his rounds of the tethering posts, freeing the buffalo and driving them along the serpentine paths. And by the time he'd gathered together a dozen or so of the beasts I finally caught up with him and gingerly prodded at their preposterous rumps with my pole, dodging the sharp swipes of their tails. Santosh didn't speak, unless you counted the clicks and whistles he directed at his herd as we reached the scrub beyond Baroo's stubbled cane fields.

But I wasn't in any mood to chat either as the buffalo fanned out to graze in the sparse grass sprouting up in the hazy shade of the ranga trees. For all I'd been through at the pondside, when I closed my eyes to the bright sun it was my mother's face that hovered before me in the speckled murk.

So much of what I could retrieve from my fevered recollection of the past few weeks seemed outlandish, especially my mother's apparition on the bottom of the pond. But there she hung in my memory, as certain as the morning chill and the red mud drying and flaking from my shins.

I looked over at Santosh and wondered again about the village's ghosts. Had my mother's wraith followed me to Bhondaripur to lurk in secret places, to see that I kept to destiny's path? Had Moonshi released her soul with his rituals after I left her ashes smoldering at the ghat, or had he betrayed her too and left her cinders to the domri's brooms?

I squatted down in the sun, wringing the water from my dhoti. Santosh listened for a while to the noises from the surrounding thicket, cocking his head around like a hoopoe, and when he seemed reassured by the steady whine and chatter of the bugs and birds, he withdrew a pipe from his waistband and began to blow upon it. He reminded me of the grave boys Nanak Chand had spirited out of the quarantine camps – bony, wary, and hollow-eyed – but his song was sweet and artful. Each of the buffalo raised its great head and looked his way, flicking its ears at the sound of his pipe, and then resumed grazing with sleepy, contented blinks. Santosh watched a kitehawk as he blew, and seemed to fashion his melody from its swoops and circlings as it tilted its forked tail and outstretched wings above us.

I stumbled and fought for breath as we wandered with the herd along the slopes of the low hills, keeping the buffalo away from the detrital, newly sown fields of winter crops. Ramesh's son came to us in the middle of the day to collect our buffalos' droppings in a basket and deliver a chapatti wrapped in cotton to Santosh, and Santosh chased away a dhangar girl with her little herd of goats who'd been cutting down peepal branches with a scythe blade banded to the end of her herder's pole. But we saw no one else all afternoon, and I suppose it was natural that even that first day a frail thread of kinship would grow between Santosh and me. Despite his grudging manner, Santosh had his father's tender heart, and when in the middle of the afternoon he unwrapped his chapatti and ate it he paused at the last scrap, squinted over at me doubtfully, and tossed it to me with a shrug. It fell to the dirt, and I wanted to leave it there, but my stomach grumbled for it and I dusted it off and chewed it as Santosh, with a faint smile, shook his head.

In the late afternoon we found ourselves near the crest of a ridge, from which we could see Gwalior's fortress rising like a cropped mountain in the pink haze, and we watched the lamps flicker on in the jumble and sprawl of the city spread out below. We lingered too long, and Santosh, scowling at me as if I were to blame, cracked his goad across the buffalos' backs and hurried them toward the village in the deepening gloom, his eyes darting about whenever we passed a thicket or a clump of trees.

It was nearly dark when we reached the pond and paused to let the buffalo drink, and by the time we had tethered them all to their posts, supper was already half over in Amma's compound.

'And where have you been, Santosh?' his mother asked as he squatted down with the other boys and his sister Ahalya fetched him chapatti and dahl.

'Did the little maharaja slow you down?' his grandmother asked, spooning dahl onto his chapatti as Ahalya stood by. 'Wouldn't even the jackals have him?'

'No,' Santosh replied, looking over at me, and whether he was replying to her first question or her last he answered in a kindly way, as if I'd been no trouble.

'Well, maharaj?' said Amma, glaring up at me as I stood by with my hands behind my back, wondering what was expected of me. 'What's the matter? The food not good enough for you?'

'N-no,' I said, quickly shaking my head, and I stepped forward. To my relief Channa's wife gave me a chapatti too, and Amma gave me dahl.

I returned to my spot beneath the swallows' nests, but my charpoy was gone, and as I squatted down and savored my little supper I wondered where I was going to sleep. When everyone had finished eating and the cooking fires were smothered, I gathered a few rags together to form a pallet where my bed had been, but Amma shooed me into the children's hut, and the children, in turn, shooed me out into the men's courtyard beyond.

I was at an utter loss by then, and stood outside the brothers' sleeping hut like a beggar, shivering in the sharp night air. But suddenly something flew toward me from behind, and I whirled around in time to see a blanket settle on the dust at my feet. It seemed to have come from the direction of the old penitent who sat by the doorway, but when I looked over at him he sat as he always sat, crosslegged, with his gray head hanging on his breast, as still as a statue. I wondered if Santosh had thrown it from within the children's hut, but it seemed too great a distance. In the end it didn't matter. I stooped down, snatched it up, and threw it over my shoulders as I searched for a place to sleep. At last, displacing a buffalo cow in a little thatched shelter built against the wall, I settled down upon the warm straw, where, as the cow had discovered, a mud trough blocked the draft. And there, at the pregnant cow's feet, with its breathing as my lullaby, I slept.

A life spent behind a buffalo's rump may be worth living, but it isn't all worth reading about, so I'll try to spare you the tedium of the months I spent goading the stupid beasts.

But every day had its highlight, its novelty, if always in isolation, like a single picture on a hallway wall. For instance, I remember one afternoon when Santosh and I were resting at the foot of a little hill north of Bhondaripur and we saw something raising dust in the distance. From where we sat all we could make out was a strange, hunched shape moving along the ground like an inchworm, so we herded the buffalo forward to investigate and found it was a lone pilgrim who, for his penance, had chosen to make his way to Varanasi by lying down in the dirt, marking where his head lay with a little trident, rising, placing his feet on the mark, lying down again, marking where his head lay again, and so on, and in this fashion grovel all the way to the Ganga. Santosh and I thought he was astonishing as we watched his progress, but he was friendly enough, asking us where he might find water and how far it was to the next village, and wishing us a good day as he rose and fell, rose and fell, off into the distance.

Some mornings we travelled all the way to the steep strand of the River Sindh and watched the dhobi women labor along the stony bank below. They clapped their twisted rolls of laundry against the rocks, the droplets forming shimmering arcs above their backs with each languid swing, and their noise, from our altitude, was like scattered applause. Here and there we would catch sight of women and girls wrapped in wet films of cotton cloth washing themselves, part by part, in the shallows. But it was always late morning by the time we reached the river, so it was hard to tell a clothed limb from a naked one in the glare and sparkle of the reflected midday sun.

Late one afternoon outside Bhondaripur, as we jogged along behind the trotting buffalo, we saw the patwari, Mangal Singh, meet a chaprasi from the city on the Gwalior Road, and receive from him, in exchange for what looked to be a fistful of coins, a little roll of paper. I think that as he sent the chaprasi away and began to unroll the paper to read it Mangal Singh caught sight of me, crushed the paper between his little hands, and hid it in his clothing, but I may have added that to the true memory long since.

For the few moments Santosh and I marvelled together at these episodes we were almost like brothers, exchanging looks of wonderment. But in the normal course of things he continued to keep his distance, as I kept mine, and we could drive the herd for hours without speaking.

It was a full two weeks before I overcame my fear of the buffalo. They were many times my bulk, after all, and heedless with their great, curved horns. I managed this only after one evening when Ramesh's naked toddler son demonstrated what cowards they were by wandering into the path of the bull buffalo's waddling, home-bound charge and bringing it to a halt by swatting it on the snout with a ladle.

But it seems that one fear always replaces another, and as soon as I stopped fearing the buffalo I realized at last what it was I should have feared all along, what it was that made Santosh's mother so fretful and solicitous when we set out each morning, what made Santosh so vigilant whenever we passed a thicket, what hurried us home when dusk approached. One evening, and I think it must have been after one of those days when we'd herded the beasts to the river, we were passing about thirty yards from a growth of tamarind on the far side of one of the low ridges that banked Bhondaripur. The buffalo were joggling along as usual at that time of day, eager to drink at the pond and eat their feed at the tethering posts, when they all suddenly stopped dead in their tracks with a sharp snort and turned their heads toward the thicket. With my newfound sense of mastery I began to shout at them at once and crack my goad across their haunches, but Santosh ordered me to be still and listened with the herd to the distant jungle, his eyes wide and keen.

'What's the matter?' I asked after a moment. 'Let's get going.'

'Shut up,' Santosh whispered back with a sharp wave. I slowly walked up behind him and stood close enough to see the gooseflesh stirring on the back of his neck. Suddenly there was a screeching sound, like a monkey's alarm, from the treetops, and a rustling in the foliage below. Santosh whirled around with a gasp and furiously began to beat at the rumps of the buffalo, though they had already sprung forward before the first blow landed.

I straggled for a moment like a calf, too dim to understand the danger, but I finally began to pound after Santosh and the herd, figuring that Santosh knew his business. Every now and then as we raced along the ridge Santosh would turn and, swiftly running backward, beat at the ground behind us with his goad, shouting 'Hut! Haa!' at the top of his voice, and none of us – not Santosh, not me, not the panic-stricken beasts – stopped running until we reached the village and splashed into the pond.

As a city boy my fear of the jungle had been no more sensible and specific than my fear of any dark and secret place. In the jungle that throbbed and rustled in my nightmares I was as likely to be devoured by demons as by tigers. But, as I was beginning to learn, for a buffalo herder on the outskirts of Maharaja Scindhia's hunting preserve these outlandish, great striped cats were a hazard of everyday life.

Up to then Baroo had been on my mind almost constantly, and I watched for him as I goaded the herd about, alert to every distant plume of dust, every treading speck on the crests of the ridges. But after the tiger scare I realized I had enough to worry about in the here and now without dwelling on my past or fretting about my future. Lying by Guli – as I called the expecting buffalo cow that shared my resting place – I stopped trying to picture my mother's face and pinning my hopes on Harigarh's welcome, and listened more closely to the jungle's song as it rose from beyond the village walls like a slow flood. It seemed to my ears as though the trees and bushes themselves advanced upon Bhondaripur those nights, as though the scrub and tangle were coiling along the rows of wheat and mustard, and I would press myself against Guli's swollen belly and will myself to sleep. It was on one such night, as I lay shutting my eyes and ears, that the patwari, Mangal Singh, sent his servant into the compound to summon me to his home.

Most of the houses I passed as I followed behind the patwari's servant were made of crude sandstone blocks mortared together and plastered over with mud and dung, roofed with thatch or sun-bleached, split, and rain-warped wooden slats.

But Mangal Singh lived in a pukka house of neatly fitted sandstone blocks with a verandah supported by Saracen columns and a roof of interlocking tiles. We entered a vast courtyard enclosing its own neem tree with a stone bench encircling its trunk like an anklet. A private well with an iron pulley lay a few steps from the doorway, and next to the house a plump cow the color of the halfmoon that shone above us stood tethered with an udder swollen to the size of a water bag. The surrounding walls were festooned with thorns, and spikes bristled from the door to the house.

As it creaked open, a deep bell sounded somewhere within. The house was dimly lit – almost pitch black, in fact, along the corridor – and I stumbled on a sleeping dog as we entered a large room in the back. The patwari sat in the weak glow of an oil lamp, on a white cotton pallet banked with purple cushions, and as the servant took his leave a second figure, wrapped in crimson, flitted briefly out of the shadowed corner and retrieved Mangal Singh's brass dinner plates. The air was still heavy with the steam from the patwari's dinner, but a thread of incense curled up from the floor, corrupting the aroma of garlic and chili and scorched ghee.

Mangal Singh looked even smaller than before among his cushions, for he sat with his legs straight out and his feet straight up, like a child. He had removed his turban, and I could see the elaborate cut and curl of his hair, which he wore in the Mahratta style, with ringlets at his ears, though Amma said he was an Ahir, just like her.

Pretending not to notice me as I stood before him, Mangal Singh busied himself with his papers, leafing through them with his ink-stained fingers and filing them into separate stacks between his toes.

'Ah, Balbeer,' he finally said, though with difficulty, for his cheeks were packed with pahn. 'The zemindar's pet.'

He had me squat down before him and looked at me askance as

he moved his papers out of the light. He began by saying how proud of me my uncle must be for my having adjusted so well to village life. I merely stared back at him, for I thought he meant my mother's brother and couldn't for the life of me figure out how Mangal Singh could have known he existed. With less irony than you might suppose, he said that considering my grave responsibilities to the buffalo it was very gracious of me to spare him some time. I couldn't help but ask him how he knew about my uncle, and still chewing his pahn and staring at me with his head turned away he shrugged and said that, after all, he'd worked for him for twenty years; who knew him better?

At last I realized that Mangal Singh thought Baroo was my uncle, and I told him that he wasn't, though my denial trailed off a little as it occurred to me that Baroo Singh *could* be my uncle for all I knew; in fact, it would have explained a lot.

Then what exactly was Baroo Singh to me, and me to him? Mangal Singh wanted to know. Friends, I was reduced to saying; and it must have sounded even more foolish to him than it did to me. Very *devoted* friends, Mangal Singh declared. And how long had we been such friends? he asked my permission to inquire, still with his sidelong stare. Long enough, I told him as he fished among his papers in the shadows beside him and withdrew a rolled document bound with black thread.

With that Mangal Singh had managed to arouse both my curiosity and my suspicions, and when he asked me to tell him again where I'd met Baroo, though I'd never told him in the first place, I shut my mouth completely and began to look around me. Gazing into the gloom to my right, I saw we were not alone. The figure in red sat silently by the kitchen doorway, and for a moment something silver on its wrist caught the light from the patwari's dim little lamp.

Quietly, practically in passing, Mangal Singh pronounced me a brave boy but a poor conversationalist as he shooed the figure away and began to unroll the document on his lap.

'That's my daughter, Sakuntala,' Mangal Singh said as I watched her rise and retreat into the kitchen. 'She's all the family I have left, Balbeer.'

Mangal Singh cleared his throat and asked about Baroo again.

He said he knew that Baroo had promised to come back for me, but he wanted to know what more he'd promised me. Though Mangal Singh asked the same way Weems had always asked his questions, as though he already knew the answer, I had long before resolved never to tell anyone about my family in Harigarh, so I finally shrugged and said, 'Nothing.'

'Nothing?' Mangal Singh persisted.

'Nothing,' I said firmly, steadying my gaze on his narrow little eyes.

The patwari looked relieved to hear this and straightened up against the cushions, folding his legs together. 'Well, Balbeer,' he said, tapping the document with each of his fingers in turn, 'I'm afraid I have some bad news for you then.'

'Sir?'

'I'm afraid our zemindar has run into a little difficulty.'

'What – what's happened?' I asked with a sinking feeling.

'I don't doubt that it's not of his own making. Probably just a misunderstanding.'

'What do you mean?'

'Well,' Mangal Singh said in his clipped little voice, sucking slightly on his lips for a moment, 'I've received this letter from him, you see, and although strangely enough it's in *English* of all things and I've had to get it translated by this babu who may have gotten some of it wrong – '

'But *I* know Eng – ' I began to say in my impatience, but I choked myself off just in time.

'What's that, Balbeer?'

'No – no, never mind,' I said.

Mangal Singh tilted his head slightly like a puzzled dog and sighed. 'Anyway,' he said, picking at his teeth for a moment with the long nail of his little finger, 'I don't think it's any reason to get excited, you understand, but it seems our zemindar has been arrested.'

I swallowed, but the walls of my throat seemed to stick together, and I had to cough them free. '*Arrested*? Arrested for what?'

The letter wasn't very clear on that point, he said, but he knew it had to be for something minor. 'In any case, as his friends we just *know* they've arrested the wrong man, don't we?' said Mangal Singh.

'*We've* never believed those rumors about him, *have* we?'

'Wh-what rumors?'

'There, you see?' Mangal Singh said with a smirk. 'You didn't even *know* about them, so how can they be true?'

'But what have they done with him? Where is he? Is he all right?'

The letter didn't answer these questions. Indeed, said Mangal Singh, it forbade us from even asking them. He guessed that Baroo was being held somewhere near Bikaneer, but he couldn't tell for sure from the translation. Besides, it didn't matter. What mattered was what was to become of me.

I longed to read the letter and draw my own conclusions, but the patwari, seeing my eyes fix upon it, set it into a little studded chest within his reach and secured it with a heavy padlock of iron and brass.

However confident we ourselves could be that Baroo would return to us, said Mangal Singh, speaking now as though reading from something he'd prepared beforehand, if the children who tilled his fields got wind of Baroo's imprisonment it could be the end of me.

I said nothing, though my despair must have been evident on my face, for I began to wonder if the time had finally come for me to set off on my own for Harigarh.

'I can tell you from experience, Balbeer,' Mangal Singh explained, 'these villagers do not trust their betters. Look at the way they've treated you, for instance. Why, they've been looking for an excuse to throw you out from the beginning, and now here's all the excuse they need. When they get wind of this business they might forget their promise to their zemindar altogether. I wouldn't be surprised if the word started to go around that Baroo Singh was *dead.*' Mangal Singh flinched slightly and shook his head. '*You* know how these silly rumors can get started. And where would they leave you?'

Tonight, I told myself with dwindling conviction. *Tonight you have to run away.*

'But, Balbeer,' the patwari said, leaning toward me with one little finger upraised, 'they don't *have* to know, *do* they?'

I looked up at Mangal Singh and held my breath.

'That's right, Balbeer,' he said proudly. 'You and I are the only ones who know. And as far as I'm concerned we're the only ones who need to know. Why upset everyone else with this news? Why disgrace and scandalize Bhondaripur? Why rob these poor peasants of their self-respect? Nothing has to change for them, or for me, for that matter. So why don't we just go about our business as before?

'You keep Pyari Lal's buffalo and I'll keep my books and together we'll keep our little secret. Oh, Mangal Singh,' he told himself, bringing his finger to his lips, 'that *was* nicely put.'

Well, for all I'd seen of life I was still small and friendless, so what choice did I have but to agree to the patwari's plan? His thinking crowded my own thoughts out, and as I sat listening to his conspiratorial singsong I could tell at last that I didn't have it in me any longer to run away on my own that night – nor, it began to seem on any night following. Even in my perilous limbo in Bhondaripur there had come times each day when, for the first time since my mother's death, I had begun to feel at home.

CHAPTER
29

Thus Mangal Singh gave me his protection, and together we left his dismal house and in the moonlight gripped the tail of his drowsy cow and swore upon it never to breathe our secret to another living soul.

I returned to my bed by the feed trough and resumed my life as a buffalo herder, and as the weeks went by I began to reconcile myself to Baroo's imprisonment, for though it meant that I might never escape Bhondaripur, it also meant that if I didn't want to leave Bhondaripur I wouldn't have to.

During the spring harvest, when the heat began to beat back up at us from the baked earth, Santosh was called away from the herd to help with the reaping. I was entrusted with driving the buffalo, though only as far as the farthest harvested field, where I could watch the whole village set to work at once: the children fetching food and water along the boundaries of the fields; the women squatting and chopping their way toward the village with their little scythes, singing songs of thanksgiving and propitiation as the men loaded their carts with the bundled wheat.

Busiest of all, in his way, was Mangal Singh, who set himself up in the shade of a tree by the threshing station, keeping track of the crop with his scale, his record books, and his quick black pen. Though he was stubborn and exacting in his duties and kept his eyebrows low to indicate the seriousness of the work at hand, he could not disguise his high spirits, for the line of his lips kept breaking into a smirk, and even when he paused to lick the tip of his nib he continued to hum a little tune.

In the evenings Mangal Singh shared his exhilaration with me by summoning me to his home and contriving to teach me a thing or two about the money. He was astonished by how quickly I grasped arithmetic (I hadn't told him, of course, about my education at Bastard Bhavan), and slowly, bit by bit, as I sat beside him in the lamplight, flicking bugs off his papers with a whisk, I was introduced to the mysteries of the village accounts.

Mangal Singh explained his system with the same wonder and gratitude with which Baroo had described his tenants. It seemed a miracle to Mangal Singh that there should have been people like Pyari Lal and his brothers who would work so hard for so little and that out of all the people in the world he had been born to collect the fruits of their labors.

And it *was* a kind of miracle. Almost half of the village's eighty acres belonged to a pair of Brahmin brothers from a distant village on the road to Morar, but the rest belonged to Baroo. Baroo rented ten of these acres to another village family, but the rest he rented out to Pyari Lal, Channa, and Ramesh, in exchange for half their revenue plus two annas of every rupee they brought in. This was profitable enough for Baroo and hard enough on Pyari Lal and his brothers as far as it went, but it went a lot further. None of Baroo's tenants could afford to buy their own tools, oxen, buffalo, and grain, so they had to turn to Mangal Singh, his agent, for a loan. Mangal Singh charged a flat fee for tools and bullocks, but loaned out seed at fifty percent interest. His profit didn't end there, however, for by switching payment from cash to kind, back and forth, year after year, he could increase his return geometrically.

Suppose he loaned Pyari Lal a fifty-pound sack of seed at planting time when it was worth two rupees. You might assume at fifty percent interest, that at harvest time Pyari Lal could have paid him back with a sack and a half. But Mangal Singh based his loans on value, not weight, and since seed was plentiful at harvest time and worth only one rupee a sack, he would demand a repayment of three sacks to make up the difference in value. When the price went back up to two rupees he would sell the three bags for six rupees and then buy six more when the price went back down. These he would loan out again when the price was up, and by the end of this third cycle he would end up with eighteen sacks worth thirty-six rupees and all on a loan of a single two-rupee sack of seed.

Everything Baroo's tenants used or occupied – carts, plow blades, even the huts they built with their own hands – belonged to Baroo. The buffalo I herded were Baroo's too, and his tenants paid him half of the profits they made from selling the milk and a fee for the milk they drank. And when you added up all of these fees and splits and repayments and included the payments in labor and barter they made to the village artisans and the donations to the local priests and the taxes they owed Scindhia's Collector on what little they did own – when you totalled it all up, as Mangal Singh did in his precious books, it was not hard to understand how Pyari Lal and his brothers could end a year of hard labor and good rains with less than nothing to show for it. And Mangal Singh's columns of figures never included the bribes he extracted for adjusting the scales in a tenant's favor or just for setting down the meagre truth, or the graft the Collector demanded in exchange for keeping his assessments just shy of ruinous.

Mangal Singh never let me see the maps he drew of the cultivated fields nor the books in which he recorded transfers of title, for these were his sacred texts and the core of his power, and his mastery of them had to be exclusive. Whatever he recorded in his maps and books, be it true or false, if it was left unchallenged and unrefuted for five years (as it was apt to be in a village of illiterates) it then became ironclad law.

I suppose I must have regarded the patwari's figuring as a kind of game, for I took so much pride and pleasure in grasping its rules that if I ever connected it those first months with the lives of the villagers I lived among it was only to marvel, like Baroo and Mangal Singh, at the riches Baroo could extract from their labor. Facts and figures, on those few occasions when I've managed to grasp any, have always tended to displace my common sense, as if in their precision they were laws unto themselves. Of course, that doesn't explain my shortsightedness, let alone excuse it, but I was only ten years old by this time, and besides, I was distracted.

Mangal Singh's daughter still clung to the shadows when I came to visit, but now and then she would let her guard down and I would look up from her chattering father's papers and catch sight of her face in a stray beam of lamplight. And at those times when I caught her looking at me and our eyes, if only for an instant, met, I lost all track of myself. Her gaze seemed to lay bare something weak and shameful within me, and I would sit breathless and insensible as her father continued his lectures beside me.

I couldn't have described her to you then, and there may not be much point now, but her beauty was exquisitely precarious, like a juggler on a pole. Her nose would have been too fine between any other pair of eyes, her lips too full above another chin. In fact her nose was the same nose that seemed so meagre on her father's face, and her lips, though unstained by betel juice and still fortified by a full set of teeth, were much the same lips that seemed so excessive above his retreating little chin. Had one feature been changed by so much as an eyelash's breadth her beauty would have lost its balance and toppled from its height.

I could go on and tell you that her eyes were like the stars and her face was like the moon and so on, but even if I could convince you with such an inventory I could never satisfy myself. Back then it seemed to me that no comparison could exalt her beauty, that the moon could hardly aspire to Sakuntala's radiance. And now, from this distance, it seems an odd way to describe a little girl who was then no more than nine years old.

No custom forbade a girl her age from showing her face to a boy my age, but she had imposed a kind of purdah on herself to please her father. Mangal Singh wore a little gold ring in the top of the shell of his right ear to protect her from gypsies, bandits, and the evil eye, and if she was, as he said, his treasure, then I suppose he believed that like the rest of his treasure she had to be hidden from view. Her purdah made her all the more haunting, of course, for it wasn't constant, like sunlight, but revealed her to me in flashes, like lightning, and her after-image lingered and swam before me every evening as I made my way back to my bed.

In the early summer Santosh and I kept the herd close to the village, for the great beasts could bear the heat only by wallowing in the shrinking village pond.

By this time I had begun to see that I had reached my limit with Santosh and his family, that the best I could expect of them was grudging acceptance. I placed more value on the patwari's attentions and even began to hope that if Baroo never returned from his captivity, Mangal Singh might take me in. And lying under the night sky with Sakuntala's face floating above me beyond the stars I might even have hoped that someday he would take me as his son-in-law, though in the morning I would hardly imagine Mangal Singh ever parting with his daughter (and the dowry her groom would demand), let alone giving her over to an orphaned herder of doubtful caste.

As we watched the beasts bluster and loll in the warm brown soup, other children sometimes joined us: Hari and Ragesh, Santosh's little brothers, and sometimes his sister Ahalya would bring him a pitcher of drinking water and sit some distance from us as he passed it around.

I missed some of the adventure of our winter herding, but even on our little daybreak grazing drives just beyond the village fields some novelties presented themselves.

One morning as we were driving the buffalo back to their wallow the herd was scattered by a thundering party of pigstickers. We didn't see the boar, though we could hear it pant and scramble through the underbrush, but I'll never forget the sight of those half-dozen British troopers galloping past on their lathered mounts, roaring and laughing and waving their lances, their faces as florid as monkeys' asses, and especially the one who nearly ran me down: all tooth and whisker like the others but with a great bloody gash across his stout calf where a boar must have slashed him with its tusk. When they'd passed by and I turned back toward the village every man within sight stood motionless, with his head bowed and his hands clasped, and remained thus until we could no longer hear the shouts and hoofbeats on the breeze.

At the end of the summer, when the heat had reached such a pitch that the men kept to their charpoys and the women ventured forth only to fetch water and sprinkle it about to keep down the dust, the buffalo pond dried up completely and Santosh and I had to set forth before daybreak and drive the reluctant, panting herd to another wallow some miles northwest of the village.

The pond lay by an abandoned baron's fort and among the twisted and overgrown remains of an old mango grove. When we first came upon it we assumed we would be chased off by herders from the village that lay well within sight of the grove, but no one bothered us and day after day we had the oasis to ourselves.

Though on one of our travels to or fro we came upon the carcass of a tiger's prey – a young nilgai with the vultures and hargila storks still plucking scraps from its bones – and though we once found pawprints from a night's prowl leading all the way up to the village gates, Santosh didn't fear the tigers so much in the summer, for in the heat of the day it took an irresistible prey to lure them out of their shaded slumber.

The grove was a peaceable place and as cool a spot as any in Gwalior, and when the monkeys that occupied the treetops were too beaten down by the heat to protest, we would pick the ripened fruit from the branches and sit in the shade, watching the dust devils career across the studded, simmering plain.

Santosh forbade me to explore the ruined fort, for he claimed it was haunted. Some days he said a yogi's ghost stalked the battlements, other days it was a mad thakur's. I didn't believe in ghosts anymore, having myself been mistaken for one, so I defied him, leaving him scowling and mute by the wallow and setting off along the base of the great wall in search of a gate.

The ground was littered with tumbled stones from the rim of the ruined wall, and I jumped from one to another as if across a shallow stream, but when I thus leapt around the corner and out of the shade and landed on the dark red stone it was like hopping onto the floor of a furnace. The soles of my feet seemed to blister, and when I fell to the ground the sun came crashing down after me like a burning timber.

If there were ghosts in the old fort they were welcome to it. I scurried back into the shade, but I wouldn't retreat all the way back to the wallow; not and give Santosh the satisfaction. So I closed my eyes and fell into one of those fevered, twilight sleeps that afflicted me on those summer days – not an escape from the heat so much as a surrender to it, so that even in my most steadfast dream the Ganga above which my mother floated began to boil, the riverbank smoldered, her voice became the hot south wind gusting against my ears.

Whether it was the quiet rustling I heard behind me in the grove or Santosh's distant, halfhearted call that awakened me, I can't say; but I jumped up in a sweat and hurried to the wallow to find Santosh calmly standing by the trembling flanks of Guli, the buffalo cow.

'You missed it,' he said with a certain satisfaction as if it served me right, and pointed down to the grass with a blood-smeared arm.

'Missed what?' I began to ask as I hurried toward him, but he grinned at me, and I saw Guli's brand-new calf raising its trembling head.

It was the homeliest thing I'd ever seen: a bony newborn bull about the size of a dog, trying now to rise from its gory landing place and stand on its long, foolish legs. The sparse yellow fur on its purple hide was wet with its mother's glue, and it mewed like a cat, stumbling sideways with its torn cord dangling.

Santosh looked so smug you would have thought he was the father as he went down to the edge of the wallow to wash the blood from his arms.

'Is it going to be all right?' I asked as the calf tottered beside me and Guli stood by, gasping for breath and chewing on the afterbirth.

'Santosh?' I said, turning toward him. 'Is it going to be all right?'

Santosh still didn't answer, nor so much as move a muscle, and following the path of his fixed gaze across the small brown pond I too saw the tiger.

It crept toward us in a mockery of stealth between the marsh grass and the depleted pool. Stopping at the edge of the water, its great yellow paws sinking into the mud, the tiger ignored both the panicked herd of buffalo now struggling out of the wallow and the tribe of monkeys shrieking and bustling in the treetops. With its long whiskers stirring and its teeth chittering and the points of its ears folded back, it seemed to see nothing but Santosh and me and the wavering calf behind us.

With a loud gasp, as if he were coming up for air, Santosh jumped over and fetched his goad. Out of instinct I followed after him, though a little vaguely, still looking back at the tiger as it now dipped one paw and then the other in the water and pushed off into the turbulent pond.

'Come on! Come on!' Santosh shouted at me, and together we beat poor old Guli to where the other buffalo had begun to regroup. For a moment they circled around in a fog of dust, waving their horns and snorting like their wild ancestors' thundering ghosts, but as soon as Santosh reached them with his pole they lost all dignity and galloped for home.

I followed them a little way but my thighs lagged and ached as if I were running through water, and then, over Santosh's shouts and the beating of the buffalo's hooves, I heard Guli's frail calf puling behind me.

'Hurry up!' Santosh called out over his shoulder, still cracking his goad across the buffalo's backs, and I wanted to; I know I did. So I still wonder why I stopped running then and turned back toward the wallow.

'Balbeer! Balbeer! What are you *doing?*' Santosh cried from the growing distance, and then the calf bawled again and I began to walk toward it.

'Balbeer! Come back! Don't you hear me? *Get back here!*'

I heard him perfectly, just as I could feel my heart struggling against my ribs as if to escape, but I was caught in a current, sweeping me back at a quickening pace, back to the edge of the wallow. I ran headlong into the tall grass, thrashing at it with my pole and hooting like an ape. In a few mad bounds I landed beside the little calf, which snorted with surprise and toppled over.

At first I couldn't see the tiger, for it was now just a tiger's mask floating toward me on the pond, but as it reached the shallows the water began to break across its long striped back and its tail rose like a snake behind it.

'Get up!' I panted at the little calf, trying to untangle its crumpled limbs. 'Please get *up*!'

I tried to hoist it to its feet without letting go of my herding pole, and still the tiger kept rising, glaring at me like an affronted king.

With one desperate heave I got the calf back to its feet, but when I tried to goad it forward it moved across the crushed grass as slowly as a crippled spider.

'Come *on*!' I pleaded, pulling it forward by its ear, but it only balked and bawled.

The tiger was no more than twenty feet from us now and creeping toward us paw by paw, crouching ever lower like a compressing spring.

I released the calf's poor ear and stood for a moment with the goad gripped in both my hands, gasping for breath. I gave a quick look back over my shoulder; there was still time to escape, for surely the tiger would satisfy itself with the tender little calf. But when I looked back at the tiger as it dug its hind claws into the dirt and gave its heavy tail a flick, a chill ran down from the top of my head to the backs of my knees and a black rage stole over me like a thunderhead.

I began to snarl and spit and stamp my feet, and before I knew it I was pounding toward the tiger and beating the ground before me with my goad.

If I've surprised you with what I did, imagine how I must have astonished that tiger. As I marched forward with my goad, howling and snarling like a mad dog, the tiger slumped down in its crouch, its ears unfolding and its coiled legs gone limp. It must have been as if a fawn were attacking it, or a rabbit – as if the whole order of nature were being stood on its head. Even when I brought the goad down across its chin it couldn't seem to do anything but lie there with its brow ruffled and struggle to puzzle me out.

Having expected, I suppose, to be dead by this point, I was so relieved to find that I was still whole that it emboldened me further and I raised the herding pole up again and brought it down across the tiger's flanks.

The indignity of this finally snapped the great beast out of its baffled stupor, and it leaped to its feet with a yowl and swiped at me once with its right claw. Now, at last, I knew that it was going to kill me, and as I shifted my grip on the herding pole my snarls turned to whimpering and I could feel urine running down my leg.

But in fact the tiger's swipe was only a gesture of concession, for with a last look at the little calf and a petulant snarl in my direction it turned around and limped back into the pool.

CHAPTER
30

You can look back at some things you've done in your youth and tell yourself you acted sensibly; you did what you had to do. But when I recall what I did that day eighty years ago I want to go back and grab that boy by the shoulders and shake him. What did he think he was doing?

As the tiger climbed up the opposite side of the pond and shook the water from its splendid coat, how could I have taken it for anything but a god, or regarded my life thereafter as anything but its gift to me? But in my delirious relief I mistook it for a vanquished foe and danced around on the grass like a peacock in full flaunt.

It's probably just as well that I had to celebrate my victory alone, got all the proud shouting and strutting over with and rinsed out my dhoti before leading the calf away, for by the time I reached Bhondaripur I was composed and dry and looked the proper hero.

Guli's calf learned to walk along the way, but faltered in the dark outside the village gate, so I carried it the last few yards with its legs gathered up like bundled twigs. When I reached the family compound I found the men's courtyard filled with people, all circled around Pyari Lal. He stood in the light from a lamp, swinging a copper ring over the mouth of a water jar as the women chanted in the shadows.

I didn't know it at the time, but they were trying to capture my ghost, for the spirit of a tiger's prey was much dreaded in Bhondaripur, as it was believed that it could lure others into its killer's clutches. I had evidently arrived at the climax, when the ring was supposed to drop into the jar as a sign that my ghost had been captured within, so no one noticed me. And it was when the ring fell in and everyone thought that my ghost had been trapped that someone – one of the brothers' wives, I think– caught sight of me and screamed.

Pyari Lal dropped the jar and gasped as it burst at his feet, and everyone whirled around, pointing and shouting and shooing their children behind them. But I was still braced by my triumph and remained calm, carrying the little calf up to Pyari Lal and setting it down among the water jar's bits and pieces. Cautiously, his brothers drew toward us, and after staring at me the longest while Channa slowly stretched his hand out to the calf, receiving a rasping lick for his trouble, and he began to laugh, and Pyari Lal, too, and finally Ramesh and the others, and they all gathered around, lightly touching me here and there to make certain I was real.

Guli croaked and strained at her tether, catching her little calf's scent on the night air. Battling the prideful smile that threatened to break across my face, I brought the calf to her, and watched as she inspected him and nudged him back toward her swollen udder. I turned to fetch my blanket and set it down beside the trough, but before I could bring it down from where it hung under the sleeping hut's eave, someone darted out of the throng, fell to his knees before me, and pressed his forehead to my foot. This was Santosh, trying to make the best of things. It must have galled him to humble himself like that, but I suppose he was only saving face, for by exalting my courage he could make his own retreat seem a little less craven.

Pyari Lal clapped his hands together behind him and ordered the women to revive the cooking fires. Channa offered me a drink from his water jar, and the children led me into their sleeping hut, making a bed for me on a freshly strung charpoy, and there I sat for an hour or so, telling and retelling the story of my battle with the tiger as Ahalya fetched my supper. Other families asked permission to pay their respects, and I must have told the story twenty times at least that night.

I didn't elaborate on the truth, but I spoke with a false reluctance and left out some things along the way. I didn't tell them that I'd been in a trance, nor that I'd lost my water when the tiger rose up at last, so I came off sounding cool and deliberate through it all. I couldn't change my story as I retold it either, for all night long Ahalya remained at the foot of my bed, gazing at me with adoring eyes.

Of course, it didn't much matter what I said, for many mouths would chew on the truth, and stretch it into outlandish proportions. If, by morning, they wanted to believe that I'd ridden the tiger like a pony or swum after it and pulled it under by its tail, it was fine by me.

Santosh drove the buffalo alone the next day, while I stayed behind to rest. He didn't go back to the wallow, for though I didn't correct much in the exalted accounts of my daring deed that circulated that morning, I did make sure everyone kept one thing straight: the tiger still lived.

I went to the patwari's that night, hoping for one last hero's welcome, but Mangal Singh took a dim view of the whole business. It wasn't that he didn't believe me; he simply couldn't fathom why I had risked so much for so little. Didn't I know how worthless the little newborn bull was, even if it happened to survive into adulthood? Hadn't I learned anything from Mangal Singh's teachings? For the rest of the evening he said no more to me, and his disapproval hung like a stench in the still air of his dim room, but I consoled myself that surely Sakuntala, listening from the kitchen, must have been impressed.

Within the week a great wind blew down from the north, sucking the loose dust up into the dark sky, and the monsoon was upon us. The buffalo pond filled up again, and Santosh and I drove the herd to our old haunts, over the newly greening hills, through rains so thick sometimes that we could barely catch our breath. The damp swelter was even harder to bear than the summer heat, but every day or two the rain would rescue us from it, and it was a relief even when it leaked down on us in the sleeping hut or washed away our path or struck us on the wind like needles.

People stopped treating me like a hero as soon as the rains came, but I never had to sleep by the trough again, nor fetch my supper for myself. It had taken an extraordinary deed to get people to treat me like anybody else, but I had finally found a place in the family.

◆———————◆

Now you may wonder how a family of cowherds could have accepted an orphan like myself, especially since villagers are supposed to be so finicky about caste.

If I had been of a lower caste they might never have taken to me at all, but remember that when Baroo left me to recuperate he gave me his protection and treated me like kin, so they all assumed I was a Rajput, just like him, which, so far as I knew, was true.

They were Ahirs, though they preferred to call themselves by their general and slightly more exalted caste name of Yadhava. Yadhavas were cowherds and came late to farming. Pyari Lal's ancestors had grazed the Gwalior countryside back during the thousand-year reign of the Phals and had turned to cultivation somewhere in the six or seven centuries since. Yadhavas themselves claimed all sorts of distinctions, from the thrones of some of the great ancient empires to the paternity of Lord Krishna himself, but nobody else thought much of them. Because they drove animals all day, out of sight and earshot of the Brahmins, they weren't trusted to keep the proper observances. And because they had to castrate bulls from time to time and sold their cows' sacred milk for cash, they were impure by definition.

Rajputs, on the other hand, stood much higher up the ladder. Nowadays every petty raja and thakur calls himself a Rajput, and no one's more status-conscious than a fraud, but back in my boyhood a true Rajput like Baroo, born in the sands of Jeysulmere, was so sure of his manifest superiority that he could afford to treat all sorts of people as his equals, even to the extent of eating their food and drinking their water.

So it wasn't a matter of my being accepted by Pyari Lal and his family so much as my accepting them – though that's not the way I looked at it back then. Wherever we stood on the ladder, they were a family and I was alone, and my caste couldn't make up for that.

During the next three years I led a life that millions of boys will lead for as long as it pleases Vishnu to preserve us, and any of them could tell you more about peasant life than I ever could: the struggles, the rituals, the timeless cycle, and all the rest of it. What matters now is where my life departed from the well-worn path.

For instance, you should know what happened to me on the last day of Dusserah toward the end of the monsoon that year. The object of worship during Dusserah varies from place to place, but in Bhondaripur it was a local goddess named Hahrti. I'm still not sure what it was about Hahrti that made her a goddess. She seems to have thrown something into a well — herself, maybe — to save her father from Mahratta soldiers (who, in the old days, used to celebrate Dusserah by wiping out a village). But then there was something about a sadhu in the story, too, and a parrot, and a donkey with an aching tooth, and I never knew for sure how it all fitted together. All I knew was that the festival meant a lot of singing and storytelling, and an improvement in the fare.

Hahrti's effigy was sculpted out of clay and decorated with dyes and whitewash on the outer wall of the women's hut, and for nine days it was the center of all the festivities, some of which extended long into the night. I joined in all the children's games and rites, but when it came time to approach the effigy to make offerings of flower petals and grain, I always held back, for there was something about her face that scared me, especially by lamplight.

On the tenth day her head was carefully removed, placed in a water jar, and floated out onto the surface of the buffalo pond, and as the women shrieked and waved their hands in ritual alarm, the boys of the village, myself included, threw stones at the jar until it finally broke and sank. There were some jokes made about my dunking almost a year before, and then, as the women broke into songs of thanks, everyone turned and marched back to the village.

If you haven't surmised by now that it had been Hahrti's face and not my mother's that had roused me from the pond's bottom, comfort yourself that I didn't realize it myself until I'd nearly fallen asleep that night. I remember suddenly sitting up in bed and smiling, for if the face I'd seen had been no more than an effigy's shard then it meant that I might not be bound any longer to the whims of my mother's ghost.

And then there was the old penitent who sat all day and night in the men's courtyard, month after month, keeping his silence by the children's hut. I must have passed him a thousand times without curiosity that first year, and it wasn't until late one wet night that I finally found out who he was.

I had been awakened by a loud spattering outside the children's hut and looked out to see that the thatched overhang that sheltered the old man had sagged and formed a kind of trough from which water flowed like a silver rope upon his poor shrouded head. I remember lying back and trying to fall asleep again, but the spattering just seemed to get louder, so I finally pulled a cloth over my head and ventured forth to see what I could do.

I tried to get the old man to move out of the way, for it was only a matter of shifting him a few inches back. But he seemed rooted to the spot, so I began to dart around the courtyard in the pouring rain, searching for something to cover the trough. At last I found a stray shake from a neighbor's roof, and setting a ladder in the courtyard mud, I climbed up and worked the little plank into the sagging thatch so that it jutted beyond the overhang and the water began to fall a foot in front of where the old man sat.

Congratulating myself on another good deed done, I began to climb down, but suddenly I felt something close on my ankles, and with the gooseflesh rising on my sopping back I looked down to see the old man's sickly, upturned face.

I wanted to scream, but managed only a strangled noise, and fell two rungs, landing with a splash on the ground. But the old man calmed me down and quietly introduced himself to me as none other than Kushal Singh, Amma's husband, Pyari Lal's father, the patriarch of the whole beleaguered family.

It took me a while to believe this, of course, for when Santosh spoke of his grandfather it was always as though he were dead, but now that I thought about it Santosh had never really said he was dead, and Amma, his wife, didn't dress like a widow, nor behave like one either.

It seems that some years back a sadhu had come to the village and cured Kushal Singh's arthritis. The holy man claimed to see something godly on Kushal Singh's forehead, and as payment for his services demanded that Kushal Singh give up all worldly things and devote the rest of his life to meditation.

The sadhu must have misread Kushal Singh's forehead, for he had never given spiritual matters much thought and left the family devotions in Amma's hands. But he was honorable, and perhaps a little weary of his toil, and so he kept his promise to the holy man, said goodbye to his family, and, lacking any desire to travel, settled down on a little wooden platform by the children's hut.

The holy life didn't suit Kushal Singh, either, for he knew little about the texts and missed his family terribly, but with the same determination with which he'd tended his crops and seen his people through drought and flood, the old man stuck to his improvised prayers and kept his silence, at least until that monsoon night.

It had been he who had watched over me those first nights, and he who'd hurled the blanket to me when I was exiled from the women's yard. The old man had taken a liking to me back when I was crazy, for his years of meditation had made him a little daft himself, and now that I'd done him a good turn he would break his silence only to speak to me.

Often I would stop on my way back from the patwari's and sit with Kushal Singh awhile as he whispered his philosophy in the night dank. He spoke rapidly, as if to make up for lost time, and liked to think he was providing me with a religious education, although most of his advice was down-to-earth and practical, with just a nod or two to the divinities.

Most of the men I knew in Bhondaripur were like that. They brought all kinds of gods and goddesses into their conversation, but mainly just as flourishes. At first I took their faith literally and struggled with its contradictions, but after a while it seemed to boil down to two sensible propositions: that the world was a divine creation, and therefore a mystery, in which one guess was as good as another; and that even if there was a hereafter it was no use fretting about it, since there was enough of heaven and hell to be had in this life.

It's hard to separate faith from habit and propriety, and I've experienced, as you will see, the strange powers of ritual, but in all my days in Bhondaripur I think I met only one village farmer who was intoxicated with religion, and everyone else thought he was crazy.

Kushal Singh tried to stick to subjects he knew something about, but sooner or later he would turn the subject to women, and since I always came to him haunted by Sakuntala's shadowy beauty I was ready to listen.

He'd divided womankind into four types, somewhat along the lines of the ancient texts but with his own special touches. He claimed that the most desirable of the four was what he called the lotus woman. She was pious and delicate and so sweet and pure that she urinated rose water (something I was sufficiently smitten to believe of Sakuntala). But it was the second type, the dove woman, whom he described with the greatest relish.

The dove woman could be vain sometimes, and mischievous, too, but her physical charms were so considerable that no man in his right mind would begrudge her little faults. Kushal Singh never tired of describing the dove woman, part by part, and though he had a weakness for similes which, in the aggregate, created images of fruits, vegetables, gems, planets, and livestock all heaped together, I learned a lot from him about the female anatomy and thus was spared, on my wedding night, some of the usual rude surprises. Kushal Singh had regarded Amma, in her youth, as a dove woman, and I suppose he'd culled most of his descriptions from his memories of her, but it was always cautionary for me to look upon her afterward as she blew water through her nose in the morning, say, or cleaned her vacant gums with a stick.

The third type was the scrub woman. Cold, courteous, and parsimonious, she had crooked toes and breasts like thorns and could hold a grudge her whole life long. And finally there was the elephant woman: as strong, docile, and hardworking as her name-sake, and almost as tall and homely.

Kushal Singh had four categories of men worked out too – the hare, the buck, the bull, and the horse – but he gave them more latitude than the women. For instance, a bull man, though he was ideally suited to the scrub woman, could marry a dove woman if he insisted, but on no account could an elephant woman marry a hare, a buck, or even a bull, as they were all above her station.

If I don't seem to take Kushal Singh seriously enough when I recollect him it's only because I'm old enough now to be the father of the Kushal Singh I knew. Back then I put a lot of stake in what he told me and worried that when I grew up I might become a bull man or a horse man and thus, for yet another reason, remain an unsuitable husband for the patwari's precious flower.

CHAPTER

31

Though I accepted Kushal Singh as my guru, I looked elsewhere, and hungrily, for a father. I admired Pyari Lal, of course, but of Kushal Singh's three sons I liked Channa the best, and whenever the families gathered I always sat among his children.

Channa was a homely man with a low brow and deep lines that ran from the corners of his eyes down to the hollows of his cheeks like extinct rivers to a vanished sea. I always imagined I could read his thoughts by tracking the courses of those lines, for he had the kind of grave and empathetic face into which you could read whatever you liked.

As a boy he'd crippled his leg by falling off his father's bullock cart and crushing his right shin under one of its great wheels. The bone had never healed correctly, and now there was an angle to his shin, almost like a second knee, which twisted his foot inward and gave him a hitched and rolling gait.

He was even-tempered, and his silences had a heavy authority about them, even as he deferred to Pyari Lal's judgment, but once every few months he would sink into a black mood and limp off into the countryside, disappearing for two or three days and then returning, always during a morning meal, mysteriously refreshed and cheerful. Those of us who loved him ascribed his melancholy to his crippled leg; but that's the worst thing about such an impairment – people think it explains everything.

I was less like a son to him than a nephew – another man's seed, another man's pride – but I hoped for more. I longed to elicit the same fond grin he flashed at Santosh when we returned in the afternoon and ran the herd into the pond, even wished for some of the same terse scoldings he gave his other children.

But how could I have expected more from Channa when I wouldn't give up my visits to Mangal Singh, his worst enemy? Sometimes I would catch Channa watching me with a wary squint as I left the compound for the patwari's house, but he never tried to stop me nor even ask me what my business was with Mangal Singh. If he had asked I probably would have told him that I was obliged to pay the patwari my respects out of courtesy to Baroo Singh: and if I'd asked myself I would have answered that I was only protecting my secrets and trying to be near Sakuntala.

But my visits meant more than that, for much as I wanted to be like Channa, Santosh, and the others, my visits always revealed how different I was. The truth was that however sweet my village years had been, they still hadn't cured me of my mother's pride, and no matter how hard I tried with the herd and goad to keep my past at bay, I knew in my bones and dreams that I had a destiny to contend with and a father to find.

My world had shrunk to a few miles of red earth and stone stretching only from the distant lights of Gwalior to the tiger-haunted wallow to the east, and in such straits my sickly pride could find no worthier crucible than the patwari's regard.

There he would sit among his cushions, smug and heavy-lidded from his nightly bhang, his sparse hair greased and pinned with little bamboo splints, and his fingers busy with his toes. There I would sit before him, massaging his legs, cleaning his pens with mineral spirits, or tearing unused scraps of paper from his old notebooks and sewing them into little pads, as he held forth on the sad, doomed, wishful follies of humankind in general and peasants in particular, and I'm sorry to say that even as he slandered Channa and Pyari Lal and the rest of my would-be family I would nod and chuckle and shake my head.

We rarely discussed our little secret, for Baroo would return when he returned and there was no use in my pinning my hopes on him until he did. It was the secret that brought Mangal Singh and me together, but a shared secret is a frail bond, for the better it's kept the sooner each confidant suspects the other of harboring some other, even more insidious secret.

Mangal Singh seemed sure that I knew as little about Baroo Singh as I claimed, but he suspected me of keeping things from him about Amma's family, which he imagined to be as prone as he to schemes and calculations. But no matter how hard he poked and prodded for new intelligence, I passed along only the most useless stuff, for my sycophancy had its limits, after all, and besides, after a day with the herd I had few real confidences to betray.

And for my part I suspected there was more to our secret than Mangal Singh had told me and more to the document he still kept hidden away in his padlocked box. He would even say as much some evenings when he'd imbibed too liberally and sleep was about to overtake him (preceded always by a volley of peculiar chirping burps). 'Poor Balbeer,' he murmured one night as his eyes closed, 'you don't know the half of it.'

He tried to pretend that I meant no more to him than a spy or a serving boy, but my information, as I say, was always meagre and his own servant could have accomplished the petty tasks he devised for me. The truth was that Mangal Singh was a lonely little man with a tortured soul, a pariah despite all his power and privilege, and I was his only friend.

I must have believed that my feeling for Sakuntala was a noble thing to which I could sacrifice a little virtue here and there without doing my honor any permanent harm. But my passion for Sakuntala was born of only a few glimpses of her in the gloom of her father's house and was yet starved for a single utterance from her perfect lips. However much she made my heart pound and my mouth go dry and all the rest of it, it wasn't love I felt for her but greed.

I couldn't know that my true love slept not five yards from me in the children's hut, nor could I recognize her when she brought my morning meal. To me Ahalya was just another of the children, though her devotion was plain enough to everyone else. Channa scolded her and Santosh teased her for being so forward, but nothing could discourage Ahalya. She called me Balho, like a lover, and when Santosh and I returned with the herd, she would meet me with a pitcher of well water.

Maybe if I'd answered her now and then with more than a grunt and a dismissive wave or returned her gaze as I ate from the bowl she brought me I would have seen that she boasted, even at the tender age of thirteen, many of the virtues her grandfather attributed to the dove woman, though later, as I got to know her, she had some of the scrub and elephant about her too.

If I responded at all it was by bristling at her attentions or barking back at anyone who teased me about her devotion, but her love seemed to feed on my indifference. I should have understood this, since it was very much like my arrangement with Sakuntala, but I didn't seem to believe I deserved a girl's love and concluded from that conviction that any girl who judged me worthy didn't deserve mine. It doesn't make much sense now that I spell it out, but there's no reasoning with a callow heart.

When your past seeks you out it can take any form it likes. In my case it was a great whirring cloud that hopped in from the barren East in the early spring of 1872, when I was almost fourteen years old.

By then Santosh had married and joined his father in the fields, and Jagdish, one of Pyari Lal's sons, had taken Santosh's place beside me. I had grown tall enough to see over a buffalo's shoulder and old enough to spill my seed in my sleep. Strangers passing through Bhondaripur would have been hard pressed to single me out from among Amma's grandchildren, for my flesh was saturated with the same fine red dust and the same harsh sun had hollowed out my face.

I was put in charge of the herd and might have enjoyed my newfound authority if Jagdish hadn't been such tiresome company. He thought the world of me and gave me every exalted title when he addressed me, but he seemed to think the world of everybody and could not stop talking – not when I begged him, not when I commanded him, not even when I tackled him once and stuffed his mouth with dust.

One day, just to get out of earshot of his babble, I climbed to the top of a ridge a mile or so west of Bhondaripur. It was a clear day and from my altitude the blue sky seemed dark and rich. Off to the west the city of Gwalior lay like scattered dice at the foot of Scindhia's fortress, and little puffs of pink dust rose from the carts on the country roads skirting the deep green fields.

Except for a hailstorm that had destroyed a portion of the cane fields, the previous monsoon had been merciful, and indeed the seasons had been kind to Bhondaripur every year since I'd arrived. This day, as I sat sighing with relief in my lofty solitude, it seemed that the good years would go on forever.

And then came Jagdish's hateful voice tripping up the stony

slope. 'Balbeer my brother! Oh, you there! Balbeer!' he called in an insistent whine whose recollection still draws my shoulders up around my ears.

I think I threw something down at him and scurried behind a rock, but his imperturbable call drew nearer.

'Hello-oh! Balbeer! Balbeer Maharaj!'

'Go away!'

'I can't, maharaj,' he piped back. 'I've got something to show you.'

I came out from behind my rock with my goad raised and shouted down at him, 'Get back with the herd! I ordered you to stay with the herd!'

'And I did, maharaj,' he said cheerfully, obliviously, as he reached the top. 'But look,' he said, pointing toward Bhondaripur. 'Don't you see?'

'I'm not going to talk with you,' I said, rearing back as if to strike. 'You go away!'

But Jagdish kept pointing and staring eastward as if I hadn't spoken, and throwing down my goad in defeat I wheeled around and followed the line of his arm into the distance.

I didn't see anything out of the ordinary at first, just the village fields full of harvest-ready wheat and mustard laid out like a map in the sunlight. But then something seemed to speckle my vision, like motes of dust, and the view grew strangely dappled.

I blinked my eyes to clear them, but the specks grew darker and something very much like a cloud, but busier and more diffuse, passed over the village, settling on it like cinders.

'You see, maharaj? What did Jagdish tell you? Locusts! Now do you see why Jagdish had to find you? Jagdish wouldn't leave the herd for nothing. Those are locusts down there. You know what that means? It — '

I knew. 'Shut up, Jagdish,' I said, retrieving my goad and running down the hillside. 'We've got to get back.'

But Jagdish kept up his chatter all the way down, and not until we'd driven the herd to the outskirts of the swarm and a stray locust whirred into his mouth did his babble finally stop.

The light turned yellow and the still fields seemed to crawl, and from every direction rank little breezes blew as the locusts flapped about. The air hummed and buzzed and the ground hissed and crackled all around us. The locusts were everywhere I looked, hundreds to every stalk of wheat, crawling one on top of another until an entire teeming column toppled over, still gnawing on the leaves and kernels. I walked among them in a daze. I'd never seen so much of anything: not stars nor raindrops nor blades of grass.

Then a single locust landed on my shoulder and clung to my flesh with its rasping feet and fixed its empty eye upon me. I cried out as if I'd been stung and slapped it away and began to stamp about, swinging my goad around me in a blind panic. They crunkled and oozed underfoot, hopped about my waist, plucked at my dhoti with their little green jaws, entangled their barbed legs in my hair.

The buffalo ran ahead and dived into the pond to escape the swarm as I marched around in aimless loops. I came upon Channa standing in the middle of the field, striking at the ground around him with a hoe, guarding a single stalk, and when I called to him and he looked up at me his eyes were filled with tears. It looked as though all the people of the village were out beating at the hordes with whatever they could find: sticks, planks, baskets, and cloth. Kites dove down through the mass and caught locusts on the wing, and here and there I came upon bloated crows with their beaks agape, so stuffed they could only flap and bump along the ground like chickens.

Ramesh's youngest son, not yet four years old, rose up in my path, covered with locusts, and beat at them with his tiny fists. I tried to help him, but he screamed at me as if possessed and ran off toward the village. I was about to chase after him when I came upon an old man lying face down on the bristling ground. I slapped the locusts from his back and turned him over. He was Kushal Singh, summoned by the calamity from his sacred roost and lying now where his loath old legs had failed him.

'Ah, Balbeer,' he said with a shamefaced look. 'Praise god.'

So I dragged him home, and though we passed rows of women and children working their way through the fields as if reaping a quick and desperate harvest, no one saw us and I got him back with his secret safe.

We killed the locusts by the hundreds, but it was all no use. The swarm left in its own good time, when there was nothing left in the village fields but a few heartbroken men standing motionless among the naked spines of the winter crop, watching the yellow cloud fly over the ridge.

The sky turned blue again and all was quiet. People began to stumble about, snatching up whatever usable scrap of vegetation they could find amid the dead locusts and broken stalks. Ramesh glared around him to find somebody to blame and finally focussed on a young sweeper who'd ventured onto the forbidden fields to join in the fight. Ramesh came at him with a hoe and chased him around the field, and he might have killed him, too, I think, if it hadn't been for a scream that suddenly rose from the buffalo pond.

Ramesh stopped in his tracks and dropped his hoe, and we all ran over to where the scream had now become a low wail. There, by the locust-littered pond, Ramesh's wife sat beside the still figure of her only son, drowned in his flight from the locust swarm.

Late in the afternoon the dead locusts began to stink along the torn rows, and Ramesh and his family set off by bullock cart to consign his little son to the river. As the village's shadow crept across the ruined fields, people sat wherever they found themselves, exhausted, their arms and legs smeared with locusts' grime, staring off across the waste. Villages not a mile away had been untouched by the swarm, and we could see the crops of Sonsa to the south, all green and gold and thriving.

Jagdish and I drove the buffalo out of the pond and were tethering them to their posts when the patwari's old servant summoned me to his master's gate. There Mangal Singh met me with a brisk nod, handed me his satchel, and led me out to the fields to assess the damage. You might suppose he was distressed by the calamity, but he seemed to take it all calmly and made his notes and calculations in a neat and steady hand.

'Here's where we're going to have to keep after these people,' he said, examining a naked stalk. 'They're going to just give up on the whole harvest if we aren't careful.'

I was ashamed to be seen in the patwari's company and longed to return to the family, but the night took forever to fall. As Mangal Singh led me along the nibbled stems and locust husks I kept gazing back to where Channa and Santosh sat together like collapsed old men.

Late that night, Mangal Singh led me into Pyari Lal's compound and called the family out of their sleeping huts.

Pyari Lal emerged with a lamp whose light made the pale scattered corpses of the locusts glow all around us. While the family gathered I stood sideways to the patwari and tried to keep my face in the shadow, as though I just happened to find myself standing next to Mangal Singh, as though his satchel had fallen into my hands from out of the starry sky.

Mangal Singh held his notes flat so as to catch the light and announced his findings. The damage was bad, he said in his piping voice, but he knew it would please everyone to hear that it wasn't as bad as they probably thought.

There were some groans from beyond the lamp, for in the upside-down world of tenant farming the grimmer a patwari's assessment was the better.

Mangal Singh pursed his lips and cleared his throat and continued to speak without raising his eyes from his notes. He reckoned that a third of the harvest remained to be reaped – from which he intended to collect the zemindar's usual percentage.

Pyari Lal hushed his family and spoke. The assessment was preposterous, he said quietly. There wasn't a tenth of the harvest left, much less a third. The zemindar's share would leave them with nothing.

Mangal Singh shrugged. He sympathized, he told them. He knew it would mean a lot of hard work on everyone's part, but he was just the zemindar's servant. How could he presume to give Shri Baroo Singh's rightful share away?

Pyari Lal asked Mangal Singh to base the zemindar's cut on whatever they collected. Baroo Singh was a fair man; he would agree to that.

And would that he could be here to agree to that, said Mangal Singh, but the zemindar had entrusted his affairs to his patwari. Now, if Pyari Lal and his family didn't want to reap a thorough harvest, that was their business, but they would be hurting only themselves.

And if they refused to harvest another speck of grain? Ramesh stepped forward to ask, his eyes brimming with tears for his poor drowned son. What would Baroo's patwari say to that?

Mangal Singh gave Ramesh a pitying look and shook his head. 'I grieve for your loss, Ramesh,' he said, 'but we mustn't let our tragedies get the best of us.' He looked back at Pyari Lal. '*You* know what would have to happen then, don't you? All your debts would come due. And my zemindar would have to find another family to work his fields. You don't want that, do you? Nobody wants that. Why do away with a long and fruitful association just because your brother's afraid of a little hard work?'

I held back as the patwari turned and walked out of the compound, wanting to throw his satchel after him, but when he commanded me to follow I obeyed and felt the family's gaze burn along my back.

After the patwari finally dismissed me for the night, I crept back into the compound like a thief. But just as I reached the door to the children's hut, Kushal Singh grabbed my ankle and pulled me to the ground.

'The time has come,' he said now with a scolding look.

'To sleep,' I snapped back, rubbing my ankle.

'No, Balbeer,' Kushal Singh said with one finger upraised. 'To choose.'

And he was right. It had. But I glared back at him and pulled myself away and spent the rest of the night thrashing about under my blanket. If I dreamed at all it was of Channa calling to me from one dark corner of the slumbering hut, Sakuntala beckoning from the other.

CHAPTER

32

In the morning I awoke with a start and acted thenceforward like someone who'd come to a decision, though for the life of me I didn't know what it was. I dressed deliberately, with a lean grace, like a hunter, and led Jagdish and the herd into the countryside while the light was only a faint promise over the eastern ridge.

A mile or so from Bhondaripur I let the nodding herd feed on roadside scrub and told Jagdish that I was going to have to leave him for the morning, promising to return to fetch him in the afternoon. Naturally, he wanted to know why, but I wouldn't say (and in any case couldn't say), and assuring him he'd be safe if he stuck to the roadside, I finally shook free, and in a great arc that took me around Sonsa and brought me within sight of Morar I stole back to Bhondaripur.

As I crept along the bramble boundaries of the decimated fields I didn't know what it was I was stalking, but I was nonetheless stealthy, silent, all business. The sun was up by then and the fields were full of people with scythes, chopping at the strange translucence of the ruined crops. It was as grim a harvest as it was meagre; not one woman sang, not one man spoke, and the littlest children sat listlessly whimpering here and there among the littered rows.

I hid for a time behind a heap of rocks sheltering one of the village shrines, and when my path was clear I darted across the crapping fields and tiptoed in among the huts. By now I was burning to know, as you may be, just what it was I was up to. But I didn't even know my destination until I reached the patwari's gate.

The carved door was bolted from within, but I made quick work of it by twisting a stick through a knothole, and opening the door a crack I squeezed into the courtyard. I looked for the patwari's servant, then remembered that every morning before his master awoke he slept in the storeroom among Baroo's sacks of grain. Now only the patwari's regal cow took notice of me as I slipped across the courtyard.

Up to then, as I said, I'd hoped that I'd eluded my destiny, but now it seemed to have me in its thrall again, for though my heart was galloping beneath my breast and the hairs bristled on the back of my neck I kept moving forward.

I ducked through the door and into the little hallway, rubbing my eyes to accustom them to the dark. Now what? I asked myself, and in answer my feet took me past the first shuttered rooms. Keeping to the darkest shadows, I slipped into the patwari's chambers and found him there asleep amid his papers. He slept like a child, all doubled over with his little feet pointy-toed, and though flies were feeding on the oil in his hair he slumbered soundly, wheezing and blustering in steady alternation.

I stood staring down at him and wondered if I still might not have to choose, for what if I were gently to waken Mangal Singh and persuade him to lower his assessment? But before I could gain the courage to disturb him, his little padlocked box caught my eye.

Mangal Singh had carelessly left it unfastened, and the brass housing of the pendulous lock gleamed in the little stripe of sunlight that had crept through the window shutter. I took a deep breath then and moved toward it as toward a beckoning star, and raising the lid of the little studded chest, I knelt down to explore its contents.

The lid opened to more lids and drawers, for the box had many compartments, in the largest of which I found the patwari's book of title records. I merely glanced at it for a moment, squinting at the figures piled along each page in the patwari's cramped little hand. In other compartments I found diaries, scrolls, registers of wells, fees, inspections, and the like, but I had to grope all the way to the bottom before I finally found the prize I now knew I'd been seeking all along: the scroll with the black thread that Mangal Singh had flourished five years before.

Mangal Singh groaned and stirred his toes a little as I untied the black thread and spread the scroll flat out on the floor. It appeared to be a legal document of some kind, with a wax seal pressed upon one corner, but if it was in English, as Mangal Singh had said, it was in a script I'd never seen before. I concentrated all my powers of recall on the lines of scrawl, but every word seemed slipslapped and contrary. It had been five years since I'd read any English, but even so, how could I have forgotten everything that Weems had taught me?

Well, as a matter of fact I hadn't, for I finally realized that in my haste I had placed the scroll upside down, and switching it around I found after a few false starts that I could read most of it straight through.

I was so pleased with this that I hardly noticed my own name when I first came upon it, nor Baroo's, but when my name came up again and then again the sense of the thing began to penetrate, for it was a will: the last will and testament of Baroo Singh himself, written on the eve of his hanging and bequeathing to me, his adopted son, all his worldly goods.

I read the scroll again and again and ever more recklessly, until I was reading it aloud and with one hand beating on the floor to the rhythm of it. And when Sakuntala came in from the kitchen and gasped at me I looked up at her and grinned, for no shock at Baroo's death nor anger at the patwari's treachery could measure up to the joy of my discovery that I, Balbeer Rao, was now her zemindar.

'Sakuntala,' I said, thus addressing her for the first time. 'Sakuntala! Now we can marry!'

But she stared down at me with perplexity, and her veil fell from her head, revealing her ears, which were not her best feature. And now she raised her voice in a shrieking spray of base oaths and spittle, thus awakening her father.

He sat up with a grunt and blinked at me, and seeing all his secrets spread out on the floor, he too began to shriek.

I snatched up the scroll, and as I leaped over his bleary form Sakuntala hurled a platter at me, but it whirred harmlessly past my brow, and I dashed down the hallway and out into the light of day.

'Channaji!' I began to shout as I raced to the fields. 'Channaji! Look!'

Everyone stood up from his labor and glared at me, for villagers hate surprises.

'Channaji!' I said, coming upon him at last in the mustard field, hefting a basket of torn pods.

'What are *you* doing here?' he wanted to know. 'Your place is with the herd.'

'No, no,' I said, catching my breath. 'You don't understand.'

Channa now stared past me, and I looked back to see Mangal Singh hurrying barefoot toward us and shaking his little fist. 'Thief!

Thief!' he was shrieking in much the same voice as his daughter's. 'Oh, you nasty little *thief*!'

'Channaji,' I said, opening the scroll and pushing it toward him. 'Look. This is the will. Baroo Singh's will. He's *dead*, Channaji! *Hanged*! And he's left his land to me!'

But Channa was a deliberate man, and everything was happening much too fast to suit him. Of course, the scroll meant nothing to him, for he couldn't read Hindi or Urdu, let alone English. But when Mangal Singh caught up with us and demanded it back, Channa knew enough not to give it to him, nor to let the patwari beat me with his satchel.

Channa asked me questions about where I'd gotten the will and how it was I could read it, the answers to which you already know, and though Mangal Singh ridiculed my claims, Channa seemed to see the anguished guilt behind the patwari's sneer.

Still, I did have to prove to Channa that I could read English and wasn't making it up as I went along. So I stood very straight and read it aloud to them all with such precision and conviction that everyone else – for by now the entire village had crowded around us – believed me. But then Mangal Singh pointed out that for all they knew I could have been reciting a memorized string of gibberish as my eyes marched from line to line. This was far-fetched, of course, but possible, and everyone became greatly consternated.

But Channa, though he was illiterate, was canny in his fashion, and devised a little test. He had me read aloud in English again, pointing with my finger at each word as I came to it, while unknown to me he memorized the location and sound (for sound was all it was to him) of a single phrase. When I was finished reading he pointed to this phrase and had me read it to him again. This I did, and when Channa heard me utter the same sounds as before, he bowed down to his new zemindar.

Pyari Lal followed suit, though a little stiffly, for I had chosen his younger brother and not him to adjudicate the matter, and Ramesh bowed too. And finally Santosh dropped down before I could stop him and touched my feet.

I suppose the patwari could have clung to his deception a little longer by claiming the will was a fake or at least demanding proof that I understood what I'd read, but Mangal Singh capitulated, pushing forward to swear his allegiance. He claimed that he'd merely been sparing me my awesome responsibilities. Hadn't he proved his good intentions by teaching me accounting and treating me like a son?

'But I would have none of this, of course, and declared the crop a total loss. Whatever the family could gather it could keep, but though I knew that he'd tried to cheat me I accepted his vows of fealty, for I was zemindar now and could afford to be magnanimous.

Such was the clamor and jubilation that afternoon that it was almost dusk by the time I remembered to send someone after Jagdish and the herd, and it wasn't until that night in the men's courtyard as everyone sat watching me feast upon Amma's best eggplant curry with garlands heaped beside me that I finally contemplated my benefactor's fate.

I asked if they knew why Baroo Singh had been hanged, and the family hemmed and hawed awhile, exchanging furtive glances, until Channa finally gave voice to what they'd only dared to whisper: that their zemindar had been the last of the great chieftains of the homicidal brotherhood of Thugs – a strangler of scores, maybe hundreds, of innocent travellers, and a fugitive from Feringhee justice ever since the Devil's Wind.

Now, as Baroo's heir I was bound to disbelieve his guilt, but even as I berated Channa and the others for believing such a thing, my belly squirmed and fluttered and I glimpsed Baroo Singh smiling down at me through the gloaming, with the pit of his eye opening like the lid to a tomb.

In turn Pyari Lal asked me what I'd been to Baroo. Was I his son? His grandson? And in the hush I told them I was neither, only a waif he'd adopted on the Ganga. I couldn't bring myself to tell them about Cawnpore and Bastard Bhavan and all the rest of it, only that I'd set out with my servant for a great westward journey, and the mystery of it so enchanted everyone that as I finished my meal they watched me eat as if I were some exotic beast whose every move was wonderful.

That night I slept in the children's hut for the last time, and though I rose at dawn as usual to herd the buffalo I was stopped along the lane by Santosh, who, diving to my feet again, begged me to allow him to take my place beside Jagdish. I tried to return to my bed, but when I got back I found Ramesh restringing it out in the courtyard, and when I tried to sit among the children to await my morning meal I was ushered out to a charpoy in the men's courtyard to eat my breakfast in regal solitude. In fact, I wasn't allowed to do anything for myself all morning, for every time I turned around there would be one of the brothers' wives waiting on me, or Ahalya with her eyes ashine.

I began to realize that I'd struck a bargain to be zemindar, trading all the little freedoms for my newfound power and privilege. I gazed imploringly at Kushal Singh as the women bustled around me, but he stared off with a hurt look, as if I'd abandoned him forever.

After my meal the men took me to the little house Baroo had occupied during his occasional visits. It was no palace. Baroo's sojourns had been brief and his tastes simple. It was constructed of stone with a tile roof, though with none of the Saracenic flourishes of the patwari's house. There were two small rooms and a verandah in the rear that led out to a little yard bounded by the patwari's compound on one side and the wall of an animal pen on the other, connected together by a low stone fence with a wooden gate which, in turn, opened out to Baroo's mustard fields.

The men struck the padlock from the door and pried open the window shutters, and as they set me and my bed out on the verandah the women went to work. They resurfaced the walls and floors with dung and clay, daubed little whitewashed images around the door-way, and singing something about new souls and the phases of the moon, they removed Baroo's effigy of Kali from an alcove in the back room and replaced it with a terracotta figure of Ganesha, benign and squat, still wet from the chitrakar's brush.

When the women were done and the sweeper had finished cleaning out the yard I called for the patwari to bring me his books, and we went over them together as the sun descended through the settling dust. On the maps of Baroo's fields and in the registry of title I saw the scratched-out places where Mangal Singh had written in his own name and left it there, hoping it would thus remain until five years' time had given it legal sanction. He seemed so relieved that the game was over that I now pretended not to notice; like his neighbors he didn't take easily to change, even change for the better, and felt more comfortable now in his familiar role. I was enough of a villager by then not to expect too much of a patwari's honor, and enough of a zemindar to know that I would need his services.

I discussed with him how we might go about easing the village's burden during the next lean months. He pretended to think this was a wonderful idea, but cautioned me against being too generous, spoiling my tenants, letting them take advantage of me, allowing personal feelings to interfere with business, and so forth. This made me all the more adamant, and I reviewed the register of debts, forgiving the astronomically compounded ones and deferring repayment on much of the rest until the next good harvest came along.

Mangal Singh looked as though he were about to weep as I struck this debt and that off the columns he'd built up over the decades, but when all his arguments had failed he bore with me, trying to soothe away his grief and horror with petty revisions in his arithmetic, turning in sorrow to his calculations like a mendicant to his mantra.

Before the patwari agreed to accompany me to the family's compound to announce these new measures, he demanded that I permit him to lend me some suitable clothing, for my dhoti and shirt were no longer seemly. I protested that if they were good enough for my tenants they were good enough for me, but I've always had my mother's weakness for clothes, and so when Mangal Singh argued that I would in fact shame the family in my herder's clothing, just as a ragged king shames his subjects, I gave in. His servant brought a selection of robes to my verandah, and Mangal Singh laid them out before me with a Kashmiri's flourishes. I chose a blue robe with ivory buttons and embroidered cuffs, and with a pained look, for it was one of his favorites, Mangal Singh asked that I accept it as a gift.

I caused quite a stir in my new attire as we walked along the village lanes, and by the time I reached the compound, children had already alerted the brothers, and now everyone, women and children included, was waiting for me as I walked through the gate.

They seemed taken aback by my new blue robe, and though they kept their distance from me now, as if I were a leper or a king, I looked around at them fondly. These people had transformed me from a mad, emaciated little city waif to a village youth with his feet on the ground, and now as their zemindar I was going to reward them.

I suppose I may not have been trying to give back so much as buy something more, for I still longed for the one thing of theirs that I didn't now possess: a true place in their family.

I asked everyone to be seated and tried to tell them what they all meant to me, but Channa gave me a disapproving and embarrassed look, and so I cut myself off and took the register from the patwari's hand. Because I owed them so much, I told them, I was going to cancel the family's debts, and with that I tore the pages from Mangal Singh's book and flung them into the air.

In a twinkling I thus gave up half of my estate and lifted a hundred years of debt from the family's shoulders. It was a grand gesture, and you would think they might have at least given a little cheer. But they just stared back at me. That I was a fool seemed plain enough to old Kushal Singh, who sat behind the others in his accustomed place, slowly shaking his head, but Channa gave me a pitying look, as if I'd lost my mind.

I was so rattled by the continuing silence that I heard myself blurting something about sharing my grain with them until the next harvest, but this only succeeded in reducing the patwari to tears beside me.

I stood around for a little while, waiting for someone to invite me to dinner, perhaps, or to share the brothers' hookah, though I would have been just as happy if they'd merely let me tend their hookah for them, like a son.

Pyari Lal finally stood up and said only, 'The zemindar is too good to us,' and so I finally turned and left.

Ahalya followed me as I returned to my exile, but Amma called her back after a few paces, and I proceeded alone with the whimpering patwari.

CHAPTER

33

I won't claim that I wasn't a little disappointed in the family for not taking me to its bosom that day, and it did seem pathetic that on my second night as zemindar I was reduced, for want of a better offer, to dining with the patwari. Mangal Singh cheered up immediately when I accepted his invitation, and by the time we reached his house his eyes were dry. He was heartened by my disappointment and thus emboldened, as he shared his cushioned pallet with me, to inquire about my future plans. I couldn't tell what he was driving at until I noticed, as the night wore on, that he kept nodding toward his daughter and leering at me hopefully.

I had already blurted my intentions to her two days before, but either in all the confusion she hadn't heard me or she hadn't yet told her father about it, for from his sly winks and insinuations (about how I was a man of substance now and should be thinking about my posterity) I could tell that he believed he'd thought of it himself.

Now, marrying Sakuntala had been my dream ever since I'd first laid eyes on her, but as so often happens when a dream's within reach, this one seemed to lose some of its mystery, and thus its power. Besides, I didn't like being rushed to any conclusion, even one as sweet as this, and so to shut him up I told him that I'd already made some plans, and thanking him for his hospitality I rose to leave.

'You won't do anything *rash* now, boy,' Mangal Singh sputtered. 'That is,' he said with a wince, remembering our changed relationship, 'I trust you've considered all the facets of the matter. If you need any assistance,' he said, folding his hands together and shuffling after me toward the door, 'I shall always be at your service.'

And so he was. An hour wouldn't go by during the next few days when he wasn't consulting with me about the accounts, arranging my meals, ordering water jars from the potter, or bringing me something for the house. The furnishings he brought were ramshackle, and I suppose they must have been items he'd replaced in his own house with furnishings he'd long ago stolen from Baroo's:

a low chair, a bathing stool, a moldy bamboo blind for the window. He tried to find a servant for me, but after a day's audition I dismissed the dimwitted boys he brought by and refused even to try the ones who looked smart enough to serve as his spies.

He became so desperate to prevent my putting my pretended plans into action that he actually camped himself in my compound, setting up his desk and pallet outside my door, and so it's no wonder that the family kept its distance. For all I know he may have shooed them away. I know Ahalya tried to see me, though I saw her only from a distance as she passed across the mustard fields in front of my verandah. But I saw nothing of the brothers or Santosh, nor did even Jagdish come by to chat.

No matter how often I spurned him, Mangal Singh grew more determined than ever to acquire through his daughter what he hadn't been able to gain by deception. When I dined with him, as I'm afraid I often did, I would always find Sakuntala dressed in her festival clothes with her little arms encased in silver bangles and her palms and soles daubed with henna. This wasn't exactly lost on me, for though I had been put off by the imperfect projection of her ears and the harsh pitch of her shriek, she remained the most beautiful woman I'd ever seen. But whatever Sakuntala accomplished with her charms, Mangal Singh undid with his persistence, smacking his lips over her curries and extolling the delights of having a woman around the house.

One night, some weeks after I came into my legacy, the patwari insisted that I join him in a draught of bhang. It tasted foul but its effect seemed benign, for when Mangal Singh again tried to turn my loneliness into bitterness by praising my generosity and damning the family's ingratitude, all the while dropping his heavy hints about Sakuntala's nubility, I merely smiled and took my leave.

I started for my little house, but the breeze was so sweet and the stars so crisp and bountiful that I continued past my gate and strolled awhile along the lanes. I stopped to loosen the bonds of the buffalo Jagdish had left tethered too tightly, and under a tree near the potter's house I found the chowkidor sneaking some sleep behind some newly turned jars. The huts I passed seemed to heave like the chests of sleeping men, and the lane before me fell off into the dark like the path of a dream.

At the family's gate I stopped to peer into the men's yard, deserted now but for Kushal Singh. I could tell from the angle of the old man's head that he was sound asleep, wrapped in his blanket against the night chill, and as I slowly made my way home in the silver light from the broad arch of stars it seemed that in all the world I was the only soul astir. Entering the dark of my house, I wondered if my father had been a chowkidor, an owl, or the shy, waning moon.

I fell into bed and seemed to drift off before I'd drawn my first breath, and when my door blew open and a scent of jasmine flew in along a silver shaft I knew I was already dreaming. I hadn't seen Sakuntala in any of my dreams since I'd stolen my legacy from her father's strongbox, but now here she was again, a spangled silhouette approaching from the doorway.

That her clothes fell from her piece by piece with each footstep I ascribed to the spell of the patwari's bhang, and as she drew back my blanket and touched me here and there with fingers slick with oil, I vowed to take a swig or two every night henceforward.

She took me in both her hands and knelt over me on the narrow bed, her hair swinging forward and trailing like a cape across my belly. I had been having such dreams for some years by then, and knew them to disintegrate just as the strength began to drain from my legs and coil in my loins. But tonight, even after I'd spent myself among her busy fingers, the dream retained its substance. There was a sheen on her upraised buttocks and her skin gave off a scent of sugar and dust, and when I finally grasped her arm to stop her quick, persistent tugging I could feel her flesh and the muscle and bone beneath.

She stood then, and moving delicately, as if the swell of her hips and breasts were heavy blooms and her legs their fragile stems, she fetched a towel and cleansed me. When she was done she backed along the dim beam of moonlight, stooping here and there to retrieve her clothes.

I lay as still as I could, not making the slightest sound for fear I might awaken myself. At the door she wrapped a blanket around her shoulders and turned as if to speak, but then there was a noise beyond the threshold, a sharp expulsion of air like a sneeze or a belch, and with one step she vanished into the night like a plume of smoke.

All night my bed seemed to tilt and turn, and I dreamed it was a raft on a headlong river, along whose bank my mother ran and stumbled, waving her arms and shouting. I raised my head to try to make out what she was saying when the roar of the river rose and I turned to see a cataract impending.

I hurtled into daylight through the misty spray, and sitting up in bed to catch my breath I could tell from the shadows that I'd slept through most of the morning.

I must have seen the towel lying by my bed where Sakuntala had dropped it, and I surely followed her footprints out the door, but I didn't give them any thought until I'd stripped down, mounted my bathing stool, and poured a jug of chill water over my head.

I wiped the water from my eyes, blinked in the morning light, started at the cawing of a crow on the patwari's wall. Still naked, and dripping water from every extremity, I stamped back to the doorway and stared down at the dusty ground. I saw my own prints, the flat-footed trail any village boy might leave, but here and there among them, and following their own path to and from my bed, were the prints of small delicate feet, joined at the threshold by a third set of prints of feet not much longer but considerably wider and favoring the toes.

'Mangal Singh!' I said aloud, and following these two sets of prints back out past the wetted dust around my bathing stool and all the way to the gate, I knew Sakuntala's visit had been no dream; Mangal Singh had led her here, commanded her inside, waited for her as she debased herself, led her home when I was spent, and following these events back to their dark origin I knew that someone must have shown her how to please me – and who else in that barren household but her dismal little father?

I donned my old clothes and marched that afternoon to the family's compound. Someone alerted Mangal Singh that I was at large, and when he saw me loose in the lanes he came chasing after me as fast as he could in his obsequious stoop. But as soon as he came within earshot I snarled at him to keep his distance, for I had something I meant to do.

'But you misjudge me!' he called after me, shrinking back to his gate. 'I only mean to serve you!'

There was the usual fuss when I rushed into the family's courtyard, but I put a stop to it by commanding everyone to sit, and when everyone had squatted down, glancing worriedly at one another, I gave a little speech.

All my life, I told them, I had wanted a family, and for the last three years I'd nearly found one. They had clothed me, fed me, taught me all the village ways. But not one among them had ever called me son. And now that I was their zemindar I seemed further from them than ever, envied and distrusted no matter what I did for them, no matter how much I gave away.

Here Pyari Lal sat up very straight and protested. Even good fortune such as mine, he said, was bound to be bittersweet, but I was a much beloved zemindar who had saved them from many hardships. There was a lot of nodding all around me, but I kept my eyes on Channa, who sighed and looked down at the ground.

Maybe so, I said, but beloved or not I was still their zemindar, and sooner or later they knew I would begin to act like one. At this Channa looked up at me and nodded.

'Where does my generosity spring from?' I asked them. 'If it's from my youth then it's doomed, and if it's from gratitude then it's bound to run dry. And what will become of us then?'

Pyari Lal blinked at me, and everyone was silent, and I confess even I had been startled by my eloquence. I told them I could do them no lasting good until our fortunes were joined, and, that said, I blurted my intentions.

I meant to have a family, I told them, and would take Ahalya for my wife.

Ahalya leaped up from among the women on the outskirts of the circle, and she looked so radiant that I had to smile, but before she could so much as gasp her grandmother yanked her veil across her face and hurried her back into the women's yard.

Pyari Lal gaped at me and Ramesh struck himself upon the forehead, but Channa stared at me gravely as he rose to his feet.

I stood too, and we faced each other as the women gabbled around us. Pyari Lal began to stammer something, but Channa raised his hand to quiet him.

'You say we taught you all our ways?' he asked with a shake of his head.

'Yes, Channaji,' I said.

'Well,' he said, 'we must have left something out, for this is no way to ask for my daughter.'

Pyari Lal gave me a conciliatory look.

'Channaji?'

'Balbeer,' Channa said (and how sweet my name sounded on his lips again), 'we have a lot to talk about.'

'Yes, Channaji,' I said.

Channa directed me to the men's hut, and there I sat with the brothers as all the rest gathered around the doorway, craning their necks to listen.

Ahalya was his hardest-working daughter, Channa said, and the apple of his eye. To part with her would be like parting with his own backbone (for all of Channa's virtues, he had no gift for metaphor). So what, exactly, could I offer as compensation?

I knew that among the Ahirs of Bhondaripur the groom paid a price for his bride, but I didn't know the going rate, so I welcomed his suggestions, and with a shy look he said two hundred pounds of grain.

'Agreed,' I replied. 'In fact, I'll make it three hundred.'

Ramesh rolled his eyes, and Pyari Lal clucked his tongue.

'No, no, no, Balbeer,' Channa said with a sigh. 'You're supposed to *bargain* with me. I'm not going to give my daughter to a fool.'

'One hundred pounds,' I said quickly.

Channa's eyes lit up. 'One hundred eighty.'

'One hundred *fifty*.'

'One hundred seventy-five pounds.'

Afraid I was giving in too early to please him, I said, 'One hundred seventy-two pounds and not one pound more.'

Channa liked that. 'Agreed,' he said. But in addition there was the traditional cash amount, and we settled on that too, bargaining our way down from his initial demand of twenty rupees to fourteen rupees and change.

Pyari Lal seemed to bristle slightly at not having a role in the negotiations so far. 'Aren't we forgetting something?' he wanted to know. 'It's bad enough you're bargaining with the groom and not the father of the groom, little brother, but has anyone thought at all about caste?'

Channa said that I'd been as good as a member of the family all these years, why bring it up now?

'Well, *you* may not care about the souls of your grandchildren,' Pyari Lal said, 'but who's going to officiate if it's a marriage out of caste?'

Channa scowled at his brother and ran his hand across his mouth.

'I hate to interfere,' Pyari Lal said sharply, and it began to occur to me that he was angry because I'd chosen Ahalya instead of one of his own daughters, 'but I say we have to consult the soothsayer.'

And so the barber was sent to fetch the jyotishi, and he set himself up on a blanket out in the courtyard with his charts and almanacs arrayed around him. This jyotishi lived on my land rent-free, so it was inevitable that his opinion, with a little persuasion, would go my way, but he took his time that afternoon, for he had so few opportunities to perform. He made a great show of listening closely as Channa and Pyari Lal outlined the problem, but made them repeat everything several times over so he could affect different cogitative poses.

The problem was that my mother had been a Rajput, and though I didn't know who my father was it was more than likely that he had been a Rajput too. This would have made me a Rajput, of course, though there seemed to be evidence to the contrary. To begin with, the Ahirs of Bhondaripur claimed to be descended from an old line of solar Rajputs to whom my mother, having been a noblewoman of the royal house of Harigarh, might well have been related. In addition, the jyotishi claimed to have traced my arrival at Bhondaripur to the conjoining of a felicitous constellation and an auspicious mansion of the moon in which the number seven figured prominently, and Bhondaripur had thrived ever after. The locusts had merely been harbingers of even greater good fortune, and if the gods had smiled for so long upon my union with the Ahirs then it must have been ordained, and by inference it could be supposed, with some safety, that my father had somehow been one of them.

It was evening before the jyotishi finally left, and I returned with the brothers to complete the negotiations. The only remaining problem was that Channa had been dickering with his sister to marry Ahalya off to his sister's son, and the negotiations had gone far enough that were Channa to back out of them now he would probably be fined by the brotherhood of his caste. I agreed to pay any such fine myself, and at that Channa abruptly stood up and said, 'All right then.'

There was a silence, and I looked to Pyari Lal for instruction. Pyari Lal stood beside me and began to whisper my lines to me, which I repeated, with difficulty, as follows:

'Gold gives no scent, flowers no gold, but your daughter gives both.'

To which Channa replied, 'Not to give life is as great a sin as taking life. Will you sow the family's dearest furrow so that I may harvest grandsons?'

Here Pyari Lal looked troubled. 'This is where a father's supposed to give him over to you for adoption, but he doesn't have a father.'

Channa sighed sharply. 'Then he can give himself up. Let's get on with this.'

So I was instructed to say, 'Father, take me as your son,' but these were the words I'd been longing to say my whole life long, and as they caught in my throat I began to sob.

Channa waited awhile for me to get hold of myself and I could hear the family whispering its concern outside the door, but I couldn't contain my tears for the longest while, and when I finally said, 'Father, take me as your son,' it was in a whisper.

Channa removed his turban and set it on my head, and I bent down and touched his feet, my father's feet, and Channa touched mine in turn and said, 'My daughter will fetch cow dung for you all the years of your life.'

And thus Ahalya and I were engaged.

CHAPTER
34

Channa bathed my feet and gave me a little silver ring to wear, and when I'd finally dried my eyes I chose Pyari Lal to play the part of my blood relation, so he went to his niece and washed her feet and daubed her forehead with powdered dye and set sweets on her lap to assure her fertility.

Now the truth was that when I asked for Ahalya's hand I did not love her. I wished I did, for she loved me, and I hankered after symmetry. But in those days people didn't construct marriages out of the passions of youth. They used firmer stuff, and trusted that out of the union of strong backs and abiding hearts, love of a kind would eventually flower.

At first it seemed to mean more to me that Channa called me son than that Ahalya would soon call me husband. The next day when I revisited the family I was afraid that despite all the ceremonies nothing would have really changed. But as soon as he saw me Channa called me son, and Santosh called me brother, and there was none of the usual fuss at the zemindar's approach.

Mangal Singh tried again and again to see me over the first few days of my engagement, at first to protest it, then to discuss it, and finally to assist me in my plans, or so he claimed, but always I sent him away. When he finally realized that my mind was made up and there was no hope of matching me with his corrupted daughter, he stopped haunting my path and hanging around my door. Indeed, when later I had to consult him and his books he was slow in answering my summons.

As for poor Sakuntala, she remained in Mangal Singh's house, across whose threshold I never stepped again. For the rest of her little father's life she was his rose, as he put it, his treasure and his doom. I always felt sorry for her, but priggishly, for her memory troubled me some nights, even as I lay in Ahalya's arms, as it troubles me still.

The jyotishi wouldn't set the date of our wedding until after the rains, for the stars were awry all summer and it was said that the gods slept through the monsoon. In the months of our engagement I never laid eyes on Ahalya, for she was always hurried off into the women's courtyard whenever I came to visit. It was a great bother for everyone, and explained why families preferred to marry their daughters to men from other villages. But for me it served an unexpected purpose. At first her absence just made it easier for me to put her out of my mind and revel in my newfound father's company, but by early summer it had bestowed upon her an air of mystery. I began to wonder about her more and more and lived off my memories of her, trying to recall how attentively she used to watch me eat, how her eyes flared up when Santosh scolded me, how she stood in the field with a water jar in her arms, waiting for me to return with the herd. Locking her away was a cruel custom, but I think now that if I had seen her day after day all those long, hot months she might never have engaged my passion.

The gods were wise to sleep through the rains that year. Clouds the color of partridge feathers held the damp heat down upon us like a blanket, and some days the rain fell so hard it seemed to shatter on the ground like ropes of glass. The winter weather broke late, and on the day of my wedding the lanes were still muddy and the sky was like tarnished silver.

Channa had ordered a hundred and fifty leaf plates and cups for the feast, though I couldn't see how we would need more than fifty, since Bhondaripur was so small to begin with and I had no blood relations to invite. But when the time came for me to set forth with Pyari Lal and Jagdish, the lanes were full of men and children, who fell into step behind us.

Pyari Lal and I rode together on a little white mare I'd bought for the occasion from a Mahratta liveryman near Morar. I itched and sweated in my costume: a new white cotton shirt and dhoti, a pink turban with a tinseled maur of peacock plumes, silk slippers, and a wool belt and blanket. I carried a crude spear in one hand and gripped the mare's mane with in the other, for though Jagdish walked in front of me with a firm grip on the mare's halter, I was certain that she would bolt when the musicians joined us, leaving me sprawled in the trampled mud.

But she must have been a veteran of these affairs, for she barely twitched an ear when the drummers played and the shenai players blew their melody in a wavering whine. Children danced around us, beating on cymbals and cooking pots to drive the evil spirits from our path, and a lone and self-important boy nearly drowned out all the others with a succession of blasts on a dented bugle he'd borrowed or stolen from a regimental band. I don't know how far behind me the procession stretched, for I was forbidden to look backward, but all along our route gaunt, moustachioed men poured into the lane, and though I can't say for certain that our racket chased away any evil spirits, it did agitate the dogs and spook the tethered buffalo.

I made the rounds of all the village shrines, offering flour and ghee to Kharak Deo, the god of the herd; sugar to Mahashi Deo, the buffalo god; rope to Matar Deo, the god of the cattle pen; flowers and milk to Krishna; grain to Lakshmi, and so on, for over an hour, until at last we reached the family's gate.

A bamboo arch festooned with flowers had been erected in the lane, and as I dismounted beneath it the women of the family approached, and many more besides – a mass of figures veiled in red and yellow lugdas sparkling with silver thread. Singing something lewd about my goad and Ahalya's lap (I could barely make it out in the din from the band), they piled garlands on my neck and daubed this and that upon my forehead.

Channa looked uneasy in his brand-new clothes. He greeted me stiffly at the gate with a halting pleasantry and a quick embrace that knocked his turban askew. I loved him all the more for his clumsiness, and as I vowed to cherish his daughter I felt as though my heart would burst.

Still singing and giggling as I stumbled among them, the women now led me to my lodgings. The brothers had constructed a new hut across from their own, which the women had whitewashed and decorated with lucky symbols drawn with chunks of brick. Here I was left with Pyari Lal and Jagdish as the women went to their quarters to finish the preparations for the feast. Pyari Lal made a great show of inspecting the hut and declaring it satisfactory as Channa looked on, while Jagdish washed my feet, babbling like a barber.

I was given some sweetened milk to calm my stomach, but I

stewed and squirmed for an hour or more, despairing over every mote of dust on my shirt and dhoti, fretting over my tinsel crown like an epicene nizam. But at last the women called me forth again and swept me along to a great open patchwork tent where the guests were already assembled and the drummers and shenai players announced my arrival with a drumroll and a fanfare.

I took my seat on a little wooden platform that elevated me above the others like a throne, and when I looked beside me at a second empty and equivalent seat my breathing grew quick and ardent. At last, I thought, I would finally see Ahalya.

The shenais swooped upward again and the drummers' hands blurred and my bride finally appeared in the parting crowd. It wouldn't have been seemly of me to look at her directly, so I strained to make her out on the periphery of my vision. She was surrounded by women – her married sister Imlia, her mother, and old Amma among them – but she looked less like the Ahalya I remembered than like a small, gaudy doll, swathed in red cotton cloth sparsely embroidered with gold thread. Indeed, she could have been almost anyone, for her face was so densely veiled that she had to be led along like a blind woman, and her arms were so thoroughly encased in bangles of ivory and glass that she could barely bend them enough to keep her clasped hands in front of her face. I was reduced to trying to see in a few stolen glimpses if there might be something familiar at least about her feet, but they were red with henna and festooned with silver bells that jangled with each step.

With the women's help she took her seat beside me and sat with her head bowed, and I thought, There's been a mistake; this can't be Ahalya; she's so burdened, humble, and frail. What did they do to her all those months in the women's quarters? But then I wondered how I must have looked to her (assuming she could see me at all) with the turban weighing down my brow and my tinsel maur awry.

What we could manage to eat of the splendid feast we ate like statues. Dish after dish was set before us on brass plates, but I could do them no justice, and the little bits of food Ahalya slowly conveyed up under her veil would return half-nibbled to her plate.

But the guests attacked the food like crows, and whenever there was a break in the music all I could hear was the rustling of sleeves, the smacking of lips, the calls for more water, more bread, more curds and curry as the women came and went with their bowls and platters. The guests faced us in several rows, the men in front, the women in back, the children racing between. I looked over at Channa as if to ask him who all these people were, but he appeared to be wondering the same thing, and winced every time someone called out for more helpings.

One of the dishes must have gone bad in the lingering heat that afternoon, for a good many of the guests spent the night retching and moaning prayers to Hulka Devi. There was some muttering about how this augured ill for the next day's nuptials, and the crowd was thinner when the family retrieved me from my lodgings in the morning.

The jyotishi had divined that the sun, stars, and moon would all be in their places in the late morning, and so I was to be wed as soon as I'd prayed before Hahrti, the family's household goddess. For this I was led into the women's quarters, having left my slippers by the door, and taken to a room I'd never before been allowed to enter. An effigy of some kind stood under a blanket, and to this little hump of cloth I offered milk and flowers and a coin or two, and prayed for a blessing. There was some stifled laughter from the women and girls crowded in the doorway that I ascribed to my clumsy supplications. But when I was done one of the children swept the blanket away to reveal that I'd been worshipping my own slippers.

There may be some who enjoy a good joke on themselves, but I'm not one of them, and when I was finally directed to Hahrti herself my offerings were few and my prayers perfunctory.

The carpenter had been one of the dinner's victims, and we had to wait a little outside the marriage shed as he weakly added some finishing touches. The shed creaked and swayed as though it might collapse at any moment, but it was made of materials that were meant to typify eternity: the posts were made of saleh wood, which when cut and sunk into the ground rooted and sprouted where it stood; and the roof was covered with the evergreen leaves of a mango tree.

When the carpenter was done the jyotishi took his place in the center of the shed, before the marriage post, around which more mango leaves were wound on a woolen thread, and Ahalya and I sat beside each other with our heads bowed as the jyotishi began to recite the texts. Repeating after him, I heard myself promise to live my life with Ahalya and her children, to confide in her, to worship with her, and finally to sleep with her on the night following her menstruation, and then I heard Ahalya's voice for the first time in all those months, subdued and hoarse beneath her veil, promising to be faithful to me, to obey me in all things, to work hard at her household duties, and finally never to travel anywhere without my say-so: the only vow, as it turned out, that she would ever break.

Then the jyotishi had us rise and bound our right hands together with saffron cloth, and with my free hand on Ahalya's shoulder I followed her seven times around the marriage post. I looked directly at Ahalya now, though it was still forbidden, and watching the gold threads glitter on her veil I thought of the last time I had circled like this, a small, bald boy with a sputtering torch. I leaned for a moment on her shoulder as we completed the final circuit, and she seemed as strong and steady as the trunk of a tree, and whether it was love or gratitude, a great wave of feeling surged through me, for it seemed that I was retrieving something I thought I'd lost forever: an abiding and consecrated friend.

CHAPTER

35

At the time of my marriage I was almost sixteen years old and Ahalya must have been about fifteen (she didn't know for sure). By modern standards we were young, and I suppose that by English standards we were children. But in Bhondaripur we were man and woman.

The custom was for the bride to remain with her family for a year or so, or until her mother, in consultation with the jyotishi, decided she was ready not only to bear her wifely duties, but also the tyranny of a mother-in-law in the isolation of a distant village. But Ahalya waited only four months, for she was moving barely a hundred paces from her mother's door, and her mother-in-law was dead. Besides, she loved me, and had longed to share her life with me ever since she was little: and it was also true that her mother knew me better than any of her other sons-in-law and had come to believe that my property and strange history had matured me beyond my years.

If I'd had to wait a year for Ahalya I think I would have gone mad. The four months I waited for her were bad enough. I bought a little pony cart in which to fetch Ahalya home, and put the mistri to work on an addition to the house, fretting over every detail. Assuming she was vain, like my mother, I sent her gifts of mirrors, combs, and jewelry and listened anxiously from the men's quarters to hear how they'd been received.

I could hardly contain my impatience with all the rituals surrounding her departure, in fitful stages, from her mother's house. It was the tradition that at first she come to visit for only a day, accompanied by Santosh, her elder brother, then to return home for a week or so, to visit again, to return home again, and so on, week after week. During each of these strange, formal visits we would sit together on the verandah while Pyari Lal or Santosh or some other escort coaxed us into conversation. Ahalya was always calm and asked about my plans to expand the courtyard or reclaim a fallow field, but my frustrated ardor made me abrupt and speechless.

When the great day came at last I hitched my mare to my little cart and helped Channa and Santosh load her trousseau aboard: clothing, pillows, quilts, mats, pots, pans, spoons and ladles, a charpoy, a noodle press, a stool, and a trunk. Ahalya wore a new working skirt, choli, and lugda and for the first time looked as I'd remembered her, walking in resolute strides to my tonga and climbing up to the seat beside me.

I was supposed to drive my cart slowly so that Ahalya's mother and Amma and the others could stagger along behind, grieving over her departure, while Ahalya, for her part, was supposed to weep and wail. But Ahalya merely sniffled, and I'd had such a fill of ritual that when the women launched into a song about how much her dolls were going to miss her I cracked a stick across the mare's rump and we trotted down the lane together.

As soon as we drew up to the house, Ahalya went to work. She carried in most of her trousseau herself, even hoisted her trunk onto her back like a coolie, and by the time I'd unhitched the mare, smoke was already rising from her cooking stove.

With her sister's help I had tried to supply the kitchen with everything Ahalya would need, but we'd forgotten a few things, and some of what we bought I had stored improperly. Ants had carried off the cumin through a chink in the spice box, the garlic had dried up, the potatoes had sprouted in their sack. The supper Ahalya improvised out of what was left was good, for she always had a knack for making do, but it grieved her to serve it to me and she miserably disbelieved my compliments when she cleared away my bowl and platter.

Kushal Singh had told me often enough what to expect that night, but there's no preparing a couple for their first union. The prospect of lying with Ahalya was so awesome that I trembled when I went to her, and could find no voice with which to murmur the endearments I had carefully rehearsed. She stood by her bed in her skirt and choli as if keeping a sacred vigil, and together we stared down at her pristine bed as if at the mouth of a chasm.

I think she must have sensed that my fear was greater than hers, for she began to whimper about the meal: how she'd disgraced herself, how I deserved so much better. Ahalya never whimpered like that again about anything, so I suspect she hoped pity might overcome my terror of touching her.

And she was right; it did. At first I stood before her like a statue, trying to reassure her: the meal had been perfect, I couldn't have asked for more. But words didn't seem to console her, and at last I managed to embrace her, clumsily patting her on the back as she leaned against me.

Even in the cold draft that gushed through the cracks in the window shutter her body was as warm as newly baked bread. I convinced myself that I was the strong one, that I would now lead us both through the night, but everything I did thereafter was in obedience to her.

I held her more firmly, though her shoulders had stopped shaking and her sobs had turned to urgent sighs. When she pressed herself against me her breasts squeezed under my ribs and to kiss me she had to stand on the tips of her toes.

I felt as though I might burst up through the roof and loom like a giant among the stars. We toppled to her bed, and I pulled at her clothes as if they'd caught fire, but just when I had tugged her choli upward and was about to affix my mouth to the tip of one plump breast, she struck me in the stomach with her knee and sent me tumbling windless to the floor.

I landed on my back and lay there for a moment, making noises like a strangling frog. Suddenly she was by my side, all apologies, cradling my head in her lap. She hadn't meant to hurt me, she said. But it wasn't seemly. It was going too fast.

Too fast for her? I croaked.

No, no, she told me. Not for her. She wanted me. She hungered for me. She'd been waiting for this night her whole life long.

I painfully sat up beside her. Couldn't she have just said something? Did she have to knee me in the belly?

She had to, she said with an anguished look. It was dustoor.

Dustoor?

Custom, she told me. Tradition. A bride must thrice spurn her groom's advances on her wedding night.

I pointed out that we were alone now, that no one would ever know if she spared me the next two assaults. But she was adamant. The gods would know, and especially Lakshmi, who knew everything, who even knew that I was urging her now to break her vow as a village bride.

I told her that I had it on the best authority that Lakshmi didn't spy on couples on their wedding nights, and as Ahalya seemed to weigh this notion, I fancied I could free her of her superstitions with sweet words and caresses. I tried to rein in my desire this time, though her pale breast still shone in my eyes like a beacon, and when I laid her back upon the bed I tried to content myself with running my insinuating fingers across her belly. But the longer I held myself in check the more it seemed as though the whole of my life were slipping by. Soon I was tugging at her clothes again, and had just succeeded in pulling her skirt down over one hip when she reached behind her, picked up a pitcher, and brought it down upon my head.

It was a flimsy little vessel and turned to dust as soon as it touched my skull, but it sent me back to the floor again, where I sat for a little while in astonished indignation. I felt like the victim of a cruel injustice, or at least a hoax, and when she knelt beside me again I shrank back a little as if she'd gone insane.

She leaned over me to inspect the small lump the pitcher had raised, and then, a little winded herself by now, she brushed her lips against my ear and breathed, 'Please, husband. Just once more.'

I started to shake my head, for though I understand that there are men whose ardor flares with such abuse, I am not one of them. But then she sat straight and slowly pulled her choli up over both of her breasts and thus lured me back to the bed, where, as my indignation melted away, she fed them to me, back and forth, one after the other, like a wet nurse, and searched me out among the folds of my dhoti.

I think she did strike me again that night, just before I entered her, but even Lakshmi might have missed it, for the blow became a soft, insistent pounding on the small of my back as we swam together through the perfumed night.

For the next week or so we barely left the house. I sent visitors away on the flimsiest pretexts and fell back into Ahalya's arms before they could reach the gate. I used to beg Ahalya not to leave me for an instant, not even to cook, and it's a good thing she disobeyed me in this or we might have starved to death.

Ahalya had an Ahir's vigilant nature and slept so lightly that even before my nightmares reached their conclusion, before my mother could begin to smoke and decay above the river's flow, Ahalya would awaken me with a caress and twine herself around me until my trembling stopped. When I awoke to find she had slipped off to her chores I would rush up and search her out like a lost child, collapsing with relief when I came upon her tending the cooking stove or dickering with the dhobi. And when I woke to find she was still asleep beside me I would stare at her for hours at a time, for she seemed like a goddess to me when she slept, and this despite her snoring, which was usually what awoke me in the first place.

The tea stalls are full of young husbands who boast about how they terrorize their poor, quaking brides. I like to think that I wouldn't have been one of them even if Bhondaripur had had a tea stall, for I knew I was no monster of virility. In fact, there were many nights when Ahalya's fires raged on long after mine had flickered out. But if I'd had my way we might both have died like voluptuaries, our emaciated bodies burned in an obscene tangle on a scented pyre, for even when my poor loins flagged, my hunger for her still surged inside me.

But this was Bhondaripur and there was work to do. After a month (though it seemed like a week), Ahalya suddenly became remote. She cleaned the house from corner to corner, sent every strip of cloth we owned out to be laundered, spread fresh dung clay on all the floors, whitewashed the threshold. I pleaded with her to return to bed with me, but she wouldn't until this or that got done, and when this or that led to something else and I finally commanded her to join me she shamed me mightily with her dutiful compliance, and even as I rooted around like a swine on her still form, I knew the bloom was off the rose.

If Ahalya and I had been allowed to live our whole lives together as wife and husband, if we lived together still — today — in whatever Bhondaripur has since become, it would have seemed a twinkling. Of all the couples in Bhondaripur, perhaps even in all of Gwalior, we were the least encumbered.

I couldn't regard my mother's death as a stroke of good fortune, but Ahalya understood how lucky we were to be living alone. She'd seen what mothers-in-law had done to her two sisters, how her own mother tyrannized Santosh's wife, how Amma had plagued her mother's life, flapping around her like an indignant old crow until the best she could look forward to was one day becoming a mother-in-law herself.

If Ahalya's sisters envied her anything, though, it was that she married a man from her own village. That I was zemindar, that I was rich compared to their tenant husbands, that Ahalya had not only known but loved me as a girl — all this mattered less than that Ahalya had had to move no further than a few doors from her father's gate, for they saw Amma's compound as a refuge to which they themselves longed to flee when their husbands beat them or illness overtook them or their mothers-in-law tormented them with particular zest.

It did please Ahalya to remain in Bhondaripur, to share her

mother's sweeper and dhobi, to know all the village women by the mere shapes of their veiled heads, to watch her cousins grow and the seedlings rise in the familiar fields. But she was the most autonomous human being I ever knew, and it was her village that gave her solace, not her family.

I know Santosh had once beaten his wife because his mother had caught her sneaking grain to her father's family, and a wife's allegiance to her father's family was the main source of strife between the husbands and wives of Bhondaripur. But Ahalya never came any closer to favoring her family over me than I came to raising my hand against her. Our first argument did concern her family, but it was she who vilified them and I who rose in their defense. She accused them of keeping a portion of my share of the harvest for themselves, and she was right, they were, for they'd been hiding away a little of the zemindar's share every season since Baroo had brought me to Bhondaripur. I'd even seen where they hid it once, in a false ceiling of one of the women's rooms. But just as Ahalya acted as though she were shocked by her own family's petty larceny, I now pretended not to know. Of course, my problem, as she saw it, wasn't that I didn't know but that I didn't care, for Ahalya's devotion to me was now total, and thus exceeded my own devotion to myself.

My memory balks like an old bullock at recollecting the differences between us, but whatever the songs may tell you, no two people are made for each other, and marriage, being a stage of life, is no paradise.

I had managed up until then to make my home an island in a sea of ritual, but I should have known I couldn't escape it forever – not with one of Bhondaripur's own daughters in residence. All those months since our engagement her mother and aunts had steeped her in their dustoor: the customs, codes, and beliefs that animated their every breath. I already had them to thank for Ahalya's attacks on our first night together, but there was more to come – so much more that I sometimes wondered if Ahalya was making it up as she went along.

Just consider the doorway, to show you what I mean. It was a simple affair that seemed to serve its purpose well enough. I'd been entering and exiting through it for a year or so by then and it had never given me any trouble. But here's what the carpenter had to do to it to satisfy Ahalya's dustoor:

First, so that lustful spirits couldn't spy on her from the lane, he had to move the door slightly to one side so that it wouldn't align with the kitchen door beyond. Then a third step had to be added to the existing two that led up to the threshold, since two steps, being evenly divisible, suggested a divided house. The lintel had to be lowered so that I had to stoop upon entering, out of respect to the household gods. For my part, I was obliged to enter the house with my right foot first, and on no account was I ever to sit or even to pause on the threshold, for that was Lakshmi's seat, which Ahalya regularly whitewashed so it might resemble the goddess's lotus throne.

Ahalya's dustoor ranged everywhere. She had the little banyan tree I'd planted removed to a spot outside the dooryard, for it was her belief that its leavings would insult Brahma and its contemplative influence might rob me of my will to make children. In its place she planted a gular tree to grant us prosperity, and by the door she installed a tulsi plant, which she wetted every morning with her bathwater.

Ahalya's path was thus littered with endless petty observances. Some days she went about her work with such speed and fury that it seemed as though a spirit had possessed her or a household god were hounding her every step.

This frenzy reached a special pitch a few months after she'd withdrawn from our marriage bed and shooed me back into the outside world. I figured she might have been menstruating, for Bhondaripur's dustoor demanded the most of women during their monthly travail. They were required to remove and wash their cotton clothing, even the cotton cords they wore in their braids, and wear wool for the duration, even in the summer weather. They were not to be seen by any man except their husbands (and not even by them in the strictest households). They were not to sleep in a bed, nor draw water, nor touch their husbands' garments, nor walk in an open place after nightfall.

But now, as if all that weren't enough, Ahalya refused to touch any blade, even a sickle or a kitchen knife. She packed away every article of red clothing she possessed and dressed entirely in green. She refused to see any of our neighbors, even her sister when she came back to Bhondaripur for one of her biannual visits. She shied away from the mare as if it carried the plague, and she scrupulously circumvented the shadow of our buffalo cow. The jyotishi began to hang about the gate with his texts and charms, and the barber's wife attended to Ahalya every morning, huddling with her in a corner of the courtyard. And every night Ahalya served me rich, elaborate, and abundant meals, pacing and coughing impatiently as I tried to finish them and then hurrying off to the kitchen to noisily devour the leftovers.

Though Ahalya implied with all her business that I too should set my hands to something, there wasn't much for me to do. I tried to make a few tours of my fields, call in Mangal Singh to review the accounts, inspect the buffalo on their evening return, but I always seemed to get in somebody's way. I suppose a lot of men would have been content to lie back and let their wives manage everything, but I never could relax when she was bustling around me, so whenever possible I tried to devise little chores for myself.

One morning I decided that a gnawed post of the mare's lean-to needed replacing, so I set forth with my ax for a stand of pipal trees. But I'd gotten no further than the dooryard gate when I came upon Ahalya squatting on the threshing ground and popping a mudball into her mouth.

Now, by this time I had given up asking Ahalya about her observances, for one question always led to another, and though her answers always had a certain charm they cast no light. I might have let even this disgusting little ritual pass, except that Ahalya, catching sight of my ax, gulped the mudball down in one swallow, and, alternately coughing and shouting 'Get away from me,' burst into tears and fled.

Believing that my young wife had gone mad, I dropped the ax on the ground and stood gaping as she disappeared into the house. The barber's wife, standing nearby, began to cackle, and the jyotishi, sitting crosslegged by the gate, smiled at me when I looked around. I began to understand from all this that Ahalya was keeping something more than her dustoor from me, and by the time I'd run after her across the whitewashed threshold I realized what it was.

I found her in her room, washing out her mouth with water, and when she saw from the smile on my face that I knew her secret she walked up to me in a stoop and touched my feet.

'And look,' she said, rising and lifting up her choli. 'It's going to be a boy, my husband. A son. For you.' And she knew this because her nipples had turned red instead of brown, and because the barber's wife had read the lines of her navel, and the jyotishi had seen it in the stars, and she herself had read it in the path of a stream of oil she'd poured upon her belly.

And she wouldn't use a blade (and had run screaming from my ax) for fear it might deform our son, and she wouldn't wear red for fear she would abort him, and she'd refused to see her sister because her sister had miscarried once, and she wouldn't go near the mare because mares carried their offspring for ten months, and she'd eaten earth from the threshing ground to stave off morning sickness, and thus with every strange observance she had been protecting my son.

I sat her down and embraced her, I pressed my ear to her belly, I commanded her to rest; I did everything a jubilant young husband might do. But in truth I was dazed by her news, or maybe it was more that her news was bringing me out of a daze, for now the fact of my manhood, my marriage, my place in the order of things became suddenly incontrovertible. I was no longer the urchin, the abandoned waif that I'd still believed myself to be, and though I was yet an orphan, what did it matter, now that I was going to be a father?

CHAPTER
36

This was in the early months of 1874, sometime around my sixteenth birthday. I know this because later that same year, when Ahalya was about to give birth, there was a great commotion in the kingdom.

Ahalya's pregnancy spanned a merciless summer and a torrential monsoon, but she never would slow down. Though her breasts and belly burgeoned like ripening fruit, her arms became sticks and her voice broke and her lovely, dark eyes seemed to shrink back into their sockets. The husband in me was ashamed that my seed fed upon her so greedily, but the father in me wanted my son to thrive, no matter what it cost Ahalya, so when I scolded her for working too hard or eating too little I could never tell if it was for her sake, or my son's.

I never interfered with Ahalya's observances again, for though they remained a great bother, much of what they required of me became second nature, and I confess that after a while her dustoor gave our domestic life a grace and order that sometimes seemed as resonant and all-embracing as nature itself. Besides, there is nothing like fatherhood to shake a man's belief, and I found that I wasn't willing to take the same risks with my son's soul as I took with mine.

And so it was with my estate. As soon as Ahalya let me know her secret, my generosity to Channa and the others dried up. My self-interest had always seemed obscure to me, and I somehow wouldn't change for Ahalya, either, for though I loved her I knew I could never match her own prudence and devotion. But for my own son's sake I bestirred myself. I toured the fields each day, even in the worst weather, directing that crops be weeded, thorn rows repaired, irrigation ditches shored up after the driving rains, and though I must have been a terrible nuisance to Channa and the others, I fancied that it made a difference to them, that it brought them out of their torpor and improved the season's yield.

Jagdish became Ahalya's link with the rest of the world, for like most women she enjoyed the company of loquacious men. Some evenings there was no escaping their conversation, for the further I tried to get from it the louder they talked, as if to assure me they were doing nothing behind my back. I found Jagdish as tiresome as ever, until just before Dusserah of that year, when he began to return from herding with stories of strange goings-on in the countryside.

It seemed that for the past few days he'd been coming upon little bands of sadhus hidden along the slopes of the eastern ridge, hard by the Kalpi Road. Ahalya was unimpressed, maintaining they were merely gathering for the mela in the city, but Jagdish maintained that these weren't like any sadhus he'd seen before. He'd found one group encamped in a little ring of boulders, like soldiers waiting in ambush.

At first they seemed to be bairajis of some kind for they wore the white garments of Vishnu's mendicants, but when Jagdish greeted them with the traditional 'Hail, Sitaram,' those who responded at all did so in a confused babble, some saying 'Good day,' which was a strange reply for a bairaji, and some saying, 'Narayan,' which is the customary greeting of a Shivaite gosain and thus stranger still.

Ahalya frowned a little at this. Maybe Jagdish had stumbled upon a new sect, pilgrims from some faraway place, bound for the Nerbudda.

But Jagdish said that when he approached them they stood all at once and he saw that two bore swords under their robes and all of them had thick necks and bowlegs, like horsemen, and their ornaments and sect marks were slapdash and contradictory. There was the crimson mark of a Sakti on one forehead, Shiva's trident on another, daubed clumsily in the wrong hues, and when Jagdish tried to engage them further in conversation, one of them began to shake his bowl at him, crying 'Apart, apart,' and another brandished his battered sword.

Now, it was no wonder to me that Jagdish might have had this effect on even the most long-suffering bairaji, and back in those days there were enough charlatans duping farmers and seducing wives to give all sadhus a bad name. But what seemed strange to me was the number of them Jagdish sighted, thirty little bands by his count, which, allowing for Jagdish's inclination to exaggerate everything, meant at least a hundred such impostors were encamped among the hills.

Ahalya decided they must all be Punjabis, for she had never seen any Punjabis and thus ascribed to them everything she found strange and inexplicable. But Channa believed there was something sinister afoot, and one night old Kushal Singh saw a crimson aureole around the sun, the likes of which he hadn't seen since the Devil's Wind first blew.

This was around the time my son was due, and for many nights I had slept fitfully, awaking at the slightest murmur from Ahalya's room and then tossing about in the heat as if the dark were taking hold of my bed and shaking it. One night I could finally bear my vigil no longer, and to divert myself for a little while I arose from bed and set forth on my mare to see the sadhus for myself.

The little mare was loath and drowsy as I goaded her toward the Kalpi Road. In the foredawn light I rode to where Jagdish had sighted the sadhus last, but there was no sign of them anywhere. At the silent hour when the night creatures had withdrawn and the day creatures still slept in their dens and nests, my mare's hooves echoed along the slopes of the purple ridges, and scolding myself for believing Jagdish and abandoning my place by Ahalya's side, I turned around for home.

The sun had not yet struck the hills around me, but above their summits I saw a pink cloud rising into the light ahead of me, and the road began to tremble like a drum. I pulled the mare to a halt and listened for a moment, and above a faint roar I mistook for an approaching wind I could hear grunts and calls like a herder's patter. I drove the mare off the road and dismounted, and suddenly there were the sadhus, just as Jagdish had described them, standing in a line along the blade of the ridge.

I tried to mount the mare again and get away, but she kept circling in a panicked sidestep as three of the sadhus now began to descend the stony slope. I clung foolishly to the pony's neck, cursing myself for being such a fool.

But the sadhus passed right by me, spread a blanket in the middle of the road, and sat upon it, facing westward. I pulled my mare behind a ranga bush and listened with them as the roar grew like a boulder rolling toward us and the dust cloud loomed ever higher. The three sadhus and their cohorts along the ridgetop watched in utter silence as around a bend in the road a great body of men approached, advancing from the distance like a porcupine. I began to make out lancers on horseback riding in ranks, soldiers marching with breechloaders, half a dozen palanquins bobbing along, a hundred villagers straggling behind, and ahead of everyone, on a jittery Iman stallion twice the size of my little mare, rode the Maharaja Aliraj Jaiaji Rao Scindhia himself.

I had never before laid eyes on the regent of Gwalior, but there was no mistaking him. He trotted impatiently ahead of his lumbering escort, and as he neared the three sadhus the morning sun cast a beam across his path. He drew his stallion to a halt in the streak of golden light, a few yards from the sadhus' station. He was a burly man with a horseman's ramrod spine and muttonchop whiskers that rimmed his wide, scowling face like a mane. He wore tinselled slippers and purple pantaloons, an orange cloak he'd hastily thrown across his shoulders, and a sweat-stained Mahratta turban that seemed to toss like a boat on the wave of his brow.

Two of the three sadhus stood and bowed, but the third remained seated, barely glancing up at the waiting king. Scindhia glowered down at the little sadhu for the longest while, cocking his head about like a perplexed lion as his escort drew to a halt behind him.

'Y-*you* are Dh-dh-dhund-d-do P-p-punt?' he asked with a grimace.

The little sadhu looked back at him evenly. He wore his hair in a knot and a white cloth was coiled around his waist and shoulders, but that was all I could see of him from where I stood. 'A true king,' he now told Scindhia, 'does not answer to his name. You ought to know that, Jaiaji.'

Scindhia gasped at this use of his familiar name as his stallion blustered and balked beneath him. 'I am S-s-s-scindhia!' he exclaimed indignantly.

'Of course you are, Jaiaji,' the sadhu replied. 'I can tell from your stammer. It's no better now than when we were boys, is it, poor fellow?'

There was a murmuring from the crowd of villagers as a wave of outrage passed along the ranks of Scindhia's guard, stirring their lances like a sudden wind.

'And I,' the sadhu continued, ' – I am Nana Sahib Peshwa, Maharaja of Bithur and descendant, if I may say so, Jaiaji, of your ancestors' master.'

Scindhia stilled his horse and stared again at the little sadhu's upturned face.

'Don't let my looks fool you, Jaiaji. I've been a miserable wanderer in my father's kingdom. But the journey's over. I am defeated. Kill me or save me, old friend. I will wander no more.'

Scindhia picked uncertainly at his nostril with his thumb and then, turning his horse sideways, he signalled to his men with one upraised fist and shouted, 'T-t-take him!'

Three of his soldiers fired their rifles skyward in quick succession, and Scindhia's guard closed around the little sadhu and dismounted. His two companions fell to their knees, and each was placed in a palanquin. There was a strange light in their companion's eyes as he was turned around and shackled, and when he disappeared into a third palanquin he was nodding to himself and smiling. Scindhia looked triumphant, and pulling a sword from one of his officers' scabbards, he cantered through the middle of his escort's ranks and led the procession back to Gwalior.

When all that remained on the road above me was a scattering of villagers, I mounted my mare and galloped for home, and looking back through my own dusty wake I saw that the host of bairajis had vanished from the ridge.

Faster than my little mare could carry me, the news spread across the countryside in bits and pieces, like shards from an explosion. The first villagers I galloped past asked if the Nana Sahib had been captured, and I called back that I thought he had, but as I rode further the questions began to change. Had Scindhia joined forces with the Nana Sahib's army? Were they advancing on the British cantonment at Morar? Was the Devil's Wind about to blow again? And when I told them no, the Nana Sahib was Scindhia's captive, they looked disappointed and scanned the horizon for another messenger who might confirm them in their panic.

When I finally reached Bhondaripur I found Channa herding the buffalo into his dooryard and Pyari Lal and Santosh dragging thorn branches up to the base of the compound wall. I tried to tell them what had happened, but they wouldn't listen, and Channa, glaring at me, suggested that even if I wasn't interested in protecting myself I might at least consider his daughter's safety. As I drove my mare down the lane I caught a glimpse of Mangal Singh pacing in his courtyard with a pistol in his hand, and at my own gate the chowkidor stood like a sentry with a pike across his shoulder. From my bewildered expression he assumed I knew nothing and informed me that the Nana Sahib had beheaded Scindhia and installed himself as Peshwa in the palace of Lashkar.

Of course, I knew otherwise, but there's nothing so contagious as a false alarm, and I ran into my house, convinced for some reason that Ahalya was in peril. But I found her in the yard behind the kitchen, scouring pans and chewing on an onion stalk. She asked me sharply where I'd been, and when I told her what I'd witnessed on the

Kalpi Road she was not impressed, for it was her belief that such things went on all the time in the outside world, and she exacted a promise from me that I wouldn't leave Bhondaripur again until our son was born.

The next day we heard that Scindhia had turned the little bairaji over to the British. The Brahmins of the kingdom, who revered the Peshwa, were outraged, and to answer them Scindhia sent his chaprasis around Gwalior with his Dusserah declaration, reminding everyone of the Nana Sahib's treachery and the vengeance that was visited upon his people for his crimes. But it was not like the Maharaja of Gwalior to try to justify himself to anyone, least of all his subjects, so his declaration only worsened the alarm, and it did not help that he had pickets posted on all the roads in case his appeal was unavailing.

Meanwhile the little bairaji's pretensions were faltering. He was whisked away to Cawnpore and examined there by Britishers who'd played billiards with the Nana Sahib before the Devil's Wind. Few of them saw any resemblance between the bairaji and the Bithur Butcher, as they called the Nana Sahib back then, even after they'd cleaned him up and dressed him in Mahratta costume. In the heat of his captors' scrutiny his claims drooped and melted away, his accounts of his wanderings doubled back on themselves, riddled with contradictions, and before too long everyone was convinced that they had a lunatic on their hands. Scindhia was slow to admit he'd been duped, for no one likes to be made to look a fool, least of all a king, and even before he made it official in a grudging declaration that the bairaji and his companions were impostors, Channa had returned the buffalo to their posts and Pyari Lal had dragged the branches back to the thorn rows.

But just as I'd been determined not to panic when the alarm was at full pitch, I now suspected that there had to have been more to the bairaji's impersonation than an audacious delusion. If he'd been just a madman, why had a hundred sadhus followed him to the Kalpi Road? And if, as Jagdish believed, those men had been soldiers and not sadhus, whom did they serve and where had they gone? Channa and Pyari Lal would hear none of this, and pleaded with me to let the matter rest, for I had so spooked Jagdish with my speculations that he refused to drive his herd out of sight of the village fields, convinced that the sadhus were spirits who now suffused the hills like a poisonous mist.

My child was born on a cool afternoon, soon after Scindhia removed his pickets from the roads. Ahalya, in her impatience, had taken various of the midwife's concoctions to speed the delivery, but ascribed our baby's sudden arrival to the ashes she'd nibbled off a lightning-struck tree.

I waited through her labor in our courtyard with Channa, Pyari Lal, Ramesh, Santosh, Jagdish – all the men of the family – in attendance. The women gathered inside as the midwife did her work, and now and again Amma or my mother-in-law would appear in the doorway and bark obscure commands: fetch a stone from a rushing stream; bring more gram flour; bring the zemindar's bathwater.

When the shadows stretched from wall to wall across the dooryard we heard a cry that sent the swallows flying up from the eaves of the roof. Channa nodded to me, and I stood up from the little hookah circle, and out came Amma with the news.

Was it a son? I blurted as I stepped forward, but Amma's eyes widened with alarm in the shade of her veil and she shook her head no.

I stopped walking, stopped breathing, for I'd come to count on a son, to believe in him in my bones.

Amma looked about her as if afraid I'd been overheard and then, in as loud a voice as she could muster, she told me that Ahalya had given birth to a one-eyed girl.

I gaped at her and reached about in the air as if to catch my fall, but suddenly Channa and Pyari Lal and all the others were dancing around me and slapping me on the back.

'At last!' Channa cried out. 'At last! At last!'

I was lurching around among them, aggrieved, appalled, convinced they'd all gone mad, when Santosh grabbed me by the shoulders and said, 'Don't you understand? Don't you know *anything*? You have a son, Balbeer! Ahalya has given you a son!'

And this was true, for by announcing the birth as a one-eyed daughter Amma had been merely confounding the envious spirits that eavesdropped on these occasions. Now my mother-in-law emerged from the doorway with my son, a squalling baby boy with a face like a fist. He stopped crying when I held him, seeming for a moment to sense the faces that hovered around him, and then he began to search with his lips for his mother's breast among the folds of his swaddle. He commenced to bawl again, and his fingers stretched outward like the petals of a spiky flower. His genitals were formidable beneath his belly's knotted stem, and his neck was as burly as a crow's. I could sense such will in his heft and such vigor in the pounding of his heels against my forearm that it struck me dumb, and Amma, mistaking my astonishment for helplessness, took him from me and carried him back to Ahalya's bed.

That night there was a great hubbub throughout Bhondaripur, for my son was the zemindar's heir, after all, the future lord of the village children, and his welfare was thus everyone's business. As Mangal Singh stood by with his record books I distributed maunds of grain that evening: to the craftsmen, to the jyotishi, to the banghi who came to play their drums, even to Mangal Singh himself. And as the men caroused in the courtyard the women sang and danced inside, and every now and then, when there was a break in the din, I could hear Ahalya weakly singing with her sisters.

There seemed to be new ceremonies to perform every day after that, and the jyotishi nearly moved in completely with his texts and charms. If you wonder how Ahalya fared, I can only say I wondered too, for during the ten days following my little boy's birth I was forbidden to see her and had only the midwife's word to go by. The midwife was a simple woman and mistook my impatience with her vague and obsequious replies for frustrated ardor, assuring me with a leer that Ahalya's loins would soon be restored for my next assault.

On the tenth day the women came in the morning to coat the floors with fresh cow dung and the barber sat me down on the verandah and shaved me bald. The jyotishi lit a small fire on the floor of the front room, and when all was ready I sat across from him and awaited Ahalya and my baby son.

They entered alone, and at the sight of them a calm came over me like a cool breeze. The old light burned in her eyes and the flesh had returned to the hollows of her cheeks, and lying in her arms beneath the swell of her bosom my little son stirred and murmured.

I wanted to leap up and embrace them both, but I played my part as patriarch and held my elation in check. While the jyotishi added incense and ghee to the little fire, wrapped ribbons around our arms and read aloud from the old texts, I wondered if in all the world there could be a man as lucky as I. As if in answer my mother flared up from the flames of the jyotishi's fire, but only for an instant, and when I looked away there was Ahalya in the saffron light, leaning her face forward to receive a daub of turmeric on her brow.

The jyotishi gave us four names to choose from for our son, all derived from the mansion of the moon on the day of his birth: Madan Mohan, Mansaram, Madhosudan, and Mahabir. When the time came, Ahalya could not choose among them and none seemed good enough to me, but then no name could have been good enough for my little boy, and we settled on Mahabir.

We brought him out into the courtyard, where the entire village was assembled, and we held him up before them, announcing his name in all directions. There was nearly as much of a racket as on my wedding day, and when evening came there was a great feast. I sat with Channa and listened to his advice about the rearing of sons as Santosh, his own son, who was as yet childless, nodded grimly by his side.

'Treat him like a king until he's six,' Channa told me, 'like a slave until he's grown, and thenceforward like a friend.'

But as at all great feasts the object of the celebration was soon forgotten, and as the families sat in little groups ordering more food from the circulating women of the family I slipped into my house and found my son sleeping among his mother's blankets. But now I could see something of Ahalya in the shape of his nostrils, something of myself around his brow. I lifted him up, and he brought his wrists together and burped as I carried him out the back of the house and down the lane to the family's compound.

There I showed him off to old Kushal Singh, who, nearly blind by now, lightly touched him with his fingers. 'He's a hare, Balbeer,' he announced. 'A beautiful boy.' And when I took my leave he touched my feet.

I carried Mahabir out of the village and into the newly reaped fields, and he lay awake in my arms, awash in the light from the tag-along moon. The bristle from the harvested mustard gave off a sharp green smell, and the insect song was so dense that it nearly drowned out the din from the distant feast. 'Yes, Mahabir,' I said as he squinted and gaped at the stars that shone about his father's head. 'All this is yours, my son. Everything you see.'

'And yours, Balbeer,' came a voice from the shade of the thorn row. 'And mine, of course.'

I pressed Mahabir against my stomach and backed away a step as a pale shape emerged from the shadows. It stopped a few feet from me, a hooded column of cloth, and I could hear its breath on the breeze that blew across the stubbled field. And then I saw in the shade of its hood a single glimmer, a solitary eye bearing down upon me like the point of a knife, and though it couldn't have been, it mustn't have been, I knew it was Baroo.

CHAPTER

37

'What's the matter?' he asked, removing his hood. 'Didn't I promise you I'd be back?'

'But – but *you*,' I said. 'You can't be – '

'But I am,' he said with his hands outstretched. 'And is this any way to greet your father?'

His voice buzzed and broke like a busted horn. He stood with a twist to his shoulders and neck, and the pit where his left eye should have been was thus cast upward as if he were hanging by it from a butcher's hook. His remaining eye flared in its socket like a lamp in a tunnel, and when he smiled at me his mouth seemed to open out onto the gloom behind him.

'Come, Balbeer,' he said, waving me forward with his bony fingers. 'Let's have a look at you.'

I shrank back, hunched over my baby son.

'Come, come,' Baroo said with a shrug. 'If I'm a ghost there's no escaping me, and if I'm not there's no danger, so where's the point in running?'

Until that moment I hadn't believed in ghosts, but now as I slowly stumbled forward to touch Baroo's feet, clutching Mahabir in one hand, I fully expected the other to pass clear through to the dust beneath him, and when it touched his skin instead and brushed against the horns of his toes the flesh squirmed along my spine.

'Balbeer,' he said, holding me by the shoulders. He hesitated for a moment as if to compose himself. 'You look *well*, Balbeer,' he said in an ardent whisper. He stared at me with such intensity that I think my knees might have given way if Mahabir hadn't diverted him with a cry.

'And this is your son?' Baroo asked, looking down into my arms. 'Mahabir, isn't it? I think I heard them shouting his name this afternoon. What a fine name for my grandson.

'Good evening, Mahabir,' he said gently, leaning close to my little boy's face. 'I am Baroo Singh, your grandfather,' And in the sway of Baroo's strange charm Mahabir stopped crying.

I swallowed hard. 'W-we heard you'd been – '

'Hanged?' Baroo interjected. 'Just so. And I tell you, Balbeer, it almost killed me.'

He put one gnarled arm across my shoulders and led me a little way further out into the field. 'You know, Balbeer,' he said with a shake of his head, 'no matter how much care you put into a plan it can only be as good as the men you choose to carry it out. My problem was that I had no choice. I was stuck with whatever was available, which in this case was a charmar halfwit hangman and a couple of gravediggers.

'You see,' Baroo said, stroking the air with his free hand, 'I had it all laid out ahead of time. Right after the trial I pretended to go over to Islam so they wouldn't burn my body after the hanging, but the damn hangman left too much slack in the rope and I broke my neck going down, and the diggers I'd paid off didn't lay enough branches in my grave before they covered it over. Only had enough air to last me a couple of hours, so I had to dig my way out before nightfall.'

Baroo gave me a searching look. 'But at least they hanged me. It could have been worse. If the Raja hadn't had some Feringhee visiting that week he wouldn't have given me such a civilized execution. Could've had my head chopped off or crushed under one of his elephants, and then where would we be?'

He said all this so gaily that I found myself nodding and cocking my head as if he were recounting some petty delay on a shopping trip.

'But Barooji,' I said finally, 'Wh-why did they hang you?'

'Why?' Baroo said with his eyebrow raised. 'You don't know why?'

'Uh, no,' I said, withering again beneath his gaze.

'That mincing little pickthank never told you?'

'Who?'

'Mangal Singh, of course. The patwari.' Baroo glowered at me for a moment. 'Or don't you think he fits that description?'

'Oh, no,' I said quickly. 'He does. I just – '

Baroo held up his hand to quiet me and paused, staring off along the thorn row. 'So he didn't tell you,' he muttered to himself, tugging at the lobe of his ear.

'Well,' he said at last with a shrug, 'what difference does it make why they hanged me? There's no accounting for a raja's justice anyway. Mustn't let a pack of lies stand between a father and son.'

Tightening his grip on my shoulder, Baroo led me further into the dark. 'But how did you like my present, Balbeer? Did I surprise you? Imagine! A zemindar at – what were you? Eight – nine years old?'

'No,' I replied haltingly. 'Fourteen, I think.'

Baroo stopped and frowned. 'Fourteen? But that's not possible. You were a mite of a lad when I left you, and they hanged me within the month.'

I could hardly reply at first, but before I knew it Baroo had coaxed forth the whole story: my madness, my immersion in the pond, my years with the buffalo, then the tiger and the locusts and the missing will. Mahabir fell asleep in my arms as I spoke, and at the end Baroo listened like a child with his mouth ajar. But when I began to tell him about Sakuntala and Ahalya he seemed to stop listening and slapped himself on the side of the face.

'Balbeer!' he exclaimed. 'My poor boy. Do you mean to tell me that you slaved away like that when all along you were the zemindar? Why, that's disgraceful. *Shameful*. That low, conniving patwari,' he said, his voice plummeting and his eye darting around in its socket.

'That scheming, preening little – '

By now he was strangling his waistcloth in his fists and spittle flew from his twisted lips, but all of a sudden he seemed to catch sight of me again and composed himself. 'But then, what can we expect, eh, Balbeer?' he asked with an abashed smile. 'A patwari's a patwari, after all, and which of us is better than he was born to be?'

Baroo's eye twitched and flared above his fixed grin as if from behind a mask. 'That Mangal Singh,' he said with a hollow chuckle. 'What a character.'

'Balbeer!' came a cry from the distance. 'Balbeer! Are you out there?'

Baroo ran a hand from his throat to his chin. 'Answer, Balbeer,' he said absently.

'We're here, Jagdish,' I called back, my voice breaking, and suddenly Baroo grabbed my shoulder.

'Shh!' he hissed through his teeth. 'Don't say *we*!'

'W-*we*,' I croaked back. 'Mahabir and I.'

Baroo looked down into my arms again and slapped his forehead. 'The *child*,' he said, 'of course. Forgive me.'

'Balbeer?' Jagdish called out again. 'Are you all right?'

'Tell him you're fine. Tell him you're coming,' Baroo said, nibbling for a moment on the point of his knuckle.

'I'm fine, Jagdish. I'll be back in a moment,' I called out, trying to keep my voice from breaking.

'All right,' Jagdish called back. 'I'll go tell the others.'

'Yes, Jagdish. You go do that.'

I looked back at Baroo and caught him grinning proudly at me and rubbing his fingers. 'So,' he said, 'when do you want to get started?'

'Started?' I said, trying to joggle Mahabir asleep, for all the shouting had wakened him.

'For Harigarh, Balbeer. Remember?'

'Harigarh?' I said. 'You want to go to Harigarh?'

'No, no, Balbeer. *You* want to go Harigarh. Remember? And I've come back to take you there.'

'B-but,' I heard myself sputter, 'I don't want to go any more. I want to stay here. My life is here.'

Baroo nodded and smiled for a moment. 'Just so,' he said. 'I knew you'd see things that way. There's nothing waiting for you there anyway. I couldn't find anyone who'd ever heard of your poor mother, and the Raja's as mad as a sunstruck Sikh. I told you this little dung heap would grow on you after a while, didn't I? So be it.

'But,' Baroo said with an upraised finger, 'there's bound to be more to your life than this. The time has come to recall your destiny, Balbeer. And believe me, Bhondaripur isn't it.'

'What do you mean?'

'Your *destiny*, Balbeer,' he said, reaching forward and pressing the tip of his finger against my brow. 'It's as sharp as the crescent moon. Bhondaripur is a resting place, son, like the nest of a hawk.'

'But *this* is my life,' I said, lifting Mahabir slightly.

'I'm sorry,' Baroo said with his eyebrows raised. 'But it isn't enough.'

'How do *you* know?' I snapped back at him now as I felt my old self, the proud widow's bastard son, stir like a ghost within me. 'You don't know me.'

'But I'm your father, Balbeer, remember?' Baroo said softly with his one eye large.

'You're not my father!' I snarled. 'I don't even *know* you!'

Baroo's chest swelled and the fire rose in his eye. 'Ah, Balbeer, Balbeer,' he said, shaking his head and approaching me. 'Maybe you're right. Maybe you *don't* know me,' and suddenly his face was so close to mine that his missing eye was like a quarry and I thought I would choke on his discarded breaths.

'But you knew me well enough when the will was read, didn't you, Balbeer? I was father enough to you when there was land to be had. But maybe you aren't the same boy I carried all the way from Jhansi. Maybe you aren't the same leaking sack of pestilence I left behind to prosper. And if you aren't, then I've made a terrible mistake in my will, haven't I, Balbeer? Giving everything away to a flat-footed, whining little village brat. Why, I'd better write myself a new one, don't you think? Give everything to Mangal Singh after all. *Then* we'll see how Bhondaripur suits you.'

I dared not breathe or blink or wipe his spittle from my face as his eyeball rolled up before me and focussed on my brow. 'But you *are* the same boy,' he said at last, leaning away with a scowl. 'The very same. I have meditated on that brow for seven years. It burned like a star in my grave. Do you think I would allow the peasant you've become to stand in the way of the prince you may yet be?'

I held Mahabir as tightly as I could and began to stagger backwards towards the village. 'You keep away from me,' I said as the blood drummed in my ears. 'I'm going back. And if you try to stop me I'll – I'll set my whole village on you.'

'*Your* whole village?' Baroo roared, matching me step for step. 'By whose grace?' He stopped and stood as straight as he could, straining against the twist in his neck and shoulders. 'Know me, Balbeer,' he said in an ominous growl that stopped me in my tracks. 'I am Baroo Singh,' he said, striking his chest with his fist. 'Supreme chieftain of the Jeysulmere Thugs. I am the last of the brotherhood, the last free Thug in all of Hindustan. Kali's sole surviving son. The rajas, the Feringhee, they have hunted me, slaughtered my family, plucked out my eye, hanged me, buried me, danced on my grave. But still I live to haunt them. I am Kali's tooth, risen from the ashes like the swordsmith's blade, so do not trifle with me, boy.

'Did you hear that, Kali?' he suddenly asked the black sky. '*His* village, he says,' and he began to chuckle and nod as if sharing a joke with someone. 'Your village,' he then snarled, poking at my chest with his finger, 'your little wife, your pup, your *life*, Balbeer. You owe *everything* to me. And if you hope to keep it you will follow me.'

Baroo stepped back, still scowling but now a little winded and faltering on his feet.

'But why me?' I heard myself whine back at him, in the voice of a child. I knew I could not stand up to the mad old man, for already I was telling myself that I would follow Baroo for Mahabir's sake, to protect his legacy.

Baroo sighed now, and his smile wearily returned to his sunken face. 'Because ever since I watched you sleep on the deck of that budgerow all those years ago, Kali has commanded me to love you. Look, Balbeer, I only want to take care of you. I'm not trying to ruin you. I don't want my land back. I don't want to cast you out on the roadside with your wife and son. No one need ever know that I'm still alive. As far as everyone's concerned, I'm dead, and I'm content to leave it that way, for death is the best disguise. But in loving you I must obey your destiny, no matter what it costs me. You'll be my heir in every way, Balbeer, or you won't be my heir at all. If you come with me now and do everything I tell you, in one month's time you may return to Bhondaripur, still zemindar, still husband, still father to your little son. Now tell me, boy. Is that too much to ask?'

I supposed it wasn't and turned around to face the village. 'But what will I say to my family?' I wondered. Here and there the moonlight caught the shape of someone heading home from my compound.

'It's simple, Balbeer,' Baroo said with a certain relish, like a craftsman showing off his dexterity. 'You came to them a stranger, didn't you? And no matter how well they think they know you, there will always be this part of you that's a stranger to them.

'So all you need to tell them is that you have to go off somewhere. Urgent business. Can't wait. Something to do with your mother's estate. Say you'll be back a wealthy man, which you just might, come to think of it. None of these sheep would ever dream of following you. Wouldn't occur to them to travel beyond Bhind, let alone all the way to Cawnpore. So you can count on everybody staying put.'

Jagdish called for me again, and Baroo shrank back into the thorn row's shade. 'Now go get your things,' he whispered. 'I'll meet you here when the moon's at its height.'

He kept pace with me a little distance as I began to stumble back across the field. 'Don't worry,' he whispered after me. 'You'll see. It's going to be all right. Kali's smiling on us. We'll be back in no time.'

I didn't dare look back at him until I'd reached the village gate. When I turned around there was no sign of Baroo anywhere, but this only made him seem to be everywhere, so that when Jagdish stepped forward to greet me in the lane I leapt back and barked like a startled dog.

'Zemindarji,' he said, 'you shouldn't go out there. The sadhus, remember? The feast is over. Everyone's gone home. Did you get something to eat? I loved the eggplant, didn't you? Amma made it herself. Nobody cooks like Amma, don't you think?'

'Goodnight, Jagdish,' I said, marching ahead of him as Mahabir began to cry again in my arms.

'Oh, all right, zemindarji,' he said, still following along. 'It *is* late, isn't it? I guess if I'm going to have to be up with the herd in the morning I'd better — '

'Good*night*!' I snapped back at him, and at last he fell back into the dark.

Ahalya said nothing to me when I approached my door, not even to ask me where I'd been. But as she retrieved my bawling son from my arms her choli was soaked with leaking milk, and there was no mistaking the anger in her eyes.

I went to my room to refine the lies I was about to tell her, but when I mouthed them they soured and curdled on my lips. Wasn't there a way out of the old man's dream? Could Baroo really change his will now that he was supposedly dead? But it was no use, I concluded. There was no escape.

That part of me which Baroo said would always be a stranger to my newfound family was by then a stranger to me as well, and when he began to waken I could barely recognize him. For seven years — the long, last years of childhood — Bhondaripur had been my universe. I had willed Cawnpore out of my memory and into my dreams, as if my mother's death, Bastard Bhavan, Moonshi's betrayal and all the rest of it were from another life, a distant incarnation of myself. But as I stood and walked to Ahalya's door I could feel this stranger taking hold, exalting my destiny, thrilling to the prospect of adventure, while the zemindar in me trembled.

Ahalya was wiping the milk from my sated little boy's chin when I entered her room. I paced about for a moment, bracing myself for the falsehoods I had to tell her, and then, holding my breath, I told her I had to leave.

The anger in her eyes now vanished, and seeing this I faltered and looked away. I told her the lie just as Baroo had fed it to me, and it was obvious from the way she looked back at me that she believed every word of it. I don't know what I'd expected from her then. I suppose I'd hoped she would see the anguish in my eyes, force the truth out of me, and rush out into the fields to chase the mad old man away.

Instead she began to cry. I tried to comfort her, but when I embraced her I too began to cry, and to hide this I had to back off into the darkness. One month, I promised her. One month and I would never leave her again.

She hurried to the kitchen to prepare my kit for the journey, overloading the satchel with potatoes, onions, sugar, chapattis, peppers, and a little vat of ghee, while I dashed over to the patwari's house to tell him I was leaving.

I found him lying half naked among his cushions, and as I stepped into his room I saw someone dart into the shadows of the kitchen. Mangal Singh was so intoxicated that I had to reach down and shake him by the shoulders. He merely rolled his eyes upward when I gave him my instructions, and dropping him back onto his pillows I said to the shadow in the kitchen, 'Tell him I'm going, Sakuntala, but only for a month. And tell him that if there's so much as a digit out of place when I get back I'll send him packing.'

I tried to savor the remaining hour or so I lingered, breathing in the sweet dung smell from the newly coated floors, listening as the chowkidor passed with his bamboo staff ticking along the lane, and watching my little boy sleep in his mother's bed. He was to look after his mother, I told him, as Ahalya now bustled about in my room. I was his father, I whispered, and I would be back, and as he squeezed my thumb and softly farted I kissed him on his glossy brow.

I had to command Ahalya to stop bustling, and then, for the longest while, we embraced in the front room, and still she asked no questions, made no pleas or protests. I felt my will draining away as I held her, the breath sucked out of me as we kissed, and before it was too late for all of us I took up my satchel and rushed out into the fields.

I was early, as it happened, for the chowkidor was still wakeful and the moon cast long shadows across the lanes. But as soon as I reached the mustard field Baroo stepped out and nodded.

'Good,' he said, slinging his satchel over his shoulder and stepping toward the western ridge. 'Let's go.'

PART FOUR

THUGGEE

CHAPTER

38

We travelled against the strange, hot wind that blew that night, and as the clouds churned by, the moon seemed to dart behind them. Baroo walked quickly through the dark fields, his old legs never faltering, no matter how deep the shadows through which we passed, while I stumbled and bloodied my shins on a host of stumps and brambles.

I wasn't sure why Baroo led me with such stealth and urgency: circumventing villages; starting at the coughing of watchmen on patrol among the huts, the distant barking of dogs, the rustling of hares and jackals along the thorn rows. I couldn't have known then and wouldn't learn until months later that when dawn next broke back in Bhondaripur, and Sakuntala dropped her bucket into the well, she would hear a shallow, unfamiliar noise from within and peering over the rim she would see, bulging up at her with horror and regret, her strangled father's eyes.

'Ah, Balbeer,' Baroo now said, pausing to urinate in the corner of a field, 'you're going to thank me.' He nodded over his shoulder at a small village in the distance. 'What a spectacle the world is from the road, with treasures abounding at every turn. See that village in the moonlight? To our eyes it looks like blocks of silver thatched with gold: all possibility, all opportunity. But to the poor beasts who sleep there it's all mud and dung and hardship. What a multitude of curses I've saved you from! What burdens I've lifted from your shoulders!'

As I stood listening, I gazed at the flying moon. It had reached its zenith and seemed to pause with us to rest.

'You're my son, Balbeer. My heir,' Baroo continued, shaking himself dry and rearranging his clothes. 'And I have so much to teach you,' he said, turning to face me. 'So much to —

'*Idiot!*' he suddenly exploded, slapping me across the face. The blow was nearly painless, but landed after so wide a sweep of his arm that I fell to the ground and tears sprang to my eyes.

'Are you crazy?' Baroo demanded to know, stepping forward and casting his shadow over me. 'Do you want to go blind?'

I gaped up at him, one hand to my cheek, and hesitantly shook my head.

'Then why do you stare at the moon like a dying pig?'

I tried to speak, but couldn't find my voice.

'Shut up!' Baroo exclaimed, shaking his fists. 'You can't be a simple village fool any longer. You're going to be a chieftain, a prince. But first you have to master the darkness. Would you stare into the sun at noon?'

I shook my head again.

'Of course not. It would burn your eyes and make you blind. And so it is with the moon. Give the moon your eye and the darkness deepens around you. Why do you think the owl can fly among the stars and spot a mouse's whisker in the brush? Why do you think I never stumble while you trip and fall and lag behind? It's because the owl and I have shunned the light and bathe ourselves in the shadows.'

Suddenly, beneath his dark, scowling brow, his mouth widened into a pitch-black grin. 'So,' Baroo said, helping me to my feet, 'your lesson begins, Balbeer. Put the light behind you,' he said, raising one ring-choked finger, 'and you will stupefy your foes.'

Baroo scanned the horizon with his one eye and shifted his satchel from one shoulder to the other. 'Come,' he said. 'We've got a long way to go and the night is half over. From now on, Balbeer, you have to remember everything I tell you, because if you lose one link in the chain of knowledge I'm going to give you it'll lead to ruination.

'Now, to begin at the beginning, a little theology,' Baroo said, clearing his throat and proceeding past the distant village. 'Tell me, Balbeer. Is God good?'

I had never been asked such a question, and in the wake of Baroo's blow it left me stammering. 'Yes,' I finally blurted. 'That is, I – '

'Good,' said Baroo, leading me along a furrow of a newly plowed field. 'And is he all-powerful?'

'I think so,' I replied. 'He must be, or he wouldn't be God.'

'*Very* good,' Baroo exclaimed. 'You're a smart boy.' Baroo paused and looked heavenward, as if something had just occurred to him. 'But Balbeer, how are we then to account for evil?'

'Evil?'

'Evil,' Baroo said with a troubled frown. 'If God is good and God is all-powerful, how do we explain evil?'

I thought this over for a moment as we passed through a row of trees and walked out onto an uncultivated plain. Actually, flattered by Baroo's assumption that I was capable of answering such a question, I thought about thinking it over, which is another matter.

'Well, Balbeer?'

'Evil,' I said, stroking my chin as if lost in thought.

'For example,' said Baroo, 'let's say a bandit comes upon a money carrier resting by the road.'

'A money carrier?'

'Yes, Balbeer. May Kali scatter them in our path. They dress as beggars and carry bankers' treasures in their tattered clothes, and they're going to be the crop of our fields.'

'The what?'

'Never mind,' Baroo said, cutting at the air with the edge of his hand. 'One lesson at a time. So,' he continued, 'a bandit comes across a money carrier — no, that's not good enough. We need someone more trusting. A dhobi's daughter. That's better. A dhobi's daughter whose beauty would dazzle the sun, whose purity would shame the Ganga at its source, washing laundry in a stream. And let's say this bandit begins to gather together her effects, and when the girl protests, he strides out into the water and slashes her with his knife and leaves her to drown.' Baroo looked at me. 'Isn't this an evil, cowardly deed?'

I swallowed hard. 'Yes,' I replied in a small voice.

'And shouldn't such a villain suffer for such a terrible crime?'

'Well, yes,' I said.

'A thousand tortures would be too good for him, wouldn't they?'

'Well . . . ' I said, trying to anticipate Baroo's next question.

'Oh, Balbeer,' Baroo exclaimed, 'you are hard-hearted! Think of that poor maiden, created to bring nothing but joy to the earth, drowning in her own blood and slipping lifelessly down the stream!'

'Yes,' I said. 'Yes, a thousand tortures *would* be too good for him.'

Baroo stopped walking and smiled at me. 'But why?'

'Why?' I asked, looking up at him.

'Yes, Balbeer. Why? What did the bandit do that was so bad?'

I inhaled sharply, my mind racing. 'He – he killed a maiden. He stole her things.'

'True,' Baroo said, walking forward again. 'Terrible crimes. But who actually committed them?'

This seemed a stupid question as I hurried to catch up with him again. 'The bandit,' I said. 'You told me the bandit committed them.'

'Yes, in a way. But who commanded him?'

'I – uh . . . *you* did?' I asked earnestly.

Baroo stopped again, his one eye glaring at me and raised his fist. 'Don't trifle with me, boy,' he sputtered through his three remaining teeth. Then, seeing my surprise, for I hadn't meant my reply as a joke, he lowered his fist and sighed. 'We're assuming this crime is *real*, Balbeer,' he said, slowly stepping forward, 'not just a fairy tale. So I'll ask you again. Who brought them together at the river?'

This time I thought carefully before replying. 'God?' I finally ventured, ready to duck.

'God,' Baroo said as if lost in thought. 'God . . . I can understand God creating the maiden in all her perfection. But the bandit?'

'But God is all-powerful,' I said. 'He creates everything.'

'Yes, Balbeer, but didn't you just tell me that God is good? Why would He have created a bandit? Why would He have put a maiden in his path? Why didn't He reach out of the earth and strike the bandit dead?'

'Maybe He was going to leave it to the police?' I asked, trying to be helpful.

Baroo glared at me and paused to control himself. 'All right then, where *were* the police?' he asked. 'Surely God at least can bring the police on time?'

'I suppose,' I said.

'So, Balbeer, how could God, who sees everything, who's all-powerful and good, close His ears to the maiden's screams when

He could have turned the bandit to ashes?'

I thought about this for several steps. 'Maybe,' I said, ' – maybe he was too busy.'

'*Idiot!*' Baroo exclaimed, and he swung at me again. But this time his garments swirled so dramatically and my eyes were so accustomed to the dark (owing to Baroo's excellent advice) that I backed out of his way at the last second and his hand swept past me like a scythe.

Glowering, Baroo stepped forward as if to strike again, but he stopped short, took a deep breath, and merely shook his head. 'Balbeer, my boy, you disappoint me. "Busy with something else"? *God*? You speak of Him as though He were a tailor lost in his stitching. This is God we're talking about. Ever-present, all-knowing, all-powerful God!'

'Well,' I suggested, 'maybe such a thing never happened, or if it did the girl was brought back to life and the bandit was destroyed.'

'A very pretty thought,' Baroo said, holding a bramble branch out of my way as we passed through a low patch of brush. 'But it has happened. I've seen it happen. And I've seen worse. And I've seen the evildoers live long lives afterward, never wanting for money or sleep or the devotion of their families. No, Balbeer. Let's not worry this example any further. Such things happen and God sees them happen and never lifts a finger. Now, why?'

I resented Baroo's leading me like a child to his foregone conclusions; I'd had my fill of it at Bastard Bhavan. 'How should I know?' I finally replied.

'Excellent!' Baroo exclaimed. 'Now we're getting somewhere. Oh, Balbeer, I was about to give up on you, and at what peril to your young life!

'Exactly right. How can we know? We only know that God is good and all-powerful. Who knows? Maybe the maiden's effects were ill-gotten and the bandit was the rightful owner's heir. Perhaps the maiden was going blind and the bandit saved her from a life of misery.'

I was relieved that I had at last pleased Baroo, but I wasn't comforted by the mitigations he was reeling off. Why, I wondered, would God have permitted any of the evils Baroo was describing? Why would He take me from my family?

'God permits what men call evil because it suits Him,' Baroo said, as if reading my mind. 'Look here,' he said, kicking aside a manure patty and, after a momentary search, snatching a dung beetle from the ground. 'Regard this poor creature,' he said, holding it close to my face. 'See how it struggles, as if there were any hope that I won't kill it.' The beetle waved its feeble limbs in the night air, and the insect cacophony seemed to rise in pitch around us.

'Can this low, pitiable vessel of a damned soul know what's in my heart? Can it know that it's about to die by my whim, merely to illustrate a point?' Baroo slowly pressed his fingers together until the beetle, with a crackling noise, was crushed. 'Of course not,' Baroo said, flicking the bug into the darkness with a snap of his fingers. 'It was only a beetle, and couldn't know my purposes.

'And Balbeer, you and I are only men and can't know God's purposes. If God were to tell me, with auguries, temptations, sudden passions, to murder you, what man could dare condemn me for obeying?'

My breathing grew constricted, and I watched Baroo with renewed wariness.

'But I'm not going to murder you, my boy,' Baroo said with a laugh and a pat on my shoulder. 'You're my son. To you, if it pleases Kali, I'm going to will my pickax.

'*Wait*,' Baroo said, stopping again and holding up his hand. 'Listen.'

I listened, but didn't hear anything above the night's incessant insect song.

'There!' Baroo said in a loud whisper. 'Don't you hear it?'

I started to shake my head, but then I began to make out a distant gurgling sound, like a hookah bubbling, somewhere in the treetops.

'Do you hear it?' Baroo asked again, and I nodded. 'Ha!' Baroo exclaimed, grinning. 'It's the goorgooria, Balbeer. The call of the tharkavi owl. Oh, Balbeer, Kali is watching, just like in the old days. I can feel her eyes upon me. She gives the tharkavi owl her voice and perches him to our right, and because I'm of the covenant I know she's warning us of enemies crossing our path ahead.'

'What enemies?'

'Be still, Balbeer,' Baroo whispered, 'and follow me.'

We hurried along the edge of an irrigation canal for almost a mile until we came to a narrow road, which we furtively crossed and then skirted some distance. At last we reached a mango grove, and here Baroo commanded me to sit. Travellers had preceded us – there were the remains of a cooking fire, and the grass had been pressed down where they had slept through the heat of the day.

'We'll wait here until the danger passes,' Baroo said, removing a pinch of powdered tobacco from his satchel and tucking it into his cheek. 'That's better,' he said, squatting on his haunches.

Baroo sighed and patted the ground beside him. 'Feel how warm the earth is, Balbeer.'

I touched the ground, and it did seem especially warm, but I ascribed it to several stones jutting out of the earth nearby. 'Those rocks must still be hot from yesterday's sun,' I said.

'No,' Baroo said good-naturedly, 'But a good guess. Only the brotherhood knows why the grove's ground is warm. I spoke of a covenant, Balbeer. Did you know what I meant?'

I sat cross-legged, like a disciple, and tried to look attentive, though my legs ached and I could barely catch my breath in the heat.

'Well, do you?' Baroo asked.

I shook my head.

'Then listen to me.

'After Brahma's work was done and the seed of man was sown, a demon walked the earth, devouring humanity as quickly as it could take root. And so Parvati transformed herself into Kali, our protector from the wrath of God and man, and attacked the demon with her sabre. Though she was like a tree, the demon like a mountain, no monster is mightier than Kali, and she prevailed.

'But this was the demon of the blood seed, and from every drop of gore another demon sprang, each more terrible than the last, until they raged across the earth in a multitude, feeding on the tender shoots of mankind with their hideous teeth. Kali fell upon these, too, and killed them, but from their blood still more demons sprang, until for all her efforts the monsters had multiplied.

'At last she rested, and out of the sweat that poured down her arms she created a new caste of men and taught them to kill bloodlessly, with the hem of her garment, and dig their victims' graves with one of her teeth. These men she called Thugs – deceivers – and they did their work perfectly, never spilling a drop of demon's blood, and thus man was saved from extinction.

'To reward her warriors, Kali granted them an eternal dispensation to sacrifice some of man's numbers for their own gain. And everywhere a demon was buried a mango grove sprouted, and there, to the sites of their ancient victories, the brotherhood brought its victims.'

Baroo spat tobacco over his shoulder. 'And that's why the ground's so warm.'

I looked down for a moment, bewildered.

'The *demons*, Balbeer,' Baroo said, stroking the dirt with his palms. 'They lie beneath us still, with their fires still flickering.'

For a moment the ground beneath my haunches seemed to lose its substance, and I saw, in a subterranean tangle of mango roots, the demons yawn and stir.

'For thousands of years the brotherhood prospered,' Baroo continued, rubbing his knuckles. 'We travelled in gangs of two, three hundred and worked the rivers and roadways of Hindustan, collecting our rewards. And could mankind *ever* repay us? Weren't we destined to prosper forever?'

Baroo's single eye grew large and wistful, and he spat out his tobacco. 'When I was a boy,' he said softly, as if he were speaking of a lost love, 'no traveller reached his destination without our say-so, no matter what kingdom he traversed, no matter how powerful and vigilant his escort. Diwans, nabobs, merchants, sepoys, bankers, even poisoners and cutthroats toppled into our graves. We spoke Ramasee, our own language, which would scald a brigand's tongue, and by the time of my boyhood our priests and chieftains had gathered together all of Kali's revelations into a code that assured our success. The calls of birds, the angle of the rain, the visits of cats and donkeys, even our own farts and sneezes warned us of danger and vouchsafed our prosperity. Let the throne of Delhi pass from Turk to

Afghani to Timurid, along the roads of Hindustan Thuggee was constant and supreme.'

Baroo stared forward for a moment, his head tilted slightly, as if listening to music.

I fidgetted in the silence and finally cleared my throat to speak. 'But how did you become a Thug?' I asked in a small voice. 'Were you born to it?'

Baroo slapped the dust from his hands and looked at me. 'Born to it? Of course I was born to it. We're all born to our professions, aren't we?'

I supposed so.

'No matter how we may struggle against them, Balbeer, our destinies are sealed at birth.'

Baroo stood and stalked for a moment through the grove, peering into the darkness and sniffing at the air. 'All right,' he said finally, sitting near me. 'We'll be safe here for a while. I was going to save my story for later, but I suppose now is as good a time as any.'

Baroo's features fell, and he slowly exhaled as if to calm himself.

'When I was a boy in Jeysulmere,' he said, his voice plummeting to the bottom of his throat, 'I saw very little of my father. My mother tried to explain why merchants of his caste had to spend long months away from home, but I was bewildered by his absences and ached for his homecomings. I was his only son and tried hard to be worthy of him. When I reached your age, Balbeer, he finally came for me and took me with him on a business trip to Bikaneer, and we travelled east with thirty servants to ease the journey and a string of camels burdened with quilted bundles.

'Along the way we met a caravan of what we took to be Kashmiris heading for the Deccan to sell their rugs and shawls. My father warned them that the road ahead was infested with Thugs, and the Kashmiris bugged their eyes and asked if they could travel with us, and thus attain security in numbers.

'My father looked troubled, for true Kashmiris are usually more wary of strangers than this, and who was to say these weren't Thugs themselves? Besides, they were travelling by bullock carts that would slow our progress.

'But in the end he agreed, and soon the Kashmiris were treating him like an old friend, for there was never a man more lovable than my father, Balbeer. He could sing songs as sweetly as the shama bird, and for every phenomenon of nature he knew a fable. After a day or so the Kashmiris were welcoming him into their tents and carts and begging him for more songs and stories.

'One evening, when the Kashmiris were crouched in prayer, my father directed a servant to take me into the surrounding jungle to collect kindling. The cook's smoke was already fragrant with onion and turmeric, and I didn't want to go. But my father told me that it was his wish, and thus my duty, and in his eyes I saw what would befall me if I argued further, so I did as I was told.

'The servant led me a little distance until we came upon a heap of brambles, which I proposed we gather. But the servant objected, saying that we were not far enough from camp.

' "What nonsense is this?" I asked him. "Why should we go any further when there's plenty of kindling here?"

'The servant's eyes grew large and he seemed very nervous, but I insisted, and we set to gathering the bramble twigs.

'After a while I began to hear the strangest noises from the camp's direction: the beating of hand drums; loud singing; interrupted shouts; grunts; a single fevered wail.

'I asked the servant what the noises were, but he denied hearing anything and began to tremble. I listened some more; for a moment all was quiet again, and then I heard a faint chopping sound.

' "Something's wrong," I said. "Something's happened to my father."

'The servant, though he looked terrified, told me I was merely being frightened by the night song. But I wouldn't listen to him, for I had never been one to imagine things.

' "I'm going back," I said, shoving him aside and running toward my father's campfire.'

Baroo looked at me searchingly. 'Oh, Balbeer,' he said. 'You're so much as I was that night: tenderhearted, headstrong, brave. I knew in my bones that my father was in danger, for hadn't he warned the Kashmiris that Thugs abounded in those parts? Could he have been certain that the Kashmiris themselves weren't Thugs, disguised in the garments of their last victims? How could I have left him in such company?

'I rushed toward the camp with my little dagger upraised – ready to die for my father, if need be, just as you, Balbeer, are ready to die for me. But when I reached a little rise in the earth and looked at last upon the camp, I saw my father seated peaceably by the fire, bundles of cloth piled all around him.

' "Father," I called out. "Are you all right?"

'My father leapt to his feet and began to shout angrily at me. Where was his servant? he wanted to know. Where was the kindling he'd commanded me to gather?

'I tried to explain, but he backed away, cursing me for my disobedience, and it was then that I saw his servants working in a circle behind him, and when they turned to look I saw that they all held knives and their knuckles were smeared black in the firelight.

'I stumbled forward, my heart kicking against my ribs, and my father stepped aside. It served me right for disobeying him, he told me. Now, in ignorance of our covenant, I was to see all at once what he had intended to show me little by little.

'His circle of servants, who weren't servants at all but his comrades – tempered Thugs with whom he shared his booty – made way for me, and there, at my feet, I saw a deep pit with a pillar of earth in its center, its banks streaming with blood. Arranged around the edge of this pit, like flower petals, lay the Kashmiris, all broken and twisted, so that at first I couldn't sort out their arms from their legs, their backs from their fronts.

'My father's comrades looked at him with their knives poised, and with an exasperated sigh he nodded back at them. "He's seen the worst of it, my brothers," he said. "Proceed. Kali must have her blood."

'And so, with shrugs, they slowly pushed the Kashmiris into the pit, calmly stabbing at their eyes, their chests, stomachs, buttocks, and thighs as the naked corpses slithered in, so that all the gore gushed into the pit and not a drop spilled onto the ground around it, and there arose from the earth such an odor of blood and bowel that it seemed to reach into my nostrils and down my throat and stir my entrails like a spoon.

' "Here, my son," my father said, pushing me forward. "If you won't gather kindling you can help our brothers here."

'He pushed me down to my knees, and a young man I was to know as Magada, my guru, grabbed my hand with the dagger in it and sank the blade into a Kashmiri's stomach, pulling it sideways so that it cut across the soft, white belly and a warm breath, like a sigh, gusted damp against my knuckles.'

Baroo paused to clear his throat. 'I didn't faint, Balbeer. Nor, though the bile roiled in my throat, did I vomit. And for my courage I was forgiven by my father and congratulated by his men.

'But how could I have understood what I'd seen? How could I not have been tortured by such bloody revelations? There stood my father and Magada appraising the booty, and there the Kashmiris were being buried, their eyes bubbling as earth tumbled down upon them, and there the quilted bundles were being opened to reveal straw: dummy cargo which they now replaced with the Kashmiris' wares. All about me there was nothing but death and deception.

'I hardly slept that night, and when I did my dreams would slap me awake, and, lying in the dark, listening to my father's snore, I entertained the strangest notions: that my father had taken a monster's form in the night, that he wasn't my father at all but a demon risen from the murk to steal me from my mother.

'But in the morning everything seemed normal again. Food was prepared; the talk was of women, kings, and destinations. I couldn't for the life of me find a trace of the Kashmiris' grave, so skillfully had it been covered over, and the camel's bundles bulged as before. I would have suspected that I'd dreamed it all up, except that my father and the others spoke of it casually as we broke camp and Magada gave me a Kashmiri's gold ring from his share of the loot.'

Baroo held his fist toward me. A thin gold band shone from one finger. 'See?' he said. 'I have it still. Even the Feringhee couldn't wrench it from my finger.

'So I knew it hadn't been a nightmare. My father and his friends had destroyed the Kashmiris and taken their treasures, and everything I'd been taught in my mother's house had told me that such deeds were wicked crimes. But my father shared his chapatti with me, tearing it with his own hand. My father loved me, and his comrades loved him, and held in his affection I still swelled with pride. If my father was a Thug, there was a reason. If he killed, it was for a purpose.

'Like God,' I heard myself say.

'Like God,' Baroo agreed. 'And though his deeds filled me with dread, I believed that when I came to understand his purpose my terror would be extinguished and I'd take my place beside him.

'So I remained with my father on his expedition, and over the next weeks many more were snared in my father's scarf. An old hadji, all puffed up with righteousness, snored his last at my father's camp, bequeathing us a sack of pearls. Three banias with their fingers stained with ink fell prey to my father's flattery on the Jodhpur Road. A troupe of Rasdaris entertained us with a pageant of Krishna's life until, at my father's signal, they were dispatched for their ornaments.

'I took no part in these killings, but kept watch beyond our night camps, and when the singing and drumming and digging stopped I'd return to assist with the burial. Once, when sepoys came near while a killing was in progress, I stumbled into their path and feigned an injury, thus detaining them until I could no longer hear the sound of Magada's pickax. For this deception I was given an extra portion of the booty, and it was determined that I was destined to become a bhurtote, a chieftain, just like my father.

'With each adventure I learned new auguries, signals, and taboos. I was an eager and retentive student, Balbeer, for just as I'd hoped, knowledge of the covenant quelled my fear and shielded me from the horrors around me.

'So I learned fast – as fast as I could – for wasn't my terror the shameful price of my disobedience? The covenant astonished me, but to all my ignorant questions Magada and my father had answers. So harmonious was Thuggee's alliance with Kali that every action, even those I thought most cruel and gratuitous – the breaking of our victims' bones, the mutilations of their flesh – were prescribed and sanctified.

'Such practices kept buried bodies from shifting, bursting, disturbing the surfaces of their graves and luring jackals with their ooze and vapors. And in return for their protection Kali was called to her meals by the crack of bone and served her beverage – blood – which she lapped from the graves with her lolling tongue like a panther drinking from a stream.

'In time I grew impatient with my nightwatches and began to pester my father for a chance to prove myself. Magada sided with me, for he believed I was a prodigy and shouldn't have been wasted on children's work. But my father wouldn't listen. I was already ahead of myself – it was time to be prudent. Murder was business, not childish sport, he said. My youth would end soon enough.

'I was frustrated by my father's cautiousness and brooded through my vigils, tying and retying my waistcloth into the shape of my father's sacred scarf and securing it with my ring.

'Toward the end of our expedition the pickings grew sparse, and for some days we passed only those whom Kali forbids us to kill: women, Sikhs, cripples, barbers, pariahs, poets. But just as Holi was approaching we came upon a small camp of Powindas, hill people who trade in condiments and wool. As a rule, Powindas are fierce, Balbeer, but easily duped, and these were no exception.

'By this time my father had put all our booty to use in his disguise. He posed as a diwan bearing gifts to his raja's allies and awed the Powindas by buying up all their wares with the hadji's pearls. They invited my father to rest in their camp, and they seemed to like me especially, for that's another thing about Powindas, Balbeer; they have a weakness for boys. To prove my skills as a deceiver, I sang them songs and giggled seductively at their indecent propositions.

'One of the Powindas was a dwarf, a melancholy man who tended the donkeys and, at his brothers' insistence, entertained us with a comic dance, and as he gravely pranced around the campfire my father signalled me to withdraw.

'I was fascinated by the dwarf's strangely solemn antics and at the same time believed I had earned the right to take part in the killing, but I slipped away and took up my vigil some distance from camp. And as I sat down to practice tying my roomal I could hear Magada's hand drum rattle and the now familiar music of murder.

'I waited a while for the din to subside, but it didn't. In fact, it grew louder, and above the usual noises I could hear angry, desperate shouts.

'I began to tremble, for now I was sure that calamity had struck my father and his comrades – *my* comrades – and I raced back toward them. But as I rushed through the black jungle I collided with something – someone – and tumbled to the ground.

'I leapt to my feet and glared down into the dark and there I saw, crawling in the dust, the little Powinda dwarf. I was thunderstruck and began to back away, but in his panic he mistook me for a local boy.

' "Save me," he exclaimed, hugging me about the waist. "Please save me. The Thugs are after me."

'I pushed him off, trying to catch my breath, and I was about to call out to my father when I felt Kali's eyes upon me.

' "Come with me," I told him. "I'll save you." And with that I ran deeper into the jungle with the dwarf stumbling at my heels.

'All around us we could hear my father's men calling to each other and beating at the brush. We reached a gully and hid there in a tangle of bushes, listening together as my comrades passed.

' "We're safe," I told the dwarf as their shouts receded. "You won't be harmed."

'The dwarf leaned his melon head against me and began to sob and wring his little hands.

' "Oh, thank you," he whined. "You're my protector," and then he told me about his brothers, and about my father's deception.'

Baroo widened his eye and ducked his head around in imitation of the panicked dwarf. 'You should've heard him babble!

' "He claimed he was a diwan!" he said. "But I knew he was lying. I knew he was a Thug! A low, murderous beast! The Thugs are fathered by vultures," he told me. "Didn't you know that? And they drink their mothers' menses. Oh, yes! This is so. I know this for a fact. And now they will roast my brothers and devour them on the spot and leave not a bone behind. And I could have been one of them. Oh, you are a beautiful boy!" he said, embracing me again. "You've saved me! Let me embrace you! We're brothers!" '

Baroo waved contemptuously at the air. 'And thus he sputtered his lies and nonsense, his tears wetting my clothes. And in his ecstasy of gratitude and relief he didn't see me twisting my waistcloth between my fists.

' "But where shall I go?" the dwarf cried, crawling about on the ground and shaking his head. "All my brothers murdered! All my people dead! Oh, I'm going to be sick! I'm going to be sick!"

'But before his gorge could rise I wrapped my cloth around his neck, pressed my knee into his back, and strangled him.'

Baroo's fists tightened. 'You'll see,' he said, looking at me. 'It's easy to kill. No one likes to admit it, Balbeer, because if it's easy to kill then it must be just as easy to be killed, and nobody likes to dwell on that. But it's like rutting, Balbeer. Remember how complicated a thing it was in prospect? Awesome, wasn't it? Almost fearsome. But in the event a very simple thing, and afterward you wondered what all the fuss was about.'

Baroo looked into the distance, his head raised as if he were tasting a delicacy. 'Yes, even that first time, with no one to instruct me, killing was an easy thing. Of course, the dwarf struggled: but absurdly, like a turtle, and I never lost control of him. In a moment he made a snoring noise, and at last, with a breaking of wind, he expired.'

Baroo glanced over and saw me shudder. 'Have I frightened you, Balbeer?' he asked through a yawn, rubbing his face with his bony fingers.

I tried to shrug as if unimpressed, but the shrug turned into another shudder, and my jaw began to tremble.

'Well, don't worry about it too much,' Baroo said. 'A perfectly natural reaction. You just haven't been initiated. I don't expect you to understand right away. All I ask is that you listen closely, Balbeer. Fear is just a limb of ignorance. I'm going to do everything in my power to keep you from being afraid, because you aren't any use to me afraid and I'd just have to kill you, and I don't want to kill you because I love you so much.'

CHAPTER

40

I suppose I should have bolted right then, but where could I have gone? I'd lost track of our route hours before, and how could I be sure that even if I managed to escape Baroo I wouldn't fall into worse hands? Well, maybe not *worse* hands; but at least this particular villain liked me, and I couldn't count on getting along so famously with the bandits and marauding soldiery who infested the country-side. I must have felt protected from evil in such evil company and thus believed somehow that villains preyed only on the innocent, not on one another. I and my family were safer, it seemed to me, in Baroo's favor than out of it.

'So where was I?' Baroo said, putting his fingers to his lips. 'Oh yes. The dwarf. I'd just killed the dwarf.'

Baroo scratched himself under the arm and coughed.

'I carried my little victim back to camp and buried him myself. My father and all his comrades wept for joy, and that night one of the Powindas' goats was sacrificed and I was given the goor – the sacred sugar – to eat and I sanctified my oaths with Magada's pickax.

'The goor transformed my universe. The sun and moon became Kali's blinding eyes. The sunset was blood running at her feet. The stars were the skulls on her crow-black breast. And when we reached home with our treasures, my mother touched my feet and set a lamp burning in my honor.

'So that's how I became a Thug, and in the years that followed I killed a hundred men by my own hand, hundreds more at my command. When my father died, he offered his command to Magada, but my guru read a few bad auguries and retired to a landlord's life in Jeysulmere. And thus, though I was much younger than some of my men, the command fell to me.

'And I was a good bhurtote too. I was never as rich or famous as some of my brethren, but the greatest treasures are conspicuous, and fame, for a Thug, is no blessing. I was careful, strict, pious, just like my father, and I would recruit only the finest men into the fold, not the pariahs, addicts and scum some bhurtotes relied upon.

'And believe this,' Baroo said, raising his finger and leaning toward me. 'All our murders were mercies. Our victims died as we all should die: quickly, with no fuss, laughing, singing, enchanted by a verse, uplifted by a prayer. A quick jerk of the scarf, and a kick in the balls to stop their senseless struggling, and it was over in a twinkling.

'Some of them might have wanted to live longer, but we all have to die sometime, and why not on one of life's peaks instead of in one of its valleys? The Hindus among them might have wished to have been cremated, but how better to serve God than provide His daughter with sustenance? I tell you, we did them all a favor.'

'A *favor*?'

'Balbeer, tell me. How would *you* prefer to die? Lying around in your usual sulk or gazing up at the heavens, praying for the soul of one of your fellow human beings? Why, I've coaxed the sweetest prayers from the most venal old banias: fat, slimy old usurers who'd never given so much as a crumb to a starving man, so that even if it was the very first time in their whole shameful lives that they'd ever had a kindly thought, they died like saints in the eyes of God.

'We never killed in Jeysulmere, and we always sold our booty to the Maharaja at bargain prices. That way he didn't have to tax his people so heavily, and everyone could prosper. So is it any wonder he gave us his protection? Even the English winked at our commerce, and in return Kali spared them our attentions.

'For many years our luck held fast and princes' fortunes were strewn across our path, but the world was changing. The new men were impatient with the covenant and eager to strike out on their own.

'It's hard for young men to lead; the old men resent you, the young have no respect. Two of our recruits, though they were bold and talented youths, questioned the importance of our auguries and ceremonies, and I spent time I should have devoted to business just trying to keep them in line.

'Maybe that is where I went wrong. Maybe if I'd been able to give both ears to the auguries I would have taken Magada's course and retired to the country.

'After my second daughter's birth I led an expedition north toward Bikaneer to prey on the Mahajans' opium trade. Kali tried to warn against it. A comrade's cousin was trampled by a camel the day before we left, and on the morning of our departure my wife had one of her nosebleeds.

'I suppose I should have obeyed these signs, but my recruits were so impatient, and after a day or so the auguries improved: women passed with pitchers full of milk, a lizard spoke to me at midnight, a crow cried from the back of a cow.

'For almost a week we travelled without seeing a soul. The desert was as bare as the moon, and my men grew discontented. *This wouldn't happen if Magada were leading us*, they grumbled. *By now we'd be straining under our sacks of booty and heading home satisfied.*

'At last I was forced to thrash one of them for his impudence and send another home for questioning the covenant. This quieted the others for a while, but I knew that if prey didn't come along soon, chaos would overtake the lot of us.

'But then, one morning, just as we were about to give up, we saw in the distance a procession of camels led by a palanquin and two mounted guards armed only with swords and lances. The sight of it made our spit run after so many days of deprivation, and we hurried to catch up.

'The guards — old, bewhiskered men in towering turbans — confronted us with their swords drawn, and we could tell from the rams' heads on their hilts that they were in the service of the Raja of Bikaneer and thus fair game.

'Some of my men were ready to slaughter them on the spot, but I silenced them and called out to the guards that we were pilgrims bound for Pushkar to worship the Creator. The old guards seemed to believe me. They confessed that they'd been lost since passing through a whirl of dust the afternoon before and asked if we could lead them back to the Jodhpur Road. I protested that we were in too great a hurry to change our course, but the guards promised a reward if we guided them, for they were escorting a dignitary of some means. We asked who the dignitary was, but the guards were sworn to secrecy and could only tell us that the dignitary was rich and highborn and could provide for us amply. I spouted a few pious protestations to quiet whatever lingering suspicions the guards may have had and then, of course, agreed to help them.

'We led them around for miles, zigzagging aimlessly across the desert, all the while seeking to know the identity of our mysterious benefactor. The two camel drivers were dim-witted, and the four palanquin bearers, quite properly, kept their mouths shut. But still it was obvious from the silk brocade and silver ornaments that before long all our waiting would be rewarded.'

Baroo listened closely to the night for a moment, sighed and shook his head. 'Can a man be so dazzled by his prey that he grows deaf and blind to the auguries? As I led that little caravan to its doom, did a jackal cry and I not hear it? Did a snake slither unseen among my pony's hooves?

'But,' Baroo said with a plaintive look, 'I was always so careful. I followed the protocol to the letter. I'd passed up far more promising prey when the omens were merely cautionary. Surely I'd have seen and heard such warnings on that empty plain. No, I can only suppose that Kali, displeased by a few among her guild, withdrew her protection from all of us and deprived creation of her voice.'

Baroo now seemed to brace himself and began to speak rapidly, his lip curled, his eye fixed on a distant point. 'We stopped for refreshment at a watering hole, a patch of muck on a stony plain. The old guards tested the water on their own palates before carrying a skin of it over to the palanquin and slipping it through the fluttering silks.

'I knew I couldn't lead them around the desert until nightfall without raising their suspicions, so I signalled to my men to take their places; there was no use putting it off any longer.

' "I think you can find your own way now," I told the guards. "Here, let me draw you a map."

'The guards and camel drivers circled around me as I drew in the dirt with my dagger. One of my men interrupted to ask if there was time to smoke a hookah, which was our code for "All is ready."

' "Yes, brother," I replied without looking up. "Bring out the tobacco," which is our signal to kill.

'With a noise like partridge flushed from the bush my brothers' scarves flew, and when I looked up I saw the guards' and drivers' empurpled faces, bug-eyed and gaping. The palanquin bearers ran off, screaming, but they were bone-weary and three of my men soon overtook them. In a moment they were all dead and we turned and set our eyes on the palanquin.

'Its frame rattled as I approached, and I could hear hard, fast breathing from within. With my dagger poised I reached out and swept the silks apart.

'Lest you judge me, Balbeer,' Baroo said, raising a hand as if to quiet me, 'remember that to that moment I'd been faithful, and faithful at a time when the brotherhood was losing faith and floundering. There were Moslems in the Punjab who confused Kali with their prophet's daughter and killed paupers, stonecutters, and oil vendors and others we're forbidden to kill. In the Bengal Thugs took to killing with guns and leaving their victims unburied, and from every drop of blood they spilled did not an English demon spring?

'It was all Kali's will, of course. The brotherhood had let her down, and even those of us who'd kept the covenant were bound to pay. So she sent the English against us with their courts and policies. Thug informed on Thug; our brotherhood festooned the gallows.

'Had we never crossed that caravan's path I might still be a bhurtote with all my comrades gathered around me, dividing our spoils by a campfire. But there's no use second-guessing fate. What happened was – must have been – Kali's mysterious pleasure.'

Baroo took a deep breath and lowered his gaze. 'So I tore open the palanquin's silks, Balbeer, and peered into the perfumed shade. There, cowering in her nurse's arms, was a little girl, as delicately beautiful a little girl as I had ever seen, dressed in the robes of the Jeysulmere court.

'We were struck dumb, paralyzed. No prey was more forbidden to us than a woman, and here trembled not only an old ayah with a dagger in her fist but a little girl, as fresh as dew – the whole arc of womanhood between them, and both the beloved of our king and protector, the Maharaja of Jeysulmere.

'What could we do? We couldn't leave them to die in the desert. And what if they somehow found their way to safety? Wouldn't the Maharaja, heretofore our understanding friend, turn against us?

'But how could we kill them? Wasn't Kali herself the avenging embodiment of Parvati, the greatest goddess of all womankind? Wouldn't the heavens shower sorrows upon us if we harmed her sisters?

' "Don't be afraid," I told the ayah. "We won't hurt you." But the old woman snarled back at us and brought her dagger to the child's throat. "Please, Mataji," I begged. "Don't be afraid. We're Thugs."

But the ayah's eyes darted about and she gripped her dagger tighter, and in an instant I could see that she had resolved to save the child from our hands by killing her.

'In that same instant I leapt into the palanquin and wrenched the child out of the ayah's arms. The child began to scream, and the ayah cried out too, but before my men could disarm the old woman she had shrieked God's name and stuck the dagger into her heart.

'The child wriggled free from me and cast herself atop her dying nurse, from whose mouth blood was gurgling into the dust. As if with one voice my men let out a moan and began to rush around in confusion, for such spilling of blood was a great curse.

'The camels and ponies raced off in all directions, and dust rose around us. Some of my men chased after them, but the stones in the earth seemed to rise up and trip them and the animals got away.

'The little girl screamed and kicked as I lifted her off her nurse's corpse. "Hush," I said, stroking her head, for I was a loving father and had a way with children. "Hush, little princess. You won't be harmed."

'But everywhere there was confusion and alarm. Some of my men kept stumbling after our animals. Others began to strike at the ground with their pickaxes. And through it all I paced about, alternately shouting commands to my men and murmuring futile reassurances to the wailing child whose clothes were fouled with her ayah's blood.

' "Hush," I kept saying. "Hush." But with increasing anger, for all our gear, our booty, our hopes were lost.

' "Kill her," one of my men said, with his scarf fluttering from his fist. "She's our ruination."

' "We can't," I told him. "We'll take her with us. I'll marry her to my son."

' "We have to kill her, Baroo," another said. "It would be merciful. She's been deranged."

' "No!" I bellowed back. "She'll calm down soon!"

'But she didn't calm down and wouldn't stop screaming, and after a time I began to hear other voices in her cries: warnings; threats; wicked, mocking laughter.

' "Quiet!" I shouted at her as my men stood by, their faces streaked with tears. "You must be quiet!"

'But perhaps the little girl was already with God, for she clawed her way out of my arms and flung herself against a stone: once, twice before I could retrieve her. The first blow crushed her nose, the second broke her teeth, and now looking down in my arms I saw not a wounded, terrified child but a demon's face, a monster's mask spraying blood with her incessant shrieks.

' "Be still!" I shouted at last, gripping her neck and shaking her. "You will be *still*!"

'And I silenced her forever.'

CHAPTER
41

If these were the memoirs of a proper hero I could now report that I fell upon the old monster and killed him then and there. But I didn't. I just sat there, listening. I hadn't been raised to think of myself as an agent of justice, which itself had been so muddled by Baroo's sophistry, by his very survival. If God hadn't seen fit to exterminate him, how could I?

Even in my terror and confusion I could tell that Baroo was testing me with his gruesome tales. I was determined to pass, and not just in order to survive, either, for Baroo's convoluted challenges had begun to snag my Rajput pride.

So as he stared back at me in the silence that followed I kept my eyes fixed on him, though sweat trickled down my brow and a chill enveloped my shoulders like a bat's wing. I think that if Baroo had had both his eyes and the moon hadn't descended behind the treetops, he would have seen the horror on my face and, taking it as one of his omens, strangled and buried me on the spot.

But instead Baroo smiled back at me with apparent satisfaction. 'Not a very nice story, is it?' he said, smoothing his moustache with the back of his hand. 'But you're a lucky boy to hear it. Why, if I'd been told such cautionary tales when I was starting out, perhaps tonight I'd still have both my eyes and a cellar full of treasure and brave men beside me at the campfire.'

Baroo reached into his satchel and withdrew a small brass jug.

'Here,' he said, uncorking it. 'You'll need a swig before we move on.'

I gulped down as much water as I could before Baroo snatched the jug from me.

'So, Balbeer,' he said, slapping the cork back into the jug, 'tell me about your father.'

I wiped the water from my chin and scowled at him. 'What?'

'Your father, Balbeer,' said Baroo. 'Who do you think he is?'

'I know who he is,' I said defiantly.

'Really? And what caste is he?'

'Ahir,' I said, for of course I meant Channa.

'What?' Baroo said, gripping my arm. 'An Ahir? But you told me you were a Rajput. I *remember*. I wouldn't have made a mistake about that.'

'Well,' I said, as his fingers closed on my bicep, 'Channa's an Ahir, and I have made him my father.'

'*Channa?*' Baroo exclaimed, releasing me. 'Your *father*? That gimpy simpleton?'

'He's not!' I snarled back at him, shocked by my own vehemence.

Baroo gave me an amused look. 'All right, Balbeer,' he said calmly. 'So he's not a simpleton. But he's not your father, either. So answer me, Balbeer. What was your father's caste?'

'I – I never knew my father,' I said, and to my shame tears sprang to my eyes.

'Poor lad,' said Baroo, patting me on the back. 'But you knew your mother, didn't you? What about her?'

'She – she was a Rajput – '

'I thought so.'

' – from a royal house.'

'*Now* I remember!' he said. 'You're a Harigarh Rajput, aren't you? Well, why didn't you say so in the first place? Balbeer, you're the most infuriating child. You've got to be more careful in your replies,' he said, shaking his finger at me and winking, as if forgiving a prank. 'If I weren't such a patient fellow I might have killed you just now, and all because you told me the first thing to pop into your head.'

I heard myself apologize.

Baroo stood and listened for a moment to the night. 'Here,' he said, throwing me his satchel. 'You carry it from now on. We can go now, but keep your eyes on the shadows, and try to keep up with me this time.'

But before I could retrieve his gear, Baroo was off into the darkness. For a moment I stood alone in the grove, wondering if I dared to escape from Baroo's mad dream. But when I slung the satchel over my shoulder I lost my balance and felt the ground shift beneath my feet as if Kali's demons were astir. With a groan I hurried after Baroo's dim, retreating figure.

When I caught up with him he was still talking, unaware that I'd fallen behind. 'What was his name?' he was asking. 'I've forgotten.'

'Wh-who?' I said, falling into step beside him.

'Your servant. At least I think he was your servant. The man who was travelling with you when I adopted you.'

'You mean Moonshi?'

'That was it. Lovely man. You must have been very close.'

'Yes,' I said, my delinquent anger growing. 'We were.'

'I could tell you were,' Baroo continued obliviously. 'I remember Moonshi very fondly. A fine singing voice, as I recall.'

'He was – ' I said, ' – he was like a father to me.'

'Was he?' Baroo said gently. 'What a lot of fathers you've had, Balbeer! Have you ever counted them up? Your father who sired you, whoever he was – that's one. Your servant – that's two. Our friend Channa, and now me. That's four! Four fathers! Well, let's see if I can't do better by you than the others did. Let's see if we can't turn your luck around.'

CHAPTER
42

We walked through a field infested with rats and had to maneuver carefully to avoid their holes. The landscape was getting drier and began to wrinkle, like a frowning brow, into shallow ravines. We descended a slope onto the marble-smooth bed of a vanished river and followed its ghostly course for several miles.

Baroo was silent for a long while and set a hard pace, but at a bend in the nullah he stopped suddenly and stared at me with a heartbroken look. 'You know,' he said in a voice that seemed on the verge of breaking, 'I wouldn't have killed that little girl in the old days. Kali would have steered me off her track.'

Baroo seemed to wipe his eye and then reached out and gripped my shoulder as if for support. 'What befell me after I plundered that little caravan will break your heart,' he said, shaking his head. 'I hate to burden you with it, Balbeer, but you've got to know about it if I'm going to make you understand your destiny.'

Baroo scowled and resumed walking. The banks of the river grew steeper as we travelled, and soon we were deep in the black shadow of a canyon. 'Remember that all our animals had fled and all our treasures with them?' Baroo asked, releasing my shoulder. 'Well, with that it seemed that Kali had doomed us all. My men lost their senses and utterly abandoned the covenant, just when they needed it most. So they drove me from them and would have stoned me to death if I hadn't outrun them. And then, without me to guide them, they left our victims unburied and our booty unclaimed.

'So it was just as Magada had foreseen. Before the hyenas could do their work that night, one of those elusive camel trains came upon the little girl's corpse, and thus the Maharaja learned of his niece's extinction, and from the marks on her escorts' throats he knew it was our work and sent his soldiers across the kingdom slaughtering Thugs and scattering their families.

'By the time I reached my village it was already known from the mewling confessions of my doomed brethren that I had led the luckless expedition, and all that remained of my wife and children was their severed heads left to greet me at the threshold.'

Baroo paused to wipe the spit from his lips. 'Oh, Balbeer, Kali's wrath is an awesome thing. She had demolished everything I'd loved, every hope, every certitude, and still she wasn't done. What did she want from me? What was I supposed to do?

'For three days I stumbled through the desert, grieving and despairing, with no auguries to guide me, like a bat floundering in the daylight. And can you believe that Baroo Singh – the bhurtote you see before you – could ever have been captured by a lone Feringhee?

'Well, I was, and by a green young Englishman at that, out for his afternoon ride. The Feringhee are our worst foe, Balbeer, but they have a soft spot for criminals. This one treated me very kindly until we reached the gates of Jeysulmere, when he handed me over to the Maharaja's guards, promising that no harm would come to me before I'd had a proper trial.

'I shouted to him that they were going to butcher me on the spot, but he shook his head and cheerfully rode back into the desert. And when he was out of sight the guards beat me with the butts of their lances and as they held me down one of them worked his thumb and forefinger around behind my eye and popped it out like a plum pit. But the Englishman heard my screams and returned with his pistol drawn taking me back into his custody in the name of his Queen and country and all the rest of it.

'He was most apologetic and grieved over my eye, but he was also ambitious, and all duty. So he chained me to a mustard cart and transported me from garrison to garrison all across Rajputana and Gwalior, until by the time we reached Jabhalpur huge crowds had gathered to gawk at Baroo Singh, the great Deceiver of the desert.

'At last the proud young Englishman brought me into the presence of Sleeman Sahib, the one they called Thuggee because he waged such war on the brotherhood. He was a priggish, impatient sort of man, and talked to me as if I were a child.

'But he knew all our ways, even our language, as if some spell protected him. He said the covenant was broken, the brotherhood doomed, but he might save me from a shameful hanging if I helped to hasten the inevitable.'

Baroo let out a bitter laugh and began to walk more deliberately, as if he were wading through a stream. 'But I knew what stock these Feringhee put in their procedures. "Gallows?" I asked him. "What gallows?" He had no proof that I was a murderer, only the rash suspicions of a grieving king. No company court would convict me on that.

'But Sleeman merely smiled and clapped his hands, and a cowering man limped into the room.

' "Tell me again, my old friend," Sleeman Sahib said to him, still smiling at me. "What do you know about Baroo Singh?"

'The cowering man slowly moved his hands away and though his hair was white and his cheeks were all caved in, I knew he was Magada.

' "He's a bhurtote," Magada answered, and he said I was the

son of Bajid Lal and succeeded my father as chief of the Jeysulmere guild.

' "And how many has he murdered?" Sleeman Sahib asked.

' "Hundreds," said Magada, and he stared at the floor.

' "And you will testify to these things?"

' "Yes," Magada said and he raised his head and saw the ragged pit where my eye used to be, and he began to weep, and I wept with him, for as surely as they'd plucked out my eye, they'd robbed my old guru of his will.

'So Magada shuffled off, and Sleeman folded his arms and told me that Kali had abandoned me, that my only hope was to help him.

'I confess to you, Balbeer, that I was tempted. Did I need more proof that Kali had abandoned me?

'But then it came to me, even as the tears flowed for my old friend.'

Baroo stopped walking and raised a quivering fist.

'When a mother abandons a child, does she keep punishing him? Why would she bother, unless it was to instruct him, to improve him, to show him that she loves him?

'No. If Kali had abandoned me she would have taken my faith with her. She was testing me, and even if all my brethren betrayed her, what would my soul have been worth if I failed her now?

'So I stood up straight and dried my tears, and I told Sleeman Sahib I would die as the best of my brothers had died, slipping the noose around my own neck with Kali's name upon my lips.

'Sleeman called me a fool and sent me off to rot in his jail until my trial. They put Magada in the cell beside me to break me down, but he was too wretched to be much use to them. He tried to offer me some of the extra food the Feringhee gave him for his services, but I refused it. Nor would I answer his questions, nor listen to his sad excuses. Only when he was sleeping would I speak to him, and this I did each night, whispering Ramasee through the bars, until Kali's spirit had swirled like a river into his upturned ear.

'It took weeks before they brought me to trial. I was to be judged with fifty other Thugs at once, as an example to the remnants of the guild that still roamed free. So one winter day we all filed out onto a parade ground, where Sleeman sat under a great orange tent and called his witness.

'Magada swore an oath on Ganga water instead of on the pickax like a true Thug, and he condemned a dozen other of my brethren before he got around to me.

'They asked him how long he'd known me, and he cleared his throat to speak, but when he opened his mouth his voice broke forth in loud barks and he fell to the floor with his head all twisted around and foam bubbling from his lips.

'Sleeman said he'd been bitten by a rabid rat in the jail, but I knew whose teeth had stilled his testimony. Without Magada to bear witness against me the judge would not hang me, so I was sentenced to live the rest of my days in prison, on exhibit, like an animal in a zoo.

'Magada died that night, and I saw how the Feringhee repaid his services: by burying him like a dog beyond the compound walls. Now I knew I'd chosen the right path. I had clung to Kali's covenant through her blackest rage and soon she would reward me.'

The riverbed grew damper now, and here and there black puddles of water reflected the stars. We walked along the edge of its banks, over smooth stones that clinked under my feet but not Baroo's – his footsteps were always silent, even when he was caught up in his story.

'I've lost count of the years I languished in the Jabhalpur jail. Five, six years, I suppose; I can't be sure. My prisonmates were all Thugs, but they'd informed and renounced the covenant and I wouldn't have anything to do with them. They wove rugs for the tourists who came to gape at us, and some of my brethren even put on shows, demonstrating their crimes with false embellishments. And though I wouldn't take part in their pantomimes or recount my adventures, I was one of the most popular attractions, for I was still Kali's unrepentant son.

'Then Sleeman Sahib departed and his successor deemed me a bad influence and sent me off in chains to Agra, casting me into the dungeon of the old palace. My cell was no more than a stone pit with an iron lid and in its eternal dark nightmares raged about me, sleeping and awake. I shared my cell with rats and vermin and my eye burned from the guard's torch when he brought me my putrid gruel.

'I might yet have surrendered to the bloodless god, too, if the guard hadn't told me in a whisper that the great Sleeman Sahib, sailing home with his wife and children, had died of a fever off the coast of Ceylon, in hell's own bubbling harbor!

'The news revived my faith: the darkness of my cell became Kali's warm, protective bosom, and in my jailmates' screams I heard the owl and the jackal singing.'

There was a faint light behind us from the advancing sun, and the insects' music was subsiding. My feet ached and my legs felt limp as I walked beside Baroo, but I was too dazed to care.

'I didn't wait long for my deliverance, for one night I found scratched on the rim of my bowl a message I could just make out in the departing glare from the guard's torch. "Soon, brother," it said, "All will be crimson."

'So that's how I learned of the Devil's Wind, and when it reached Agra it blew open the hatch of my cell, and there was Kali, waiting for me at the prison gate.

'Of course, in my condition I wasn't much use to the rebellion, and I collapsed on the march to Delhi. But it was just as well, for once again Kali had spared me the company of fools. When the Feringhee struck back the old Moghul wet his throne, and everywhere the Feringhee marched the trees bore bloody fruit.

'I passed through one village where they'd hanged every man and boy and gathered the women and children in the panchayat and burned them alive. And I passed through places where men had been blown from guns and lay in pieces like butchered meat, and you couldn't see the earth for the vultures and you couldn't see the vultures for the smoke.

'But I stayed ahead of the slaughter by travelling southwest, to Bundi, where I fell in with a poor old Mahratta who was on the run himself. We travelled together for a while, but he was tiresome company, always bewailing his circumstances like an overthrown king. I trotted out all my songs and stories to cheer him up, but it was no use, and one morning, when we stopped to rest by the Pindari Bridge on the Kotah Road, I began to taste the sugar in my spit and determined he should die.

'But just when I was about to strangle him, all unbeknownst to him, of course, a ridiculous pair of Mang riffraff came along with daggers upraised, demanding all our goods.

'Well, it was just a matter of kicking the first one in the balls and the second in the windbag and there was an end to their adventure, but the Mahratta took me for a hero. He confided that back in Gwalior he'd been a man of means, with a spice shop and a family and a little jagir out in the countryside. But now the shop was burned up and his sons were dead in the Jhansi siege and the Feringhee were hunting him down for selling sweetmeats to the sepoys. He'd been planning to disappear into one of the desert states and from there sell his Gwalior jagir, but now he said he'd lost all heart for worldly things, and to reward me for saving his life, which he proposed to devote to Shiva, he gave me the deed to his land.

'Well, I was in no position to turn him down, so we went to a babu in Bundi to have the transfer witnessed and recorded. But with all due respect to Shiva it seemed to me that Kali deserved the old man more, so a couple of nights later I strangled him for her and offered him up with all the proper observances.

'I suppose you've guessed what the old man's jagir turned out to be – the very land you will pass along to your little son, Balbeer. But it turned out that he'd been mistaken about his sons, for one of them still lived, and his terror of the Feringhee had been unfounded, for no one had taken the slightest interest in his commerce with the rebels. Of course, his son was not glad to see me. It wasn't my fault that his father had given me his legacy, but what was done was done, and I still expect people, no matter how often they may disappoint me, to accept their lot with a little grace. I offered to share with him, for that's the kind of man I am, Balbeer, but he wouldn't be satisfied and put up all kinds of fuss, and in the end I finally had to throw him out of Bhondaripur.'

Baroo sighed and smacked his lips. 'And there was an end to it, at least for the time being. It turned out Mangal Singh had been goading the lad all along, for he'd been robbing the family blind for twenty years or so. But one look at me and Mangal Singh knew I was not a fearful old fool like the Mahratta.

'Bhondaripur was a shambles when I got there, with half its fields burned off and its tenants nearly starved. But I put things right. If Kali had chosen to reward my faith with a quiet life as an eccentric old Rajput in a cluster of dung heaps and Ahirs, then I would make the most of it.

'But I had such trouble sleeping. I kept hearing auguries at night:

wolves whimpering, donkeys sneezing, cats hissing, crows, tigers, all
the beasts of the jungle and the field breaking into song. Sometimes
the omens were so momentous that I would rise off my bed and
follow them into the countryside, and as the nights wore on the
auguries led me further and further away and I'd be gone for days,
weeks at a stretch, searching for my destiny like a heartsick boy,
pricking my ears to Kali's whisper. And then came that night I found
you on the budgerow moored at Bithur and I knew at last where Kali
was leading me, how I'd survived all my brethren, how her fire still
burned in my breast. It was all for you, Balbeer. For the future.'

Moved, Baroo swallowed hard and looked away. 'Don't you
understand?' he asked, and the question seemed to catch in his
throat.

I didn't quite, but I felt a strange pity for Baroo now and a
pained affection that was no longer merely reciprocal, so I nodded
back to reassure him.

'I was saved so that Thuggee might live on,' Baroo said, looking
at me hopefully and blinking back a tear. 'I've been spared to plant
Kali's black seed.

'You, Balbeer,' Baroo said, gripping me by the shoulders.
'You're to be the prince who sprouts and blossoms in the dark.
You'll be as keen and merciless as an owl when I'm through with
you. Oh yes,' he said as he saw the fear and doubt stir my features.
'Yes, Balbeer. *You*. You'll be pious and pure and exquisite in your
deceits. Your scarf is going to fly unseen, like vapor, and your pickax
will break the earth without a whisper and you'll collect mankind's
debt to Kali's guild.'

Baroo leaned in close, steadying his eye as if taking aim, and
then, with a great sigh, released my shoulders.

'You can do it, Balbeer,' Baroo said softly. He looked up into the
sky. Half the stars had disappeared in the sun's precursive glow.

'Besides,' he said through a sudden yawn, 'you must.'

CHAPTER

43

The wind stopped as soon as the sun began to strike the low hills ahead of us. We continued along the riverbank and passed among a group of bald and quizzical storks feeding on bloated toads: an omen, Baroo assured me, of good things to come.

'How are you doing with that satchel?' Baroo asked with a sympathetic look.

Too winded to reply, I nodded back at him and groaned.

'I know it's heavy,' Baroo said, 'but Kali's going to love you all the more for carrying it. It's full of gifts for her — odds and ends, really, not like the treasures I used to lay at her feet. But,' Baroo said, lowering his voice almost to a whisper, 'Kali's a woman, after all, and with women it's the thought that counts.'

Quick brown martins peppered the sky, their cries overwhelming the music of the retreating night, as Baroo led me across the riverbed and stopped amid a cluster of boulders.

'From here it's half a day's walk,' Baroo said, rubbing his face with his bony fingers.

I set the satchel down and stood for a moment with my hands on my knees, trying to catch my breath. 'Where . . . ' I finally asked as the sweat dropped from my forehead to the dust at my feet, 'are we going?'

'First to Kali's house, Balbeer,' Baroo said. 'We have terrible work to do, and for that we need Kali's approval. She's abandoned all her shrines but one, and it's still a good distance. Can you make it?'

I didn't think I could, but, swallowing hard, I lied to please him.

'Well,' Baroo said, 'maybe *you* can, but I need to rest. We'll sleep here until the sun begins to decline. That way we should get there just as they're opening for business. How does that sound to you?'

'Good,' I said, collapsing to the ground.

'We won't have to keep watch around here,' Baroo said, fitting himself into the skug of a boulder. 'The locals think this place is haunted.'

It was, I thought, and by us. 'But what about tigers and snakes?' I asked, looking around at the interstices and ledges above us.

'Tigers and snakes never bother Thugs,' Baroo said, closing his eye and sighing. 'It's the scorpions I worry about. Now get some sleep. You'll need your strength tonight.'

I remember feeling strangely exposed in the light that morning. The sun made the world look vacant after the lush and spectral darkness through which we'd travelled, and I caught myself longing for night to return. What was happening to me? I wondered as I lay down some distance from Baroo. Could he have already so changed me that I cringed in the sunshine like a mole?

I stared at the blue sky for a while, trying to reaccustom myself to the daylight, and wondered about Ahalya and my baby son. She would already be awake by now and wondering how far away I was. I imagined my son at Ahalya's breast as she stoked the cooking fire, saw his little fingers uncurl, watched the village slowly stir as the sun caught the tops of the trees. But before the tears could well up in my eyes I was fast asleep.

'Get up, Balbeer. It's time to go.'

I don't know what I'd been dreaming when Baroo awakened me, only that it made me leap to my feet with my eyes wild and my heart racing.

'Balbeer!' Baroo shouted, shaking me by the shoulders. 'Snap out of it!'

I jerked free of his grip and stood staring at him, glimpsing in a moment before I regained my senses a vision of the disaster that was soon to overtake us.

'Are you all right?' Baroo asked, frowning at me.

With a gasping breath I shut my eyes and nodded.

'Now don't go crazy, Balbeer,' Baroo said, slowly tearing off a piece of bread he was eating and handing it to me. 'You're going to need your wits about you.'

I took the bread and squinted around in the light. It was past noon, and the lines of the far off hills wavered in the heat. 'I'm all right,' I replied, taking a bite out of the chapatti.

'All right,' Baroo said, walking out from among the sheltering rocks. 'Let's go, then.'

Baroo was silent all afternoon as we trudged on, and when his breathing grew labored and his shoulders began to sag I remembered that he was an old man after all and wondered if his omniscience and vigor had been illusions of the concealing night. He stopped often for water and rest, pretending it was for my benefit, and though I welcomed each respite I could tell it was out of his necessity, not mine.

We reached the hills in the late afternoon and snaked our way among them. Each symmetrical hill stood some distance from the others, like a tidy pile of grain on a merchant's tray. The flat plain on which they stood was sandy and barren, but the slopes of the hills were tufted with scrub and small, stubborn trees whose foliage was more gray than green. Walking around one of these hummocks we surprised three snouty, bristled boars, which screamed and snorted their alarm and scrambled off in a bank of suspended dust.

Just as the sun began to funnel down between two hills we reached a little structure set against a stony slope, the first sign of human habitation we'd seen since dawn.

'Well, here it is,' Baroo said with a grand sweep of his arm. 'Kali's house at last.'

It was the humblest destination imaginable, a small stone building with the mortar crumbling away, its roof atilt, its door a crude crisscross of weathered planks secured with a padlock.

'It may not look like much to you,' Baroo said as I gaped in bewilderment, 'but Kali's a goddess of particular tastes. This is the last temple in Hindustan where she still deigns to make herself flesh. All the others have been defiled by muddlers and reformers.' Baroo reached forward and ran his fingers over the huge iron padlock.

'But we're early,' he said, looking toward a dense thicket of brush some yards off. 'We'll hide over there until the others show up. Can't be too careful; the Feringhee have been looking for this place for thirty years.'

We lay back behind the thicket to wait. As dusk fell and the night creatures began their songs and whispers, a light seemed to rise in Baroo's eye, and he started to nod, mutter, and chuckle to himself, as if conversing.

'Just listen to that music,' Baroo said at last with a contented sigh. 'Even the stars are singing.'

Baroo looked at me and grinned. 'Balbeer,' he said, 'I envy you. Tonight you're going to see what a pale and empty life you've been leading, what vain prayers you've been babbling.'

Baroo's grin fell for a moment, and he sat up to peer through the brush. 'That is, if they ever get here.'

'Who are we waiting for?' I asked, tentatively peering with him.

'Mata, the priest,' Baroo replied. 'And the supplicants, and the virgin, of course.'

'The virgin?'

'Yes,' Baroo said, 'and the goats.'

'Goats?'

'Hush,' Baroo said. 'I think I hear something.'

We listened closely for a moment, and I began to make out a distant jingling, like a string of cowbells.

'There they are,' Baroo whispered.

A lamplight appeared from around a hillside, illuminating six hooded figures leading two angular goats. 'It's about time,' Baroo said, climbing a little way up the slope for a better look.

As they neared the temple I could hear them chanting something to the tap of a shallow drum. A plume of dust rose behind them, silvery in the moonlight, and the pierced tin lantern cast a crown of light upon their path.

'Come with me,' Baroo said, sliding down on his haunches. 'And don't say a word.'

'Hail the Mother Goddess!' Baroo called out as the hooded throng stopped in front of the temple.

'Baroo Singh?' came a dry, cracked voice. 'Is that you?'

'Yes, Mata,' Baroo replied in a hearty voice. 'At last!'

Baroo led me forward until we stood blinking in the lamplight.

'Baroo Singh,' Mata said from the shadow of his hood. 'You look awful.'

Baroo knelt and touched Mata's feet, irritably signalling me to follow suit. 'What did you expect, Mata?' he asked. 'It's been ten years.'

'And who's this?' Mata asked, leaning down as I touched his feet.

'This is Balbeer,' Baroo said, grabbing a fistful of the back of my shirt and pulling me to my feet. 'The boy I wrote you about.'

Mata leaned toward me for a closer look, and peering fearfully from under my brows I could just make out his features beneath his hood: a parched face, all peaks and hollows, with a streak of crimson grease from the bridge of his nose to his thick, slack lips.

'And this bumpkin is to be your prince?' Mata asked with a sneer.

'He's no bumpkin,' Baroo said, his smile stiffening. 'He's an orphan of noble blood with glory written on his forehead.'

'Will you keep it down?' Mata suddenly barked at his chanting entourage. 'I can't hear myself think.'

Mata stared dubiously at me for a moment more and then lowered his lamp and shrugged. 'If you say so,' he said, heading for the door to the temple. 'It looks like a pretty ordinary forehead to me.'

'Don't worry,' Baroo whispered to me as Mata turned and walked up to the door. 'Mata never could read a forehead.'

Mata handed his lamp to one of the others and began to pat at his robes. 'The key,' he muttered. 'Where's the damn key?' He searched a little longer and then whirled around to glare at his disciples. 'Well?' he demanded. 'You heard me. Where's the bloody key?'

The others turned and began to search their clothing, grumbling accusations.

'You had it.'

'No, you had it last.'

'I never had it. He gave it to you.'

'Liar! Mata gave it to you.'

'He never gave it to me. You – '

'Silence!' Mata shouted as he pulled the key out of his waistcloth and shoved his nearest disciple, sending them all stumbling backwards and causing the goats to bleat.

'Five of you following after me and none of you could find the key,' he snarled, grabbing the padlock. 'I suppose I have to do everything myself.'

Mata inserted the key and wrestled with it for a while, finally jerking at the padlock with such violence that the whole latch came off in his hands and the door itself, after teetering for a moment, tore loose from its rusted hinges and fell forward in a puff of dust.

'When are you going to fix this thing?' Mata snarled at the man from whom he now retrieved his lamp. 'You've been promising to take care of it for months.'

'I know,' the man replied, almost sobbing, 'I'm sorry. I don't know what's wrong with me. I should be beaten. Why do you put up with me?'

'Oh, shut up,' Mata said, stepping onto the fallen door and holding up his lamp. 'Don't be such a wretch.'

Baroo pulled me forward, and we all followed Mata through the doorway. He seemed to proceed an impossible distance into the little building, until I realized that it had been constructed over the mouth of a cave. As we entered, squealing bats flupped past us to escape the lamplight.

The temple let out a foul breath, and as I stood choking just inside the doorway the others squeezed by and bustled about, lighting mustard lamps and muttering incantations and making themselves at home.

'Here it is, then,' Baroo said softly. 'You're in Kali's house, Balbeer.'

A huge canopy hung from the ceiling, directly beneath which the floor was black and glossy like marble but beyond whose shelter everything was encrusted with bat guano. Far in front of us, where Mata now knelt to light a row of torches, was a huge, rounded stone, like a half-embedded grinding wheel, over which a statue of Kali glistened and glowered in the intensifying light.

With a sharp intake of breath Baroo fell to his knees. 'Beautiful,' he whispered to himself. 'Horrible. Magnificent.'

Maybe it was my exhaustion, or the way the torches cast their wavering light, but the statue seemed not inanimate so much as suspended, as if frozen in the middle of some horrific assault. I didn't dare move for fear I might break the spell and send her careening forward, slaughtering everything in her path.

Her hair and four arms were entwined with snakes, and in her hands she held a sword, a dagger, a lotus, and a skull. All her anklets, bracelets, and rings were coiled cobras, and around her head she wore a diadem of skulls and bones. Her breasts were like spearheads, her tongue hung like a slab of meat from her gaping, fanged maw, and her red eyes bulged in demented indignation.

'Isn't she wonderful?' Baroo asked as I stared. 'Isn't she everything I said she was?'

I felt as if I might faint, and shutting my eyes to the sight of her I fell to my knees beside Baroo.

'That's my boy,' Baroo said. 'Oh, son, this is a dream come true. To kneel with you in Kali's house.

'Isn't he perfect?' Baroo called out to Kali's figure. 'Haven't we chosen well, my mother?'

'Quiet down,' Mata said. 'Nothing's ready. Nothing's ready. Who was supposed to clean up after the last time?' he asked, carrying a little heap of bones to the doorway and tossing them out into the night.

'Madoo,' someone said. 'It was Madoo's turn.'

'Madoo?' Mata said, slapping the dirt from his hands. 'Might as well leave it to the rats as Madoo.'

'I do my work,' one of them piped in a wounded voice. 'I just wasn't feeling well.'

' "I just wasn't feeling well," ' Mata mimicked. 'It's always something, isn't it, Madoo? What's it going to be today? A headache?'

'No,' Madoo said. 'I don't have a headache.'

'Of course not,' Mata said, addressing the others. 'Madoo never has a headache *before* we pass around the bhang and penetrate the virgin. Only afterwards, when there's work to be done.'

Mata rubbed his eyes and turned toward Baroo. 'Oh, Baroo Singh,' he said with an exasperated sigh. 'It's not like the old days, is it? Remember this place before the Feringhee came? Remember the Raja's visits? Remember when you and the gang would show up in procession and heap jewels in the doorway?'

'Those were great days,' Baroo said, rising to his feet. 'But they'll come again, Mata. Balbeer's going to see to that.'

Mata gave me a doubtful look. 'Does he know our rituals?' he asked, narrowing his eyes.

'No,' Baroo said, patting my back. 'You might say he's a virgin.'

'Well,' Mata said, pushing off his hood. 'At least that makes one virgin for the ceremony.'

'What do you mean by "one"?' Baroo said, looking back through the doorway at the lone figure standing outside with the goats.

'Now don't get excited,' Mata said, signalling to the figure to enter. 'She's a virgin all right, in a manner of speaking.'

'In a manner of speaking?' Baroo asked, glowering at Mata. 'Either she's a virgin or she's not, and if she's not I want my money back.'

'Look,' Mata said, stopping the hooded figure and passing the goats' lead ropes to one of the others. 'She's the best I could get. The market's all dried up. You think it's easy finding virgins in this day and age? Baroo Singh, I admire your spirit, but you've got to make a few concessions now and again. This new Raja of ours doesn't donate girls to us any more, and the Feringhee have run our suppliers out of the kingdom. Besides,' Mata said, 'the rest have grown sort of attached to her.

'And you've got to admit,' Mata said, suddenly reaching around and opening the girl's robe, 'she isn't hard to look at.'

The girl made no move to cover herself as her clothing fell to the floor, but merely stood with a downcast look in the glow from the lamps and torches.

'Turn around,' Mata gently told her as Baroo and I stared, and she slowly revolved about, the light and shadows slipping along her body's slopes and valleys. She was what old Kushal Singh had described to me as a dove woman, with strong hips and large, round breasts.

'See what I mean?' Mata asked. 'And none of your skin and bones, like some of them. You know how much it costs me to keep her like this?'

Baroo, his one eye burning, slowly shook his head.

'With some women you give them a chapatti and they blow up like a bladder. But you could feed her enough for an army and she wouldn't put on a kilo.

'Still,' Mata said, giving her a light pat on the buttocks, 'when she does put it on it's in the right places.'

Baroo, trying to recover some of his irritation, shook his head. 'She doesn't look like a virgin to me,' he muttered. 'I don't know if — '

'And what's a virgin supposed to look like?' Mata asked, raising the girl's chin. 'Look at this face. Demure. Innocent. Have you ever seen anything more pure?'

Baroo shrugged and turned around to feign his displeasure. 'Well, I just don't know,' he said, wringing his hands together and staring up at Kali.

'What did you want, an infant?' Mata asked imploringly. 'She's a woman, Baroo Singh. Sure, she may have been through all this a couple of times but it hasn't affected her a bit. She's still the modest little fawn she was when I found her.'

As Mata and Baroo bickered, the girl raised her eyes and, when Mata wasn't looking, winked at me, running the tip of her long, lewd tongue around her lips.

'Well,' Baroo was saying, 'if you say so. It just seems to me — '

'Look,' Mata said, leading the girl to the altar. 'The way I figure it, a virgin stays a virgin just so long as she confines herself to these ceremonies, because during these ceremonies she becomes the vessel of Kali, right? And when Kali's spirit departs she becomes a virgin all over again.'

'But,' Baroo said, his eyes fixed on her as she walked with the graceful sway of an elephant, just as Kushal Singh had told me, 'we are going to sacrifice her, aren't we?'

'*Sacrifice* her?' Madoo exclaimed. 'What is he talking about?'

'Well,' Mata said, helping the girl up onto the stone, 'that's what I wanted to talk to you about, Baroo . . . '

'Oh, no,' Baroo said, emphatically shaking his head. 'No you don't.'

'The trouble is,' Mata said, 'this one here is kind of special to us, and frankly we just don't have the kind of momey it takes to replace her.'

'What do you mean?' Baroo said. 'I sent you money to cover all your expenses.'

'It wasn't enough.'

'It always used to be enough,' Baroo snarled.

◆————————◆

'Are you comfortable?' Mata asked the girl as she lay back on the curved stone. 'Are you too chilly?'

'Mata!' Baroo shouted, and the others shrank back against the walls of the cave.

'Baroo Singh,' Mata said evenly, 'it was enough twenty years ago, maybe. But not today. Twenty years ago we could sacrifice a child every week, we could cover the walls with leopard skins, we could carry Kali's image through the streets.'

'Mata,' Baroo growled, stepping forward with his fists clenched.

'Very well, Baroo Singh,' Mata said, 'If you must know the truth, she's – ' Mata took a deep breath. 'She's my niece.'

'All right, everybody,' Mata called out to the others with a clap of his hands as Baroo gaped back at him. 'Let's get naked.'

I still maintain that I'm a modest man, despite my performance that night (and disregarding some of my subsequent adventures, pursued as they were under the influence of opiates, spirits, and the threat of death). Even if I had been accustomed to such rampant nakedness as was now revealed and Mata and his disciples hadn't been strangers to me I still would have stood paralyzed with shame as they disrobed around me. For the plain truth was that however much the sight of the girl's body arched over the stone had aroused me I was no match for the endowments of that lurid congregation.

'Well,' Baroo said, resignedly unfastening his clothes, 'this isn't exactly what I had in mind, but I guess there's no point in bickering. Mata knows his business.'

Baroo pulled off his shirt and grinned at me. 'What's the matter?' he asked in a loud whisper. 'Is she too much a woman for you after that sparrow you've been married to?'

I glared at Baroo, my hands tightening into fists.

Baroo obliviously unwound his waistcloth. 'Come on, Balbeer,' he said. 'Kali's not going to wait all night.'

Beneath Kali's frenzied image the girl stretched and yawned and absently began to pick at her fingernails.

I fumbled vaguely with my waistcloth until it at last came loose, but before it could fall to the floor I clasped it to my groin and stepped back, as if to shrink into the shadows.

'Balbeer, what is the matter with you?' Baroo asked earnestly. 'Is it your manhood you're worried about?'

Mata, standing pale and naked at Kali's feet, clapped his hands again. 'Hurry up, Baroo Singh,' he called out. 'Let's get on with it.'

'In a moment, Mata,' Baroo said. 'Look,' he whispered to me, 'are you afraid you're not going to measure up to their equipment? Is that it?'

I merely stood stock still, swallowing hard.

'Because if that's all that's bothering you, take a look at me. Am I so endowed as to make you feel ashamed?'

I glanced briefly at Baroo's scarred and scrawny body.

'Well? Am I?'

I looked again. He wasn't.

'And I wouldn't have it any other way. Don't you know what these supplicants go through to attain such proportions?'

I slowly shook my head.

'Hell. That's what they go through. Pendulation, nettles, alum, peppercorns. And listen,' Baroo said, pointing as the others walked up to the girl and knelt around her. 'Do you hear that ringing?'

The jingling sound was louder now than when I'd first heard it outside the temple and seemed to conform to the congregation's every movement.

'Can't you tell where it comes from?' Baroo asked. 'Look carefully.'

I stared for a moment, trying to find the source, when Mata stamped his foot with impatience and I saw a small, round brass bell glitter from his foreskin.

'How'd you like to wear bells like that for the rest of your life?' Baroo asked. 'Wouldn't *that* come in handy when you're sneaking up on prey? And all for what? To be a low bull of a man? To terrorize your little wife?'

'Baroo!' Mata called. 'You get over here this instant or we'll start without you!'

'Right away,' Baroo said, gently coaxing me out of the shadows. 'Come on, Balbeer. We've got nothing to be ashamed of.'

I let go of my waistcloth, and we walked upon the cool, smooth floor to kneel with the others.

'Well, it's about time,' Mata declared as I looked at him across the slow billowing of the girl's stomach. 'Now then,' Mata said with a sneer, 'you young prince, Baroo Singh's pride and joy. Do you know why you've been brought to this place?'

'Yes,' I said with my head bowed.

'Then tell me,' Mata said.

'For Kali's blessing,' I said with a fearful look in Baroo's direction.

'For Kali's blessing. Right you are,' Mata said. 'But Kali doesn't give her blessing easily, boy. She's got a million other things she'd rather do tonight, terrible things you don't even want to think about. So we've got to —

'Madoo!' Mata suddenly shouted, and a hand darted back from the girl's thigh. 'Madoo, you're a bat's eyelash from getting thrown out of here,' Mata said to the small, scowling man beside me. 'So keep it up, Madoo, just keep it up.'

'There was a fly,' Madoo muttered. 'I was only — '

'Shut up,' Mata said, 'and be still.'

The girl grinned up at me complicitously as Madoo pouted floorward, covering himself with his hands.

'Come here, boy,' Mata said to me with a wave.

I looked to Baroo for reassurance, and he nodded to me to obey.

'We have an initiate with us tonight,' Mata said as I stepped up to the altar, 'so we're going to have to be a little more patient than usual.' Mata frowned at Madoo. 'A lot more patient in your case,' he said, smiling as the others, the girl included, snickered.

'Gaze upon her,' Mata said to me, abruptly speaking in a monotone. 'Feast your eyes upon her beauty.'

I looked down at the girl on the stone, who flicked her tongue at me again and lightly ran one hand along her stomach.

'Not her, idiot!' Mata hissed, spinning me around to face Kali. 'I mean her! Kali! The Mother Goddess!'

I stared up at Kali's twisted figure, trying not to flinch as my eyes collided with her horrific gaze. She seemed to drain the strength from my knees, and I felt Mata's hands pressing down on my shoulders and forcing me to kneel.

'Oh, Mother Goddess,' Mata intoned, picking up a small clay pipe and raising it over his head, 'we thank thee.'

'Oh, Mother Goddess, we thank thee,' his disciples droned

behind me, and over them I could hear Baroo's voice, charged with conviction.

They all chanted a hymn together, thanking Kali for everything for which sane men curse creation: pestilence, ignorance, war, poverty, and death. Their hymn had them longing to dance with Kali on the burning ground, and claiming every sort of benefit from her worship. As his disciples repeated each verse Mata puffed away on the pipe, and as he introduced new verses his voice slowed and deepened.

'My heart is your burning ground,' Mata chanted, now handing the pipe to me and signalling me to draw smoke from it. 'My heartbeat is the drumming of your feet.'

I inhaled deeply, as on a hookah, and filled my lungs with the dense, sweet smoke.

'And when I close my eyes I see you flying to me in a cloud of ashes,' Mata drawled, nodding to me to give the pipe another puff.

I drew in a second breath of smoke, wondering when it would begin to affect me, and as I brought the pipe away from my lips its fumes stung my eyes and I began to blink back tears.

'Now drink this,' Mata whispered to me as the others droned their ragged repetition. He handed me a small metal cup whose contents I decided not to examine before downing it all in one gulp.

'Brave boy,' Mata muttered as I proceeded to choke on the burning, viscous beverage.

'Take this youth into thy womb,' Mata chanted, helping me to my feet.

'If it be thy will,' the others answered.

'Give us a sign,' Mata said, turning me around to face the others.

'If it be thy will.'

I rubbed my eyes and shook my head to clear my vision, and when I looked down at the others they were no longer kneeling but standing over the girl, rubbing a black paste into her flesh.

'Give us a sign,' Mata said again, raising his hands above his head.

'If it be thy will,' the others answered.

Mata paused and gave the girl an exasperated look. 'I *said*,' he hissed, 'give us a *sign!*'

The girl seemed to be daydreaming, oblivious to the hands

passing over her, but then, as if suddenly remembering her cue, she put her hands over her head, raised her legs into the air and let out a long, high, unearthly whine.

'Oh, Kali, you are made flesh!' Mata exclaimed, pressing his palms together. 'Prepare thyself to accept this youth's devotion!'

'Oh, Kali, you are made flesh! Prepare thyself to accept this youth's devotion!' the others cried, grasping the girl's legs and stretching them apart.

By this time the bhang and the spirits were having their effect, and when Mata prodded me forward I stumbled dizzily and the room seemed to swirl about with the girl's body as its axis. My eyes fixed on her loins, whose mouth was daubed with henna, and I felt my heart begin to pound against my ribs as if for release.

Mata prodded me again, and I fell against the stone. As I knelt, paralyzed, at the girl's loins, a hand reached between my legs and with one movement applied a substance to my member that caused it immediately to stiffen and swell.

'We surrender ourselves to your worship!' Mata chanted as he stood over me. 'Take our child into thy womb!'

Baroo was so moved that the pit of his missing eye leaked tears as he nodded vigorously to me to do what was expected.

I shut my eyes and tried to calm my breathing, and flung myself between the girl's outstretched limbs, entering her with one blind thrust.

Now, lust without love is dead-ended, but the act itself is so familiar that there passes between any man and woman so engaged a sense of kinship. Up to that night I had ascribed this sensation to the love I felt for Ahalya when we first lay together in Bhondaripur. But when the girl wrapped her arms around my shoulders and pressed her plump breasts against my chest, I felt safe, as in a harbor.

I kept my eyes closed, and she rocked beneath me to the rising chant as the flesh prickled along my spine. To hasten my release I withdrew and thrust again with all my might, and just as I could feel myself about to burst I opened my eyes and screamed.

Not out of ecstasy, as you might suppose, but out of bald horror. For when I looked beneath me I saw not the fraudulent young virgin but Kali herself, her eyes rolling, her hair writhing, her tongue slithering like an eel among her bloody fangs.

I jerked back, trying to escape, but she gripped me as if in a slippery fist and began to milk me dry. I shut my eyes and screamed again and felt myself shrink, felt her swell up all around me and suck me bodily into the cavern of her black womb.

'*Kali, Kunkali, Kali, Kunkali,*' came a low, insistent chant from somewhere beyond the darkness, and as I kicked and bucked against the walls of Kali's womb I felt someone grasp my ankles and drag me back out into the light.

CHAPTER
44

I can't say for certain what happened next. The ceremony must have proceeded for a while afterward, and then I think I was dragged outside, for my heels were scraped when I awoke. I was laid down by the busted door to Kali's cave, and I remember how lightly I lay on the ground, how the stars swirled overhead, how my ears rang and roared.

But I don't know when the others departed, only that they were gone in the morning when I finally sat up. Baroo squatted nearby with his back to me, chuckling and chanting by a quartered goat whose blood reflected the dull haze. I called to him, but he waved his hand behind him as if to keep me from spooking some prey. He held a pickax up to the dim western sky, whispering to it like a lover, and gently setting it on a blanket as if laying a baby down to rest, he turned around and faced me.

If I'd been entertaining any hopes that I might outlast Baroo, I gave them up now. He looked a good ten years younger, and even the twist in his neck seemed almost righted. His eye was bloodshot but quick and wakeful, and when he spoke now his voice was deep and strong.

'Everything's perfect!' he exclaimed. 'Better than I'd ever dared to dream! Come, Balbeer,' he said, waving back at me. 'Kneel beside me.'

But I seemed to know before he spoke that I was to come to him, and I was already standing, still naked and shivering in the damp. I stumbled over to Baroo like a drunken man, for the earth kept tilting about underfoot and the horizon seemed to revolve like the rim of a cup.

'That's my boy,' Baroo said, and when I was huddled next to him he began to rummage around in my satchel.

He withdrew the little tin of ghee Ahalya had packed for me and threw it off into the shadows, and thus he disposed of the sugar she'd given me, and the salt and turmeric too, and soon my goods were fountaining up around us and clattering off into the dust. At last, when the satchel was all but empty, he threw it down before me and said, 'There. That's better. For the next seven days, Balbeer, you shall eat next to nothing. No ghee, no meat, no fish, no sugar. I'm going to purge you of all the world's corruptions. You won't shave. You won't give scraps to dogs or jackals. You won't indulge yourself in any act of charity. You won't rut with women nor clean your teeth nor wash your waistcloth. Only when I've freed you of all entanglements can I bestow upon you all the black secrets of Kali's heart. Do you understand?'

I did understand, for I still seemed to hear him even before he moved his lips. But my quick nod must have been lost in my shivering, for he cracked his knuckles against my crown and, still smiling, asked again if I understood.

'Y-yes, Barooji,' I quickly replied, ducking my head between my arms.

'No, Balbeer,' Baroo said with an irritated sigh. 'Not "Barooji". Don't you see? Everything's changed. From now on you call me *guru*.

'Now look,' he said, reaching forward and stroking the handle of his pickax. 'This is Khusi, Balbeer, Kali's tooth and the standard of the brotherhood. Khusi, this is Balbeer.'

The pickax was a simple affair, like a shepherd's hatchet. One end of its head was curved and pointed like a woodpecker's beak, the other end flat and newly sharpened. Its only decoration was a line of red spots running from the handle to the head, which seemed to be blackened as if by fire.

'Mata and I consecrated her last night, Balbeer,' Baroo said, lifting it now and holding it in both hands. 'In my grandfather's day they would drop Khusi into a well each night, and in the morning she would leap back up and alight in Grandpa's arms.'

'By magic?' I asked.

'Magic!' he exclaimed. 'Don't you think a thousand generations of Thugs could tell the difference between a magician's trick and a miracle of God? Isn't there a world of difference between them?' Baroo grimaced and shrugged. 'But that's all right, Balbeer. Such things are second nature to me, but they're bound to be a wonder to you. Besides, Khusi stopped leaping for the brotherhood in my father's day. That was your first warning to us, wasn't it, my mother?' Baroo asked, smiling sadly at the sky.

'Maybe someday Khusi will leap for you,' he said, and he looked at me for a moment, or through me; it was hard to tell.

'Now remember,' he said, suddenly all business, 'if any man falsely swears on Khusi he will die horribly. His face will turn around to his back and he'll choke to death on his own bowels. I've seen it happen. Khusi's more sacred than Ganga water to us, and why not? She's Kali's tooth! And as she digs her graves for us, only we can hear her song,' and here Baroo pretended to strike at the ground with the pickax, murmuring, 'Khuruk,' with each stroke.

He told me how she was consecrated, and how she was to be reconsecrated if she ever fell from our hands. The shadow of no living thing could pass over her, and each night she was to be wrapped in a white cloth and buried with her head pointing the way for the next day's journey. No animal or unclean thing could ever touch her, no man could set foot on her bed.

Baroo thus wrapped the pickax and set it down, slowly withdrawing his hand from it as if he'd balanced it like a juggler. 'Can you remember all that?' he asked, squinting at me.

'Yes, Ba – Guruji,' I stammered back.

'Good,' Baroo said with a firm nod. 'I believe you. Now this,' he then said, plucking a yellow scarf from his waistcloth, 'this is our roomal, Balbeer. Kali's hem. The brotherhood's banner.'

He tugged it upward and released it, and as it opened and began to drift down flat, he plucked it up again with his deft fingers. Holding it by one corner, he flapped it before my eyes, and in that instant a little knot appeared on the opposite corner, attached to a thick silver ring, and as I gaped at his sleight of hand he suddenly sent the knotted end flying around my extended neck.

'Got you!' he whispered with a wild grin, and then just as I was about to struggle he flicked it off again and there was a second knot tied a foot and a half from the first.

'See?' he said, flourishing the scarf in front of me. 'That's the sugar knot. We learned it at Kali's knee. Watch,' he said, untying and retying the knot for me. 'See? Now you try it.'

I was in such a state of awe and dread by this time that my movements were mere twitches and shudders.

'No, no, boy,' he said, snatching it from me after I'd fumbled with it for a while. 'Like *this*,' and again he showed me. 'Now try it again,' he said, handing it back.

I somehow managed to tie it on the second attempt, and Baroo fondly stroked the stubble on my head. 'Good boy. Now from here on you're to practice it at every opportunity,' he said, and he showed how he used to practice knotting his roomal by wrapping it around his bony old knee.

Drawn by the reeking quartered goat, kites and vultures reeled above us as Baroo instructed me in the strangler's craft. He dressed me in clothes like his, which he called *seep*, complete with a Rajput turban. On no account was I to allow the turban to fall from my head or catch fire at camp, for it was a grave augury that would require us to delay our expedition for seven days.

He told me that a good strangling was all in the wrists, as long as the knots were right. Once the scarf was in place all it took was digging your fists into the victim's neck and with the knots anchoring your grip, rocking your knuckles outward. I was not to be alarmed if my victim snored as I strangled him. This was what he called the *setna*, which he likened to the tolling of a bell. And he warned me to expect that in their pitiful throes our poor prey usually fouled their dhotis, raising a stink he called the 'bloom.'

'In the sway of the holy sugar it's sweeter than jasmine,' he assured me, and I nodded blankly, like a monkey on a leash.

He demonstrated his murderous craft every which way. Sometimes I would play the victim, sometimes he. When I was the prey

Baroo had to coax me to pretend to struggle, and when he was the victim he had to order me to tighten the scarf around his throat, for through it all I seemed to float like a cloud.

I don't know what it was I'd left behind in Kali's womb; maybe just my backbone. But as I drew my scarf around Baroo's throat I knew I could never kill him. I was too proud when the old man praised me, too hungry for his favor, and it was as if I'd become both myself and my mother in one of my old nightmares: one self running along the riverbank, distraught and appalled and warning of catastrophe, the other riding headlong on the rushing stream and thrilling to his prospects.

I won't tell you everything Baroo taught me that day, for it's better that some things die with me. He showed me places where a little poking or prodding with the tip of a finger could paralyze your limbs or strike you dumb or addle your wits forever. By the end of the afternoon we'd been over all manner of things, from strangling to burying prey, and Baroo was pleased with how quickly I seemed to learn.

In the evening we gave the vultures their due and walked a mile or so to a deep nullah to camp for the night. Baroo buried the pickax under some stones and ate an early supper out of what was left in my satchel, throwing me a measly scrap of bread as I practiced the sugar knot. We prayed to Kali as the sky turned black, or in any case Baroo prayed while I knelt beside him, imitating all his moves. I dreaded sleeping that night and struggled against it as Baroo kept watch, but as if to confirm that he was leading me on a predestined path my sleep was immediate and untroubled.

The next morning Baroo gave me no breakfast, just a swig or two from his waterskin, and we unearthed Khusi and set off westward, as she bade us, through a desolation fit only for scorpions and hyenas.

All the while, Baroo lectured me on the auguries, without a knowledge of which all the skills I'd learned the day before were worthless. He himself had learned them gradually and naturally during the course of his apprenticeship, but now he proposed to teach them to me all at once. For this we were perfectly matched, because when it came to rote memorization I was a disaster — one of the Reverend's ruins — and when it came to orderly exposition, Baroo was hopeless. Maybe it was his age, or maybe there was simply no order anyone could impose on Thuggee's fearful code, but his lectures gushed forth like muddy water and ran off in all directions.

'Now then, Balbeer,' he'd say after a grudging pause for breath, 'never set forth when your daughter's menstruating, nor within seven days after your wife menstruates or after the death of any weaned member of a Thug family. But if you should come upon a bride weeping along the path of her husband's house it's a good sign, just as it's good to come upon a corpse from another village, but if you should hear mourners weeping in your own village you should turn back, and the same goes for the birth of a daughter, a colt, a lamb, or a calf, except a buffalo calf, of course, unless it dies.'

Not even Dileep could have kept up with him. He could go on like that for hours, skittering about from beast to beast and circumstance to circumstance, pausing only to say, 'Right?' or 'But that's just good common sense.'

I tried hard to concentrate, but I couldn't keep my mind off my shrinking stomach, and even when I managed to memorize a fragment of his lessons I would end up missing a dozen more. I didn't dare ask him to repeat anything, for I'd been nodding along with him for miles.

Now he was saying a jackal was a good omen crossing right to left but a bad omen crossing left to right. But hadn't he just said that two jackals crossing from right to left meant chains and dungeon bars? Or were those wolves? He'd said *something* about wolves. A wolf's howl was good by night and bad by day. That was it. Or was it bad by night and good by day? And a wolf's dung was good in the evening but bad by moonlight. Or was that dog dung? How could you tell the difference, anyway? Kite dung was good, though, wasn't it? Or did it mean you had to discard your clothes? No, that was if a lizard fell on you. But the call of a lizard was good.

And now he was saying something about the call of a hare. It was terrible. Meant you were going to die horribly and hares would drink rainwater from your skull. I could remember that. But I'd never heard hares cry. I didn't even know they had voices. So how would I know when I heard one? How would even Baroo know if he heard one? — because obviously *he'd* never heard one or the hares would have drunk rainwater from *his* skull.

Let no one tell you that the Thugs were a fearless bunch, for though by Baroo's account they could peacefully sleep atop their victim's fresh graves and commit every kind of atrocity without troubling their souls, it seems to me now that all they'd managed to do was name their fears, not conquer them. The uninitiated might fear the call of an owl in the middle of the night, but just because a Thug would have a name for it, and impose a meaning on its timing and position, it wasn't any less dreadful.

The auguries took up two days of travel, and only at the end did Baroo attempt to give me a few general rules. He said Kali gave two kinds of signals: the *pilhau* on the right and the *thibau* on the left. Generally speaking, the *pilhau* was favorable and the *thibau* unfavorable at the start of an expedition, but at the end the converse was true.

'But of course,' Baroo added as he settled into his blanket for the night, 'there are exceptions.'

On the third night I welcomed sleep as a respite from Baroo's instruction, but it didn't come as easily as before. The sounds of the night, which had once spoken to me in one soothing, encompassing voice, became many voices, all babbling urgently, like strangers in a dream. A jackal yipped and howled among the hills, something rustled lightly in the brush beyond our campfire's glow, a kuraya owl gave a low, clinking call, like chains dragging in mud. I tried to think of Ahalya, but when I closed my eyes to picture her there was Kali, standing guard at the door to my old life, her slack lips shifting with each night sound. She was trying to steer me with her voices, as my mother used to steer me through the press of a crowd. And now they circumfused the night together, Kali and my mother, and I fell into a sleep as deep and black as a midnight well.

The next day Baroo tried to teach me Ramasee, but with no more success than before, for his instruction was as random and furious as ever. You could never hope to see an old man more exhilarated than

Baroo on that fourth day. As we forded a ryth in the Chambal River
and climbed like crocodiles up the bank and into the hills of Tonk, he
seemed to burst with all his dismal secrets.

There's little point to my recalling all the words he tried to teach
me as we trudged along in our sopping clothes, for they aren't mine
to recall. I remember that a *bydha* was a maimed man and *bani* was
blood, but I've forgotten most of the rest of what little I managed to
learn.

Some of the signals Baroo taught me explained what I'd thought
were Baroo's own quirks, like his habit of running his hand from his
throat to his chin when he was unimpressed by something, or how he
always hawked up phlegm whenever we set forth. These were two of
a hundred signals the Thugs employed to hide their grim intentions
from their prey: two of maybe five I can now recall.

By the sixth day my stomach had finally given up all hope of a
decent meal and had shrunk to the size of a withered plum. I couldn't
seem to remember how Ahalya's meals tasted, nor how anything
tasted except the dusty scraps of stale chapatti Baroo fed me. This
gave me an exalted feeling, an ascetic's delusion that I had somehow
mastered my hunger by force of will. My panic gave way to a crazed
conviction that just by hearing Baroo's teachings I'd committed them
to memory. I suppose I was counting on Baroo's promise that in the
end the goor, the consecrated sugar I was to eat in my initiation,
would turn me from an addled boy into a prince of deceit and calm
the muddy flood of Baroo's teachings into a limpid pool.

So, finally, as Baroo talked I listened idly, as if to music,
enjoying the rustle and lilt of his whisper, for his speech had become
so riddled with Ramasee that it was as if it were shot through holes
and all its meaning leaking out.

'In Tonk there's a *baee*, Balbeer, rich with the Jaipur trade. The
burkha of this region was a *Khosman* and kept a man in the Nawab's
court to monitor the caravans. He once showed me where his *bileeas*
lay, *nissar*. The *karhoo* hanged him, too, and most of his *kous* with
him, and now the *bitous* come and go without fear. There's a *bilgari*
skirting the *baee* that's as tangled as a *churaji's* locks, and there we'll
seek a solitary *jhoosa* for our first *gharnakhna*.'

Of course, that's an approximation of how he'd taken to
speaking, for it isn't in my power to duplicate it. But it no longer

mattered to me that I didn't understand it, for I heard it as an incantation.

On the evening of the sixth day Baroo recited the taboos for me, reeling off so many kinds of men we couldn't kill – musicians, water carriers, stonecutters, pariahs, riverbound mourners with their loved ones' bones, pilgrims bearing offerings, goldsmiths, dhobis, shoemakers, chucklers, carpenters, lepers, starving men, hermaphrodites, cripples, amputees, to name a few – that I was hard put to think of anyone he'd left out.

He had a special horror of killing the maimed, perhaps because he was maimed himself, and believed that any Thug who violated this clause of Kali's covenant would fall to pieces and spend his afterlife with all his severed parts stuck together higgledy-piggledy.

We reached our destination that night, and from the look of it I guessed that the *baee* Baroo spoke of must have meant a well-travelled road, and the *bilgari* signified the deep, adjacent jungle. Ever since that night at Kali's temple all I'd seen of my fellow man – besides Baroo – was a few figures creeping like bugs on the distant hills. Baroo had steered us clear of the shepherds and ascetics who inhabited that region, like a captain navigating a rocky strait.

But now when we crossed the Banas River and set our feet on the Bundi Road we passed within a few yards of two caravans encamping for the night. I could hardly recognize the sweet aroma from their cooking fires, and shrank back from the dull gaze of the camel drivers as they unloaded their blustering beasts, but Baroo strode right by, shouting his greetings to all and sundry. We were unwashed and gaunt with hunger but for all that a no doubt unexceptional-looking pair in those parts: a father and son, a guru and his disciple, a pilgrim and his servant: to one way of thinking or another we were all of these. But I saw suspicion in every eye, and if Baroo hadn't been so hearty I might have betrayed us both with my skulking tread.

Baroo led me off the road and along an oblique path that took us into a tangled wood. He was reassured by the cry of a crane as we approached the river, and chose the nearest spot to camp: a grassy hollow beneath an overarching neem. It must have rained in those parts not long before, for the grass was soft and green where we bedded down.

There was nothing much left of Baroo's old voice after those six days of teaching. It ground along like a carpenter's rasp as we prayed together that night, but lying back beneath his blanket he continued to speak even as he drifted off, like a child singing himself to sleep.

'Tomorrow, tomorrow, tomorrow,' he murmured as his eye slowly closed, and for a moment he seemed to sleep. But then his eye opened again and he peered up through the branches.

'Have I left anything out?' he asked with a doubtful look, raising his head slightly from the grass. But within a moment some little creature chattered at us from the surrounding tangle and Baroo nodded and smiled.

'I didn't think so,' he said, and he lay back and fell asleep, as if at the close of some great labor.

CHAPTER

45

'Wake up, Balbeer,' Baroo whispered to me in the morning. 'It's the seventh day!'

He declared this as if it were wondrous news that the seventh day should follow the sixth.

'Wh-what?' I asked as his eye hovered over me.

'Whew, Balbeer,' Baroo said, wrinkling up his nose and turning his face away. 'Your hunger's poisoned your breath, boy. But never mind. The fast is over. Today we feast.'

I felt my stomach weakly jump beneath my ribs. 'We do?'

'Yes,' he said, rolling up his blanket. 'Eventually. If all goes well. But like all sacred feasts this one is going to require certain — sacrifices, shall we say.'

Baroo drew a little brass jug out of his satchel and stood, and I could hear his joints pop and click as he tried to straighten his twisted back.

My throat tightened in anticipation of a drink, but Baroo

stepped past me. 'You wait here,' he said as he began to beat his way toward the river. 'We need fresh water for the *jeetjana*.'

I must have gaped back at him, for I didn't know what a *jeetjana* was, but Baroo must have mistook my confusion for wonderstruck anticipation.

'Yes, Balbeer,' he said, turning for a moment to smile at me. 'This is the big day. Everything we've been working for. By tonight we should know what kind of teacher I've been, what sort of stuff you're made of,' and with that he disappeared into the jungle.

This still didn't explain what a *jeetjana* was, but I thought of the goor again as he tromped off, and assured myself that I would find out soon enough.

In all that time Baroo had never let me out of his sight, not even to obey the call of nature, and now as the noise of his progress faded away I fidgeted shyly in my own solitary company. Like mice after a hawk had passed, my instincts began to brave the air again, and as Baroo's absence wore on I paced the camp, daring myself to flee and daring myself to stay in desperate alternation, lurching back and forth, back and forth, until I was giddy and winded. Muttering to myself, I took out my roomal and began to tie the sugar knot on my knee, shaking my head to the clamoring within and chanting loudly to drown it out.

But I didn't know what it was I was chanting until Baroo reappeared in the little clearing carrying his dripping pitcher and, with a proud grin at his faithful disciple, chanted along with me in his sandy voice, '*Kali, Kunkali, Kali, Kunkali . . .*'

'Oh son,' he said, reaching down to touch me with his wetted hand, 'you make me so proud.'

I looked up at him then, and the din receded into a dull hum. He brought a small yellow sack out of his waistband and emptied its contents onto my blanket. There were silver and copper coins, a bit of turmeric, and other odds and ends, which he now instructed me to enclose in a series of knots in the pickax's cloth.

'A few treats for Kali,' he said as I accomplished this, and when I was done he said, 'Good,' and holding the pickax against his breast with one hand and the little jug in the other, he stood as straight as he could and closed his eyes, as if awaiting a dreaded summons.

Suddenly he lurched eastward and began to march in a straight line out of the clearing and into a thicket of brambles, like a blind man on a tether.

I stayed behind at first, but before he'd disappeared from sight he called out to me to follow, for Khusi was leading him to a sacred spot. So I rushed after him, scratching myself on the brambles that snapped back in his wake. We came to a tangle of trees uprooted by the flood, and there Baroo heard a crow cry, an auspicious sign within sight of a river, as we now were.

He spread his blanket on a tilted stone and knelt upon it, facing the flow. With his eyes heavenward he said, 'Great goddess, mother of us all! If our plan pleases you, give us your protection and smile upon us with a sign.'

I knelt down at the base of Baroo's crude throne and watched with him for an augury to manifest itself.

'Just one sign, Mother Goddess,' he suggested helpfully.

After half an hour's vigil Baroo began to mutter, 'Please, Mother Goddess. You've brought us this far. I've done everything you asked. What more can I do? Please, Mother Goddess. Just this once,' and so on, and it did seem to me cruel of Kali to bring Baroo this far just to disappoint him.

'Kali,' I heard myself say to the brightening winter sky. 'You do what he asks.'

At this Baroo gasped, and stared down at me. '*Balbeer*!' he whispered with his eye bugged out. 'Are you trying to get us *killed*?'

'But look,' I said, pointing across the river, for in that moment a black buck ventured forth to drink on the opposite bank.

Baroo peered outward, hunched down as if against a wind, and then leaped up to his feet.

'Ha!' he exclaimed, breaking into a little dance on the slanted stone. 'I knew it! I knew I could count on her!' And as the buck now bolted at the sight of him he bid me dance alongside him. This I did for a while, though gravely, like a bear, and then Baroo stopped me and aimed his eye at me again and said, 'I never heard anyone talk that way to her before. Not once in all my days. And look what she does for you. It's a miracle, Balbeer. *You're* a miracle. You snap your fingers and she speaks! Ha!' he exclaimed again, and held me for a moment against his sharp ribs.

'Now, Balbeer,' he said, patting his chest to calm himself. 'Here's what I must do.' He raised a finger and shook it at me, but his face broke into a grin, and when he spoke he had to swallow back an excited chuckle. 'I must abstract myself. I have to sit here on this rock for seven hours, Balbeer. Seven hours thinking on Kali's glory. But meanwhile I want you to go back and pack our things and wait. Will you do that for me?'

'Yes,' I said firmly, exulting in his joy and pride. 'Whatever you say.'

'I know, Balbeer,' he said, embracing me again. 'I know you will. Now go,' he said, releasing me, 'and when I get back we'll taste the holy goor together.'

So I left Baroo on the riverbank and ran headlong into the tangled wood. That Kali had listened to me – no, *obeyed* me – was proof enough for me that I was born to be her prince. As I thrashed my way toward the clearing I imagined that the brush was making way for me and the birds I flushed up were shrieking my praises.

But pausing to free my waistband from a stray thorny branch, I realized that Baroo and I had left no path to follow back. I tried to shrug this off at first – after all, Kali was bound to lead her boy back to camp. A bluejay croaked somewhere ahead of me, and I nodded, for it had to be my mother's beckoning voice, but no sooner had I gone ten paces more into the jungle than the bluejay began to fuss with another in the treetops and jays were chuckling and cawing all around me.

And then as I stopped to puzzle out Kali's babble, I heard heavy footsteps falling from somewhere beyond the dull-green tope. I held my breath as they drew closer, and stood still, but as my eyes darted around the dapple I heard a blustering moan and saw, in the instant I shut my eyes, Genda the giant's homely face.

I gave out a cry and ran as fast as I could, but the footfall kept gaining on me as I struggled through the brambles, and the ground trembled like a drum. Just as they seemed about to overtake me I broke through onto the Bundi Road and stood dazed and torn in the sunshine, and before I could fathom where I was, my pursuer crashed through the brush behind me: a little herd of buffalo still muddy from the river, goaded forward by a mild boy the spit and image of myself.

'Praise God,' he said in a high, husky voice, and cheerfully drove his beasts right by me.

But I backed away from him as from a ghost, and running as fast as I could I somehow found the oblique path Baroo and I had taken and dashed back to the clearing.

Not even one of Baroo's seven hours had passed, but already the hum was rising in my ears again and bursting into a hundred contentious voices. I tried to busy myself with the packing, but there was nothing to it but throwing a few stray articles into Baroo's satchel and hiding it in the brush. I hid myself as well, crouching under the low spread of the neem tree and practicing the sugar knot.

I drowned out the voices for a while with Kali's name, rocking back and forth like a sadhu, and when some voice penetrated my mantra and begged me to flee I reminded myself of the goor again: the sacred sugar would save me.

Save you from what? the voices asked. *And for what?*

From my cowardice, I told them. *For my destiny.*

From your conscience, they answered, *and for a madman's dream.*

I stood and paced around the clearing again, breathing fitfully, like a hare.

Run! the voices cried. *Run while you've still got time!*

Yes, I said aloud, shaking my scarf in my fist. I'll run. I'll run so fast he can never catch me. I'll run back to Bhondaripur, and if he dares to follow me there I'll turn him in, or kill him if I have to. That's what I should have done in the first place. Kill the old monster. It's what he deserves.

But for all this resolution I kept circling the clearing, around and around until I'd tromped a trail in the soft green grass. I searched along the edge of the dappled wood for a path to take that he could not follow, but he knew the little trail to the Bundi Road, and I couldn't remember where he'd set forth through the brush for the river.

I've got to think, I told myself, shutting my ears with my hands and stooping toward the neem tree. I crawled back into the shade, curling up on my side like a wounded worm and falling into a dream.

I saw the men of my family gathered in my courtyard in the apricot evening light, awaiting my return. There was Channa passing the hookah to Pyari Lal, and old Kushal Singh, freed from his post by the women's quarters, spitting against the compound wall, and Santosh, whom I did not know I loved until I saw him now among the others, and likewise Jagdish. I seemed to float toward them, as if I were riding my mare, and travelled around to the back of my house, where Ahalya sat, resting for a moment as the chapatti baked, gently slapping the flour from her hands and staring out along the rows of seedlings in the mustard field. She didn't see me, nor hear me when I spoke, but Mahabir did and chuckled up at me from his rumpled quilt.

I wanted to climb down and embrace them, but something seemed to grip my feet, and when I looked down I saw it wasn't my mare I was riding but an owl. It carried me past Ahalya now, and Mahabir began to cry, and as it rushed me along the thorn rows, toward a gloom that spread down the sky like ink, the dust flew from its feathered neck. I began to struggle, but its talons were like shackles on my legs and its wings flapped like rags in a wind. It carried me into the sky, over the fields and ridges, across rivers and towns and vast wastes, until at last we hovered over a great black maw in the earth below, and the owl began to descend in a lazy spiral.

I begged it to take me back, but it only turned its great head about and winked one opal eye. I grabbed the owl around its neck, and it laughed at me with its little black beak and folded up its scraggly wings, and we both began to fall.

I leapt up from my resting place and struck my head so hard on the branch of the neem tree that if it hadn't been for my turban it would have knocked me cold. As it was, the dappled clearing seemed to revolve in the sun like a crystal, blinding me with each flashing facet. I stumbled out into the center of it, holding my head in my hands, and though you might think I'd have known from my nightmare that there was no use in running, all I brought back from my fevered sleep was a cold, bald terror.

I had no way of knowing how long I'd been asleep nor how long it would be before Baroo returned, but in my panic all this meant to me was that I had no time to lose. So with a deep breath I rushed into the jungle and thrashed about again among the thorns. I turned a deaf ear to Kali's voices and tried to steer a straight course outward between the river and the road. I don't know how long I scrambled about, but it seemed like an eternity, and when I finally glimpsed some open ground I made for it with a blind lunge and found myself back by the river again, not five yards from Baroo.

I let out a gasping cry at the sight of him, but he didn't turn around at first, only sat there with his back to me, his legs crossed, his hands upturned on his knees, his head upraised on his crooked neck. But something about his shoulders told me he knew I was behind him, and after a moment he pivoted his head all the way around and winked his missing eye.

'Quite an effect, isn't it?' Baroo said, pointing to his neck. 'Been able to do this ever since the hanging.'

'So,' he said, standing and yawning and arching his back. 'Seven hours up already? I must have lost count. Never could read the shadows right.'

He stepped down from the tilted stone and shaking loose his drowsiness, smiled at me again. 'Nice of you to come back for me,' he said. 'But try to be more careful in the brambles. Look at you. You're all scratched up.'

I hadn't moved a step since I'd emerged from the tope, though my bones shook as if to free themselves from my foolish hide.

'Hope you got a chance to rest,' Baroo said, putting his arm around me and leading me back into the woods. 'I've been thinking about your first *gharnakhna*. Seems to me we've got to choose him with care. We need somebody from another caste, or better yet, another creed. Somebody awful. Somebody whose own mother wouldn't care if he lived or died. A low, scheming humbug to break you in. How does that sound?'

'Uh, good, Ba – uh – guruji,' I said as he led me directly back to the clearing.

'I thought you'd like it. And the way things have been going I think we can count on the Mother to place just such a *beeto* in our path. Oh, Balbeer, that meditation did me a lot of good. I'm as clear as glass.' He gave a little hop and raised his clasped hands to the sky. 'I feel like I'm the one who's getting his first taste of the *goor* today, not you.'

He looked at me as I stood stooped and defeated by the neem tree. 'But I'm forgetting,' he said, separating his hands and shaking his head. 'This is serious business. You're right to be so sober about it, Balbeer. Sometimes I've got to scold my own high spirits.' He nodded at that and took a deep breath.

'Now then,' he said, striding toward me with an earnest frown. 'Where did you put my kit?'

I fetched it for him from the brush, and he sat down in the middle of the clearing and rummaged around in his satchel for a while. He nodded to me, and I sat down before him, and in his fond smile I saw something that gave me pained hope: not for escape or courage or even good luck, but hope for absolution.

Baroo seemed to find what he was looking for, but before he would bring it out he had me clasp my hands and shut my eyes. I could hear the rustling of paper and then a sigh, and suddenly Baroo was speaking to me in a voice I'd never heard before: deep and priestly, like bubbles in mud.

His prayer was so dense with the Ramasee that I can't recall a word. He called Kali a dozen names, summoned her in all her ghastly manifestations, smacked his lips over the blood that flowed off her tongue, clapped his hands to the music of the skulls knocking together along her necklace, and as he hummed and chuckled and moaned I peeked at him through the mesh of my eyelashes, afraid the sun had burned out or Baroo had multiplied into a hundred chanting Thugs. But all I saw through the haze between my lids was his old neck puffed and swaying like a lizard's wattle and his one eye rolled upward, pink as milk from a bleeding teat.

I shut my eyes tight, praying I might never have to open them again. My stomach twitched and murmured, and I pressed my tongue back against my throat to keep my gorge from rising. *Just hold on,* I told myself. *The sugar will save you.*

Baroo's chants and moans kept plummeting until they shook my ribs and buzzed my nose, and then suddenly he cut off his incantation and gripped my forehead in his iron hand. I could hear his panting, broken here and there as if he were swallowing back sobs.

'Now,' he said in a whisper as paper rustled in his lap. 'Eat.'

I dropped my jaw, and Baroo said, 'Banish, banish, banish,' in a rising chant, and popped a ball of sugar between my lips.

At last, I told myself, at last, and I began to chew on the sacred lump of goor.

'No, no,' Baroo said, pressing his hand up against my chin. 'Let it melt. Let it flood your mouth . . .

'Banish, banish, banish,' he growled. 'All mercy. All fear. It is death, it is death, it is death.'

My sugared spit ran like a spring and swirled down my throat. Darkness slipped behind my eyes, smothered the bursting sparks from the sun's veiled light, stopped up my ears, singed my nostrils, turned my red blood black.

My stomach bucked against the sweet flood, but as my gorge began to rise again Baroo clamped his hand over my mouth, and I choked it back, swallowing the remaining lump in one gulp.

As it plummeted down my throat I popped open my eyes, and Baroo, nodding, removed his hands from my mouth and brow.

I sat wavering, staring around me like a blind man healed. It was almost evening, and the light gave the dull leaves a golden sheen, but it was the underside I saw now as I slowly rose to my feet: the silken, blossoming shadows. The sugar seeped into my entrails like the gloaming, and the eastern sky seemed veined and purple. My breaths were leisurely, and when I put my hand over my heart it beat slowly, resolutely, unafraid.

'Yes, Balbeer,' Baroo said, rising now and sniffing back a tear. 'It's Kali's world.'

CHAPTER
46

I looked down at my hands and flexed them into fists. They were all sinew and steel, and my feet were articulate, like a monkey's, in the press of the grass.

Baroo watched me for a moment and began to cry, stopping here and there to gasp, 'I'm sorry,' or, 'I can't help it,' or, 'You don't know what this means to me,' and then bursting into tears all over again.

I stared at him from a little distance, watching the tears fall along the wrinkles in his battered old face, and wondering how I could ever have been afraid of him. I didn't mean this fondly, either – afraid of such an old fool was what I meant. My gaze must have been as pitiless as the frost, but it seemed to warm the old man's heart, and he staggered up with a wet grin and embraced me.

'Where's this feast you promised?' I heard myself ask as he clung to me.

He let me go and wiped the tears from his hanging cheeks with the backs of his hands. 'The feast,' he said with a shake of his finger. 'Of course. Right away.'

He hurried over to his kit again and drew out packets of little brass canisters and set them out on his blanket. He scurried about like a servant, scolding himself when he spilled something or fumbled with a lid. When everything was ready he escorted me to the blanket and showed me where to sit, and upon asking Kali's blessing and thanking her for this and that, he served me my evening meal.

There was pickled brinjal and a hot, salty curry of potato and peas, a dollop of ghee, and a little stack of chapatti: food he'd been carrying with him all week. He served it to me and sat back like a wife, watching me eat. 'Good, eh?' he asked as I chewed and swallowed. 'You want some more? More bread? Here, take more. Eat up. Isn't that better? Doesn't that taste good?'

I ate as much as I could, which wasn't much; my stomach had shrivelled so. And when I was done Baroo ate a little something himself and packed the canisters back in his kit. 'What a day,' he said, shaking out his blanket. 'I don't know about you, Balbeer, but I'm exhausted.'

'No, Baroo,' I said with my newfound calm. 'There isn't time.'

Baroo squinted at me. 'What's that, Balbeer?'

'There isn't time,' I said. 'We have to go.'

Baroo laughed inadvertently and then covered his mouth. 'Go?' he asked. 'Go where?'

'To the next *bileea*,' I heard myself say, and there it was, the Ramasee, tripping off my tongue.

'The next *bileea*?' he said with an appalled look. 'Who made you *bhurtote*?'

'At the next *bileea* we'll find the *dudh* you described. He's a *Khosman*. He's waiting for us now,' I said, and hearing it I believed myself, or whoever it was whose voice issued from my mouth.

'Oh, *is* he?' Baroo said with faltering sarcasm. 'And where is the next *bileea*?'

I waited for the answer, and when none occurred to me I stood and said, 'I don't know.'

'Ah,' Baroo said. 'You don't – '

'But you do,' I said, and I began to walk.

'Balbeer!' Baroo called out as I stepped onto the path, heading for the Bundi Road. 'Balbeer! Get back here!'

But I kept marching forward with my eyes set straight ahead, and I didn't look back, even when I heard his footsteps behind me.

'Damn you, Balbeer!' Baroo said, grabbing me by the shoulder. 'You're still a cheyla! You don't tell me – '

But when he pulled me around to face him he saw the heat in my eyes and squirmed away. 'I'll – ' he stammered, his eye still fixed on me, 'I'll just – get my things.'

I turned back around and continued marching along the path. Baroo caught up with me on the road, winded, shifting his satchel on his old shoulders. 'Down this way,' he panted. 'About three miles. Not a *bilgaree* like this, but lots of concealment among the stones. There's an old cenotaph nearby. Locals won't go near it. We'll make our *thap* there and wait for your *dudh*.'

'We won't have to wait,' I told him. 'He's already there.'

Baroo kept glancing over at me as we made our way down the road, past the encampment of oil pressers, one of them an obsequious albino, and a party of Mangs glowering at us from the shadows, and this time it was I who greeted them and Baroo who hung behind, averting his face.

'Now, Balbeer,' he said, trotting along to keep up. 'This may be precipitate. You only just took the goor, after all. Why don't we sleep on this tonight? See how we feel in the morning.'

'How much further is it?' I asked, for the tope had thinned out along the roadside and the ground had a clawed, churned-up look, with sharp rocks rising from the meagre scrub.

'I don't know,' Baroo said. 'Another mile, I think. But you haven't been listening to me. What do you say? Don't you think we'd better wait an hour or so? Just to check the auguries?'

But I pretended not to hear him, nor the voices, now mere whispers, that spoke to me, begging me to turn back. I had never felt so substantial. I could feel the dirt road give a little with each of my steps, the night air part in my path like an adoring crowd. The shadows fluttered ahead of me like ribbons and hung like banners along the road.

I won't blame you if you don't believe that when we took a path off the road and followed it past a cenotaph to a *bileea* set among a circle of upturned stones we caught sight of an old *Khosman* — Ramasee for Moslem — sitting by a fire. Baroo didn't believe it either, and at the first sight of him shrank back, pulling me with him before I could shout my greeting.

'Balbeer,' Baroo whispered, holding me by the shirtfront. 'This is going too fast. What's gotten into you, boy? I can't keep up with you. How did you know he was going to be here? Is this some kind of trick? Have you turned against me?'

But I found the old man's suspicions pitiful and shook him off. 'You brought me to Kali,' I said, leaning toward him, 'and she's brought me here.'

Baroo's eye rolled about for a moment as if searching her out. 'I've made these prophecies myself, you know,' he said uncertainly. And then he said, as if to himself, 'But not so young . . . '

He looked over at the old Moslem now and cogitated, worrying his lip with his teeth. 'Must be a scribe by the looks of him,' he muttered as I squatted down beside him. 'Sixty years old. That's a dolpari cap in the Lucknow fashion. He's no hadji, so he's probably not a pilgrim. Probably just making his rounds.'

All this Baroo surmised from the old man's head, for the rest of him was wrapped in a blanket. To my cold, corrupted eyes he looked like nothing more than a heap of dung with a head attached, pale and poorly shaven.

Baroo shook his head once and looked off into the sky. 'I need a sign, Balbeer. A whisper. A glimpse. Just to be sure.'

'Kali?' I said without raising my head. 'Show him.'

And as soon as I'd spoken a lizard chittered behind us.

Baroo whirled around with his eye wide, for this was an augury of rare auspiciousness.

'Praise Kali,' he gasped. 'It's the *bara mutti*. How did you *do* that?'

But I merely shrugged and busied myself with my roomal around my knee.

'All right, all right, Balbeer,' Baroo whispered. 'It shall be as you say. You can take him. But remember this,' he said sternly, shaking his finger at me. 'No matter how much our mother may favor you, there's an *art* to this thing. You shall *gharna* this *Khosman* when I give the *jhirnee*. But keep your mouth shut and leave the *townaree* to me. I'm going to *karthi kurna* the old *dudh* with a fable, and when I say "Fill your pipe," you must set to. Remember, now. "Fill your pipe." That's your *jhirnee*.'

'Yes, yes,' I said as I tightened the anchor knot. 'Whatever you say.' And with that I stood and shouted, 'Peace be unto you,' to my prey.

Baroo gave out a little cry and tried to grab my ankle as I stepped forward, but he snatched at the air and scrambled along behind me.

'Who's there?' the Moslem croaked back, ducking his head around and peering into the dark.

'Peace be unto you,' Baroo called back, glaring at me as he pushed ahead.

'And blessings,' the old man replied uncertainly, still unable to spot us beyond his little fire's glow.

'Here we are, brother,' Baroo said as we finally came into view.

The old man curled his wrinkled lip at the sight of us, but Baroo stepped daintily around the little patches of spit the Moslem had dispensed on the ground around him and stooped over the fire to warm his hands. 'Thank the stars we found you.' he said, rubbing his fingers together. 'Never travelled this road before. I don't mind telling you, brother, it scares us to death.'

'Indeed,' the Moslem muttered, pouting toward the fire.

'What a dreadful country,' Baroo said. 'I may be a Bhatti Rajput born and bred, but I can't stand this desolation. If God didn't abide in every thorn and stone my soul would petrify.'

The Moslem shook his head and spat into the fire.

'You're not afraid?' Baroo asked like a child as I joined him by the fire.

I thought he was asking me, and I began to reply, but Baroo surreptitiously kicked my ankle.

'That's not it,' the old man said. 'It's that thorn and stone business. God watches us, but not from here.'

'Ah,' Baroo said, looking intrigued. 'He's apart, is He?'

'Of course,' the Moslem said. 'What do you think? God is His own creation?'

'I see,' Baroo said, nodding respectfully. 'Yes, I can see what you mean.'

The old man reached his left hand out of his blanket and picked up a stick with which to poke his fire.

'You know,' said Baroo, 'I have my faith and it has served me well enough. But the contradictions — I must say, they gall me sometimes. I've always admired the way you children of Islam see right through to the heart of things. It's a faith with an edge to it.'

'It's a sword,' the old man piped.

'A sword!' said Baroo, squatting down now. 'That's beautifully put.'

'I've no extra food for you,' the Moslem said abruptly. 'I'm a poor man, as it pleases almighty God.'

Baroo gaped at the Moslem as if this were the furthest thing from his mind. 'Food?' he exclaimed. 'No, no. We want nothing. It's just such a relief to find a friendly face on this dark road. Just a share of your fire's warmth is all I ask, if that's all right with you.'

The old man squinted suspiciously at me as I squatted nearby. I could taste the sugar rising in my mouth like a venom, and all I could see of the old Moslem was his shy, turtle's neck about the blanket.

'This your son?'

'Him?' said Baroo. 'No, no, no. He's just a servant, and a little dim at that.'

It was strange, for I knew this was only a ruse, but Baroo hurt me with that, and I glowered at him for a moment.

'All my sons are grown,' Baroo continued cheerfully.

'Mine also,' the Moslem said, raising this chin.

'Oh? And how many do you have?'

The old man twisted his head around slightly and said, 'Five.'

'Five sons!' Baroo said. 'And I was glad for my three!'

The old man smirked and shrugged.

'But then,' Baroo said mildly, 'I've had only the one wife to mother them.'

The Moslem's eyes flared a little at this, but Baroo quickly changed the subject.

'You know,' he said, affecting an elegant sonority in imitation of the Moslem, 'I've been almost everywhere north of the Deccan in my day. I've seen Amber and Marwar and Mewar, and admired their ferocious beauty. And there's nothing more exalted than the ramparts of Jeysulmere, Delhi, and Bundi, or grander than Scindhia's roost. But there was only one paradise on this earth.'

Baroo paused, and the Moslem tried for a moment to hide his curiosity. 'Indeed?' he finally said. 'And where was that?'

'Pardon me?' Baroo said, pretending not to hear.

'Where was this paradise?'

'Well,' Baroo said, duckwalking a couple of steps toward the Moslem and lowering his voice, 'this may strike you as strange, coming from a Rajput, but I would have to say it was' – and here he whispered reverently – 'Lucknow.'

The old man snapped his head around and gaped at Baroo. 'Lucknow!' he said. 'You know Lucknow?'

'Oh yes,' Baroo said. 'But before the Devil's Wind. Before the Feringhee got hold of it. Back when it was still the poet's dream.'

'Lucknow,' the old man murmured. 'Oh, yes. It was so.'

'Don't tell me you've been there too?' Baroo said with an astonished look.

'Been there?' the Moslem exclaimed. 'I was *raised* there!'

'Ah,' Baroo said. 'Of course. I should have guessed. I knew there was something about you. That lilt in your speech, and – forgive me – the dreamer's look around your eyes.'

'Ah, the Moti Bagh . . . ' the Moslem said softly.

'And the Imambara,' Baroo chimed in.

'And the songbirds in the old chauk, remember?'

'And the confections,' Baroo said with a smack of his lips. 'The best in the world.'

'In the universe,' the old man said.

'But what was the secret?' Baroo wondered. 'There were richer kingdoms. And better locales. What raised Lucknow above all the others?'

The old man, lost in his memories, only shook his head and stared at the fire. His old neck looked flimsy and repulsive, like a caterpillar's trunk to my impatient eyes.

'You know,' said Baroo, 'I was pondering that very question one day in the old chauk, and I wondered if the answer might not have been written all over the city, for everywhere I looked there were lofty mottoes and ethical verses, all in the most artful Nastaliq script. Why, a man couldn't take a step without reading a katbas or a qatat so sublime it would infuse his day with beauty and virtue.'

At this the Moslem began to sob, and seeing his helplessness I started to reach for my roomal and draw it from my waistband, but Baroo glowered at me and shook his head, for he was only warming up.

'What is it, brother?' he asked with his eyebrows high. 'I didn't mean to cause you sorrow.'

'No, no,' the old man said. 'It isn't you that sorrows me but my wretched kismat. If you took me for a lowly clerk I would not blame you, for that is all I am.'

'Ah, but clerks are never lowly — ' Baroo began to say, but the old man held up his hand.

'A lowly clerk,' the Moslem insisted. 'That's what I am. But it wasn't always this way. Before the Wind, in the reign of Wajid Ali Shah, upon whose memory I press my brow, I was apprentice to Mir Bandey Ali, the greatest of all calligraphers, whose katbas and qatats adorned the walls of every mansion and palace, whose art was the very soul of Avadh.'

'The heart and soul,' Baroo agreed.

The Moslem nodded and sighed. 'And in those days I was his favorite. I fashioned the finest and supplest quills, mixed ink as pure as blood, drew curves as felicitous as a houri's breast. My old master maintained that my gift was divinely bestowed, for though my hand was as firm as iron yet its touch was so light it would not bruise a butterfly's wing. The master would not begrudge me this, but another apprentice was envious and conspired against me.

'One day this apprentice and I accompanied my master to the home of Nabob Agha Hasan Khan, an eminent patron who had commissioned a Nastaliq script. The master had permitted me to help him with the verses along the border and thus was eager to introduce me to his patron as his heir. I had never seen so grand a home as the Nabob's palace. It was harmonious in every proportion, exquisitely ornamented, free of vulgarity and pretense. We passed through a hall lined with ivory screens and a menagerie of jade statuary and waited for the Nabob in the anteroom. This second apprentice, knowing how anxious the master was that I make a good impression, straightened my clothing for me as we waited, claiming the pleats in the back of my waistcoat were all awry.

'We were then led into the Nabob's chamber. He extolled my master's work, and was astonished by the perfection of my small contribution. To reward us he doubled my master's fee and fed us delicacies from his own kitchen.

'But as we were about to take our leave, there was a hubbub in the hall. A servant had discovered that one of the jade pieces was missing. The Nabob apologized to us for the inconvenience, but ordered that no one leave his palace until the statue was found, and when all the servants had been searched, and every guard, and every corner of the house, the Nabob concluded that there was nothing for it but to search his guests. He began with the other apprentice, apologizing most profusely to our master all the while, and when he found nothing there my turn came, and as his servant searched through my pockets I accepted the Nabob's apologies too, but then his servant's hand paused in my waistcoat and slowly brought forth the little green falcon.'

'No,' Baroo said, slapping his forehead. 'You don't mean – '

'Yes. The apprentice, that lost soul, that Companion of the Left, had planted it on me in the anteroom. My master fainted dead away, and I am told he died soon after from the shame of it. And the apprentice cursed me with a smirk, and the Nabob had me taken to be tried by the mullahs. They punished me as the Law prescribed, and exiled me from Lucknow, from my family, from everything I held dear, and I became a kitabat, a copier of documents, circling among the little villages of Tonk.'

The Moslem closed his eyes and shook his head.

'But,' Baroo said, 'surely you still had your gift, your touch. No one could take that away from you.'

'Oh yes they could, my friend,' the old man murmured. 'And they did.'

Baroo stuck a finger into the pit of his missing eye as if to tuck back a tear. 'That is the saddest tale I ever heard,' he said, giving me a surreptitious glance.

Now, this may have been the saddest tale that I had ever heard as well, but I was utterly unmoved, as if my heart were encased in a cold sugar crystal. I could taste the goor from the tip of my tongue to the pit of my stomach, and fidgeted with the tail of my roomal.

Baroo gave the *khokhee*, the signal for me to take my place, by hawking up phlegm and holding it in his mouth. I thus duckwalked around behind the Moslem, with my eyes pinned to the absurd thread of the old man's throat.

Such was my clumsiness that even in the depths of his reverie the old man noticed me and turned his head with a puzzled look.

'What is he doing?' he asked Baroo with a squint as I stared back at him.

'Oh him?' Baroo said, and he spat the phlegm into the fire. 'Don't mind him. He's restless. I think he likes you. He thinks he's protecting you back there. Watching out for danger — that sort of thing. I hope you don't mind humoring him.'

The Moslem shrugged and looked back at the fire.

'Have you ever wondered at your good fortune?' Baroo asked suddenly, standing as if to stretch his legs.

'My what?'

'Your good fortune,' said Baroo. 'Brother, with all due respect, don't you see what you were spared? In your memory Lucknow is a paradise, a garden of songbirds. But you got out just in time. Why, it's a ruin now. A ghost of itself. I've been there recently. The maiden is a battered old harlot now. The apprentice inherited nothing but ashes. There are no qatats and katbas, only common calendars and graven images. No, for you, and you alone, she is still a virgin; she still makes music among the flowers, along the hallways lined with jade.'

The old man looked ashamed and began to slowly nod at the crackling fire.

'Luck is a question of recognition,' Baroo said. 'It is dispensed equitably among men, but only a few are given the capacity to make the best of it. In this Lucknow you and I remember I heard a story-teller relate a fable to this effect. Oh, he was such a master that people would sit in the marketplace and listen to him hour upon hour.'

Baroo arched his back slightly with a groan, and the Moslem waited a moment for him to continue. 'A fable?' he said. 'I love fables. Tell it to me.'

'Me?' Baroo asked, raising his hands in demurral. 'I would be overreaching. No Rajput could ever do it justice.'

I gave Baroo a pleading look, for the goor's flood seemed about to crest, but he tugged at his earlobe to say, *Not yet.*

'Please, brother,' the old man begged. 'I haven't heard a good story in ever so long.'

Baroo scratched his jaw for a moment and shrugged. 'Well,' he said, 'I suppose I can try. But in my own crude tongue if you don't mind. My Urdu shames me.'

'Yes, yes,' the Moslem piped back.

Oh no, I muttered to myself. Not another story.

The Moslem raised his head high, stretching his feeble neck as Baroo began to pace before the fire. Now? I wanted to ask. Can't I take him now? But I held myself in check, not daring to move my lips lest the sugar seep away.

'In Persia,' Baroo began, gesturing grandly with his loosely sleeved arm, 'in the time of Umar, when the footprints of the Prophet, blessings and peace be upon him, still ornamented the sands and his perfume yet lingered in his wake, there lived a boy named Khazim who desired a jeweller's daughter.'

The Moslem sighed and began to rock slightly on his haunches.

'He had only glimpsed her once, by chance, in passing, but in that instant she stole away his wind. She was her father's hidden pearl, moon-faced, chaste, and pure, and the most exalted princes vied for her. But the jeweller would part with her only in exchange for the greatest diamond in creation. Her suitors brought treasure boxes brimming with every kind of gem, but the father could not be satisfied.

'Now,' Baroo said, beginning to pace by the fire, 'Khazim was but a cobbler's son who had never beheld even a particle of diamond, and he despaired, and the more he despaired the more he desired the jeweller's daughter, for such is the pairing of ardor and hopelessness. One day a saint, passing by his shop, divined the boy's condition and took pity on him.

' "Women aren't worth such despondency," he gently told Khazim. "Their beauty is fleeting. Save such passion for the virgins of heaven, when you shall have all eternity to expend it."

'But would Khazim heed such wisdom?' Baroo asked, pacing rapidly now and gesturing with his hands and shoulders.

The Moslem shook his head, and in my fever I thought it might topple from his shoulders.

'Of course not,' Baroo said. 'He begged the saint to help him find such a gem as the jeweller demanded, and seeing there was no quenching Khazim's fire the kindly saint pointed to a star in the sky and bade him follow it for a hundred nights, and though it might lead him across oceans and mountains and deserts he was not to speak to anyone he passed, nor seek to know his situation. At the end of a hundred nights he would come to a stone shaped like a bull and there the heavens would reward him.'

The Moslem shifted slightly in his blanket, and now I drew out my roomal behind him.

'And so Khazim took leave of his family and did as the saint said,' Baroo continued with a quick glance in my direction, for I was kneeling now behind the oblivious old man with my roomal in my hands.

Baroo recounted the little cobbler's travels, and I tried to keep my ears pricked for the *jhirnee*: 'Fill your pipe.' But as the star led Khazim over mountains, through valleys and across the beds of vanished seas, something in the fable began to resonate like a small, far-off bell. I seemed to travel with Khazim, only backward, to Bhondaripur, to the buffalos grazing on the ridge, to the pond, to my invalid throne in the women's quarters, back to my fevered journey out of Cawnpore, where my memory floundered in a fog of dreams.

'And on the hundredth day,' Baroo was saying now, 'in a bleak waste, Khazim came at last to the bull rock and climbed upon its back and begged the heavens for a diamond of such size and beauty as to wrest his beloved from her father's house.'

The sacred syrup ebbed and the hum rose again in my ears, and in the fog I saw myself lying by a campfire, with Moonshi and Baroo attending.

'And no sooner had Khazim's plea ceased to echo in that waste,' said Baroo, kicking a stone into the fire, 'than the star that had led him there began to tremble and tear loose from the sky and float down into his arms, a bright, cold diamond the size of a water jar.'

'Ah,' the Moslem sighed as sparks soared up into the dark.

'Khazim's heart leapt and the waste was verdant with his prayers of thanksgiving,' Baroo said, frowning at me through the curtain of flying cinders. 'But when his jubilation was spent and he climbed down from the bull and turned around from home, he saw that without the star to guide him there was no returning.'

'No returning,' the Moslem murmured, following the sparks as they flared above him.

I gaped at Baroo now as the sugar soured in my throat. Moonshi had never abandoned me. How could I have believed it? He'd *loved* me. He'd *abided*.

'And for the rest of his days,' Baroo said, speaking deliberately, 'he wandered that waste, meditating upon the old saint's lesson: greed, lust, ambition; what can they gain you if you lose the bearings of your soul?'

It was Baroo! I told myself now. Baroo had beguiled Moonshi just like this and strangled him, and in my fever I had confused it with a dream!

'And now, Balbeer,' he said in a near whisper, his one eye twitching, 'fill your pipe.'

That was it, I told myself, trying to clear my head. The *jhirnee*. *Do it. Do it now!*

But I couldn't move. I saw Moonshi sink back into the fog, pleading with me, begging me to save him, and the resolution leaked from my arms like blood.

'The *pipe*, Balbeer,' Baroo now snarled. '*Fill the pipe!*'

At this the old Moslem came out of his trance, and turning his head around he saw my roomal pulled taut between my trembling fists and shrieked.

I couldn't stand the sound of it, for so many voices were already screaming in my ears, and if only to silence this one I fumbled my scarf around his neck.

By now Baroo had fallen upon him too, and for a moment we struggled together to subdue him, but then he rose and rose to an impossible height, lifting both of us off our feet, and he began to whirl around, clawing at his throat.

'Murderer!' I panted as Baroo and I spun around like twirlers. 'You killed Moonshi! You *murdered* him!'

'Shut up!' Baroo hissed, holding his end of my roomal in both hands.

I tried to grab at Baroo, but only managed to lose my grip on my roomal and fly off onto the ground, and Baroo, still holding firm to the empty scarf, tumbled through the fire.

He sprang to his feet with his clothes smoldering, but when he faced the old Moslem now his eye drooped among the fountaining sparks, and every sinew seemed to sag, for now the old man's blanket had fallen away and there stood before us not a feeble old clerk but a Pathan as tall as a tree, with a brass club strapped to the stump of his arm where the mullahs had severed his writing hand.

'*Maimed!*' Baroo gasped, dropping his hands to his sides, and the Moslem reared back from his great height and brought his stump down upon Baroo's old head. Baroo didn't flinch or stumble, but his turban, as if to confirm the curse of the maimed that had befallen him, dropped from his bald head and into the fire.

The Moslem stood back for a moment, astonished that after such a mighty blow Baroo could still be standing there, wavering, and turning around to face me.

'Oh my son,' Baroo said, staggering toward me, 'now look what you've done.'

But before he could reach me with his outstretched hands, the Moslem raised his stump again and shattered Baroo's skull with one swift stroke.

The Pathan's club tore loose from his arm and flew by me as Baroo teetered overhead, his crown caved in like a sack of glass. I thought I heard Kali's name on his breath as he toppled onto me, but then his eye brimmed with blood and I began to shriek.

The old Pathan stood back for a moment, digging for something in the waist of his trousers. I struggled under Baroo's dead weight, but before I could roll his body off my legs the Pathan was advancing upon me.

'No, no!' I stammered up at him. 'You don't understand! He killed my servant! I was – '

'Pig!' the Pathan growled. 'You bloody little pig!'

I saw right away that there was no talking to him, and finally heaved Baroo off me. I tried to rise to my feet, but slipped in Baroo's warm slick and felt the Pathan's fist strike my side. I fell forward as he drew back again, but now he too slipped in Baroo's gore, and landed hard on his brittle old rump as I limped into the dark.

'That's right!' he shouted after me. 'Run! But I'll get you! I'll hunt you down!'

For the longest while I didn't dare look behind me as I stumbled and staggered among the rocks and shadows. But even after the old Pathan's threats and curses had faded off I kept my eyes straight ahead, for it wasn't the Pathan I was afraid I might see behind me, but Baroo Singh himself: a little twisted still from his hanging, a little battered from the Pathan's assault, but otherwise none the worse for wear, floating after me across the stones.

PART FIVE

HARIGARH

CHAPTER

47

I ran all night, or what was left of it, and heard my doom in every shadow's whisper. A stench seemed to follow after me, as of hides set out to cure, but it wasn't until twilight that I saw it was Baroo's blood that raised it. His gore caked my shirt and waistband and still seemed to trickle down my leg.

In the morning I came to a little river – the Banas again, I suppose, or maybe one of its tributaries – and I threw myself into it, discarding my ruined dhoti and scrubbing at myself with the river mud. But when I reached around to clean my aching side I nearly swooned, for the stitch from my running seemed to flare, and looking under my ribs I saw a hole where the Pathan's knife had entered, and my own blood leaking out. I cast myself up onto the muddy bank and crawled under a ledge in the low scarp that ran along the riverside. I plastered my wound with handfuls of mud, but to no purpose, for I knew I was going to die, and good riddance, too, with Baroo's sweet venom still lurking among my vitals. As I lay back on the sandy floor and shut my eyes, it seemed to me that death could take me no further from Ahalya and my little son than I had already come.

Dhobi women, climbing down the crag with their bundles of laundry, were the first to find me, but it was their children who wakened me, murmuring, 'I go to Narayan' in their high, husky voices.

I sat up too quickly, for the pain flashed in my side like gunpowder, and my startled groan sent the children fleeing in all directions. I scrambled deeper under the ledge as they ran to their mothers and turned to gape at me. Flower petals spilled from my naked lap, and all about me little heaps of flower and salt had been carefully set out on patches of cloth.

Now it was no wonder that they had taken me for a holy man of some kind, for had I found a scrawny, wild-eyed naked man sleeping by a river, covered with mud, his head barely stubbled over, I might have made the same surmise. But it's a wonder how long it took me to comprehend my circumstances, and the advantages they offered to a fugitive like me.

I cowered all day in that dusty skug, glaring at whoever tried to come near and snatching up little handfuls of their offerings on the sly. My wound hadn't leaked a single drop of blood since my brief sleep, and it began to dawn on me that I might live. By this time death seemed a mercy and survival a useless complication, but as I forced my memory past my contamination and back to Bhondaripur I feebly dared to hope that all was not yet lost.

I tried to take stock of my situation, but to begin with I had only the dimmest notion of where I was. I supposed I had to be somewhere in Rajputana, but for me that was like saying I was somewhere in nowhere, for all I knew about Rajputana was what Moonshi had told me long ago: that it was far to the west of Cawnpore, and unimaginably vast.

I flinched at Moonshi's memory then and cursed myself for ever having believed Baroo's lies about him. But the truth of his murder opened out onto strangely sweet memories of my boyhood which I thought I'd locked away forever: the press of the bazaars, the kite wars, the confectioner's treats, the temple by the ruined ghat, my mother singing in the glow of a mustard lamp, the city's clatter rising to my rooftop roost like a flock of birds.

All this reminiscing must have given me just the right aspect for my newfound disciples, for over the next few days word seemed to circulate that a mendicant of rare austerity and abstraction had come to rest by their humble stream. Bigger crowds than the immediate desolation could generate gathered to partake of my darshan, and by evening my vicinity would be cluttered with their offerings and the ledges sparkling with lamps.

As it turned out I couldn't have chosen a better resting place, for the locals had seen few ascetics in those parts. They mistook me for a bairaji of the Manbao sect, or some exotic variation, and called me Dinji Boa, the humble one. It ws the local belief that the rocks that ranged along the river, hung here and there with hornets' nests, were the remains of divinities petrified by Brahma for their arrogance. Thus humility of the sort I seemed to embody was regarded in this region as the highest virtue, and newcomers to the throngs that stood all about were told that I had wounded myself in a recent frenzy (some even claimed to have witnessed it) and that I had been led by a vision to their river to intercede with the gods on their behalf.

I never said a word to anybody, nor even pretended to pray, but like a temple statue I was infused with the aspirations of the faithful: to the few men who paid me homage I bore a hope of better grazing for their miserable sheep; to the children I seemed to offer protection from the evil eye.

But to the women – the majority of my public – I was an agent of fertility, as I was to discover one night when I awoke from one lascivious dream into another as a beefy village woman with feet like great scuffed boots lowered herself upon my dusty pud.

Now by that time my wound had closed, but I was by no means robust, and when I awoke my loins had already summoned so much of my strength that I could only grunt with surprise and then lie back stock still until she finished. Of course it wasn't my children she wanted but her husband's, so she, like her sisters who followed her one after another through that long night, merely dipped me into herself for a stroke or two, dismounted like a syce, and scurried back to her husband's bed.

They came to me all night long, and I didn't refuse a single one, for it seemed to me now that my life depended on doing whatever was expected, even late in the night when there was nothing left of me but a sore, withered thing which the last of them had to stuff between her thighs with her calloused fingers.

Not a few scoundrels have undertaken the sadhu's life to taste just such fruits, but by the third night my recuperation had begun to stall, and I knew that if I didn't move on soon one of these fretful shepherd's wives, or her shamed husband, was going to kill me.

So I fashioned a travelling bag out of the scraps of cotton that had been set around me, and claiming a shepherd's goad as my staff I

set forth at dawn with a fresh coat of mud to keep the police and the
bugs away. I followed the stream as far as I could, heading eastward,
into the sun, but the rocky channel grew steeper and narrower and
the flow became tempestuous, so I climbed up from the riverside and
marched a few miles among the adjacent hills.

The region was abounding in chinkara gazelles, and I kept
coming upon drowsy herds of five or six taking their rest in the
nullahs. I seemed to raise no alarm among them, and as I passed
within a few feet of the little speckled bucks and does I wondered if
my muddy coat had disguised my scent or if sadhus had been passing
through those parts for so long that the chinkaras no longer saw
them as men but as gentle, kindred apes.

I kept Ahalya's image before me like a simmering shape on a
desert horizon and stumbled toward her step after step, stroking my
side to mollify the pain. I reached a road and followed it a little
distance, until a pair of lancers appeared, mounted on bony old
horses and dressed fantastically, with plumed helmets and studded
shields. I dared myself to stride right by them as any sadhu would,
but I was still hunched over the gash in my side, and lest they'd been
sent forth by some local raja to search for the old Thug's wounded
apprentice I ducked behind a boulder before they could catch sight of
me.

My legs gave out in the early afternoon, and I encamped by a
little tank within distant view of a fortified town. The hills were
gentler here, the rocks retreating into the dull-green grass that
bristled up like sparse fur from a thin hide of topsoil. A great jumbled
palace rose huggermugger on the face of a cliff overlooking the
whitewashed town. Walls coiled and fattened about the fortress and
then stretched out like a sleeping snake all the way down to the plain
beyond, though aside from the palace they didn't seem to protect
anything; the land on the high side of the walled slopes was as barren
as the low side, and nowhere within my broad view was there a single
patch of cultivated ground.

I didn't know it then, but I had somehow blundered my way
southeastward, into Bundi. From my altitude I could hear a burble
from the bazaars, punctuated by shouts of barking dogs and an
occasional rooster's crow, all of it ebbing and flowing as the wind
blew this way and that about my ears.

I revived an ember from an abandoned campfire and fried a little flour and ghee on a stone I worked loose from the rim of the crumbling tank. My mud coat had flaked down to a dusty film, which I amplified with ashes, and gripping my goad in one hand I settled myself down to eat my supper at the base of a little peepal tree that had set its roots in the damp cracks of the tank's wall. A kite swooped down from the hilltop and soared out over the city, on a level with the uppermost battlements of the cliffside fortress. I could make out a few figures retreating into the city for the night. Some led little herds of goats or sheep – from my altitude it was hard to tell.

But as the lights grew brighter and more numerous in the gloaming, a solitary figure began to make his way out from the city, zigzagging up the slope. He was low but substantial in raggedy silhouette, and lumbered along like a bear. At first I watched him with detachment, as if I could have reached out and flicked him aside. But then I began to hear him, clinking and clanging like a gypsy wagon on a katcha road, and I began to pray for him to veer off his crooked path, skirt my hill, and pass on into the range beyond.

But I waited too long, so that by the time it was plain that his destination was the tank, I had nowhere to run. I could only hold my breath as he approached, striking the ground before him with the nub of his trident staff. He seemed consternated by the fire and peered around him, sniffing at the smoke.

'Har Nerbudda?' he called out uncertainly, catching sight of me at last.

He was a gosain of some kind, as the trident bespoke, but I'd never seen his like before. He wore a latticed iron collar around his neck, as if he'd caught his head in a window grating, and from this hung shells, feathers, bells, and scraps of fur. A leopard skin was draped across his shoulders, piled high with necklaces of basil beads and rudraksha berries, all entangled with his whiskers. Sacks hung like weaverbird nests from his shoulders and his sheepskin belt, bumping among dangling pitchers and bowls, firetongs and lacquered calabashes. He carried some kind of scroll under one arm, and had tucked a woollen blanket under the other, and his arms and legs were half encased in stacks of metal hoops and bands, and speckled with tattoos. His headdress was a precarious heap of braided cloth studded with trident stickpins; his matted locks stuck out at all angles, as dense as horn; and as he turned toward me now the stretched and shredded lobes of his ears danced and dangled like a chicken's wattle.

'Har Nerbudda,' he said again, but more firmly, looming over me now against the dusky sky, a walking heap of bric-à-brac.

I knew from this particular greeting that he had performed the perikrama – walked the whole course of the Nerbudda from mouth to source to mouth again – and weakly replied, 'Victory to Mother Nerbudda,' as was the custom.

He nodded at this, starting a clattering among his necklaces and ornaments, and leaned toward me for a better look.

'Now let me guess,' he said finally. 'Digambara, am I right? Sky-clad.'

I rose to my feet with both hands on my goad.

'No? . . . Aughar jogi, then,' he said. 'That's got to be it.'

I stepped around him, ready to strike if he made a move against me, and began to back off along the edge of the tank, figuring that any gosain who'd performed the perikrama could quickly see me for a fraud.

'I can't – I can't quite make out your sect mark,' he said, stepping toward me. 'But wait. I've got it. Dandi. That's it, isn't it?'

By now I was a couple of yards from him, moving back into the dark, and finally catching on to my terror he said, 'No need to go, brother. I don't mean to chase you away. A brother of the spirit, that's all I am. Stay. Please. Look,' he said, rummaging for a moment in one of the appalling sacks that hung from his shoulders. 'I picked up some leftovers from the brass workers. I'll share them with you. I didn't mean to scare you.'

'You didn't scare me,' I said, lowering my goad for a moment. My own voice startled me, for I hadn't heard from myself since I'd sputtered up at the old Pathan.

'Well, good,' the gosain said. 'That's a relief. I keep forgetting how I must look to some people. I've picked up all – all *this* so gradually, you see, it's like it grew on me,' he said, giving his collar a shake. 'Sometimes it's all I can do to lug myself around.'

I kept peering back at him, alert for the slightest sign of treachery. He made an awful racket just standing there, and smelled like a vulture on the cold breeze that blew up the hill, but he was as cheerful as a toddler. He had a meagre sort of beard, like a Sikh's first growth, and a great red sect mark smeared upon his forehead, but for all his shabby mass his features were delicate, and when he caught me staring at him he grinned a little and batted his eyelashes like a girl.

'Come, come,' he said now, leading me back to the little fire. 'No point in freezing out there. We shall be friends. I can tell. I'm going to call you maharaj. But look here,' he said as I slowly followed after him, watching him in a sidelong fashion, 'you've let your sect mark go. There's nothing left of it, maharaj. Here,' he said, 'permit me,' and he reached into yet another sack and brought forth a lidded copper vessel full of greasy white clay. He dipped two fingers into it and brought them up to my forehead, his bracelets clattering down his arm.

I pulled away from him for a moment and gripped my goad again, but he gently reached further forward, as if offering a tidbit to a wild creature, and I held still as he drew a crescent on my brow and daubed a little white dot – Shiva's eye, he said – on the bridge of my nose.

'There,' he said with a proud nod. 'That's better. There are austerities and there are austerities, maharaj. But how is God going to recognize you if you don't keep up your sect mark?'

He suddenly drew a sharp breath through his teeth and gaped at me, and believing he had finally found me out I began to edge away from him again. But then he put on a shamed expression. 'But maybe you don't wear a sect mark?' he said. 'Oh, there you go again, Nanda,' he told himself. 'Always jumping to conclusions. Think you know everything, don't you?'

'Uh,' I said, in spite of myself, 'it's all right.'

'No it's not,' he said. 'I'm *always* doing that.'

'But – but you were right,' I said. 'I'd let it go. You know – in my meditations and all. I get careless. Forgetful.'

'You too?' he asked cautiously. 'You're not just trying to make me feel better?'

'No, not at all. I'm glad you reminded me.'

'Well,' he said, letting his shoulders droop, 'that's a relief. Mind you, I never saw a sadhu who didn't wear a tilak. But you never know. If I live to be a thousand I will never see every variety of our kind. You've probably noticed,' he said, bending back one of his horrid locks, 'but I haven't quite settled into anything just yet. You might say I'm still feeling it out. I know where I'm headed, you understand. No question about it. But how to get there, what path to take. That's the crux of the matter, isn't it?'

He brought forth iron tongs as long as his arm and began to arrange the glowing coals into a tidy circle. 'But then look who I'm asking. You obviously haven't had any problem choosing a path. Have you come from the tank as well?' he asked. 'I didn't see you down there.'

'No,' I said. 'I've come from – uh, Tonk,' I said, and cursed myself for opening my mouth. 'A little shrine there I like to visit.'

'Oh?' Nanda asked. 'What shrine is that?'

'A local shrine,' I said, trying to shrug off the subejct. 'A little lingam by a stream. All very crude. But venerable.'

'And quiet?'

'Oh yes,' I said. 'Very quiet.'

'Ah,' he said with a nod that sent his earlobes flying. 'Lovely. Just the thing.' But then he grimaced and said, 'And there you go *again*, Nanda. Just who do you think you're fooling? You *hate* the quiet.

'I hate the quiet,' he said, turning toward me. 'It's a problem for someone of my vocation. But never mind. I like bustle,' he said with his eyes brightening. 'I love a crowd.'

'Well,' I said, 'that's all right. Better to hurry through Tonk anyway.'

'Yes,' he said, smiling back at me. 'Pindaris all through those parts. They'd steal the whiskers off a corpse.'

'The lice off the whiskers,' I said, nodding.

'The fleas off the lice,' he said with an expectant look.

'And the whiskers,' I said, 'off the fleas.'

We stared at each other for a moment and then Nanda burst out laughing, clanking and clattering as he ducked his head around, and I joined him and we laughed together out of all proportion, our voices dancing among the gloomy hills. I don't know what set him off, but I laughed out of relief, and not just because my ruse was working. Just talking to another human being lifted my spirits above the particulars, which were that I was a fugitive and a fraud, wounded and lost and telling lies.

We talked for another hour or so and decided to travel together awhile. I had trouble dozing off that night, for in his sleep Nanda was as noisy as a Dusserah procession. He slept seated, with his head slumped down upon his collar, and every time he twitched and started he would set off his bells and rattle his beads and his bowls would clop like tumbling coconuts. My only comfort in this was knowing that if he was not as friendly as he seemed and really meant to do me harm, at least he could never take me by surprise.

He didn't notice my wound until morning, when he woke to find me replenishing my coating with the cold ashes from the expired fire. He was appalled to see me applying them unrefined, and insisted on filtering them several times through a cotton rag until he'd achieved a powder as fine as talc and almost as soothing to my abraded flesh. In the course of this he came upon my wound and fretted over it as my mother might have, concocting a balm for it out of dung and leaves and powders he withdrew from his sundry sacks and baskets.

He scolded me for mutilating myself like that, and exacted a promise from me that I wouldn't tear myself in his company, a vow I took with a great show of reluctance – for how, I asked him, could I guarantee that the gods would spare me this divine compulsion? Nevertheless, he said, if we were to remain friends I was to treat myself as kindly as I treated him.

I followed my new friend down the hillside and into Bundi, where we begged for a while among the Kasars, the brassworkers, near the silver market. Bundi was a beautiful city then, as it may be still, banked by the Raja's ramparts, which rose behind the bazaars like a backdrop in a portrait gallery. The paintings that made it famous adorned every wall, arch and doorway, depicting moon-faced Bundi kings, as poised as stone, riding after leopards and boars on their grand stallions and elephants, in colors as keen as the morning light.

We caused little stir in the bazaars that choked the lane to the palace gate, for the crowds were thick with holy men chanting by the tea stalls, blessing the banias, and awaiting their due from the faithful. I tried to bear my nakedness as grandly as Nanda bore his clattering rig. He begged in the usual fashion, by standing outside windows and doors, crying 'Apart! Apart!' and shaking himself all over, and when someone came to the door to dispense a little fistful of salt or a wad of leftover bread he would hop in place and bestow a blessing or two, fidgeting with his rosaries. I hopped along with him at the first few houses, but in motion my nakedness seemed to me even more conspicuous than Nanda's clang and clatter, and I took to falling back and looking saintly, as if I were above the whole business.

CHAPTER

48

We left Bundi on the Kota Road, with enough provisions to get us through the day. Nanda was in high spirits at first and sang as we marched along, clattering a rhythm on his fire tongs. I was still weak from my wound, and after a few miles the flickering pain slowed me down, but it was Nanda who slowed us down the most. In the daylight I saw that he was more delicate than lean, and his trinkets weighed heavily on his slender frame. He stopped every mile or so, ostensibly to worship by some sacred well or auspicious tree, but as the day wore on he took to praying at the most unlikely places, gasping prayers before boulders, milestones and whatever else was handy.

We might have made more progress if Nanda had stopped talking once in a while, for it seemed to take a lot out of him. But in my lonely state I would have listened to even Jagdish with fascination, so I did nothing to shut him up.

At first he felt called upon to wax philosophical. He maintained that the only path to the eternal was meditation. He claimed that in his trances and comas he had learned endurance from the earth, abstraction from the sky, equanimity from the unchanging sea. I had to agree with him, of course, for meditation was my ostensible stock in trade, but to me it all sounded tidy, halfhearted and secondhand, and Nanda was as relieved as I when the subject changed to his hapless history.

He told me very little about his childhood as we limped along, but from the incidentals I surmised that he'd been a Bhopal bania's first-born son who'd renounced his father's ways and set forth, as a young man, to overcome the world.

'I studied under a great Paramahansa who lived in the cliffs of the Vindhya range. He hadn't eaten anything in twelve years, and some even said he hadn't drunk anything either, except when it rained. He had such a powerful aura that it gave off a scent – almost like a flower, once you got used to it. He only spoke in conjunction with certain mansions of the moon, and then only if he had something to say. With his austerities he'd appropriated all kinds of power from the celestials. He could dive into the earth and contemplate whole worlds at a glance, and naturally I wanted to be just like him.

'I did everything I could to please him, but it was hard to know exactly what he wanted. Mostly he just sat on a ledge he'd claimed for himself and paid me no attention. Now the celestials may have been generous enough to him, but I knew they weren't going to give anything up to the likes of me without a struggle, so I set to performing the gravest austerities I could devise.

'If my guru didn't eat, I wouldn't eat either. If he sat naked in a chill rain, then I would immerse myself in freezing water. If he sat out in the sun then I would build fires around me and meditate in the scorching smoke.

'The difference was that while he was meditating on the eternal, I was meditating on him. I kept looking up to see how I was doing, but he'd just sit there, not even shaking his head, and after a while it drove me crazy.

'I took to whipping myself with sticks, sleeping in brambles, even chewing live coals after morning puja. Once he seemed to wince a little, another time I think he shrugged, but pretty soon I was too far gone to care. I remember I spent two days under a dripping water pot, and another day I recall beating my feet with fire tongs.

'Then one day he gave a great sigh that tumbled stones from the distant mountainsides, and he climbed down from his ledge. I can't remember what it was that finally wore him down. I think I was lying in the dust, trying to drive a spike through my cheek. Whatever it was, he put a stop to it, and ministered to me most kindly until I was ready to travel, and then he sent me away.

'He was very sweet about it, but very firm. What I was doing was penance, he said, and the way he saw it penance was just arrogance stood on its head. My brand of asceticism was fit only for faqirs who maim themselves with spikes and chains to gain admittance to the whorehouse – and that's what he called it, the whorehouse – that their prophet called paradise.

'He was right, of course. Asceticism was supposed to separate the soul from the body and reattach it to God. But what God was going to want a soul in such torment?'

So Nanda limped up into Rajgarh and tried to join the Kanphata jogis. 'They were so nice to me,' he said. 'Tolerated all my flaws. "It will come," they used to say. "It will come." "What will come?" I wondered sometimes, but never mind.

'My guru was two hundred years old. Lived in the jungle near Saugor. Highly esteemed by all the others. Not just his cheylas, either. Even the elect used to gather alms for him. That was the life. Never even had to leave his shrine.

'I studied under him for nine months. Ate his leftovers, drank his bathwater. He taught me some mantras and texts and sometime around Diwali he smiled on me and declared me fit for initiation. And I made it through without a hitch, too, up until the time came to insert the great glass Kanphata rings through my ears. As you can see, the rings didn't hold. They tore right through my earlobes and fell into the dust, and you should have seen the fuss everyone made.

'My guru cursed me and beat me with his umbrella, and he had quite an arm on him too, for a two-hundred-year-old. He called me a fraud and a devil and other things too vile to repeat, and it was what I deserved, I suppose. Overreaching again. But never mind. It could have been worse. If your ears tore in the old days they used to bury you alive.'

Nanda fell in with a Sanyasi after that, and changed his name to Bharti, after his guru's order. 'My guru was Swami Bhaskarananda Bharti. *The* Swami Bhaskarananda Bharti. Maybe you heard of him? He could fly. Just for show you understand. Preferred to walk like the rest of us. Didn't ask much of me. Collected his own alms, filtered his own ashes. All I really had to do was follow him around.

'The rules were simple enough, too: never wear white, never nap, never ride a horse, never think about women, and never get agitated – oh, and never sleep on a couch; that was an easy one. "Love nothing, hate nothing," that was his motto, and I thought, fair enough.

'But then one day while I was out pissing in the woods, a leopard came along and ate Swami Bhaskarananda Bharti. And do you know what he did? He retained the lotus position through the whole business! Imagine! He could have flown off anytime he liked. But no, he just sat there with this odd little smile and as the cat ripped his bowels away, I thought to myself, "Well, what's the use? I'll never be up to this." So I quit.'

He nearly gave up after that, but one day a farmer offered to sell him a cow with a fifth leg. 'He took me for a Nandia jogi, and I thought to myself, Well, maybe I *am* a Nandia jogi, so I bought it from him. Got such a good deal it was almost unseemly, but I suppose I wasn't a bania's son for nothing. That extra leg was really just a little fin with a lump of bone in it. Hung out from one shoulder like a tortoise's foot. But it was a wonderment to pilgrims, and even after splitting my alms two ways – between me and the cow – I prospered. Not that prosperity was the point, I realize. Needless to say, I shared my alms with everybody. And that cow earned more than her share, I can tell you. She left everything green in her path. Rain followed us in the middle of summer, barren old women bore sons.

'It got so that word would travel ahead of us and we'd be greeted by the village priests and put up in the finest serais. Children used to sell her dung to the faithful, Brahmins would come and bottle her piss. I was hard put to figure where austerity fit into all this, until one day we were climbing through a barbed-wire fence to visit a Feringhee's servants outside Jabhalpur, when the wire snapped up and sheared my little cow's extra leg away.

'Well, it had never been held up by much, and once the bleeding stopped it hardly left a mark. I didn't know what to do, but I didn't want to disappoint anybody, so I took a thorn and some string and sort of sewed the little leg back on.

'It seemed to work just fine, and when I reached the servants' quarters everyone revered my little cow, just as before. I imagine that given enough time that leg might have grown back on, too, but then the burra sahib came marching into the quarters. He was as big as a house, with orange hair all ruffled up from sleep, and he took one look at my little cow and shouted, "Fraud!" and tore that extra leg right off.

'I tried to explain, but he laid claim to my cow and promised it to whoever could chase me out of the compound, so there was an end to my Nandia days.'

Decked out now in all his Nandia gear, plus a few trinkets from his terms with the Paramahansa, the Kanphata, and the Sanyasi, he made his way to the Nerbudda to soothe his spirits in the holy stream.

'When the rains came I found myself stuck in Hushangabad. The city was full of real sadhus who'd been in the life for decades, and they took me for a charlatan in my slipshod rig.

'Except for one old saint I met by the ghats. He was a sun worshipper. Blind as the stone by the time I knew him, but he was still at it, following the warmth of the sun from one horizon to the other. I told him my story up to that point, and he took pity on me. I thought I'd learned my lesson – no more gurus – but he was such a nice old man, and not a mute like the others. Talked your ear off if you let him, but always with his old head tilted up to the sun. Needed a cheyla to help him keep his head aimed right on cloudy days, so I settled in with him, and lived off what he could spare from his alms.

'One day I was down in the river shallows performing my morning ablutions when the wind blew up and I caught sight of something jutting up between the waves. So I waded out to it and pulled up this collar. It was iron and it had been there a while, but the odd thing was that there wasn't a speck of rust on it. I decided to pop my head through and carry it to shore, but a thunderhead came roaring up the river with the lightning lashing all along the ghats and I suppose I panicked. I felt myself sinking in the mud, choking and sputtering as the rain swept down, and no matter how I struggled I couldn't get the collar off from around my neck.

'But just as I was about to drown, the wind raised a mournful song from my collar, like a poor lost soul's, and this strange force seemed to lift me out of the mud and return me to the old saint's side.

' "Ah," he said, touching the collar with his fingers, "then the wheel has chosen you."

'Of course, that was easy for him to say. The collar wasn't

chewing *his* neck raw, or bearing down on his shoulders like the sins of the earth.

'But I kept it. And when the wind blows I still hear those poor souls wail. In all the years I've walked the Nerbudda, nobody's been able to tell me what the collar signified, and I still wonder sometimes if it's a sadhu's rig at all or just something that fell off a steamer. But it's been a great curiosity to the faithful, and quite an austerity, so I make the best of it.'

Thus Nanda assembled his gear around his iron collar and set forth to perform the perikrama like a proper gosain, stopping at every holy place he came upon along the Nerbudda's course and festooning himself with souvenirs from Broach to Amarkantak. In the process he became the Nanda I met in the Bundi hills, a one-man sect trying to live by all his gurus' teachings, though they clashed in his soul as loudly as the gewgaws and fetishes that dangled from his weary frame.

He told me all this, and more besides, in our long days of fitful travel. We passed many of his kind along the road, and rested among them by the tanks and temples. There were gosains and bairajis, faqirs and jogis and yatis of every description, for it was still travelling season. I once saw a bairaji strike a gosain over a question of bathing order on the banks of the Chambal, and two jogis came to blows one afternoon over something to do with lineage, but all in all they were a peaceable lot and gave each other their due.

I saw faqirs at Hindu shrines, gosains at Vishnuite temples, bairajis at Shivaite, and yatis interspersed among them all. Yatis were Jain ascetics who'd taken the matter of reincarnation to such an extreme that they wouldn't wear clothes lest washing them might kill a louse, nor bathe in a river lest they might trample a fish, nor light a fire lest it incinerate a moth. They believed that if you killed a bug in this life you would become a bug in the next, so they bathed in cooking water from other folks' kitchens and hunkered down by other folks' fires, more or less leaving the risk of an abysmal afterlife to their benighted benefactors. If a yati was careful enough he could circumvent reincarnation altogether and attain eternal peace, and thus the midget yati I once encountered bound for Mount Abu, who'd woven the hairs of his beard and moustache together to filter out flies and swept the path before him with a soft cotton broom.

I suppose you could say that the Moslem ascetics didn't really hurt anyone but themselves, but they were a trial to the sensibilities. The Madari faqirs lashed their legs with whips and dragged great heavy lengths of chain. One night a few of us were huddled around a fire when one Madari suddenly tramped through it and hopped off into the night, shouting 'Aam Madar!' at his smoking feet. The Jalalia faqirs liked to horsewhip themselves on the hand and eat live scorpions with particular ostentation, and the Rafai faqirs hit themselves on the cheeks with iron maces. We once met a Rafai who'd already lost an eye to this practice, and spent half a night praying to his instrument not to claim the other one. But even more distressing were the Sada, the Brides of Hussan: men who dressed in women's clothing and spoke in fluttery falsettos, but never clipped their whiskers.

I found nothing to recommend these Moslem sects, but I did admire a Nakshbandia faqir I chanced upon one night in Gaintha, bestowing blessings on the children – Moslem and Hindu alike – who flocked around his lantern. He had what Nanda called 'mahst,' a kind of benign melancholy, and smiled down at his small disciples as he dignified their brows with lampblack.

I lost count of the weeks we travelled along the Chambal, zigzagging from shrine to shrine, catching this festival or that, taking our places along the village lanes and begging alms from the pilgrims. I stole a bell from a bullock and attached it to the end of my staff, and fretted over my appearance like an actor, powdering myself with ashes at every campfire, perfecting my sect mark in the little English hand mirror that hung from the back of Nanda's collar. Nanda was right; if you lived to be a thousand you could never know every kind of holy man. There seemed to be infinite numbers of sects, and within each sect countless divisions and subdivisions. And then of course there were the charlatans and the fugitives like me, and the eccentrics like Nanda who cut their own path to paradise. Most sadhus were too set in their ways to take much interest in one another, and in the weeks I spent among them no one ever challenged my masquerade.

But it pained me to deceive Nanda, for he was always so trusting and so truthful, if it is truthful to favor the harshest truths about yourself. He was always deferring to me in matters of philosophy, and exalting whatever tortured epigrams I managed to stammer back at him. Like most talkative men he admired reticence, and read all kinds of wisdom in my silences. I had a longing to confess everything to him, which usually struck me with its full force at night, as he sat snoring and clattering beside me. I know he would have shrugged it off, for his code forbade him to pass judgment. But back then I trusted no one.

As the weeks and miles went by, my fear of capture receded. I'd made good my escape from the old Pathan, but Baroo haunted me still, drifting through my sleep like the sugary steam from the confectioners' stall. He was dead for sure, I told myself. No man could live with his skull caved in. I recollected his death a hundred times to convince myself of that.

But then he would rise up in my dreams, straight and youthful, with his missing eye restored, welcoming me home at Bhondaripur's gate. He floated about my house, extolling Ahalya's cooking, chucking Mahabir under the chin, delighting Channa with his fables. I tried to warn them he was murderous and mad, but it was as if I were a lunatic; no one heard me, no one saw me but Baroo himself. He winked at me now and fondled Ahalya, crabbing his hand under her white skirt as she suckled my baby son. I cried out, but my voice was eerie and distant, like an owl's hoot, and then Mahabir raised his little fists and wound his blanket around Ahalya's throat.

I awoke from this dream gasping, with a sickly taste in my mouth. I suspected this was a trace of the venomous goor, flowing like a tide when I slept. And so as we left the dwindling Chambal and veered eastward into Gwalior, it wasn't Baroo I feared any more, nor the Pathan, nor even the police. It was the Thug I carried within me: Kali's serpent coiled in my soul.

In early March, I think it was, Nanda's circuit finally brought us to Gwalior to partake of the alms that poured forth from the faithful on the festival of Makar Sankrant. We reached the outskirts of the city on the afternoon before the mela was to begin, and joined an old yati at a crumbling Jain shrine on a hillside near the fort. The yati was a shade aloof, and pitied us for the afterlives we faced because of our reckless practices, but Nanda admired old sadhus on general principles and charmed the sage with his good manners.

According to Nanda, the sun had been travelling southward for the past two months. 'But tomorrow,' he said as he polished his gewgaws for the next day's begging, 'it turns from its deathbound path and arights itself. Just you watch – everything changes.'

More than you know, I wanted to tell him as I searched the view for Bhondaripur. There must have been a dozen villages laid out before me that crystalline afternoon, but I had to climb higher up the hillside to catch a glimpse of my own harvested fields beyond the remotest ridge.

Nanda watched me as I darted from one vantage point to another, anxiously squinting off into the distance, but he ascribed my restlessness to Sankranti's approach.

'The days of the gods begin tomorrow,' he said that evening.

'And the nights of the demons,' the old yati said, his voice muffled by the cotton mesh he wore about his lips.

'Yes, of course, Bapuji,' Nanda said. 'But the days of the gods more than compensate, wouldn't you say?'

'No matter,' the yati replied with a tilt of his head. 'It is all different. It is all the same.'

I'd been putting up with hundreds of conversations like this, and spouting just such pieties when the need arose. But tonight I had no patience for it. I had planned to lose Nanda in the city the next day and proceed from there to Bhondaripur, but my heart tapped at me like a herder's goad. I yearned for my wife and son sleeping now within a few hours' walk from where I sat, and at last I could wait no longer, and resolved to go home that very night.

I think I must have willed the sun to set that evening. Nanda fell asleep almost as soon as the night had fallen, but the old yati stayed up for hours, reciting to himself from the Pakrit text he carried with him in a thick, soiled scroll. I listened to him in an agony, watched him with a murderous glare, shut my ears to his unceasing drone.

The moon was already past its zenith when the yati finally dozed off. As I rose from my resting place, Nanda frowned and stirred a little, clattering like a tambourine. I had the same old urge to waken him and tell him everything, or at least to repay him somehow for his companionship, but all I could do was leave my bell-topped staff at his feet and bid him goodbye in a whisper.

◆————————◆

CHAPTER

49

I moved in a stealthy zigzag as I crept down into the city, but by the time I'd passed safely through the dark bazaars and into the outskirts beyond I became like a warrior charmed by the ardor of his quest, whom neither bullet nor blade can injure, and my path had grown as straight as a bowstring. If a pond stood between my family and me I forded it, if a hill I climbed it, if a thorn row I scrambled through it, and had I the power I would have leapt across the roofs of the houses in my path, and flown across the fields.

I reached the old mango grove where the tiger had spared my life, and the night breeze set the treetops to jubilating as I strode through.

It was dawn by the time I climbed to the top of the saddleback ridge that overlooked my fields, and the swallows were flying up from the eaves of the houses to greet me. I paused a moment to catch my breath, leaning my hands against my knees, and my eyes veered along the paths and lanes until they finally found my house, still shaded by the ridge to the east. There was no smoke as yet from Ahalya's breakfast fire, and not even a rooster's crow broke the silence.

'Home,' I said aloud, and began the last descent, stepping with care over the rubble of the hillside, when who should appear rounding a great boulder but Jagdish and his herd of buffalo.

We stood and faced each other not ten feet apart, and I raised my hand and grinned, trying to muster the wind to greet him. He stopped dead in his tracks as the buffalo passed by me with their horned brows nodding, and his jaw hung down like a ladle.

'Jagdish!' I finally called to him. 'It's me! I'm back!'

'I – ' he stammered back, 'I go to Narayan.'

I took a step toward him with my arms outstretched, then I saw the ashes on my flesh and remembered my disguise.

'No, no,' I said with a laugh. 'I'm no sadhu, Jagdish. It's me! Balbeer!'

I waited for this to penetrate, for a smile of recognition to flicker across his gaping lips, but his jaw only dropped lower and his eyes bulged out from their sockets, and suddenly he turned around and ran.

'Jagdish!' I called, stumbling after him. 'It's me! Don't you recognize me? Come back here!'

But Jagdish just raced ahead, throwing down his goad, and if he hadn't looked back and tripped over a stone I would never have caught up to him.

'Damn it, Jagdish,' I said, reaching him before he could rise to his feet. 'What's the matter with you? Aren't you glad to see me?'

But as I looked into his horror-struck face I remembered his fear of the spectral sadhus he'd come upon before Mahabir's birth. 'Look,' I said now, spitting on my hand and wiping at my cheek. 'I'm no ghost. See? It's only ashes.'

'Ashes,' he mumbled back, cringing at my feet.

'That's right,' I said. 'Just ashes.'

He slowly nodded up at me, staring hard at my features, but the terror never left his eyes, and every time I shifted my feet he cowered like a slave.

'Yes, Jagdish,' I said, leaning down toward him. 'It *is* me. It's Balbeer. I've come home.'

Jagdish closed his eyes and turned his head away, and from his shoulders I could tell he was weeping.

'There, now,' I said, choking back a sob myself and touching him on the shoulder. 'It's all right, Jagdish. I'm home for good.'

But Jagdish gripped his hair and shook his head. 'Oh, zemindar-ji,' he said, his eyes still shut to the sight of me. 'You can't be. You mustn't be back.'

'Well, that's a fine welcome,' I muttered, straightening up and staring down at my house. 'Get up,' I snapped at him. 'Get up and greet me like a friend.'

Jagdish slowly got to his feet, hiding his face in the crook of one arm. I yanked his arm down and stared into his anguished eyes. 'What is it, Jagdish? What's wrong?'

'You know what's wrong, zemindarji,' he said, still sobbing. 'You must know what's wrong.'

'But I *don't* know, God damn it,' I barked back. 'So tell me.'

'The *patwari*, zemindarji,' Jagdish said, averting his eyes. '*You* know.'

'Mangal Singh? What's he done? Damn it, I warned him,' I said, shaking one fist.

Jagdish hesitantly turned and glanced at me.

'But he's – he's *dead*, zemindarji. Remember? He was murdered. The night – the night you left.'

'*Murdered*? Mangal Singh? What are you talking about?'

Jagdish shook his head slightly as if I were mad. 'He was strangled. The very night you left. They say – '

'Baroo!' I cried out, stumbling back a step.

'Zemindarji?' said Jagdish, cocking his head.

I covered my face and stared into my palms, trying to recollect that last evening. I saw myself standing over Mangal Singh, shaking him, barking my commands. 'What?' I said, uncovering my face again. '*What* do they say?'

'Well, naturally, zemindarji,' Jagdish said, sniffling back his tears. 'They say you killed him.'

'*Who* says this?' I wanted to know, raising my fist to him.

'Uh, *everyone*, zemindarji. The tahsildar. The suba and all his agents. And Sakuntala. She – she says she saw you.'

'But that's – that's impossible . . . ' I mumbled, still trying to envision that night. She'd been sitting in the kitchen, in the shadows. And her father was alive when I left him. Wasn't he? He was sleeping. Drunk with bhang. But then I saw him in my grip with his head rolling back. Was he already dead by then? I asked myself, gaping at Jagdish. Had Baroo already paid his visit?

I gripped Jagdish's shoulders in my cold hands. 'You've – you've got to believe me, Jagdish. It wasn't me. I didn't even know. It was – it was Baroo Singh,' I said, but my voice trailed off again as faith gave way to doubt and terror on Jagdish's tear-streaked face.

'Baroo Singh?' he asked in a high, humoring voice, trying to step away. 'It was Baroo Singh, you say?'

'That's right,' I said, pulling him back toward me. 'It was Baroo Singh. He came for me that night. It must have been him, don't you see? While I was saying goodbye to Ahalya.'

But he didn't see, and his chin began to tremble. 'Please, zemindarji,' he said. 'Please don't kill me too.'

'Shut up!' I shouted down at him as he drooped at my feet like a sopping cloth. 'I haven't killed anybody. It was Baroo, I tell you. Don't you understand?'

'Yes, zemindarji,' he whimpered, with his hands clasped over the back of his neck. 'Just don't kill me. I'll never tell them you were here.'

'Ahalya,' I said, giving up on poor Jagdish. 'She'll believe me,' I muttered, pushing Jagdish aside and stepping past. 'She's got to believe me.'

'No, wait!' Jagdish called out. 'You can't go there!'

'I'm going *home*, Jagdish,' I shouted back at him. 'I'm going to see my wife and son.'

'No, zemindarji!' he cried out as I dashed to the bottom of the slope, 'they're – '

But I'd heard enough, and covered up my ears as I tore through the thorn row. By now the sun had reached the rooftops, and I could hear people hawking and spitting in the lanes as I neared the gate. I kept running, still naked and ashen in my disguise, pounding along the path to my house. Someone – a potter, I think – stepped into the lane just as I ran by, and we collided, but as he spun down into the dust I regained my balance and pushed open my gate with my shoulder.

'Ahalya!' I shouted, 'I'm back! I'm back!' I raced to the door and burst through it, banging my head on Lakshmi's lintel. 'Ahalya!' I called again. 'Ahalya, it's me! I'm back!'

But the rooms were empty, not only of my wife and child, but of all our possessions as well. Not a bed, not a pot, not a scrap of cloth in any room.

I tore through to the verandah in back, still calling out her name, but it was bare as well, and all the walls were cracked and untended. I staggered back through the house, trying to tame my breathing. There was something I'd forgotten. Another room, perhaps. Or her family. That was it! She'd moved back to Channa's house.

But just as I made for the front door, Channa himself appeared in it, flanked by Santosh and Pyari Lal, all winded by the dash from their house.

'Father!' I gasped at him. 'It's me! Balbeer! Where are they? Where are my wife and son?'

Channa stepped forward, glaring at me.

'Tell him,' said Santosh through his teeth. 'Tell the zemindar.'

'The zemindar,' Channa repeated grimly, looking me up and down. 'In all his glory.'

I glanced at each of them in turn, trying to catch something kindred in their eyes, but their gaze was harsh and bitter.

'Don't you recognize me?' I asked faintly. 'It's me. It's Balbeer,' and I touched Channa's twisted foot.

Channa stepped back a little at this, and his glower seemed to falter. 'We know who you are,' he said. 'And we know what you did.'

I stood up again. 'No, Father,' I said, slowly shaking my head. 'You don't know what I did.'

'We know,' said Pyari Lal, stepping forward. 'The whole kingdom knows.'

'I didn't kill him, Father,' I said, my eyes fixed on Channa. 'I swear to you I didn't.'

'You swear on what?' snapped Santosh. 'On what do you stake your soul, zemindar?'

I glared at Santosh now with all the rage that I could muster, and standing tall with my ribs stuck out I said, 'I swear on the life of my son.'

Channa groaned a little, and Pyari Lal turned his head away.

'And what's that worth to you, zemindar?' Santosh said with a sneer. 'What's it worth to anybody?' He moved forward as if to strike me, but his eyes filled with tears and he staggered back, sobbing against Pyari Lal's shoulder.

I reached forward out of instinct to console him. 'What is it, Santosh?' I said. 'What's happened?'

Beyond Channa I could see a crowd begin to gather in the courtyard; children, mostly, a few veiled women, and Ramesh working his way through them toward my door.

'Ahalya. Mahabir,' Pyari Lal said as Channa turned his face

away. 'They're gone.'

I stumbled then as I turned to face him, and gripped his arm to keep from falling. Now he too lost his courage and slumped back against the doorframe.

Then I heard Channa's voice as I remembered it, gentle, deliberate. 'She believed you, Balbeer. It didn't matter what Sakuntala told her, or the tahsildar. I told her to move back with me, but she wouldn't. Said you'd promised you'd be back in a month. Waited for you calmly, without a whisper of doubt.' Channa nodded with pride at this. 'And even — ' he said, raising one finger, 'even when that month had passed and everyone told her you'd run away for good, she still believed you, and divined that you'd been injured.'

'But I *was*,' I said, pointing to the scar on my side. 'Stabbed. Right here. Look.'

Channa glanced evenly at the old wound. 'Just so,' he said, nodding slightly. 'She always had a gift for those things.'

Santosh squatted down on the floor and sniffed back a tear.

'So one night when we were sleeping — '

'The chowkidor deeper than anybody,' Santosh piped in.

'One night,' Channa began again, 'when we were all sleeping, she picked up Mahabir and packed a few things and set forth to find you.'

'When, father?' I said as Ramesh joined us, gaping at the sight of me.

'Weeks ago,' said Pyari Lal. 'I don't know exactly.'

'But didn't you look for her?' I began to shout. 'Didn't you try to find her?'

Channa glared at me anew and stepped toward me with his fists at his sides. 'I'm her *father*,' he growled back at me. 'He's my *grandson*. Don't you think I would try to find her?'

'We all tried,' said Ramesh.

'But Channa was gone for days,' said Pyari Lal. 'Looked high and low.'

'And?' I asked Channa.

Channa's glare faded again and he shook his head. 'Nothing. Not a trace. I might have come close up in Kerowlee. A shepherd claimed he'd seen them. But I never did.'

'She'll be back,' Ramesh said with a firm nod. 'I keep telling them. She can't wander around out there forever.'

The others hardly looked up. 'No,' said Santosh as Pyari Lal shook his head. 'She won't be back. She won't give up until she finds him. You know how she is. Head of stone and heart of fire.'

'I'll find her then,' I said. 'I'll find them both.'

Channa looked at me with a faint spark of hope in his eyes. 'But where will you look? I looked everywhere.'

I was awash in doubt, and could hardly make my sore legs move. I heard my mother whisper that my wife and son were dead. *Forget them, forget them,* she seemed to chant. But I found myself consoling Channa and the others, patting their backs, reassuring them that all would be well. 'I'll find them, Father,' I said. 'Believe me. I'll know where to look.'

My words were relayed back out to the crowd in the courtyard, and the women nodded and embraced each other. Channa stared into my eyes for the longest while as if seeking out the boy he'd raised. 'Yes,' he said finally. 'All right. But only send us word when you find her. Don't come back. Never come back, son. They'll hang you if you do.'

The commotion among the women grew louder as I gaped at Channa and reached down to touch his feet again. 'But I didn't do it,' I said. 'I couldn't kill anybody. You know that. It wasn't me, Father. That night when I left I lied to everybody. I had to. I wasn't going to Cawnpore. I had no business there. It was Baroo that dragged me off that night. Baroo Singh the Thug.'

Santosh stood up, and the others stepped back from me with their mouths hanging open.

'No, it's true,' I began to sputter. 'They didn't kill him. He wouldn't die.'

Suddenly a woman glided into the room parting the gathering crowd like a figure in a procession. She was veiled and slight, and for an idiotic moment I thought she was Ahalya, but then she raised her arm and her veil fell down and I recognized Sakuntala. I stumbled backward, as much in terror of her black eyes all rimmed in red as of the dagger she held high in her small fist.

'Murderer!' she screeched, and there was that voice again, like a blade slashing at stone. 'You killed him! You killed my *father*!'

But she seemed to choke and falter on his name, and didn't lunge at me so much as fall forward in a near faint, sobbing weakly as Channa grabbed her wrist.

'Killed him, killed him, killed him,' she chanted feverishly, rolling her head about as Channa pulled her back into a corner of the room.

'Please, Sakuntala,' I said, stepping toward her. 'I didn't. I didn't kill your father.'

'Go now, son,' Channa said over her delirious incantation as her dagger fell to the floor. 'She'll have sent for the tahsildar.'

I made as if to embrace him, but he sharply shook his head as Sakuntala began to flail in his grip.

'I'll come back,' I said as I stepped toward the rear door.

'No,' said Pyari Lal. 'There's nothing for you here. The suba's taken your land away. Find Ahalya. Give us word when you can. But don't ever come back to Bhondaripur.'

'But I – '

'Go!' cried Channa, and when I hesitated in the doorway Santosh shoved me out toward the mustard fields.

'Come on,' he said, running after me. 'I'll lead you to the ridge.'

He took me through the densest rubble on the slope of the eastern ridge, along a path we must have followed a thousand times in the days when we drove the buffalo together. I lingered on the blade of the ridge with a sinking heart, gazing down at the fields and houses, and then Santosh and I embraced like brothers now that I was no longer his lord.

CHAPTER 50

I circled around Bhondaripur and made my way westward, resting that night in a little mango grove halfway between Gwalior and Morar. I could hardly raise my eyes as I rushed along, for the world stretched out so far in so many directions. Ahalya could have been anywhere within a month's walk from where I lay that night – even farther if she'd caught a ride somehow. I closed my eyes and tried to think like her. If I'd told her that I was going to Harigarh, and if she remembered it, and if she knew Harigarh was in Rajputana, and if she knew where Rajputana was, then I would look for her there, but my thinking wasn't even as clear as that may sound, for with every 'if' my mind would stagger in despair.

Now while I'd been darting around the countryside that day, Nanda had been out searching for me. I thought I'd done everything I could to keep out of sight, but maybe in some secret hope that the tahsildar would find me and put an end to my preposterous quest, I travelled carelessly, for a citybound sadhu told Nanda he'd spotted me filching some water from a field well, and from there a pair of oil pressers directed him to the mango grove, where he found me sleeping, dreaming of my lost wife and son.

In this dream I sat eating supper with Ahalya and Mahabir, simply and peaceably, so it was a wrench to be brought back into the desolate night by Nanda's call and clatter, but when I recognized him, standing a little way off in the dappled moonlight, I leapt to my feet and embraced him, knocking my chin against his collar.

'Maharaj?' he said, tentatively patting my ashen back as I began to sob like a baby against him. 'Are you all right?'

There was nothing for it now but to tell him, for it all weighed on me too heavily, so I had him sit before me in the grove and I confessed everything: blubbering that I was no gosain but a Thug's disciple, a fugitive in two kingdoms who'd tried to strangle an old scribe, who stood accused of murdering his own patwari, who'd broken his vow to his wife and son, and all the rest of my sorry history. I kept pausing and glancing over at Nanda to see if he'd had his fill of me yet, but he sat utterly still, with all his ornaments quiet, his face hidden in the shadows. When I was finished I slumped, defeated, not even bothering to brace myself for the berating I deserved for deceiving him all those weeks and then deserting him to boot.

There was a silence, and then his collar softly rattled. 'Ah, maharaj,' he said, shaking his head. 'What a shame.'

'I know, I know,' I sputtered back, the tears spilling down my cheeks again. 'I'm sorry, Nanda. You've been so good to me. I didn't want to lie to you.'

I went on sobbing about how sorry I was, how ashamed I was, but he just stared back at me with the look of someone approaching a major decision, and finally raised his hand to silence me.

'Shame?' he asked when I was quiet. 'You want me to tell you about shame?' And he told me this story.

'When my father and mother were married, my mother had no luck bearing children. She lost two before they'd even swollen her womb, and a third was stillborn. My grandmother told my father to get rid of her, but he loved my mother, and gave her one more year to produce. She'd already tried every cure she could think of: sherbets, powders, even her pregnant sister's piss, but all for nothing. So finally in desperation she turned to Mahadeo, the destroyer, and struck a terrible bargain, and sure enough, it worked. Nine months later she gave birth to me, and to another boy the next year, and yet another the year after that, until my father had sired three sons to share his bounty.

'Needless to say, as the oldest son, I stood to inherit all my father's lands and businesses, but it was his next oldest son, my brother Samir, who was my father's pride and joy. And there was no doubt about it; he was a beautiful boy with a real head for business. He could bargain with customers at the age of three, and held his own with the Mahajans at five. Still, I did what I could to please my father. Once when he was ill I ran all his businesses for him and never lost track of a single pice. But no matter what I did, it was always Samir my father trotted out to show off to the guests and customers, while I drudged away in the back.

' "But never mind," I'd tell myself. "Someday all this is going to be yours and poor Samir's going to have to work for you," and I'd scold myself for my jealousy.

'Then one day when I was almost grown I noticed that not only Samir but Madan, the youngest, were already engaged, and yet no arrangements had been made for me. So I went to my father and asked him about it and he looked me up and down and sort of smacked his lips and said, "Nanda, go to your mother. Tell her the time has come."

'Well, finally! I thought, so I went to my mother and told her the time had come, but my mother just turned around and began to pack me a travelling kit.

'For the time had come not for my marriage but to make good on her end of her bargain with Mahadeo. What she'd done, it turned out, back when she was barren, was promise Mahadeo her firstborn son in exchange for the rest of her children. So I was supposed to go to a festival they held every January on a cliff in the Sathpore range and pray at Mahadeo's temple, and then, when the priests gave the signal, jump off the cliff.

'Well, as you can imagine, I was distressed by these instructions. But in the end I tried to look at it this way: if my life was Mahadeo's to give, then it was his to take. My father gave me enough cash for a one-way trip to the Nerbudda, and my mother called out to me, "Be careful," as I set out toward my doom.

'It was November when I left and the mela fell on the first moon in January, so I should have been able to reach the cliff on time, but I guess I must have dawdled, because by the time I reached the Sathpore range it was almost February and the priests told me I'd have to come back the next year.

'You should have seen that place, maharaj. Cliff must have been a hundred, two hundred feet high, and down below, if you dared to look, you could make out all these bones scattered on the rocks.

'I tried to linger there, to sort of prepare myself for the next year's festivities, but that only seemed to make the prospect worse. So I set off to better myself spiritually, and that's when I took up with the Paramahansa, remember?

'Well, I'd fully intended to go back to the mela the next year, but I don't know, it sort of slipped my mind, what with the Kanphatas taking to me so kindly. I guess I figured I'd be worth more to Mahadeo if I stepped off the cliff as a saint than as a bania's boy. Or maybe it was just the cliff itself. I know the whole point was to just fall off, but the thing is, I have this horror of heights. Can't even stand up on a chair without getting dizzy.

'So, in short, maharaj, I never did make it back to that cliff.'

Nanda stopped here and sighed.

'That's it?' I exclaimed then. 'You're ashamed because you wouldn't jump off a damn cliff? Are you crazy?'

Nanda looked over at me now, and his chin began to quiver.

'Your mother sends you off to kill yourself and you're ashamed because you choose to live?'

'You really aren't a gosain, are you?' Nanda said, rattling his ornaments as he shook his head. 'Can't you guess the rest of my story?'

'What are you talking about, Nanda?'

Nanda's shoulders now began to shake as if with sobs, though he seemed to cut them off at the throat, for his voice was clear and steady. 'The *rest* of my story, maharaj. Don't you understand? This is Mahadeo I'm talking about. Mahadeo the merciless.'

'So?'

'So I went home, maharaj, after I missed the mela a second time. Figured my mother would find out anyway, so I might as well tell her. Well, she should have known, for on the first moon of January the year before, Madan had been carried off by the ague, and a year later as I'd been sucking up to the Swami, little Samir, my father's pride and joy, had been crushed to death by a sack of squash.'

'But, Nanda,' I said hesitantly, 'that was just . . . *coincidence.*'

Nanda gave me a nauseated look and turned away to compose himself. 'Now you might have thought my mother would have killed me on the spot for breaking her bargain, struck my skull with her skillet for disobeying her. But no, maharaj, she was overjoyed to see me, covered me with kisses, and my father embraced me and fed me with his own hand, for now I was all they had left, you see. I could have burned my mendicant's robes and become my father's favorite, just as I'd always dreamed, but I couldn't bear the shame of it, maharaj, and I fled Bhopal forever.'

I argued with him half the night about the meaning of all this, forgetting my own predicament again, but all my reassurances only depressed him more, as if reason itself were shameful. 'Excuses, excuses,' he kept mumbling back, and then he nodded off to sleep for a little while, flinching and whimpering like a dreaming dog as I sat up beside him, trying to mark my route on the amorphous map that was forming in my brain.

But when Nanda awoke, not an hour later, he was his cheerful self again, and charged with resolution. There was no use arguing with him; he was my friend, and he was going to help me find my family.

Now that I'd been recognized in my ashes by the people back in Bhondaripur, I needed a new disguise, and this Nanda fashioned out of the junk he carried with him in his stinking sacks. He laid a saffron cloth over my head and wrapped another around my waist, fussing over the folds like a tailor, and when we ventured out of the mango grove and braved the road that cupped Morar and the king's palaces at Lashkar, I was dressed as a jogi of some kind, with a calabash and my old jingling staff and a rolled-up text tucked under my arm like a newspaper. Nanda made me promise I'd give this guise a little more consideration than the other – a little more respect.

'Freshen up your sect mark, maharaj,' he told me. 'Say a mantra every now and then. Beg a little. You never know – the life might grow on you after a while.'

We continued through the little towns that lay west of Gwalior, and at Sewar we shared a ferry across the Chambal with three homebound sepoys from the garrison at Morar: upright modern men who scoffed at the two of us for our backward ways and never suspected I was on the run. Once we'd crossed the Chambal into Karauli we began to ask after Ahalya, and in three days we must have met twenty helpful souls who claimed they'd seen her.

In Machilpur we were told that a woman answering her description had taken up with a woodturner in Hindaun. In Hindaun we were told she'd last been seen travelling by palanquin toward Patunda, and in Patunda they said she was back in Machilpur, searching for me among the inmates of the local jail.

I stopped believing any of this, but I think most of those we approached weren't trying to trick us, exactly – they just wanted to help. Losing a wife and son was an awful thing to contemplate, and it was always felicitous to help out a holy man, so if they'd seen any woman carrying a baby along the road in the last six months they told me she must have been Ahalya and sent me off in search of her. South of Jaipur an old baluchi told me she'd drowned in a flood, though it hadn't rained once since I'd set off with Baroo. But then he burst into tears and we figured he must have been talking about his own wife.

But the most common thing we came up against was people telling us that Ahalya was ahead of us, sometimes even before we'd had a chance to describe here. 'Straight ahead,' they'd say, pointing down the road, without another word of explanation, and finally we decided they didn't mean this geographically so much as philosophically. 'Whatever you seek must lie ahead' was what they meant, but it would have been a mercy if they hadn't said anything at all.

Now Nanda did everything he could to lift my spirits as we followed one false lead after another, setting forth and doubling back and lurching from village to village in crazy loops and zigzags. A sweeper might tell him that Ahalya had passed by two months ago, following in the wake of a caravan of Mahajans, and Nanda would run up to me with his ornaments crashing like cymbals and declare, 'I think we're on to something this time,' or, 'This is just the lead we've been waiting for.' Lacking much hope of my own, I tried to cling to his, but after a few weeks, as the hot weather advanced upon us, I began to trail behind him, and it was I who insisted we pause at the temples, cenotaphs, and tanks that littered the countryside.

I think it was the day we searched for Ahalya in a little town east of Kishangarh that I knew I would never find her. A weaver had told us he'd seen Ahalya not five days before, half starved, with a baby on her hip, walking like a ghost along the Mashi River. He told me she was no Rajput woman, but a drab Ahir from the East, searching for her husband among the bleak hills. It was a fitting enough description to lure out my last frail hope, and we followed the Mashi to its source and climbed through the low hills toward Kishangarh, coming to a little town whose name I've since forgotten – one of those intermittent market towns you come across in the remotest places, of no consequence to anyone but the villagers in its vicinity. Nanda and I limped into it a week or so after Holi, and the dusty brick was still stained with splashes of dye. By this time I'd taken to joining Nanda in his begging, and it was as I was about to approach an old Jain's textile shop that I saw Ahalya striding down the center of the town with Mahabir on her hip.

I let out a great cry and threw down all my gear and ran straight for them as Nanda stumbled along behind.

'Nanda!' I shouted to him. 'I've found them!' And then, when I reached them, 'I've found you! Ahalya! Mahabir! I've found you at last!'

But of course I hadn't, for when I reached Ahalya and yanked at her veil, she and my son turned into strangers – terrified strangers – shrieking at me as I drew my hands away.

I suppose it must have been a market day, for in my memory the street was filled with people, so many of them women in drab dress carrying babies on their hips, and as Nanda hurried me out of town, my last frail hope expired.

Nanda could have led me anywhere after that, for all the real searching I did. My eyes never left the ground before me, and when we paused here and there to plan the next leg of our quest my mind would drift off somewhere — not backward, now that I think of it, but to some blank and distant plane. I took to entertaining little riddles as we trudged along, and I could ponder Nanda's lyrics for days at a time. I began to say my mantras just as Nanda bade me, and paid attention to my guise, fussing with the sparse beard that had sprouted from my chin.

Some time in the summer months Ahalya and Mahabir disappeared from my dreams, supplanted by my mother, who carried me now on the bone of her hip along the simmering, wavering road. Accustomed as he was to failure of the most chronic kind, Nanda took naturally to my quest, and even in the worst of the heat, when the sweat that dripped from his beard hissed and steamed on his iron collar, he never lost heart. Asking passersby if they'd seen Ahalya, weighing each kindly lie against the others, drawing our route in the dust of some temple courtyard, stocking up on alms in the market towns — the whole business became a kind of ritual for him: another penance, but with a nice earthbound goal.

But I don't have any more stomach for my quest now than I did back then. I became a sort of addled expert on the southeastern kingdoms of Rajputana, or their underside, anyway. We walked in so many circles and curlicues that it wouldn't have surprised me if we'd met up with ourselves somewhere along the way. In the summer months we saw more beasts than people on our journey, and once, in the hunting preserve of the Maharao of Kotah, we even came upon a lion, which Nanda mistook for a god, though it was too heat-stricken to lift its head. And one evening (somewhere near Ajmere, I think it was, for we were among lush hills, and a cool breeze was blowing), I walked right by the old one-armed Pathan I'd almost murdered, but he never recognized me, nor did I realize who he was until he was well past us, for I was too intoxicated with ganja.

And there's the truth of it, finally, out in the open. I'm ashamed to admit it, but as we stumbled around Rajputana, trying to find my wife and son, I surrendered my will to the smoke that the sadhus shared at our resting places.

Among certain varieties of sadhus, ganja was a staple, and ever since I'd first taken up with Nanda and his kind, sadhus had been offering us puffs on their little clay pipes and sips from their little cups of bhang. Nanda always accepted, just to be companionable, but he saw ganja as a cheat, a short cut to the abode of bliss, and never made a habit of it. When I still held out hope that I might yet find Ahalya and Mahabir I refused their offers. But by late summer, when my hope was gone, ganja seemed to feed into my thinking, which had become despairing and dead-ended.

I might have paused to gaze at young women bathing by a well, or gaped at the stars spread out above me, but the only song I heard amid the glories of creation was *What's the use? What's the use?* My grief had dulled to an ache, and my despair had degenerated into a kind of abstraction that centered itself on the futile circuitousness of life. The ganja helped to confirm me in this state of mind, for once the initial elation receded, with all its dizzy hopes and insights, I could content myself with the mere contemplation of my autonomy and convince myself, as I puffed away by some sacred stream, that it was somehow more likely that Ahalya would find me if I stayed put than that I would find her if I wandered all over Hindustan for the rest of my worthless life.

I tried to make Nanda understand this, but he had no patience with my indolent addiction, and kept goading me along from village to village. Some days I was so foggy with ganja that I couldn't see my own two feet, and kept up with Nanda only by staggering after the sound of his ornaments clattering ahead of me. If we had passed Ahalya herself one of those late-summer days I wouldn't have seen her, nor would she have seen her husband in the ratty, threadbare, glassy-eyed ascetic he'd become.

CHAPTER

51

During the last of those six months Nanda led me around I must have been miserable company. But no matter how much I lagged and whined and wheedled, Nanda bore with me. He ascribed my equable periods to my true nature, and blamed my black moods on the ganja, though in fact I was always more serene when I was full of smoke, and blackest when it cleared.

Of course, we both had our crotchets. When the ganja wore off Nanda's habits grated on me intolerably. The half-dozen songs he knew had long ago ceased to charm me, and his incessant accompaniment on his clacking fire tongs positively scrabbled at my spine.

But it was his morning ablutions that bothered me the most. His filthiest practices were all pursued in the name of health and hygiene. He never took what you would call a proper bath in all the time I knew him, but he was a stickler about his orifices. A day couldn't begin for him without his cleaning out his nasal passages by means of a stringy rag he used to work up his nose and into his mouth and then tug back and forth a few strokes, first through one nostril, then the other. Every few days he would ream out various of his other passages with knotted strips of cloth, and some mornings nosebleeds were the least of his afflictions when we set out on the road.

We didn't travel much during the monsoon, and I got used to sitting around this or that hermitage with my brethren, smoking ganja and sharing alms and counting the beads on my necklace. It didn't matter to me where we were any more, even when it still occurred to me to seek my family, and I began to regard my indifference as seemly, considering I was probably destined to spend the rest of my days as a gosain. Nanda had begun to integrate our search with the cycle of festivals, so that if one villager suggested we look in Jaipur, where there was to be a mela, and another told us to look in Sambhar, where there was not, we would head for Jaipur.

The last great rain found us in a thatch shelter some gosains had erected under a neem tree overlooking a broad tank somewhere in the Chitor range. Nanda had broken a toe climbing down the rain-slick steps of a nearby temple, so we remained there for more than a week while he rested his foot in a little clay cast.

Three holy men shared the shelter with us. The first was an Urdhamuki who spent half the day hanging like a bat from a little pole frame. He was a sour and raggedy man, as I remember him, who suffered from terrible headaches. (In fact, I don't think I ever met a sadhu who was healthier for the stunts he performed.) The second wasn't a sadhu exactly but a pilgrim who was making his way from Baroda to Varanasi by means of sashtang dandawat, just like the pilgrim you may remember Santosh and I encountered, crawling like an inchworm among the Gwalior hills early in my herding period. This pilgrim was all calluses, bruises, and scabs from his prostrations, but he was determined to reach Varanasi in ten years' time, barring too many wrong turns. I remember that he had a horror of snakes, and always laid a hoop of coarse rope on the ground around himself to ward them off at night.

The third holy man was an Urdhabahu gosain whose disciple had recently abandoned him. The Urdhabahus begin their careers by binding their arms to little bamboo poles and sticking them over their heads, leaving them there until they atrophy. By doing this they believe they can appropriate power from the gods, notably from Shiva, who was said to be very much relieved, along with everybody else, when an Urdhabahu died. But for all their powers the practice renders them helpless, and they must rely on pilgrims and disciples for their earthly needs.

This Urdhabahu had compounded his austerity by keeping his hands closed in a fist, and by the time I met him the nails on his fingers had grown clear through his palms, between the bones and out the backs of his hands. He had tried to persuade the poor, scuffed-up pilgrim to serve him until the cool weather brought the faithful back to his shrine, but the pilgrim took forever hunching back and forth between the shelter and the nearest village, and the Urdhamuki was too busy with his hanging and headaches to be much use.

Thus, with Nanda broken down, it fell to me to collect alms for everybody. In exchange for my services the others gave me portions of hemp, both in the form of ganja and in a greasy concentrate the

Urdhamuki used to make by boiling the leaves in a mixture of butter and water. He took this for his headaches, but a little mixed into a cup of water was enough to cast me into a blind fog. My delusions were always vivid and various when the hemp took hold, but beside the point. I think smoking ganja is like stirring a lake with a paddle; you can cause quite a commotion on the surface, but the depths aren't disturbed a bit. If I dreamed about my mother as I slept under the dripping thatch, or looked out at the rain and envisioned my wife and son drowning in the flood, it was just a sign to me that I was sobering up and needed another dose.

I begged for everyone in a little village a mile or so from our haven, and it's a wonder to me now that I could find my way back and forth in my condition. The villagers were forest folk, and seemed to be mightily impressed by the way I staggered around, for they were generous with their alms. I found that even after the heaviest doses of hemp I could always wax philosophical, though by the time Nanda's toe had mended I had no idea where I was or how long I'd been there, and I think if you'd asked me who I was I would have been hard put to say.

All I knew was that I didn't like seeing Nanda up and around again, for all it could mean was that we would have to resume our quest. I kept trying to tell him that it was hopeless, but that made him all the more determined, of course, for the hopelessness of it was what made it such perfect penance for the both of us. The Urdhabahu kept begging us to stay, at least until another disciple came along, for he was helpless with his kindling arms and depended on my services. But the Urdhamuki couldn't wait to see us go, especially Nanda, whose clatter aggravated his headaches. He was always making sport of Nanda's maverick creed, and Nanda would just sit there, staring across the pattered tank with this trapped smile, nodding at every jibe that suited his sense of shame.

There was dignity in this, I suppose, but I couldn't see it at the time. I think I may have hated Nanda a little for his imperturbability, and joined in with the Urdhamuki sometimes, but I was so addled by then that I can't say for certain.

My memories of the morning we left together are brief and fitful, like glimpses of sky among churning clouds. I know I griped and whined as Nanda packed his gear, and threatened to part

company, for I would have been content to live the rest of my days
beneath that thatch, and shorten their number with my unwholesome habits. But when Nanda finally bade farewell to the pitiable
Urdhabahu and the jubilant Urdhamuki, and limped off into the
countryside, I followed after him, for the truth was that the ganja had
made me sheepish and indifferent to my circumstances.

I carried my own stock of hemp in my sack, and I remember that
the pilgrim accompanied us a little distance by means of his
prostrations, but he progressed too slowly even for Nanda, and we
finally had to pull away. It was Nanda's plan to take in the Dusserah
festival in the nearest kingdom, which proved to be a two-day walk
through the verdant countryside.

A city gate looms up in my memory now, its portals bristling
with spikes, and the Maharao's kettledrums boom as Nanda and I
pass through. But I can't believe I took note of any of it back then, for
I hadn't even bothered to ask Nanda the name of the kingdom, and it
was all I could do to keep up with him as we walked through the
throngs to an old sandstone temple where our fellows had assembled.
The women in their festival best, the men in their teetering turbans
and their beards all parted and curlicued were a red-and-orange blur
as I stumbled along behind Nanda, but they made way for us, as
people do for holy men, on account of our aroma.

The first thing I did when we finally settled among the little
island of sadhus seated in the street was light up my pipe to calm my
nerves. Soldiers dressed in ancient armor shoved the crowds back to
the edge of the street with their black bucklers and absently struck
some of the persistent with the butts of their lances. Some bald priests
in saffron robes stood at the temple gate anointing a tethered buffalo
with this and that, and I caught myself nodding at the purple bull as
if at some kindred spirit. But when my thoughts began to fumble
their way back toward Bhondaripur I shut my eyes for a moment and
drew as deep a puff as I could manage from my little clay pipe.

Then Nanda said, 'Look. Now he comes,' and pointed to our
left.

Around a corner of the street a host of jogis appeared, all
dressed in white shifts and smeared with orange dye from head to
toe. Their hair ran in coils down their backs, and their beards
reached to their waists, as tangled as birds' nests, and as they hopped

and stomped toward us, bugging their eyes and chanting, some among them threw red powder into the air so that they seemed to float along in a crimson fog as they brandished their spears and broadswords.

'The Naga,' Nanda told me. 'Shiva's troops.'

There was a great slapping of drums and a groaning of horns, and in the red cloud's wake an old tusker slouched into view. He was a full storey high, and draped with mirrored blankets, and on his great potato of a head a silver maur wobbled. The mahout was a Naga too, and poked his jewelled ankh behind the elephant's ears, rocking from his hips to the old beast's sway.

Behind the mahout an old man rode in a silver howdah, and now as the elephant approached I could see that his blankets were studded not with mirrors but gems. The old man was naked and scrawny but sleek, with his old flesh newly washed and oiled and his hair falling freely to his waist.

'The Maharao?' I asked Nanda as the elephant came to a halt before the temple and the Naga jogis tipped their weapons in tribute.

'No, no,' Nanda said. 'He's the Raja Jogi. The high priest. Here comes the Maharao.'

And around the corner the horn blowers came, and the drummers, and a row of shenai players, and men with cymbals and gongs as big as tonga wheels, all making their noises as eunuchs sashayed among them, tossing flower petals into the air. Next, rank upon rank of nobles pressed into the street, some no more than tiny boys, all clad in breastplates and silken pantaloons and grandiose turbans stuck with heron plumes and bits of shrubbery. A few rode horses, two wavered on camels, but the rest walked with their matchlocks of brass and steel and silver-handled swords in velvet scabbards. A little platform had been raised for nobles of the first rank, while the rest of the Maharao's vassals arranged themselves in rows where the soldiers were holding back the populace.

The cheer that arose as the Maharao finally appeared, seated upon his travelling throne some eight feet above his bearers' shoulders, was muted with reverence and nearly drowned out by the royal musicians' cacophony. The throne leaned outward on its great carved struts as the bearers rounded the corner, and seemed about to topple amid the blue and yellow pennants that waved up from out of the kicked-up dust. It seemed so even to the Maharao himself, who gripped the arms of his throne and leaned counterwise, but the bearers scrambled sideways just in time to right it and the Maharao jutted his parted whiskers to show his unconcern.

I couldn't count the bearers for all the dust they raised, but there must have been twenty of them at least, and still each of them grunted and struggled under his burden. The gold throne must have been heavy enough with its polished iron poles, but the Maharao weighed upon them more. He was a sulky man in his middle years, and as round as his ancestor, the sun, from whom he now hid beneath a teetering silken parasol.

He stared off at some middle distance with studied indifference, but his eyes had a latent fire about them, set beneath eyebrows that had been trimmed and pencilled to resemble fishhooks. His face was powdered white, with his black beard spraying outward like cat whiskers along his burnsides and then flowing symmetrically over his breast like a fountain of ink.

Below the part in his whiskers was a collar of great square emeralds and a cascade of pearls was looped all the way down to his belly. He sported epaulets of beaten gold, and a pink sash littered with medallions, and diamond garters on the sleeves of his tight white blouse. Below a wide belt of gold chain mail he wore an apron of purple silk shot through with gold, and he sat with his legs crossed beneath a heap of white pleated skirts. And atop all this, above the crimson sect mark on his brow, he wore an anticlimactic cap, an heirloom from some diminutive ancestor, that sat on his head like a drinking cup.

Now of course I couldn't have taken all this in at once, but that is how I recollect him nonetheless, in a memory compounded by the subsequent Dusserahs I passed in his kingdom. At the time he was a gilded blur floating on a cloud of dust, and in fact my eyes kept wandering from him to the poor quaking buffalo tugging at its tether.

The Maharao's retainers began to circulate among us sadhus, handing out sweetmeats. I gave my share to Nanda, for I had sworn off sugar since taking the goor. But neighboring holy men derided Nanda for accepting it, and he looked so miserably ashamed that I took it back and tucked it into my satchel.

The bearers hoisted their regent within range of the Raja Jogi's howdah, and as his ascetic troops danced and jubilated, the Maharao placed a tinsel garland around the old man's neck. Now the musicians increased their racket, and everywhere priests were shaking whisks or chanting canticles or freeing what looked to be jays from silver cages. Someone set off flashpowder at the feet of the buffalo, and little puffs of yellow smoke mingled with the dust and dye.

Suddenly the drumming and the hornblowing stopped as the Raja Jogi presented a bow and arrow to the Maharao, and the crowd parted to form a little lane between the Maharao and the buffalo. The crowd was quiet too, and the priests, and as the Maharao took aim at the beast from his travelling throne, the street was so still that you could hear the bow creak as the Maharao pulled back on the string and a dull strum as he fired.

The arrow flew under the buffalo's nose and stuck in the shin of an attending priest, so the musicians started up again as he was carried off and a new arrow fetched for the Maharao. The bearers were directed to move him a little closer, and one of the soldiers began to beat an old man with his shield for distracting the Maharao with a sneeze. The crowd was silent again, and the Maharao had better luck on his second shot, for at least the arrow didn't strike anyone, but stuck in the tethering post with a resounding twang.

The buffalo was beside himself by now, and despite the priests' best efforts presented the Maharao with a moving target, so as the second arrow was unstuck and returned to him, his throne was moved a few feet closer.

This time the Maharao took more care, biting down on his tongue, and though his arm trembled with the strain, he managed to sink the arrow into the buffalo's shoulder all the way up to the feather. As the great beast honked and staggered and fell, the crowd gave a sigh and the musicians resumed their clamor.

I thought of Guli and her calf, and turning away from the buffalo's throes I found myself facing the nobles assembled on the platform behind me and gazing up at my mother's face. And it *was* her face, I could have sworn it was, and she was radiant with relief at the Maharao's success.

I gasped and turned forward again, shutting my eyes and

fumbling my pipe to my lips. But its ember had gone cold, and when I opened my eyes and slowly turned around again, my mother was still there, though she was now moustachioed and clad in a turban and tunic.

'Nanda,' I said, slowly rising to my feet. 'Nanda, where are we?'

'Get down, maharaj,' he said, jerking at my arm. 'We're not supposed to stand. Only the Naga are allowed to stand.'

'Nanda!' I shouted, trying to shake him off. 'What place is this?'

'Harigarh, of course,' Nanda said, grabbing at my arm again. 'Now sit down.'

But I couldn't sit, for now I knew who it was on the dais behind me.

'Uncle!' I began to chant, stepping toward him among the indignant sadhus, and by the time I'd reached the outskirts of the congregation, with Nanda crawling after me, clattering and clanging amidst his brethren, my chant had become a shout, and I was running toward him with my arms outstretched.

CHAPTER

52

I think one of the guards struck me first, with the butt end of his lance, but the Naga joined in soon enough, and I tumbled down among them, still crying out to my mother's brother.

I came to in a black and trickling cavern with my legs shackled to a long iron bar that ran the length of the earthen floor. It wasn't much comfort to find Nanda lying beside me in the dark, for as best as I could tell he'd been beaten too, and his collar bent and dented.

My neighbor to my right was an old Bheel who winked and leered at me when I looked over at him, and said something to me I was just as glad I didn't understand.

Nanda had a lump over his eye as big as a mango, and it took me an hour to rouse him. He begged me to keep away from him, though of course I couldn't under the circumstances, and when he saw that his sacks and tongs and walking sticks were gone, and discovered the damage to his collar, he burst into tears.

There wasn't much I could do for him except apologize and try
to explain about my mother and her girlhood in the Harigarh court.
He listened with his back to me, whimpering and sniffling in the
dank, but as I filled in all the details I could remember, whispering all
the while in case the old Bheel knew his Hindustani, Nanda slowly
turned around and stared back at me with his blackened eyes.

'So you see I *know* he's my uncle,' I concluded. 'He's got to be.
He's my mother's spit and image.'

Nanda gaped at me a little longer and said, 'And this isn't just
the ganja talking, maharaj?'

'No, no,' I said, realizing for the first time that I was sober. 'It's —
it's worn off.'

'Because,' said Nanda, 'you really shouldn't smoke, maharaj.
You just can't handle it.'

'I know, Nanda,' I said. 'I'm sorry.'

'Well,' he said, beginning to weep again, 'I'm sorry too,
maharaj. This latest business — right in the middle of Dusserah! — it
was so . . . so *crazy*.'

I won't tire you with an account of how I convinced Nanda of
what you already know to be true, for all I really did was appeal to
his natural credulity. In the end he accepted my story out of
friendship, as yet another act of faith, and embraced our predicament
as a new test: a sure sign that the gods, at long last, were paying us
attention.

I promised Nanda I would get us out of the Maharao's jail, but it
was just as well that he never asked me how. Our fellows were a low
variety of criminal — Bheels, as I've said, and hapless dacoits and even
a stray Pindari or two — who met my inquiries with spit and derision.
I convinced Nanda to keep his mantras to himself as the sun went
down, and dispense with his dietary scruples when the guard came by
with supper.

The mouth of the cavern was a vast grate with a barred door,
beyond which guards stood drowsy watch. When the night fell a stiff
draft came skittering along the floor, and as I lay shivering, trying to
devise a plan, I was almost tempted to accept the old Bheel's indecent
invitations, just to keep warm.

My mother seemed to share that cavern with me, fluttering

against the bars like a caged sparrow. But my dreams were of Ahalya, stumbling back over the ridges with Mahabir astride her hip, and returning defeated to her father's house. By the time I awoke this dream had become a conviction, and I told myself that there could be no life for me in Bhonaripur any more, and no happiness for my wife and son if I returned. I'm ashamed to say I concluded this with amazing calm, though I suppose I must have exhausted the sorrow of it in the intervening months.

In the morning we were loaded into a bullock cart to labor on the roads. The jail stood on a low hill within distant view of the Maharao's palace, and as I dragged my manacles out into the light and climbed into the awaiting cart I had my first real look at the Maharao's dominion.

The city was fortified by a ring of sharp ridges whose defiles had been filled in with great stone walls that were so pocked and weathered you had to blink to distinguish them from the adjacent cliffs. The palace had been carved out of the steep slope of the highest ridge, and the city, spread out at its feet, seemed to be constructed from its tumbled leavings, so that at a distance Harigarh looked like a quarry of rosy quartz, with here and there a vein of marble catching the sharp morning sun. Beyond the circle of ridges, walls ran to the east and west, but lost interest a half mile from town and fell off into rubble.

We were taken to a tree-lined stretch of road that led to the Maharao's hunting preserve and set to work repairing the damage from the recent rains. The monsoons were a ruination to the kingdom's roads, and here there were pools where nearby ponds had overflowed, and ruts and potholes where the trampled clay had dried, so we filled the potholes and smoothed the ruts and drained the puddles where we could.

The hunting season was almost upon us, and you might think the guards would have driven us hard, but they were a lazy pair who longed to linger in the cool shade and fetch pahn and tobacco from the nearby village, and one of them even barked at Nanda, for whom labor was a novelty, for working too fast. I flirted for a while with trying to explain my situation to them, but figured I would only be beaten again for it, and to no account.

We labored all day with our shovels and baskets, and suffered the jibes of the children who came to watch, but the only real hardship was the murmur of a nearby stream that almost drove us mad with thirst. The road was little travelled, for the hunting preserve was forbidden to the locals and stocked with panthers.

But in the quiet of the early afternoon an Englishman and his servant came riding along on scrawny old horses. The Englishman was a slight man with freckles turned nearly black by the sun. He wore a turban in the Rajput style and baggy cotton trousers tucked into knee-high boots, and carried a little rifle strapped over one shoulder.

The guards bestirred themselves as he approached, and had us line up along the roadside. But he gave us a brief, irritated nod, and hardly raised his eyes from the notes he was making on a little bound pad.

Immediately I saw how he might fit into my efforts to make myself known to my uncle, but I gave myself the afternoon to perfect my plans. I figured he would pay me attention if I spoke to him in English, but it had been eight years since I'd spoken it, if you don't count my fitful reading of Baroo's will three years before.

I struggled to remember something of what Weems had taught me, and at first I could only remember a few broken quotations from the Bible. But slowly as I patched the potholes that afternoon, listening to the distant crackle of the Englishman's rifle, I began to construct a little speech.

It wasn't until the end of the day, as the doves bathed in the roadside dust and we were climbing back into the bullock cart, that the Englishman finally reappeared, still jotting his notes, but now with his net sack filled with little crumpled songbirds. Nanda must have seen the heat rise in my eyes as the Englishman approached, for he cowered as we settled into the cart, and begged me to keep quiet.

I nodded to him to calm him down, but then just as the Englishman passed I jumped to my feet and shouted.

'English!' I cried. 'I talking my name Balbeer Rao! I son to Natholi Rao, Cawnpore side, my mother, please! Lord God Almighty, the Diwan my uncle, sir! I was lost, I am found, amen! Jesus Christ believe in me!'

It was such an astonishing performance that even the guards were paralyzed, and the only sound was Nanda's despairing groan and the clatter of his collar as he hid his head.

The Englishman halted his old horse and looked up from his notes, his eyes hidden by the shimmer of his spectacles.

'I'm sorry?' he said, tilting his head. 'Were you addressing me?'

It was strange, considering how clumsily I spoke, but I understood every word he said, and tried to reply with vigor.

'The Diwan name Rao. I name Balbeer Rao, sir! Oh, by Jove, he is my uncle! Oh Lord of Hosts,' I declared, pressing my hands together and gazing at the sky. 'It is so, amen!'

'Do you mean Bhulwant Rao? The Diwan?' the Englishman asked, raising his chin.

'Praise the Lord, sir, yes!'

'You are his nephew?'

'*Nephew!*' I exclaimed, for I hadn't been able to dredge up the word. 'Yes, quite so, by Jove! I his *nephew!*'

I stood to attention and grinned as the Englishman spurred his horse a few steps forward and looked me up and down.

You know how I must have looked, still grey with ash, half naked, all scrag and bone, and with one eye puffed up from the day before, but as he stared now into my face I was jubilant with hope.

'The nephew of Bhulwant Rao,' the Englishman finally said, stroking the faint stubble on his chin. 'How utterly preposterous.' And with that he turned his horse toward town.

'Please, sir! You tell him, please!' I desperately called after him as the guards closed in. 'Please, you tell him I am come!'

The guards didn't beat me too badly, for they were still a little awestruck by my speech, and at least they left Nanda alone this time, but as I sank back into the rumbling cart he glared at me, and wouldn't speak to me the whole ride back.

Harigarh was a glory in the evening light, and I remember how clouds of parrots flew in an emerald blur toward the golden ramparts of the Maharao's palace, but to me it seemed like a figment of my despair, as unobtainable as a mirage, and I hoped for nothing more than a puff or two of ganja whenever the Maharao let us go.

The Dusserah festival went on for several more days. At night in the cavern we could hear the beat and blare of the Maharao's musicians and in the morning as we climbed into our cart a few of the lamps that had lined the Maharao's route to and from the palace would still be flickering from the night before.

To compensate for their missing out on the festivities, the guards treated themselves to a full week of overseeing our labor on that shady stretch of road, and even after we'd shovelled and raked that road as smooth as paper, they would find false fault with what we'd done, and order us to start all over.

With his heavy collar bearing down on his slight frame, Nanda suffered that week, and though the air dried and cooled with the winter breeze, the sun beat on his poor bruised head, and by the end of each morning he was staggering under his basketloads of dirt and gravel. I and another prisoner, a stout greengrocer imprisoned for giving short weight, did our best to help him, but he always shook us off.

To his overturned way of thinking, of course, the worse off he was the better, but there seemed to be a new edge to his penance, an unfamiliar ostentation. At my most impatient I accused him of merely trying to shame me: punish me for all the hardship I had caused him.

If he wanted to kill himself, I said, that was his business, not mine.

But he would just look pained and thoughtful, and set to work with renewed desperation.

As I've said, sadhus in general are an unhealthy breed, and it was not long before Nanda began to lose his wind. He never coughed the way my mother did, but some mornings he could hardly catch his breath. His ribs seemed to close on his backbone, and by evening there would be blood in his spit.

I began to brood about all the loved ones I'd lost in my brief life – my mother, Moonshi, Dileep, Ahalya, Mahabir, even old Baroo Singh (at least the Baroo Singh who had loved me in his fashion) – and I resolved that I wouldn't let Nanda join them. But no matter what I said, no matter how I tried to help him, he grew ever more frail and fey.

One night I awoke from my habitual nightmare to find Nanda lying back on the ground with his head lolling from his collar and clutching at his sunken chest. I scrambled over to him and cradled his scraggly head in my arms and saw, even in that cave's deep darkness, a faint, surrendering light.

I tried to call the guards, but he reached one bony hand up and pressed it to my lips, shaking his head. 'No, no,' he croaked. 'I am dead. I'm finished. I go to God.'

My eyes began to burn and tear, and I swallowed back a sob. 'No, Nanda,' I said. 'Don't die. I'm sorry. I'm so sorry. I didn't mean to drag you into this.'

'Oh, no,' he said with his odd little smile. 'It is all a circle, maharaj. It's not our doing. We are all of us but grains of sand. Shiva calls, and I must go. Do not despair. We are all one.'

Now as I have told you I never had much patience with talk like that, least of all from Nanda, and as he ran on in this vein, heaping one epigram on top of another, as if trying to be certain his last words would be lofty, I suddenly lost my temper.

'No you don't, Nanda,' I said, grabbing his collar and shaking him. 'You're not going to let yourself off that easily.'

Nanda gaped up at me and groaned. 'Please, maharaj!' he said, grabbing me by the shoulders. 'Please let me alone!'

By now we'd awakened everyone, including the greengrocer, who'd been sleeping to Nanda's left, but I ignored their protestations and drew my face down to Nanda's.

'Aren't you forgetting something?' I whispered at him.

'F-forgetting?'

'Your *shame*, Nanda. You're *Mahadeo's* boy, remember? Mahadeo's firstborn son. You think you can just lie down and die? What about the cliff, God damn you? What about your shame?'

Of course, these were awful things to say to a dying man, and I can't be sure I meant them kindly, but you should have seen the fire flare in my poor friend's eyes, and his chest fill up with breath.

'Oh, God,' he wailed, lifting himself up out of my arms. 'You're right, you're right, you're always right! I'm a coward! I'm a worm! When am I ever going to learn?'

And suddenly there he was again, my old friend Nanda, sitting up as good as new and thrilling to his shame.

Without a trial, without so much as a glimpse of the kotwal or any of his agents, we were released the next day and ordered out of the kingdom. The guards returned most of our gear, for it was a sin to pilfer a holy man's effects, but they kept the ganja, for which I hungered again, and Nanda's fire tongs, for which I nearly thanked them.

Nanda was delighted to be back on the road, and full of resolution. We would go to Pushkar, he said, and consult with Brahma at his temple there, the only such temple in all of Hindustan. And then we would resume our search for Ahalya, only this time we would let the stars guide us, and all our dreams and visions.

There was such bounce in his step as we found the Kotah Road, and this but a few hours after he'd almost passed away, that I didn't have the heart to tell him that for me the quest was over. I can't say exactly what my plans were then, but I knew I had to shake Nanda loose, for his sake as much as mine. I reckoned I would follow Nanda for a few days more, and then go my separate way to the coast of Gujarat, perhaps, or down to the mouth of the Nerbudda to begin the perikrama. I don't really know if I'd resolved to become a holy man in earnest now that the world had shut its doors to me, for I was still no more inclined to the spiritual than before and could only have gone through the motions, out of pitiable default.

But not an hour outside of Harigarh, as Nanda begged for alms from a little camp of gypsy smiths, a soldier rode up on a splendid lathered stallion and searched me out in the shade of a ranga bush.

'You there,' he called out. 'Are you the one who claims to be Balbeer Rao?'

By this time I had had my fill of Harigarh, and expected nothing but trouble from life, so I said no, I wasn't. I was a man of God, I told him, bound for the abode of bliss.

The soldier was the most martial man I ever saw, with a back as straight as a flagpole and whiskers waxed into place. He and his stallion snorted at my little speech, and as he inspected me with his hard grey eyes he rubbed the hilt of his sheathed sword, working the muscles bunched in his bare forearms.

'No,' he said finally, climbing down from his saddle. 'You're the one, all right. You must come with me.'

Though there was no point in trying to flee from such a knight, I backed away a step or two and shook my head in vague denial.

'Come with me, now, maharaj,' he said, grabbing my arm in his iron hand and leading me back to his horse.

Nanda emerged now from the gypsy camp and began to trot toward us, waving his staff, while the soldier hoisted me into his saddle as if I were a small boy.

'Maharaj!' Nanda cried, clattering up to us. 'What's happening?'

I looked down at him then as the soldier climbed up behind me on his stallion's back. 'I have to go back,' I said as calmly as I could manage, for I knew the time had come to say goodbye.

'But why?' he said, grabbing at the stallion's halter. 'They can't take you away. We're not in Harigarh any more.'

But the soldier jerked his horse's head away and turned him around with a click of his tongue.

'You let him down!' Nanda said, recovering his balance and raising his staff over his head as if to strike, but before it could complete its arc the soldier drew his sword and lopped it in two.

'Goodbye, Nanda,' I called back as the stallion trotted down the road.

He wavered a moment, gaping at his cleanly severed staff, and then gave chase, drawing up alongside with all his trinkets clattering. 'I'll wait for you,' he panted.

'No, Nanda,' I said. 'you go on. I'll find you when the time comes. Goodbye, brother. I'm going to miss you.'

'Goodbye, then, maharaj!' he cried, losing his wind and falling back, and the last I ever saw of Nanda was his raggedy shape receding in the dust we raised, and if he ever did reach Mahadeo's cliff I'm proud of him, and if he never did I'm glad.

CHAPTER

53

Now it turned out that the little freckled Englishman happened to be the British Resident and tutor to the Maharao's son, and as I'd been shaming Nanda back to life the night before, he'd happened to mention to Diwan Bhulwant Rao a curiously haunting episode on the

Rajshikari Road. A scruffy little sadhu, of all things, speaking in a mongrel tongue, had suddenly piped up from the convict cart that he was none other than Balbeer Rao: the Diwan's long-lost nephew: the son of his dead sister, Natholi Rao of Cawnpore.

The Maharao, citing poor Scindhia's experience, declared it remarkable that I hadn't claimed to be the Nana Sahib as well. This had been greeted with general hilarity, in which Bhulwant Rao joined, but when the evening's nautch was over and the Maharao had been seen safely to bed, the Diwan summoned his most trusted guard and commanded him to fetch me.

The guard was ruthless with his stallion, whipping the wheezing beast back into the city and up the steep approach to the palace gate. If I'd had my wits about me I might have feared for my life, for those were the days of unfixed principles, when maharaos could execute subjects for much less consequential crimes than posing as a nobleman's lost relation.

But I saw the palace with my mother's eyes, nodded at the passing scene as if it confirmed some vagrant memory, and when we passed through a series of courtyards filled with fruit trees and pavilions, such was the pertinacity of the conceit she'd instilled all those years ago that I fancied I was finally taking my rightful place in my mother's old dominion.

The guard lifted me out of his saddle and led me up a wide flight of marble steps, through a garden filled with petitioners, and into a darkened hall of audience, where my uncle was waiting on a low bolstered bench.

Though I was sober now, and saw the manly lines upon his forehead and the stiff moustache spiralling up from his lip, my mother yet haunted his face: about the sharp nose, the resolute chin, the quick dark eyes. I fell to my knees and tried to touch his feet, but the soldier held me back, and the Diwan averted his nose and sniffed at a perfumed scarf, for as you remember I was coated in dung and ashes and still a little ripe.

'Do you know who I am?' he asked, and in the gloom behind him I could see his servants and secretaries arrayed in a row.

I couldn't answer for a moment, for my mother haunted his voice as well.

'Do you?' he said, glancing down at me impatiently and fidgeting with his sleeves.

'Diwan — Rao, sahib,' I answered finally, still kneeling before him.

'Brilliant,' the Diwan answered with a sigh, raising his eyebrows and inspecting his fingernails. 'Perks!' he called out without lifting his gaze. 'Perks, my friend. Please do come in.'

The little Englishman I'd confronted now appeared beside the Diwan's bench and squinted at me through his glasses.

'Tell me, Perks, old friend,' said the Diwan. 'Is he the one?'

The Englishman tilted his head slightly and then abruptly removed his glasses and nodded. 'Yes, Diwan,' he replied quietly. 'I think so.'

'Very well,' said Bhulwant Rao with a wave of his fingers. 'You may go.

'Tell me again, holy one,' Bhulwant Rao said as the Englishman departed. 'Who am I?'

Now I had never seen an Indian thus dismiss an Englishman, and for a moment I was dumbfounded. 'My uncle,' I managed to say at last, as firmly as I could.

'Am I?'

'Yes, Diwan Sahib.'

'Your uncle. . . . And what makes you think so?'

'My mother was your sister,' I said, and all through the room there was the sound of pen points scraping on paper.

'And this sister's name? What was it again? I forget.'

'Natholi,' I said. 'Natholi Rao.'

The Diwan looked unimpressed. 'And what might *your* name be?' he asked, looking back at his servants with a smirk.

'Balbeer,' I replied, slowly rising to my feet. 'I am Balbeer Rao.'

The Diwan looked me up and down, and held a brass cup out for a servant to fill. 'And your father, Balbeer. Does he have a name as well?'

I sagged a little. 'I don't know,' I said. 'She never told me.'

Again the Diwan looked unmoved. 'Well then, tell me about your mother, Balbeer Rao. Now, as you no doubt must have heard in a bazaar somewhere, I did have a sister, and by God her name was

Natholi Rao. I loved her dearly, you understand, but she was a gimpy, gap-toothed girl when we finally married her off. Tell me, Balbeer Rao, how did you find her?'

Gimpy and gap-toothed? If he searched for a flicker of doubt in my eyes I'm sure I didn't disappoint him.

'Well?'

'N-no, Diwan Sahib,' I said, swallowing slowly. 'She was never lame, and she had all her teeth. She was small, slender. She was beautiful. She looked – she looked like you.'

I thought I saw him falter for an instant, but then he smirked again, this time at an old servant who stood nearby with a pitcher of water. 'Very flattering, Balbeer Rao,' he said. 'And may I ask where you were born? In Lucknow, wasn't it?'

'No, sahib,' I said. 'Cawnpore. We lived in Cawnpore.'

'Ah, Cawnpore,' said the Diwan, tapping his chin with his forefinger. 'Now what do you suppose my sister was doing in a place like that?'

'She – she was a widow,' I said. 'She had no place else to go.'

'Nowhere else?' the Diwan asked with a mocking shrug. 'But why didn't she just come here? Wasn't this her home?'

I lifted my eyes to his and glared at him. 'Because you wouldn't take her in,' I said as slowly as I could, though my heart was racing.

'Nonsense!' he blustered and then reined himself in, shaking his head with sly admiration as if I'd nearly tricked him.

'Now, you say I look like your mother, is that right?' he said, his gaze ranging across my face.

'Yes, sahib,' I said with a deep breath. 'That's how I knew you were – '

'Indeed?' he cut in, leaning back with his eyebrows arched. 'And yet you, your mother's son, look nothing like me. Can you explain that? I don't see a single kindred feature. Do you, Bansi Lal?' he asked, turning to the servant again.

The old man stiffened and cleared his throat. 'No, sahib,' he said in a servile whine I'd heard somewhere before.

Now what the Diwan had said was true; I looked nothing like my mother, and yet for all my fretting on the subject this had never occurred to me before. My knees wobbled a little as I wondered, could I favor my father so? Was Natholi Rao my mother? Was I *anybody's* son? And there my audience might have ended if I hadn't gazed back at the old servant's face.

'And yet you would have us believe –' the Diwan was saying, when suddenly I heard my voice cut in, as if it were answering a question in the old man's eyes.

'He's dead,' I said, and the servant started.

'Wh-what?' the Diwan asked, leaning forward a little.

'Moonshi Lal,' I said slowly, gently, for the old man's sake, because now I knew he was Moonshi's father. 'My mother's servant. My servant. My best friend.'

The Diwan glanced back at the old man, whose Adam's apple bobbed on his long, shy throat. 'Very well,' he said, jutting his chin. 'Describe him to us.'

'He stood this tall,' I said, taking a step forward and raising my hand to the bridge of my nose. 'And – and his eyes were all contrary, but the right eye always met your gaze if you waited for it. He had no chin to speak of,' I said, shutting my eyes a second to envision him. 'Skinny. Stooped. Always kept a towel over one shoulder. Bet his wages on partridge fights. Couldn't waken him with a cannon. But he taught me how to fly a kite, and he always stood by us, no matter what. Served my mother from the day she was born. Tried to bring me home, even when I was as good as dead. Carried me a hundred miles on his back. And he would have brought me home, too, but he was murdered.'

'Oh, murdered?' the old man groaned with his bristled chin trembling. '*Murdered*, sahib? How did they murder my little boy?'

'Strangled him, Bansi Lal,' I said. 'An old Thug tricked him and strangled him and there was nothing I could do.'

Bansi Lal and I began to weep together, and the Diwan looked back and forth at us, trying to catch his breath.

'Wait, wait,' he said, incensed at being so easily circumvented. 'What about your mother?' he demanded with his brow astir. 'What became of her?'

'Her lungs,' I said, wiping at my tears with my dusty wrist. 'Her wind gave out. But you know that. You knew she was sick, and you did nothing.'

The Diwan began to explain himself again and then rushed to his feet and shouted, 'Silence!' And when Bansi Lal kept whimpering behind him he shouted to silence him too.

'You're pretending!' he said quickly, panting for breath. 'Maybe you knew my sister, and my nephew too! But they're dead. Long dead. We have burned them in our hearts. And here you come with your false tears and your slimy masquerade, trampling on our grief.'

'But I didn't die, Uncle,' I gently told him, for suddenly, in his fury, he looked more like my mother than ever, with his head thrown back and his eyes as black as pitch. 'I live. I've come home.'

'No, no, no,' he said with sharp shakes of his head, standing now and hurriedly stepping into his slippers.

'Please don't turn me away,' I called out as he made for the door.

'These are all lies,' he growled, whirling around and facing me. 'Take him away! Run him out of the kingdom!'

A strange, hot breeze puffed into the hall as the doors opened for him, and in a voice that was familiar but not my own I said, 'Go, then, Bhulwant Rao. Forsake your own blood, as you forsook my mother. But may her embers set your roof ablaze, and her ashes choke your well!'

I'd merely adapted an old sadhu's curse the Urdhabahu had taught me, but the voice seemed to rise from my vitals, as disembodied as an echo, and froze my uncle in the doorway.

CHAPTER
54

My uncle ordered everyone out but the guard and me and locked the door behind him with a thick brass bolt. I supposed from this that my little speech was about to cost me my head, but then as my uncle approached I again saw my mother, fierce and frail, in his brimming eyes.

'Nephew,' he said hoarsely, hugging me to him: but he seemed to be in a terrible confusion, for almost immediately he pushed me back and turned away, and then, with a groan, wheeled around and slapped me across the jaw.

'Never speak to your uncle like that again!' he exclaimed, marching back to the bolstered bench and ducking his head about.

'Th-then – you believe me?' I asked, rubbing my stinging cheek.

'Yes, yes,' he said, wringing his hands as if to wash them. 'I knew it from the start. I was merely . . . *testing* you,' he said with an uncertain glance in the guard's direction. 'Just wanted to see what my nephew was made of. Now then, Balbeer,' he said, gripping his knees and jutting his chin. 'What can I do for you?'

I realized for the first time that he could do everything for me – answer all my lifelong questions – but I shrank from it, and merely stuttered a hope that he might put me up for a while.

'Well,' he said with a shrug, 'of course we can always find lodgings for you here. God knows we've got room.'

'Thank you, Uncle,' I said and bowed slightly, trying to marshal my courage to ask him for more.

'But what brings you here after all this time?' he asked evenly. 'Why have you sought me out?'

I couldn't tell him that I'd merely stumbled upon him in a stupor. 'So much has happened,' I began to say. 'There's so much I –'

'Well, no matter,' he declared, abruptly rising to his feet and unbolting the door. 'All that matters now, nephew,' he said as his clerks filed in, 'is that you have a bath.'

Bansi Lal led me outside the Hall of Audience to a little adobe bungalow set against the hem of the wall that flanked the palace. There, in the courtyard, I was given a bar of soap and a bottle of kerosene for my hair. The soap seemed to peel a layer of skin away with the dust and ashes, and disenchanted lice fell from my head as I rinsed myself with well water. A barber shaved my beard and waxed my moustache into little spirals, and Bansi Lal helped me into a clean white shirt and tight trousers, and wrapped a courtier's turban around my head.

Itching in my unaccustomed cleanliness like a man with the pox, I was then transported by palanquin along endless levels of ramps, drives, and courtyards to my uncle's quarters in the House of the Turtle, the oldest in the Maharao's complex of palaces.

The House of the Turtle was in the purest Rajput style, utterly free of Moghul influence. There wasn't a true arch in the whole house; the doors and windows had squared frames whose upper corners were embellished with carved elephants pressing their trunks against the lintels. Balconies jutted out from every window, supported by brackets in the shapes of fish and snakes, and each roof was bowed with drooping eaves like the brim of a solar topee.

Bansi Lal led me up several flights of stone steps to my room, a large but sparsely furnished chamber whose sole ornamentation was a row of European tiles set along the baseboards depicting the Stations of the Cross. A punkah hung from the ceiling; and a Kashmiri screen with a kicked-in panel stood in a corner, shielding a stack of steamer trunks; and on the wall above a mildewed chair someone had installed a shrine to Hanuman. The bed was big enough for a sizeable horse, with mosquito netting draped around it that billowed like a ghostly sail in the sharp breeze from the window.

Bansi Lal left me to rest from my transformation, but I couldn't sleep in the sinking fluff of the great bed and sat out on the balcony to take in the view.

Terrace upon terrace of orchards and gardens ornamented with fountains, tanks, and pavilions lay just below me, each shielded from the next by a crocodile spine of wall, with a few stray sentries squatting with their hookahs along the ramparts. The lush green of a Maharao's palace fell off abruptly for some eight storeys of bare scar to the band of untended scrub that lay between the palace façade and the surrounding fortifications, at whose base the whitewashed city lay in a haze of evening smoke, with red chilis and newly dyed cloth set out to dry upon the rooftops, and temple spires jutting up from the jumble of guttering candles.

Some twenty yards to my right, on the palace's towering façade, a balcony with a carved stone screen hung out over the gardens, and as the sun fell behind it I could make out a woman's figure silhouetted among the facets, gazing across the town. It could have been from that selfsame balcony that my mother watched the wives of the Maharao, Zalim Singh's grandfather, climb upon his pyre, for within full view, on the slope of the western ridge, stood what looked to be a complex of royal cenotaphs, falling into shadow now as the sun descended. And maybe she'd played in the garden below on Holi days, squirting dye at her brother in the Maharao's orchards.

I was where my mother had begged poor Moonshi to take me, hoisted to safety from my foes and terrors, where all the mysteries could be laid to rest. And yet as Harigarh slipped into the gloaming below me, all I heard was the sadhu's refrain, *What's the use? What's the use?* still whining in my ears.

I was summoned downstairs after dark, and brought into a great hall of the house with a thirty-foot banquet table lined with chairs. The table was empty, and so seemed the room until I walked to the other end and found my uncle and his sons seated on bolsters around a low, circular table by the kitchen door. There were great mismatched chandeliers overhead, but they'd been left unlit, and gave the room a frigid, cavernous air.

My uncle nodded to me in the dim light from a single lantern set on an English plant stand, and beyond its glow servants stood along the wall like spectral sentries. He introduced me to his two sons, the younger of whom looked even more like my mother than his father did, and squirmed a little as I stared. The older, Pratap Rao, was my age but didn't look it, for he was shorter than I, with a plump, callow face. He greeted me stiffly and without curiosity, rising and bowing as I took my seat beside his father.

We ate in almost total silence, and though I ascribed this to my unfamiliar presence that night, it seemed that my uncle had no small talk around his sons. He regarded his home as a haven from conversation, great and small, and there was a heavy authority to his silences which made the younger son fidget and Pratap Rao brood.

The supper was lamb and saffron rice decorated with silver leaf, yogurt flavored with coconut, cheese and peas in a lentil gravy, and I ate until I thought my shrunken gut would burst. After the finger bowls were passed around, his two sons took their leave, bowing to me, touching their father's feet, and my uncle and I walked out into the garden to take pahn in an old pavilion.

'Do you like your room?' he asked wearily, rubbing his eyes as the servants prepared a cushioned sitting place for the two of us.

'Oh, yes,' I said. 'It's more than I –'

'Good,' he cut in with an odd snort, sitting down and patting the pillow beside him. He took a portion of pahn from Bansi Lal's tray and sprinkled it with rose water, nodding to Bansi Lal to pass the tray to me, and I took my portion in turn, though I never had a taste for taking pahn; it has always seemed like chewing a sachet.

'Now tell me, Balbeer,' he said, signalling to the servants to withdraw. 'What is your plan?'

'I – '

'You do have one, don't you?'

'Well, yes,' I said, working the wad of pahn into one cheek. 'That is, you see, I'd given up all hope of – '

'Ah,' said my uncle with a sigh, 'that's to be expected. Happens to the best of us.'

'I've been wandering for so long, I – '

'Well, Balbeer,' my uncle said, 'I can't say I pity you for that. I think some days I might renounce everything, just as you did. Trade all this for the pilgrim road.' He chewed thoughtfully for a moment. 'So what you're saying is that you don't have any plans, is that it?' he asked, looking up at me suddenly as if I'd just materialized beside him.

'Yes, Uncle,' I said. 'I guess that's so. You see, this was all an accident. I'd given up – '

' – hope. Yes, you told me that already. Well, I think you're going to find this an odd place to recover your hope, Balbeer, if you don't mind my saying so.'

'Uncle?'

'Harigarh,' he said. 'Home. I tell you, Balbeer, it isn't what it once was.'

'Ah, but what is?' I heard myself blurt, lapsing into my sadhu's parlance.

My uncle looked at me and rubbed his nose. 'Please, Balbeer,' he said quietly. 'Spare me.'

There was a silence as he stared off again along the tidy row of trees that stood against the scalloped wall.

'My sister,' he said suddenly. 'Did she suffer very much?'

I glanced at the stars arrayed above the wall, and decided not to be merciful.'

'Well, it was consumption, you know,' I said. 'It takes a long time.'

My uncle ducked his head and stared at his shadowed lap, and for a moment he was so still I thought I'd somehow put him to sleep. 'Did I ever tell you the story of Surat Singhji?' he asked absurdly, as if we'd often sat like this before.

'Uh, no, Uncle,' I said, looking over at him and seeing that he'd been crying.

'Then I shall,' he said, sniffing and blinking back a tear, and he told me this story:

Maharao Surat Singh of Harigarh had lived during the reign of the Moghul Jehangir. It seems that during a durbar one morning he'd cut a Moghul emissary in half for making an idle suggestion about the maintenance of the Maharao's favorite cannon, a Portuguese siege gun Surat Singh and his nagas worshipped like a lingam.

Jehangir was willing to forgive and forget, but not Surat Singh, for whom anyone's forgiveness, even the Grand Moghul's, was the basest insult, and so he declared war forthwith, and slaughtered all his Moslem subjects.

Jehangir sent an expedition to punish Surat Singh, but as I've said, Harigarh was as perfectly fortified as any citadel in Rajputana, and though the Moghul's general laid siege with all his might, his cannon balls bounced off the walls like marbles, his battering rams never reached the gates, his catapults could make no breach, and six months later, for all his efforts, his army was still baking on the plain while Surat Singh snacked on peaches in his garden.

This proved such an embarrassment to Jehangir that he sent orders that if his troops failed to take Harigarh in the next two weeks they were to kill themselves, even the officers, and forget their places in paradise. But though they redoubled their efforts with their ladders and lances, by the end of the first week they were still no closer to victory. So finally Jehangir's desperate general proposed a pitiable gambit. He would have his men erect a mock fortress out of mud and wood, stock it with a few of his own soldiers dressed as Rajputs, storm it, raise Jehangir's standard above the rickety battlements, and declare themselves the victors.

So they did that, and with but the faintest hope that they'd somehow circumvented Jehangir's wrath, the general and his army broke camp.

But no sooner had they begun their march to Delhi than they

heard a clatter and a creaking behind them, and looked around to see the great spiked portals of Harigarh open.

For it seemed that Surat Singh, having watched all this from the safety of his palace, had been outraged by the fraudulent assault. Commanding his wives and concubines to incinerate themselves in the treasury and donning saffron robes, he now led his little army of jogis and guardsmen in a furious charge on Jehangir's dumbfounded troops.

Of course, Surat Singh was hacked to pieces, his warriors slaughtered, his wives duly immolated, the city razed, and its populace enslaved, and yet here was my uncle singing his praises with his eyes bugging out, like an awestruck schoolboy.

'Understand that story and you understand Harigarh,' he exclaimed, reaching out and gripping my knee. 'Glory! Chivalry! Honor! A maharao's born to be a warrior, first and foremost. To be proud, brave, noble, quick to take offense.

'And I,' he continued, shaking a finger at himself, 'I was born to be a warrior's diwan. I should be marshalling his army. Rationing the stores. Calling forth our clansmen. Unfurling my kingdom's banner.

'But look at me,' he said, speaking in the faintest whisper, 'pricking my ears to every treacherous whisper, prying a damning confidence from a widow's dupe, sorting the truths from the half-truths and the half-truths from the outnumbering lies: the plots and depravities in the zenana, the mutinies in the guard, the larceny among the priests, the bribes tucked into the charan's charts, the gemstones missing from the Maharao's throne. Night and day I wade through the filth of the kingdom, the dynasty's rot. And for what? So my king can dance on an English leash? So the Empress can have her precious stability? So Pratap Rao can take my place when they murder me at last?'

My uncle wiped the flecks of spit from his lips and glowered at me a moment, as if affronted by my innocence. 'See what you've gotten yourself into? Think perhaps you should have stayed in Cawnpore?'

'No, Uncle,' I said, meeting his gaze.

'No? And why not?'

'Because,' I heard myself reply, 'this is my home.'

My uncle stared at me a little longer and then rose to his feet, arching his back.

'Poor Balbeer,' he said with a groan, leading me back toward the house. 'I suppose you're right, God help you. Well then, let's try to make the best of it.'

CHAPTER

55

The next morning my education began with a visit to Maharao Zalim Singh himself. With Pratap Rao in tow, my uncle escorted me on the walk to the royal residence, and as gunfire echoed down the maze of porticos and passageways he nervously cited an old Persian saw: 'If your king says the day be night, reply, "Behold the moon and stars." '

We found his highness in the uppermost garden of the palace, shooting at fish with a brace of silver pistols. He sat on a raised marble terrace, under a blue-and-white canopy bordered in gold brocade. On the terrace steps a pair of hunting leopards lay preening themselves on the end of a bronze chain, hardly blinking as the pistol balls whirred over their heads and slapped at the water below. To either side of the Maharao gentle fountains raised little cones of water in which oranges were balanced, bobbing and spinning in the cool spray.

As we entered the garden two sweepers were hastily carting away the cheetahs' dung. A shikari stood nearby, reloading the Maharao's pistols, and the usual body servants hovered about the terrace with parasols and whisks, trays and pitchers. In a corner of the garden petitioners were gathered for the morning durbar, giving a little hopeful cheer with each of the Maharao's shots.

A herald announced my uncle's arrival, but he could hardly be heard over the charan bard who stood at the edge of the turbulent pool, reciting the titles of Zalim Singh's ancestors. Beyond the terrace stood a row of trees pruned into the shapes of elephants and bearing a singular fruit: perforated clay balls in which the Maharao's peaches ripened, safe from the monkeys now screeching at the cheetahs from the surrounding wall.

I waited among the petitioners as my uncle approached Zalim Singh in a low stoop, murmuring some flattery about the Maharao's aim. Zalim Singh returned his greeting with a grudging wave of his hand from the level of his waist. It was customary for him to thus indicate the status of his visitors; princes of equal rank earned a wave from the level of his heart, the rest of us from various points below.

Kettledrums resounded to mark the hour, and with a sour expression, Zalim Singh returned his pistols to his shikari and signalled his herald to begin the durbar, washing the pistol soot from his hands on sculpted ice as retainers fetched the few dead and dying carp from the bloodstained pool. His face was blotched with powder, his hair fell in scrags, and his beard was all akimbo, as if he hadn't bathed or changed since rising.

My uncle always assigned the least-favored petitioners to the head of the line, for the Maharao, still irritated by the interruption of his morning's recreation, was harshest on the first few cases. It was my uncle's plan to try to fit me in after Zalim Singh had expended his wrath but before he could imbibe his khusamba, an opium concoction which sometimes made him euphoric but usually murderously glum.

The durbar got off to a macabre start with the case of a petty thief of the Mang caste who'd been caught trying to steal a mango from a greengrocer. This would have been unremarkable except that the Mang was lacking not only his right hand but his left arm to the elbow, his right leg to the knee, his left foot, his nose, his upper lip, and both eyes, all removed at one time or another for past offenses.

The kotwal, a fretful, monocled man with a betel-red moustache that drooped down to his collarbone, confessed to his sovereign that he was at an utter loss as to how further to punish the Mang, who sat in a little cart with a cheerful smile, awaiting the Maharao's judgment.

Zalim Singh wondered if he had to do everything himself. Was the kotwal *totally* lacking in ingenuity? It was simple: remove the wretched Mang's tongue – that would teach him.

But the kotwal had the Mang open his mouth to show that this had already been done some years before.

Very well then, said the Maharao. Remove his private parts.

But here the kotwal had to restrain the Mang from fumbling out of his waistcloth.

Then *kill* him, the Maharao thundered, striking his knee with a fat fist. Drag him from an elephant. Roll him in coals.

The Mang seemed to see the sense in this, but the kotwal wondered if perhaps execution might be a little extreme, considering that the Mang had merely attempted to snatch a mango.

Zalim Singh roared and threw a pillow at the kotwal, which the kotwal ducked into so it would reach its target and then stumbled back so as to demonstrate the force of his excellency's arm.

All right then, the Maharao declared, suddenly calm. Paint the Mang's face half black, half white, and send him around town seated backwards on a donkey.

At this the Mang gave a cry, fell forward out of his little cart, and seemed to beg in his tongueless fashion for mercy, but the kotwal looked relieved and grateful, and returned the pillow to the Maharao's terrace, thanking his excellency profusely.

A hapless bania of no account was called forth next to have his parasol approved. During Dusserah the Maharao had noticed that some of his subroyal subjects had sported parasols and palanquins of an elegance far exceeding their stations in life, and so a decree had gone out that all such paraphernalia had to be reviewed by the Maharao himself. This little bania's parasol seemed humble enough, and its only decoration was a hymn to Zalim Singh stitched along the fringe, but his highness was in an awful temper after the Mang business, and besides had little use for banias anyway, having only the dimmest notion of what they did.

So he resolved to make an example of this one. He ordered two guards to set the parasol ablaze and pitch it over the wall, and fined the bania some exorbitant sum, for which the trembling merchant counted himself lucky, and kissed the ground with gratitude.

As the next petitioner crept forward my mouth went dry, for I was to follow in the favored fourth spot, though the Maharao's mood showed no improvement. The third supplicant was a sword-smith who'd been offered a position in the armory of the Maharao of Bundi, Zalim Singh's distant cousin. No vassal of the tradesman castes could move out of the kingdom without first gaining his

Maharao's permission. Zalim Singh liked tradesmen, admired the way they were always making things; and he seemed to soften a little as the swordsmith pleaded his case.

Oh, very well, he said. He wouldn't begrudge Maharao Raghubir Singh the swordsmith's services.

To show his gratitude, the swordsmith presented Zalim Singh with a curved Khorrassain blade with a solid silver Ram's head hilt.

Zalim Singh was delighted with the sword and ranged around the terrace for a while, swinging at the bobbing oranges suspended in the fountains.

On second thought, the Maharao declared, raising his new toy overhead, the swordsmith had better stay — Harigarh could ill afford to lose so fine a craftsman. But just to show how pleased he was with the swordsmith's gift, he announced, he would keep it and treasure it always.

And now as the swordsmith slouched out of the garden my uncle beckoned me forward, and I approached the Maharao in a low stoop and touched the bottom stair, as the others had done, which brought me so close to the drowsy leopards that I could smell their rank breath and see the fleas hopping on their dappled coats.

Zalim Singh was still standing, turning the blade of his new sword this way and that, as my uncle introduced me.

'Your highness,' he said, half bowed, with one arm outstretched in my direction, 'this fine young man is Balbeer Rao, late of Cawnpore, and my dear dead sister's son. For many years I thought he was dead. But behold, he lives!'

'Bhulwant Rao,' the Maharao said, wiping the orange juice off the blade with the awning drapes. 'Have you ever seen a finer sword than this?'

'Uh, no, your excellency,' said my uncle, sagging a little. 'Never.'

'It's a Bikaneer motif, isn't it? Dungar Singhji has a birthday coming up, doesn't he? He should have one. Arrange it for me.'

'Immediately, your highness.'

'Good,' said Zalim Singh, settling back into his pillows and crisping his fingers at a servant. 'Now then, who have we here?'

My uncle took a deep breath and began again. 'Your highness,' he said, 'this is Balbeer Rao, late of Cawnpore, and my dear — '

' — dead sister's son,' said the Maharao with an unaccountable wink. 'I remember. I'm not deaf. Is he the little sadhu Perks encountered?'

'Why, yes, he is, your highness,' said my uncle. 'And miracle of miracles – '

'He turns out to be your nephew after all. Isn't that something? And what have you been up to all these years?' he asked me expansively. 'Looking for the Abode of Bliss?'

'Yes, your highness,' I replied in a choked voice. 'And now I've found it.'

For a moment my uncle seemed to hold his breath, but then a servant handed the Maharao his goblet of khusamba and Zalim Singh laughed abruptly. 'Well said, Balbeer Rao,' he declared, raising a finger studded with gems. 'Welcome to Harigarh. Are you staying with us long?'

I glanced again at my relieved uncle, who furtively mouthed, 'Yes, your highness,' with a slight nod.

'Yes, your highness,' I said. 'I – I'm going to live in my uncle's house.'

My uncle looked sharply pained and said, 'That is his *hope*, your highness. That is his *dream*. But of course only *you* can make such dreams come true.'

But the Maharao had already chosen to be amused by my inadvertent presumption and slyly wagged a finger at me. 'There's something I like about this fellow,' he said, sipping his opium. 'Something refreshing.'

'Thank you, your highness,' said my uncle, motioning to me to bow lower, for I'd allowed my posture to straighten.

The Maharao gulped down some khusamba and sat still for a moment, smacking his lips, as if awaiting an explosion.

'So what is he?' he asked, licking at his moustache. 'About my age, would you say?'

My uncle looked uneasy, for even in my withered state I was obviously young enough to be Zalim Singh's son. 'Uh, not quite, your highness,' he said. 'A tad younger, perhaps.'

'I thought so. You know,' he declared. 'I love these sadhus. One of these days I'm going to renounce the world myself,' he said, belching loudly. 'I really am.'

'Oh, your highness,' my uncle began. 'And deprive your subjects of – '

'I've an idea,' the Maharao interjected. 'Yes,' he said, raising one plump hand. 'A lovely idea. Bhulwant Rao?'

'Yes, your highness?'

'The Crown Prince, Rai Singh – he still needs a companion, doesn't he?'

'Well, your highness,' said my uncle with a fretful glance in my direction, 'I believe that when last we met we agreed that Pratap Rao – '

'Who?' the Maharao asked impatiently.

'Uh, Pratap Rao,' said my uncle with a wan smile. 'That is, my son.'

'Oh, *him*. Yes, well, of course he has *him*. But *he's* not much of a companion, is he?'

'Oh, your highness, Pratap Rao *adores* the prince. Why he positively *worships* – '

'Who doesn't?' the Maharao asked petulantly. 'Everyone adores my . . . uh, *son*, don't they?'

'Oh, yes,' said my uncle, 'for the Prince is flesh of your flesh, your highness, blood of your blood.'

'Yes, well,' said Zalim Singh, 'I've heard rumors to that effect. But the point is, your son can't be much of a companion to Rai Singh, can he? I mean,' he said, with a mischievous look at the latticed balcony that hung out over the garden, 'Pratap Rao is such a cipher, Bhulwant Rao. Such a pallid little drudge.'

'He's – he's *serious*, your highness,' said my uncle with a miserable shrug, wringing his hands before him.

'Well, he's no companion. No more than you're my companion, Bhulwant Rao. It's impossible,' said the Maharao, with a certain kindliness.

'But your nephew here,' he said, 'is something else again. He's been places. A messenger from another realm, that's what he is. Have you taken a good look at him, Bhulwant Rao? It's an interesting face.'

My uncle gazed at me with his sovereign as the blood rushed to the tips of my ears.

'But wait,' Zalim Singh suddenly called out, crisping his fingers at his clerks. 'I'm feeling . . . poetic!'

My uncle contained a sigh and feigned an expectant look as the Maharao's clerks readied their pens along the garden wall.

'Let's see,' the Maharao muttered, conducting for a moment with one stubby finger. 'Yes,' he said, raising his head as if to sing. 'Now take this down.

> *'He stands before us from a distant land:*
> *Another empire by Nerbudda's strand.'*

He paused, looking pleased, and closed his eyes for the next surge of inspiration. A drummer hurried into the garden and began to tap in rhythm to his composition.

> *'Ashes,'* he continued, *'not talcum, pales his face;*
> *Sorrow, not lampblack, leaves about his eyes its trace.*
> *What does his saintly gaze evince?*
> *What counsel shall he bring his Prince?'*

I've got to admit I was flattered by all this. No one had ever called my gaze saintly before, and I resolved that as soon as the audience was over I would find myself a mirror and see what his highness was talking about.

Zalim Singh was silent for a while, rocking slightly with his eyes shut tight.

'Beautiful,' my uncle ventured finally as the drummer stopped tapping behind us. 'Truly extraordinary. Once again, if I may say so, your highness has managed to capture not only the – '

But the Maharao wasn't finished.

'What counsel shall he bring his Prince?' he suddenly repeated, rising to his feet.

'Bring news of all his subjects' woes,' he said, glaring now at the latticed balcony.

> *'Forewarn him of encircling foes.*
> *Pray with him to the sentry star*
> *That watches over Harigarh,*
> *That he might be half so great a king*
> *As Maharao Zalim Singh!'*

And with that he reared back and threw his cup of khusamba up at the latticed balcony and laughed as a tiger might, with a rib-shaking roar, trailing a smattering of chuckles from his terrified court.

My uncle waited him out, nodding and smiling as best he could between frightened glances at the balcony, now lightly spattered with khusamba.

'Oh,' Zalim Singh gasped, wiping at his tears with the pavilion drapes. 'Oh, I can't stand it. It's *too* droll. I want it illuminated!' he shouted to his clerks. 'Yes,' he said, turning back to my uncle, 'illuminated and bound and borne to the zenana. You see to it, Bhulwant Rao. It's my gift.

'My gift!' he bellowed up at the balcony. 'Did you hear that, Tarra Bai? My gift to my beloved Queen!'

But at the word 'beloved' the glee went out of him, and he glared at me as if I'd appeared out of nowhere.

'And *this*,' he sneered, pointing at me with his new sword. 'This *creature* you call a nephew.'

'His name,' said my uncle helpfully, 'is Bal — '

'I don't care what his name is,' said the Maharao, stepping out from among his cushions. 'I want him to stick to my son like a shadow. I want his stink in the Prince's nostrils. Do you understand me, Bhulwant Rao?'

'Yes, but your highness,' said my uncle, all reasonableness, his shoulders high about his ears, 'is he really suitable? I mean, as you say, he's just a — '

'*Silence*, you old hen,' Zalim Singh hissed, advancing upon us down the steps. 'I know what you're up to, you and my Queen. You and my *love*, my *adoring little wife*. Well, you haven't pecked the old lion to death yet, have you? Not just *yet*,' he said, bringing the swordpoint to my uncle's chin.

'Not yet, eh, Tarra Bai?' he called up toward the balcony. 'There're still a few teeth in the old lion's bite!'

'We — we are inexpressibly grateful, your highness,' said my uncle, staring down the Maharao's sword and stumbling backward toward the gate. 'I only hope my nephew will prove w-worthy of your generosity. R-right, Balbeer?'

'Uh, yes — yes,' I stammered. 'Th-thank you, your highness.'

But the Maharao had lost all interest in us, and stopped beneath the balcony, gazing upward with heartbreak in his wild eyes as the khusamba dripped like nectar on his brow.

·CHAPTER·
56

'It was the khusamba talking,' my uncle declared when we'd escaped from the Maharao's garden. 'It puts him out of sorts,' he said, speaking at the top of his voice as if to make himself heard by the nagas at the gate and the petitioners who streamed out around us. 'And why wouldn't he be out of sorts?' he went on, leading me away. 'My goodness, with all he has to worry about?'

But as we walked out of earshot of the others the heat rose in his eyes and he dabbed with a kerchief at the dent the Maharao's sword had left in the flesh of his chin. 'Oh God, am I bleeding?' he asked, his voice dropping almost to a whisper as he inspected his kerchief.

'No, Uncle.'

'No, of course not,' he muttered, trying now to catch his breath. 'The blood never shows.

'See, nephew?' he said, leading me up a series of stone steps and landings. 'See what you've stepped into? I tell you, Balbeer – go back to the sadhu's road. This is no place for you. This is no place for any of us.'

I followed him up along the course of a wall overhung with balconies and gazed out at the amber city. I remember it was a clear winter's day, and beyond the town's reaches the scrubby stone hills seemed to extend forever to the west and rose into steep cliffs to the north and south. This was the only place in the whole world left to me, I wanted to say, but I tried instead to change the subject.

'This Tarra Bai,' I asked, all matter-of-fact. 'Who is she?'

My uncle whirled about and gripped my arm. 'Keep your voice down, for God's sake,' he hissed, pulling me along. 'The zenana,' he whispered, surreptitiously pointing up at the balconies, 'is everywhere.'

His whisper was so much like my mother's that I started as he jerked me forward. 'Is – is she the Maharani?'

My uncle didn't reply until we'd turned a corner and reached an alcove black with soot where we couldn't be seen or overheard.

'I fear for you, nephew,' he said quickly, still whispering and craning his head about, on the alert for eavesdroppers. 'I fear I can't teach you in time to save you.'

Whereupon he told me about the Queen.

Before my birth, Harigarh had been ruled by Bhijay Singh, Zalim Singh's adoptive father, an imbecile, as my uncle allowed, who dressed in women's clothing and danced so convincingly at his nautches that his nobles finally had him strangled one night with his own brassière, a gift from the Maharaja of Alwar.

By the time of his accession, Zalim Singh had already proved himself his father's opposite, and wore out wives as quickly as my grandfather, his diwan, could recruit them. There were none among them that Zalim Singh would recognize as his true queen until my grandfather, searching through the zenana of the royal house of Kishengarh, plucked a rare flower for his Maharao called Tarra Bai who charmed the Maharao with her wit, beguiled him with her beauty, and matched Zalim Singh with her appetites.

But it was two years before she bore him a son, Rai Singh, and by then another of his wives had given birth to two. These two plump scions stood ahead of Rai Singh in the line of succession until his eighth year, when Zalim Singh was believed to be dying of apoplexy after a fall from a camel. First the eldest son was found suffocated in the smoke from a smoldering screen, and then the second was fatally stung by a centipede in his bath.

So when the Maharao finally recovered from his delirium he found not his two plump, familiar sons by his bedside, but Rai Singh, Tarra Bai's slender darling, in whose aura Zalim Singh would skulk and squint ever after.

Rai Singh looked so little like Zalim Singh that half the court believed Tarra Bai had conceived him with another man, while the other half was convinced she'd faked her pregnancy and adopted Rai Singh on the sly.

The death of his sons put an end to Zalim Singh's love for Tarra Bai, and a poisonous loathing arose between them. But for all that, Tarra Bai remained his formidable queen, and ruled the zenana as her personal fief.

'These balconies, windows, screens,' said my uncle, almost inaudible now as he pressed himself further into the alcove's shadow. 'They're everywhere. And all connected to the zenana by secret halls and passageways. The palace is as labyrinthine as her purposes, nephew. Nothing escapes her notice.'

'Even here?' I asked, glancing out into the light.

'Even here. Somewhere she's waiting, playing cards, counting her pearls, wondering what I'm telling you. But she'll find out soon enough,' he said wearily. 'She always does.'

'But how?'

My uncle looked at me evenly. 'One of us will tell her.'

'But I won't tell her,' I said, inadvertently raising my voice.

'Well,' said my uncle with a sigh, placing a hand on my shoulder, 'then I suppose I'll have to.'

I looked at him in confusion as he led me back out into the light.

'So, nephew,' he said full-voice, leading me past an old sentry in rusted mail. 'Companion to the Crown Prince! Imagine!'

He talked heartily for a while, leading me between two generations of palace wall and up a steep lane as I searched among the facets of the pierced stone windows above us for signs of the Maharani and her agents.

We came to the gate of an improvised garden walled in brick, set like one of Cawnpore's British compounds around an annex of the old palace.

'Now let's have a look at you,' said my uncle, inspecting my attire. 'The Prince is a stickler about appearances.'

He reached up and straightened my turban slightly and directed me to tighten my sash about my waist.

'Well,' he said as a chowkidor trotted up to open the gate for us, 'you will have to do.'

We walked along a little cobbled path that led us under several trellises hung with roses. 'This is the home of Mr Spencer Perks, our British Resident,' he said. 'The Prince takes his lessons with Perks Sahib every morning, as you shall.

'You there,' he called to the chowkidor, 'fetch me my son.' And as the chowkidor complied, my uncle pulled me close to him for a moment and whispered again.

'You serve the Crown Prince well,' he said fervently. 'Look after him. He promises Harigarh a golden age. But *remember*, Balbeer,' he said now with a worried scowl. 'It's *Pratap Rao* he must favor, not you. Pratap Rao must be diwan.'

Now I never regarded myself as a winning personality, but the unlikeliness of my uncle's proposition was obvious enough to me as Pratap Rao now emerged from Perks's house, with his strange, shuffling gait, and his pimpled brow hanging heavily upon his narrow, sidelong eyes. It seemed to me even then that the prince would favor anyone, even me, over Pratap Rao, but I don't know if I already felt ambition swelling in my breast, or saw the chance that the Diwan's office might some day be mine for the taking.

My uncle explained to Pratap Rao about the Maharao's decision and bade me farewell at the door to Perks's house, leaving Pratap Rao to escort me in wounded silence.

Spencer Perks's home had once been a guesthouse reserved for Englishmen of marginal repute who now frequented the new hotel in the city. He took his pedagogy more seriously than his political duties, which, after all, were few, and turned his parlor into a formal classroom, complete with English study desks, maps, historical tables, chalkboards, a lectern, and a gallery of portraits of all the governors-general and viceroys of India, arranged in chronological order between the windows.

But he never used this classroom, preferring instead to conduct his classes in his library, his garden, his laboratory, his darkroom, even his closets and lavatory — wherever the day's lessons might take him.

That morning we found him in his laboratory, breaking the wings of a bulbul's corpse and stuffing its throat with tow.

'Ah, Pratap Rao,' he said, glancing at us briefly over his scratched and dusty spectacles. 'Just in time. Look here — fetch me that scalpel, will you? There's a good lad.'

Pratap Rao made no attempt to introduce me, but fetched Perks's scalpel for him as I stood poised in the doorway.

'Isn't she a beauty?' Perks asked, folding back one broken wing. 'Downed her yesterday evening. And look here — perfect shot, right through the heart. I'll just make my incision,' he said briskly, inserting his scalpel into the bullet hole.

Along the tops of the bookshelves behind him, little mounted birds stood on a long brass bar with tags hanging from their feet. The shelves themselves were half-filled with books and littered here and there with folios and scrolls. Books and papers lay all about the room as if shot from guns, and every spare surface was covered with test tubes, beakers, jars, astrolabes, telescopes, lenses, cameras, chemical trays, impaled insects, scraps of vegetation pressed in glass. On one wall there was a menagerie of stuffed lizards he'd collected, and I jumped a little when a gecko in their vicinity suddenly scrambled for the window.

'Now then,' said Perks as Pratap Rao stood by with a sickened look. 'I'll just snip this right here,' and he severed the wing bone and peeled the feathered flesh away, humming to himself.

A black curtain hung across the door to his darkroom, and I could see an easel standing in an adjoining verandah that served as Perks's studio. The air had such a brackish smell from all the jars left open, the test tubes left unwashed, and the sad little skins left out to cure, that not a single fly braved the atmosphere.

'Now, Pratap Rao,' Perks asked without looking up as he freed the skin from the back and breast. 'Who have we here?'

My cousin glanced at me a moment and sniffed. 'He is Balbeer Rao,' he said. 'My father's sister's son.'

Perks peered at me. 'Your cousin, then? Is he indeed? Not the little beggar I encountered on the Rajshikari Road?'

Pratap Rao merely shrugged, so I stepped forward with my hands pressed before me. 'The same, sahib,' I said.

'Why, isn't that remarkable? Isn't that wonderful?' Perks asked Pratap Rao. 'And I thought he was an impostor for certain. Well, well, well,' he said boyishly, putting down his scalpel and wiping his hands on his apron. 'How do you do?'

'I am well, thank you, sahib,' I said, bowing down.

'Well, I do apologize for not believing you,' he said. 'But you must admit, you didn't look the part.'

He began to tell how he'd mentioned me at the Maharao's banquet, but then a clock chimed on the bookshelf and he fumbled under his apron for his pocket watch.

'The Prince is late,' he muttered, fretfully clicking it open and frowning at its clouded face.

'Will you be studying with me as well?' he asked mildly, returning to his work.

'Yes, sahib,' I said.

'Well, splendid,' he said, snipping the bone of the second wing. 'Look here,' he said, '– will you fetch me the arsenical soap?'

But as I stepped toward it there was a swift padding and shuffling in the hallway, and ranks of barefoot servants scurried into the laboratory: two stooped sweepers first, duckwalking with their brooms; then a tall, languid boy with a horsetail whisk; a coolie toting a purple tasseled hassock; and a kitmadgar with a silver cup and pitcher on an enamelled tray.

Each successive servant – there must have been half a dozen in the first wave – was dressed more gloriously than the last, but nothing could have prepared me for Rai Singh himself, the Crown Prince of Harigarh, as he burst through the doorway, along a hastily rolled-out carpet.

'Ah,' said Perks, 'there you are.'

The Prince stood stock still at the sight of me, poised with his silken sleeves extended like one of Perks's impaled butterflies, and then he composed himself and strode in, trailing a few more of his retinue.

'Oh, Professor, am I *awfully* late?' he wondered in a high, melodious voice, pressing one finger to his cheek.

He was a little shorter than I, but in his stupefying splendor he seemed to tower over the rest of us. He wore tight green leggings and a great ruffled skirt with immaculate white pleats and a jacket of saffron silk that was lambent in the shadows and gave off constellations of light as Rai Singh passed along the windows. His face was clean-shaven and his delicate features were almost oriental, like the Buddha's, except that his gaze was not serene but quick and restless.

It may have only been the servants who crowded in with him in Perks's laboratory, but Rai Singh seemed to suck all the air out of the room as he glided about, and I would still have to say that he was the most beautiful human being, man or woman, that I've ever seen.

Pratap Rao bowed low, and I followed suit, but Perks, thanks to his office, remained more or less upright.

'Professor,' Rai Singh cried, giving me the merest passing glance.

'Please don't scold me. You know I couldn't bear it. Can you forgive me? Here,' he said with a wave to his most senior servant, 'please honor me by accepting this merest token of my regret.'

The servant advanced upon Perks carrying a narrow carved box on a satin pillow.

'These gifts,' Perks said, struggling to sound grave as he plucked up the box with his pale fingers. 'Really, your excellency. There's no need – '

The box contained an exquisite mother-of-pearl pen with a silver clip and a golden nib which Perks extracted with an inadvertent gasp, shaking his balding, freckled head.

'Your excellency,' he muttered. 'You really shouldn't – '

'There, there, old fellow,' said Rai Singh, pointing to one of the Professor's pens amid the clutter on the table. A second servant trotted up and held it by his shoulder like a tiny javelin. 'Do you think,' said Rai Singh, 'that I could allow my guru to record his wisdom with such a humble instrument as this? Never!' he said, pointing to the window, and the servant pitched the old pen into the garden.

Perks gazed wistfully out the window. 'Your excellency is too kind.'

'Nonsense,' said Rai Singh, suddenly stepping up to me. 'Now tell me, please – who in the world is this?'

Pratap Rao, speaking with his father's suppliance, as if to a dangerous beast, replied that I was his cousin.

Rai Singh clasped his hands behind him and circled around me, pouting at this and that unseemly feature of my person, twitching one fine, penciled eyebrow at my spread, scuffed sadhu's feet, as his senior servant trudged behind him, poised to do his bidding.

'As a matter of fact,' said Perks, reaming out the bulbul's head, 'your father has arranged for him to join your excellency's retinue. Isn't that so, Pratap Rao?'

As I fetched Perks his arsenical soap, Pratap Rao straightened up from his bow. 'Yes, Professor Sahib,' he allowed with a furtive sneer.

Rai Singh drew his face closer to mine and fingered the pearls on his necklace. Nowhere had I ever felt so brutish as in Rai Singh's elegant proximity. My folded hands were still grey from the dust and ashes of the sadhu's road, and my bare toes stuck out like blunt horns on the cold stone floor.

'Straighten up,' he casually commanded, for I was still bowed low before him, and he stared deep into my eyes for a moment, tapping the thumb of his right hand with each of his delicate fingers.

'*I* know what this is!' he suddenly exclaimed, turning to Perks with his linen pleats brushing against me. 'It's a joke, *isn't* it?'

'Well, your excellency,' said Perks uncomfortably, 'it's certainly not *my* idea of a joke.'

'Yes, yes,' said Rai Singh, raising his hand. 'It's a joke. It's my father's joke. It's my father's joke on my mother! Isn't it, Pratap Rao. Come on, isn't that so?'

Pratap Rao gave the Prince a grim, hesitant smile.

Rai Singh stamped one foot and laughed, slapping his knees. 'Oh, Mother isn't going to like this,' he said gleefully. 'Not one bit. Her beautiful son,' he said, meaning himself, of course, 'companion to a peasant!'

I usually wouldn't have minded being called a peasant, for to me it was no insult, but to the Prince it was, and out of embarrassment more than outrage, I suppose, I scowled at Rai Singh and began to shuffle slowly from the room.

Pratap Rao furtively urged me on against my own best interests, pointing to the door, but the Prince came after me and stationed himself upon the threshold, blocking my way.

'I – I fear your highness has offended him,' the Professor said, draping his tiny feathered skin over a drawer handle and wiping his hands on his apron.

'Offended *him*?' asked Rai Singh in astonishment. 'How?'

'Well, your excellency,' Perks gently suggested, 'the – ah, peasant business.'

'But he *is* a peasant. You *are* a peasant, aren't you?' he asked me now with confounded innocence.

I turned to Perks for an answer, for the truth was that I was as much in the dark as Rai Singh.

'Well, your excellency,' said Perks, removing his apron now and washing his hands in the laboratory basin, 'one can never tell. He may be a diamond in the rough.'

CHAPTER 57

Perks chipped away at the rough for a week or so, trying me out in a dozen subjects, as an object lesson to the Prince in the deceptivity of appearances. As much to my astonishment as everyone else's, my peasant's hand could still form a tidy English script, and with a little prompting I could recite an entire psalm from memory. I also discovered that I was reasonably competent in arithmetic, owing, I suppose, to the patwari's accounts.

Perks didn't really test me that week, however, at least not in the Reverend's sense. He seemed to think that examining us would have been ungracious, like testing dinner guests on an evening's conversation. I eventually came to recognize that Perks's greatest gift was the trust he put in us, but in the beginning I didn't know what to make of him. Maybe the Reverend had permanently soured me on education, or perhaps I was just too old to play the eager pupil, but I so distrusted myself that I mistook the Professor for a fool.

Back in my Christian period, Dileep once told me a parable about an archery guru giving his pupils their first test. He asked the first boy what he saw before him, and the boy described the view: the sky, the plain, the tree blossoming in the distance. 'You will never do,' said the guru, and called forth the second boy, who said he thought he saw a sparrow perched in the tree. 'Better,' said the guru, 'but not good enough,' and he called the third boy forward.

'I see the dot in the centre of the sparrow's eye,' declared the third boy, and the guru embraced him as his disciple, and I think he grew up to be Arjuna, or maybe it was Lord Rama – one of the two.

Now Dileep told this story as another example of a teacher's witless trick: any schoolboy knows the disadvantage of being called on first, and by the third turn any idiot could have guessed the guru's drift.

But I tell it to explain why Perks so confounded the Maharao's court. To my uncle's way of thinking, culture depended on the sparrow's eye: the strictest investment of a man's entire being in a single pursuit. This might produce musicians, painters, and soldiers who were helpless in almost every other respect, all the way down to washing their own feet, but it also gave rise to the most elaborate and expressive music, the most exquisite painting, and the most heroic traditions on earth.

And now along came Spencer Perks, describing himself, with some pride, as an amateur's amateur, a student of the world. Naturalist, historian, taxidermist, photographer, astronomer, watercolorist, poet, linguist, anthropologist, archaeologist – he was all these things. And why not? Life was short.

About five years before I stumbled on the scene, Perks had snagged himself on the Maharao's fancy while conducting field research for one of his many unfinished works: a definitive study of the ruling houses of Rajputana tentatively titled *Sovereigns of the Sun and Moon.*

All the other Rajput houses employed a Feringhee, and Zalim Singh wanted one too, so he beguiled Perks into signing on as the Prince's tutor, paying the little man an exorbitant sum to support him in all his avocations, and outfitting his quarters with all the furnishings of an English country cottage. The Maharao was delighted by Perks, as by a gadget of many uses, and when the British Resident died he petitioned Northbrook, the Viceroy, to name Perks the new Resident, which Northbrook did, as a gesture of appreciation for Harigarh's loyalty during the Devil's Wind.

The Professor was an intuitive teacher who spun his lessons out of circumstance, and I still think how much he and Dileep would have enjoyed each other. Let one of us happen to remark upon the weather and he would flourish barometers and thermometers in the laboratory, demonstrate principles of evaporation in the darkroom, or usher us out to observe the clouds. Let us inquire what time it was and he might make a sundial in the garden, or uncover the works of his hunting watch, or hike with us up to the Maharao's old water clock high above the Durbar Hall.

On the sadhu road I'd been blundering toward the bleak conclusion that I was but a grain of sand in a storm, or a bit of flotsam on an endless sea. But Perks seemed to believe that each of us was part of a comprehensible order, and a necessary part, like a tooth on a gear in his pocket watch, without which time would limp a little, the universe would stagger.

'Someday you must tell me all about meditation, Balbeer,' he told me early on. 'For my part, it has always seemed such a waste of my brief time on earth to contemplate a nothingness which, by most credible accounts, I shall occupy soon enough.'

As far as my uncle was concerned, this was a degraded and wayward philosophy, and he warned me against it when we dined together.

'And you see to it that the Prince doesn't fall prey to this preposterous English arrogance,' he told Pratap Rao and me one evening, out of the blue, with his cheek bulging with pahn.

I can't say Perks was wasted on me – not, at least, as entirely as he was wasted on Pratap Rao, who, like John Christopher, saw no wonder in life, only chores and opportunities. Perks's attention drew me out of the fog, if only for the Prince's sake, and I saw Harigarh the clearer for it.

I won't say Perks was wasted on Rai Singh, either, for the Prince could be alert and retentive in his selective fashion. But his servants kept him an arm's length from almost everything. I told you that we hiked up to the Maharao's water clock one day, but the truth is that the rest of us hiked up while the Prince rode in his palanquin, consuming lassi and sweets in the curtained shade.

If a lesson called on him actually to write something, his servants would place his elaborate and largely useless Kashmiri lap desk (useless because the Maharao had caused his seal to be carved deeply into the top), and as a body servant massaged Rai Singh's fingers, a bearer would secure a parchment scroll, dip his golden pen into his crystal English inkwell, and present it to him on a tray. If after all that the Prince actually did scratch something down, another of his servants would duck in after every few characters with a jade blotter. And when Rai Singh tired of his exercises his practice sheets would be hurried off to be copied down in several languages and finally bound in velvet folios and whisked off to his mother's apartments.

It was ridiculous on the face of it, but after a while I began to see the pathos of it. Rai Singh's privileges simultaneously exalted and trivialized his accomplishments, which, academically speaking, weren't even a match for mine, and sometimes, at his most vigorous, he would curse and swat at his servants, peering around as if to glimpse the world beyond them.

But perhaps on this subject, as I'll try to explain, I'm not to be trusted.

It has always amazed me the way people tend to pity their betters. I've known beggars in the street who worried terribly if the Maharao looked a little peaked passing by, and I've seen poor, squalid sweepers rejoice when their fat thakur had made a lucrative match for his youngest son.

I suppose you might argue that all this is in their interest: a sullen king might make life difficult for a beggar, a little of the baron's dowry might trickle down the gutter into the sweepers' reach. But I've noticed that when people have no hope they have a way of standing their thinking on its head, so that where you would expect to find envy and hatred you're likely to find pity and even a kind of tortured affection.

And so it was with me. I kept seeing Rai Singh's extreme good fortune as an affliction he suffered for the kingdom's sake. He may have been living a lazy man's dream, but was it his own dream, I wondered, or was he somehow caught, like the rest of us, in the wrong dream?

Rai Singh's dilemma will not cost me any sleep tonight, but in my waning youth it preyed on a weakness of mine for men of power and wealth that I mistook for an affinitive strength. I fancied that I had some mystical bond with my betters: an ineffable and immediate rapport. I regarded men of influence – 'dignitaries' as Moonshi used to call them – as I'm afraid I still regard beautiful women, which is as if I, alone among men, comprehend the awful burden of their beauty.

I suppose I have my mother to thank for this crippling notion, but my pity for Rai Singh was all that my pride could sustain as I now joined the flatterers, sycophants, and spies who trailed behind the heir apparent. Perhaps I hoped my pity might shield me a little from the shame of my lowliness in that strange, whisper-ridden, labyrinthine house the stars had made my home.

I've probably told you too much about Professor Perks. His lessons were the ballast of the day, but they counted for only a couple of hours or so, depending on Rai Singh's mood. For the rest of the day I waited on the Prince, and waited, and waited. And for what? I sometimes wondered.

His apartments were in Zalim Singh's own wing of the palace. The Maharao himself slept outside in a tent so elaborate it was more like a parchment house with two storeys supported by great carved posts all guyed with silken ropes shot through with golden thread. Here he slept to confound a jyotishi's benign prediction that Zalim Singh would die in his sleep, under his own roof.

But the Prince slept in a suite of rooms shimmering with mirrorwork and overlooking a tiered pleasure tank his father frequented on hot summer evenings. Here the son could catch the father at his manly revels; and the Queen, as always, could keep track of them both from behind her screens and spyholes.

Pratap Rao had the right of entry to Rai Singh's suite, but I had to wait on a little upholstered bench in the hall outside the door. I remember that the walls had been lined with decorative French paper that had bubbled and mildewed in the weather, and a line of ancestral portraits ran the whole length of the hall, accounting for every Maharao of Harigarh, from Zalim Singh all the way back to the dimpled moon itself.

Rai Singh's habits were regular enough. He liked the night hours, and stayed in bed until almost noon, at which time he would begin a toilette, including bath, shampoo, and massage, that lasted another hour or so. Then the doors of his suite would burst open and out would spill his servants, preparing his path to the Professor's apartments; whereupon Rai Singh would emerge with a perfumed flourish and climb into his brocade palanquin, bobbing off, languidly snacking on dates, as Pratap Rao, in grave impersonation of his father, fretfully trotted alongside, reminding the Prince of his appointments.

Rai Singh had been banished from his father's daily audiences, but halfway up the lane to Perks's cottage a squat Moslem functionary named Amiya always met him to report at a breathless trot on his highness's latest rulings. Rai Singh listened fondly, chuckling at his father's excesses or sadly shaking his head at the Maharao's posturing.

'Really, Father, you shouldn't have done that,' he would mutter, with feeling, gazing off as we reached the Professor's gate. 'That was not a kingly thing to do.'

After class Rai Singh would hurry back to his apartments to rest, and for the first few days I spent my afternoons on the upholstered bench, waiting for him to rise, but eventually returning to my own room to doze through the afternoon hours in my engulfing bed.

By the way, I don't mean to sound too lofty about Rai Singh's servants, for I too had more than my share. My uncle had a palanquin made available for my use, with six bearers to trot me about, and in addition to the usual complement of sweepers, water carriers, punkah wallas, and the like, a sorry second cousin of Moonshi was assigned to me as a body servant — a leering boy named Bisi who had mossy teeth and foul breath and a palsy that kept his head in constant nutation.

Toward the end of the afternoon Bisi would awaken me, and I would hurry back to await the Prince's emergence. His evenings were occupied by a whole range of occasions: banquets; nautches; fireworks displays; the opening of festivals; the anointing, on the Maharao's behalf, of the siege cannon, the fruit in the orchard, or the blind old rhinoceros, symbol of Harigarh's strength, that was kept chained by the city gates.

The most tedious evenings were spent at the banquets the Maharao was fond of throwing for whoever happened to be passing through the kingdom. Any rumpled white who stumbled into the hotel in town was a fair candidate for guest of honor at these affairs, but if he turned out to be someone of really dismal insignificance, the Maharao would duck out before the soup course, leaving his guests to eat course after course in wounded and bewildered silence.

It was at one of these affairs that my fancied affinity for dignitaries got me into trouble. I'd already noticed that when I began to attend the various gatherings of Zalim Singh's court and listened to some visiting personage — a railway engineer, a noble, a police inspector on holiday — I developed this sure conviction that he was addressing his remarks directly to me.

On this particular evening, not two weeks into my companionship to the Prince, I was standing in my accustomed place, behind Rai Singh's chair, when the guest of honor, a portraitist named Prinsep, interrupted his witless toast to the absent Maharao to complain that I had been impudently nodding and smiling as he spoke. Not only had I not meant anything by it, I hadn't even known I was doing it; but my uncle immediately banished me from the hall, and later lectured me on the value of composure.

But something in me was outraged that the querimonious little painter hadn't realized whom he'd been dealing with: a dignitary in his own right, a kindred spirit in servant's costume.

CHAPTER
58

My uncle sustained a pained and dutiful affection for his dead sister's son, and in addition to providing me with servants he paid me an allowance of five rupees a week – an enormous sum, it seemed to me, especially since I did nothing to earn it.

My mother's ghost occupied my uncle's house like a mist, and in the dark corridors her sorrow clung to me like dew. I looked for her among the framed photographs that littered my uncle's drawing room (an English affectation the Maharao had imposed on my uncle's house during one of his highness's Anglophile periods), but I found no sign of her, of course, nor of any other woman of the family: only tinted portraits of the Maharao and camera-wary cousins from neighboring kingdoms, gravures of the Queen Empress and various viceroys, group studies of the Maharao's cabinet, his thakurs, and his English guests arranged in sporting gear on the palace steps with a tiger or two laid out at their feet. Nor could I find any among all those faces that bore a fatherly resemblance to me.

I furtively cornered various servants, including Bansi Lal, Moonshi's father, and coaxed them into recalling my mother and the circumstances of her exile, but all I could pump from them was a few generic anecdotes – how beautiful she was as a little girl, how she skylarked in the orchard with her brother, how she was always gracious, truthful, and kindly. It seemed that as soon as she was nubile the household lost its memory, for there wasn't a soul in my uncle's house who would recollect for me why she departed and with whom.

I learned quickly never to raise the matter with my uncle, for it only pained him to hear my mother mentioned, and he would rise up and snap at me in wounded indignation.

Didn't I live in his house like a son? he asked me once, pounding the dinner table. Did I have to worry the wounds in his old heart as well? Did I have to drag the river for my mother's ashes? What would it tell me? What would it prove? Why would a young man with his whole life ahead of him seek his fate in the distant past?

This eventually shut me up, but I was never convinced by any of it. The gratitude I felt toward my uncle was as pained and dutiful as his affection for me, for in my heart I knew his was not my family; my real family still sought me out along the road. Otherwise why didn't he introduce me to his wife – my aunt – or any of his daughters, as if I were a true relation?

And for my part, how could I forgive my uncle for my mother's banishment when he still exiled her from his household's memory? I couldn't, and thus, despite all my uncle's hospitality, I set out to find my own place in the Maharao's palace, even if it might destroy my uncle's dreams.

So sometime in those first few months in Harigarh, I deemed Pratap Rao an unworthy rival for Rai Singh's affections, and resolved to become the most accomplished courtier in the Prince's entourage. Already my feet were losing their calluses and the hollows in my cheeks were filling in again, and thanks to Bisi's oil massages my skin grew sleek. I began to pay exorbitant attention to my appearance, and instructed Bisi to awaken me an hour earlier than before so I could devote that much more time to my toilette. It shames me to recall how I fussed over my whiskers and scolded the dhobi if he missed a wrinkle in my kammerband, but I suppose I needed all the confidence that a pleasing appearance could give me.

As the Prince napped in the afternoon I would climb into my palanquin and ride down into the city to spend my allowance on ornaments, with my bearers chuffing along fore and aft and Bisi singing my praises to clear our path.

'Shri Balbeer Rao Sahib approaches!' he'd call in his palsied voice, shaking a whisk at the traffic. 'Beloved nephew of esteemed Diwan Bhulwant Rao! Honored companion of the Crown Prince himself!'

People would lift their heads to see what all the bother was about at that sleepy hour of day, and a few would bow down as I trotted by. But I caused no particular stir, for the townspeople knew one noble from another and I didn't count for much.

The palace walls sent sound scuttering across the city, but Harigarh had no mills or factories, so there was none of Cawnpore's throb and hum. As in the country, sounds were always distinct and intimate. Close your eyes and you could hear a cock crow on one block, a tinker hammering on another. Here the confectioners' cauldrons bubbled, there a donkey blustered, a petty zemindar's camel padded across the paving stones; and you were just as apt to hear a kestrel give its stuttering cry hundreds of feet above the rooftops as see it poised on the crisp evening wind.

Near the brass workers' alley I stopped and dickered with the Moslem jewellers in their row of shops lined with white linen, haggling over ear studs and bracelets and medallions. And with whatever money I had left I would then proceed to the silk merchants' stalls in Shivaganj, where, as bolts of cloth were unravelled for my inspection, I could watch the elephants come down to bathe.

When the afternoon heat slackened off and the light along the surrounding cliffs turned gold, a bell would sound from the Maharao's ramparts and the townspeople, without so much as a break in their conversation, would casually clear the thoroughfare leading from the palace gates to Shiva's tank. And then the spiked gates would groan open and down would thunder an avalanche of elephants, dust puffing up from their parched backs along the whitewashed walls, trumpeting and pounding until they hurtled into the green soup of the sacred tank to loll and sigh as their mahouts climbed about, scrubbing their hides with brushes.

I saw more of the women of the palace in the market than in the palace itself, which is to say I stole a few glimpses of their sparkling silhouettes sometimes as their palanquins parked near mine, and occasionally, at a merchant's stall, would see a lady delicately point at a display case or hold up a few beringed fingers as she bargained for a bracelet or a wisp of embroidered veil, and the warm air would sweeten with the scent of jasmine and patchouli.

I didn't realize it at the time, but all I'd managed to do with my finery and ornaments was to render myself ever more invisible to the Prince, for my only distinction, after all, had been my vulgarity. I would have been hard pressed to say what Rai Singh thought of me after the first few months, if he thought of me at all. I suppose I remained a mild curiosity to him in Perks's class, and sometimes an irritation, for the Professor was always urging him to appreciate my attributes, which Rai Singh naturally resisted. He didn't seem any more interested in Pratap Rao, but he always turned to my cousin as his adviser, or at least his sounding board, if only out of habit.

Now I've already demonstrated my weakness for unrequited love, and though you might have hoped I'd learned my lesson with Sakuntala and been cured forever by Ahalya's undisguised affection, it seemed to remain a stubborn weakness in my character. It's not too much to say that I was infatuated with Rai Singh, and my obsession deepened with every hint of his indifference to me. I am a fool for beauty, and Rai Singh was beautiful: not only in appearance but in manner and speech. He always spoke with perfect poise, and his gaze was as unblinking as a baby's.

I had never had a passion for a man before, and this troubled me deeply, but sometimes, gazing at him as he practiced tabla in the garden, or frowned handsomely over his exercise books, or fed his stallion from his own hand, I yearned to win his heart as if he were a woman.

The only virtue of my station by the Prince's door was that it at least afforded me a view of some of the palace's inner traffic. There were always servants bustling about, but the traffic didn't really pick up until late at night, when the Maharao banished everyone from his revels but his latest importation of courtesans, and my uncle would station himself in the hall of private audience and receive the barons of Harigarh, who paced and skulked along the corridors, whispering and haggling and hatching plots.

The Maharao's thakurs had once been loyal and ferocious

clansmen whose exploits against the Afghanis and Timurids were legendary. One of my own ancestors, Bika Rao, pursued his foe so single-mindedly that even after he'd been decapitated his head chewed through a foot soldier's jugular while his body climbed up the side of an elephant and drove a spear through his mahout.

But then the Moghul and the Mahratta empires crumbled, and in all of Rajputana it was as if the gates of a menagerie had been thrown down and every beast let loose. The maharaos ran out of proper thakurs and traded their jagirs for the protection of moneylenders and bandit chieftains. By the time the British stepped in, all but one of Harigarh's seven jagirs (seven if you counted Jagat Deo's realm, which had shrunk in my time to a brothel on the outskirts of Shivaganj) had fallen into the hands of banias and scoundrels.

The Maharao detested them, and one of his entertainments was to humiliate them whenever possible at his morning durbars, and refuse all that they asked, no matter how reasonable. Had he been a gifted king he would have seen that this played into his wife's hands, for the barons soon learned to send their wives into the zenana to plead their cases with the queen. Tarra Bai would then dispatch one of the Maharao's serving girls – always the youngest of the bunch, I'm afraid, for such were the Maharao's tastes – with orders to use her every wile to persuade his highness to change his mind.

The one exception was Madho Bhau, the last of the Maharao's clansman thakurs. He rarely left his bleak jagir on the edge of the Thar to visit the capital, but he always made memories when he did. One evening I was dozing on my upholstered bench when I heard the unaccountable clatter of horse's hoofs down the hall, and sure enough, skidding around the corner along the polished marble floor came Madho Bhau himself on his old charger, chasing stray courtiers with a battle cry on his lips and a battered scimitar upraised.

Everywhere Madho Bhau passed the townsfolk would cheer him and the sentries along the ramparts would seem to come alive. Zalim Singh loved Madho Bhau as if the old man were his father (which, for all I knew, he may have been) and forgave him all his quirks, even when, during a nautch I witnessed from my uncle's house, the old man stood up, all battle scars and whiskers, and raged up at Tarra

Bai's window, declaring it wasn't pearls she wore about her pretty neck but the testicles of Harigarh's nobility, and drunkenly dropping his trousers to prove that his, at least, were still intact.

For nearly a year I trailed forlornly behind my splendid Prince, and by the following winter I had just about given up hope of ever impressing Rai Singh.

Then one hot morning the Professor had us sit outside in his garden while he tried to explain the economics of farming. I remember I had a headache, for I'd drunk some of the Professor's port the evening before, following another of the Maharao's inscrutable banquets.

Perks was having no luck making Rai Singh understand the difference between subsistence farming and farming for profit, and seemed just about ready to tear at his hair in frustration when I suggested I might help. It had occurred to me that Rai Singh not only didn't know the difference between subsistence and profit, he didn't know, exactly, what farming was. In fact, as I demonstrated with a few quick questions, he had no idea where most of his food came from, the exceptions being game, which he shot, and fruit, which grew in his father's orchard.

He had no inkling, for instance, that bread was made from flour, which, in turn, was made from wheat, and I had to explain, as Perks sat by, all about plowing and sowing and harvesting, threshing and grinding and all the rest of it.

Rai Singh was astounded that people would work so hard for so simple a thing as bread, and his ignorance afforded me a perfect opportunity to show off my knowledge of a world unknown to him. But as I described all that labor to a prince who'd never worked at anything, as far as I could tell, and I recalled how Channa used to toil in the fields around Bhondaripur, trusting that Scindhia, his king, watched over him like a father, I grew vehement, and ended by saying, 'And *that's* how you get your fancy cakes, your excellency — from the sweat of your people!'

Well, no sooner were these words out of my lips than I was trying to swallow them back again.

'It – it's the sun, your excellency. This headache. I'm afraid I've spoken too –'

But already Rai Singh had risen from his bolsters and stamped his slippered foot.

'You are excused from my company, Balbeer Rao,' he said, tugging at the lace of his collar.

'Y-your excellency,' I stammered, rising to my knees and bowing as Rai Singh's servants swarmed about, snatching up his cushions. 'I meant no – '

'Pratap Rao?' he snapped, turning his back to me. 'We must go.'

And with that he crisped his fingers at his bustling servants and marched off to his palanquin.

I assumed from Pratap Rao's victorious smirk as he trotted off beside his prince that my political ambitions, if that's what they were, now lay in ruins.

'Pity,' was all I gave the Professor time to say as I hurried out of the garden and stumbled back to my uncle's house in a fog of shame and hopelessness.

Within an hour of my return to my dim room I had sent Bisi out to buy me a packet of the best ganja he could find, and through the interminable afternoon I puffed on my hubble-bubble until, as in my mendicant days, the hemp fog had obscured my despair. Perhaps I might yet rejoin Nanda on the road to bliss, I thought as Bisi undressed me and dragged me up into bed, and I dozed off into the most confounding dream.

CHAPTER

59

I dreamed I was curled up on a barge amid a heap of cushions, floating along a river. It was nighttime, but the sky was bright from a great conflagration along the bank. A pig sat at the helm, squealing at the distant flames, and then I rose and touched his shoulder and he turned toward me, and his face was not a pig's face any longer but my own, and the barge began to rock and spin, throwing me into the stream.

I fought against the current, trying to swim toward the ashen shore, and that's how Rai Singh found me, scrambling and gasping in my sheets.

He jabbed me awake with a riding crop and stood over me in a beam of moonlight, glaring down in his purple silks.

'Get dressed,' he snapped, and stood impatiently out on the balcony, slapping at his boots with his black quirt as I fumbled into my clothes.

So this was how I was to be banished, I thought, taking a final look around my room as he silently led me into the hall, stepping over Bisi, asleep on the threshold.

I staggered after him down the stairs and out into my uncle's courtyard, where Hala Deo, the guard who'd first brought me to the palace, awaited with three moonstruck stallions. Rai Singh and Hala Deo leapt onto their mounts, and the Prince commanded me to mount the other.

'B-but, your excellency,' I said, slowly climbing on the stallion's back. 'My uncle. I should tell him goodbye.'

'No time for that, *maharaj*,' he sneered, as if addressing a fraudulent sadhu, and laid his crop across my stallion's backside.

We clattered out of my uncle's yard and down the steep, cobbled incline to the palace gates, where the Prince's chief bearer waited in ambush, struggling into his clothes. But before he could catch hold of Rai Singh's bridle the Prince had spurred past him with a joyous shout and we hurtled through the city, scattering the jackals that roamed the deserted streets.

Now I was no horseman, despite my rides on my little country mare back in Bhondaripur, but my stallion had a smooth gait, and followed Rai Singh like a dog as Hala Deo galloped behind us both.

The town fell back into desolation, and we turned off the main road onto a little lane that twisted so sharply through hills of stone that I had to cling for dear life to my stallion's neck.

The lane straightened out into a broad road that led us finally onto a plain. In the moonlight up ahead I could see a village, and a farmer plowing with his bullocks in the middle of a desultory field, raising a dusty ghost behind him.

Rai Singh turned off the road, leapt a culvert, and headed straight across the field, reining his stallion to a halt before the astonished farmer, who fell prostrate before him.

My stallion stopped with Rai Singh's, and just as suddenly, and I toppled over his thick neck and tumbled headlong onto the broken ground.

Now as you know I had often before believed my time had come, but now I was sure of it. 'All I ask,' I said, rising to my feet as Hala Deo advanced upon me with his hand on the hilt of his scimitar, 'all I ask is that you be quick about it.'

But Rai Singh wasn't listening, nor even looking in my direction. He was stepping over the whimpering farmer and peering at the bullock team.

'Now what is this?' he asked, running his hand along the stock of the plow.

In the far distance I could see people gathering at the edge of the village, and heard them muttering, though they all held back.

I stood as straight as I could to receive Hala Deo's blade, glad at least that someone would witness my execution, gladder still that they were villagers.

'Balbeer, maharaj,' said Rai Singh, circling the bullocks and the plow, 'I asked you a question.'

I dared to glance at Hala Deo and saw him standing with his sword yet undrawn. 'Y-your excellency?' I said weakly.

'Is it a *plow?*' asked Rai Singh with a light flaring in his eyes. 'Is *this* what you were talking about?'

I took a tentative step toward Rai Singh as Hala Deo nodded to me to answer.

'Uh, yes,' I said, meeting Rai Singh's delighted gaze.

'A plow . . . ' he murmured, running his quirt along a bullock's spine. 'And with this they make all these furrows?'

'Yes,' I said, recovering my breath. 'That's right.'

'How?' asked Rai Singh. 'Show me how.'

'Show you how, your excellency?'

'Yes, maharaj,' he said. 'You think you know so much. Show me how to use this thing.'

I paused a moment longer. Could that be all this was about? A midnight's diversion for the Crown Prince?

'Well?' said Rai Singh, sticking his riding crop under his kammerband and grabbing hold of the plow.

'Well,' I said, picking up the farmer's goad where he'd dropped it. 'First of all, you have to loop the reins around your shoulder.'

'Like so?' he asked, but he fumbled with the reins and I had to untangle them for him.

'Now press down on the stock so that the blade digs in,' I said, warming to my instruction.

'Yes,' said Rai Singh. 'I have it. Now what?'

'Now,' I said, handing him the farmer's goad, 'just give them a crack across the rump.'

'Like so?' asked Rai Singh, striking the bullocks, and suddenly he was off, bumping through the field.

Anyone who's ever driven a team and plow can tell you it isn't easy. Guiding two reluctant bullocks on a straight course while you're stumbling over great hard clods of upturned earth and pressing with all your weight to keep the blade from slipping out of the sun-baked crust is the most grueling labor there is, so it was no wonder, especially in the dark, that after a few yards Rai Singh fell and was dragged along, clinging to the plow's stock.

So Hala Deo and I chased after the bullocks as they veered off toward the village with the plow bumping along and Rai Singh still holding tight in a tangle of reins.

We finally pulled them to a halt not a hundred feet from the village throng. There was a hush as the slender Prince painfully rose to his feet, with his silks all caked and torn, and then a great cheer arose as he rigged himself up over our protests and tried again, albeit on a lateral course across the field, and fell again, and tried again to master the team, until he'd scribbled furrows all up and down the little field and finally collapsed, laughing like a schoolboy, on the broken ground.

'So, maharaj?' he asked me as Hala Deo and I pulled him to his feet. 'Do you see how Rai Singh labors for his fancy cakes?'

'Yes, your excellency,' I said, bowing low, and I could feel my love for him set like mortar.

He was alive with questions as the villagers gathered around – children first, then their fathers and grandfathers, and then the women lined up along an outer circle.

'Why in God's name do you plow at night?' he asked an old farmer, who took a while to find his voice.

'I'm an old man, huzoor,' he said. 'In the old days we plowed at night to hide from the Pindaris. Now it's a habit, and spares me the heat of the day.'

'And the land here,' said Rai Singh, slapping the dust from his sleeves. 'Is it any good?'

The farmer shrugged. 'Not any more, huzoor,' he said.

'No? Why not?'

'Forgive me, huzoor,' said the farmer as the villagers pressed closer to listen. 'But it's these Feringhee. In the old days we were always being raided. First the Mahrattas, then the Pindaris – always somebody. So a lot of land was left uncultivated. That made it fertile. Now there's no more raids, so we cultivate too much.'

'It's true,' said another old farmer, stepping forward. He stood as straight as a latthi and looked evenly into Rai Singh's face, so I assume he must have been the headman. 'And the Feringhee make men swear on Ganga water, and on the Koran, and even on their own black book, and all kinds of lies are told upon them, and they rob the land of the blessings of God!'

He seemed to startle himself with this outburst and melted back into the throng as Rai Singh paced awhile, contemplating all he'd heard.

'And what do you think, maharaj?' he said, turning to me.

I looked around at the villagers. 'I think these are Rajputs, your excellency,' I said. 'And I'd no more try to turn a Rajput into a farmer than a bow into a pestle.'

It was an old saw, but everybody laughed, the Prince included, and we drank opium with the elders on charpoys set out for us on the broken field, and then we climbed on our horses and galloped off, chasing down the sinking moon.

It was a night beyond imagining, and I suspect, though all the principals but me are dead, that somewhere in that country, even as I write, a villager is offering incense to Rai Singh, the Farmer's Prince, in painted effigy.

Rai Singh and I rode in tandem through the awakening town, laughing and singing on a wave of opium, and I rode like such a true Rajput, said the Prince, that he made me a gift of my stallion and dubbed him Hunza at the palace steps.

He took me with him to his apartments, and caused a great commotion in his filthy, tattered silks. The two of us bathed amid a swarm of horrified servants who gasped at every bruise and scratch they found upon him, and clothed me in one of his sets of shirt and trousers, cut in the Moghul style.

They installed us in an alcove lined with mirrorwork that cast the morning light upon us in shimmering constellations as we breakfasted on fruits of all kinds, and a yogurt pudding I still remember that was mixed with saffron and pistachios, and curried partridge that the Prince had bagged himself on the Rajshikari Road. Through a window framed in Punjabi lace we could see the aftermath of the Maharao's revels, the waters of his pleasure tank littered with petals and candles, slippers and strips of silk. And all through breakfast Rai Singh and I chattered like reunited friends, recalling the night's adventure.

Now I hope I'll be forgiven for dwelling for a moment on the look on Pratap Rao's face when he arrived that morning at his usual hour to find me dining with his prince. At first his face still bore the marks of smug satisfaction at my downfall in the Professor's garden, which he must have savoured all night. And then he saw me, and his eyebrows bunched up his pimpled forehead and his dull eyes flinched and his jaw dropped slowly, like a drawbridge.

'Pratap Rao,' said Rai Singh, oblivious to my cousin's dismay. 'Come join us. We were just discussing plows. Balbeer tells me that in his country they are fitted with iron blades. Isn't that so, Balbeer? While our people are still using wood. Something to think about, wouldn't you say, Pratap Rao? Make a note of it, will you?'

Pratap Rao still gaped at me and slowly raised the ledger he carried, crisping his fingers for a pen.

'And this jowar they're planting. Balbeer says they plant too much of it. Should be sowing more wheat, and we should be storing it for them against the next famine. Does my father know? Has he made plans for this?'

Pratap Rao swallowed and tried to regroup his wits. 'Uh, why, yes, your excellency. That is, I'm not certain. You see, he – '

'Well, I think he should know about it. All this fodder they're growing – you'd think our people were still nomads, herding sheep. We have other mouths to feed. Cash crops – that's what you said, isn't it, Balbeer?'

'Yes, your excellency,' I said, showing off my familiarity. 'But I thought you were too drunk to remember.'

Pratap Rao jammed his nib into a page of his ledger as Rai Singh laughed, slapping his knees and abruptly rising to his feet. 'Oh, Pratap Rao, what a night I've had. I've got to tell old Perks about it!'

And with that he was hurrying out into the sunshine with me by his side, as Pratap trailed among the servants.

Perks was delighted to see me resurrected, for he'd always been my champion, and listened proudly to Rai Singh's chatter.

'See, I *knew* you'd be friends, you two,' he said. 'It was bound to happen.'

CHAPTER
60

For some reason Perks imagined I would be a healthy influence on Rai Singh, and I suppose I was. But I still wonder if he was a good influence on me, or more to the point, if I was a good influence on myself.

We became inseparable — like lovers, it was mischievously whispered, though there was no truth to that — but our mutual devotion was unequal in at least one respect, for I found that the more I had to lose, the more circumspect I became about my past. I knew Rai Singh in all his aspects, for he kept nothing from me, not even the counsel of his mother, Tarra Bai, when he returned from his daily pilgrimages to her apartments. But he knew Balbeer Rao only as an aspiring courtier with a mysterious past out of which I could conjure all manner of knowledge, from methods of irrigation to the habits of the Aghoris, the carrion sadhus who haunted the palace gates. No matter how hard he tried to pry my history from me, I clung to my precious mystique.

As I strove to better myself, all my old mother-borne conceits were confirmed, and I acquired a proprietary air in my progress along the palace corridors, flourishing my sleeves and barking at the servants, including poor, palsied Bisi, who was much taken by my self-importance and became deferential to the point of reverence as he ministered to me.

On those mornings when I didn't awaken in the Prince's apartments themselves I would often find Bisi waiting with a new set of clothes for me, courtesy of Rai Singh, and I would dress quickly, with less fretting and fussing as my confidence grew, and hurry to the Prince's apartments in time to awaken him and marshal his servants through his languid toilette.

Every morning, as servants bathed and bedecked him as if he were a sacred idol, the Prince received the humbug gurus it amused the Maharao to send along for the Prince's instruction. Having been a charlatan sadhu myself, I had no patience with them, but Rai Singh was promiscuous in his philosophy and equably entertained, at least for the moment, whatever notions they were peddling.

There were jogis who came in smelling of camphor and sandal-wood to promulgate their theories about the life force and the illusion of existence and the all-seeing inner eye and all the rest of it, and exalt their cosmic insignificance. Some were supple men who would deliver their lectures only from the most appalling postures, with their limbs all twisted about and their heads upside down. Others were more specific in their austerities, and ran spikes through their tongues and cheeks without bleeding (with luck; one of them — a nervous, pockmarked youth from Jhansi — bled so profusely from his tongue that the barber had to be summoned to cauterize it).

A favorite of the Prince's was Ommi, a middle-aged jogi from Gujarat, who used to set himself up on the middle of the floor and tie his private parts into various decorative knots, and then dress them up like puppets, depicting different scenes from the life of Shiva. And in something of the same vein, there was a nameless Sakti from the Vindhya range who reminded me of old Mata and his disciples. He was the Prince's chief instructor in the art of love, though he made it sound like more of a chore, if you ask me, and mixed up his theology with carnality.

As far as he was concerned, sex had no value unless the woman suggested in her nudity the 'revelation of the cosmic mystery.' Like Nanda, he had womankind all dissected and quantified, but puffed them up with pious imagery, so that his description of a woman's pubis, for instance, consisted of a sacrificial altar covered with kusa grass. Lying with a woman was supposed to be an act of spiritual enlightenment, embodying a kind of dream state where everything became one. He also took a lot of stock in not spilling one's seed, which he suggested Rai Singh accomplish by meditating, when necessary, on a deity's flaccid pud.

I don't mean to suggest that Rai Singh wasn't manly, but he had an awfully detached attitude toward women, if you don't count his mother among them. The Sakti appealed to him, I think, because he legitimized the Prince's own obliviousness to the other sex. I believe this was a consequence of Rai Singh's own beauty, which few maidens could match, but he never hungered after any of the girls his father sent him, only serviced them dutifully and sent them on their way.

He taught me how to ride Hunza in the true Rajput manner, kicking off the stirrups and dropping the reins and guiding him about with my heels. As we rode out into the villages of the kingdom I used to lecture him on the evils of the thakurs' rule, though as zemindar of Bhondaripur I'd been a kind of petty thakur myself. Rai Singh's simple insistence that the universe make sense, as Perks promised us it should, was the key to his better nature; and as we rode home from the sowing and the harvesting he railed against the larcenous barons who truly ruled his people, and we would lie around his apartments some evenings and plot their downfall with righteousness and ardor as the Prince's servants brought us our khusamba.

Rai Singh imported a kite maker from Delhi so I could teach his excellency the art of flying battle kites. But the artisan was a snobbish old Moslem who refused to make the humble kites I remembered from my rooftop wars in Cawnpore, and instead fashioned ever more elaborate contraptions I could barely control. Still, Rai Singh and I spent many hours together flying the artisan's creations from the roof of the Hall of Audience, and I remember one Diwali when the kite maker presented us with a huge flying lantern that we sailed out among the stars, with the townspeople cheering from the illuminated streets below.

I taught Rai Singh to swim just as I had learned, in a buffalo wallow we chanced upon one hot afternoon, and thereafter we sometimes dived from the Prince's balcony into the Maharao's tank below, and searched the bottom for the trinkets that accumulated there from his father's revels.

We went hunting in the wintertime, along the borderlands of the Maharao's hunting preserve, with a shikar and a few beaters and the Prince's servants following with lunch. We hunted black buck and cheetah and whatever else the beaters scared up, with twin Belgian shotguns.

I was a poor shot, perhaps because I had so little heart for sport, and most especially for the death throes of the Prince's prey. But this is not to say I was more merciful, for there was nothing merciful about my bungled shots; on occasion the shikari would have to chase for miles after some poor beast I'd wounded, and finish him with a clean shot to the heart.

The Maharao brought the Prince and me along on only one grand shikar, and that at the insistence of his weekend guest, the Governor of Rajputana, a great, florid former public-school head-master who shared Perks's hopes for Rai Singh's accession but terrified everyone with his bellowed lectures on hygienic food preparation at the banquet in his honor.

The shikar was not a success. We started off in grand fashion, with the Maharao's hunting leopards, a dozen elephants, an army of beaters, and a city of tents erected out among the ruins of a thakur's fortress, equipped with all the modern conveniences, even a stone fireplace for the Governor's tent, with a brace of express rifles mounted over the Queen's portrait on the mantel. The beaters managed to corral a fair number of panicked game near a little defile a mile or so from camp. But by then the morning had already been ruined.

The Governor had brought along his favorite retriever and his wife, both of whom he doted on, stroking their heads and speaking to them in baby talk, like an ayah. But when the Maharao ordered his cheetahs let loose they mistook the retriever for a deer, I think, and promptly killed it. The Governor tearfully demanded that the cheetahs be destroyed, but the Maharao refused, and sent the beasts back to the palace, encouraging the Governor to vent his grief on the prey that now darted into view. But the Governor's wife, who unaccountably shared my howdah, panicked as a boar ran by and fired her shotgun into the bush, striking Balu Singh, the eldest shikari, in the shoulder.

At the hunting dinner that night the Maharao tried to cheer the Governor with a toast, commending him for the purity of his devotion to his wife. 'I myself am too coarse,' he said, 'to love such a homely woman.'

Rai Singh was pained by his father's boorishness, and at these moments I could see him straining to keep from interceding. Zalim Singh had his vestigial, ancestral sense that he was an autonomous king, beholden to no one, least of all a pallid distant queen. However much he tried to impress her agents, and vie for their attention with his fellow princes, he was the Maharao of Harigarh – which was not much smaller than England itself – and tried to regard Victoria as his equal.

But Rai Singh didn't share his father's resentment of the English. I never heard him speak of them as gora or even Feringhee. To him they were simply the English, and a worthy power to answer to.

I suppose the British thanked Perks's benign influence for this, but the truth was that Rai Singh was too secure to be ambitious in the usual sense. He believed he'd been born to rule Harigarh – a conviction his mother did everything in her power to reinforce – but I don't think he would have deigned to struggle for the throne if he'd had to.

Of course, he didn't have to, for to everyone but his father his destiny was manifest, and his mother was his protecting star.

In the summer the Maharao languished among his fountains, defeating the heat in the tepid draft that was drawn up from the palace cellars through a system of stone shafts engineered hundreds of years before by Zalim Singh's ancestors. But the rest of us were left to swelter in our apartments, with nothing but doused, moldy punkahs and window shutters with which to battle the harsh Rajput sun. Perks was so afflicted with prickly heat that one day he actually had to be bound in wet sheets to keep from scratching himself to death, and only the choking fumes of incense coiling through the Prince's chambers could keep the flies at bay.

The heat had been worse in Bhondaripur, but there was something about the indolence of palace life, the expectation of comfort and convenience, that made it all the more unbearable, and by late June I was urging the Prince to retreat to the Maharao's summer palace in Mt. Abu. His mother opposed the idea, because for her purposes she needed to have both her despised husband and her beloved son in one place, where she could keep an eye on them.

Perhaps it was the sadhu in me that longed for a change of scene, but I felt I would suffocate if I had to stay in Harigarh any longer, wallowing in the Prince's tub, sleeping in wet sheets, staring up at the punkah as it stirred the air overhead. So I presented the idea as a challenge to Rai Singh's autonomy. When was he going to stop listening to his mother? I asked him. When was he going to be his own man?

And so Rai Singh petitioned his father for permission, which Zalim Singh granted, and good riddance, and we set off by train for the summer palace.

As we rode in a special coach lent to us by the Maharaja of Jodhpur, Rai Singh grew more and more fretful and talked incessantly about his mother, but I was too fascinated by Jodhpur's coach to listen. It was outfitted with English parlor furniture and gilt gas lamps and a special Kashmiri carpet woven to fit around the desks and tables that had been bolted to the floor. Poor Perks came with us, but he spent the journey in a salted bath to soothe his prickly heat, and Pratap Rao was relegated to a little open vestibule where he rode in mortal terror of the roar of the locomotive and the lurch and clatter of the tracks as we sped across Rajputana.

The summer palace was in fact a rambling English frame house set on the slope of a hill and overlooking a broad tank, purchased, on a whim, from a Mewar thakur of declining fortunes.

Mt. Abu was Rajputana's hill station, for though it was never as cool as Simla or Mussoorie, it was easily reached and there was always a breeze blowing across the lake. I revelled in the crisp air of the palace gardens, and led Rai Singh among the shrubs and flowers, enjoying our freedom from Harigarh's oppression. But Rai Singh was little cheered, and our first night I awoke to find him hunched over his desk in his apartments, writing to his mother.

Mt. Abu was frequented by many Rajput princes, who vied for the favor of the Raj with balls and banquets. Even at his most sullen and homesick, Rai Singh was a great favorite at these affairs, and such was his beauty and his grasp of English that he could charm even the lipless memsahibs from the civil service who shied away from native princes.

It was on one of these occasions that I met the future Maharaja of Bikaneer, who spoke in an accent he claimed was Greek, owing, he said, to his descent from Alexander the Great, who'd passed through his kingdom in his campaign across the Indus. And I conversed one evening with the Raja of Tonk, a pinched little man who wore a mantel clock in his turban with reversed face and works so that he could tell the time with a pocket mirror.

There was another whose name I can't recall just now, but who had recently invited one hundred thousand paying guests to the wedding of a pebble to a bush, employing a dozen elephants, hundreds of camels and horses, and costing hundreds of thousands of rupees. My dinner partner one evening was the sinister Raja of Ludora, who'd accumulated great wealth by hiring his richest subjects as diwans, promptly executing them for transgressions, and thereupon seizing their estates.

'You are well on your way to the prime ministership!' he told me over sherbet, and it was the one time I faltered in my campaign to become diwan.

And another evening the Prince and I were entertained by the future Maharaja of Alwar, whose grandfather had given the imbecile Maharao Bhijay Singh his fatal brassière. Assuming, I suppose, that Bhijay Singh's inclinations had been passed along to his grandson, the Maharajkumar offered Rai Singh first a hermaphrodite, then two pubescent Kashmiri boys, and finally the services of a lewd, shaved monkey, all of which Rai Singh politely declined, pleading constipation.

Rai Singh didn't take much interest in anything except the Maharao's broad, turtle-shaped barge, which we would take out in the evening to cruise the lake as nautch girls entertained us from the bow. 'Girls' was what the English called them, but in fact these were rather elderly, and I always found their dancing a little dreary.

But the Prince's interest in them was purely musical, anyway, and he found much solace in their song as he accompanied them on tabla. And to the tug and gurgle of the boatmen's oars I would dream of the day when I would become the Diwan of Harigarh, as Pratap Rao watched forlornly from the shore. I would move the court to Mt. Abu and make my Prince of the Plow the glory of his people.

CHAPTER 61

Late one year the Maharao was invited to Delhi to attend the grand
review in honor of Albert Edward, the Prince of Wales, who was
touring his mother's empire. But the Maharao's astrologer forbade
him to travel on account of an impending collision in his highness's
stars, so Zalim Singh invited the Prince to visit Harigarh instead.

But the best Perks could manage was to arrange for the Prince's
train to pause somewhere in Harigarh's vicinity on its way to Jaipur.
So a great pavilion was erected in the wastes that lay where the
Rajputana line looped down twenty miles or so from town, and there
he gathered his court on a dry and windy February day. The
Maharao sat on his travelling throne in the center of the pavilion,
with a long Turkish carpet leading to the tracks. At Perks's insistence, Rai Singh stood beside him, joined at my uncle's insistence by
Pratap Rao, and at Rai Singh's insistence by me. The barons, even
including old Madho Bhau, flanked us with their respective suites,
and behind them stood the balance of the court, flanked, in turn, by a
row of the Maharao's elephants, with bards and conch blowers
intermingling and a vast crowd of the Maharao's subjects spread
across the hillsides. Cannon were set up to fire the salute from a
nearby peak, and the Maharao's soldiers stood along the track in
whatever they'd managed to find in the palace armory: a variety of
chain mail, shields, harness, and spiked basinets. For all the dust the
crowd kicked up and the elephants raised with their impatient snorts
and swaying, we must have been a splendid tableau out there among
the barren hills, awaiting Victoria's son.

Perks paced and fretted in blue-and-red livery a size too big and
a white plumed helmet jammed down above his spectacles. Gifts for
the Prince of Wales lined the Turkestani carpet: astronomical
instruments, a volume of Scottish poems illustrated by the Maharao's
own portraitist and set on a silver bookstand, a small jade cannon, a
rifle disguised as a spear, swords, shields, chests, models of the

palace, and a gilded armilary globe with jewels representing the celestial spheres.

But evidently this was not enough, as Perks found out a minute or so before the train was due, when he happened to spy something trembling beneath the Maharao's throne and dragged out a little figure cloaked in spangled silks.

'Your highness,' said Perks, clutching his pocket watch and backing off from the sparkling apparition as it knelt down before him, 'What is *this*?'

'Merely a gift for Albert Edward,' replied the Maharao, pouting a little now that the surprise was spoiled.

'Wh-what kind of gift?' asked Perks, gaping down the track as a puff of smoke rose in the distance.

'The best kind,' said Zalim Singh with a broad wink. 'A little something for Bertie, man to man.'

Perks seemed to turn grey as the train whistle blew and the crowd behind us began to cheer. 'You − you can't mean − a *concubine*?'

'A concubine?' asked Zalim Singh, looking hurt. 'Not yet, I should say not. She's the sweetest flower of the lot. I've never laid a hand on her. She'll be Bertie's flower to pluck.'

'Bertie's flower to pluck,' Perks mumbled back, staring down at the trembling figure as the train pulled into view.

'But this is *impossible*, your highness,' he squeaked, with his helmet all awry.

'For Maharao Zalim Singh,' said my uncle, suddenly darting forward, '*nothing* is impossible!'

'*Thank* you, Bhulwant Rao,' said Zalim Singh, primly inspecting himself in a hand mirror.

By now we could see the banners that festooned the locomotive. The conch blowers began to play, and many dancing drummers, and the bards chanted their eulogiums as countrymen fired their muskets into the sky.

Perks glanced back and forth between the concubine and the impending train, and then his eyes fixed on the little signalmen who stood nearby, semaphoring to the engineer, and I could see the Professor arrive at a desperate decision.

As the train began to slow between the rows of pickets, Perks threw his watch to the pavilion floor and wrested the flags from the signalman, and standing tall, with his helmet falling from his speckled head, he waved the royal coaches past.

And all we saw of the Prince of Wales was a bearded man peering through the window at our stupefied tableau, like a plump prawn in a crystal bowl.

Perks watched as the train ground by, and slowly turned to face the Maharao. And here is how I shall always remember him, standing at frail attention in the dust and cinders, with his pocket watch at his feet, all shattered and sprung.

Rai Singh blamed his father, not Perks, for spoiling the reception, and for myself I thought Perks had done a noble thing, sparing both of his employers. But the humiliation plunged Zalim Singh into a murderous rage, and he charged home on his elephant, ordering his guards to set fire to the pavilion.

Rai Singh and I rode our stallions off the road and into the hills, losing Pratap Rao after a mile or so, and reaching the palace before any of the rest of the Maharao's suite. The Prince trembled for Professor Perks, for the only time he'd seen his father in such a state was about six years before when his polo team had been defeated by Alwar's lancers. For days afterward the Maharao had been utterly silent, and it wasn't until half his team had disappeared from the kingdom and a fire had broken out in the pony stables, with many mounts lost, that Zalim Singh was his merry old self again.

Rai Singh and I were too dispirited to dine together that evening, and I returned to my room in my uncle's house, now heaped with trunks full of Rai Singh's gifts and decorated with heroic frescoes at the Prince's own expense. As I fell off to sleep I vowed I would stand by Perks in the morning, no matter how ferocious the Maharao's rage.

I slept fitfully, and had such dreams that I couldn't tell if I heard wails of laughter on the air that night, screams or song trailing the cold, sharp wind. An hour before dawn I gave up on sleep and was sitting on my bed, tossing cowrie shells against the footboard to divine my luck, when I heard something shift across the floor.

It was still dark enough that I had to stare hard into the corner of the room to see one of the studded trunks slipping along like a ship.

I stood up on my bed, knocking my head on the netting frame. 'Wh-who is it?' I cried out. 'What are you?'

The trunk abruptly stopped, and I could hear a childish whimpering rising from its shadow.

I bent down and fumbled under my pillow for my dagger.

'Please, huzoor,' someone whispered behind the trunk.

'Show yourself!' I commanded, finding the dagger at last and pulling it from its sheath.

'Yes, huzoor,' came the reply, and up rose Albert Edward's concubine, cowering in what was left of her spangled silks.

She was taller than she'd seemed at the pavilion, and stood with her henna hands pressed together and her dark eyes downcast, as if in prayer. Under the torn remains of her cloak she wore a dancer's gauze pantaloons and a thin choli in the Gujarati style that left the undersides of her breasts exposed.

'How did you get in here?' I asked, lowering my dagger somewhat.

'Please, huzoor,' she said, kneeling down. 'Don't tell them I'm here.'

I warily stepped around her and peered into the space where the trunk had been, and there I found a hole in the wall, disguised by a panel coated with plaster and painted to match the surrounding wall.

'Where does this lead?'

She dared to glance back at me for a moment, and her eyes flashed with tears in the gathering light. 'T-to the labyrinth, huzoor,' she said. 'I'll go back. Just don't tell the Queen.'

She made as if to return to the hole in the wall, but I blocked her path and called for Bisi, still gripping my dagger before her.

She gasped with a hunted look about her and lunged for the balcony, as if to cast herself down the palace wall, but I caught her wrist as she tried to pass and flung her into the overstuffed chair, where she sat glaring at me in a cloud of dust that rose from the seat cushion.

'You can't go out there,' I said. 'Someone will see you.'

'Please, huzoor,' she said, suddenly abject again, and I have to confess that she aroused me a little with this attitude. 'Don't tell them

I came to you. Let me rest here. *Please*. I'll do anything.'

I caught myself staring at her and pondering the possibilities she presented, but I tried to shake them off, pacing a moment around her.

'What do you want with me?' I finally asked. 'Why did you come here?'

'For-forgive me, huzoor,' she said, rising from the chair and bowing to me. 'I didn't mean to. I didn't know where I was going. The Maharao fell asleep at last. I had to get away.'

'The Maharao? You were with the Maharao?'

She shuddered and raised her face to me, and now I could see a tiny rivulet of blood at the side of her lips, and then I caught sight of the little abrasion on her throat, as if someone had ripped a necklace from her, and then a bruise in the flesh of her waist: all rather artful, as in a miniature, now that I think back on it, but appalling at the time.

'And *he* did this?' I asked, gently, inadvertently reaching toward her.

She flinched and crouched down as if in sudden pain, and I led her to the bed and fetched her a wet cloth from my bathing bowl.

She allowed me to dab gently at her mouth and her long, pale neck as she curled up on her side and told me all about her night with the Maharao.

She said her name was Meera, and her father had traded her to the Maharao in exchange for a franchise to sell opium to the guard. She'd been kept in the zenana for some months as a treat the Maharao was saving up for himself when Holi came around. But only two days ago he had changed his mind, and bade his wives to prepare Meera for presentation to the Prince of Wales.

Upon returning that evening from the débâcle by the tracks, the Maharao had summoned Bertie's intended gift to his own sleeping tent, and there vented his rage on her person. Meera went into elaborate detail about all the things he did to her, which I shall not recount, for there's no reason that your pity should be corrupted, as mine was, by lust.

When she finished her story she was lying back among my bedclothes, sleepily whispering her thanks, and though my poor loins ached at the sight of her I moved away, seating myself in the dusty armchair as she trustfully dozed off.

She was actually a little plump for my taste, and there was a keenness about her nose that, even in sleep, gave her a slightly predatory look, but she was a splendid apparition in the morning light, and so peaceable that she drew me with her into sleep, and when I awoke, to Bisi's knocking, she was gone.

Perks cancelled our classes the next morning, and refused to see us when we came calling, citing, through a servant, a digestive ailment. But at the Maharao's insistence he attended an impromptu banquet that evening, where, having wreaked his vengeance on Meera, Zalim Singh was his old, expansive self, and made a conspicuous show of forgiving Perks in a rhyming toast and dismissing the entire affair as another of his ingenious pranks.

'Let the rest of them toady for the Empress's pup,' he declared as his steward filled his chalice with port. 'I know no regent till the sun comes up!'

The Maharao exchanged a dozen toasts with Perks that evening until at last, after a conciliatory toast to Prince Albert himself, the Professor toppled over drunk, and had to be carried from the hall by Rai Singh's servants.

We escorted him back to his cottage, laughing as he lifted his quavering voice in song, but when he was helped out of his palanquin and set tottering on his garden path, he was suddenly grave, and waved a finger at the Prince.

'Very mag-a-mani-nous, your father,' he slurred earnestly. 'A f-forgiving nature, *that's* the truest test of a born king. And you –' he said, shaking off the servants as he reached his door. 'You are a noble in the truest sense too, your excel-cency. And you too, Balbeer. True,' he panted, running out of air, 'true, too, too true,' and with that he fell unconscious into his servant's arms.

'Maharaj,' Rai Singh whispered as we walked to his apartments, 'why did you glare at my father so?'

'Did I?' I asked innocently. 'I didn't realize.'

But of course I did realize it, for all evening long I thought I would burst with the awful knowledge of how Zalim Singh had assuaged his wrath.

I was poor company that night, and refused for the first time Rai Singh's invitation to sleep in his apartments, for in my imagination my own room in my uncle's house had become an enchanted place, as if some new apparition might emerge from my wall at any moment.

I sat up half the night with the door bolted shut and the passageway opened and cleared of trunks, awaiting Meera's return. Of course, she'd never actually promised to return, and no doubt couldn't have even if she wanted to, but it was as if I'd divined some implicit pledge in the trust she showed me, dozing off like that in her tattered silks.

I stared down the black passageway, wondering how even the Maharani's labyrinth could reach from the vicinity of the Maharao's tent to my uncle's house, halfway up the cliff. I even stuck my head inside for a moment, as if to crawl down to search for Meera, but the passageway gave off a dank perfume and I recoiled, retreating to my bed.

I heard another scream in my sleep that cloudy night, but awoke to find it must have merely been the song of the Maharao's shenai rising again from his pleasure tank. I remained awake until morning, praying to God that Meera was safe from Zalim Singh's attentions, though lust still sullied my indignation when I pictured what he might be doing to her still, even then, as I lay alone in the gathering light.

The jackals had already had at Professor Perks when a grass cutter found his broken corpse the next morning, all crumpled up at the base of the palace wall. Whoever pushed him must have hoped to make it appear as though he'd fallen while observing the stars the night before, for his telescope and assorted other of his astronomical instruments were littered all around him.

By the time Bisi had led me to the scene, Perks's body was already being carried in a bloody sling to the Maharao's garden. Zalim burst out of his tent in his nightgown and made a grand display of shock and grief, weeping real tears over the Professor's eviscerated corpse, but he didn't fool me, and my own tears dried up in the heat of my outrage.

I broke the news to Rai Singh before Pratap Rao could reach him, and stayed with him through the morning as he grieved in the Professor's cottage, among all his beloved paraphernalia. Perks was buried the next day, and it fell to me to recite a psalm, even as I glared at the attending Maharao, who wept so piteously that even I could see that his guilt was sickly with contemptible remorse.

As for my own grief, it seemed to be suspended, as if saving itself for some greater loss. I owed Perks so much better, but something in me must have divined his fate as soon as he'd befriended me, for look what had become of all my other champions.

The Viceroy sent an inspector to Harigarh to investigate Perks's death, but it didn't seem to matter to him that the clouds had obscured the sky the night Perks was supposed to have ventured forth with his telescope, or that there'd been more equipment scattered around his corpse than he could possibly have been carrying when he fell. After a few polite inquiries, a banquet, and an afternoon of pigsticking on the Maharao's hunting grounds, the inspector returned to Calcutta to report that Spencer Perks had indeed been the victim of an unfortunate accident.

None of this surprised my uncle. 'He was never one of their own, you see,' he explained. 'He was always his highness's man. Now they can appoint a career man to the residency.'

I could tell from Rai Singh's manner that he shared my suspicion about his father, but I did nothing to foster it, for it was always an odd feature of my friendship that I always tried to protect him from his worst fears, even when I shared them.

Rai Singh and I vowed to continue our education in Perks's cottage as a sort of tribute to him. We even included Pratap Rao in the project, and tried to treat him better, just as the Professor would have wanted. But none of us had Perks's gift for animating the forbidding books and instruments that cluttered his cottage, and Pratap Rao remained such a tiresome prig, especially when it came his turn to teach, that after a week or so we gave up the tired and mournful ritual and shuttered up his rooms.

CHAPTER 62

Now through all this I could not stop thinking about Meera, and slept in my room in my uncle's house whenever I was able. I must have been a miserable companion to the Prince, who mistook my lickerish perplexity for grief, and sought to divert me with elegant gifts and pastimes.

He gave me a pair of tipait pigeons – tiny, iridescent birds from the Afghani hills – which we flew some mornings from Rai Singh's balcony, high above the jumbled town. Another gift was a Gujarati bow with which we shot at catfish trapped in beaters' nets along the shallows of the Chambal. He ordered my favorite dishes from the palace kitchens, including the yogurt pudding I mentioned, but I had no appetite for any of it, however much its recollection now makes my spit run. And one evening he offered me the loan of a local courtesan he'd taken a fancy to, which I once would have declined for Ahalya's sake, but now declined for Meera's.

I will not blame you if you abandon the history of a man who could cast his wife and son from his heart to make way for a sybaritic dream. But remember how I'd contended with the mystique of the zenana for four years: seen the nautch girls whirl in the Maharao's garden, heard the jingling and giggling that tripped down from the stone screens, smelled the perfume that wafted from the women's palanquins. In all that time I'd never once succumbed to temptation, and yet my circumstances conspired to lure me back to a callow ideal of desire, made all the more potent by my abstinence and my despair of ever seeing Ahalya again.

I would like to think that it was out of that despair that I turned to the ever more elaborate opium beverages Rai Singh served in the late evenings, concocted of lime, honey, cinnamon, saffron, and imported liqueurs in various combinations. I downed great goblets of the stuff, and when the Prince dozed off I would stagger back to my uncle's house (though I would have sworn to you I flew), singing, bellowing, reaching into the air to touch the pinprick stars.

If I happened to chance upon my uncle he would always brush by without a word, and Pratap Rao would smirk. One night I came upon them both in the vestibule, father and son, earnestly hatching plots together, and I burst into tears at the sight of them, shouting Ahalya's name, but I don't remember this; I've only got Pratap Rao's gleeful account to go on.

On one such night in the late spring of what must have been 1879, I stumbled up the stairs to my room as always, tiptoed past Bisi asleep on the landing, bolted my door, opened the passageway with a little prayer, and stumbled into bed. I don't know if I ever did doze off, for the opium cleared a path between consciousness and sleep along which I seemed able to travel back and forth at will.

The moon was full that night, and I listened for a while to the faint whine of shenai rising from the orchard, and stared out through the balcony door at the strange, torn clouds that passed like widows before the Maharao's regent.

There was a creaking sound, like a cricket's call, in the shadows near my bed, and when I turned my head to look, a cloud seemed to follow, swirling down from the moon to gather itself in a nimbus around the dark shape padding toward me.

'Meera?' I whispered foolishly, casting off my coverlet and rising from bed. 'Is – is it you?'

'Please, huzoor,' she said, bowing down to touch my feet. She was trembling in a simple white shift with her hair hanging in a loose braid and a single silver anklet her only ornament. 'I'm so frightened.'

I led her to the edge of my bed and promised her she'd be safe with me, though no sooner had we reached my bed than I was caressing her. I told her I adored her, and we lay together in a writhing embrace, but I proved a clumsy lover. It took little more than the warmth of her beneath my coverlet, her aromatic breath, the perfume that arose from her as she slipped out of her shift, to bring me to satiety. But she quickly went to work on me with most practiced dexterity, and within an hour I'd done her better justice, though it was all I could do to keep up with her, for she was double-jointed everywhere and adopted unimaginable poses. At one point it was as if I were in bed with three women instead of one, for she could gather several parts in impossible proximity and put them all to use at once.

Now I could attest that she bore no more marks from the Maharao's attentions, but just as soon as I had given her the last of my essence and we fell back in a tangle on my dishevelled bed, she began to sob again, just as before.

I'd never felt so contented since I'd carried Mahabir out into the mustard field, so I was not in a mood for Meera's tears.

'What is it?' I asked, rising to my elbows. 'Is it the Maharao? Did he hurt you again?'

She swallowed and shook her head, daintily dabbing at her tears with the sheet.

'That doesn't matter,' she sniffled, lifting her perfect chin. 'None of that matters now.'

I didn't know what she was talking about, but I sighed with admiration at her selflessness, and on the next inhale savored her dense perfume.

'What do you mean it doesn't matter? It matters now more than ever.'

She shuddered and suddenly turned away, burying her face in one of my pillows, with the tangled bedding puffing up around her.

She moaned something, but it was muffled, and my attention strayed to the lambent curve of her upturned hip.

'What?' I asked softly, touching the hollow of her waist.

'The *Prince*,' she said, lifting her face toward mine.

'What about the Prince?' I said, and then I started and gaped at her. 'You don't mean the Prince abused you?' I said, kneeling over her. And before she could reply I was off the bed and stamping around the room. 'Rai Singh? My friend? It can't be. He wouldn't – '

She glowered at me, drumming her fingers as if I were falling behind some schedule. 'No, no, no,' she said, suddenly very businesslike. 'The Prince has never touched me. He's never even *seen* me, huzoor.'

I stopped marching about and glared at her with foolish, thwarted rage. 'Then what *is* it, Meera?' I said, climbing back beside her. 'What about the Prince?'

She sat up, with her breasts swaying in the dim light. 'Oh,

huzoor,' she said pityingly, touching my cheek with her fingers. 'He's doomed.'

I gripped her wrist. 'What do you mean, doomed?'

'His highness – ' she began to say, startled by my sudden stare.

'You mean the Maharao?'

'Yes, huzoor. The Maharao is going to kill him.'

I pulled away from her, and a chill spread between my shoulder blades. 'How do you know this?' .

'He – he *told* me, huzoor,' she said, moving toward me with a light flaring in her eyes.

'How? When did he tell you?'

She ducked her head modestly for a moment and sat very straight, like a nautch girl preparing to sing.

'A week ago I was called to keep him company,' she said. 'He was in such a strange mood, much uplifted by his khusamba, but when I lay with him his passion was feeble and unavailing, though I tried everything, even sticking – '

'Never mind that!' I exclaimed, wanting to strike her for her shamelessness. Didn't she know I loved her?

'I'm sorry, huzoor,' she said, pausing as if turning a page to the next passage. 'Anyway, he got all sloppy and confessional. Told me he knew what people said about him. He wasn't deaf and blind. But they'd see who ruled Harigarh soon enough. They'd see what Zalim Singh was made of.'

'How? What did he mean?'

'He said killing the Professor was just the beginning.'

'He said that? Oh, God, Meera,' I said, striking my brow. 'Then it's true?'

'Yes, huzoor,' said Meera enthusiastically. 'And then he spoke in verse. Let me see,' she said, staring at the ceiling and stroking her throat.

> *'I'll scour the kingdom till it's clean,*
> *First the boy and then the Queen.'*

'Those were his exact words, Meera? "First the boy"?'

' "And then the Queen." Yes, huzoor,' she said.

'He'd kill his own son?'

'But he said he isn't his son,' said Meera. 'Listen:

'Stolen from another's lap,
To suckle at the Rani's pap.
No blade could ever find his heart.
He has no guts to tear apart.
No brains to dash
No veins to slash
He's but a ghost in gold and silk,
So let him drown in anchar milk.'

The poetry was awful, even by the Maharao's standards, but I was flabbergasted by Meera's recollection.

'I have an ear for these things,' she explained with a brief, shy smile.

'What's anchar milk?'

'Oh, it's strychnine, huzoor,' she said, as if it were perfectly obvious.

'I've — I've got to save him,' I said, walking about now and fetching my robe.

'Oh, no, huzoor,' said Meera, pressing her hands together. 'Please. He'll kill us both if you try.'

'I've got to,' I said. 'The Prince is my friend, I've got to warn him.'

'But the Maharao will find out, huzoor. And he'll find out I told you. And what would become of me then? Do you know what he keeps in his dungeon, huzoor? A domri dwarf with a skinner's blade, and he peels his prisoners to the bone, bit by bit, and it takes them weeks to die.'

There was again a strange relish in the way she spoke, and goosebumps rose on her bosom. But she was right; none of us was safe from the Maharao's wrath.

'You can do nothing, huzoor,' she said, hugging herself as if against the cold. 'Unless . . . '

'Unless? Unless what?'

'No, huzoor,' she said with a shudder, drawing the coverlet over her thighs. 'It's too dangerous.'

'Meera? What are you saying?' I asked, stepping toward her.

She bit her lip a moment and straightened up again. 'Unless we kill him first,' she said, and evenly, too, like a judge pronouncing sentence.

I could feel my spit sweetening and my insides stir as I gazed down at her.

'Every morning he goes to his lavatory, where a pitcher of lassi awaits him by his tub. On the wall just behind the tub there's a loose tile, mounted on hinges, that connects to the Maharani's labyrinth.' She beckoned me to her, casting her coverlet aside as I passed through the mosquito netting. 'He always dozes in a bath of salts,' she said, and I read the hard gleam of vengeance in her dark eyes. 'He likes his privacy, so the guards keep outside, and only one servant stirs his lassi.'

She ran her hand down my chest, and I could feel the serpent uncoiling further in my belly.

'I could show you the way,' she said, taking hold of me, 'and when the servant steps out . . . '

'But I can't, Meera,' I said, gazing along her supple back as she bent over me.

'Oh, huzoor,' she said, her breath like a warm dew upon my lap. 'Have courage,' and with that she tugged upon me with her lips, arching into another of her lewd knots, and we consummated our lethal alliance as the morning light stole down the whitewashed wall.

CHAPTER
63

As the goor still swirled on my tongue I resolved to assassinate the Maharao and scurried off on shaking legs through the shadows of the Professor's garden to steal into his dusty, abandoned apartments. I found my poison bobbling in a bottle of quicksilver on the darkroom shelf and tucked it into my robe, returning undetected to my room. Meera had waited, as she'd promised, just inside the passageway, and sending Bisi off on a phantom errand I bolted my door and climbed down the musty, narrow corridor, black as pitch, holding Meera's hand as she led me along the smooth, greasy walls.

There were steps and inclines and here and there a crack of light, as at the base of a door, and as my eyes grew accustomed I could just make out Meera's ghostly form ahead of me. I desperately wished I'd had another dose of the Prince's khusamba before I'd ventured forth, for I could feel my courage flagging with each stumbling step. But what choice did I have but to kill the Maharao? Beyond all that I owed Rai Singh and the dead Professor, what would my life be worth if the Prince was murdered? And what would become of Meera? The Maharao would swat us like flies.

But the goor was ebbing on my tongue as we turned down a curling flight of steps and tiptoed toward a crack of light, and I could feel the serpent in my stomach slacken. All that gave me heart was Meera's perfumed wake as she resolutely led me forward.

'Now, huzoor,' she said, pausing and bending down to touch my feet. 'Save us,' she whispered. 'Save us all, huzoor.'

I embraced her hard, as if she might absorb my trembling terror, and then she gently pulled away.

'Feel this string,' she said, handing me the end of a length of cord. 'Follow it back through the corridors and it will lead you out of the labyrinth.'

'But what about you?' I asked, reaching toward her.

'And here,' she said, stooping down to retrieve her anklet and placing it on my wrist. 'Take this for luck, huzoor.'

She backed away, turning from a pale ghost to a black, amorphous shadow, but for her eyes, bright as candles, floating up the corridor.

'Wait for me, Meera,' I called out as loudly as I dared.

'I will,' she whispered back. 'Have courage, huzoor.'

I watched her disappear around a corner and then turned toward the crack of light. I felt in my kammerband for the Professor's vial, hoping I might have dropped it along the way, but alas it was still secure. I closed my eyes a moment, trying to summon Baroo's homicidal spirit to guide me, but his only visitation was a cold, damp draft that sifted by as a door closed somewhere deep in the Queen's labyrinth.

I felt along the crack of light until my fingers fell upon a metal latch, and holding my breath I gave it a turn, slow as death, and pushed the little door ajar.

The view was just as Meera had described it. There was a tub, not a yard from where I crouched, and beside it a little brass pedestal with a goblet and pitcher and a plate of pahn, which a servant was tending with his back to me, humming tunelessly to himself.

The room was all tile and marble, and water gushed into the tub from a copper gargoyle. There was a punkah overhead, wafting the steam from the porcelain tub, and linen towels were stacked on an English table much warped by the lavatory damp.

The servant rose and turned, facing me as I pulled my head back from the tiny opening. I could see him scoop a handful of bathing salts from a clay jar and stir them into the water, and then, as he dried his arm on the tail of his shirt, he did a peculiar thing: with his highness groaning and yawning outside the door, the servant generously spat into the steaming tub.

The Maharao entered, wrapped in a cotton robe and beating on his great chest as if to clear his lungs. He seemed like such a huge thing to kill as he dropped his robe. The thatch at his loins had been trimmed with a razor into the shape of a trident, over which his belly loomed like a bhisti's sack as he delicately stepped into his tub. His bulk displaced great bucketfuls of water over the porcelain rim, and all I could see of him was his broad, bristled back and his heavy topknot as he leaned against a sopping cushion for his daily wallow.

Now as I told you, the pitcher was within my reach, but the trouble was that the Maharao's face was turned away from me, and I would have to stretch my arm over his head to spill the mercury into the goblet. By now my brow was as cold as ice and my palms tingled and itched, and I would have abandoned my desperate mission right then and floundered back to my bed, when my gaze alighted on the brutal trunk of Zalim Singh's neck, where a pink boil was flowering, and then strayed to the black epaulets of hair on his dimpled shoulders, and I thought not of Meera, nor myself nor the endangered Prince, but of poor, trusting Spencer Perks.

No doubt the Maharao had hired some badmash to slaughter my little champion, but all the same it was Zalim Singh's own shoulders I now envisioned shoving Perks to the edge of the wall, and his own fat hands casting him down to his death.

The servant padded about the room awhile, fussing here and there, and I knew that before long the parboiled king would want his lassi.

'Leave us,' I mouthed, drawing the vial from my kammerband as the servant dawdled, refolding a towel or two. But then the Maharao himself grumbled at him in dismissal, and suddenly I was alone with Zalim Singh.

I had no time to lose, but I watched and listened for his breaths to slow, and when his chest was heaving peacefully beneath his beaded, haywire beard, and his breaths cleared a channel through the rising steam, I opened the little door and ventured my arm out with the vial gripped in my shaking hand, and emptied Perks's quicksilver into the Maharao's goblet.

I didn't spill even a drop, and jerked my arm back into the passageway, rejoicing that the deed was done. But somehow I caught my sleeve on the latch and the little door slammed shut. There was a loud, interrogatory grunt beyond the wall, and a great sucking noise as the startled Maharao rose from his bath.

'Jagal?' I heard him roar. 'What was that?'

I desperately wrenched at my snagged sleeve, dropping the vial and setting the tile to chattering.

'Look!' shouted the Maharao. 'The wall!'

I could hear footsteps hurry toward me, and then something sharp jabbed at the edge of the tile.

In the course of my struggles I'd somehow secured the little latch, at least, so they had to chip at the tile to loosen it, and as a great alarm arose I finally tore myself free and searched the floor for Meera's cord.

'Meera!' I called out, knocking from wall to wall with the guards' jabs and shouts echoing all about me, as if I were crawling through a crowd.

At last I found the cord and grabbed hold, pulling myself through Tarra Bai's labyrinth as the little tile popped open.

I stepped into the pitch dark above a set of stairs and tumbled down, knocking my shoulder on the cold stone floor. The cord led me along yet another corridor, with here and there more cracks of light along the wall.

'Meera! Where are you?' I cried, stumbling as the passageway twisted about, with lesser hallways leading off in all directions.

I came to the base of a set of stairs that spiralled upward, with rods of sunlight shining through little spyholes along the way, as if I were ascending a tower. But where I should have reached a parapet I found myself following the cord along an ever-narrowing corridor that sloped slightly downward, where the air turned foul and the floor crunched underfoot and here and there something flapped and screeched around my shoulders.

I ducked down as the corridor seemed to funnel to a dead end, and behind me, against the little windows set high along the wall, I could see panicked fruit bats whirling about.

'Meera!' I called again, but heard no reply above the bats' screaming. I leaned back against the wall in despair, but the wall seemed to evaporate behind me, and I fell flatlong through a crimson curtain. And thus I found myself in a bare and shuttered chamber, gaping back in astonishment at Rai Singh.

'Your – your excellency!'

'Balbeer!' he gasped. 'What's the meaning of this?'

I slowly rose to my feet and saw we were not alone. A frail figure in a dingy veil sat motionless behind him, cross-legged on a humble charpoy with a few frayed bolsters for support. Wavering strands of smoke rose from joss sticks set about her in little dingy urns, and long jute ropes hung down from little pulleys in the ceiling.

'Your excellency, I – '

'Answer me, Balbeer,' said Rai Singh, moving as if to protect her and gripping the handle of his dagger. 'What are you doing in my mother's chamber?'

'It's – it's the Maharao,' I finally blurted. 'He was going to murder you. I was – '

'Get out of here, Balbeer,' he said. 'Leave us at once.'

'No – *listen* to me,' I pleaded, stepping toward him with my hands outstretched. 'You don't understand. I'm trying to save you. The concubine, remember her? Albert Edward's gift? She came to me last night.'

Rai Singh glanced behind him at the Maharani, and I could see her slowly shake her head.

'You're lying to me, Balbeer. Why are you lying to me?'

'No, no,' I said. 'I'm not lying. I'm telling the truth. I tell you, she came to me. She told me the Maharao was plotting against you.'

The little Queen sighed and gently nudged her son aside. 'But what brings you here?' she asked equably. 'Don't you know it's forbidden?'

Her voice had a strange quaver, almost like Bisi's.

'Maharaniji,' I said, falling to my knees. 'She led me into the labyrinth. I gave poison to the Maharao. I followed the cord and it brought me . . . here,' and my voice trailed off, as if I were awakening from a dream; how could I convince them of any of this when it no longer made sense to me?

'You gave poison to the Maharao?' asked Rai Singh, drawing his dagger and advancing on me (a tad melodramatically, now that I look back on it). 'You mean you've killed my *father*?'

But again the Queen restrained him. 'You gave my husband poison?' she asked simply.

'Yes, Maharaniji,' I said, my head swimming now in the musty air.

'And did you succeed?' she asked with a certain urgency, leaning her veiled face forward.

'No, Maharaniji,' I said, 'I don't think so.' And we both sagged a little.

Tarra Bai slowly shook her head, as if in sadness, and beckoned to her son to sit beside her.

'Oh, my baby,' she said as he slowly settled beside her, still gripping his dagger and glowering at me. 'These are such bitter lessons I must teach you.'

Her veil was dark over her mouth, and flapped limply as she spoke.

'It's not the Maharao he's come to kill,' she said, stroking his cheek. 'It's you, my baby.'

Rai Singh straightened up and gaped at me again.

'No,' I snarled back at her. 'Never! You can't believe it, your excellency! I'm your friend!'

But he could believe it; I could see it in his dark eyes.

'I've told you again and again, my baby,' she said. 'Kings can have no friends.'

'Your excellency,' I said as his eyes filled with tears. 'Don't listen to her.'

'You were going to poison us both, weren't you, Balbeer?' she asked quietly. 'You were going to poison our breakfast, weren't you?'

'Never,' I said, and then I tried to match wits with her, standing very straight. 'With what?' I wanted to know. 'I carry no poison.'

Rai Singh seemed to brighten slightly as the Maharani beckoned me forward.

And I came forward, too, for in all my life I never knew anyone who could exude such power. In fact, as soon as she crooked her finger at me I was crawling forward, with my hands clasped before me, and prostrating myself before her.

But it wasn't my obedience that interested her; it was the anklet Meera had given me, which the Queen now snatched from my wrist.

'You have no poison?' she asked, shaking her head again.

'No, Maharaniji,' I said, hesitantly lifting my face from the straw mat. 'I used it all on the Maharao.'

'Then what,' she asked, 'can this be?' And she unscrewed a floweret from the anklet's hinge to reveal a little compartment filled with powder.

'But Meera – she gave it to me,' I blurted, rising to my knees.
'Meera?'
'The concubine.'
'Ah.'
'I *swear* to you, I didn't know ... '
'Ah, yes,' said the Queen with more sad shakes of her head as she reached up and pulled at one of the ropes.

I gave Rai Singh an imploring look, but he turned his face away, and his shoulders shook with sobs.

'It's not your fault, you know,' said the Queen cheerfully, sorting through a cloth bag, such as a lowly clerk might carry. 'It was in your stars, Balbeer, from the very start. Such conflict. Such hopeless disarray.'

She withdrew a little picture in a frame and cleaned it with her sari's hem.

'But I think that once you know the truth, you'll see why all your schemes were unavailing.'

It was my uncle she'd summoned with the rope, and now he hurried in through a doorway, glancing at me without surprise, and Pratap Rao trailing in his shadow.

'Uncle,' I said, but he grimly raised his hand to silence me and stood behind the Maharani's charpoy with his hands clasped behind him.

She offered me the picture now, but I was afraid to take it and gazed again at the Prince. I swear he seemed to lose twenty years at his mother's side, and was now whimpering against her breast like a baby.

'Take it,' she commanded, and I obeyed, and found myself holding a photograph of an Englishman in white linen, standing beside a veiled woman in a wedding sari.

'Your mother . . . ' said the Maharani, pointing with a sharp nail to the woman.

'And,' she said, sliding her nail toward the Feringhee, 'your father.'

I dropped the photograph as if lightning had struck it, and gaped about at everyone. 'No,' I said, and I chanted it a few times more. 'No. It can't be. It's a lie.'

'When were they married, Bhulwant Rao?' asked the Queen, turning slightly toward my uncle. '1856, wasn't it?'

'Yes, your highness,' replied my uncle with a sad nod.

'She'd misbehaved so badly, your mother. No one would marry her until the Feringhee came along.'

Hala Deo now entered from a door behind me and stood with his sword unsheathed, and I wanted to die like this, denying my mother's disgrace.

'This – this *woman*,' I gasped, retrieving the picture and glaring at it. 'She could be anyone.'

'Oh, but she's not. You know she's not. She's your mother,' said the Queen. 'You won't deny your own mother, will you?'

'It's a lie,' I said once more, and yet I peered at it again, drinking in the Feringhee's face, searching for a single kindred feature.

'You refuse to believe us?' asked the Queen, clasping the back of Rai Singh's neck. 'Then find out for yourself.'

'What do you mean?' I demanded to know.

'In Cawnpore, in the Memorial Gardens,' said the Queen, plucking back the picture. 'He's buried there, you know.'

'Who?'

'Your *father*, Balbeer,' said Bhulwant Rao, as gently as the Queen allowed.

'John – what is it?' the Queen asked with relish.

'Willard,' said my uncle softly, ducking his head now.

'Ah, yes. That's it. John Willard. He took her there, you know. Lucky girl. I knew your mother, did you know that?' said the Queen, patting her son's back.

I stood there, trying to fit all the pieces together as Hala Deo took hold of my arm in his steel fist.

'Let him keep his stallion,' the Queen told him. 'But see he's out of the kingdom by noon.'

'Yes, your highness,' said Hala Deo.

'You see, Balbeer Rao?' she said. 'You're no danger to anyone when you know the truth. You'll hatch no more plots against us. There's nothing here for a cheechee.'

And so Hala Deo led me away – past Pratap Rao, past my remorseful uncle, past my whimpering, infantile Prince.

But when I reached the door I gave Tarra Bai one last look and she slowly turned her head around.

'Have courage, huzoor,' she called after me, and there was Meera's face peering back at me from the shadow of the Queen's dark veil.

PART SIX

RĂO

CHAPTER
64

Hala Deo rode with me to the border and set me on the Jaipur Road. I drove poor Hunza hard all night to the bastions of Dausa, where I sold him to a liveryman and bought a ticket to Cawnpore on the Agra railway line. At the counter, dust puffed up from my sleeves and streaked my trousers where Hunza's lather had wetted them through, but I still wore my silver dagger in my kammerband and Rai Singh's solar medallion still shone from my sash, and taking me for a noble, the agent sold me a berth in a second-class car, the highest class natives could travel.

The train chuffed into the little station at ten in the morning, as the distant fort swam in the rising heat, and I found my compartment occupied by three Englishmen who'd overflowed the first-class cars. They'd been travelling since Jodhpur, and groaned and sneered as I silently entered, but perhaps seeing my dagger, or the heat in my eyes, they made no protest as I took my place by the slatted window and turned my face to the hot, dust-and-cinder wind.

Civil servants bound for the hill stations to join their families, the three Englishmen ate tinned fruit and drank brandy from their tiffin kits as we lurched eastward, and as the light glared in they ordered a block of ice from first class, which one of their servants, stationed out in the aisle, was called in to fan, all to no effect but a spreading puddle on the dusty floor.

Assuming I knew no English, they talked variously about inconvenience, incompetence and ingratitude. The largest of the three, who'd rolled his trouser legs up over his great mottled calves, speculated as to how a friend of theirs who was boarding the train at

Bhartpur was going to take a second-class berth, especially now that I was aboard.

'A tad too dem-o-cratic for old Thorny, don't you think?' he said, rolling his eyes in my direction.

'A tad, yes. I should say so,' said the youngest. 'Remind me, old man. Who was that poor babu who offered to share his ekka with old Thorny? Remember? Quoted Shakespeare right to Thorny's face.'

' "To be being or not be being, that is being the *kves*-tion," ' the fat one said in a singsong, waggling his head.

'Precisely. But tell me, has anyone explained the babu's infernal hankering after the participle?'

'Something to do with the Welsh, I think,' said the fat one, gravely sipping his brandy.

'No, no, no,' said the third, a bald man who made sport of the greenflies with a rolled-up paper. 'I'll tell you.'

'Indeed?' grumbled the fat one.

'Of course. You see, by employing the participle, he need never conjugate any verb but "to be." And secondly, he employs this construction because it's *passive*.'

'Ah, yes. There you are,' said the youngest, raising his tumbler.

'Passive, of course,' agreed the fat one. 'But go on. What about this babu?'

'Well, Thorny caned him, of course,' said the youngest.

'Very fond of Shakespeare, is he?'

'Caned him soundly?' asked the bald man, poised to strike a fly on the arm of his seat.

'Quite soundly. Fractured the hippo's collar bone.'

'Bloodied his patent-leathers.'

'Smashed his umbrella, I should think,' the bald man piped in.

'And do you know what Surrey Hippo Sillabub did?' asked the youngest.

'Not complain, surely,' said the fat one.

'Precisely. And to the police, as a matter of fact.'

'Oh,' said the bald man. 'Foolish hippo.'

'And when that was unavailing, he wrote a letter of protest to the local hippo gazette. Spelled it all out, but in language that was so intemperate — '

'Lost our composure, did we?' asked the fat man.

'So intemperate, as I say, that he was tried for sedition and given six months' hard labor.'

'Do him good, I should think,' said the fat one, snorting into his glass.

'Yes,' sighed the bald one. 'Hard labor for a change.'

At every station more greenflies flew in to bedevil the bald man. No one embarked or disembarked at most of the little stops we made, and after Kherli an Englishman circulated with his topee extended, collecting rupees, to bribe the engineer to proceed nonstop to Bhartpur, and when a Mahajan and his servant had to jump from third class past his stop at Nadbai Helak, a cheer rose up from first class.

Thornhill was as his friends so fondly described him. He howled at the sight of me, and shook his twisted cane, and as I rose from my rightful seat and followed the stationmaster to a third-class carriage I comforted myself that even if Tarra Bai was right about my father, at least I was only *half* English.

As the train pulled out of Bhartpur I found a place on the upper tier of the triple-decked seats, and sat hunched under the ceiling, raising my face to the wind that blew in from the clerestory roof. There must have been a hundred of us packed into that car – women, children and old folks mostly – and I wondered where the young men were until I heard the ceiling thump and creak as they shifted about out on the carriage top. Every now and then a hand would swing down into one of the open windows, and a wife would fetch it tobacco or pahn or a freshly wetted rag.

I wondered then as I wonder now how far Tarra Bai's plot extended. I suspect it must have begun with the courtesan by the tracks, and when Perks saved Zalim Singh from disgracing himself it was she who had Perks murdered, and then when the Raj declined to prosecute the Maharao she came to me. But I sometimes wonder if Tarra Bai's plot hadn't hatched as soon as I stumbled into Harigarh, as if she were some avatar of Kali herself. I counted myself lucky, I suppose, to be alive, but I had to wonder if my life had been a gift or just a loan until her purposes were served.

In the rattling, hurtling henhouse of a car, Brahmin sat by Moslem, Pathan by Sikh, babu by Rajput, all grudgingly joined together as we rushed across the boundaries. Somewhere on the outskirts of Etawah the Jamuna came into view, and we all craned our necks to see it in the evening's mustard light.

I was tired enough to sleep even on that hard, vibrating bench, but I didn't dare close my eyes for fear that like a poor old hadji who had dozed through Etawah, I might miss my stop. My countrymen prepared their suppers on whatever spare patches of floor they could claim. A Brahmin's servant even built a little cooking fire between the cars. A Marwar Rajput shared his water with me, but not his food, and I turned my face to the clerestory as the dinner hour wore on. A halfmoon followed us out of Etawah and silvered the passing plain. As the women drew their children into their laps to sleep, and the old people sat by, silent and wakeful, I marched my memory back with each mile, from the palace to the prison to the pilgrim road, back to Bhondaripur and the buffalo and the budgerow's puddled deck, through Bastard Bhavan and the burning ghats, until it collapsed at last in my mother's room, and I watched her preen beside her smoking lamp and set forth into the mystery of the empty city streets.

I left my place on the upper tier and made my way among the sleeping bodies to the window, gasping in the whispering wind. I could jump, I told myself, staring down at the blurred gravel grade, and if the fall didn't kill me, I could always scrabble back to the mendicant's life. Why dignify Tarra Bai's lie with this miserable journey? What could it prove after all these years? As if it shared my misgivings the locomotive stopped more often the closer we came to Cawnpore, snorting and shuddering at every town like a balking bull.

But I never budged from the window until the engine blew its keen whistle and we began to pass by the city's mills, all aglow in the middle of the night. The train pulled into the old East India Company station west of the cantonment, and I stumbled out with half the carload, and dodged the young men who now dropped down from the carriage tops to seek work in the city.

I asked the coolie how to find the Memorial Gardens, but he knew them as Company Bagh, and told me they were sacred to the British, and no Indian was allowed to enter. But I pretended I was merely seeking someone who lived in their vicinity, and he sent me across the Grand Trunk Road, and up along the canal until I came to a road I recognized from Weems's Mutiny tour, and followed it westward across the canal and into the old bazaar.

The night was still, but dust hung in the air like fog, suspended in the waves of heat still rising from the road. I caught the familiar smell from the harness factory to the north, and among the hasty proliferation of workers' hutments, tea stalls, and temples, I caught sight of the arch where my mother used to buy her flowers, and the bridge where I'd been beaten, and the little lane where Sayideen once lived, now all turned to miniature against the scale of my boyhood recollection. When I came to the turn for my old street I felt as though I might choke, and my eyes stung from the floating dust. I forced my way past, and began to run, nearly stumbling on the men who lay sleeping here and there along the road.

In my panic I found myself on an unfamiliar street lined with European shops – a portrait studio, a dress shop, a chemist's – and had to ask directions of an old man I found sitting up under a lamppost, in a clutter of dizzy bugs. He bid me stand closer, and peered up at me through a swarm of moths.

'Maharaja,' he said suddenly, with his eyes lit up. 'Maharaj-ji!'

'Where's Company Bagh?' I asked again, trying to catch my breath.

But still transfixed as if by some apoplectic delusion he threw himself at my feet and cried, 'Jai maharaj!' as I ran on.

The shops gave way on my right to a small park with a statue of the Queen Empress, and then the road ended in a fork, and I found myself pausing at the gate to the garden itself.

Two Highlander guards sat on little stools, dipping towels into a bucket of water and mopping their empurpled faces. I shrank back at the sight of their rifles, and in their kilts, with cigars smoking from under their brown beards, they looked to me like monstrous women. One of them watched me as I turned onto the left fork and began to slink along the high, spiked wrought-iron fence that enclosed the Company's shrine.

'You there!' he called out, half rising from his stool.

I pretended not to hear, and kept walking in the shadows of the overarching trees that lined the sidewalk.

'Bloody hell!' the soldier exclaimed. 'You there! Halt! Fetch us some water!'

'Aw, Jesus,' said his partner. 'What are you going to do now, Brian — shoot the little wog?'

'I said, halt!' the first cried out, dropping heavily back down on his stool. 'Bloody cheek,' he muttered defeatedly.

'Or bloody deaf,' his partner sighed.

I circled around the garden, slipping past the guards at a second gate. From there the fence seemed to curve around forever without a break, across from the harness factory and back toward the Queen's park. I had paused to rest at the gardeners' quarters behind the park, trying to work up the courage to climb the wrought-iron fence, when a small boy padded out to urinate in the gutter.

I called him over and told him I had to get into the garden. Did he know a way?

'Not allowed,' he said, all matter-of-fact.

'I know that,' I said, bringing out some coins from my kammer-band. 'But *you* know a way, don't you?'

He accepted the bribe with a city boy's shrug. 'Wait here,' he said, and padded back to his house.

'No, wait,' I tried to call after him, but I didn't dare raise my voice.

After a while the boy returned with his father, a middle-aged man with a stubbled chin, buttoning his green mali's trousers. He introduced himself as Leela and asked what he could do for me.

'The garden,' I said cautiously. 'Can you get me in?'

'Ah, sahib,' he said hoarsely. 'I don't blame you.' He sniffed at the hot night air for a moment. 'Just from the aroma you can imagine how beautiful it is. Even now, in this weather, it's a mass of blossoms. But even I, Leela, chief gardener — even I can't claim it's worth getting shot for.'

'But it's not the flowers,' I said. 'It's a grave I've come to see.'

The mali shooed his son away and stared at me a moment. 'Whose grave, sahib?'

I hesitated, but there was something in the mali's eyes that engendered trust, and I said, 'An Englishman. John Willard.'

The mali's eyebrows twitched, and he led me two steps deeper into the shadows. 'Who are you?' he asked in a whisper.

'Never mind who I am,' I said. 'Look, I can pay you. Can you get me in?'

The mali seemed to chew on this proposition for a moment. 'I know who you are,' he said. 'You're the Rao boy, aren't you? You're Shrimati Natholi Rao's son.'

I lost my breath for a moment and drew away from him. 'Wh-what makes you think that?'

Leela looked me up and down a moment. 'The Rajput dress. You're about the right age, too, I should say. And who else would seek Willard Sahib's grave?'

'You knew my mother?'

'Of course I knew your mother, sahib,' he said.

'But how?'

'How, sahib? Why, I brought her to Willard Sahib's grave every Itewar.'

'Then it *is* true,' I said aloud, stepping back.

'Sahib?'

I gaped back at the fence. 'Where – where is he?'

'Sahib?'

'*Willard*,' I said, gripping his arm. 'My *father*!' And there it was – I'd said it. I'd finally found my father.

The mali stared at me a moment, stroking his stubble. 'All right,' he said with a quick nod. 'I'll help you.'

He peered up and down the street for a moment and led me across to a point in the iron fence that was obscured by a firebox, where he removed a bar as if by magic, and led me into Company Bagh.

There was a slight glow in the eastern sky, and the distant streetlamps cast faint combs of light along the fence, but the garden itself was in shadow as we crept from bush to bush and then along a scalloped hedge that lined a cobbled footpath. Marble angels and crosses glowed among the flower beds, marshalling the dim, ambient light. The air was sweet and heavy, and the grass was warm and sopping underfoot from the dribbling black hoses the malis had set out for the night.

'The House of the Women,' Leela whispered, pointing up a broad lane to the Cawnpore Well, the garden's centerpiece, where the butchered women and children lay buried, but all I saw of it was an angel's shadow behind a granite screen.

'This way,' said Leela, darting along a row of potted flowers, and I scrambled after him to a sandstone obelisk on an open triangle of grass, where Leela left me for the moment to keep watch from under a flowering bush.

I crawled to the base and tried to read the inscription. It identified the spot as the site of the Nana Sahib's headquarters during the Devil's Wind, where many of his prisoners were put to death. It said that their remains had been left scattered about by the fleeing rebels, but later gathered together and interred by a survivor named Shepherd.

There followed a list of the Nana Sahib's victims arranged in order of their death, and not six names down the very first row I came upon my father's name.

John S. Willard, Engineer, Died June 7th

I reached out and ran my finger along the black, inlaid letters, and I don't think I ever felt so calm, before or since.

'John S.,' I caught myself thinking. 'I wonder what the "S" stands for?'

I read the names of eight others killed that same day, and then read my father's name again and again, and then I stood and stared down at the soft, wet grass at my feet. Here was why my mother dressed in widow's robes. Here was her destination on those midnight forays into the city. Here was why she could never return to Harigarh and never breathed my father's name to me. What would have become of me if she had? What was going to become of me now?

'Sahib!' Leela whispered from somewhere out of sight.

'Shh, Leela,' I replied. 'It's all right. I've found him,' and I began to pull flowers up from the garden.

'Rao Sahib! No!' he croaked, rustling about in his hiding place.

'Oh, hush,' I said. 'You can spare a few flowers, can't you?' And I placed a little bunch on the ledge beneath my father's name.

'No, sahib!' Leela called out. 'Get away!'

But it was too late, for by the time I saw the Highlander he'd already dropped his bucket and leapt toward me with his green kilt flying.

He pinned me to the ground like a boulder and ripped my

dagger and sheath from my waist. My turban rolled off, unravelling like twine, and though my head was half submerged in the sopping grass I still caught sight of Leela darting away to safety.

CHAPTER
65

The Highlanders didn't beat me exactly, but they dragged me like a sack of rags between them, and I think they must have kept my dagger for themselves, for I never saw it again. They were too triumphant over my capture to ask me to explain myself, and I don't know what I would have told them if they had, for though I was in no mood to lie, I had to wonder where the truth would lead me.

They took me to a nearby compound and placed me in the custody of an English constable stationed on the verandah of a stately bungalow. A Punjabi in a khaki uniform manacled my hands behind my back and made me kneel at the base of the verandah steps, on the sharp quartz gravel of the driveway.

The constable sat at a rickety desk, puffing on a brown cigarette to keep the bugs away. Glancing at me with no more interest than a hotel night clerk might take in a late-arriving guest, he removed a form from a slotted box, dipped his nib into an inkwell, and asked me my name.

I told him my real name (though I suddenly wondered now if it wasn't really Balbeer Rao Willard) and gave Harigarh as my address. He frowned at this and stared at me a moment, working the muscles in his jaw.

'Wait here,' he said, rising from his desk and walking into the house, and I was suddenly gripped by the fear that by some miracle of English book-keeping the drowsy constable had connected me with Balbeer Rao of Bhondaripur, wanted for the murder of the patwari, Mangal Singh.

After a few minutes he reappeared in the doorway and bid the Punjabi bring me in. In an anteroom of the dark house I was ordered to stand before a desk that was enveloped in a tent of mosquito netting, whose occupant now seemed to materialize as he turned up the flame of his oil lamp.

He was a bald and elderly Englishman with narrow spectacles and yellowish-white sideburns all awry from sleep. His nightdress was soaked through with sweat, and his neck was livid with prickly heat. He read the constable's report once or twice, raising his chin and blinking as if to shake off his drowsiness.

'Balbeer . . . Rao,' he asked in Hindi, cocking one eyebrow. 'Is that correct?'

'Yes,' I said in English. 'That's correct.'

'Ah, forgive me,' he said, glancing up at me. 'A babu. Very well then, Balbeer Rao. What the devil were you doing in the Memorial Gardens?'

'Visiting,' I said.

'Visiting? Visiting whom, sir?'

I could feel my knees wobble, and I let out a great breath. 'I'm very tired,' I said.

'Constable,' the old man said, 'may we have a chair for Mr Rao?'

The Punjabi pushed a stool up behind me, and I slowly sat down.

'Are you new to Cawnpore, Mr Rao?' the old man asked as a bead of sweat dropped from his eyebrow and rolled down one lens of his spectacles.

'No, not exactly,' I said.

'No?'

'I – I was born here.'

'*Were* you?' he said, wiping his spectacles with a handkerchief. 'And when was that, if I may ask?'

'I don't know,' I sighed. 'After the Devil's Wind, I think. Look,' I said, 'what does it matter? I was in the gardens; you caught me. I'm guilty.'

'And do you live here now?' he asked, ignoring me.

'No,' I snapped. 'In Harigarh, just as I told the constable.'

'Then perhaps you didn't know, Mr Rao, that the Memorial Gardens are hallowed and no native is allowed to set foot there?'

'Except the malis, of course,' I muttered back at him. 'Who else would do the dirty work?'

The old man squinted at me and seemed to sigh to quiet his irritation. 'Yes, of course,' he said, untying the ribbon on a bundled, dusty file. 'But you aren't a mali, by the looks of you, are you, Mr Rao?'

I leaned over on the stool then and wiped my forehead with my knee as he shuffled through a little pile of papers.

'Now, unless I am very much mistaken, Mr Rao, you are the son of one Natholi Rao of Harigarh,' he said, running a finger along one of his papers. 'I believe she died in 1864, is that about right?'

Oh God, I thought, he knows everything. My heart began to pound, and I must have nodded despite myself, for he smiled back at me and continued.

'Now, as I understand it, upon her death you attended the Mission Society for the Propagation of the Revealed Word et cetera, et cetera, for nearly four years, and ran away in the midst of an epidemic. Am I correct so far?'

My mouth had gone dry, and I swallowed, glancing around now at the constable and the Punjabi.

'Mr Rao?'

'I'm – I'm not saying,' I mumbled back.

The old man peered at me a moment with his grey eyes, and grimly nodded at the Punjabi, who approached me with a sneer. I shut my eyes as he reached toward me, but suddenly my manacles fell away from my hands with a sharp click, and when I blinked my eyes open I was alone with the old man, who was smiling at me.

'I imagine you must wonder how I know so much about you, Mr Rao,' he said as I rubbed my wrists. There was a creaking above us, and the punkah began to wave, stirring the air around us. 'Well, it's very simple,' he said. 'You had a servant named Moonshi Lal, didn't you, Mr Rao?'

I sat up straight and nodded.

'Well, Moonshi was my servant too. Mine and Mrs Harris's, of course, God rest her soul.'

'Harris!'

'So he told you about us, did he?' he said, brightening. 'Yes, I hired him after that absurd business with the hakeem. Never did find the killer. Certainly wasn't Moonshi. Such a hapless fellow, I thought, but Mrs Harris took to him. Must have been in our employ for two, three years. But then he left us most precipitately. Never gave us a moment's notice. We surmised he'd fled with you. Back to Harigarh, I suppose?'

'Yes,' I said. 'Back to Harigarh.'

'Oh good,' he said. 'Tell him I'm very cross with him, will you? But give him my best?'

I probably owed him the truth, at least for Moonshi's sake, but I couldn't bring myself to tell him. 'I shall,' was all I said.

He nodded and frowned down at his file for a moment. 'Now what about this trespass, Mr Rao? What was *that* all about?'

I looked down at my hands, so dark against my white trousers, and tried to look contrite. 'I – I'm sorry, sir,' I said.

'You seem a very sober young man,' Harris said with some perplexity. 'I even sense a certain moral core. I can't imagine it was just a lark.'

I kept silent and shrugged ashamedly.

'Well, Mr Rao, we cannot have native gentlemen of any stripe violating our gardens at will. Ordinarily I would order you imprisoned; however, owing to our mutual fondness for Moonshi Lal, to our concomitant bond, if you will, I shall exact only your most solemn promise that you will never invade the gardens again. Is that understood?'

I hesitated at this, for how could I promise never to visit my father again? But I'd lied to Harris once already, why not a second time? 'Yes, sir,' I said finally.

'Good,' said Harris, closing his file with a dusty slap. 'Now tell me,' he said, turning down his lamp, for the morning sun had risen, 'where are you staying in town?'

'Uh – nowhere, sir,' I said. 'I – I just arrived last night.'

'Do you have – people left in the city?'

'No, sir.'

'Oh dear,' Harris said, leaning back with a troubled look. 'That won't do.' He stared for a moment at the slowly swinging punkah. 'Ah, I have it. Constable!' he called out suddenly, dropping his file into a desk drawer and slamming it shut.

'Yes sir?' said the Constable with a paramilitary quickstep through the door.

'Constable,' said Harris, 'I am releasing Mr Rao.'

'Thank you, sir,' I said, rising to my feet.

'*Releasing*, sir?' asked the Constable.

'Yes, Constable,' said Harris with an amused look. 'I don't think Mr Rao will be troubling us any further. I am releasing him into the custody of the old Mission Society Asylum Something-or-Other.'

'S-sir,' I broke in. 'I don't think – that is – '

Harris's smile began to falter. 'Yes, Mr Rao?'

'Sir,' I said, trying to control myself. 'That is, they don't know me there any more. They won't take me in.'

'Oh yes they will,' said Harris, standing now and stretching his back. 'They took you in before. They'll do what they're told. They're a damn nuisance, if you ask me. They can make themselves useful for a change. I want to see you in a week, Mr Rao, for I have certain inquiries to make from other districts. I take it I can trust you to remain within reach?'

I could see his patience was exhausted. 'Yes, sir,' I said.

'Good,' said Harris. 'In the meantime, I hope you will keep out of mischief, Mr Rao.'

'Yes, sir. Thank you, sir.'

'Constable?' said Harris. 'Send Harish around to – Bastard Bhavan,' he said with a wink in my direction. 'Have them come fetch Mr Rao.'

'Very good, sir.'

'In the meantime have some tea, Mr Rao,' said Harris, stepping through the netting. 'And a biscuit, perhaps.'

'Thank you, sir,' I said weakly.

'See to it, will you, Constable?' Harris said, returning to his room. 'I'm late for my morning ride.'

The constable led me out to the verandah, where a second constable was waiting, a bucktoothed man with a briar pipe who'd come to begin his day shift.

'Who do we have here, John?' he asked, slowly looking me up and down.

'Caught him in the gardens last night,' said the first, sitting me down by the punkah walla.

'How dreadful. What's his sentence, then?'

The night constable rolled his eyes and sniffed. 'None. He's to be released.'

'Harish!' he called out with a clap of his hands, and a cowering man with slipslapping sandals came hurrying out from behind the house.

'Sahib?'

'Harish, you're to go to the Mission Society for the Propagation of — oh, never mind,' said the night constable with a wave of his hand. 'Go to Bastard Bhavan, Harish. Find whoever's in charge. Bring him here.'

'In . . . charge?'

'The muckamuck. Mission maharaj,' the constable said, kicking at the cowering man. 'Now *quickly!*'

The day constable squinted down at me. 'The old man gone soft again, John?'

'I do what I'm told, I don't tell what I do, that's my motto,' said the night constable, stiffly locking a desk drawer and stepping into the driveway.

'I've left no backlog, Alan,' he said, striding off. 'So I'll expect none this evening.'

'Right you are,' said the day constable, settling down at the desk. 'Sleep well.'

The departing constable grunted and paused at the gate. 'And fetch his highness there some tea,' he called back. 'Old man's orders.'

'I shall, John.'

A servant brought me tea and biscuits, which the day constable had me consume on the lawn, in the intensifying sun, as he leaned back in his chair and languidly searched his pockets for matches. The tea raised a sweat on my forehead that the weak morning breeze slightly cooled as I awaited Weems, trying to assure myself that he could have no power over me now that I was a man.

I finished my tea and ate the biscuits as delicately as I could manage, and when the day constable fell asleep I returned to my place beside the punkah walla. I was dead tired, and in the whine of the greenflies and the creak of the punkah walla's rope I was soon fast asleep, and suffering through my old nightmare again. Even as I dreamed that morning, even as I saw my mother burst into flames and turned to see the stranger on the bank behind me, I expected to see Willard's face, my father's face at last. But as always I awoke too soon.

I must have awakened with a cry, for the punkah walla was staring at me as I tried to catch my breath, and then the chowkidor opened the compound gate and a tonga drawn by a swayback horse rolled up the drive.

As the constable shook himself awake, a man in a black suit stepped out of the tonga, and rising to my feet I saw he wasn't Weems but Mr Peter, with a face as brown as saddle leather, and then, as he stepped up to the verandah and removed his topee, I saw he wasn't Mr Peter, either, but Dileep.

CHAPTER
66

'I am Peter John,' he said, approaching the desk, and I thought my heart would burst.

'Are you indeed?' sniffed the constable.

'I believe his honor wishes to see me?'

'His honor is out,' said the constable. 'He's left orders for you to take this ruffian into your custody.'

Dileep glanced over at me without recognition, but I was struck dumb by the look in his eyes.

'And may I ask why?' he asked evenly.

'You may ask all you like, *Reverend,*' said the constable, sucking on his cold pipe. 'It doesn't matter. Those are his honor's orders, and that's all you need to know.'

Dileep gave up on the constable then and slowly approached me, and all I could do was nod encouragingly, for I'd lost all my wind at the sight of him. He was still taller than I, though he stood with his shoulders curved forward, which gave him a sunken look about the chest. His face still bore traces of his cholera; his cheeks were hollow and his mouth straight and thin. But in his eyes I saw the Dileep I'd known: stalwart, quick, and kindly.

'Who are you?' he asked, though even before his words were out a little flame of recognition seemed to flicker in his eyes.

'Dileep,' I whispered, stepping toward him. 'Dileep, don't you know me?'

I lurched forward to embrace him, but he recoiled for a moment and grabbed my forearms. 'Diwan?' he asked, pushing me back for a better look. 'Is it you?'

'Yes, Dileep,' I said, finally regaining my voice.

He gaped at me a moment longer and then embraced me stiffly. 'I never thought I'd see you again,' he said quietly, slowly shaking his head.

'I say, Reverend, sign here, if you will,' said the constable, flourishing a form and smiling to himself as if our embrace had confirmed one of his fondest suspicions.

Dileep released me and bowed his head to compose himself. 'Where, Constable?' he said, returning to the desk.

'There . . . and there, and . . . there,' said the constable leafing through the triplicate form.

Dileep rubbed his nose and sniffed between signatures. 'Will that be all?'

'Yes, Reverend,' said the constable. 'He's yours.'

Dileep nodded to me and led me to the carriage, replacing his topee as we stepped into the summer glare. He drove his old horse gently out the gate and down the road past the police lines.

He kept glancing over at me, and then looking away when I returned his glance, and neither of us spoke until we'd passed the Moslem burial grounds.

'I thought you were dead, Diwan,' he said at last, fixing his gaze straight ahead between the hutments that lined the broad road.

'I know.'

'We'd heard you'd died in the city.'

'From Nanak Chand?'

Dileep nodded uneasily.

I told him about my flight from Bastard Bhavan, realizing,

halfway through, how selective I was being. I never mentioned Baroo's profession, nor even Bhondaripur's name, nor any other detail anyone could track. I suppose I did this out of habit at first, but as I kept glancing at my old friend in his black suit and oversized topee, I became ever more cautious. He looked elderly, somehow, and remote, and listened to me politely, without a single interruption.

I ended my account with my arrival in Bhondaripur, and then we drove a little way in silence.

'Diwan,' he said casually as we passed the Muir Cotton Mill, now engulfed in workers' hutments, 'did you ever marry?'

I hesitated a moment. 'Yes,' I said.

'Any children?'

He asked this in such an odd little singsong that I looked over at him and frowned. 'Yes,' I said. 'A son.'

'And where are they now?' Dileep asked, tilting his head slightly. 'Harigarh, I suppose?'

I looked away and shook my head. What was the use in telling him the truth? 'No,' I said finally, 'they're dead.'

Dileep nodded, but with a look of consternation, as if afraid to ask more questions. We slowly passed a row of bullock carts hauling cotton bales, their drivers sleeping under little rag tents.

I looked over at my old friend. 'You've changed, Dileep,' I said foolishly.

Dileep shouted at one of the bullock drivers to wake him, and the man lurched up, knocking his tent down around him.

'We lose more drivers to that,' he muttered as the man shook his goad and cursed us. 'They doze off and get crushed under the wheels.'

'So what are you now?' I asked, steeling myself a little as I caught a glimpse of Bastard Bhavan in the distance, behind a little rise now covered with a colony of workers' hutments. 'Redeemer Walla's assistant?'

Dileep swallowed hard, patting the dust from his sleeves. 'No,' he said.

'Good.'

'*I'm* Redeemer Walla,' he said quietly. 'The Reverend is dead.'

At first all I felt was relief that I wouldn't have to face the Reverend, but as Dileep explained how he died my relief gave way to an unexpected sorrow.

'He passed away four months ago. It was a stroke, just when the hot season began. He'd had one before that froze up his left side, but he carried on. Went around in a wheelchair the boys made for him. He died in the middle of chapel, humming a hymn.'

I fought back against my strange grief and forced a little chuckle.

'So,' I said, leaning back in my seat, '*you're* Redeemer Walla now.'

'Yes,' said Dileep. 'For the time being.'

'Until?'

'Until the board finds a replacement.'

'An *English* replacement.'

Dileep shook his head as he used to when I disappointed him. 'I'm too young, Diwan,' he said stiffly. 'They need a man of experience.'

'You mean you're too brown,' I muttered, 'and they need an *English*man of experience.'

'Oh, Diwan,' Dileep blurted, his old self surfacing for a moment, 'there you go again. Jumping to conclusions.'

But I was not my old self, and wouldn't be cowed. 'What conclusions?'

I could see Dileep think better of whatever he'd intended to say. 'What are you doing here, Diwan?' he asked abruptly. 'The servant said they caught you in the gardens.'

I nodded.

'What were you doing there?'

'Looking,' I said, gazing off at the roadside.

'Looking for what?'

'For my father,' I said.

Dileep shrugged at this, and I remembered how he used to scold me for hankering after my father so much. 'And did you find him?' he asked me now.

'I did,' I said, reaching over and touching his shoulder. 'And you know what?'

'What?' asked Dileep with a worried look.

'He was *English*.'

Dileep's eyes suddenly came alive. 'No,' he said with a gasp.

'Yes,' I said. 'It's true. He was John S. Willard, Engineer. Died in the Devil's Wind. Buried in the Gardens. I'm eight annas, Dileep. I'm a cheechee.'

We stared at each other for a moment and then both burst out laughing at once.

'I know,' he said, removing his topee and placing it on my head. '*You* can be the Reverend's replacement.'

The school grounds now lay in a sea of makeshift dwellings, and a Moslem chowkidor with a sword in his belt opened the gate for us and salaamed, perplexed by our laughter.

The Reverend's beloved perfect lawn was now all stubble and scrub, studded with the droppings of goats and lean cows that roamed at will among the buildings. The kilns were overgrown with weeds, and against one wall of the main building lay a heap of broken pottery.

Dileep said that the pottery works had closed down two or three years after I left – not enough boys to keep it going, not enough demand to turn a profit. But a local mill owner gave the mission a yearly grant in the name of his son, who'd been killed on the Northwest Frontier. Some of this money had gone to reroofing the main building with red tile, erecting a gothic spire where the wooden cross had once been strapped to the chimney, and installing a modest stained-glass window in the old shell hole in the chapel.

A ragged syce grabbed the horse's bridle at the entrance, and for his sake we tried to sober up.

'*Servants*, Dileep?' I muttered as we stepped down from the carriage.

'Look,' said Dileep, retrieving his hat from my head, 'from now on I want you to call me by my Christian name.'

'Peter?'

'Yes,' said Dileep, clearing his throat.

'But I can't do that.'

'It's my name, Diwan,' he said quietly, pausing at the door.

I stared up at him a moment and sighed, thinking of the Reverend's stubborn little sheep.

'All right, Peter,' I said.

I could already hear a dull schoolboy chant, and passing through the little hallway I found myself standing among a dozen or so boys seated at the old study tables. They were dressed not in uniforms but in shirts and dhotis, and one of their number was conducting the class. They all seemed to brighten at the sight of Dileep, who smiled easily around at them and introduced me to the class.

'This is Shri Balbeer Rao,' he said. 'My old friend, remember?'

'The one you called Diwan?' a little boy asked without so much as raising his hand.

I winced a little, for in my day he would have been punished for speaking out of turn, but Dileep smiled back and said, 'That's right. Good boy, Amiya. You remember.'

'The one who ran away?'

'That's right, Samuel. You remember too,' and the second boy beamed.

Dileep smiled at me sheepishly. 'I tell them about you in my lessons sometimes.'

'Rao Sahib,' asked the first boy, 'why did you run away?'

Dileep gave me a worried look, and for a moment I saw him staggering out into the rain that morning ten years before.

'Because,' I said, ' . . . because I didn't have such a good teacher as Mr John.'

Dileep looked relieved as the boys nodded and giggled. 'Now back to your lesson,' he said, brushing his hand across one boy's head, 'while I introduce Shri Rao to the others.'

He led me on into the kitchen, where six small boys, the youngest about three and the oldest six or so, were helping a serving woman make chapattis. Dileep stood by and fidgeted with an odd expectancy as I nodded to the little boys, one by one. They looked at me without interest, but I paused to pat the head of one four-year-old, so much like myself when I first came to Bastard Bhavan, who was now rolling dough into little balls and setting them out on a floured platter.

When I looked back at Dileep he was staring at me intently as if waiting for me to speak. 'You know,' I said, 'it's strange. I'd been dreading coming back here, but it feels like home.'

Dileep smiled a little and sighed, and led me to Weems's old rooms to wash. He gave me a new shirt to wear from a trunk of old clothes one of the society's members had sent from Calcutta, and I joined him in the Reverend's office for tea. It was as Weems had left it, with the rows of bookshelved Bibles and the Queen's portrait now speckled with bugs trapped behind the glass. Dileep looked serene, somehow, as if I'd passed a crucial test, lived up to some long-standing expectation.

We sat on the cool stone floor before the Reverend's desk and talked of this and that as the serving woman brought us our tea. I tried to steer clear of the subject of Dileep's conversion, but it rose in the current of our conversation like a rock in a river, and I knew we would strike it eventually.

I remembered what a gifted teacher Dileep had always been, and told him now how pleased I was to see that his boys loved him.

'It's as you say,' he said simply. 'This is home.'

I had Dileep try to account for everyone I'd known in the old days. He said Mr Peter had deserted the Reverend to clerk in Twoomy's apothecary, but Dhanda was still around, though he was out today on an errand, and had named himself Ezekiel Weems. Copy, Mark, Jahangir, and one of the other Moslem boys had died within a week of John Christopher's burial. Matthew and Luke had found work in the cantonment, and Ralph had run away.

'The Reverend prayed every day that Ralph would come back,' said Dileep. 'All the way to the grave.'

'Redeemer Walla never would let go, would he?' I said idly, finishing my tea.

'No. In fact, he never really gave up on you, either. Say what you will about him, his faith was a mighty rock.'

I sensed a sermon in the making and attempted to cut it off. 'His ambition, you mean,' I said, trying to smile back at Dileep, who had that pitying look Weems himself had once employed.

'No,' he quietly insisted. 'I mean his faith. He was a believer.'

'God knows,' I said.

'He was a – '

'Fool,' I cut in.

Dileep sat still for a moment and nodded. 'Perhaps,' he said imperturbably. 'But he was God's fool.'

I looked away and wiped my forehead with my sleeve, for I

could feel the heat rising in my blood. 'Is this going to be one of Redeemer Walla's little talks?' I asked. 'What's next, Dileep? The parable or the warm milk?'

Dileep smiled slightly, as if at my obviousness. 'No, Diwan,' he said quietly.

'Good,' I said, rising abruptly and going to the window. Outside, beyond the ruined kilns, a goat grazed among a little group of stone crosses enclosed by a low brick wall. I wanted to say something pleasant to diffuse my impatience with my old friend's piety, but the best I could do was to say, 'I see everyone had a nice Christian burial.'

Dileep rose and walked to his desk. 'Yes,' he said, frowning at a stack of papers. 'The one in the middle is the Reverend's.'

I stared a moment at the first cross, where John Christopher was buried, and at last it seemed the time to ask, 'What happened to you, Dileep? Why did you desert me?'

I slowly turned to face him, but he kept staring down at the clutter on his desk. 'As I recall,' he said stiffly, 'you deserted me.'

'Answer me, Dileep,' I said, stepping toward him. 'Why did you give him your soul?'

'I didn't,' he said, glaring at me. 'I gave my soul to God.'

'*His* God.'

'No, not his God,' said Dileep. 'God wasn't his, God isn't anybody's. We are all – '

' – God's creatures,' I muttered, turning away and leaning for a moment against the bookshelves.

'If only you'd stayed, Diwan,' he said. 'I could have taught you so much. I was reborn in Jesus Christ. I heard him speaking to me in the dark.'

'That wasn't Jesus Christ, Dileep,' I said, walking away from him. 'That was Redeemer Walla chanting all that stuff in your ear about the resurrection and the life. Drumming it into you when you were down. When you couldn't defend your soul.'

'The Lord works in mysterious ways,' Dileep said, wearily sitting in the Reverend's chair.

'The Lord's a bully,' I said, 'and a cheat.'

Dileep gave me a besieged look and bit at his lip. 'Perhaps,' he said, 'but he makes a better God than I did.'

I made no reply to this, and at last sat across from him in a mildewed chair, listening for a moment to the crows, the flies, the far-off mills pounding like the summer's pulse.

'Don't hate me, Diwan,' said Dileep.

I raised a hand and shook my head. 'I don't,' I said. 'I can't hate you, Dileep.'

'Uh, *Peter*, remember?' he said with a tired smile.

'*Peter*,' I said. 'Peter John, God's fool.'

'Yes,' said Dileep, and for a minute we sagged into our chairs like two old men, pondering the distance between us.

'What's become of the babu?' I finally asked.

'Nanak Chand?'

' "The Bengali ass with the English bray," remember?'

Dileep stood and paced before me for a moment, tapping a finger against his lip as if composing what he was about to say.

'Not another sermon, Peter,' I sighed up at him.

'Nanak Chand,' he said, ignoring me. 'You know, I was just getting around to telling you about him.'

'Oh?'

'Yes,' he said, sitting down again and leaning back. 'You know, after Nanak Chand brought us those three boys with cholera the Reverend turned against him, and he fell on hard times. We heard awful rumors about him. Surrounded himself with criminals. Turned profits on his fellows' woes.'

'Nothing new in that,' I said, settling further into the chair.

Dileep shrugged a little and clasped his hands over his head. 'But every now and then he'd turn up demanding this or that of the Reverend, maintaining we owed him something for his services, for all the boys he'd brought into the fold. I guess he thought of us as his nest egg, Diwan. But the Reverend always chased him away.

'Eventually he gave up, and we didn't see him for the longest while, and then about two years ago, after the Reverend's stroke, after Mr Peter had deserted us and I was trying to shoulder some of the burden, Nanak Chand turned up at the door with a child in his arms. And I tell you, Diwan, he was a changed man. He was gracious. He was humble. He was contrite. He begged our forgiveness for all the misery he'd brought us. And please, in the name of Jesus Christ, our Lord and Saviour, would we take the child into our keeping?'

Dileep ran his finger across his teeth for a moment and shrugged. 'He told us the child's father had disappeared, and the mother had died whoring for the soldiers. He said he himself had no means of providing for the child, for his own lot was now so miserable, and he had nowhere else to turn.

'This was not the Nanak Chand I knew,' said Dileep. 'I could see that the Lord had softened his heart, and I could only rejoice in his salvation and accept the boy into our fold.'

Dileep cocked his head and smiled. 'We didn't know the boy's real name, Diwan, so we called him Jacob. He was half starved when Nanak Chand brought him to us, but he bloomed in our keeping. He was the hardiest little soul you'd ever hope to see. The Reverend took to him especially, for even at three Jacob had a keen interest in books, and used to sit by and listen to the older boys' lessons for hours on end.'

Dileep leaned forward with a bewildered look. 'Then one morning, I'd say more than a year ago, I heard a lot of shouting and wailing in the yard, and I came out to find that a chowkidor had caught a woman trying to sneak onto the grounds. She wouldn't tell us her name, or what she wanted, though I could tell from her baubles what she did for a living. But when I was about to send her away the boys came out to garden with little Jacob in tow, and at the sight of him the woman tore loose of the chowkidor's grip and snatched Jacob up in her arms.

'It took Jacob a little while to recognize her,' said Dileep, studying my face, 'but I know a mother's love when I see it. I begged her to forgive us; we'd been told she was dead. And I cursed myself for believing Nanak Chand's lie. I told her that though we loved Jacob she could take him home, but she shrank back from this and shook her head, and she said the strangest thing, Diwan.'

He stared another moment and set his hands flat atop his desk. 'She said her husband had lived here once, and she knew we would take good care of his son, and all she asked was that we call him by his rightful name.'

'Mahabir,' I whispered, gripping the arms of my chair.

'Mahabir, that's right, Diwan,' Dileep said. 'How did you —'

'Where is he?' I said, jumping up from the chair. 'Where's my son?'

'But you said — '

'Mahabir!' I shouted now, stumbling toward the kitchen, and there I found him, the little boy I'd patted an hour before, standing up from the others with his hands all white with flour.

CHAPTER

67

Mahabir bore with my sudden embrace, glancing across at Dileep for reassurance as my tears puddled up between us. He had such heft to him as I carried him out the kitchen door and into the hiss of the simmering sun. I kept holding him out for a moment to drink in his quick, dark eyes, dust the flour from his perfect hands, trace his brow with my fingers, and then hugging him to me again and pacing about, whispering his name.

'You told me they were dead,' said Dileep, following me at a little distance with his arms crossed.

'Yes,' I told him, fixing my gaze on Mahabir's face. He was a beautiful boy, with his mother's fine chin and broad mouth. 'I'm sorry, Dileep.'

'But why did you lie to me?' he asked simply, without reproach.

I shook my head and pressed Mahabir to me again. 'Habit,' I said, though I knew I owed Dileep better than that.

'Mahabir,' I said, finally letting him down. 'Look at me closely. My name is Balbeer Rao, and I'm your father.'

Mahabir looked over at Dileep for a moment and then stared back up at me, his eyes darting from one side of my face to the other as if to fix me in his memory, and then he reared back one foot and kicked me on the shin.

Dileep scolded him as he ran back to the kitchen, but I told him to leave Mahabir be. A little kick was the least I deserved.

As Dileep pumped fresh water into the bathing trough, I washed the muddy tears from my face and began to tell him everything: about Baroo, about the Pathan and Mangal Singh and my months among the sadhus. He made one of his leaps of faith and believed me, even consoled me about my abandoning Ahalya's trail back in Rajputana. No one would ever have guessed my simple village wife could have travelled all the way to Cawnpore.

He'd never seen her again after that morning a year ago, and she'd never told him where she had come from or where she was going. But he reminded me, as gently as possible, that he had guessed from her ornaments that she was a vaishya, and advised me to seek her in the regimental brothels of Generalganj.

No, I told him flatly, all wounded righteousness. I knew Ahalya. She could never become a whore. She would die first. *Better she were dead*, I heard myself tell Dileep as he stood by, waiting me out, and I suppose I meant it too, for I'd grieved for her already, and by dying she might have spared me the truth.

But when my indignation was expended, Dileep fed me a meal in the Reverend's old potting shed, now shaded by a flourishing tree, and bade me recall her for him, recount our courtship, our marriage, Mahabir's birth, and thus coaxed my hope awake: an old hope I thought I'd smothered to death with ganja all those years before. And so I left my son in my old friend's care and set forth to find Ahalya.

I walked southward from Bastard Bhavan, along the route I used to take with John Christopher on Redeemer Walla's Mutiny tours. A swarm of yellow buntings seemed to materialize out of the dust cloud that billowed overhead like a scrim, and I cast no shadow on the fine dun powder that lay ankle-deep along the roadside.

The chowkidors slept at the gates to the little English bungalows I passed, their memsahibs and babalogues now safe in the cool hill stations for the duration of the hot weather, and here and there along the compound walls lizards basked and dozed.

My old neighborhood was shuttered up against the heat, and

when I paused to stare up at the window to my boyhood home, there was no one in the confectioner's shop below to take notice of me but a small, pockmarked boy who squatted by the trays of sweetmeats, waving a whisk against the flies. Even the Street of Silver was half deserted, but as I turned into the narrow lanes of Ram Ganj, I had the sensation of being followed, though I never heard any footsteps nor caught a glimpse of anyone darting behind me, only felt a faint stirring of my hackles as I plodded along the cluttered street.

I was just approaching the canal bridge that led to the cantonment bazaars of Generalganj when an old widow woman stood up from the gutter at the sight of me and began to jubilate, following along beside me in an impossible stoop and chanting 'Jai Maharaj! Jai Maharaj!' like the mad old man the night before.

Taking her for a beggar, I flung a few coins at her and broke into a run across the street, but she took no notice of the coins, even when two boys leapt out and snatched them up around her, but stood gasping for breath with her eyes shut tight, clasping her hands over her poor shaved head.

The military cantonment stretched for five miles between the Ganga and the Grand Trunk Road. It was laid out like a park, with vast distances separating the canteens, barracks, officers' quarters, churches, hospitals, and all the rest. But between the Commissariat Yard and the Avadh and Rohilkhand line the regimental bazaars were as dense as Ram Ganj. The shops were in army-issue buildings set like barracks in tidy rows, but their proprietors had added so many lean-tos and awnings that on its outskirts Generalganj would have blended imperceptibly into the jumbled bazaars of Ram Ganj, but for the bounding canal.

Generalganj was beginning to stir from its afternoon doldrums as I entered the cantonment among a trio of elephants in chain harness headed for the artillery lines. I walked along a grid of little streets, passing groups of shops in gradual declension, from a row of stationers and booksellers to provisioners and greengrocers, used-furniture dealers, coppersmiths, harnessmakers, cobblers, and butchers.

I asked a sweeper to point the way to the Gora Chakla, where the British soldiers kept their whores, and he pointed down a long narrow lane to a katra separated from the rest of the bazaar by a block of razed ground. The walls were almost twenty feet high, and a single door, guarded by a soldier with a wooden staff, led to the courtyard inside.

On my march from Bastard Bhavan I had tried to brace myself for anything, but in my imagination I'd expected a gaudier apparition, like the chaklas I had passed through with Nanda, where girls with painted faces stood out on balconies and rooftops, boasting of their proficiencies to the men below. But this chakla was so austere from the outside that if it hadn't been for the sherbet shops in the vicinity I might have taken it for a dispensary or a jail.

I squatted in the ruined block for an hour or so, contemplating the katra's entrance and despairing of ever getting past the guard. But in the late afternoon, as the sherbet sellers set out their tables and benches for the evening trade, Hindu youths began to appear at the door, show something to the English guard, and gain entry to the Gora Chakla.

So I stationed myself in a doorway at the far end of the little lane and waited a few minutes until a similar youth passed in that direction, and I snatched him up and covered his mouth and dragged him into the shadows.

I pinned him down among the rubble, and with all the ferocity I could muster I whispered, 'Now you listen to me, you little pimp. If you struggle, I'll kill you. If you help me, I'll pay you. Which is it going to be?'

Of course, with my hand over his mouth I might have asked a yes-or-no question, but I gathered from his hopeful nod that he'd decided to live, and I slowly brought my hand away from his sneering lips.

He was a sorry-looking brat with a deep scar in his scalp, and he stared up with a leer that seemed to be permanent.

'Those boys,' I said, nodding my head down the lane. 'What is it they show the guard?'

'Ticket,' he said, squirming a little beneath me.

'What do they *do* in there?' I asked, leaning in close to his face.

The boy's eyes lit up a little and he gave me a thin grin, like a snake. 'You want to jiggy-jig, maharaj?' he asked. 'Gora Chakla's very good for jiggy-jig. But no Hindu gentlemen allowed at night. You come in the morning. I'll get you in. You try my girl. She's number twenty-five. Brand-new. You'll like her very much.'

His breath was like soured milk, but as I listened I tasted something sweet boiling in the back of my throat and clamped my hand over his mouth again, glaring at him so hard that my eyes began to ache.

'Shut up,' I told him. 'Shut up and answer me this. Why do they let you in the Gora Chakla? What is it you do?'

I uncovered his mouth again and wiped his spit on my shirt. He swallowed, as if to sober himself, and said, 'It – it's the hot time, maharaj. The Feringhee soldiers boil. My number twenty-five is first-class quality. She's got number one punkah boy.'

'You're her punkah walla?'

'That's right, maharaj,' he said. 'I'm the number one punkah walla. I see through a hole, and when they start I pull slowly and when they finish I pull fast. Very scientific. And the soldiers pay me a pice. Sometimes two. You try in the morning, maharaj. Number twenty-five likes Hindu men so much better. She's going to like you, maharaj. But tonight, only English soldiers – '

'Is there – is there a woman there named Ahalya?' I asked, peering out at the katra walls.

'Maybe so, maharaj. Could be. Lots of girls in Gora Chakla. All got numbers.'

'She's small,' I said. 'Dark. Ahir, from Gwalior.'

But the boy could only give me a confused shrug.

'Your ticket,' I said, leaning my forearm against his throat. 'Give me your ticket.'

The boy glanced sideways. 'I – I don't have a ticket,' he muttered, twisting his chin about, trying to breathe against my weight.

But now I caught sight of his clenched fist, and when I pried it open a little tin medallion stamped '25' fell to the ground beside him.

'Please, maharaj,' the boy said with a panicked look. 'I can't work without my ticket.'

'No,' I said, slipping it into my kammerband. 'But I can.'

I paid him a rupee, the equivalent of sixty-four of his miserable fees, and told him to retrieve his token at Bastard Bhavan in the morning. But if he cried out now or reported me to anyone, my friends, I said, would cut his throat.

He seemed to believe me, and his eyes darted about as I climbed off him. 'Now, go!' I barked, and he slipped back into the lane and with his rupee clenched in his skinny fist, he ran off toward the canal.

I found a barber a block or so away, across from the dhobis' stalls, and paid him to shave my moustache and cut my hair to the punkah boy's length. I hid myself in the rubble of the empty lot and tore my trousers into strips, knotting them together and wrapping them around my loins like a dhoti. By early evening the crows and adjutant birds had already gathered to beg from the soldiers who sat in twos and threes in the sherbet shops. A Moslem peddler, obviously lost, lurched around the corner of the katra wall, and the guard chased after him, whacking his staff against the ground as the soldiers cheered him on.

I closed my eyes and tried to fortify myself with some recollection of Ahalya, and then, when it was almost dark, I stood and began to run toward the gate, waving my tin medallion and shouting, 'Late, sahib! Late, sahib!' at the top of my voice.

The guard jammed his staff across the doorway and snarled at me as I came to a halt before him. He was as square as a brick in his red coat, and his face and eyes were as devoid of color as the sweat that dripped from his pale yellow whiskers. He was bareheaded, with a flat, squashed nose and one ear all chewed away.

'And who in bloody hell are you?' he wanted to know, looking me up and down.

I couldn't bear the sight of him and rolled my eyes around like a simpleton. 'Late, sahib! I number twenty-five cousin. He sick, sahib. Not work tonight. I come pull punkah number twenty-five.'

'His cousin, are you?' he asked, tapping me lightly on the shoulder with his metal-tipped staff.

'Y-yes, sahib,' I said, crossing my eyes now and biting on my tongue.

'You're a little old for a chakla punkah boy, ain't you?'

'Oh, yes, sahib,' I replied, grinning around like a fool. 'I older cousin, yes. Pull for number twenty-five.'

The sergeant stared at me a moment and then snatched the medallion out of my hand and delicately inspected it in the light from the little lamp that burned over the doorway.

'This ain't no proper token,' he muttered to himself, bending it slightly between his fingers.

'Aw, come on, sarge,' cried a lean soldier from one of the sherbet shops, uncapping a flask. 'I got number twenty-five tonight. I'll die in there without a proper punkah.'

'The cupid's itch'll get you first, Jeffries,' said the sergeant, still frowning at the little token.

'I'll vouch for the little nigger, sarge,' called another. 'He's a good nigger, he is.'

'Go vouch for your grandma,' replied the sergeant, staring at me now with his glassy eyes.

'Oh, yes, sahib!' I said quickly, before my legs gave way beneath me. 'I very good nigger. Pull slow. Pull fast. Keep you cool you jiggy-jig.'

The sergeant grinned at me, baring a broken tooth or two, and tossed the medallion over his shoulder and into the courtyard.

'Well?' he asked as I stood dumbfounded before him. 'What are you waiting for?' And he booted me through the door.

I scrambled after the little token and found myself surrounded by mud-and-plaster huts with tile roofs, each with a number painted over the door. Before I drew too many stares from the women and soldiers walking to and fro across the courtyard, I ducked into the hut marked 25, and settled myself down in the passageway between the door and the curtained-off room, giving the punkah rope a tentative pull.

'Bhanu,' a girl's voice called out from within. 'Get in here!'

I wondered for a moment if Ahalya's voice could have changed so much, from the soft husky tone I remembered to this harsh, imperious whine.

'I'm not Bhanu, memsahib,' I called back through the curtain. 'I'm Bhanu's cousin. Bhanu's sick tonight.'

There was a long silence, and I thought first, What if Bhanu has no cousins? And then I thought, What if number twenty-five really is Ahalya and she recognizes my voice? But then she sighed and said,

'Did you check in with the mahaldar?'

The mahaldar! I said to myself. I'd forgotten these places had proprietors.

'Boy?'

'Yes, memsahib,' I said finally.

'Good. But you're late. What's your name?'

'Uh – Puran, memsahib,' I said.

'Well, you already missed one, Puran. You pull extra hard for the next one or I'll tell the mahaldar.'

'Yes, memsahib,' I said, still in my simpleton's voice, and then the lean soldier was suddenly standing in the doorway, wavering on his feet.

'This number twenty-five?' he asked, wobbling a little as he extracted a string of glass beads from his red coat.

'Yes, sahib,' I said, turning my face away from the whiskey vapors on his breath.

'All right then,' he said, stepping forward through the curtain. 'You pull that bloody punkah good tonight.'

I squatted down under the rope and began to pull on it as number twenty-five and the tipsy soldier set the bed to creaking.

I leaned forward to peer up and down the row of huts across the way. There must have been forty of them. How in God's name was I ever going to find her? How did I even know she was here? On the strength of Dileep's hunch I was playing punkah boy in a regimental brothel! What could Dileep know about women? What did he know about the world?

But then something struck me as strange about one of the huts that faced me: strange and familiar all at once. Where all the others had two steps leading up to them, this one had three, and the lintel of the door was set a good foot lower than the others, so that anyone entering had to bow down low.

'The *punkah*, boy!' the soldier gasped from behind the curtain, and I sank back into the passageway and jerked at the rope. But after a while I had to peer out again at the wonder of Ahalya's dustoor, transposed to the brothels of Generalganj.

The soldier staggered out through the dingy curtain with his coat unbuttoned and his shirt untucked, and kicked at me with a dusty boot.

'Bloody useless wog,' he slurred, wobbling out into the courtyard.

There was no sound from within but a faint trickle of water. I let go the rope, and peering through the punkah walla's spyhole I saw number twenty-five squatting on the floor by her bed, wringing a towel over a pan of soapy water.

I crawled out into the shadows to find the courtyard nearly deserted. It was not yet nightfall, and at the far end of the katra a barber manned a bathing station, heating an assortment of battered kettles over a brick stove, and a small boy with a torch was making the rounds of the lamps that hung here and there from the doors to the huts.

I stared hard at Ahalya's door for a moment, daring myself to move. She might not even be there any more, I tried to tell myself. She could have been banished to the Kala Chakla in Ram Ganj with the pox. But then I spotted a little potted tulsi plant thriving by the steps, and I willed myself across the courtyard.

I could see a flaring ember bob in the darkened doorway, and stooped my way into the little passage to find a punkah boy smoking a bidi by the entrance to Ahalya's chamber, pulling the rope with his curled toes. The air smelled of tobacco and incense, rose water and sweat, and from behind the thin blue curtain that hung from the lintel I could hear an Englishman softly droning.

The boy couldn't have been more than six years old, but he looked up at me with a complicitous nod. 'Bhai?' he asked. 'You new here?'

'Yes,' I whispered, staring at the flickering light that played upon the curtain. 'Look,' I said, still devising my plan as I spoke. 'I'm Bhanu's cousin. Number twenty-five. The mahaldar, he wants you to switch with me tonight. Says you're the best. Needs you for some special customers.'

The boy made no move, squinting up at me through the smoke of his cigarette. 'Number twenty-five? Are you sure?'

'Yes,' I said, trying to keep from throwing him out the door. 'The whole night?'

'Yes,' I said, clenching my fists. 'The whole night.'

'But twenty-five's good business,' he muttered, rubbing a hand across his lips. 'This one takes all night.'

'Look,' I whispered, grabbing at his rope now. 'The mahaldar says hurry!'

'I'm going,' said the boy, rising from his squat. 'Watch you pull straight,' he said, departing into the yard. 'The pulley's loose.'

I took his place by the curtain and closed my eyes, breathing through my mouth so I wouldn't be dizzied by the perfumed air, and then, with a groan, and the sweat pouring off me like rain, I stood up and stepped into the room.

And there was my long-lost wife, Ahalya, and for all my horror and shame, my heart nearly burst at the sight of her. She sat on a charpoy, bare to the waist, across from a young soldier reading to her by candlelight from a book of verse. Neither of them saw me enter, for the soldier sat with his back to me and Ahalya idly picked at her nails with her painted face downcast and her breasts hanging heavily in the heat.

The soldier was fully clothed, and read to Ahalya in a martial meter, holding his little book out at arm's length as if it might explode.

'Sahib!' I said loudly, for now I couldn't seem to keep myself from shouting. 'Sahib, mahaldar apologizing! Number thirty-two must be coming quickly! Officer is calling for her! Very big matter!'

The soldier peered around, a new recruit with a baby's face, heartbroken at the sight of me.

'Oh, dear,' he said, closing his book. 'Yes, of course. Well, it *is* awfully late,' he said, standing from his chair and clicking his heels together, nearly toppling the iron candlestick.

'M-may I call on you again?' he asked, turning back toward Ahalya. 'This has been a lovely evening. I so hope I shall see you again. Well, goodnight,' he said, backing into me, and then, turning stiffly about-face, he marched out of the room.

Through all this Ahalya stared at me, frozen where she sat, with her eyes encircled with lampblack and her painted lips agape.

She called me 'Balho,' and then 'husband,' and when I stepped toward her she flung herself down and touched my feet and wept, crossing her arms over her breasts. I begged her forgiveness, but she rose and across my lips she placed her hand, now so soft and smooth, and begged me to forgive her, and when I embraced her she seemed to cower out of shame.

'Ahalya,' I said as the voices rose in the courtyard. 'I've come for you. We've got to go.'

She covered her face in her hands as I quickly draped a blanket over her shoulders and led her toward the door, but she squirmed free when we reached the curtain and darted into the corner.

I pulled her back to her feet, and snatching up the candlestick, I dragged her by the wrist into the courtyard. Out of the corner of my eye I saw there was a commotion at the bathing station, but I hurried Ahalya to the gate. The guard was not at his station, but refreshing himself in one of the sherbet shops across the way.

'Hello? What's *this* now?' he called out, rising from a rickety chair and taking up his stick.

I forced my legs to pause and turned around to face him, crossing my eyes again and agitating my head.

'Uh – number twenty-five, sahib,' I sputtered. 'She's getting bad menses troubles. Too much blood. Must be taking Lock Hospital.'

He crossed the lane and stared at Ahalya's tear-streaked face under the veil of her blanket.

'Where's Nanak Chand the mahaldar?' he wanted to know. '*He* should take care of this.'

I gaped a moment at Nanak Chand's mention. 'Yes, sahib,' I said, beginning to pull Ahalya along again. 'He so busy, sahib. Send me take number twenty-five Lock Hospital.'

He paused to ponder this as we stumbled around the corner now and along the katra's wall.

'But wait,' he said, following after us. 'That ain't the way to the Lock Hospital.'

I pulled Ahalya into the crook of a wall and ducked my head around. There was no one else in sight but a shoeshine boy hurrying to the sherbet shops around the corner.

'And what're you doing with that candlestick?' the sergeant demanded to know, shifting his grip on his staff.

Ahalya gasped as I answered him by stepping forward and raising the candlestick over my head.

The sergeant grinned and hunched down, striking at my knees to fell me, but as the staff arched around with an evil hum I somehow hopped over it, and caught him on his backswing with a chop to his bare crown.

He dropped his staff and fell to one knee with the blood pouring black as ink between his astounded eyes, and he paused there, as if in prayer, as I jerked Ahalya away.

She begged me to forget her, to leave her behind and save myself, struggling every few yards to shake me loose. But then she looked back and saw the guard stand and retrieve his stick, and she lifted her sari above her knees and ran with me like a village girl.

The sergeant raised no alarm, but pounded along behind us in his great boots, gaining on us as we stumbled over the railroad tracks and dashed the quarter mile to the depleted canal. I pushed Ahalya down the embankment and commanded her to go on to Bastard Bhavan while I lured him off her trail.

She refused and began to scramble back up to me, but as the sergeant's footfall grew heavier behind me I shouted to her that Mahabir was deathly ill. She believed this desperate lie, and with a groan she turned and squattered through the water, begging me to follow.

I watched until the dark closed around her, and I turned back toward the tracks. I could see the sergeant clearly now, slouching down the road some thirty yards distant, and I ran to the Commissariat Yard and pulled myself up onto the wall, dancing and hooting like an ape until he finally turned off Ahalya's path and ran straight for me with his staff upraised.

He struck at my feet, but I leapt out of the way and landed in the yard, dashing into a herd of pack camels. The sergeant climbed over the wall, landing heavily behind me, and ranged along the yard's perimeter, following the wave of panic I raised as I stumbled through a forest of camels' legs.

Soon I was half blind in the dust the camels kicked up with their dung-caked hoofs, and I bumped against their knobby limbs, all hide and bone. I meant to cross into the bullock yard and circle around to the canal, but I must have lost my bearings, and almost suffocating now on the sour dust, I fell out from among the honking, blustering herd into a corner of the yard where the top of the wall rose out of reach to meet the roof of a shed, and whirling around I found myself not ten feet from the advancing sergeant.

The camels sniggered and pranced as he plodded toward me, his brow rent and swollen and his pale eyes burning in their gory sockets.

'She was my wife,' I said, and not to appeal to the sergeant's decency either, but just so he'd know before he killed me, as I knew he would, for I had no weapon and he, for his part, had no witnesses.

He chuffed like a locomotive and snarled at me in a strange tongue, raising his thick staff in both his hands. I fell to my knees and prepared for death as best I could, whispering goodbyes to my wife and son. Gazing beyond my advancing executioner, I saw death approach like a great shadow out from among the pack camels, but it enveloped the sergeant, not me, and hurled him like a broken doll under the camels' trample.

'Genda!' I said as the shadow paused above me.

'Rao Sahib,' it rumbled back with a slow bow, and through the dust I saw the great pocked face protrude, and the heavy hands reach forward to lift me to my feet.

As the camels kicked the sergeant's corpse about, Genda led me over the wall, and I followed after him down to the canal like a child.

'My wife,' I said, trotting along to keep up with him, though his steps were slow and stately. 'She ran ahead.'

'She'll be safe,' he said with the finality of fate, stepping down to the edge of the canal where a small thatched boat was beached.

Genda bade me sit on the prow of the boat and heaved it out into the shallow water. He waded a little way, pushing the boat ahead of him until the water grew deeper, and then pulled himself onto the deck, nearly submerging the rear and lifting me high off the water until he'd settled himself in the middle and taken up the oars.

He rowed us past Generalganj and up through Old Nauchgar toward the Ganga, one giant foot set like a leathery cushion against the frame of the thatch roof.

'Where are we going, Genda?' I asked, daring now to lay my head upon the deck as he rowed us along with leisurely strokes.

'Sleep, Rao Sahib,' he said in a voice that gently trembled the deckboards. 'I'm taking you home.'

CHAPTER
69

We floated to the mouth of the canal and turned upriver, between sandbars littered with turtles. A faint breeze grazed the water, and as we pulled out into the moonstruck river the city's clamor subsided into a dull pulse from the mills and the ringing of a bell on the railroad bridge.

Rolling onto my back and gazing up at the dim stars as they slipped behind the thatch, I soon fell asleep to the gurgle of Genda's oars in the silver flow. I hadn't had a night's sleep since Harigarh, and I slumbered soundly, for when I awoke I was still lying on my back, and the stars had turned to swallows in a purple sky.

I looked around at Genda, still rowing us along in the broad stream, and rubbed my eyes.

'How long have I been asleep?' I asked, sitting up and blinking around at the sandy shore.

Genda hawked and spat over the side. 'All night, Rao Sahib,' he said with a yawn that clinked and groaned like a drawbridge.

'All night?'

'Yes, Rao Sahib,' he said, shrugging his shoulders. 'It's good. You need your strength.'

'But we should be home by now,' I said, meaning Bastard Bhavan, as I searched the banks behind us for Cawnpore's stacks and spires.

'We're almost there,' said Genda, sliding a sack to me. 'Eat now, Rao Sahib, before we reach the shore.'

I saw no sign of the city, only a few huts along the farthest bank, and realized with a start that we were slipping along the northern bank, on the Lucknow side of the river.

'Genda,' I said, staring over at him now. 'Where are we? Where are you taking me?'

Genda shrugged his lips and gazed off at a flock of spoonbills feeding along the shore.

'Genda,' I said, reaching forward to stay his oar. 'Answer me.'

'Home, Rao Sahib,' he said quietly, and though I pulled hard on one oar he kept rowing without difficulty, and I merely bobbed around for a few strokes as if caught on an engine's piston.

'Genda,' I said finally, sitting back and gaping up at him. 'Who are you?'

Genda sniffed and smacked his lips a moment, laying his matchstick oars across his lap. 'I'm your servant, Rao Sahib,' he said, 'I'm your protector.'

'You saved my life,' I said, 'and I thank you for it. But who sent you to watch over me?'

Genda gazed off again and dipped his oars back in the water. 'Genda?'

He sighed, and his shirt seemed to billow like a sail. 'Have a little faith in me, Rao Sahib. That's all I ask. I do not wish you harm.'

I rushed to my feet and gripped the thatch, looking back downriver.

'Genda,' I said, 'Take me back. Take me home to my wife and son.'

'I can't, Rao Sahib,' he said mournfully. 'Later I will. Afterward. But not now.'

'Afterward? After what?'

Genda held his breath a moment and shrugged. 'After you know the truth.'

'About what, Genda?' I cried. 'About you?'

'No, sahib,' he said with a worried look, as if afraid he was overstepping his bounds. 'About your father.'

'My father!' I said. 'But I *know* about my father.'

'Ah,' he said with a kindly look, 'Company Bagh. No, Rao Sahib,' he said, looking off toward shore. 'That's only half a truth.'

'It – it's enough for me,' I said, as an old fear fluttered through my belly.

'It's *nothing!*' Genda suddenly exclaimed, glaring at me.

I swallowed and gasped, pressing my back against the rickety roof. 'Please, Genda,' I said. 'Take me back to Bastard Bhavan. Leave me be.'

Genda looked away as if embarrassed for me and shook his head.

'If you don't,' I said, taking a step toward the edge of the boat, 'I'll jump.'

'Then I will have to pull you out,' he said simply, counter-balancing my weight by the merest shift of his huge leg.

'I mean it, Genda,' I said, raising one foot over the water.

'I know, Rao Sahib,' he said patiently. 'You're a brave man. You proved that in the Gora Chakla. But look at the current here. See how it curls around? See how I must pull against it? Even if you got away from me you'd drown, and what would be the point of that, Rao Sahib, when I mean you no harm?'

I stood poised a moment longer and collapsed on the deck, trying to keep from weeping as he drew the boat to shore. 'Then I'll run away from you,' I said as the hull hissed to a halt on the sandy bank.

'Then I'll catch you, Rao Sahib,' he said, standing and pitching the oars off into the water. 'And if you try to kill me I will stop you. And if you try to trick me, well, I won't be fooled. No matter what you do I'll abide by you, and take you to your fate.'

So there was nothing for it but to slouch after Genda and do what I was told. If I disappoint you in this, if you imagine I should have stood up to him, I only wish you could have been there to see how easily he pushed the boat back into the stream, or how the elevated planks that traversed the mudflats bowed beneath him and jumped and clattered in his trail.

As the boat slowly spun out into the current, we walked to a grove of trees that leaned bare-rooted along the flood line, where an albino syce was waiting with a scrawny brown gelding already laden with provisions. Genda lifted me onto its back and gripped its bridle, leading us northward onto the blistering plain as the syce danced in our dust for a mile or so, chanting and shaking a string of beads.

My guess is that we'd begun our journey south of Kanauj, just opposite where the boatmen had thrown me off their budgerow all those years before. But it's only a guess, because Genda wouldn't tell me any more about our whereabouts than he would say about our destination, and I never spoke to another soul in the whole two weeks we travelled.

The sun did rise on my right and fall on my left for the first few days, so I suppose we must have travelled straight up the stretch of Avadh that lies between Sitapur and Lucknow, though we never came close to either city. In fact, we skirted the towns altogether, and slept in desolate places to the calling of leopards and jackals.

The satchels that hung from my loath old pony were well stocked with provisions, and we carried five-gallon bottles of water wrapped in straw, but I had no appetite in the never-ending heat, and the sound of the water sloshing all around me was a torture. Genda gave me a loose tunic to wear, and a turban wrapped in the Mahratta style, but the sun burned through like acid as we plodded across Avadh.

For the first day or so I tried to occupy myself by memorizing landmarks along our path, for I think I still idly contemplated escape. But the only landmarks were the efflorescent beds of vanished tanks, some nearly half a mile across, and the ruined villages with their bricks all heaped and charred, where the rebels and the British had passed through twenty years before, and I saw these in such numbers that I soon lost track of their sequence.

I tried to engage Genda in a little conversation, but his lot, of course, was worse by far than mine, and he seemed to march before me in a trance. So by the morning of the third day I too had fallen silent, and stared down at my pony for so many miles that I can still picture the disposition of its mane and the constellation of fly bites along its lathered neck.

We crossed two rivers, the Sarda on the fourth day and the Gogra on the evening of the fifth – names I learned only a week or so ago, when I was packing up your maps. I dozed off when I could, and often as not I dreamed about my mother, except that now she kept raising her smoldering arm and pointing down a whitewashed road, and when I half awoke one afternoon to see a dust devil hopping by in the distance, peppered with whirling debris, I cried out and jumped down from my pony's back, refusing to go another step until Genda gently lifted me back again.

We cast blankets over a few low bushes and slept beneath them through the worst heat of the sixth day. As we set forth that night Genda warned me to be silent, for we were passing through a taluk that had been bestowed upon the loyal Maharaja of Kapurthala, who jealously guarded it with patrols on all its boundaries.

But we never saw a single soldier the whole night, nor any other living soul, and by dawn we'd crossed out of Avadh and into a stretch of Nepal that was known back then as the Land of Twenty-two Kings. Here the plain began to heave and crack into ridges and ravines, and a faint bank of hills rose up from the horizon all lush with shade trees.

But the trees might as well have been a mirage, for all they marked was the edge of the terai, Nepal's bulwark, the three-hundred-mile band of pestilential swamp and jungle that lay rotting at the Himalayas' feet. The sodden trees turned the heat of the plains to steam, and as we climbed the tangled slopes the dust and clay became a thick, begrudging muck.

We slept in shifts to keep watch against the tigers we could hear rumbling out among the sal trees, for the firewood Genda gathered was too wet to raise more than a foul brown smoke. Genda slumbered deeply, snoring like a quake with his great jaw drooping, but escape never seemed more futile. Hopelessness hung over the terai like a sopping shroud, and by morning I'd be half mad from the mocking treetop squawk and chatter; the sulfur stench of the marsh; the whine of the mosquitoes, fat as bees, that braved the campfire smoke.

In the worst of the swamps I dismounted to keep the pony's legs from sinking above the knees, and two or three days beyond the border a snake attached itself to my pony's leg. The serpent thrashed like an eel as Genda stabbed at it with a stick, but it must not have been venomous, for once we'd bound the pony's leg she merely limped a little. Still, it seemed to trouble Genda, and that evening he admitted to me his belief that snakes of the terai carried the ayul on their breaths — the virulent fever that infested the swamplands.

Now in the days it took us to cross through the terai I must have seen a score of snakes, including a python we came upon ingesting a pig, and a cobra that rose up from among our water bottles one night. And all manner of vile creatures dropped upon us from the trees, including a centipede as long as my forearm. In some places you couldn't stand still for an instant lest the ants overtake you, and I opened one of our sacks one morning to find three black scorpions in residence.

But the leeches terrorized me most. The mosquitoes stung when they struck, and the ants gave a tickle when they scurried up my legs, but I could wade for miles and never know the leeches had attached themselves to me until I reached dry land and saw the green worms studding my legs or felt my blood trickling from the fine, triangular wounds they inflicted. Even after Genda had singed them off, I could feel their ghosts stretch and flex in a trail of slime across my puckered flesh.

I think Genda burned with fever from the fourth to the sixth day we slogged through the terai, for his eyes swam when he looked at me and here and there he would break into an astonishing song. But he would never admit to the ague, and staggered along as always.

After six days of rain and muck the grade grew steeper and we climbed up beyond the clouds into dry, narrow valleys set amid ridges and spurs. Pines and flowering mimosa intruded on the sal forests, and here and there, on an outcropping of stone, a cool, dry breeze cut into the damp heat, and in the deepening blue sky the sun began to lose its aureole.

In a few of these valleys we came upon settlements of the most miserable human beings I ever saw. They lived in little clusters of brick hovels with excrement heaped by every door and the muddy lanes littered with bones and offal from their blood sacrifices.

They were a nasty-looking lot. In some places it seemed as though there must have been a decree that any man who wasn't a cretin had to be a drunk, and any woman lacking a goitre had to have her nose removed. They were stout, with faces as flat as drumheads and calves like cannonballs, and everyone, men and women alike, had moustaches.

I don't know what religion they claimed to practice; I hope it wasn't Hindu. They seemed to sacrifice some poor creature every time they turned around, and in one village the headman greeted us by offering us a drink of chicken's blood, twisting the head off a little rooster as you might uncork a bottle and taking a swig himself of the jetting gore.

The men wore broad swords which they flourished at each other whenever their poor wives passed with their conical basketloads of kindling and dung, and in two villages we passed the bodies of young men slain by jealous husbands, or of husbands slain by jealous young men. Genda wasn't sure.

Genda claimed he understood the random clicks and whines that composed their speech, but I still hope he misunderstood the man who, according to Genda's translation, offered to exchange his baby daughter for a chance to lie with my pony, though I suppose I have to give this some credence when I recall how he leered and whistled as we passed.

Early in what must have been the third week of our journey, Genda led me through a narrow pass so obscured by vegetation that it seemed at first as though he were leading me directly into the mountainside. The crooked defile brought us out into a vast, uncultivated valley, where Genda left our pony in a shepherd's keeping, slinging what was left of our provisions over his shoulder and leading me up the steep slope of an adjoining mountain.

My saddle-weary legs ached and trembled as we climbed together, and Genda's great bulk loosened avalanches of gravel as he stepped from ledge to ledge. He moved before me with astounding grace, and here and there reached back down to pull me up beside him.

After a day or so the trees became sparse and dwarfed, and the thin air burned like liquor in my throat. We would reach one peak only to ascend another, and I kept gasping up at Genda's back and demanding to know, 'Where are you taking me? Where are we going?'

'Soon, Rao Sahib,' was all he would say. 'We'll be there soon.'

I vomited up the meals he served me at our little camps, and I couldn't distinguish my exhaustion from my deepening terror. In my sleep I gasped for air, and on the windy ledges I began to hear my mother's howl. Despair stripped my legs of all their sinew, and at the slightest recollection of my wife and son I would stagger and sob and lag behind, until at last I could go no farther, and Genda carried me on his shoulders down the slope and on into a great pine wood.

He set me down in a shallow gorge and washed my clothes in the stream as I shuddered and mumbled on a bank of moss. He forced me to drink a sweet broth he prepared from his store of provisions, and I kept it down somehow, though it roiled in my throat as the darkness fell.

I thrashed through the night like a man floundering in a river, slipping into sleep and then scrambling out again, gasping for breath, at the first glimpse of the beasts that lurked in the depths of my dreams. I dreamed I was in Company Bagh, digging around my father's obelisk with a mali's spade, and unearthing Baroo's twisted cadaver, and Mangal Singh's and Moonshi's, and the Reverend's, and the old hakeem's, all folded like puppets, and when I came to Willard's it turned to dust, and I looked up to see that the obelisk had now become Shiva's smoking, beckoning worm.

CHAPTER

70

At dawn Genda shaved the stubble from my face and scalp and dunked me in a frigid pool to wash the hairs away. I barely had the strength to stand as he dressed me in my newly laundered clothes.

'This is the day, isn't it, Genda?' I asked as he wrapped my turban for me.

'Yes, Rao Sahib,' he said, tucking my turban's tail into the tight coil and standing back with an appraising squint.

'But is it much further?'

'Come, Rao Sahib,' was his only answer as he hefted our sacks and bottles.

'You'll have to carry me, Genda,' I said, raising my arms to him like a toddler.

'No, Rao Sahib,' he said, striking out along the rapids. 'Not today. It wouldn't be seemly.'

'But I can't walk!' I called after him.

'You're going to have to try,' he said without so much as a glance back as he disappeared around a bend in the stream.

'But I can't, Genda,' I shouted, crossing my arms, 'and I won't!'

I waited awhile for Genda to capitulate, and nodded confidently when I heard his rumble in the woods behind me. But then I caught a glimpse of him far downstream, still plodding along, and looking behind me I saw something lumbering among the shadows, and before Genda's figure had disappeared in the spray that flew from the cataracts and flumes I bounded after him, and for all my exhaustion I caught up with him just as he cut away from the stream and into the dark wood.

We followed a vague, undulating trail through stands of towering pines inhabited by tiny, bucktoothed deer that scattered at our approach, barking like dogs. We left the trail around noon and zigzagged along the warm, dappled floor, littered with cones and needles, until we came to an elephant's skeleton moldering in a little clearing, with its long-bow ribs covered over with moss.

Here Genda set down his kit and pointed to a steep, jagged hill veiled in clouds.

'This is as far as I take you, Rao Sahib,' he said. 'You must go the rest of the way alone.'

'The rest of the way to where?' I wanted to know as he hung one of his satchels on my shoulder.

'At the end of the clearing you will find a path marked with tridents. Follow it as far as it leads.'

'But Genda,' I said, 'you can't send me off like this.'

'Just follow the tridents, Rao Sahib,' he said, pushing me forward. 'You'll see. You won't get lost.'

'Won't get lost? I'm *already* lost! Forget it, Genda,' I said, stepping toward him. 'I'm not going anywhere without you.'

Genda sighed and placed his hand on my head. 'You must, Rao Sahib,' he said quietly.

'Well, I won't,' I piped back.

But then he began to close his fingers around my skull as if inspecting an orange. I think he meant it as a gentle admonition, but when he released me I shrank back from him with the stubble bumped up on the back of my neck.

'Now go, Rao Sahib,' he said, picking up his kit. 'I'll come back for you soon.'

I turned around and held my breath a moment, clasping the satchel and peering up at the enshrouded hill.

'Please, Genda,' I said. 'Can't you at least — '

But when I turned around to plead with him he was gone. I called out for him and thrashed along the clearing's edge awhile, but it was as though he'd vanished into the ground or flown up into the gathering clouds.

So I did as I was told and finally crossed the clearing in search of the trident path. I saw no sign of it at first, and reeled into the wood, panting like a panther's prey, but casting my eyes upward I caught a glimpse of a row of saplings to my right whose branches had been pruned into tines. Catching my breath and drawing the spit back into my mouth, I followed the row into the deep woods and up the base of a mountain.

The path gently zigzagged along the mountain's face until it took a steeper course marked by small, whittled tridents stuck in little heaps of stone. I followed these up into the belly of the clouds, where the trees became stunted and windblown and finally gave way to mean brush and weathered rock. The clouds dampened my waistcloth and beaded the hairs on my arms as I clambered along from stone to stone and collapsed at last on a broad ledge shrouded in mist.

I hunched against the wind awhile and rubbed my arms and bruised feet, searching the slope for the next leg of the trident path. Then suddenly there was a great thump, and another, and another, like the dull beat of a slack drum.

I rose to my feet and stared hard into the mist that blew along the ledge and thought I saw something move in faint adumbration.

'This way!' someone called through the fog in a hoarse drone, like an old charan. 'This way to the durbar!'

I slowly stepped forward and after a few paces found myself standing at the mouth of a cave. An iron trident, rusted in the mountain damp, jutted up above the entrance, on a spire fashioned from the schist that lay strewn along the mountainside. Chains and buckles hung here and there like an elephant's tackle, and shreds, as of rotted yellow tent, drooped from a webbing of rope along the ceiling. A small fire smoldered in the vestibule, and a few feet into the cavern rose a crude stone wall with a curtained portal.

'Sit! Sit!' the voice croaked from within, and I slowly knelt down by the fire, across from a heap of decaying mats and bolsters.

There was a clattering noise from behind the curtain and a few muttered curses, and then the rattle of a hand drum.

'Life and glory everlasting,' the voice now called out, 'to Shrimunt Maharaj Dhiraj Dhundoo Punt Nana Sahib Punt Purdhan Peshwa Bahadur!'

And out the portal shuffled the strangest old man I ever saw. His bloodshot eyes burned in a face all coated in ashes, like a sadhu, or a mad clown. He wore a brocade tunic turned green with mold, and a silken turban in the Mahratta style, but half unravelled on one side with bare peacock quills poking out along the crown. He held a sceptre of some kind in one hand that might well have been gold, but with its gemstones pried away, and in the other hand he flourished a tasseled scroll.

I rose instinctively as he stopped and stared at me awhile, and for a moment I thought I recognized him from somewhere.

'The spit and image,' he whispered to himself. 'The very spit and image.'

'Who are you?' I blurted, stepping back as he shuffled past me to the heap of moldering pillows.

'Who am I, the boy asks,' he muttered sidelong, as if to a courtier's ghost, as he painfully settled in among his bolsters. 'Don't you listen?' he asked petulantly. 'Do we have to repeat everything? I am the Nana Sahib, boy. I am Punt Purdhan Peshwa Bahadur!'

I gave out a laugh, as you might well have too, for he was a sorry sight in his filthy cave, about as regal as a nag or a poor, starved mouse. But then I suddenly thought of the elephant's skeleton in the clearing below, and my laughter trailed off. This *couldn't* be the Nana Sahib, I told myself, but even that seemed to double back on me, for I remembered what the Reverend had said of him all those years ago on his Mutiny tour. Dhundoo Punt, the Nana Sahib, the Beast of Cawnpore, the Bithur Butcher, 'condemned to wander in the wilderness, where there is no way.'

'Did you bring the ghee?' the old man asked in an ardent whisper, fixing his eyes on my satchel.

'Wh-what?'

'The *ghee*, boy,' he said. 'Didn't you bring it?'

I stared at him a moment longer. Under all his ashes, wrinkles, and rotting finery lurked someone I'd seen before.

'I – I don't know,' I said, gripping the satchel.

'Well, look in your sack, boy,' he snapped. 'Don't keep me waiting.'

I slowly reached into the satchel and brought out a tin which he ordered me to bring to him, plucking it out of my hand when I obeyed. He turned away from me and protectively, like a beggar shielding his alms, pried open the tin with his sceptre and dipped in a finger to sample its contents.

'Ah,' he said, smacking his lips and cackling. 'Real ghee. No more of that muck from the shepherds. Goat piss and tallow – that's what it was,' he muttered, snapping back the lid and tucking the jar between his legs.

'Now tell me, boy,' he said, 'how did Genda talk you into coming all this way?'

'He – he told me you knew the truth,' I said, returning to my place by the fire.

'The truth?' he said, glancing around as if at an audience. 'The boy must be a proper fool to come so far for such a meagre thing as the truth.'

He ducked his head modestly, as if to subdue the approbation of his spectral retinue.

'Maharaj-ji,' I said with grudging respect, 'Genda said you – '

'Everyone wants *something* from me,' he said obliviously with a pompous sigh.

'Maharaj-ji,' I persisted, 'do you know about my father?'

The old man smiled mordantly to his left. 'Do I know about his father, the boy wants to know.

'Of *course* I know about your father,' he said with a smirk. 'And your mother, too, for that matter. Ah, yes. Yes I do,' he said, casting a few gnarled chunks of wood into his fire.

'Then tell me about him, maharaji-ji,' I said. 'I have to know how he died. Was he in the Entrenchment?'

'Ah, you know about the siege?' he asked, his eyes brightening.

'Was he slaughtered with the Fatehgarh refugees?' I pressed on. 'Or did he survive the massacre at Sati Chowra?'

'*Slaughtered?*' the old man exploded, pounding his fists upon his cushions. '*Massacre?* How dare you throw those words at me! What about Neill? What about Renaud? *There's* a butcher for you! Didn't he slaughter? Didn't he massacre my people?'

He seemed to puff up with indignation, and exhibited some vestigial corpulence around the jowls.

'I only meant – '

'Only meant! Only meant!' he muttered, clasping his hand to his brow. 'I knew it,' he said with his voice breaking. 'I *knew* it would be this way. Why did I ever send for you? I was in such a good mood this morning, and now look at me. I've got a splitting headache.'

With that he gave a dramatic sigh and collapsed among his pillows. His face was gaunt and he seemed to be lean under his tunic, but there was still some mottled heft to his thighs, and he lay back like a fat man, with his arms extended, his short legs crossed at the ankles.

He fumbled with the tin for a moment and began to work a little ghee into his temples, revealing a pale complexion underneath the smear.

'Good, good,' he murmured, shutting his eyes. 'Just the thing.'

Rain began to fall from the passing clouds. 'That's better,' he said as the wood chunks began to catch. 'Much better.'

He opened his eyes and stared at me a moment as if for the first time. 'You are an aggravating boy,' he said. 'A very impatient boy.'

He mumbled a moment, tilting his head and gravely nodding, as if someone were whispering in his ear.

'Yes, good,' he said, lifting his head slightly and peering at me along his blunt nose.

'Your mother, boy – what did she tell you about me?'

'About – the Nana Sahib?' I asked.

'The same,' he said, nodding slightly.

'Uh, nothing,' I said with a confounded shrug.

'Oh, come now, boy,' he said, smiling as if this were impossible. '*Nothing?*'

'No, maharaj-ji,' I said with dim and unaccountable satisfaction. 'Nothing.'

He pouted at this and looked away, fidgeting with the frayed embroidered cuffs of his tunic. Then it was as if someone were whispering to him again, and once more he peered at me and cleared his throat.

'And Willard?' he asked. 'Did she mention him?'

I grudgingly shook my head.

'Ah,' he said, giving a furtive, conspiratorial nod to the vacancy beside him. 'Always discreet, your mother.'

Sensing an insult prowling in that remark, I quickly said, 'But she visited his grave every week. The mali told me. He used to sneak her in.'

This displeased the old man, and he smacked his lips and irritably raised a hand as if to silence his phantom attendants.

I felt something begin to turn in my stomach as it finally began to dawn on me that if this old man really was the Nana Sahib then he was my father's murderer.

'Willard worked for me, you know,' he said with his nose upraised again. 'I employed several Feringhee in the old days. I took him on as a favor to Harigarh. He dug a tunnel for me from my palace to the bathing ghats at Bithur. Very scientific. No posts. Big enough for my elephant to pass through. I was quite pleased. Spared me the sun, you see. I can't bear too much sunshine. I'm not dark like you,' he said with a little sneer.

'I paid Willard a generous stipend. More than he could ever have earned with the railway. See?' he suddenly exclaimed, glancing from point to point around the cavern. 'There's *another* example! See how generous I was? And to one of theirs! And still they cut me off without a pice! Without a title! And all because I didn't pop out of Baji Rao's loins?'

He shrugged and sighed, shaking his head as if refusing to listen to silent, consoling voices.

'He . . . worked for you?' I asked, glancing around to see if someone was lurking in the shadows after all – Genda, maybe, or the old charan.

He gazed off into the rain for a moment, and his eyelids drooped. Water dripped from the cavern's mouth and pooled upon the ledge. 'I gave him a bungalow, too,' he said softly. 'He and your mother lived right by my aviary. I used to call him Weaverbird. He was always so ingenious. He was going to build a sewage system for my menagerie. Showed me his plans on the billiard table . . . ' he said, his voice trailing off.

'They killed all my beasts, didn't they, boy?' he said, glancing over at me. 'My apes, my rhinoceros, my old lions.'

I waited a moment as he sniffed back a tear. 'What about my

mother?' I asked gently. 'How did they meet?'

The old man suddenly grinned to either side of himself and exclaimed, 'Oh, now boy. You must know by now. Didn't your brother tell you?'

'My – what?' I croaked, slowly rising to my feet.

'Sit down, boy,' he said, and I fell back as if my legs had turned to water.

'My *brother*?'

'Well, your half brother, of course. He was *her* son, after all.'

'Wh-*who* was her son?'

'Why, Rai Singh, of course,' he said with another appalled smile.

'But it can't be,' I mumbled, glancing around the cavern floor as if I'd dropped something. 'How could – '

'Didn't you even know that?'

'But how – '

'Why do you think she left Harigarh in the first place? Don't you see, boy? Tarra Bai was barren and needed a prince to fulfill her ambitions, and your grandfather needed an ally. So when your mother's baby was born it was given over to Tarra Bai.'

'But who – '

'– was the father? Don't ask me. Your mother was scrupulously discreet, remember?'

'Was he Willard?'

'Willard, he says!' the old man exclaimed, turning to his side again with a conspiratorial chuckle. 'No, no, no. This was *before* Willard. What would Tarra Bai have wanted with a cheechee prince? No, no,' he said, combing his fingers through his beard. 'The rumor was that he was sired by Tarra Bai's brother. That would have made her the little bastard's mother *and* aunt, wouldn't it? A very degraded house, Harigarh. Too shut off. Why, when my father wanted sons he gave up on the zenana. Adopted my brother and me out in the open, with all the proper ceremonies. But which did the English honor? To which of us did they extend the privy purse?'

He ranted on in that vein for a little while, but I shut my ears and tried to conjure Rai Singh's face. Had it been my mother I'd seen in those dark, fond eyes?

'Of course, your mother couldn't stay in Harigarh,' he said, abruptly returning to the point. 'Not with her own son playing in the halls. She couldn't have kept away from him for long. Such a *ferocious* woman, your mother. So your grandfather married her off as best he could, which turned out to be Willard, of all people. He was a lonely widower and didn't mind the complications. So they set off together, with her servant in tow, and that's when I hired him. Now do you finally see, boy? It's really very simple.'

But I couldn't seem to picture my mother with her Englishman, my father, keeping house in Bithur. In my memory she remained a widow, haunted and besieged, and the harder I tried to place her in the Nana Sahib's garden the further she receded, floating off in a trail of smoke.

'It's a lie,' I muttered, glaring over at the old man. 'It's all a lie. Why did you send for me? What is it that you want?'

He shook his head back at me and crisped his tongue, tapping his scroll against his temple.

'If you're the Nana Sahib,' I snapped back, 'then tell me why you murdered him.'

'*Murdered him*, the boy says,' he declared, glancing around his durbar cave again. 'He doesn't know anything, does he?'

He shifted slightly in his seat, straightening his back and shrugging his shoulders and glaring around as if to quiet his ghostly court.

'I was his *friend*, boy,' he said with a shake of his scroll. 'When the word reached us of the uprisings in Delhi and Meerut it was I who put him and your mother on a boat for Allahabad. I was a better friend to him than he was to himself. He said his place was with his countrymen, in the entrenchment. Can you imagine that? After everything we'd meant to each other? What had his countrymen ever done for him? No, I told him, you get on that boat and get away from this place.

'Now tell me,' he asked with an innocent shrug, 'was that the act of a butcher? Of a beast?'

'Never,' the fire must have whispered back, for he shrugged again with a helpless sigh in its direction.

'How could I have known it was already too late? The first bodies didn't begin to float by my bathing ghat until he and your mother were well out of sight. I must have counted twenty while I was performing my puja, but only one came close enough to identify,' he said, wrinkling his nose and smacking his tongue in disgust. 'A little English boy, it was, crawling with turtles.

'Where did they come from, Bala?' he asked, turning to his left, and speaking, I think, to his long-dead brother. '*Fatehgarh*, that's right,' he said with a grateful nod.

'But you know, boy?' he said, glancing back at me now. 'It was as if the wind had swept them into the river, and the Ganga was flushing them into the sea. I felt something tear at the sight of those white corpses, felt something cut loose and drift away forever.

'And when the wind came I opened my wings to it, didn't I, Bala?' he said, flapping his arms. 'And it lifted me up to my father's perch, and I was Punt Pardhan Peshwa Bahadur!' he sang out, rising to his feet now and marching onto the ledge with his sceptre upraised, as if conducting his own echo. 'They cheered me! They swore allegiance to me! Even the Moslems! Imagine! And I don't even *like* Moslems!'

He danced around on the ledge awhile, stiffly kicking up his feet.

'When the entrenchment fell, soldiers poured in from all over. Chauhans, Gaurs, Gautams marched before me in review. I promised them each a gold bangle, and we must have fed a thousand Brahmins to the jowls. The celebration went on for six days, and what a glory it was! The feasts! The nautches! The grand processions to and fro!'

But then he faltered in his dance, as if someone had laid a restraining hand on his shoulder, and he turned around and frowned, trying to regain his composure.

'But about that business at Sati Chowra,' he said, hurrying back to his dingy throne. 'I want you to know I had no hand in that, boy. I was going to let them go and good riddance. Let the Ganga take them away. I had enough prisoners to dispose of already.

'We tried to lay down a code about them. The Christians and half-breeds we gave over to the Moslems to convert or execute, depending. The Chinese we exterminated, of course. What were they doing here in the first place? The babus we flogged, unless they'd been caught using English, in which case they were killed. Hoarders we fined and imprisoned, and flogged sometimes, as a lesson to the banias, and the spies we maimed and beheaded. All perfectly sensible.

'But it was hard to know where the English fit into all this. We decided to kill all the males, except for Mr Greenway, whom we held for ransom, but at first even that was hard for me to stomach.

'I remember the first one they brought before me was Mr Owen. Found him in a pig's hovel somewhere. He'd been my houseguest at Bithur on several occasions. I had many English visitors, you know. Such ungrateful guests! They sniggered at the feasts I served them, pocketed the silverware for "souvenirs," defiled my carriages with their adulteries, littered my gardens with their bottles and cigars.

'But Mr Owen was one of the better ones. Complained about the guesthouse linens, but admired my topiary. And now here he was on the first day of my rule, dressed in muddy pyjamas and stained with walnut juice. What was I supposed to do with Mr Owen?

' "Kill him," Bala told me, and Azimullah too. Easy enough for the two of you, though, wasn't it?' he called out suddenly. '*You* didn't have to make the decision. Nobody was being killed in *your* name.

'What a business,' he sighed, 'being king.

'Well,' he said, turning back to me, 'I told Mr Owen how very nice it was to see him, and even asked after Mrs Owen, but straightaway he denounced me as a scoundrel and a murderer. I tried to calm him down, for he was just making things more difficult, but he couldn't help himself. Sounded off as though *his* troops surrounded us, not mine. Well, he just couldn't seem to help himself, and obviously neither could I. I couldn't let anyone speak to the Peshwa like that, not in front of all the others, so I ordered a sepoy to cut off his head.

'And wouldn't you know it? The sepoy refused! Insisted we give Mr Owen a sword so he could go down fighting. Well, this was typical sepoy thinking. What was Mr Owen going to do with a sword? He could barely stand up. So Genda did the job in a few quick strokes.'

The Nana Sahib sputtered his lips like a horse and scratched himself under one arm. 'The most trying business was what to do with the memsahibs and babalogues. Bala here wanted to do away with them, like a nest of newborn kraits.'

He peered over in his brother's direction, crisping his tongue, and then Bala must have said something displeasing, for the Nana

Sahib's eyes flashed. 'I know, I know,' he snapped. 'I'm getting to that.

'So many prisoners,' he sighed, rubbing his temples. 'A *plague* of prisoners. Wretched, filthy, sunstruck, starving. Some of the women were too miserable to save. Half dead anyway, and deranged by grief. After the Fatehgarh refugees arrived we had fifty, sixty women and children under guard, and after Sati Chowra another two hundred stumbled in. We put them all in the Bhibigar, near my headquarters, where I could protect them from Teekha Singh's troops. I sent them brandy and let them take the air out on the verandah every evening. I even assigned a maidservant to look after their needs, but all they did was complain. The bread was too coarse, the dahl was too thin, the straw was stale, the water was dirty. *Memsahibs!'*

'But maharaj-ji,' I said as he paused now to straighten his turban, 'what about my father?'

The wet wind curled into the mouth of the cave and bestirred the embers in the fire's bed. The old man seemed to consult for a moment with his long-lost courtiers, silently working his mouth and holding the scroll against his chest.

'Well, I did what I could about Willard,' he said, nodding grimly. 'But they never did reach Allahabad. He and your mother ran aground somewhere near Mauhar, I think. A zemindar took them in and offered them his protection. But when word reached him that we'd vanquished the English, he brought them to me as a gift.

'Your mother was all right,' he said with a yawn. 'But poor Willard was a shadow of himself. The zemindar had treated him badly. One eye was all puffed closed and he had a sabre cut across his shin, and fleas, and prickly heat, and dysentery too.

'I looked him up and down. "Dear, foolish Weaverbird," I said to him, "*now* will you accept my protection?"

'But he just pointed to your mother and spoke in a whisper, with his lips all blistered up. "Protect Natholi," he said, "but my place is with the others."

'I gently tried to remind him that the "others" he spoke of were dead.

'But he knew that, of course. "Then slaughter me as you slaughtered the others," he said to me.'

The Nana Sahib hesitated, tugging at his lower lip, and when our eyes met I could feel something uncoiling in my entrails and seeking the path to my throat.

He looked away and sniffed slightly. 'Well, there was no talking to him. After everything we'd meant to each other he could talk to me like that. What do you do with such people? I'll tell you what you do. You give them what they want.'

The Nana Sahib flicked his beard with his fingers. 'And do you know what he said to me just before Genda's sword descended? He said, "Dhundoo Punt, you're no sportsman!" *You're no sportsman!*' He laughed abruptly and then cut himself off with a snap of his head.

'But your mother was so *noble*, boy. So proud. Never spoke, never shed a tear, never even blinked. And as she was taken off to Bhibigar the crowd parted for her silently, and I wouldn't let the soldiers practice with their swords on Willard's trunk until she'd passed from sight.'

I tried to force a tear at least for the murdered father I never knew, but my eyes were cold and stubborn. 'Then you *did* kill my father!' I shouted. 'You *did* murder him!'

The Nana Sahib gave me a look of such exquisite boredom and disgust it froze me where I stood. 'Oh, shut up, boy,' he said, reaching out a hand as if to hold back his brother. 'How can you be so stupid?'

I stood wavering a moment, as if waiting for my grief to call me to vengeance, but all I felt was the constant slithering in my belly and a vapor rising like a bubble in my throat.

'Sit down, boy,' he commanded, and I slumped down in defeat. The flames rose high between us, and the wood chunks popped and crackled.

'You stupid boy,' he said, shaking his scroll at me now. 'Do you think I brought you all this way to tell you the story of Willard's death? Don't you understand *anything*?'

I gaped at him now, for somehow, through the wavering yellow flames that flickered between us, his face looked even more familiar than before.

'You don't see it *yet*? he asked, incredulous, rolling his eyes upward to the black ceiling. 'Would it help if I told you that Willard was an old man when he died?'

'M-maharaj-ji?'

'Old. Seventy or so. *Too* old, don't you see?'

'Too old?'

'Yes, boy,' he said, throwing the scroll to me. 'Too old to be your *father!*'

The scroll tumbled by me, and I slowly fetched it, though with my eyes still fixed on the old man's face.

'Go on, boy,' he said. 'Open it.'

The ribbon disintegrated into purple dust as I fumbled it open and tipped it into the firelight.

It was a horoscope, yellowed and brittle, with its corners all worn down. Gods and goddesses paraded along its margins, and Ganesha sat at the head of them, over a column of charts and Sanskrit script.

It took me a moment to decipher the characters, for they'd been brushed on in a rushed hand and my own hands shook. But then I came upon my name, Balbeer Rao, and then my horoscopic name, Baba Sahib Panwar, scrawled at Ganesha's feet.

'Did you find it yet?' the Nana Sahib asked, gazing out at the intensifying rain.

'I – I see my name . . . ' I said, still working through the script in the wavering glow.

'No, no,' he said, glaring at me impatiently. 'Not that.'

Next I came to my mother's name and began to read it aloud. '. . . Natholi – no,' I said, leaning closer to the fire. 'Nathubai. Saubhagwati Nathubai.'

'Yes, yes. That's your mother's proper name.' he said with a disgusted smirk. 'But what about your father, boy? Look for your father's name.'

I skimmed up and down the columns, hunting for Willard's name or some Sanskrit transliteration, but the only other name I could find, brushed haltingly, where the jyotishi himself must have faltered out of dread and astonishment, was Dhundoo Punt.

I looked up at Dhundoo Punt, the Nana Sahib, Punt Purdhan Peshwa Bahadur, and began to see whose face it was lurking beneath all the ash and wrinkles. It was my face, grinning back at me as from a filthy mirror.

'See the resemblance?' he asked cheerfully.

'*You!*' I gasped.

'Ahhh, now,' said the Nana Sahib with a satisfied sigh. 'There you have it. The truth at last.'

I brushed the scroll out of my lap as if it had caught fire.

'No,' I said, 'It can't be. It's a trick. This isn't my horoscope. You're just trying to – '

'Oh, but it most certainly *is* your horoscope,' he said equably. 'Genda fetched it for me from your mother's trunk. Had to kill the old hakeem to get it.'

So that was why Sayideen was murdered, I told myself, gaping back at him through the flames.

'Well, we couldn't let it fall into the wrong hands, could we? I only had your interest at heart, boy. Imagine if the English had found out you were my son! Why, they'd have shot you in cold blood, just as they did Khan Bahadur's boys.'

'B-but – what about Willard?' I stammered. 'My mother . . . '

'Well, what about him? He was no husband to her, boy. He wasn't fit. How could he have been, an old widower like that? Really, it was such a waste.'

'But how – '

He yawned conspicuously, and shot his wrists out of his brocade sleeves. 'Ruling is a lonely business – a miserable business, really. I gave up everything for my people; asked so little in return.'

He shrugged a little, leaning back on one arm and gesticulating with the other. 'Women,' he said wistfully. 'You have no idea how I've missed them.' He shook his head a little and gazed out as the rain persisted into the gloaming.

'I wouldn't defile myself with the memsahibs of Bhibigar, you know. Wouldn't let my soldiers, either. Not that they were tempted.

'But your mother – now, she was different. I'd always admired her, you know. There was that ferocity about her which suffering only seemed to feed. God, she was beautiful in her fashion, and highborn, too.'

He shuddered as if from a chill, and hunched over his crossed arms. 'Bala returned from battle one evening, wounded, all covered with dust. Wouldn't give me a moment's peace. "The English have crossed the Pandu Nadi," he says, "and they're fighting like demons to save the memsahibs and babalogues."

'And Azimullah here says, "Wouldn't they fight a little less like demons if there were no one left to save?"'

'I was surprised at you, Azimullah, of all people,' he said, shaking his head like a schoolmaster. 'And after all the memsahibs you conquered in London.

'I tell you, it made me sick. I wouldn't hear of it. But they insisted – Bala, Azimullah, and all the others. And I was so tired, boy. So tired of making decisions. So finally I said, "Go on, then. Do what you must. But have the sepoys do it. Let them earn their keep for a change."

'But I didn't forget your mother, boy, or the promise I'd made to Willard. So I had her brought to me safe and sound, and we listened together for the sepoys' guns.

'They fired their guns all right, but merely into the ceiling! And you should have heard the wail that arose from Bhibigar.

'But no,' he said, covering his ears. 'No one should ever have to hear such things.'

He ran a shaking hand across his brow, and my gaze fell from his face to the grey wattle of his neck.

'So,' he said, clearing his throat and spitting, 'I sent Genda in with some of my guards. I could always count on Genda. Told them to use swords, knives, anything to hold down the noise.

'But they took all evening, boy,' he said, with his eyes darting about the cave. 'It was awful, terrible. The sobbing and shrieking.

'So I ordered a nautch to drown out the nightmare and led your mother up to my apartments.'

'Stop it,' I wanted to shout. 'Don't tell me any more.' But my jaw was clenched and stubborn as a sickly sweetness seeped along my gums.

'I wouldn't have troubled her,' he said, glancing across at me. 'But Adla, my favorite – well, she was unclean. And all the others were back in Bithur. And your mother was so inspiring, so uplifting, even in her rags.

'All I wanted was companionship,' he said plaintively, wringing his hands. 'Just on that one night, that one night out of all the nights of my glorious reign.'

He brightened a little and smacked his lips. 'And you know,' he said fondly, with his eyebrows raised, 'I think she understood me, boy. Understood what it meant to me that night. Not at first, of course,' he said, his voice trailing off. 'But afterwards . . . later . . .

'Oh God,' he sighed, 'it was all so . . . trying.'

He caught my gaze then and must have seen a dreadful rage gripping my features like a frost, for he tried to regain his composure, sitting up straight and swallowing.

'But don't you see?' he said, wiping his palms on his legs. 'I saved her, boy. Brought her back with me to Bithur. Put her on my barge with my womenfolk. But she threw herself into the river as we cast off for Avadh. And even with everything that was happening to me I found the time to grieve for her, boy, for I truly believed she had drowned.'

He sniffed in a great breath of air and shut his eyes for a moment like a jogi. 'But her servant saved her. Don't you see? She couldn't drown,' he said, puffing up with pride. 'She was carrying the Peshwa's seed.'

He stared at me now with his eyes half-lidded. 'You, boy,' he said, tucking his chin against his throat. 'She was carrying *you*.

'Now come, Baba Sahib,' he said with his arms outstretched. 'Come and greet your father.'

And there he was at last, my father, reaching out to embrace me in his stinking robes. I think I meant to obey him and fall into his arms, but as I rose to my feet something popped and hissed in the bonfire, and when I glanced down into the flames I saw my mother's smoking skull and heard her urgent whisper and felt Kali's serpent writhing along my arms.

I slowly reached up and removed my turban, for it was seemly to approach my father bareheaded.

'You've been such a comfort to me, boy,' he was saying as the turban unravelled in my hands and the sacred goor now flooded my mouth like honey.

He struggled at first, and thrashed about as I pulled the cloth tight around his neck, but for all that it was a simple thing, just as Baroo had promised. I stared steadfastly into my father's eyes as the rain washed him clean, and as he jerked beneath me and snored his last breath into the trickling chill it was my mouth gaping up at me, my eyes staring back from the puddled ground.

◆———————◆

With all his ghosts attending, I heaped up my father's treasures and effects and burned his body in the fire that night, keeping vigil like a loving son until his skull burst amid the embers.

I waited all morning for Genda to come and kill me, and finally fell asleep by my father's ashes. In my dreams my mother vanished from the river shallows, never to haunt my sleep again, and I awoke peaceably in the late afternoon to find Genda standing over me with my father's sceptre in his hand.

I asked only that he be quick about my execution, but he gave me the sceptre and touched his great forehead to my feet, hailing his new lord and master, Shrimunt Maharaj Dhiraj Balbeer Rao Baba Sahib Purdhan Peshwa Bahadur.

So I followed my bloody slave down the mountainside and back through the forests and foothills, and not until we reached the terai did I finally escape him, leaving him slumbering by a smoldering fire and casting my sceptre into the consuming swamp.

The ayul caught up with me on the outskirts of Bahraich and it was two long months before I could stagger back to Bastard Bhavan.

I'll tell you that in my fashion I abided by my wife and son, but what became of them thereafter is better left untold, for I always strove to spare Ahalya any further shame on my account, and save my son from the Peshwa's dream.

But remember that it was I, Balbeer Rao, who slew the Nana Sahib, and if someday, when I'm long dead, you return my history to my countrymen, let them read it at least as a cautionary tale should they ever again yearn for the rule of kings.

EPILOGUE

In February of 1954 I returned with my wife to India aboard the S.S. *Strathmore* and travelled by train from Bombay straightaway to Cawnpore. It was my intention to attempt to discover what became of Moonshi, whose own fate he had so willfully consigned to obscurity at the close of his confessions. I had devoted all the time I had reserved for my own memoirs to coaxing Balbeer's story into English, and it has often seemed to me since as though Moonshi has become my master, I his servant.

Even as our train hurtled through the dust of Uttar Pradesh, I still wondered why Moonshi had entrusted his story to me, to whom he had never demonstrated more than token affection and respect. Perhaps I had meant more to him than I had thought; I was, it seemed, the closest approximation to a family he had left.

But much as I wanted to think that Moonshi had harbored some deep feeling for me, I suspected that he had simply recognized in me the sense of duty that has characterized us Cuthbertsons since the Norman invasion. He could at least be certain that once I had accepted his gift I would honor it. Who among his countrymen, reeling then from the throes of their nation's independence, would have welcomed his chronicle, with its black horrors and ambivalences? At the very least he could assure himself that his story would not make itself known to me until I was at sea, and that in his own country, during what little time he had left, his secrets would be safe.

Moonshi had tried to resign himself to a servant's life, a master's whims, and for years it seems he had succeeded. But his history, Balbeer Rao's life, still had too much momentum left to permit Moonshi the oblivion he so desperately sought. After all he had suffered and lost, someone had to know who he had been and what he had done. So at last, surrendering himself to the spirits of his past, he lit his lamp and wrote.

In Cawnpore I came upon the Reverend Weems's grave in a churchyard adjacent to the old Mission School, and nearby Judith uncovered the overgrown headstones of Copy, John Christopher, and Peter John (or Dileep, as Balbeer insisted upon calling him), who died, as best we could ascertain from the crumbled inscription, in 1905. Of Willard's obelisk we could find no trace, though the Memorial Gardens, now officially dubbed Nana Rao Gardens, were littered with the remains of monuments and headstones destroyed by the mobs that burst into the sacred confines on the eve of Indian independence.

Reverend Weems's school was now a post office, and yet some of its files remained tucked away in what must have been the Reverend's room. Its present occupant, Mr V. K. Bannerji, was most helpful and gracious, but the only trace I could find of Mahabir was a reference to a boy named Jacob on a bit of undated correspondence listing him among a dozen other boys as a grateful recipient of a shipment of secondhand shoes.

Mr A. N. Singh, Assistant Superintendent of Police, was most helpful in confirming, from his records, much of Balbeer's story, and I believe I managed to locate his boyhood home, as he described it, with the confectioner's shop still occupying the ground floor.

We then proceeded to Gwalior, where the Collector, Mr D. R. Mankenkar, greeted us and escorted us by car to Bhondaripur. Ahalya's family still labored for the local zemindar, but all the principals were long dead. Pyari Lal's grandson was head of the household now, and the story of Balbeer Rao the Thug, with the inevitable embellishments, was now a local legend. Balbeer's house and compound were being maintained by a single servant for the infrequent visits of the present zemindar, a bania from the city whose great-grandfather had evidently been awarded Balbeer's lands after Balbeer's conviction, in absentia, for the murder of the patwari, Mangal Singh.

The reader will look in vain, as I did, for a Rajput kingdom named Harigarh, but from my investigations it would appear that it is only the name that is a falsehood, not the kingdom. If I have guessed its true name correctly, and thus the names of its rulers, then I have ascertained that Tarra Bai finally succeeded in poisoning Maharao Zalim Singh and placing Rai Singh upon the throne. However, Rai Singh and his mother seem to have had a falling-out, and she had him poisoned as well when he attempted to banish her to the foothills of the Himalayas. I suspect that Balbeer disguised these principals to protect Rai Singh's grandson, the present Maharao of 'Harigarh,' who, after all, is Balbeer's grandnephew. Whatever Balbeer's reasons, I feel duty bound to honor them.

Upon my return to Jullunder, I was told by my most able successor, District Magistrate Solanki, that none of my servants had remained in his employ. However, I did manage to locate our old dhobi, Om Prakash, who informed me that Balbeer Rao had left our compound within a week of our departure, declaring himself free of servitude now that the burra sahibs were gone, and vanishing northward into the maelstrom of partition.

And that, it seemed, was that. However, on my last afternoon in Jullunder I took it into my head to attempt to interview the old widow woman who used to bring Balbeer his meals. She'd lived in a little settlement of dairy workers a mile or so from our compound.

The settlement was now quite extensive, filled with uprooted Hindu refugees from Pakistan, and it took me an hour to find anyone who remembered her. He was a bania of some sort, and rather too eager to demonstrate his English, but he informed me that just after Independence she too had moved away.

It seemed that there, at last, was an end to it, but on an unaccountable impulse I asked anyway that I be allowed to see her hut, and found it to boast, alone among all the others, a low lintel and three steps to the door.

Hugh W. Cuthbertson
I.C.S., Retired
Cheltenham, Gloucester
October 1955

GLOSSARY

The following definitions are based primarily on *Hobson-Jobson*, Yule and Burnell's classic Anglo-Indian etymological glossary; *Ramaseeana*, William 'Thuggee' Sleeman's own dictionary of the Thugs' language; *The Mystics, Ascetics and Saints of India* by Oman; *Castes and Tribes of Central India* by Russell; *Lucknow: The Last Phase of Oriental Culture* by Abdul Halim Sharar; and the author's own experience on Balbeer's trail. Thug terms from *Ramaseeana* are followed by an (R).

adjutant birds: Large carrion cranes, so-called because they were such a common sight feeding with the vultures on the battlefield dead.

Aghoris: Shivaite sadhus who testify to their pantheism by eating tidbits of human waste and exhumed corpses.

Ahirs: A subdivision of the herding caste.

Akalis: The zealots of Sikhdom; fundamentalist followers of Govind Singh, the most martial of the founding gurus.

Anglo-Indian: Any long-term British resident of India.

ankh: A short, hooked metal goad used by elephant drivers.

anna: One-sixteenth of a rupee.

Arjuna: A semidivine hero of the Hindu epic *The Mahabharata*.

Aughar: A low-caste jogi identified by the wooden pipe he plays before eating and drinking.

Avadh: Sometimes spelled *Oudh*: one of the Northwest Provinces. An autonomous Moslem state whose capital, Lucknow, was the great center of Moslem Indian culture. Its annexation by the British in 1856 helped to spark the Mutiny of 1857.

avatar: The reincarnation of a divinity.

ayah: Nursemaid; governess.

ayul: A virulent malaria that infested the swamps of the terai.

babalogues: Small folk; children.

babu: A clerk; often connotes pompous self-importance.

badmash: A ruffian or thief.

bagh: Garden.

Bahadur: Title given to kings, meaning hero or champion.

bairaji: Refers here to a holy man who worships Vishnu and his avatars.

Baluchis: Natives of Baluchistan, a Moslem division of British India, situated between Persia and the Punjab.

balu shahi: Moist, round, syrupy sweets.

banghi: Derogatory slang for an untouchable.

bania: A Hindu merchant or moneylender.

bearer: A domestic servant, equivalent to a butler.

Begum: The title given to a Moslem queen.

Bengali: A native of the northeastern coastal province of Bengal.

bhai: Brother.

bhang: The dried leaves and stalks of intoxicating hemp, here referring specifically to the form ingested with beverages and sweetmeats, as opposed to ganja, which is smoked.

Bhatti Rajputs: A clan descended from Punjabi tribesmen who were pushed southward into Jeysulmere sometime before the tenth century.

Bheels: Inhabitants of the forests and hills of the Vindhya and Malwa ranges and the northwestern Deccan; believed by some to be the aborigines of Rajputana.

Bhibigar: Cawnpore's House of Sorrow or House of Women, where the women and children were murdered during the Devil's Wind.

bhisti: Water carrier.

bhurtote: A master Thug; a chieftain. (R)

bidi: Indian cigarettes made from rolled tobacco leaves secured with string.

bileea: A resting place, usually a grove; the preferred murder site among Thugs. (R)

Brahma: The Creator; the least worshipped of the Hindu trinity.

Brahmin: A Hindu of the highest priestly caste.

brinjal: Eggplant.

budgerow: A keelless sailing barge used on the Ganges.

bulbul: A small green songbird; India's poetic equivalent of the nightingale.

burra sahib: Great master; applied to the master of a house, or the highest-ranking European of a district.

cantonment: British residential area.

caste: From *casta*, Portuguese for the hereditary occupational divisions of Hindu society.

chakla: A red-light district.

chamar: An outcaste leatherworker.

chapatti: A flat, round, unleavened bread baked on a griddle.

chappals: Sandals.

chaprasis: Servants who function as heralds, couriers, and doormen.

Charans: A caste of historians, genealogists, and bards.

charpoy: The standard Indian bedstead; a wooden frame strung with rope or cotton ribbon.

cheechee: Derogatory slang for anyone of mixed Indian and European blood.

cheyla: A disciple; pupil.

chick: A window blind made of bamboo splints laced with twine.

chinkara: The Indian gazelle.

chitraker: An artist; painter.

chowkidor: A watchman, especially a nightwatchman.

chowra: Glass wedding bangles.

choultry: A resting place for travellers.

Civil Lines: British civil cantonment.

Collector: The chief administrative officer of a district.

Company: See *East India Company*.

dacoits: The dreaded banditti of North and Central India.

dahl: A spiced lentil porridge; the mainstay of rural India's diet.

Dandis: A sect of jogis identified by the staffs they carry.

darshan: The beneficent presence of a great saint.

deodar: A cedar tree common to the Himalayas.

Devil's Wind: Balbeer's name for the Sepoy Rebellion or Great Mutiny of 1857, in which soldiers of the East India Company's army, in league with some of North India's nobles and landlords, rose up to drive the British out of India.

dhobi: A washerman.

dhoon: A flat valley lying between the Himalayas and its foothills.

dhoti: The common Hindu loincloth, loosely wrapped around and between the upper legs.

Digambaras: Literally 'sky-clad'; a sect of yatis or Jain ascetics who go naked.

Diwali: An autumnal festival of lights celebrated by Hindus with illuminations and fireworks.

diwan: The principal officer of a native state; prime minister.

dolpari cap: A cap that consists of two strips of cloth with a seam at the top, similar to the Congress cap; in Lucknow it is elegantly embroidered.

domri: The scavenger caste that disposes of carrion and tends the pyres at Hindu funerals (individually known as a *dom*).

doob: Nutritious creeping grass prized by grasscutters as horse feed.

dudh: A non-Thug; anyone eligible for strangulation. (R)

durbar: Assembly before a king, either of nobles and chieftains or subjects with petitions.

Dusserah: The ten-day festival celebrating Rama's defeat of the devil Ravenna.

dustoor: The amalgam of customs and superstitions that permeates Indian village culture.

East India Company: The primary British mercantile concern in India, under whose auspices the British ruled India from 1757 until it was displaced by the British government in 1858, when Queen Victoria became Empress of India.

eight annas: Derogatory term for anyone half Indian and half European: eight annas equals half a rupee.

ekka: A small, two-wheeled, one-horse cab.

Eurasian: Here used to mean a person of mixed European and Indian ancestry, as opposed to an Anglo-Indian, which here refers to a longtime British resident of India.

Faithfulganj: A central section of Cawnpore's military cantonment.

faqir: A Moslem holy man.

Feringhee: A Britisher or, more loosely, any European.

garh: House.

Ganesha: Shiva's son; the potbellied, elephant-headed God of sagacity and prudence.

Ganga: The Ganges River; most sacred river in India.

ganj: Suffix meaning 'market.'

ganja: Here refers to the smoked form of hemp, as opposed to *bhang*, which is ingested.

Generalganj: The native market adjacent to Cawnpore's military cantonment.

gharna: To strangle. (R)

ghat: A landing place, especially any riverbank steps leading down to the water.

ghee: Clarified butter.

godown: A warehouse or storeroom.

gola: A granary.

goor: Unrefined sugar used in Thug rituals.

gora: A low-class white.

Gora Chakla: Red-light district frequented by low-class whites, especially army privates.

gosain: Used here to refer to any holy man who worships Shiva and his avatars.

Gujarati: Native of the northwestern coastal state of Gujarat.

hadji: Any Moslem who has made the pilgrimage to Mecca, identifiable by his beard, *sans* moustache, often dyed red.

Hahrti: Local goddess of Bhondaripur.

hakeem: A Moslem doctor.

Hanuman: The monkey god, extensively worshipped as Lord Rama's faithful ally in the epic *Ramayana*.

hardaur: Mound of earth studded with banners erected to ward off evil.

Hindustani: Nanak Chand, a Bengali, applies this derisively to any Hindu who is not a Bengali.

Holi: Spring festival in honor of Krishna during which people dust and spray each other with dye.

hookah: A water pipe in which smoke is drawn from a bowl of burning tobacco down a pipe to a water-filled chamber and up a second pipe to the mouthpiece.

hoopoe: A small crested bird with a long, curved bill, onomatopoically named for its song.

houri: One of the exquisite maidens who await devout Moslems in paradise.

hubble-bubble: Onomatopoeic name for a water pipe (see *hookah*).

Hulka Devi: The goddess of vomit.

huzoor: A respectful form of address applied to any exalted personage.

Imambara: Lucknow's House of the Imams, a spectacular brick-and-limestone Moslem place of worship damaged in the Mutiny and since restored.

Iman: A variety of Arabian horse.

jagir: A hereditary assignment of land.

Jains: The most influential sect of heretics opposed to the Brahminical traditions of Hinduism; they arose out of the teachings of Vaddhamana during the theological struggles of the fifth and sixth centuries B.C.

jawar: A tall millet whose stalks are used for fodder.

jeel: A lake.

jelabi: A deep-fried sweet made from a cord of spiced dough and soaked in sugar syrup.

Jeysulmere: A desert kingdom of Rajputana, inhabited by the Bhatti Rajputs.

jhirnee: Signal. (R)

-ji: A respectful and sometimes affectionate suffix appended to names and titles.

jyotishi: Astrologer and village priest.

kala: Native; literally 'black.'

Kala Chakla: Red-light district frequented by natives.

Kali: The goddess of destruction and death and an avatar of Parvati, Shiva's wife.

Kanphatas: An especially rigorous sect of jogis, known by their saffron robes, shaved heads, and oversized earrings.

karthi kurna: Beguile. (R)

katbas: A stylized writing of a verse from the Koran or other lofty aphorism used to decorate Moslem households.

katcha: Unpaved, crude; opposite of *pukka*.

katra: A market or complex of apartments in a walled enclosure.

Khosman: A Moslem. (R)

khusamba: Opium beverage popular among Rajputs.

kitabat: The copying of Moslem documents and manuscripts.

kite: The common Indian carrion hawk.

kitmadgar: A table servant.

kotwal: Superintendent of police in native states, sometimes doubling as a magistrate.

Krishna: The cowherd avatar of Vishnu and hero of the *Mahabharata*.

kukri: A short sword, like a cutlass.

kuraya owl: The barn or screech owl.

lassi: A cool yogurt drink seasoned with sugar, salt, and pepper.

latthi: A bludgeon, usually a long bamboo pole wrapped here and there with iron bands and carried by watchmen and police.

lingam: The priapic symbol of Shiva.

lota: A small, spheroidal brass pot used for drinking water, cooking, and worship.

Lucknow: Capital city of the old kingdom of Avadh and the Athens of Moslem North India.

lugda: A turban, often with a sash running down from behind.

Mahadeo: Shiva, the Destroyer.

Mahajans: A subcaste of bankers and merchants.

mahaldar: Here refers to a brothel-keeper.

maharaj: Common form of address for nobles, rich men, and holy men; also a mocking title for the self-important.

maharajkumar: Crown prince.

maharana: Kingly title in some Rajput states.

maharani: Of a king's many wives, the pre-eminent queen ruler of the zenana.

maharao: Kingly title in some Rajput states, including Harigarh.

mahout: An elephant driver or trainer.

Mahrattas: The ferocious race of Hindu warriors who overthrew the Moghul Empire only to be overwhelmed by the British in the early 1800s.

Makar Sankrant: A festival marking the transit of the sun along the Tropic of Capricorn, when the sun ceases to move toward the inauspicious South. It is marked by much alms-giving and the ritual settling of family disputes.

mali: Gardener.

Manbaos: A sect of bairajis adamantly opposed to Brahminism.

Mang: A low caste, originally of musicians. The women were often midwives, the men nightwatchmen and castrators of livestock, but widely regarded as hard-hearted thieves.

Marvaris: A subcaste of cowherds.

Marwar: Rajput kingdom of Jodhpur.

Mataji: Respectful form of address for 'mother.'

maund: A varying measure of weight, here equal to about 25 pounds.

maur: A tinsel crown worn by Hindu grooms.

mela: A religious festival.

Mewar: Rajput kingdom of Udaipur.

mistri: Any kind of technician, here specifically applied to a carpenter.

Moti Bagh: A beautiful park set within Lucknow's market square.

nabob: A Moslem term for a ruler or noble, sometimes applied to influential Anglo-Indians.

Naga: The warrior gosains of Rajputana.

Nandias: Mendicant jogis who lead sacred cows (blessed with various birth defects), collecting alms.

Nastaliq: A refined script developed by the calligrapher Mir Ali Tabrizi.

nautch: An entertainment performed by female singers and dancers (nautch girls), sometimes bawdy but usually sedate, which invariably followed banquets in Indian royal houses.

neem: A common tree throughout India endowed by Hindus with medicinal and mystical powers.

Nerbudda: The most sacred river in Central India.

nilgai: An ungainly, short-horned deer, about the size of a cow.

nizam: Originally the title given to the Moghuls' provincial governors, but later applied to the ruler of Hyderabad when the province became an autonomous Moslem state.

nullah: A dry watercourse.

pahn: Betel leaf, usually taken wrapped around a nugget of betel nuts, anise, and other spices as a digestive aid after meals.

pakoras: Spiced pieces of vegetables dipped in batter and deep fried.

Pakrit: An ancient script used in early Jain texts.

palanquin: A travelling box litter with a pole running through, borne on the shoulders of four to six men.

pandies: Derogatory term for native troops derived from Mangal Pandy, a sepoy who was reputed to have fired the first shot of the Devil's Wind.

Paramahansas: A superior order of scholarly sadhus who, after a twelve-year apprenticeship, practice extreme austerities, worshiping themselves as embodiments of the divine.

Parvati: Shiva's wife, of whom Kali is an avatar.

Pathan: A native of the Afghani lands bordering British India; a fierce, towering Moslem stalwart much feared in battle.

patwari: Village accountant.

perikrama: The holy pilgrimage along the course of the Nerbudda, required of many sects of sadhus.

Peshwa: Originally the title of the chief minister of the Mahratta king, until the Peshwa himself became ruler of the Mahratta Empire; the most potent of all the Nana Sahib's titles.

phog bush: A low, rugged bush that grows in the Indian desert.

pice: One sixty-fourth of a rupee; one quarter of an anna.

Pindaris: A subcaste of the Mangs; a hill tribe of bandits and warriors who plagued the kingdoms of Rajputana.

pinnace: A modified budgerow rigged like a brigantine.

puja: Hindu worship, prayer.

pujari: Officiating priests at a Hindu temple.

punkah: A large, swinging mat fan, hooked to a ceiling and pulled with a rope, usually by a boy (*punkah walla*) stationed outside the door.

purdah: The custom of shielding women from public view, either by sequestering them or by keeping them heavily veiled; originally Moslem but adopted by many North Indian Hindus.

qatat: A four-line verse in calligraphy, much revered as decorations in Moslem households.

Raj: The British Imperial administration in India; the Indian Empire.

Rajputs: The great warrior race of Hindus famed for their fiercely independent, chivalric kingdoms in Rajputana.

Rajputana: The great feudal province of North India, lying to the west of Delhi; renamed Rajasthan after independence.

Rama: An avatar of Vishnu and the hero of the epic *Ramayana*.

Ramasee: The secret language of the Thugs.

ranga: A common roadside bush with fine leaves that give it a hazy appearance.

rani: Queen; less exalted version of maharani.

rao: King; also a common surname in Rajputana.

Rasdaris: Travelling troupes of actors who perform pageants of Krishna's life.

Resident: The chief British civil officer at a native court.

roomal: A scarf; in Ramasee, the consecrated scarf used by Thugs to strangle their victims.

ryth: Shallow part of a river used as a ford.

sadhu: A generic term for any Hindu holy man.

sahib: Form of address for a respectable white man; also a title affixed generically to Indians of rank, such as the Nana Sahib.

Sakti: A Hindu sect that worships the life force in all its manifestations.

Sankranti: See *Makar Sankrant.*

Sanyasi: A Hindu in the fourth and final stage of life who retires from the world to renounce all earthly pleasures and depend on charity.

sashtang dandawat: A pilgimage made exclusively by means of repeated prostrations along the ground.

sati: The Hindu rite of widow-burning, outlawed by the British in the early 1800s.

Savada House: Headquarters of the Nana Sahib during the siege of the Cawnpore garrison.

sepoy: A native soldier in the Indian Army.

shama bird: Cousin of the magpie, with a loud, clear song.

shenai: The classical Indian reed instrument, similar to an oboe, regarded as auspicious at weddings, births, and housewarmings.

shikar: A hunt.

shikari: A hunting guide.

Shiva: The Destroyer; in his many incarnations the most widely worshipped of the Hindu trinity in North India.

Shri: Roughly equivalent to Mr.

Shrimati: Mrs or Madame.

Sikhs: Followers of a sect founded in the sixteenth century by Guru Nanak as a bridge between Hinduism and Islam, but which became a warrior sect in defense against the later Moghuls who persecuted them. Identified by their distinctive obovoid turbans, hair and whiskers left uncut, ever-present blade, and bangle.

Sikh Wars: The British campaigns against the Sikh rulers of the Punjab, first in 1845–46, then in 1848–49, ending in the British takeover of the Punjab.

Singh: Literally 'lion'; a common name in North India, especially in the Northwest provinces, Rajputana, and the Punjab. (All Sikhs are named Singh, but not all Singhs are Sikhs.)

skug: A declivity in a hill; a shelter.

solar Rajputs: Rajputs whose royal lines are believed to be descended from the sun.

solar topee: A pith helmet, more properly *sola* topee, after the plant from which they were originally made.

sowar: A private in the Indian cavalry.

suba: Chief of police in some native states.

Sudras: The lowest artisan caste of Hindus.

syce: A livery boy; a groom.

tabla: Here refers to a pair of drums, the higher-pitched *tabla* and the bass *banya* used in lyric North Indian music.

tahsildar: A revenue officer; in some princely states the chief civil officer of a subdivision.

taluk: A large estate, in this case bestowed by the Raj to the Maharaja of Kapurthala to reward his loyalty during the Devil's Wind.

tank: Any dammed or excavated reservoir, lake, or pool.

terai: The 300 miles of pestilental, desolate swamp that lies between Avadh and the Nepalese Himalayas.

thakur: Rajput equivalent of a baron.

Thar: The great desert of Rajputana.

Thug: Literally 'deceiver'; a member of the ritualistic sect (Thuggee) of stranglers who preyed on the roads and rivers of Hindustan until the early nineteenth century.

tilak: A mark worn on the forehead, here referring to a sadhu's sect mark.

Timurids: The Turkestani forebears of the Moghuls.

tonga: A two-wheeled, horse-drawn cab of lighter construction than an ekka.

tope: A grove or orchard.

townaree: Seduction or deception. (R)

tulsi: The basil plant, sacred to Hindus.

Urdhabahu: A gosain who suspends his arms overhead until they atrophy.

Urdhamuki: A shivaite sadhu whose austerities include hanging upside down for long periods.

Uttar Pradesh: Upper Provinces; present name of the state composed primarily of the Northwest Provinces of the British Raj.

vaishya: Here refers to a prostitute.

vakeel: An attorney.

Varanasi: Benares; the most sacred Hindu city, situated on the Ganges.

Vishnu: The Preserver; much worshipped in his many avatars, including Rama, Krishna, and Buddha.

walla: A man connected with a particular function (such as a *punkah walla*, one who operates a punkah).

yati: A Jain holy man.

Yunani: Greek; a Yunani hakeem is a Moslem doctor who practices in the ancient Greek tradition, diagnosing on the basis of pulse.

zemindar: A landlord.

zenana: The apartments of a house or palace where women live in seclusion.

ACKNOWLEDGMENTS

I wish to thank my parents for bringing me to India in 1954 when I was young enough to accept it, and my late grandparents Ward for returning me to India in 1968 when I was old enough to appreciate it. I am indebted to Dr. Douglas Ensminger and my brother Geoff for giving me the opportunity to tour India as a photographer; Harish Chander Bector for being such a true friend and resourceful guide through North India; the people of Hoshangabad village, to whom Part III of this book is dedicated, and especially its headman, Pyari Lal, and Balbeer, son of the sweeper Puran; Mrs. Sajni Thukral and her family for putting up with me during my anguished tour of Balbeer's world; His Highness the Maharaja of Gwalior for introducing me to his very helpful press secretary, Mr. P.B.L. Agnihotri, and his gracious and hospitable family; Mr. Gulab Singh, Companion to His Highness's late father, for his reminiscences of life at court; the people of Sonsa village; Mrs. Muriel Wasi for her guidance and assistance; Mr. J.T.M. Gibson of Ajmer for his help and hospitality; His Holiness Pirzada Saqib Khanooni for sharing his knowledge of Moslem medicine; Dinesh Chandra Nautiyal for his assistance in the city of Gwalior; the Urdu poet Mohammed Farooq Ahson of Cawnpore; Shri M. M. Kapoor of Sati Chowra Ghat; Mr. A.K.S. Solanki, District Magistrate of Cawnpore; the staff of the Memorial (Christ) Church on the grounds of the old entrenchment in Cawnpore; Mr. Khusheed Alam Khan, Chief Minister of Tourism and Civil Aviation in India; Mr. Jaswant Singh, M.P.; Mr. Dinesh Khosla; Mrs. S. Jagannathan, Western and Southern Regional Director of the Government of India Tourist Office; Mrs. Pallavi Shah of Air India in New York; and all those in India, Great Britain, and the United States who put up with my obsessive interrogations about nineteenth-century India.

ACKNOWLEDGMENTS

I wish especially to thank my godfather, Professor Emeritus Andrew Bongiorno of Oberlin College, for his steadfast belief in me and this book, and for his exhaustive assistance in the preparation of this manuscript; and my friend, Michael Finley, for all his criticisms, scoldings, pep talks, and advice.

Thanks also to the wondrous Yale University Library, without which this book could not have been written; and Dr. R. J. Bingle of the India Office Library in London for his gracious and pertinent assistance. I wish also to thank the authors, living and dead, of the histories, biographies, guidebooks, albums, atlases, anthropological studies, surveys, memoirs, travelogues, portfolios, glossaries, manuals, and encyclopaedias I consulted while researching this book.

I am indebted to Robert and Katherine Huntington for their abiding faith in my enterprises and for watching over my family during my Indian tour in 1982. I owe many thanks also to John Hawkins, Tom Rosenthal, and Alan Williams for their early support and enthusiasm for this project; Dr. Victor Altshul for his help over many hurdles; Nan Norene for her careful early readings of the manuscript; my sister Helen; and Hugh Walls Cuthbertson, Esquire, for the loan of his name.

I wish to thank my children, Jake and Casey, for always seeming to trust, despite overwhelming evidence to the contrary, that their father knew what he was doing.

This book is dedicated with all my love to my wife, Debbie, who saw me through six years of crazy labor, and who always knows a false note from a true.

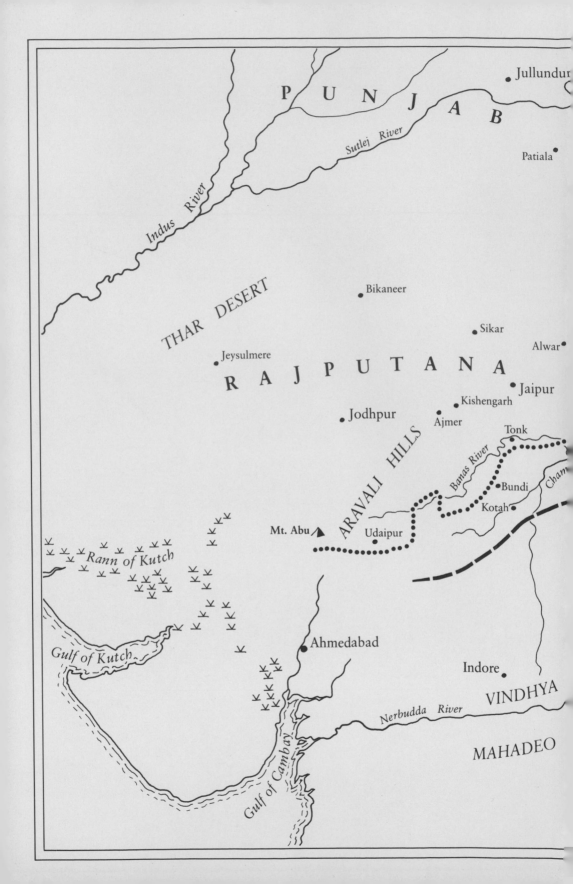